The Nature of Monsters

ALSO BY CLARE CLARK

The Great Stink

The
NATURE
of
MONSTERS

Clare Clark

HARCOURT, INC.

Orlando   Austin   New York   San Diego   Toronto   London

www.HarcourtBooks.com

Library of Congress Cataloging-in-Publication Data
Clark, Clare.
The nature of monsters/Clare Clark.—1st ed.
p.   cm.
1. Women domestics—Fiction.   2. Pregnant women—Fiction.   3. Pharmacists—Fiction.
4. London (England)—Fiction.   5. Psychological fiction.   I. Title.
PR6103.L3725N38   2007
823'.92—dc22   2006019666
ISBN 978-0-15-101206-0

Text set in Dante MT
Designed by April Ward

Printed in the United States of America

First edition
A C E G I K J H F D B

For Charlie. Just Charlie.

The Nature of Monsters

SEPTEMBER 1666

Everyone was agreed that the fire would burn itself out before it reached Swan-street. In Tower-street they had embarked upon the blowing up of houses for a fire-break. She had felt the shocks of the explosions in the soles of her feet as she bent over her mending, but although the glass rattled in the windows, she had not been alarmed. On the contrary, her mood had been one of tranquillity, even contentment. The pains that had dogged her throughout her seventh month had eased. When the child kicked, she had stroked the dome of her belly with the palms of her hands, moving them in reassuring circles, her lips shaping lullabies so old and familiar that they felt as much a part of her as her own breath. That night she slept deeply, without dreams. Even when the night-lanthorn thundered upon the door of the shop, shouting that the fire was coming, that those who remained abed would surely burn alive, she remained untroubled. Quietly, she eased herself to her feet and settled her shawl about her shoulders. For all that it had been a hot, dry summer, it would do the infant no good if she was to take a chill.

The bird must have sought refuge in the chimney. Its high-pitched cry caught in the mortar, setting the irons shrilling in echo before it plunged into the empty grate, its wings brilliant with fire, setting wild shadows thrashing against the wall. Bright scraps of flame spiralled upwards as it lashed and twisted, its eyes lacquered with terror. Beside the grate the stuff spilled from her sewing basket, spangled with sparks. Languidly, as though wearied by the very notion of combustion, a pale scrap of muslin smouldered. When at last it caught, it did so with a burst of flame and a sucked-in gasp of surprise. The blaze took quickly. From beneath the stink of burning feathers came the distinct smell of roasting meat.

Then she was down the stairs, outside, running, the skirts of her nightgown bundled in her arms. The streets were filled with people, twisting, screaming, pushing. Above them the fire was a vast arch, grimed with oily black smoke. The wind bayed and twisted amongst the flames like a pack of dogs, goading the blaze, urging it onwards. Suddenly she turned. Mr. Black. It had not occurred to her to think of her husband. Sparks gusted upwards, swarming like bees round her face. In their frames panes of glass shrivelled to yellow parchment. Someone screamed, falling against her with such force she was almost knocked to the ground. Hardly thinking where she ran, she stumbled away, fighting against the current of people spilling downhill towards the silver sanctuary of the river. Above her birds wheeled and shrieked, twisting arcs of flame. The dust and smoke burned her eyes and throat. It hurt to breathe.

On the great thoroughfare of Cheap-side, the kennel ran scarlet with molten lead, the liquefied roof of the mighty church of St. Paul's. The noise was deafening, her cries drowned out by the crowds and the screams of horses and the crack and rumble of falling houses and the howl of the wind as it spurred the flames forwards. Behind her the wooden beams of a church tower ruptured with a terrible crack. Time ceased as she turned, her hands before her face. A column of fire, as high as the mast of a ship, swayed above her. The flames billowed out behind it like a sail. There was a rolling roar of thunder, like a pause, before it groaned and fell in an explosion of red-gold and black, throwing thousands of brilliant fire-feathers into the air.

The fit of terror that possessed her then palsied her limbs and shrivelled the thoughts in her head to ash. She could do nothing, think nothing. The breath smouldered in her lungs. In her belly, the child thrashed madly, but though its elbows were sharp against her flesh, it could not rouse her. All sense and impulse banished, she stood as though bewitched, her eyes empty of expression, her face, fire-flushed, tipped upwards towards the flames. Had it not been for the butcher's wife who grasped her arm with one rough red hand and dragged her bodily to the quay, she would doubtless have stayed there and burned.

Years later, on one of the few occasions that he had permitted himself to speak of her, his father had told him that afterwards, when it was all over, she had confessed that she had thought herself dreaming, so detached was she from the physical mechanism of her body and the peril of her predicament. In the extremity of her fear, she had ceased to occupy herself but had gazed down upon her own petrified body, observing with something akin to detachment the calamity that must certainly ensue and waiting, knowingly waiting, to discover precisely the nature of the agonies that awaited her.

She had waited, but she had not prayed. For she had known then, as surely as she had known that she must perish in this searing scarlet Hell, that God was not her Father in heaven but a pillar of fire, vengeful and quite without mercy.

I

1718

Afterwards, when I knew that I had not loved him at all, the shock was all in my stomach, like the feeling when you miscount going upstairs in the dark and climb a step that is not there. It was not my heart that was upset but rather my balance. I had not yet learned that it was possible to desire a man so and not love him a little.

Oh, I longed for him. When he was not there, the hours passed so slowly that it seemed that the sun had fallen asleep in the sky. I would wait at the window for whole days for the first glimpse of him. Every time a figure rounded the corner out of the trees, my heart leapt, my skin feverish with hope even as my eyes determined it to be someone to whom he bore not the slightest resemblance. Even Slack the butcher, a man of no more than five feet in height and several times that around the middle, whose arms were so pitifully short they could barely insert the tips of his fingers into the pockets of his coat. I turned my face away hurriedly then, my cheeks hot, caught between shame and laughter. How that beer-soaked dumpling would have licked his lips to imagine the tumbling in my belly at the sight of him, the hot rush of longing between my thighs that made my fingers curl into my palms and set the nape of my neck prickling with delicious anticipation.

In the dusty half-light of the upper room, breathless against the wall, I lifted my skirts then and pressed my hand against the slick muskiness within. The lips parted instantly, the swollen mouth sucking greedily at my fingers, gripping them with muscular ardour. When at last I lifted my hand to my mouth and licked it, remembering the arching fervour of his tongue, the perfect private taste of myself on his hot red mouth, I had to bite down hard upon my knuckles to prevent myself from crying out with the unbearable force of it.

Oh yes, I was alive with desire for him, every inch of me crawling with it. A whiff of the orange water he favoured, the touch of his silk handkerchief against my cheek, the remembrance of the golden fringe of his eyelashes or the delicate whorl of his ear, any of these and less could dry my mouth and melt the flesh between my legs to liquid honey. When he was with me, my sharp tongue softened to butter. I, who had always mocked the other girls for their foolish passions, could hardly breathe. The weaknesses in his face — the girlish pinkness of his damp lips, the irresolute cast of his chin — did nothing to cool my ardour. On the contrary, their vulnerability inflamed me. Whenever I was near him, I thought only of touching him, possessing him. There was something about the untarnished lustre of his skin that drew my fingertips towards him, determining their movements as the earth commands the sun. I had to clasp them in my lap to hold them steady.

The longing intoxicated me so I could barely look at him. We sat together in front of the empty fireplace, I in the bentwood chair, he upon a footstool at my feet. My mother's knitting needles clicked away the hour, although she kept her face turned resolutely towards the wall. For myself I watched his hands, which were narrow with long delicate fingers and nails like pink shells. They dangled impatiently between his legs, twisting themselves into complicated knots.

It never occurred to me to offer him my hand to hold. Slowly, as though I wished only to make myself more comfortable, I adjusted my skirt, exposing the white flesh of my calves. His hands twitched and jumped. I lifted my petticoats a little higher then. The fingers of his right hand stretched outwards, hesitating for only a moment. I could feel the heat of them although he did not touch me. My legs trembled. And then his fingertips reached out and caressed the tender cleft behind my knee.

The ungovernable swell of desire that surged in my belly knocked the breath from my lungs and I gasped, despite myself. Silently he brought his other hand up to cover my mouth. I kissed it, licked it, bit it. He groaned softly. Beneath my skirts his right hand moved deftly over my skin so that the fine hairs upon my thighs burst into tiny flowers of flame. I slid down towards him, my legs parted, and closed my eyes, inhaling the leather smell of his hand on my face. Every nerve in my body strained towards his touch as inexorably, miraculously, his hand moved upwards.

Unhooked by longing, my body arched towards him. When at last he reached in to touch me, there was nothing else left, nothing in the world but his fingers and the delirious incoherent frenzy of pure sensation they sent spiralling through me, as though I were an instrument vibrating with the exquisite hymns of the angels. Did that make him an angel? My toes clenched in my boots, and my belly held itself aloft in a moment of stillness as the flame quivered, perfectly bright. I held my breath. In the explosion I lost sight of myself. I was a million brilliant fragments, the darkness of my belly alive with stars. When at last I opened my eyes to look at him, my lashes shone with tears. He raised a finger to his lips and smiled.

Oh, that smile! When he smiled, his mouth curved higher on one side than the other, dimpling his right cheek. That dimple spoke to me more eloquently than his eyes, for all their untroubled blueness. And it was surely one hundred times more fluent than his speech, which was halting at the best of times and rutted with hiccupping and frequently incomprehensible exclamations. Even now, when so much time has passed and I must squint to recognise the girl in the bentwood chair, the recollection of that tiny indentation can unsettle me. Back in those days, it was as if, within its perfect crease, there was concealed a secret, a secret of unimaginable wonder that might be known only to me. For like everyone who falls for the first time under the spell of corporeal desire, I believed myself a pioneer, the discoverer of something never before identified, something perfectly extraordinary. I was godlike, omnipotent, an alchemist who had taken vulgar flesh and somehow, magically, rendered it gold.

Had you asked me then, I would have said I loved him. How else to explain how desperately, ferociously alive he made me feel? It was only afterwards, when the lust had cooled, that I saw that I was in love not with him at all but rather with myself, with what I became when he touched me. I had never thought myself handsome. My lips were too full, my nose insufficiently imperious, my eyes with their heavy brows set too wide apart. I was denied the porcelain complexion I secretly longed for. Instead, my face seemed always to have a sleepy, bruised look about it, as if I had just awoken. But when he touched me, I was beautiful. It was only afterwards, as he offered his compliments to my mother and prepared to return home, that I became a girl once more, commonplace, cumbersome, rooted by my clumsy boots to the cold stone floor.

He patronised my mother from the beginning, his address to her exaggeratedly courteous, a pastiche of itself. As for her, she bridled at every unctuous insincerity, her habitually suspicious face as eager as a girl's.

"I am but your humble servant, madam. There could be no greater privilege than to oblige you," he would say, bowing deeply before throwing himself into the bentwood chair and allowing my mother to loosen his boots. He did not trouble to look at her as he spoke. His tongue was already moistening his lips as he smiled his lazy smile at me, his eyes stroking my neck and the slope of my breasts.

I'm ashamed to say that at those moments I cared not a jot for her humiliation. He could have called my mother a whore or the Queen of Sheba, it would have been all the same to me. The pleasantries were a necessary chore to be endured, but my heart beat so loudly in my ears I hardly heard them. I thought only of the tug of my breath inside my chest, the shimmering anticipation between my thighs. As long as he touched me, as long as he smiled at me and caressed me, his fingers drawing a quivering music from my tightly strung nerves, my mother's dignity was not a matter of the least concern. As long as that tiny indentation in the corner of his mouth whispered its secrets to my heart and to my privities, he might have unsheathed his sword and sliced off my mother's head and I would have found reason to hold her responsible for his offence.

If I allowed my desire for him to obscure his failings, then so, too, did my mother, though her desires swelled not between her thighs but in the dark recesses of her purse. They were at least as powerful as my own, and they sent her into shivers of breathless anticipation. Once, just once, I mocked him for his creaking courtliness. Well, I was peeved. He always refused my mother's offers of food, declaring himself quite without appetite while gazing at me with a greed he did not trouble to disguise. On this occasion, however, he smiled at her—at her!—and set about the plate of victuals she put before him with gusto and extravagant praise.

"The finest mutton you have ever eaten?" I echoed scornfully. "Do you think us such knuckle-headed rustics that we would swallow such claptrap? Still, I suppose we should be grateful to have anything to swallow at all. A handful of empty compliments—shall we make a dinner of them, Mother, now the meat is gone?"

He said nothing, only raised a languid eyebrow and continued to eat, his chin greasy with meat. But my mother shot me a look of such brutal force that it might have brought an eagle down from the sky.

Afterwards, when he was gone, she struck me about the head and told me angrily that it was time I learned to hold my tongue. Was it beyond me to learn a little humility? The boy was the son of the wealthy Newcastle merchant Josiah Campling, whose own father had made a notable fortune in the shipping of coal to the port of London and who himself had expanded the family business to include the more lucrative trade in Negro slaves. This was not his heir, it was true, but there was enough money to ensure that he would be settled well. The family lived in a fine new house, some five miles from our village. It was close by there that I had met him for the first time, when he had dismounted from his horse to watch the bringing in of the first harvest. The day had grown hot, and when we stopped to take our midday meal beneath the shade of the oak trees, the dust from the threshed corn hung like a gauzy shawl against the blue sky. Laughing, he had called out that he was parched and surely

we could find it in our hearts to spare him something by way of re-
freshment. When one of the girls offered him a drink of apple cider,
he took it, his eyes fixed upon me as his lips caressed the neck of the
earthenware bottle. Determined not to blush, I held his gaze. When
at last he lowered the bottle, he smiled. I knew then that I was lost.
That evening, as dusk silted the hedgerows, he walked with me
along the white lane and kissed me. Around us cow parsley floated
on the deepening darkness like soap bubbles, exhaling its thick licen-
tious scent. He did not tell me his name. He did not need to. I knew
who he was. We all did. We knew about the collection of Chinese
porcelain that the maids were expected to dust daily. We knew their
livery, their carriage, that they owned a lake stocked with exotic
golden fish. We knew that all of the children would be expected to
make propitious marriages.

As for us, my mother was but the village midwife, respected and
respectable still then, her hand clasped by the curate after the Sunday service and a few words exchanged as to the weather, but as foreign to the Camplings as a tiger to a fly. My father had been curate
himself until he died, and my mother had always struggled to manage the expenses of a family on his meagre stipend. She had been
helped in this by the unwitting co-operation of my seven brothers
and sisters, who, perhaps more sympathetic to her difficulties than
I, had none of them chosen to burden her for long. I alone amongst
her children had persisted in life beyond my fifth birthday. I remember my father as an anxious face beneath the shadow of a round-
brimmed hat and a voice that clung to the cold stone of the church
like cobwebs. He was no sermoniser. Instead, he spoke of God with
wary circumspection, as an exhausted manservant might speak of
his capricious master. More than anything he feared enthusiasm and
religious fervour, reserving particular abhorrence for the onion-
munching papist peasants of France. When he died, succumbing to
a pleurisy when I was perhaps seven years old, and my mother told
me that God had taken him up into Heaven, I felt a little sorry for
him. Despite my mother's insistence that Heaven was a paradise of
eternal joy, I could not shift the picture I had of my father, his face

creased into its usual expression of weary fortitude as he coaxed flames from the Heavenly fires and sponged the angels' starched wings ready for them to put on in the morning.

After that it was only my mother and me. Ma Tally, as she was commonly known, was more than just a midwife. Renowned for the efficacy of her medicines, she was consulted frequently when conventional physick had failed to bring the patient to health. She mixed her recipes from herbs, roots, and waters that she gathered herself, mindful of the very best time and place to collect each one and knowing instinctively, without recourse to scales and measures, the precise amount of each ingredient required for each of her numerous draughts and ointments. So effective were many of them, that she might, if she had been a man, have become rich upon the profits of them.

As it was, however, she was like all midwives of her sex prevented by law from charging for her services and was forced to rely upon presents from her patrons, a precarious business since their generosity was inclined to run in inverse proportion to the fullness of their pockets. From time to time, there had been money enough to allow me to attend the village school. I learned my alphabet and the rudiments of reading. By the time I was grown, I had mastered the words in all of the school's small library of chapbooks and my handwriting was adequate, if not elegant. But there had never been anything to spare for a dowry. In her more cheerful moods, my mother gave me to believe it did not matter. My face, she observed consideringly, might not be handsome in a conventional manner, but it had a wantonness about it that might serve me well, if I used it carefully. Fine-looking girls, she asserted, might be divided into two categories: those that men liked to display in glass cabinets like figurines and those that they preferred to handle. I, my mother assured me, was one of the latter type. A man might do a great deal against his better judgement on the promise of a face like mine.

I believed her less because I thought her right than because I had little or no interest in the matter. I had thought nothing of marriage before I met him. What dreams I had were all of Newcastle, a magnificent town many miles from the petty limits of our small parish. I was perhaps sixteen, a woman who should perhaps already have been pushed out to make her own way in the world had my mother been ready to relinquish me. Headstrong and opinionated, I was nonetheless young for my years and had yet to learn the shaded skills of subtlety or prudence. I occupied the present moment entirely; my mood was jubilant or it was desolate, and there was little of anything in between. It was easy for a girl of that nature to pin such extremes of feeling upon the simplest of precepts and I did. With him I was joyfully, entirely alive; without him the days dragged, as bleak and dreary as winter fields. The simplicity of it entranced me.

It occurred to neither of us to speak of the future. He declared me enchanting, delightful, delicious, and I placed my finger upon his lips, wishing them only warm and insistent against mine. He brought me gifts of clothes, but it was my mother who clapped her hands with astonished glee when she saw them, a scarlet cloth petticoat with a broad silver galloon lace to it and a black scarf lined with blue velvet. She hung them in the press, and her brown face creased like an old apple. As for the sonnet he penned in my name, which I hastened to burn before I might find some clumsiness in it to offend me, she insisted upon folding it in a clean rag and placing it in the tin box on the dresser.

"We shall have him," she murmured to herself, the words ripe with triumph. "Oh, my girl, we shall have him, all right."

It was a gamble for her; I understand that now, and I do not blame her for it. She knew that the risks were considerable and that the price of failure was high. But she knew, too, that time was running out, for her as well as for me. They had already begun, you see, the whispers and the nudges that were to be her undoing. It was not unusual, when a woman grew old and sour and there were fears she might become a burden on the parish. My mother sought no charity, but the gravel in her urine made her snappish and disagreeable. Even her own carefully pounded preparations did little to ease her discomfort.

It should have surprised neither of us that fingers began to be pointed in the direction of our cottage. Already some of the village children had been strangely affected with unknown distempers. One, the son of the baker with whom my mother had exchanged angry curses, had vomited pins; another was frightened almost to death by nightly apparitions of cats which all of a sudden would vanish away.

It made no difference that the second was a child my mother barely knew and with whom she had no quarrel. There were rumours that she kept a lead casket beneath her bed in which she concealed the caul and afterbirth of infants she had delivered so that she might use them to revenge herself against those who crossed her. Osborn the grocer claimed that the balance of the scales in his shop was sent awry whenever she set foot in the store. It was not long before several of the village women who could afford the extra expense contrived to send for the man-midwife when it came to their lying-in. When one of the infants refused to suckle, it did not take long for the gossips to agree that it was Ma Tally who, in a fit of jealous temper, had stolen away its appetite.

Not everyone shunned her. Her remedy for dropsy—made to a secret recipe that claimed seventeen ingredients including elder, betony, and foxglove—remained sought after. But there was a wariness now, a faint sharp whiff of fear and suspicion that rose up off our neighbours like the smell of unwashed skin from a child sewn too long into its winter clothing. My mother dismissed such foolishness, declaring that words were only words and could not harm her, but she was too shrewd not to be afraid. And so it was that she narrowed her eyes and set about securing her future, hers and mine together. An opportunity like the Campling boy came along once in a lifetime and then only if you were very lucky. She had no intention of losing him.

The second harvest was brought in, despite heavy rains. His lips grew hungrier, his hands more insistent, and I strained towards him, crushing myself into his embrace. Beneath the canopy of her shoulders, my mother's knitting needles clicked faster, louder, the whistling of her breath almost a hum. Then, one blowy afternoon, he cleared his throat and suggested she find something with which to occupy herself in the other room. My mother turned, her expression unnaturally bland, her knitting needles held aloft.

"But what of my daughter's virtue?" she asked placidly. "Of course, sir, there is another way."

The ceremony took place less than a week later. He did as he was bid but made no attempt to conceal his amusement. My mother fixed him with a beady gaze as she spoke the necessary words. As a midwife she had baptised many infants too weak to cling on to life until the parson might be brought. Over the years she had perfected a tone of affecting piety that might have put many a loose-toothed Sunday sermoniser to shame. My mother's cousin, who acted as landlady at a half-respectable inn on the turnpike a few miles north of our village, had been persuaded to leave the business for a day or two and sat as witness in the window-seat, her wattles shaking appreciatively as she pressed her handkerchief against her mouth. I wore my scarlet petticoat and a bodice that my mother had cut down and re-trimmed so that it might show the pale swell of my breasts to best advantage. Even as my mother laid the broom upon the floor and we jumped backwards over it, our fingers woven together, my palms were damp and I could think only of his mouth upon my nipple, his hand between my thighs. Afterwards we drank the French champagne he had brought. As the wine took hold of me, trailing its golden fingers over my skin, I desired him so acutely I could barely stand. My mother begged him to say a few words, but he shook his head, declaring her charming country ritual observance enough. Instead, he bent to kiss me. His eyes were blurry with lust, and I saw myself reflected in them as I melted against him. Then, bowing to the two old women, he took my arm and, guiding me to the adjoining room, the bedchamber I shared with my mother, he closed the door.

I had once overheard an aunt mutter to my mother that it was worth enduring the indignity of marriage only so that one might enjoy the privileges of widowhood. When I recalled those words, as

I tore off my petticoats, I pitied her. She had never had a husband for whom she ached with unrestrained longing. She did not know what it meant to take a husband into her arms, so that she might close her eyes and lose herself, time and again, in the perfect sphere of her own private ecstasy.

My memories of that afternoon are sharp-edged, bright and deceptive as the shards of a broken looking-glass. I remember it grew dark, and he lit a rushlight which he set upon the floor, casting strange shadows upon the draperies that hung around the bed. I remember the salty reek of the burning fat, saved from the skimmings of the bacon pot, and the sweet scent of the bed-linen, which I myself had laundered and starched and set to stand in the pine chest with bunches of drying lavender. Most of all I remember the dismal twist in my belly as I saw him naked for the first time. As girls we had liked to hide by the river on summer evenings so that we might spy upon the farmers' boys as they stripped to swim. Their bodies had been hard and wiry, the round muscles moving like unripe fruit beneath the sunburnt skin of their arms. The apricot sunlight had dappled their brown shoulders and tangled itself in the dark triangles between their legs.

He by contrast was pale as milk, his flesh as pliable as a child's. The hair upon his groin was blond and sparse, and from it his yard rose thick and pink as a stalk of rhubarb. I closed my eyes hurriedly, pulling him beneath the covers, straining for the explosive rush of lust in my belly in which I had come to place my faith. The flesh of his buttocks was yielding and slightly sticky, like bread dough. I caressed them warily. I had never touched his skin before. Now he barely touched me. He was greedy and rough, and it was quickly over. Soon afterwards he returned home, where business associates of his father's were expected for supper.

We were married.

The night-lanthorn calls eleven of the clock, I should to bed. My hand aches & my stomach too (the calomel has not eased it & my turds were hard as gravel) but not my heart, not tonight, despite the lateness of the hour. My discourse sits before me virtually complete, the title page so creamy bright in the glow of the candle it seems that the light comes from within the pages themselves.

UPON THE MOTHER'S IMAGINATION: A TREATISE BY GRAYSON BLACK.

How it thrills me to think of it in the hands of fellow men of science, its meticulously chosen words pondered, deliberated, &—let it please God—praised. If modesty permits me, I must confess to believing the analysis of the physiological effects of imagination masterly. Of course the raised temperature of a woman's blood when in a violent passion must heat the fluid parts of the body. & of course, when those passions duly weaken, the salts contained within those fluids must be deposited within the body, precisely as salt marks the interior of a cooling cooking pot. Where else could they then collect but <u>in the unshed blood of the menses</u>? It is inevitable, then, that when the menstrual blood is ingested by the child for nourishment, the salts impress themselves upon the as yet unhardened muscle & bone of the foetus. & so the child bears the imprint of the mother's passions as sealing wax receives the imprint of a stamp.

There is a beauty in the simplicity of it that touches me even as I write. Does the thesis not share the characteristics of the greatest scientific discoveries: so lucid, so plain, that it seems impossible, once it is set down, that it was not always known?

Of course I cannot deny that there remain imperfections, though hardly of my making. My fieldwork in the parish has yielded little but frustration. The difficulties lay in the women themselves, who, despite my repeated imprecations, seem unable to remember the particulars of their activities from one moment to the next & are as careless of their hours as flies. For all that I tell myself that I must be patient, that the nature of such women can never be altered, I confess I grow discour-

aged. It was with some considerable envy that I watched on Friday last the anatomisation of a live dog at the College of Surgeons, while I seem unable to compel my women so much as to open their mouths. Surely the exchange of one for another, appreciated by so very many, would be regretted by none!

II

It was an abundant autumn. But as the fruits swelled and sweetened upon the hedgerows, our encounters grew brusquer and more tart. The uneasy distaste I felt for his white fleshiness had not so much diminished my appetites as honed them, ground them to a sharper point. I set about their gratification resolutely and without any pretence at affection. I no longer kissed him, indeed I barely touched him, but, far from displeasing him, my coolness served only to provoke his desire. He gripped my arms, trapping them painfully above my head as he thrust deep inside me, biting at my neck, goading me to cry out. When I wrapped my feet round his buttocks, spurring him with my heels, forcing him deeper, harder, his face twisted with an ardour that was close to hatred. Fierce though they were, our lusts were quickly sated. We grew adept at securing our own private pleasure. The heat could be relied upon to explode through my belly, although it cooled more rapidly on each occasion. But though I longed for him to be gone, I sulked as he dressed, heavy with a resentment I could neither alter nor understand. When I called him husband, maliciously, insistently, knowing that it agitated him, he laughed without smiling and the lump in his throat bobbed.

He laughed in the same manner when my mother requested an interview with his family. His father was a man of sanguine humour, he told her, with the red face and popping eyes characteristic of those with an abundance of blood. Even in the most favourable of circumstances, the old man was given to outbursts of strong temper, and the circumstances at the present time were far from favourable. A ship in which the merchant had had a substantial interest had recently been lost, attacked by Portuguese privateers before it had the chance to exchange its cargo of silver for Negro slaves. Given the profits that its investors had sought to realise from the venture, it had not been considered economic to insure either the ship or its consignment. This unwelcome intelligence had been communicated in a letter delivered to the breakfast table, and the old man's roar had echoed so violently through the house that the Chinese vases had chimed together like bells.

Since then the slightest provocation was likely to produce in the merchant an attack of splenetic fury that had the veins upon his forehead standing out in purple ropes. The household tiptoed around him, fearful he would find his dish of coffee too hot or his coat inadequately brushed. One of his sisters had waited more than a week before she dared approach him for a new gown, and then his howl of outrage had been enough to bring the last of the rose petals tumbling from the bushes beyond the window. It was hardly a judicious time for a son, even a son as well loved as he, to present to him as a prospect a girl with no family nor fortune of any kind to recommend her.

It was my mother who saw the signs first. Unused to illness, I had thought myself struck down by a cold which filled my head with fog and left my limbs heavy and disobliging. I longed to sleep. When he lay heavily upon me, biting at my breasts, I cried out in real pain. My distress inflamed him. He bit harder, burying his nails in the soft flesh of my arms, forcing himself with painful abruptness between my legs. I said nothing as he dressed but hunched my back against him and closed my eyes, sunk in soreness and despondency. I did not answer him when he bid me good night. Although I had a powerful need to urinate, I could barely summon the strength to drag myself from the bed. When at last I squatted on the pot, the quilt wrapped clumsily round my shoulders, I had to drop my head between my knees, so certain was I that I should faint.

My mother discovered me in that position some minutes later. She considered me for a moment, her head on one side, her mouth puckered. Then she left the room. I heard the clank of the kettle over the fire. When she returned, she carried a cup of steaming liquid which she held out to me.

"Drink this, Eliza," she instructed. "It will revive you."

I took the cup. The liquid was dark green with the harsh aroma of sage. The queasiness roiled in my stomach and I swayed, slopping the hot tea over my fingers.

"Hold it still, you clumsy baggage! You will spill it."

Snatching the cup from me, my mother held it to my lips and ordered me to drink.

"This will help with the sickness. It will also stay the child." Her face softened and she stroked my arm a little, as though it was a cat. "You have done well, my dear. This will bring this boy out like a blister."

It shocked him, you could tell, although he turned the twist in his knees into a swagger as he steadied himself against the back of the bentwood chair.

"A child? But—"

The astonishment in his voice was undeniable. I felt the coarse rub of irritation against my chest. What did he expect to have sired, a calf? My mother gripped my hand painfully, warning me to remain silent. I bit my tongue, but I stared at him beadily, daring him to show discomposure. He himself kept his gaze on the floor. His cheeks were the bluish white of skim milk. For a moment I thought he would swoon, and the sharp tang of dislike flooded my mouth, souring my saliva.

"I—but—I never—"

"You never what, exactly?" I demanded, aiming at haughtiness, but my voice came out reedy and strained. He looked at me for a moment, blinking rapidly, his lips trembling, his hand groping at his waist for the hilt of his sword. It was a moment before he understood that he did not wear it, that it sprawled instead upon the floor, where he had discarded it shortly after his arrival. His fingers flexed as he regarded it. Then, stiff-backed, he turned to my mother and jutted out his chin.

"Given your daughter's proclivities, how can I be sure that the child is mine?" he drawled.

My mother clenched my hand so hard it was a miracle that the bones did not break.

"How do you dare speak so before your own wife?" she hissed. "I had thought you a gentleman, sir. You have shamed my daughter enough by your refusal to acknowledge your vows to her before your family. Would you tarnish her virtue further by doubting her fidelity?"

The boy raised one eyebrow. I noticed then how like glass marbles his eyes were, protruding a little too far from their sockets. I had a sudden powerful urge to shake him with all my strength until they fell from his head and rolled upon the floor. The thought of his plump fingers palpating my flesh, insinuating themselves between my legs—the goose-flesh rose upon my chest and neck, twisting the skin away from its bones. Despite the warmth of the day, I shivered.

"My wife?" he echoed mockingly. "My wife? I fear you are mistaken, madam. I have no wife. I have taken no vows. None, that is, that might be regarded as such by any civilised person. Or by the law."

"What—?"

"Quiet," Ma Tally barked at me, jerking my hand. She glared at the boy, her eyes hooked into his face. "If anyone is mistaken here, sir, it is your good self. You see, I was there. I officiated at the ceremony. There was also a witness, if you care to recall."

"You claim that superstitious rustic gibberish to be a binding contract of marriage!" he sneered. "Jumping over a broom? Really! I hate to disappoint you, madam, but there is not a magistrate in the land that would consider me legally wed. Jumping over a broom, I ask you!"

A spike of bile rose at the back of my throat. Dizzily I tugged at my hand, certain I would vomit, but my mother only tightened her grip. The tip of her nose sharpened to a white point.

"Ah, but that is where you are wrong, sir," she said smoothly. "You see, my husband was a curate before he died, so I know a bit of something about these things. Maybe a magistrate might have his niggles with what we done in the legal way but not the Church, not for a minute. The Church considers you married before God, good as though you made your promises in St. Bede's itself. You ask Reverend Salt if you doubt me. He'll tell you just the same. Cottage or cathedral, it don't matter to the Archbishop—he don't see a jot of difference. You're married, you are, no question about it. The two of you's bound together for life now, for better or worse. Married, fair and square."

The boy opened his mouth to object, but Ma Tally knew when to press her advantage. On and on she went, until I was so chill and giddy that I heard only the roaring in my own ears.

The boy blinked and bit his lip. His thrust chin began to quiver. Then, at last, to my shame and disgust, he burst into noisy sobs. It was hard to distinguish his words, but the sense was unmistakable. He had made a mistake. It had been only a bit of amusement. He had never intended matters to run so out of control. I was a harlot, a sixpenny whore who was out for her own gratification. He had given me presents, had he not? He had honoured his obligations, had behaved like a gentleman. It was I who had lured him on, encouraged him, tricked him. This child, well, he doubted it even existed. He had always made it perfectly clear that there was not the slightest possibility of marriage. His father would never in a thousand years entertain the prospect of a union with a girl of my kind. He would see both of us dead first. And if he so much as attempted to defy his father's wishes, the old man would not hesitate to cut him off without a penny. He would be thrown out into the streets, forbidden to see his mother and sisters. He would lose everything.

As for me, I could think of nothing but my own nausea. I saw the expression upon my mother's face, I understood its meaning, but I gave only the scantiest consideration to the scandal that would certainly follow, to my own ruin. I could think only of the sickness, the sickness and the disgust, coiling and curdling in my stomach. I could hardly bring myself to look at him, at his weak sticky face and his streaming nose, which he wiped on the back of his cuff like a child. If he had tried to touch me, I think I would have struck him.

He had addressed not a single word to me since the interview had begun.

I clenched my eyes tight shut, willing him gone. Inside me the child twisted like a worm, its marble eyes peering into my private darkness, its hooked claws clutching and squeezing at my stomach as, piece by tiny piece, it devoured me. I would have torn into my own abdomen and ripped it out with my fingernails, there and then, I would have flung its tiny bloody corpse in his face and exulted in his horrified revulsion, I would have stood over him as he gagged and kicked my boot into the soft parts of his stomach, if I had only had the strength. But it was too late. The worm had no intention of relinquishing its grip. It would see me dead first. Already it had sucked the animal spirits from me like the juice from a plum so that I was shrivelled to nothing, nothing but a stone wrapped in dried-up skin. I wanted to die.

My mother, on the other hand, was aflame with righteous fury. She danced about the room as though the floor beneath her feet was a grate of hot coals. The boy watched with growing horror as she took his letter from the tin on the dresser, gathered together her wrap, her cloak, her pattens, and thrust his coat and hat into his arms. He would not tolerate it, he stammered desperately, blowing his nose with attempted authority and almost dropping his hat. He would brook no interference in his affairs. No, indeed not. It would behove Ma Tally to remember her position. He demanded she respect his wishes. Of course his father would never condescend to see her, he sputtered. She was a fool if she thought he would permit her to place so much as a toe across his threshold.

My mother said nothing. Instead, she smoothed her hair in front of our scrap of glass and placed her bonnet upon her head, pulling its strings together with a smart tug. Then, picking up his discarded sword, she spun round to face him so abruptly that its jewelled hilt grazed against his nose. His voice wobbled as he snatched it from her. If she was to be granted an interview, what then? His father was a malevolent, rancorous old man. Surely she could not be such a fool to expect a sympathetic hearing. The merchant would have

mother and daughter thrown in the pillory for lewdness and insolence, horse-whipped at the cart's tail. He would not rest until they
were drummed out of the parish in disgrace. Was Ma Tally so comfortably settled that she could afford to be stripped of her right to
parish relief in her dotage? Or did she truly believe that the village
would move to defend her against the old man's wrath? If she did,
she was even more soft in the head than she appeared. For he knew
without doubt that they would be only too happy to be rid of her.
Did she not know that there were many out there who had already
declared her a witch?

Ma Tally fixed him with a look then that might have shattered
stone. His mouth opened and closed, but no words came. Afterwards I wondered if this speechlessness was a curse she set upon
him, but I think it unlikely. My mother was a wise bird and would
have known it quite unnecessary. He was cursed enough already
without her efforts, cursed with vanity and stupidity and the simple-
minded greed that comes with a lifetime of having the idlest of your
fancies indulged.

"I shall be back in due time," she barked at me over the sag of
his shoulder as she pushed him out into the darkening afternoon.
"When things are settled."

I said nothing but stared miserably at the floor. She slammed the
door. The faint tang of orange water quivered in the air, wistful as
dust in a slice of sunlight. I breathed it in. Everything was still. Then
the blackness rushed back in.

Seizing a bowl from the kitchen table, I vomited.

My mother did not return that night. I did not think to worry about
where she might be. I seemed barely capable of thought at all. I lay
alone upon our bed, without troubling to undress. I did not weep.
My heart was leaden, the hundreds of words I had failed to speak
heaped heavily upon my chest, but my skin prickled and twitched
and my fingers were taut with restlessness. To quiet them, I wrung
the rough blanket between my hands until my palms ached. The
rawness comforted me.

When I woke, a bright rent of light slit the bed-hangings. I blinked, my eyes still bleary with slumber, and raised myself onto one elbow. I wore a nightgown I had owned as a little girl, white cotton trimmed with lace, presented to my mother at the christening of one of her charges by a grateful godparent. Although the gown had long since been worn into rags, I felt no surprise to be wearing it. The fabric was soft as a kiss, and I shivered, my belly flushed with sleep-warm desire.

I pushed back the curtains. The room was filled with light. He was not there. I felt a sharp tug of apprehension, even as I chided myself for expecting him. He never came before dinner. Instead, my mother stood at the window, her back to me, pouring water into the cracked yellow bowl. She wore a muslin cap I did not recognise, its lappets loose over her ears. I called out to her. She turned round. The cap was edged with a frill of such startling whiteness I had to shade my eyes. When I looked again, I saw that it was not my mother at all. Instead, it was his golden curls that writhed beneath the cap, coiling sinuously round his shadowed face. His face and at the same time not his but something far more brutish, sharp-featured with the textured coarseness of thick dark fur. I saw the gleam of teeth as he lifted the ewer high above his head and poured its contents upon the floor. Not water, now, but blood, a terrible unstoppable stream of blood, lumpy with large black fibrous clumps that fell in splatters upon the flagged floor.

I struggled to sit up, my heart pounding, the scream caught in my throat like a fish bone. It was still dark. My bodice squeezed my chest until I could hardly breathe. I reached round to pull loose the lacing, my hand shaking. The skin between my shoulder blades was slippery with sweat. Gobbets of blood flashed and slithered in the shadowed folds of the bed drapes. I ground my fists into my own eyes until the redness blurred. But I knew what I had seen. I could not pretend to misunderstand it. I had made a covenant with the Devil, and the Devil, who must always betray those that deal with him, had staked his claim upon me. I might escape him for as long as I lived upon this Earth, but he had come to tell me, without equivocation, that my soul belonged to him. I had sinned against God and against goodness, and no number of petitions for forgiveness could restore me to grace. I was damned, and I would burn for eternity in the sulphurous flames of Hell.

I write these words calmly now, my quill quite steady. I am older now and have seen too much of the world to be so sure of either the truthfulness of dreams or the Old Testament apoplexies of a pitiless and vengeful God. It is harder, surely, to forgive yourself for your own follies and failures than it must be for Him, who has so many cases to consider. But then I was young and ignorant and awash with emotions so violent I might, I think, be forgiven for imagining them real. I considered myself worldly, after all. I had more education than many of my acquaintance and could read tolerably well and even write a little. I had a wide knowledge of the plants and herbs to be found in our district. And I had known a man, had felt in my stomach and the soles of my feet the pyrotechnic thrill of ecstasy. It is not then surprising, perhaps, that I believed my instincts were to be trusted.

What armour did I have then against fear? Only the sooty flame of a rushlight, which I huddled over until a hard white dawn set about scouring the darkness from the hem of the sky, forcing its bleached fingers through the last of the leaves beyond my window.

What an evening! Indeed, I hardly care that, despite my express in-
struction, that damned drab of a girl has once again failed to light my
fire. Who cares that this room is colder than a tomb! Tonight I can even
overlook the full inch of dust upon the chimney-piece, although she
shall surely find me in less indulgent temper on the morrow. Not only
is she the idlest creature on God's Earth, but she flaunts herself before
the fat apprentice like a twopenny whore. But enough, enough. After
an evening of such eminence, even the vexations of that foolish strum-
pet shall not tarnish my high spirits.

The Royal Society, how the words thrill upon my pen. The Presi-
dent of the Society himself, the distinguished Mr. Sloane, was present
& all the most prominent men of science, gathered together in a room
hardly larger than a parlour. What was more, Mr. Johanssen, at whose
invitation I attended, introduced me to several illustrious Fellows,
amongst them Mr. Halley, the astronomist, who described to me a case,
personally witnessed, of an animal resembling a whelp delivered by the
anus of a male greyhound. He promised to send me his account of it,
or at least to have the Secretary at the Society do so as it is already pub-
lished in the <u>Transactions.</u> *In my turn I told him of the Dog-headed*
race of savages known as the Tartars whose physiognomy results from
the godless practice of fornication <u>more canino.</u> *He was most interested*
& encouraged me to send to him the latest draft of my thesis. Imagine
if he were to endorse it, Mr. Halley himself, & propose it for presenta-
tion at the Society! I should like to see Simpson's face then, & the faces
of all those stationers who would reduce the art of science to nought
but shock & sensation. The thought of it is intoxicating.

As for the debate itself, it was only through the exercise of strenu-
ous self-discipline that I obeyed Mr. Johanssen's stricture that guests
must remain silent during the proceedings. For, to my delight, the thrust
of that night's discussions turned upon that matter essential to my
work: if indeed the body is, as Descartes would have it, mechanical in
its structure & workings, with all God-created beings obeying the rules
of immutable rules of mathematics, who or what drives the machine?

23

The debate that followed was most vigorous. There were those who asserted animation as a matter for God alone, & others who argued for a nerve-juice issued from the brain which moved the heart, but it was the eminent Mr. Tabor who in my view put forward the most powerful argument. His doctrine, recently published, contrives an ingenious blend of a soul & an external & divine principle that guides motion, an arrangement that combines gravitation, subtle matter, & the intervention of the Almighty to direct the heart to throw blood to the ends of the arteries & thereby drive circulation.

When he was finished speaking, there was violent applause for some ten seconds before the debate broke out once more with redoubled force. I was amongst those who rose to their feet & cannot describe to you the powerful feelings it roused in my breast to stand as an equal amongst these men & imagine myself the subject of such applause. I fear I paid little heed to the remaining experiments of the evening, so giddy was I with all that had already taken place & the certainty that one day I shall stand before them & they shall stamp & huzzah & I shall know that the work I was placed upon this Earth to do has indeed been satisfactorily done.

I only wish I could say the same for that good-for-nothing harlot of a maid. I have swallowed a purge but fear it comes too late. My stomach tortures me & the cold sets my teeth to chattering so violently I fear I shall take a chill. How dare she make me ill with her carelessness, when she has been told so many times of the delicacy of my constitution & of the grave demands placed upon me by the rigours of my work. When I rebuke her, she pouts those lips & smirks & thrusts her hips at me in her harlot way, but I shall not be put off so. I have half a mind to go to her now, while she sleeps, so that I might acquaint her with the full extent of my displeasure. Let her see how she likes it, to stand before me on such a night in nought but her thin nightgown. A whipping & a night in the coal cellar would surely serve to improve her memory & subdue her unruly spirit.

III

Naturally I blamed my mother. She was all that was left. Besides, it is easiest to strike out at those who make no effort to defend themselves. Their very passivity drives one to greater fury, to more violent assault. Our Lord Jesus understood this. Consider His instruction that, struck by our enemies, we should turn the other cheek. Only a fool would mistake this for the meek acceptance of injustice. On the contrary, turning the other cheek is a considered act of aggression. It is distressingly, brilliantly cruel. For if, despite the frenzy of your beatings, your victim refuses to express his pain, what then must become of your own, bloating and blackening inside you? It must tear open the very crown of your skull.

When at last Ma Tally returned, a little after dinner time the next day, her skirt was ruffled with dust and she looked weary, her face collapsed somehow, as though the bones that buttressed it had rotted and crumbled beneath the wrinkled skin. She did not greet me. Without taking off her cloak, she sank into the chair by the empty fireplace and closed her eyes. In the endless hours of the night, I had thought myself quite without hope. But some faint desperate flickers of optimism must have persisted in me, for it was only when I saw my mother's face and the leaden way in which she dragged her feet across the floor, that those last feeble glimmers were snuffed out. My heart clenched like a fist and my nose prickled, but I did not cry.

Instead, I was flooded with a bitter, venomous anger. I wanted to hurl my stool at her, to bite her, kick her, smash my fist into her nose. I wanted to shake her by her shoulders until the few teeth she had left were jolted from her gums. Everything in her posture incited me to violence. But I did not move. I peered grimly at her from under my cap, my head resolutely lowered, and I said nothing. Even as the tide of rage swelled inside me, a part of me congratulated myself on my control. Let her be the first to break the silence. Demands for news would serve only to dignify her condition and implicate me in her failure. I had no intention of doing either. It was she, after all, who had contrived this devilish venture, she who had put up my virtue for a wager. My reputation had been all my fortune. Now, with a single throw of the dice, it was gone. My life was over. I would hate my mother forever.

Ma Tally sighed, sinking lower in the chair. Her chin sagged onto her chest. I clenched my teeth together. Let her say it. Let her say: *I have failed you. I have ruined us both.*

"Sage tea," she whispered, without opening her eyes. "Brew me some sage tea, girl. I have had a long walk and no breakfast."

I dragged myself over to the grate, pushing the black kettle over the flames with such force that the iron bracket struck the chimney. Ma Tally flinched, but she said nothing. We watched in silence as the water grew hot and the stump of a spout let out a feathery shriek of steam.

"So?" The word belched from me before I could swallow it.

"So," echoed my mother, staring at the gnarled roots of her hands in her lap.

I laughed then, a high choke in the back of my throat, as I sloshed boiling water into the teapot, scalding my fingers.

"Don't bother to tell me," I spat, shaking my hand furiously. "I have no interest in the pitiful future you have brokered me. Why should I concern myself with such foolishness, now that I am ruined?"

My mother did not reply. Her face was impassive as she watched me clatter a single cup from the shelf. The tea was weak and fragments of dried sage leaf floated on its surface. I slopped the cup at her feet and turned away to the fire. My face burned and unshed tears clumped behind my nose. I would not give her the satisfaction of seeing me cry. Slowly, as though the movement pained her, she reached down to pick up her cup. I heard her suck at the hot liquid. Her slurping disgusted me.

"You go to London on the stage, Market Day next," she said quietly.

I wheeled round.

"That's right, child," she said, her face bent over her cup. "London. There's a position for you there. With an apothecary. A respectable man."

"But—"

"They'll know what needs doing. All the necessary expenses have been agreed and a little extra to ease your passage. We settled on a year, longer if they like you. That way there'll be no arousing suspicion. Three pound a year and a new gown too, which isn't bad, considering."

Ma Tally raised her head to look at me. Her smile was lopsided, and her little eyes were unusually bright. I put it down to the mention of money. She was a greedy little magpie, my mother, and never happier than when presented with something shiny. Abruptly I felt the dizziness return. I grasped the chimney-breast to steady myself and rested my forehead against the cool stone.

"And how much did he pay you, Mother?" I whispered. "That you would sell me?"

Ma Tally pretended not to hear me.

"As for that boy, he is sent to Newcastle this morning." She scowled at the floor. "He's to sail immediately for the colonies. We will pray God his ship may sink and the fishes make a fine dinner of him."

Shakily I drew myself up to glare at her.

"I shan't have you speak that way of my husband," I said, but my lips were white and stiff and formed the words only with difficulty.

"There is no husband, not any more. In London you will be a widow, your husband lost at sea. It's best. There you'll be free to begin again. Your pay will do for a portion. They say London husbands don't come cheap."

Her voice wavered then, and she buried her face in her cup.

"He would've had you sent by the waggon, the tight-fisted scoundrel, but I wasn't having none of it," she mumbled into her tea. "I will not be bullied by such a dog, for all his rich man's bluster."

"I am a married woman," I said more desperately. "My husband lives, whatever you say. You can't sell me like a Negro."

Ma Tally slammed her cup down.

"Don't tell me what I can and cannot do, girl. You will go to London and forget what's been, and you will be thankful for your good fortune. There's not many gets a second chance."

And so it was that I found myself cast off, abandoned not only by my erstwhile husband but by my own mother too. She might have helped me herself, if she had wished to. She had long since been sought out by women of the parish who found themselves inconvenienced and had secured something of a reputation for her belly-ache teas. But she refused. She even had the effrontery to chide me for my foolishness. For all that the situation had not come out in the way that we had wished it, there was profit to be made from it and profit I would, if it was the last thing she made me do. She protested that she had no wish to be parted from me but that there was nothing to be gained by keeping me where I was and much to be lost. In London I might find myself a better future, better perhaps even than the one I had already glimpsed.

For a while I was stupid enough to muse upon her words, to imagine that she might care for me as a mother should, that she did indeed have my best interests at heart. For a few days we were gentler with each other. She made me savoury broths to ease my nausea and rubbed my shoulders to loosen them. She bound a hare's foot to a thong of leather so that I might wear it about my neck for good luck. For my part I accepted her kindnesses with something close to gratitude. I no longer blamed her quite so completely for my misfortunes. I remembered the passion with which she had defended me, and I felt a warm twist of affection for it. It occurred to me that I might even miss her a little when it came time for me to go. At night, when I found her hand upon my shoulder as she slept, I did not throw it off.

And then I found them. I hadn't been searching, not specifically. Or not for that. When I lifted the loose floorboard and felt to the back of the damp press, I had no intention of taking anything that was not mine. I was simply curious and I was running out of time. My life was to take a new course in an unknown city. Most people never came back. If I was never to see the cottage again, I wanted to be sure I took its secrets with me. I knew my mother's business. Women came to the cottage with child; they left alone. I felt a thrill of awful anticipation as I fumbled in the loose brickwork in the chimney. My fingers touched something stiff and slightly greasy above the ledge where we set the bacon to smoke. It was a package, wrapped in a piece of oilcloth. It occurred to me then that I could leave it, dust my hands off on my apron, and put it out of my mind.

Except that I couldn't. My hand trembled as I reached it, pulled it down, and unwrapped it. And there they were. Rolled up like a slab of meat, like a corpse in a winding-sheet, four shiny golden guineas. *Profit we would.* How she must have cackled to herself as she watched me softening towards her. How she must have longed me gone, so that she could lay them out in a row upon the bed and trace the shiny implacable shape of them with the tip of one avaricious finger. A victory, then, in the end. Her only child's future traded to soften her own.

For my remaining nights at the cottage, I slept wrapped in a blanket on the floor and woke with my limbs stiff and cold. I refused to answer her, to acknowledge her. I could barely stand so much as to look at her. The creak of her leather stays or the trace of her old-woman smell was enough to send me into a blind, black fury.

When the time came for me to leave the cottage and the waggoner hoisted my box into the cart that would take me to the staging inn, I looked directly ahead, my eyes fixed upon the flat white sky. My mother hesitated as though she intended to speak. Then she turned and went back into the cottage, closing the door quietly behind her. Sharply, I urged the waggoner to hurry. He shrugged indolently, scratching his balls and hawking with slow deliberation into the ditch before finally hauling his bulk up beside me. He nudged me then and I frowned. Laughing, he slapped the reins against the horse's withers, and with a jolt we moved off.

I had sewn the guineas into the lining of my padded petticoat, along with my hare's foot for good luck. I liked to imagine the soft paw patting each one in turn like children, keeping them steady. All the same, the coins dragged at the fabric so that my skirts caught against the splintery wooden bench of the waggon. If I moved suddenly, I could feel them shifting, their muffled edges bumping the side of the cart. Inside the oilcloth I had left four round flat stones. It had taken me a full afternoon to find four of precisely the right shape and thickness, and I had polished each one upon an old rag to bring it to something close to a shine before replacing the bundle in its hiding place in the chimney. I felt a sour shiver of satisfaction in my bowels when I pictured how her face would fall when she discovered the treasure gone, her greedy smile shrivelling faster than a slug sprinkled with salt.

I smiled grimly to myself to think of it, perhaps I even laughed, for the waggoner gave me a sly sideways glance and shifted his thigh so that it touched against mine. Disdainfully, I moved away, turning my shoulders from him, but the smile still twitched grimly at my lips. I was determined never to see Ma Tally again, but I wished her to remember, long after she had stamped out the last embers of my existence, that I was the kind of person who was not to be trifled with.

To Mr. Grayson Black
Apothecary at the sign of the Unicorn in Swan-street

Grayson, my dear fellow,

I beg you to accept my apologies for my tardiness in responding to you with regard to your manuscript. Business has proved uncommon brisk these past months & there has been little time for the mountain of manuscripts that await my attention.

I have now had the opportunity to consider yours, perhaps the weightiest of the lot, & I am obliged to confess that I can see no market for it at present. While the subject is of considerable interest to many of my customers, those volumes that have proved themselves most in demand are principally illustrated compendia of examples of the many strange creatures born of woman around the globe. I have had particular success with Swammerdam's <u>Uteri muliebris fabrica</u>—amongst his many fascinating examples, I would cite in particular the tale of the pregnant woman who took care to wash herself after being greatly frightened by a Negro so that the ill effects of her imagination might be reversed, only to discover her child born black in those places she was unable to reach.

Where then are the similarly intriguing cases in your account? An idiot girl & a child born with uncommonly large moles as a result of her mother's affection for currants hardly satisfy. I would add here that Swammerdam's book contains many fine illustrations, while your volume is more notable for the very considerable number of pages you commend to scientific discourse of a frequently opaque nature. I fear my customers have not the inclination to read so great a quantity of words—nor I the ink for them neither!

I regret that I cannot help you further. As an old acquaintance, I would only enquire whether you had considered finding a patron, perhaps a physician or other educated man of science, to assist you in the promotion of your efforts? You might find both the standing & the counsel of such a man of considerable value.

Please extend my warmest regards to Mrs. Black. I enclose the page you requested & remain, sir, your loyal friend & servant,

SEPTIMUS GAULE   2nd day of July 1718

Extract of a letter, written from Paris,
containing an Account of a Monstrous Birth
& Published in the PHILOSOPHICAL
TRANSACTIONS OF THE ROYAL
SOCIETY in the year of our Lord
Sixteen hundred & sixty-six

In the house of M. Bourdelots was showed a
monster in the form of an ape, having all over its
shoulders, almost to his middle, a mass of flesh,
that came from the hinder part of its head, &
hung down in the form of a little cloak. The
report is that the woman that brought it forth
had seen on stage an ape so clothed: the most
remarkable thing was, that the said mass of flesh
was divided in four parts, correspondent to the
coat the ape did carry. The woman, upon enquiry,
was found to have gone five months with Child,
before she had met with the accident of that
unhappy fight. Many questions were on this occasion agitated: viz. about the Power of Imagination
& whether this creature was endowed with a
human soul; & if not, what became of the soul of
the embryo, that was five months old.

IV

I had never travelled in a coach before, and my first experience of it was uncomfortable enough for me to wish never to have to do so again.

It rained incessantly for the nine days it took us to drive to London, sheets of molten clouds that thundered against the roof of the carriage and turned the road to swamp. The horses made slow progress. On more than one occasion, we lost the road altogether and had to traverse some miles out of our way to rejoin it. Frequently we were required to stop so that the wheels might be dug out from the mud. The coach moaned and buckled as though every rut and puddle in the path were an agony to it. I had thought myself fortunate to have secured a seat facing forwards for the length of the journey, but our trunks, tumbled any which way in an iron basket suspended on bars upon the rear of the coach, struck against the wall behind my head with a barrage of such ferocious blows that I was certain they must burst clean through it.

The ceaseless bangings were not the only inconvenience to the passengers inside. The weather required us to keep the tin windows raised so that the rain might not come pouring in. In the closed space, the air quickly became stale and brackish with the powerful smell of bodies and wet wool. The only illumination came from a pattern of holes punched in the metal and a thin tear of light where the plate of the window did not quite fit in its frame. The draught from this gap spread a veil of tiny droplets across our laps, but it conceded only the most grudging suggestion of daylight. The darkness was intensified by the dull black leather that covered the interior of the coach, studded with grimy broad-headed nails which were, I supposed, intended by way of ornament and instead gave it a faintly menacing atmosphere. It would not have been possible, had

I cared to, for me to make out any more than the vaguest features of my fellow passengers.

I did not care to. In the inn, as we took breakfast prior to departure, I noticed one woman, a buxom madam with a yellowed cap and a scarlet complexion, who picked at her teeth with her fork and clucked disapprovingly at everything her husband had cause to say. The chariot's occupants were mostly men in their middle years travelling alone, and when it came time for us to take up our seats, I took care to position myself beside her. She enquired my name that first morning but, finding me to be uncongenial company, promptly forgot it and occupied herself instead with the joint pleasures of a bag of sugary pastries and incessant admonition.

Her husband, a man even wider than she, seemed to take offence at neither the crumbs nor the criticisms. Indeed, on the few occasions that a remark of his passed uncensured, he took care to repeat it so that she might have a second opportunity to find something about it that displeased her. Otherwise, the conversation proceeded as it always must amongst men, with long silences punctuated with grunts and curses or, more frequently, gusts of flatulence and immoderate laughter. I curled myself into my corner and wished only to be left unmolested. At night, when we disembarked to take supper and lodgings in yet another roadside inn, I declined to accompany the others into the parlour.

Instead, I took myself directly to bed, requesting my meal be brought to my room on a tray, although I seldom ate it. The worm inside me was fattening itself, tightening its grip on my guts and sickening me even as the worms of my childhood had sickened me. My appetite failed. I had a dry cough and a poor colour, and my eyes were hollow and bruised with dark shadows. Even the treacly black rage that had sustained me in the first miles of the journey had begun to ebb away, leaving only a sooty scum that smeared the inside of my chest and tasted bitter on my tongue. I felt empty, bereft, my dress hanging from my thin shoulders like a child's, poorly altered. I refused to think of my mother, but when in the long, dreary hours my head fell forwards in a chilled half-sleep, it was the image of the door of our cottage quietly closing that jerked me back into consciousness. In the seat opposite to mine, a man sucked incessantly on a long clay pipe. The smoke caught in my throat and stung my eyes until they watered.

The jolting movement and stuffy interior of the coach compounded my already uncertain stomach and rendered me weak with nausea. Each morning, when I was roused at dawn to take my place once more in the carriage, I vomited so violently that I was sure I must turn myself inside out. But, for all the miseries of the journey, I longed for it never to end. I had met only one person who had been as far as London in all my life, a baker's apprentice, who, his face pale with flour, swore an oath that he would never return. He had remained there only a month, and in that month, he claimed, he had been daily taunted, admonished, jostled, pissed upon, and frequently stripped of his money. There had been not an inch of space to think, not even a sip of clear, clean air to breathe. The clamour of the streets had been insufferable, the choking fogs that pervaded them foul with disease, the famous river no more than a stinking brown ditch of rotting shit. London itself was a vast and fiendish carnival, an endless Hell stinking of tainted meat and swarming with footpads, swindlers, and whores. A place of the damned, he had muttered grimly. There was no kindness to be found there, no trace of sympathy for one's fellow man. One might wander forever as one street twisted into another, on and on, pressed on all sides by the rush of people until one fell, exhausted, to the ground. And when you did, no one would think to stretch out a hand to help you. You would be trampled instead beneath the heedless feet and irritated curses of a thousand strangers.

London. The very name had the whiff of brimstone about it. A city the size of twenty Newcastles? It was unimaginable, horrible. As the days passed and the miles grudgingly gave themselves up beneath our wheels, the airless, lightless clamour of the coach in which I endured from hour to hour took on the awful tension of a purgatory from which, however much I prostrated myself and begged forgiveness for my sins, there might be no deliverance. My fate was already decided. All too soon I would be cast out into London's fiery and pitiless abyss.

There would be nobody there who would wish to deliver me. I harboured no false hopes of sympathy from the apothecary and his family. It was plain that they would despise me and mistreat me cruelly because, quite aside from the satisfaction it affords a man of means to abuse a servant, it would, as associates of the merchant, surely profit them to do so. I could hardly expect kindness from a master who, paid to unyoke me from my troubles, knew the full extent of my shame. My sins would not be forgiven. God Himself would smile with fatherly approval upon the resourcefulness of his chastisements and buttress his thrashing arm. But he would rid me of the worm, thank God. He would give me something that would flush it out as a clyster purges a stubborn turd from the bowel, and, like a turd, it would be tipped away, buried in one of the stinking cesspits that city houses grew upon. It cheered me a little to think upon it, the white worm in the rank darkness of a foul cellar, sucking desperately, hopelessly for air as it drowned, abandoned in a filthy mess of shit.

Early on the eighth day, I was startled to be roused from a thin doze by the brisk shouts of ostlers. The coach had come to a stop, and I saw when I opened my eyes that I was its only remaining occupant. The stillness of the carriage was startling. It was no longer raining. The door stood open, and the air had the green river taste of freshly washed skies. Tentatively, I allowed my limbs to relax.

"We are arrived at Hampstead Hill."

I looked up to see the fat woman's husband standing in the doorway of the chariot. He had a kind face, brick-red, with deep grooves into which a smile might be conveniently slotted.

"You are indisposed, I know, but the waters here are well-known for their medicinal properties. Perhaps you might feel a little stronger if you took some."

He proffered his hand, but I shook my head. Fatigue knotted my limbs and made my neck ache. The fat man opened his mouth to say something. I closed my eyes. There was a pause.

"Sleep well, my dear," he murmured.

His heels clattered on the cobblestones as he walked away. I squeezed my eyes shut, leaning back against the musty-smelling seat, but the noises of the morning pressed in upon me. The horses' harnesses rattled against the struts of the carriage as the animals were unhitched. Metal buckets clanked against stone. Voices called out orders. A dog barked. Several clocks competed to chime the hour. Nearby someone was striking a hammer against wood. There was a warm reek of fresh horse manure. I opened my eyes. Beyond the open door, there was a courtyard and, beyond that, its thatched roof frayed with watery sunshine, a long, low inn. I was thirsty and I realised that I needed urgently to piss. Slowly I swung out one leg, groping with my foot for the step. My legs were weak with hunger. Holding tightly to the iron rail so that I should not fall, I climbed down.

And there it was. I shall never forget it. The clamour of the yard, which until that moment had clanged and echoed inside my skull, seemed to cease, so that even the twitters of the birds fell silent in the face of it. There was no building, no wall to break up the prospect, only a slope that curved away, its scrubby turf scabbed with churned mud. Beyond the hill it stretched away into forever, a glittering carpet of low black-tinted mist pierced by the sharpened points of innumerable spires and unrolled like a gift at my feet. London. And, in its centre, triumphantly, rose up a mighty orbed mass, a dome of unimaginable majesty, its silvered patina shadowed with midnight's inky blue. For all its immensity, it seemed to float above the city, borne up on a solemn wreath of cloud. As I stared, a thin shaft of sunlight broke through the mottled sky above it, striking the lantern at its crown and turning its apex to liquid gold. My heart constricted, but something deeper inside me stirred. It was faint but unmistakable, the warm quiver that ran through my belly. I clenched my fists then, for safety, but I could not take my eyes from the city. It glistened in the pale light like a promise. Even as I watched, it seemed to grow, as all around it and beyond it, smoke curled endlessly and proprietarily upwards from a thousand chimneys to join with the clouds and claim ownership of the heavens themselves. The noise, too, the noise rose up from it like the shimmer of heat from sand, a hollow roar like the echo of a vast and distant ocean, eternal and unceasing. It seemed to me that the force of it moved the spires like the sea-swell of a tide, sucking at the pebbles of where I stood, pulling me onwards.

I did not go in but stood at the swell of the hill until the coachman summoned his passengers for the final stage of the journey. As I climbed into the carriage, one of my fellow passengers enquired what it was that amused me. It was only then that I realised I was smiling.

At last I am well enough once again to take up my pen. My indisposition was severe but never, I think now, grave, a chill which took hold first in my chest before moving to my abdomen, where it lingered, keeping me to my bed these full twelve days. But today I am much recovered in strength, owing to a new tincture of my own devising, that mixes two grains of opium with five of rhubarb pounded with a little camphor & taken in a tumbler of Canary wine, blood warm. It has proved uncommonly effective in relieving the pain. It is some years since I felt so powerful an energy surge within me. Tonight the candle shall give out before I do.

It is an unseasonably mild evening in London & I sit before the window, careless of the draught through the casement, with a bottle of Portugal wine at my elbow. Of course such pleasure does require that I am obliged to gaze upon the monstrous dome of our new cathedral. It is truly a grotesque creation, the vainglorious grandiosity of its design trumpeting a popish enthusiasm that is an affront to any sober Anglican. Can the burghers of this city have already forgotten that it was those heretics who set the fire that destroyed the great Cathedral upon whose hallowed ground this vile boil now swells? Resurgam, indeed! It is nothing but a pustulous wen on the face of the city, a monument to corruption & to superstition & of course to Mr. Wren himself, who charges a scandalous 4 shillings for entry to the place &, it is said, squats like Moloch in the nave on Saturdays, receiving guests as though it were his own parlour. It matters not to him that it was our taxes that paid for its erection, nor that the place is not yet even complete & painters continue to swarm over the inside of his dome like spiders on their ropes. On the contrary, I am sure he demands a considerable share of the admissions. The man's vanity is outlandish. I do not doubt he would erect an altar there in his own honour if he could only manage it.

How my quill flies across the page! The wine I have taken would seem to have an intoxicating effect quite at odds with the quantities I have consumed. The letter from Samuel Marlowe rests beneath my elbow & sends a thrill of anticipation directly into the pit of my arm.

Surely it is a sign, the answer to my prayers. The prospect of uninterrupted study is matchless &, from what Marlowe writes, the subject ideal, shaped of precisely the manner of crude clay most suggestible to stimulation. Oh, praise be to the Lord God, who, in His wisdom, has chosen me, His faithful servant, & has placed the flaming torch of Truth in my hand so that I may light the way. May His glorious will be done!

V

There was a warning shout and the coach came to a sudden stop.

"The New Road already?"

Yawning, the man opposite me reached up to lower the window and peered out. Pallid sunshine powdered his short wig. I glimpsed a jostle of smoking chimneys and the hazy orange of an open fire before I was overcome by a powerful stink of pig shit and rotting refuse and something harsh and chemical like burning hair. I swallowed and pressed my hand over my mouth as the man brought his head sharply back into the coach, struggling to raise the window as he did so. But even as he wrenched at the strap, a blackened hand pressed down upon it and a grey face loomed at the window. Male or female, it was impossible to know. Its hair was long and straggled and coated with a thick white dust. Its yellow eyeballs rolled like egg yolks in their deep sockets. The hand clawed at the air and the mouth opened. Its two remaining teeth, set together in its lower jaw, were skewed and mossy as old gravestones. Beside me the fat woman gave a little shriek.

"Come, kind sir, a little something—"

There was a shout from the coachman, the sharp crack of a whip, the jingle of harnesses. Then, with a sudden jerk, the carriage leapt forwards, almost throwing me from my seat.

"What the Devil—?" demanded the fat woman's husband, leaning forwards to settle his buttocks more categorically across the bench. His wife swallowed and pressed a pastry hurriedly into her mouth. Her upper lip was bristly with sugar.

"Thieves?" one of the gentlemen enquired anxiously.

"Damned beggars," said the one at the window. "Bed themselves down in the ash-heaps out here full winter through. Acquaintance of mine owns a brick field out here. Isn't a damned thing he can do about it. It's the kilns, of course. Warmth draws 'em out like lice."

Relieved to have escaped a robbery, the men fell to a pleasurable complaining. I did not listen. So this was it. We would soon be there. Our progress had slowed to a crawl. There were other coaches alongside us. I could hear the lascivious suck of mud upon their wheels, the shouts of the coachmen as they traded curses. Horses whinnied and danced. Herds of cattle on their way to market blocked the road, bellowing their reluctance. The foul stench grew stronger. Several of the gentlemen held handkerchiefs to their mouths. At last I begged the gentleman opposite me to lower the window so that we might all breathe some fresher air, but he only snorted. It was the air out there I should be worried about, he retorted. Where did I think the stink was coming from, anyway? Besides, the ditches along this road were several feet deep and so full of malodorous filth that, with the windows open, we would be knee-deep in rancid mud before we'd gone a half-mile.

"First time to London, then," he said. He was a thin man with hunched shoulders and bony legs that folded beneath him like a grasshopper's.

I nodded curtly, not wishing to prolong the exchange.

"Come up to snare yourself a city husband, I don't doubt." He leaned forwards to peer into my face. "Quite a comely little baggage, aren't you?"

I replied stiffly that I was recently married and was to take up a position with the family of a relative while my husband attended some necessary business in the Indies. The rest of the carriage had been occupied in their own conversations. Now, to my displeasure, they turned their attention to me.

"Man must be a knuckle-head," said his neighbor, a milk pudding of a man with protruding teeth who showered the carriage's occupants with spittle as he spoke. "Sending a lonesome wife to London, of all places? The bastard'll be sprouting a cuckold's horns afore his ship's so much as hoist anchor."

"It is you, sir, who is the knuckle-head if you think—"

The grasshopper leered.

"My, a spirited little vixen, isn't she?" he observed, with no little spite.

"Anger becomes her," drawled the milk pudding. "Brings a pretty colour to those pale cheeks. Say, if it is a position you seek, why not come and work for me? I can think of at least one hundred positions I might be able to offer you, and each one more gratifying than the last."

I blushed angrily as the other men laughed.

"The greatest gratification you could give me, sir," I replied with as much dignity as I could muster, "would be to drop down dead."

The fat woman's husband chuckled approvingly and leaned across his wife to pat my leg. She slapped his hand hard, sending up a cloud of sugar.

"The girl should be welcome in our house, should she not, madam?" he said equably to his wife as he inspected the damage to the back of his hand. Before she might empty her mouth to speak, he turned back to the other gentlemen, his round belly shaking with laughter.

"My wife could not countenance a handsome girl about the place. Last maid she hired was blind in one eye and so much disfigured with the smallpox, 'twas a wonder I did not mistake her for a strawberry and eat her with cream. Mrs. Tomlin is a green-eyed harridan when it comes to servants, is that not so, my dear?"

His wife shook her jowls crossly, choking on her pastry.

"It's a wise woman who doesn't trust her husband," the milk pudding declared.

"And a weak-minded fool of a husband who permits his household to be ruled by a shrewish wife," sneered the grasshopper.

The fat woman's husband smiled without rancour.

"I assure you, sir, that my wife is as obedient and dutiful as any man might wish and is invariably in agreement with me. It is simply," he added, with a twinkle in his eye, "that I am not always cognisant of my views upon certain matters until she informs me of them."

There was a burst of laughter amongst the assembled company. The atmosphere was suddenly convivial, the passengers expansive with one another now that the journey was almost over.

I alone remained silent. We had descended Hampstead Hill some time earlier. With every uncomfortable turn of the wheels, my spirits rose and fell, and with each jolt of the carriage, I felt the breath suck and shiver in my chest and the grip of the worm in my belly tighten and relax, as though in the first pains of labour. We were in it now, the cloudland I had seen from on high, and every moment brought me closer to its centre, to the place where the dome ascended skywards and the door stood open upon my grim sentence of servitude.

A satisfactory day.

My stomach is easier, though there is an alarming bruise beneath the surface of the skin close by the right hip bone. I have taken comfrey to disperse the congealed blood & applied a poultice of the same to draw the obstruction outwards. It is imperative that my blood & juices be kept in a due state of thinness & fluidity, whereby they may be able to make those rounds & circulations through those animal fibres with the least resistance that may be, or I shall grow stale & sluggish. To that end, I bleed myself weekly & continue to swallow three grains of opium each day, for not only does the poppy relieve pain in the severest degree, but it harmonises the whole constitution, so that each part may act in just proportion to the other. Truly I have never worked so quickly nor with such clarity.

Everything is arranged. A matter of days, only days, & then at last—at last I shall set about the essential elements of my proof.

It occurs to me, suddenly, that I understand precisely how, in utero, it is decided whether an infant be violently deranged or, as in this case, inertly idiotic. I must commit it to paper before it is lost & yet it is so plain to me I cannot believe I have not seen it before. Surely, this is decided by the nature of the maternal passions, so that violent madness results from those passions which manifest themselves violently through bulging eyes, distended veins, redness of face, hard pulse such as anger or excessive sexual appetites. Idiocy, by contrast, must be the result of those strong emotions evidenced by paleness of features, dead faints, coldness of extremities, irregular pulse such as excessive fright.

It is quite plain, plain & undeniable. Not for the first time, I find myself elated & yet calm, quite without doubt. The opium works like a whetstone on the blade of my intellect, sharpening it until it slices through ambiguity & ignorance like an anatomist's knife, revealing all its secrets.

I shall have Mrs. Black bring the idiot to me forthwith so that I may examine her further. Surely her injury is mended now, for it was hardly a violent blow & her childish bones are too waxy to break easily. She must learn to endure. With my powers of perception exalted so, I can afford to waste not a single moment.

VI

And so it was one dishwater afternoon in January in the year of our Lord 1719 that I set my foot for the first time upon London's tainted and abundant soil. The coach set us down at an inn in Holborn. I hardly knew where to look, so astonishing was the clamour and the bustle of travellers and coaches and horses, but from what I could make out, each one of the inn's seven coach houses might have provided ample accommodations for the most discerning of country squires.

As for the inn itself with its fine columned porch and its rows of grand windows, each fashioned from a single great sheet of glass, I could not imagine that the King himself could live in a palace more magnificent. I stared around me, my mouth hanging open, unable to take it all in, until a coachman drove his horses so tightly alongside me that I could feel the heat rising from their flanks and might have felt the tang of the whip across my cheek if I had not stepped backwards into a puddle. Moments later a man in a tight black coat instructed me to close my mouth and move on before he stopped the hole himself with the bung he kept handy between his legs. By the time I had thought up an appropriately scornful reply, he was gone. Everyone arriving in London, it appeared, was intent upon business so urgent that the loss of even a minute would have the direst of consequences.

It was barely past dinner time, and already the afternoon was grey as dusk. From inside the long lower windows of the inn, there came the supple glow of clustered candles, the red blush of a fire. Heavy with exhaustion, I felt the clutch of hiccups at my chest and gripped my left thumb in my right hand as tightly as I could; I could not risk ill fortune on such a day. For a moment I thought to secrete myself inside the snug golden belly of the Eagle and Child for as long as I could contrive it, perhaps forever, but before I could take one step towards the door, a messenger boy ran up to me. Asking if I was come in on the Newcastle stage, he informed me that the apothecary had sent him so as he might bring me back to his house without misadventure. I was not to trouble myself about my box. Instructions had been left for it to be sent on with a porter later that afternoon. We could leave immediately.

The boy's face was stained purple around the mouth and his hands were dirty, but his eyes were bright and he looked well-fed enough. Remembering the warnings of the baker's boy, I drew myself up and demanded how I was to know that he was indeed sent by my employer. I had no intention, I declared, of allowing myself to be gulled out of my possessions by a common thief. This little speech had sounded impressive as I composed it in my head, but for all my bluster, I made a poor job of delivering it. Fatigue caused my voice to tremble. To my great vexation, I realised I was not far from tears. The boy shrugged and rubbed the back of his hand against his nose, leaving a bubbled trail in the dirt.

"It was Mrs. Black had me come. Said you was like to get yerself lost or somefink, not having been to London before. Said you'd be glad of someone to show you the way. Gived me sixpence and all." He scuffed a toe in the mud, then looked up with a sudden grin. His teeth were startlingly strong and white. "Said you might give me somefink too, if I minded me manners and let you take the wall."

The unexpected kindness of Mrs. Black was too much for me. The tears spilled over and rolled down my cheeks. I yawned widely and rubbed my fists against my eyes, so that the boy might not see them and pity me.

"But it don' matter," the boy said anxiously, reaching out a hand towards me. I glared. Changing his mind, he plunged it instead into his pocket and shrugged. "I was only sayin'. You don' 'ave to fret yerself 'bout the extra, not if you ain't got it."

If this was a trick, then it was a very superior one. I had neither the spirit nor the inclination to resist further. I shrugged and followed him.

Outside the street was paved in stone and so broad across a farmer's hay waggon might have turned itself quite around in a single manoeuvre had it not been for the impenetrable press of traffic. As it was, I had never seen so many vehicles gathered together in one place, chaises and chairs and carts and coaches and waggons, crowded together three deep, each blocking the next, their wheels rattling in their sockets and their drivers engaged in a ceaseless exchange of shouts and curses. Frequently an irate passenger would thrust his head out of his conveyance and yell his own abuse, fist aloft. Above this clamour, horses stamped their hooves, pedestrians called to one another, street vendors cried their wares, and bells sounded out the hour from what must have been one hundred church steeples. At the corner of one street, a street organ creaked out its tune, a moth-eaten monkey in a plush skull cap crouched atop it, while only a few feet farther on a ragged fiddler sawed out an Irish jig, accompanied by a tiny ragged girl with a tambourine. A trumpeter commanded the crowd to see a calf with six legs and a topknot. A tinker banged a frying pan with a tin spoon, singing out his business and calling for kettles and skillets to mend. The fish-man's bawled chant collided with the oyster-lad's and clattered against the ditty of the pudding-man: *Two for a groat, and four for six-pence!* The cry of the milk-maid pierced them all, her long shriek like the wail of a dying cat. A man in an ancient tricorn hat carried a cage of birds slung round his neck, each one frenziedly chirruping and flapping its wings against the flimsy metal bars. Parsons, lawyers, porters, excise-men, water-carriers, milk-girls, and pedlars of all kinds elbowed their way through the throng without looking, their heads lowered in the headlong rush. Doors banged, taverns and coffee-houses belching raucous groups of men out into the street. And, without pause, children wove like flying needles in and out of the crowd, their shrieks streaming behind them. They leapt across the kennel, a stinking slurry of refuse of every imaginable kind which in places was close on three feet across, ignoring the stones that had been set into it by way of a crossing, and dodged between wheels taller than they, which creaked ominously over them as they disappeared. Their heels threw up sprays of mud, splattering the beggars who squatted, grimy with dust and soot, amongst the heaped-up rubbish in the shelter of doorways and, plucking at the hems of passers-by, implored them to spare a few pence.

It was like an enormous, extravagant puppet show. I watched agape, aching to lift the joiner's sawdusty hat for a better look at his seamed face, to finger the flashing silver buttons upon a dandy's coat, to feel the coarse texture of an old man's campaign wig. I wanted to raise my own voice and add it to the clamour, so that I might become part of it. I would have been content just to linger and stare about me, but even that was impossible. I was carried along by the relentless tide of people. I could not stop. Besides, I dared not lose sight of the boy, who slipped ahead of me with the sinuous assurance of an eel.

Determined to arrive at the apothecary's house with my dress unsoiled, I refused to give up the wall, though it bore the grimy trail of a thousand skirts at hip height smeared along its length. I surrendered my privilege only when a sooty chimney-sweep with elbows like a pair of folded umbrellas walked directly up to me and, refusing to budge, stood with his arms akimbo, rolling his creamy white eyes in his blackened face, until I was forced to step out into the road, where directly a nut-seller rammed his wheelbarrow hard against my shins and several chairmen cursed at me to clear out of their way. Alarmed, I pressed myself back against the wall, but as I passed the entrance to a narrow courtyard, two mangy curs un-leashed themselves at each other, twisting themselves into a growl-ing eight-legged blur of teeth and drool. I screamed, stumbling away, my heart pounding against my ribs and my head filled with a kind of blind roaring. The boy turned impatiently, gesturing at me to follow. I clenched my fists, struggling to regain my composure. Once, as a girl, I had been badly bitten by a dog, and I retained a powerful fear of them. Reflexively I reached up to touch my scar, a ragged purple seam where the nape of my neck met my shoulder. I called for the boy to slow down, to walk with me, but he was too far ahead to hear me above the racket. Biting my lip, I hastened to catch him, my legs shaky and treacherous.

I was almost abreast of him when, ahead of us, a gentleman with red-heeled shoes and a sword two feet long was jostled by a greasy porter pushing a barrow of boxes. Wheeling round with a yell of outrage, the gentleman threw the startled porter headfirst into the gutter. Immediately a mob clotted around the pair, laughing and jeering and urging them to a fight. Meat-faced men and urchins pushed roughly around me, angling for a better view. The stale smell of beer and old sweat mixed with the mouse-nest reek of breath and bodies and greasy clothing. A boot came down heavily on one of my feet. Yelping, I tried to squeeze between the men as they crowded forwards, but they pressed together like roof slates, one overlapping another, allowing no opening. Their rough coats grazed my cheeks. Behind me there was the dull inhaled thwack of a nose crumpling beneath a fist. The men cheered but, for all their outward high spirits, there was something ugly about their faces now, something gaunt and greedy. There was another punch, a piglet's shrill squeal. A roar went up from the crowd. The men jostled harder. For a moment I lost my footing and feared I would fall. Scrabbling upright I pushed again, turning myself sideways to slip out. The bodies pushed back. Someone cursed. I felt the castellated knuckles of a clenched fist against my ribs. Another hand plucked at my cloak. Out of the corner of my eye, I saw the flash of a drawn blade. I felt the scream swelling in my chest.

"Come on."

The voice was low and clear, like a voice from a dream. Someone seized my hand. Against my chilled skin, the fingers were warm and insistent. Comforting. Furiously I tried to pull my hand away.

"Get your hands off me, you thieving good-for-nothing!"

The hand tightened its grip, wrenching at my arm. The men shoved against me so that my ears twisted painfully against the scrape of their sleeves. I twisted my hand to try and escape. Then, abruptly, I was free. Behind me the crowd, tiring of spectatorship, set quickly upon one another in a barrage of blows and curses. Blood splattered shiny red across the dull grey stones of the kennel. The messenger boy glanced up at me as he dropped my hand.

"Come on," he said again, and pointed across the road. I followed him through the perilous press of vehicles, my hands shaking, my face hot with fear and anger. The fear I dismissed as no more than the panicky apprehensions common to those weakened by tiredness and hunger. Had the contemptible maggot in my belly not insisted upon draining me of my habitual strength and vigour, I would doubtless have found myself less susceptible to foolish fancies. The anger, however, I clung to gratefully. I fumed at the boy as he turned into a narrow lane, gesturing at me to remain close to him. It was too late for such niceties now, I muttered angrily to myself. Surely he could not expect a gratuity from me after such a thorough-going display of carelessness. It was true that I had never really been in danger. But all the same, I told myself firmly, if I had been alone, I would have more quickly understood the possible risks of the situation and taken steps to avoid it. I was not worldly, exactly, having been denied the rich man's pleasure of travel, but as the daughter of a cunning woman, I had met many of the diverse and devious characters who populated that world and lent it its flavour. My mother had taught me to listen to what people did not say, to winkle out the meanings that concealed themselves inside the hard shells of words. In the village I had been known to be sharp-witted and sharp-tongued. Only once had I allowed my passions to rule my instincts, and I had paid a very great price for my folly. I had no intention of making such a mistake again. There would not be many in London who would contrive to get the better of me.

There was considerable comfort to be derived from these assurances. As I walked, I repeated them to myself until my heart ceased its frantic knockings. When at last we stopped in front of a door and I realised that we were finally arrived, I spat once upon the ground, for luck, and dismissed the messenger boy with only a casual sneer as a gratuity.

He did not leave, however, but lingered beside me as I rang the bell. It jangled within the shop and fell silent. No one came. There was a small latched flap in the door through which customers might be examined before being admitted but it remained closed. Feeling my heart quickening once again, I stepped to the window and peered through. The inside of the shop was not lit, but behind the glass the ledge was crowded with dark-coloured glass bottles and jars. Between them I could make out a large volume placed upon a low stand, set open. Beside it was a tray of coloured stones strung upon strips of leather and a yellowed skull. Beyond the ledge I could make out the outline of a counter set with more, larger bottles and, behind it, an open doorway, leading into another room. I leaned closer to the glass so that I might have a better view. I made out the shape of something long and ridged suspended from the ceiling before my breath misted the glass. I rubbed it with my sleeve and looked again. Beside me someone cleared her throat.

"Mrs. Campling?"

Startled, I stepped backwards, glancing over my shoulder. My foot sank into a puddle of mud, but there was no one behind me.

"Mrs. Campling?" the voice said again. "I am Mrs. Black."

A woman stood in the doorway of the shop, her arms crossed, a woman made entirely of precisely ruled lines. Her face was long and stern, its planes sharpened by iron-grey hair pulled tightly back from the crown. Above the two angles of her cheek-bones, her eyes were curt incisions, while her nose was a narrow triangle, pinched to a white tip. Her plain white cap was so crisply starched it might have been folded from paper, while beneath the jutting lines of her collar-bones, the rigid bodice of her plain dark dress made another precise triangle of her chest, permitting no softness or curvature of flesh. It was impossible to imagine her sighing with pleasure when her stays were finally loosened at the end of the day. It was impossible to imagine her sighing with pleasure at all. A man would cut himself one hundred times before he so much as got his buttons unfastened.

Mrs. Black considered me, her bone fingers drumming upon her sleeves. I looked anxiously over my shoulder. Apart from the messenger boy who still waited, shifting from foot to foot, we were quite alone. The bunch of iron keys at her waist clanked a little as she drummed. Beside them, on a separate loop, a birch switch dangled, its leather handle worn to the shape of a hand.

"You are Mrs. Campling, are you not?"

Still I hesitated. Perhaps it was a trick. If I answered in the affirmative, would punishment follow? After all, it was his family who had arranged my position. They had despatched me to this place not as the wife of their son, never that. The Campling name must not, under any circumstances, be besmirched. I was no more than soiled sheets to them, a musty ill-used bundle which must be bleached clean of ignoble stains. The expenses of the laundry had been met. That, as far as they were concerned, would be the end of it.

And yet the apothecary's wife addressed me with his name. Eliza Campling. The anticipation of it caused the saliva to leap in my mouth. I swallowed, tasting excitement and disgust. Often I had imagined myself taking his name, owning it—what girl in my position would not have?—but it had always been like a new dress that belonged to someone else, something to be admired, stroked a little perhaps, but never taken out of its paper, never put on, for fear of spoiling it. Now I thrust my arms roughly into its sleeves, wrenching it over my shoulders. Who cared if it ripped? I would wear it with as much destructive pride as I could muster. I would eat in it, sleep in it, and when at last I was rid of the vile worm, I would bleed in triumphant scarlet across it. If there was to be punishment, let it come. It would have been worth it. For a bright fleeting moment, I would have taken what was rightfully mine.

"Yes," I said firmly. "I am Mrs. Campling."

That first evening, when Mrs. Black saw the bare finger on my left hand, she gave me a brass ring to wear and chided me for being careless with my own. There was not the faintest trace of archness in her voice. Indeed, in all the time I knew her, Mrs. Black never once betrayed, by the slightest gesture, any knowledge of my true circumstances. To her I was always someone's wife, always Eliza Campling.

And I was fool enough to be glad of it.

She is here.

I can hear her lumbering feet as they thunder up the stairs, her strangling northern inflections as she does battle with the rudiments of the English language. I shiver a little as I imagine the effects of this great metropolis upon her undeveloped sensibilities. I know of no stranger not bewildered & disturbed by the glare & clamour of it, be they perfectly familiar with European cities of some considerable size. How powerful a provocation, therefore, must it prove to a rustic sprung only days ago from a mire of mud? Indeed, I have ordered Mrs. Black to warn her repeatedly of the city's dangers, for a dread of unseen horrors beyond her immediate environs must surely stimulate a heightened state of imagination which shall serve the work to its considerable advantage.

So, too, with myself. Though the particulars of the situation contrive to blur the line between the domestic sphere & the precision of the laboratory, it is imperative that I maintain a rigorous distance between subject & examiner. I shall neither acknowledge her outside this room nor address her upon any matter not pertaining directly to the study in question. There must be no easing of formality, no moderation of the strict & objective rules of science. This is not simply a matter of correct procedure, although the objectivity of my observations shall gain from such rigour, but a part of the work itself, for fear & unease are as vital as the subject's intrinsic susceptibility to the success of the enterprise. My work with the parish women has shown me clearly that the low faculty of imagination that so dominates women is brought most effectively to the fore by the cultivation of such fear. It weakens the solids & fibres of the body, already so much feebler than those of the male, so that they are at their most receptive to impression.

On no account may she be permitted to grow comfortable.

VII

Mrs. Black took me first to the kitchen, a dark low-ceilinged room tucked beneath the street. A small fire burned in the wide grate, and by the window a linnet bounced on its perch in a wire cage. I could smell meat roasting with rosemary and the shitty reek of the cesspit in the cellar beneath. A muddle of boots and hooves and wheels hustled through the upper panes of the grimy window. The rain had once more begun to fall, and the kitchen was thick with shadow. In the half-darkness a girl busied herself kneading dough, her face bent low over the table. Flour danced in a dust round her, blurring her outlines, while round her ankles a yellow cat made a sinuous figure of eight, its tail hempy as a length of rope.

"Mary!"

At the sound of her mistress's voice, the girl startled backwards, bumping into a ladder-backed chair, which fell with a crash against the stone flags, sending the yellow cat streaking away into a corner. The girl giggled and then tried to swallow her laughter, covering her mouth with a floury hand. Mrs. Black sucked in her breath but said nothing. Instead, she set the chair once again on its feet and taking a taper to the range, lit the stick of candles on the kitchen table. The girl did not attempt to assist her. She blinked in the light, tracing a large circle on the floor with one foot. Her large head hung a little to one side as though its weight was too much for her. She wore no cap, and her amber hair was caught at the nape of her neck with a scrap of ribbon. It was not a modish colour, but it glowed like polished copper in the candlelight and for a moment I almost envied it. Then I saw that there was a bald patch the size of a man's palm on the right side of her scalp. Its lower rim was crusted with a dark black scab.

"Mary," Mrs. Black said more harshly. "This is Mrs. Campling. She is to stay with us awhile, remember?"

With an effort Mary lifted her head. I saw immediately that she was an idiot. Although her face lacked none of the individual features requisite to its construction, it had all the same an unfinished air about it, a slackness as though the clay that fashioned it had been too wet. The mouth hung open and so, too, did the eyes, pink and lashless as a rabbit's. Naked and oddly vulnerable, they bulged from their flattened sockets, their swift sliding movements giving the unsettling impression that they were able to look in two directions at once. Their gaze slid over my shoulder and across the top of my head before, together, they came to settle upon the smudge of flour that whitened the bridge of her indistinct nose. Her cheeks were an inflamed red in her pale face. Meanwhile her fingers busied themselves in her mouth, her large wet tongue probing at the lumps of uncooked dough caught in her bitten fingernails. She mumbled something inaudible. Bubbles of saliva gathered at the corners of her mouth.

"Fetch Mrs. Campling some water," Mrs. Black instructed. "She will be thirsty after her long journey."

Slowly Mary dragged her hand from her mouth. Her upper lip was cleft from the base of her nose so that it fell in two loose flaps over her protruding front teeth, exposing a slice of wet white-pink gum. Blinking her rabbit eyes, she smiled in my approximate direction, a slack lopsided grin. Her chin was crusted with a paste of spittle and flour. Several of her bottom teeth were missing. I shook my head firmly.

"Thanks all the same, but I don't think—"

Mary rolled her head around, her bulky tongue struggling to form a word. Then, with painstaking slowness, she took down a wooden dipper from a nail on the wall and a cup from the narrow dresser and carefully scooped a dipperful of water from a bucket by the range. When I took the cup from her, its belly was scummy with dough. She waited expectantly, her loose eyes slithering round me and over me and through me until I could stand it no longer. I took a hurried sip and set the cup upon the table. The water was unpleasantly warm and had a brackish taste. I forced myself to swallow it. Mary clapped her hands together and smiled so widely that her tongue fell from between her lips and her rabbit eyes disappeared into two curved slits. Her delight was obvious.

It was also repulsive. Quickly I looked away. What could possibly have possessed Mrs. Black to hire such a freak I had no idea. The girl's mother must have had a hare run across her path when she was with child, or maybe even eaten hare meat. It was well-known in my village that if no action was taken to reverse such damage, the child would be born marked by the animal. My mother had favoured tearing the dress of the mother, which, if done directly, was known to neutralise the hare's abominable influence. Clearly the mother of this moon-calf had been something of a half-wit herself.

"You will do your utmost to speak clearly," Mrs. Black informed me crisply. "Or you will struggle to be understood. I fear we have a rather more gracious way of speaking in London than you are used to in the provinces."

Outraged, I opened my mouth to protest. Me, harder to understand than this rattle-head who could barely squeeze out a grunt without falling over with the effort? Mrs. Black pinched her face together and studied me, her eyes somehow angry and impervious at the same time. Very gently her fingertips plucked at the switch that hung at her belt.

I closed my mouth.

"As to the arrangements here," she continued, "you are to sleep with Mary in the garret. I'm sure you will be comfortable. Come, let me acquaint you with the house. Then you may rest before supper."

So there was to be punishment after all, I muttered to myself as we made our way up the dark wooden staircase. I was to be forced to sleep with an addle-headed idiot of a maid who could barely utter a syllable and who would doubtless piss in the mattress and dribble into my hair. I thought of my mother, her curled body compact as a walnut in the bed beside me, and my heart squeezed. Once again those vexing tears, whose foolishnesses I had been obliged to check all day, threatened to fall. I rubbed my nose with the back of my hand, biting down hard on my tongue. There was no future in such nonsense. My mother had betrayed me. I would shed no tears for her.

Instead, I forced my attention towards the particulars of my new home as Mrs. Black briskly pointed out its arrangement. It was considerably larger than I had expected. The ground floor was mostly taken up with the shop and the laboratory, the first looking out over the street, the latter over a small patch of yard to the back of the house. I would be required to assist when necessary in the shop, Mrs. Black informed me, but the laboratory was kept locked. I would be permitted to enter it only with her authority, and then I was to touch none of the apothecary's scientific equipment. Any breakages would be deducted directly from my wages. Behind the shop was also a narrow dining-room where the apothecary and his wife took their meals.

On the first floor, Mrs. Black pointed towards the private chambers of herself and her husband. Both doors were firmly closed. On the second floor, she paused. As on the floor below, there were two doors, set at right angles to one another. Again both were closed. The one on the left, Mrs. Black informed me, led to the room occupied by the apothecary's apprentice, a Mr. Pettigrew. The other was the door to the apothecary's study. As she spoke, she placed herself firmly between it and me, as though to block my path.

"You are never to lay so much as a finger upon the handle of this door, do you understand me? The apothecary will countenance no intrusion." She spoke severely, as though to a wicked child. I felt a flush of resentment warm my neck. "Mr. Black is engaged upon a work of extreme importance. He will not endure his papers to be disturbed. Even Mary is bid never to enter. If there is cleaning to be done, then I will undertake it myself. If he calls for victuals, you will knock to announce yourself and leave the plate outside the door. You will not tread heavily in your chamber nor make any other noises that might upset him. You will remove your shoes as you go up and down the stairs. It is your duty and responsibility while remaining in his house to guarantee the apothecary the privacy and silence that his work necessitates. If he finds even the least cause for complaint, you may expect no leniency in his treatment of you. Do I make myself clear?"

She glared at me. I shrugged. The pretence seemed ridiculous to me, ridiculous and futile. The apothecary might wish to keep the more unsavoury particulars of his business a secret from the prying eyes of the Justice, but it seemed a little far-fetched to attempt to deny the existence of such services to those who sought to profit from them. After all, for what other reason had I been despatched here?

"Answer me, girl," she barked, skewering me with her gaze.

So much for Mrs. Campling, then.

"Yes, madam," I muttered sulkily, staring at the floor. If she considered the time for courtesies concluded, then so did I. As I followed her up the splintery wooden stairs to the garret, I let my feet strike the boards with as much force as I could muster.

Ahead of me Mrs. Black bent to open the low door and stepped back so that I might enter. I set one foot across the threshold and gasped, my ill temper quite forgotten. The room contained a large bed, furnished with a heap of rugs and a flock mattress and hung with heavy dust-coloured drapes, and in the corner a rickety three-legged stool propped up under the eaves and bearing a chamber-stick and a small leather book. But it was only later that I noticed them at all. If the room had boasted no more than a pile of greasy rags to sleep on, I would still have been unable to prevent myself from crying out with the sheer wonder of it. For the enchantment of that room was not contained within its four sloping walls but framed by the plain peeling border of its single window.

In a moment I was across the room and throwing open the casement. The houses on the west side of the lane were rather less tall than their neighbours opposite them, and the roof of the house across the street sloped down towards me, so close that, had I looked, I might have seen the brown streaks in the white splatters of bird dung, the soft mouse-grey balls of lichen that nestled amongst its slates. But I did not look. I did not see the shop signs beneath me as they shifted and creaked on their rusting brackets, distorting the noise from the street below. I vaguely heard Mrs. Black calling out to someone on the stairs, but I did not turn. I could not tear my eyes away.

For there, above my head, rising with glorious disregard from a low jumble of roofs and smoking chimneys, was the dome I had seen from Hampstead, only now it soared before me, its vaulting magnificence held aloft by a vast coronet of pillars. The columned lantern at its summit reached upwards into the smoke-bruised sky like Jack's beanstalk in the chapbooks at the village school. A golden balcony encircled it, and at its top, triumphantly, it held aloft a vast golden orb and cross, burnished bronze in the twilight. There was nothing of supplication in its appeal to Heaven, nothing of the humility before God so beloved of the Bible. On the contrary, it rose from the mud as a magnificent testament to the boundless ambitions of men, realised in all their inexorable glory. It was flanked by two great towers, like a pair of footmen in splendid livery. One bore the most enormous clock I had ever seen.

I could hardly bear to blink my eyes and lose the sight of it, even for a moment. As I stared the bells pealed out the quarter-hour, rattling the slates of the roof about my ears. In all my life, I had never dreamed that such a thing might exist. Beside it I felt tiny, as irksome and inconsequential as a louse, but at the same time it filled me with a rush of excitement. My heart quickened. And for all that I urged myself to fear what was to become of me in the apothecary's house, as I stared at the dome, I felt once again the faint stirrings of anticipation in my chest. In the shadow of this magnificence, I felt somehow safe, cheerful even. Who cared about the idiot maid, about the trials I was about to endure? I was not so much a fool to be careless of the pain ahead. I had heard the terrible moans of the women who sought out my mother's bellyache tea. Afterwards I had washed the blood from the twisted linen. I knew that the next few days would be fearsome and dangerous, but when the time came to purge me of the vile worm, I would take my chances in this room. I would drink whatever they gave me and rejoice. If I could but gaze through this window as my body racked and cramped, then I might tolerate the pain. All the perils and injustices of the world would be powerless to harm me while a structure of such majesty stood sentinel against my slice of the London sky.

NOTES FOR OBSERVATIONS UPON A CONGENITAL IDIOT

1. PHYSICAL EVIDENCE that solid fibres of body significantly <u>weakened</u> by effects of the mother's imagination: slack assemblage of limbs & muscle; cleft lip & palate; very large head [circumference about twenty-four inches & a quarter]; small eyes with weakened eyesight; very large tongue of a full five inches in length; unusually small ears (no more than two inches in length); flattish nose prone to blockage; sparse hair; urine thick & with sweetish taste [deficiency of salts? though tears appear to contain customary amount]

2. CALLOUS ORGANS OF SENSATION: slow to thought & insensible/dull to small pains [pinching/pin/candle flame applied to skin of arm]; stronger stimulus [physical blows/knife/hot coal]➤   surprise & confusion—BUT NOT ROUSED TO ANGER

3. MEAGRE POWERS OF REASONING matched by EXCESSIVE EMOTION: deficient grasp of logic e.g., patterns, basic mathematics; little stimulation required to produce foolish laughter/abundant tears; unreasonable terror of darkness; superfluous response to sudden noise—screaming, dropping of held items [weakness of solid fibres?]

4. GODLESSNESS: poor grasp of rudiments of faith; refusal to repeat [recall?] simple prayers/oft-repeated verses; lack of conscience; moved by self-interest over virtue [NOTE: **<u>Is an idiot in possession of a soul?</u>**]

↓

LOOSENING OF NERVE-STRINGS
LIKE STRINGS UPON A VIOLIN:
RESPONSES SLOW, SENSATION DULL,
REASONING SLACK & CARELESS

VIII

Those first nights at Swan-street I lay awake, my fist closed round the hare's foot beneath my pillow, certain I should never sleep again. At home the nights were silent, disturbed only by the straining of tree branches in the wind or the distant muffled bark of a fox. But in London the noise of the city never ceased. The darkness was alive with yells and shouts and whistles, shrill with anger or drunkenness or desperation, I could not tell which, and with the rattling of coaches and the groaning of shop signs and the impatient tolling of bells quarrelling amongst themselves. When at last I contrived through sheer exhaustion to sink into an uneasy drowse, I was roused every hour with the fearful din of the watchman thundering at every door, bawling out the hour and the threat of rain. By dawn, when the shutters of the shops clattered open and the waggons laboured up the lane on their way to the market at Smithfield, churning up the chill grey air with their great wheels and drowning out the birds with the lowing of bullocks and the neighing of horses and the foolish gurgling frenzy of forlorn flocks of sheep, the day was once more begun.

Beside me the idiot girl stirred in her sleep. Tugging the rugs roughly over my shoulder, I rolled as far away from her as I could manage. The sickness was worst when I lay down, the night-blackened room lurching and rolling beneath me. Something bit at the back of my right knee. I cursed softly, humping myself upwards so that I might scratch it better.

The sudden movement cramped my belly, and I dug my finger-nails into my flesh, pressing downwards and squeezing as though I could tear the contemptible worm clean from my flesh. I saw it clearly, its blind eyes blank as it ground into my belly, stabbing its claws yet deeper into my flesh. Each day it grew stronger, more implacable, and yet, since my arrival, nothing had been said, nothing done. At first I thought the tea we drank in the mornings bitter and assumed it to be a preparation of sabine or some other such herb that might dispose of my troubles, but Mary drank it too, chipping extra sugar from the loaf to stir into it when Mrs. Black left the kitchen. When I carefully enquired about it, Mrs. Black informed me that I was privileged enough to be drinking tea made from leaves brought all the way from India, which was steeped first for the apothecary and then a second time for our breakfasts. This tea was so precious it was kept not in the pantry with the other provisions but in a locked canister in the dining-room to which only Mrs. Black had the key.

"It is something the apothecary wishes to do for Mary," Mrs. Black said with an expression that was neither frown nor smile but a curious mixture of both. "He claims she has a fondness for it, although how he can tell—" She cleared her throat. "Doubtless you will develop one too. I've found that girls who marry above themselves are not slow to acquire expensive tastes."

And so I drank the bitter purposeless tea and I waited. Although it had never sat comfortably with me, I attempted to learn patience. I told myself that it was a matter of waiting for the right time. There was the alignment of the moon to consider, I knew, and doubtless there were others who had waited longer. Neither would it be prudent if I fell ill immediately upon my arrival in London. It would favour us all not in the least if the neighbours were roused to suspicion. Besides, and surely most decisively, I had been hired by my mistress as a servant, on full and proper pay. Our agreement ensured that I would remain in her household for a full year, regardless of what else it was that went on beneath her roof. She made it clear from the outset that she meant to make as good a maid of me as she could manage.

The routine of my new life was rigid and unchanging. On every day except Sunday, I rose with Mary when the watchman called six o'clock. When we were dressed and the bed straightened, Mrs. Black would unlock the door to our chamber. When she was persuaded that both we and the room were in satisfactory order, she would take our pulses and demand view of the contents of our chamber-pots before she permitted us downstairs. She studied the turds as though they were tea leaves, swirling them round in the pots with her eyes narrowed in concentration. On several occasions in my first weeks, she had me deposit my pot, still full, outside the door of the apothecary's study so that he might subject it to a further examination. She would not have a girl of hers taken ill, she told me sternly. It did not look well, not in an apothecary's house. To that end she also insisted upon sniffing about me like a dog, peering into my eyes and ears, and ordering me to open my mouth so that she might count my teeth. On one occasion she even took measurements of my brow and the circumference of my skull, tapping my forehead hard with her pencil when I fidgeted.

When these formalities were completed and their conclusions noted in the big book Mrs. Black kept for this express purpose, I then assisted Mary in the daily duties of the house while Mrs. Black went to the market for the day's provisions. I pitied the unfortunate tradesmen forced to bargain with her. She knew nothing of compromise or concession. Certainly she took no account of the fact that the very air of London was suffused with a sticky soot that blackened everything on which it lit, so that it required unceasing vigilance to maintain the appearance of cleanliness. Even a plate, untouched for a week, would, when finally lifted from the shelf, instantly begrime a clean apron and stain the tips of your fingers to bruises. If the mistress discovered such a thing, the punishment was swift and severe.

The work was hard, monotonous, and wearisome, and each night I fell into bed barely able to stand for fatigue. But, for all that, to begin with at least, even the most commonplace of the tasks assigned to me were brightened by the gleam of novelty. I had never before seen a house with so many possessions in it, and I liked to touch them. It gave me a quiver of greedy pleasure to beat the dining-room carpet and see its riot of colours revive, to rub a cloth over the abundance of varnished wood and pewter and glazed Fulhamware and discover the rich gloss that lurked beneath their veil of grease and soot. Every time I passed the looking-glass in the dining-room, the perfect precision of my reflection made me start. I could not bear for that reflection to be smudged or smeared. I polished that glass until it shone like a white winter sun on its dark wall.

The only duty I refused to have anything to do with was the emptying of the chamber-pots and close-stools. I left those to Mary. She never objected, although I resolved to misunderstand her if she ever tried. We were under instruction to empty them in the vault beneath the house once their contents had been examined and recorded, but if Mrs. Black was not yet returned from shopping, Mary would giggle at me, her eyes leaping in her skull like marionettes and, slopping the pots with gleeful abandon, would throw the contents out of the window. We would both wait for the splash, hoping for a cry of outrage from a passer-by. On the occasions that it came, I laughed, too, but slyly, snorting in my throat, for if I showed my amusement too openly, Mary would tug like a delighted child upon my sleeve and bring her great slack face up to mine until our noses almost touched. Her chin was chapped raw with saliva, and her breath was foul. I preferred to keep her at a distance.

When the first round of chores was completed and a meal prepared for the apothecary and his wife, we were permitted to take a breakfast of bread, cheese, and small beer in the kitchen. Mary chewed loudly, with her mouth open. Above us we could hear the occasional jangle of the shop bell and the clunk of a customer's footsteps across the floor. On the rare occasion when the shop was busy, I was required to assist with fetching and carrying and with the wrapping of packages.

I liked the shop. It did not have the dark, sealed-up airlessness of the rest of the house. Although the door was kept closed, even on warm days, the thick round panes of glass of the windows caught sunlight like syrup in the bottom of a bottle, showing the auburn tints in the wooden floor. I liked the flap in the door that allowed you to peruse a customer before permitting them in. I liked the shop's smell, the harvest scents of dried flowers and herbs dancing over the sharp reek of vinegar and the exotic resin of the Oriental medicines. I liked the stretch of polished counter in which you could see the pale gleam of your eyes, the wide shallow drawers with brass handles shaped like shells, the walls lined with shelves and crowded with bottles and jars: the blue and white ones on the lower sills fat and ponderous as aldermen, the amber stoppered flasks like petrified drops of medicine, the green glass jars that glowed emerald when struck by the early morning sun. I liked the chatter of the customers, the tilt and clunk of the brass scales as Mrs. Black weighed out tea and tobacco. I even liked the strange prehistoric creature called an alligator that hung from the ceiling, his hide cracked, his teeth brown and dull as wood chips in his parted jaws.

The only thing that discomfited me was the skull upon the table. It had a habit of grinning, as if taking comfort from the knowledge that although its own decease had been grisly enough, yours would be much worse. I refused to look at it, examining instead the living faces of the customers for marks of the great capital. But to my disappointment, apart from their accents, which required them to speak in a penetrating but frequently incomprehensible shout, I could see little difference between them and the villagers I had grown up with. I had hoped for much more.

I comforted myself that I saw hardly enough of them to judge. I was never permitted to go out, except to the stand-pipe and to church on Sundays. To begin with I had no strong objection to these arrangements. The stand-pipe was located close enough at the top of the lane, and I liked the short walk for there were diversions enough to lighten the weight of the buckets. When I wished to see more of the city, I crept up to our attic and gazed out of the window. The sight of the dome, flanked by its two magnificent towers, never failed to lift my spirits. It presided over the smoke and the filth and the chaos of the city like a king, careless of its power. It never looked down. All might fall into the mud around it, and still it would continue to stare away towards the smudged brown hills of Surrey, enormous and immutable. It was impossible to believe that it had been built by the men who scuttled in its shadows. I preferred to imagine it, complete and perfect, pushing its way up from a city beneath this one, a city of untold magnificence and splendour, where men as tall as houses strode the jewelled streets arrayed in coats of gold. I liked to imagine the moment that its golden cross had shattered the crust of London's tainted earth, the rising dome scattering the tiny citizens of the metropolis and their matchwood houses with glorious disregard. On cloudy days it seemed the dome was rising still.

On my first Sunday at Swan-street, I accompanied Mrs. Black to church. She warned me to stay close to her, for the city, she claimed with a warning frown, was quick to devour the unwary, but I lingered all the same, agreeably confused by the noise and the jostle of the streets. In London, at least, God appeared to make an exception to his Sabbath strictures. As for the church, it was grander by far than any I had ever before encountered, almost a cathedral, with an aisle twice the width of my father's and pillars fatter than a mayor. The parson was a nervous man with a curd-cheese complexion and a permanent frog in his throat, which afforded the unexpected amusement of words that sometimes escaped him in a shrill squeak and at other times failed to emerge altogether, causing him to blush scarlet as a girl. When I grew tired of such pleasures, I diverted myself by studying the congregation. There was one woman in particular who caught my attention, since she had the habit of mouthing to herself in silent echo every word that the parson uttered. When a word slipped away from him, she craned forwards, her mouth open, as though she hoped to catch it like a communion wafer on her tongue. Such amusements turned out to be poor compensation, however, for the hour or more I was required to spend with Mrs. Black afterwards as she read aloud from the Bible. Occasionally she asked me to repeat verses after her, so that she might correct my pronunciation. Mary, lucky sow, was allowed the day off, which she took in bed. That night the bed was hot and tumbled and coarse with crumbs. I cursed her violently for her carelessness, but in truth the night was bitter and I was grateful for the fusty warmth of it.

There was no shop-keeping on a Sunday as a matter of principle, as the master was devout. The house was even darker then, with the shutters locked and shades made of cambric pulled down over the shelves of bottles and jars. I thought such pi-jaw hardly necessary. For most of my first week, the shop might just as well have been closed. Customers came only infrequently, and there were days at a time when the shop bell did not sound at all. On those days, if the mistress was out, the apothecary's apprentice, whose name was Edgar Pettigrew, would come down to the kitchen and warm himself in front of the range.

Edgar was a flabby youth with plump hands and a pale complexion that put me in mind of a softly set junket. His buttocks and thighs were soft as dough in his tight breeches, and his uncut hair hung in sausage curls around his ears. Even his voice was plump, fatty with cheese and self-satisfaction. He had a habit, at meals, of leaning over my shoulder and helping himself to the tastiest morsel on my plate. When I slapped his hand away, he only laughed, closing his fat fist around whatever he had chosen and pressing it hurriedly into his mouth. In the laboratory—a narrow dreary room with shelves on all four walls and a deal table in the centre crowded with books, flasks, and ferocious-looking metal contraptions—all of the glass cups and flasks were smudged with his fingerprints.

"You impudent sluttikin," he goaded, the words greased with butter. "I have a mind to take you over my knee and paddle your bare arse for your insolence."

"Try it and I'll hack off whatever it is you keep in your codpiece," I retorted hotly, brandishing my knife.

Mary squawked unhappily, banging her fists upon the table. Edgar's presence always unsettled her.

"Such sauciness," he murmured. With an insinuating finger, he lifted a stray curl of hair from the back of my neck. I twisted my head away. Unmoved he slid his round bottom onto the edge of the table and took another fragment of buttered biscuit from my plate.

He chewed slowly, like a cow, his eyes fixed upon my chest. In the past month, my figure had swollen extravagantly and now my bosom rose in a white bow above the brim of my stays.

Edgar licked his lips.

"So the master does not object to his idle apprentice keeping his customers waiting?" I demanded, scraping my chair back and turning away towards the sink.

Edgar shrugged.

"What customers? I have better things to do than freeze myself half to death waiting for business that will never come. Why, doubtless you can think of a few yourself, Eliza, my brazen little puss. You must have offered entertainment enough for some wag-tailed dog to find yourself as you do."

Before I could answer, he grabbed my waist and, spinning me around, pressed his tongue into my ear. I wriggled ferociously, but he held me tight. Mary whimpered.

"Besides," he whispered, his lips wet against my ear. "Mr. Black is gone out. Seeking 'the company of fellow scientists,' self-deluding fool, as if there are any in London that would so much as pass the time of day with a worthless quack like him. Still, he is gone and what he does not see will not grieve him. It seems a pity to waste that vulgar mouth of yours on words, when we might persuade it into action."

"I'd fuck a dog before I'd let you lay a finger on me," I hissed, trying to free myself. "You let go this instant or, I swear it, you'll get a pair of black eyes for your trouble. I am a married woman."

He released me then and smiled, his cheeks plumping into two pillows.

"Oh, yes," he purred. "A married woman. Of course."

Displaying a remarkable nimbleness for a man of his size, he skipped round me, lowering his mouth to my bosom and biting me hard. As I yelped in pain and rage, Mary gave a whimper and covered her face with her hands.

"Edgar?"

Edgar did not trouble to answer the mistress's summons. Instead, he rolled his eyes at me, stretching up his arms in an exaggerated yawn. He lowered them only as Mrs. Black opened the kitchen door.

"Madam," he drawled, executing an unctuous bow. There was a smudge of coal dust on one of his stockings. "What is your pleasure?"

"Edgar," she said again, and to my astonishment, her mouth turned up a little at its edges. Upon the sharp points of her cheek-bones, two faint blushes of pink had bloomed. "If you will. I require your assistance."

"You flatter me," Edgar replied. "I am, of course, entirely at your disposal."

"Of course."

Mrs. Black's fingers fluttered at her sides. She appeared a little out of breath. The blade of her Adam's apple sliced up and down her throat, several times in quick succession as if it would cut the flesh in two. Edgar bowed again, gesturing at her to ascend the stairs ahead of him. Then, over Edgar's shoulder, she observed me. On my breast the bitten skin reddened. Hastily I placed a hand over the mark.

"What do you think you are looking at, missy?" she snapped, her face folding into its habitual crisp lines. "And cover yourself up, if you please. This is a respectable house, not a bagnio. I will not tol-erate any girl of mine disporting herself like a sixpenny strumpet. Any more of that and you shall find yourself in the cellar."

She swept up the stairs. Edgar bared his teeth at me in a silent growl, raising his fat hands like claws. Then, smirking, he followed her. Furiously I hurled my plate into the sink. Mary, who until then had kept her face hidden, rose and came over to me. Very carefully she reached out to touch the bruise on my breast with one finger. The nail was bitten so low that the tip of her finger looked fat and swollen, but her touch was cool, light as a moth. Impatiently I pushed her hand away. Mary said nothing but blinked at me, her mouth slack.

"What?" I demanded angrily. "Cat got your tongue?"

Above our heads the bell of the shop jangled. There was work to be done. But as I slammed out of the kitchen, my heart was

heavy. I banged my mop against the dark boards of the hall, slosh-
ing too much water from the bucket. I knew Mrs. Black would rebuke me for squandering it, but I did not care. If I was to be
friendless in London, I might at least grant myself the dignity of believing that it was a matter of my own personal choosing.

Every long dark day of that first week, I told myself firmly that neither the waiting nor the disagreeable nature of my fellows were
matters of the slightest consequence to me. I declared myself careless of the strangeness of the new house and the strictness of my
mistress. I was not in London to please myself, after all, but for a
purpose, and I determined to see that purpose resolved. I had only
to execute my duties and avoid punishment and, when the time
came, to pray for a safe deliverance. A year would soon be over.
Then this page of my life would be torn from the record and a fresh
one begun. I would be at liberty to do what I wished, to go where I
pleased, to take another position, perhaps, or even to return home.
I tried not to think of my mother's face as she closed the door of
the cottage. I was no longer her concern nor she mine, treacherous, double-dealing, foul-smelling crone that she was. I missed my
mother not one jot.

No, there was nothing at Swan-street that unsettled me. What
did it concern me that I never once laid eyes upon my master? After
all, this was not a country cottage, with everyone heaped one on top
of the other like puppies. It was doubtless quite usual in a London
household with many rooms that a maid might go weeks at a time
without encountering her master. It was not as if he was not spoken
of frequently. On the contrary, his requirements and desires were
discussed and worried over, his health and comfort a source of unceasing concern.

Nor was his authority in doubt. Mary was afraid of him, thrusting the tray in my hands when it was time to take his dinner up to
him, pushing me out of the kitchen with her head turned away and
her eyes squeezed shut. I rolled my eyes at her, but all the same my
knees trembled a little as I bent to place the tray before the closed

door. When later I returned, the smeared dishes gleamed in the half-light, their contents gone, the folded napkin twisted and marked with wine and gravy. Each day I washed his dirty plates, brushed his coat and wig, rinsed out his worn white stockings. Sometimes in the mornings, there were signs that he had walked about the house while we slept. I smelled the burnt sweetness of his tobacco when I shook out the rug in the parlour, gathered up the curls of orange peel discarded in the grate, rubbed with a cloth at the pale grey mark on the wall above his chair where he liked to lean his head. Often, as I lay in bed, I heard him pacing the room beneath me, his feet drawing figures of eight on the varnished boards, round and round, his voice a taut black thread pulling the darkness into folds. Then I held on to my hare's foot a little tighter and rebuked myself for being absurd.

And still I did not see him. I grew uneasy, peering round door-ways and jumping at shadows. For it was not quite true that there was no mystery at all about my master. On my very first day at Swan-street, before my box had so much as been brought to the door, Mrs. Black had commanded me that I was never under any cir-cumstances to look directly at the apothecary nor was I to express any surprise or dismay at his appearance. If I chanced to encounter him on the stairs, I was to keep my eyes to the floor. If I disobeyed her in this, I might expect harsh and certain punishment. She pro-vided no other explanation except to pull Mary's sleeve from her shoulder and show to me a line of dark purple bruises that blotched her pale skin.

I never dared ask why. It was almost as though I feared the taste of the question in my mouth. My master was as present and yet as invisible in the house in Swan-street as God Himself was in church, except that, as Mrs. Black and the frog-voiced parson liked to in-struct me, God was the one true Light. My master, on the other hand, seemed to me to be composed of darkness, of shadows and locked doors and windowless stairwells and the sour black smoke of extinguished candles. In the gloom of the house, his absence was unyielding. It clung to the murky corners of every closed-up room, as sticky and persistent as cobwebs.

It was to be a full eleven days before I saw my master for the first time. I was sweeping the stairs when the door opened and he entered the house. The landing was dark and he did not see me. When he paused in the hall to peer at his reflection in the mirror, his shoulders and the crown of his hat caught the dusty sunlight from the high slice of window behind his head. At first glance he appeared almost comically ordinary. He was of unexceptional height and build. His hat was round, of the kind favoured by country curates. He wore a black frock-coat with a stiff skirt grown slick and greenish with age, and old-fashioned square-toed shoes with buckles. The silver was tarnished, the leather cracked. The cuffs of his shirt were marked with ink. The overall impression was commonplace, drab even. Despite myself, I felt a stab of disappointment.

Then he turned to face me. I squinted so that I might see him better. My knees buckled. He moved towards me. Steadying myself against the wall, I forced myself to keep my gaze fixed upon his approaching shoes, to observe the smear of mud upon one leg of his breeches, how his pale stockings had a shapeless grey patch across the front of his ankle as though he had put them on upside down. The wooden heels of the shoes struck hollowly against the wooden floor. A far-off part of me noted that one of the boards was loose and would need nailing. He was at the bottom of the stairs now. Screams bubbled in my lungs, my ribs pulled so tight together I could barely breathe.

In all my imaginings, I had never dreamed that my master would have no face at all.

I closed my eyes, my fingernails digging into the palms of my hand, but I could not shift the image, the round hat and beneath it the moving patch of dark shadow, the blank of blackness with holes for eyes that loomed between two fogged slabs of wig. Where there should have been nose, cheeks, mouth there was nothing but darkness, swirling darkness that shifted and moved, devouring the light, draining its warmth. The wall behind my shoulders was cold as a corpse. What would one touch if one reached out to such a face? Would it strip the flesh from your fingers, shrivel the bones to ash? I whimpered, the darkness of my closed lids spangled with silver dust. Beyond the roaring in my ears, all the commonplace daytime noises had ceased, as though the house was holding its breath.

At the bottom of the stairs, the shoes paused. I heard the knock of the wooden letter-box, the hiss of something being dropped onto the cherrywood table, the leathery creak of a fart, each noise sharp as a spoon against a glass so that the silence vibrated with its echo. Then he began to climb. I pressed myself flatter against the wall, clutching my broom against my chest with both hands, wishing myself invisible. Usually I would have done anything I could to avoid the ill luck that must surely come from passing another person on the stairs. I only wanted him past me, gone, disappeared once more behind the safety of a locked door. He drew closer, so close I could smell ink, the lingering reek of tobacco and spilled wine, the stale powder of his wig. I squeezed my eyes shut, concentrating all my attention on willing him gone.

Suddenly I felt the press of his fingers round my jaw. My stomach fell away.

"Good," he murmured. "It is time. We shall begin tomorrow."

His grip tightened. Hot tears swelled behind my eyelids. Then, abruptly, he released me. My head jerked forwards.

"Mary! Have your mistress come to me directly. And sponge my hat. Those rooks are become a plaguey nuisance."

Then he was gone, his shoes clattering up the stairs to the next floor. I heard the scrape of the key in the lock, the slam of the door. Then silence. As it settled softly about me, my legs began to shake. I slid down the wall, huddled into my dark corner, pulling the gloom about me like a quilt, letting the tears slide unheeded down my cheeks.

My master was no apothecary. He was a fiend, a demon, the faceless agent of the Devil himself.

What kind of Hell was it that I had come to?

In her belly it floats, conceived in perfection by the father but as yet imprecise in form, its limbs soft as wax. A male child perhaps but, born of woman, powerless against the violent passions roused by the ardent nature of the female imagination & the failure of the weak & suggestible female body to resist the effects of such passions.

Suspended in milky darkness, it grows dimly aware of the raised temperature of the liquid in which it floats, the irregular palpitations of the muscular heart located directly above it, the strong paroxysmal movements of the organs of respiration & the convulsions of the fibres & the nerve-strings of the body as breath comes faster & more wildly. Already it senses that the more rapid respiration during a seizure of imagination is driving the heated blood more violently than is usual through the woman's body, hurling it to her extremities so that the womb pitches in her belly like a boat on a stormy sea.

The storm abates. The blood steadies & cools. The foetus settles, resuming its curled slumber, soothed once more by the unshed blood of the menses, which provides its nourishment. It cannot taste the difference in its composition nor turn away its mouth, for the blood enters its body without its compliance, by means of the navel string. It cannot know that the high temperature of blood has heated the fluid parts of the body & that, even now, as these parts cool, the contents of those fluids are deposited in the woman's body, as salt marks the interior of a cooling cooking pot, & collect in the same pool of menstrual blood that provides its sustenance.

& so it is begun. The salts in the blood impress themselves upon the waxiness of the foetus, before muscle & bone might have the opportunity to harden. It can only endure, as the force of her passions press into its tiny form the embodiment of its vilest extremities.

I stare into the glass & the opium sharpens my eyes so that I see every detail of my damaged cheek with perfect clarity, every tiny flake & hair & hole in the skin as though I examine it beneath a microscope. It seems to spread as I look, each scarlet scale of skin its own betrayal, repository of another's sins, the weakness & imprudence of woman imprinted without mercy upon the innocent flesh of a child, the truth not a balm but an agitator, its message simple & incontrovertible: the absolute impossibility of forgiveness.

IX

I cannot say precisely how long I remained there, crouched on the landing. Certainly it grew dark, the light draining from the glass pane above the door until it closed over, shut tight. The clamour of the lane leaked into the house as though strained through muslin, pure drips of sound without sense or substance. Nothing felt real, not even the cold plaster of the wall against my back or the coarse bristles of the brush that grazed my shins. My hands made pale shapes upon its splintery handle, ghosts that drifted free of my arms in the twilight. Around me the house contracted, distilling into night, pooling everywhere into eye sockets and gashes of mouths and the brimstone whiff of demon breath. I did not dare to move, although I thought longingly of the hare's foot concealed beneath my mattress. Instead, I observed the worsening cramps in my legs distantly, without curiosity. Inside my belly the worm stretched and squirmed. For a brief, bright moment, like the spark of a tinder-box, I was lit with a kind of desperate comradeship.

It is time. We shall begin tomorrow.

The spark went out. I pressed my knuckles against my belly, pushing them together. Something moved within it, a faint twist of resistance. I pushed harder. Suddenly, below me, the shop door opened, discharging voices and a puddle of yellow light. The ordinariness of it was startling, shocking. Shadows leapt against the walls of the stairs as someone carried a candle into the hall. Light crept up the stairs, catching the peaks of my knees, the lappets of my cap. I longed to crawl into it and away from it at the same time.

"You are mistaken, madam. He is come home already. His hat is—well, that's a pretty sight, I must say."

Edgar stood at the bottom of the stairs, the candle held aloft. Narrowing his eyes, he tilted his head to get a better view. Awkwardly I pressed my legs together and tried to stand, but my cramped muscles refused to oblige me and I stumbled, jabbing myself painfully in the chest with the handle of my broom. Edgar's mouth twitched. When Mrs. Black called something to him from within the shop, he shook his head at me, running his tongue lazily over his lips.

"I imagine you shall require that shiftless chit of a maid to work it over, madam," he called back without taking his eyes from me. "It would appear that birds have made something of a cesspit of the brim. Do you wish me to fetch her for you?"

Mrs. Black must have concurred, for Edgar gestured at me and then at the hat that lay upon the cherrywood table.

"Eliza!" he feigned, his hands cupped round his mouth. "Eliza, where are you?" And then in a low hiss, "It may be customary for a maidservant to sleep upon the floor in whatever God-forsaken corner it is you come from, but I should warn you that in civilised society, it is considerably frowned upon. I would advise you to get down here before I am obliged to inform your mistress of your insufferable idleness."

Scowling, I limped down the stairs, my broom bumping behind me. A slice of light came from beneath the shop door. I could hear my mistress conversing with a customer and, from downstairs, the clattering of pots as Mary prepared the supper. An ordinary evening. I refused to look behind Edgar where the tall clock threw a looming shadow and the glass pane above the door was black and bottomless as a well.

"I was not sleeping," I muttered, and my voice tasted sour on my tongue. "I—I was—"

"What?" Edgar reached out and pinched my cheek. I twisted my face away, my eyes on the ground. "Indisposed? And why would that be, I wonder?"

Before I could answer, the door to the shop opened and Mrs. Black leaned out, vexation whetting her sharp features. Edgar's hand vanished into his pocket.

"Edgar, those pills, if you please. Mr. Butterfield is waiting."

"Madam."

"As for you, girl, what are you doing lurking about? Get to the kitchen, and quick about it. There's supper to be got and a thousand other things besides. And take the master's hat with you. If it is left any longer, that stain shall mark."

The hat squatted on the table, dark, malignant, a wide white streak across its crown. In the laboratory a drawer slammed and Edgar cursed loudly. Mrs. Black watched me, her arms crossed, her fingers drumming upon her forearms. Summoning all my courage, I snatched up the hat. As I lifted it from the table, something soft and dark fell out from the crown, a swath of congealed shadow that clung to the felt brim. I gasped and almost dropped it. Impatiently my mistress seized the hat from me and peered at it.

"Damned birds. Use soap. And wash the veil separately. It is perfectly filthy. Ah, Edgar, at last. Mr. Butterfield, I am so sorry to have kept you."

Placing both hands lightly on the small of Edgar's back, she pushed him before her into the shop, closing the door behind her. As for me, I barely noticed the immodesty of the gesture. I stumbled down the stone steps to the kitchen as though my legs were made of wood. Mary blinked at me as I pushed open the door. She held a wooden spoon in her fist, and her face was flushed pink with exertion.

"Help Mar'?" she asked tentatively, waving her spoon so that splashes of gravy hissed on the hot metal of the range.

I did not answer. Instead, I half-threw the hat upon the kitchen table. It was then that I saw it properly for the first time. The hat had a veil. The dark gauzy fabric was perhaps a foot or more in length and attached to the crown with a series of small black hooks so that it fell over the brim to the shoulders, protecting the face in the manner favoured by bee-keepers. The hem of the veil was blurred grey with dust. Streaked across the crown of the hat, and clotted in the brim, was a thick trail of bird shit. I bent over, my shoulders seized with a fit of shaking.

Mary's hand was soft and warm upon my shoulder.

"Ill?" she whispered.

I shook my head impatiently, stepping away, but still I could not stop the shaking.

"Laugh?" Mary persisted, following me. "Is joke?"

"For the love of peace—!"

I wheeled round and thrust the fouled hat in her face. Mary stumbled backwards, her hands flapping and her mouth working with alarm. I glared at her. She blinked back. I sucked in a long, ragged breath. Then dropping the hat onto the floor at her feet, I smoothed my skirts and walked slowly around her and over to the sink.

After supper Mrs. Black informed me that the master wished to see me the next morning, directly after breakfast. When in my confusion I choked and had to press my hands over my mouth, she gave me a narrow look and warned me that she would tolerate no impudence. If my master informed her that I had been anything other than entirely obliging, she would have no hesitation but to use the birch.

That night I lay awake in the darkness. My head ached with exhaustion, but I could not sleep. At last, when the night-lanthorn called midnight, I rolled over and dug Mary in the ribs. She muttered, sucking on her tongue as though it were a sweetmeat. The sound of it disgusted me. I poked her again, more harshly this time. She groaned.

"Mary," I hissed. "Mary, wake up!"

"Wha—?" she mumbled, humping herself over onto her side.

I pulled her hair. She yelped in surprise. I could see the whites of her eyes as she squinted at me in the darkness, the gleam of her irregular teeth.

"Have you ever seen it? The master's face?"

"Mn."

"So? What is it?"

"Red. Fire," Mary mumbled, humping her back from me. "Sleep."

"Burned?" I shuddered, imagining livid flesh melted into waxy folds.

"No burn. Red." The words were muffled, slurred with sleep. "Stain. Fire stain."

I turned on my back, gazing up into the darkness. Fire stain. Could a commonplace red stain upon his face be the extent of the master's terrible secret? The pettiness of it soothed and agitated me at the same time. Beside me the idiot burrowed deeper into the bed, flatulent snores snagging in her throat. The sound filled me with a murderous irritation. Was idiocy contagious? What nature of fool was I to trust the word of a tom noddy, who could hardly tell a fart from a farthing? Kicking off the covers, I rose and went to the window, pressing my face against the cool glass. Beyond the casement the mighty dome held sway against a moon-metalled sky, indifferent to the dark jumble of roofs that cringed before it, reaching up their chimney-pots like arms in supplication. There had been a farmer's boy in our village who'd had a crimson stain across his brow and down one side of his face. The marked skin was raised and rough, its surface studded all over with little yellow pimples. His ear on that side was always scarlet, as though mortified to be appended to so unsightly a blemish. We had tormented him and called him names, but my mother had always been kind to him.

"It's hardly the poor child's fault," she said and sighed, shaking her head. "That mother of his, she's been a greedy lass her whole life. Longing for strawberries in February? She must have known it would mark the boy."

A responsible mother, she told me firmly, controlled her appetites or if she could not, made sure to satisfy them. Otherwise, they grew so powerful that they took her over, burning themselves into the flesh of her unborn child. Was that how it had been for my master? On my first day at Swan-street, my mistress had warned me against profligacy, insisting candles and coal be used when strictly necessary. I had a sudden picture of a woman, large with child and wrapped about with a shawl, her lips blue with cold, crouched shivering before the empty brick hearth in the kitchen as the ice glazed the low window and she dreamed of a fire so high that it stung her cheeks and caused the infant in her womb to thrash with the heat of it. I shivered, all at once aware of my cold feet, the goose-flesh on my arms, but still I lingered at the window, staring out into the darkness towards the invisible smudge of the hills. In nearby streets and houses, lights still burned despite the lateness of the hour, but it seemed to me that, beneath the endless roofs, the thousands of voracious city mouths sucked in what remained of warmth and light, exhaling in return a darkness blacker than any darkness known to night, so that, with each vast polluted sigh, another light died in a curl of sooty smoke. As for the first pale shell tints of dawn, they would be drained from the sky before they could pink the lowest of the red rooftops. It would be night forever.

The cold had penetrated my bones so that my teeth chattered together. Chafing my skin with my hands, I climbed back into bed. Mary murmured and rolled against me, her slack body warm as a muffin. I did not push her away. I did not permit myself to think of her protruding eyes, the way her tongue lolled wetly in her mouth. Instead, I tucked my cold feet into the snug bend of her knees.

In the darkness she could have been anyone.

I am so beside myself with outrage that I can hardly hold my quill. I remind myself that a man of science must always remain dispassionate, but there are surely circumstances in which such an expectation is neither reasonable nor desirable. The body of a man may operate by mechanic principles, but he is not a machine.

The evening began well enough. I dined with Wright at the chophouse & was comforted by his opinion of Gaule, the odious bookseller. It was Wright who reminded me, after all, that even the distinguished Mr. Harvey was compelled, long after his proof of the circulation of the blood, to continue to teach to his students the Galenic principles which his discoveries had emphatically disproved. Despite the company he keeps, Wright is a fine & decent gentleman.

It was at the Folley that we encountered the insufferable Simpson. To my annoyance, Wright greeted him heartily & called for more wine, which Simpson & his companion fell upon like locusts. Sodden with liquor, the dog then began an account of a paper he had recently read into the science of physiognomy & ways in which the particulars of anatomy reveal the hidden heart of a man.

New experiments made in Germany, he informed us, had proved beyond doubt that it was no longer appropriate to assign the defects of babies to the passions of the mother, since women lacked the authority to make anything distinctive of their own without male agency. Instead, the source of such deficiencies could be traced directly to the <u>intrinsic corruptions of the child</u>. A hump, therefore, reflected not the exposure of the pregnant mother to a crippled man but rather the affected child's inability to bear responsibility, while a hare lip revealed the loose mouth of one who might not be trusted & two Siamese twins, conjoined at the waist & sharing only a single vagina, had been shown then to harbour depraved & deplorable sexual desires. As for facial staining—& here he fixed me with his reptilian eye—it was attributable to vile thoughts, thoughts that would cause a respectable man to blush.

Perhaps I should be grateful that Wright intervened to prevent injury, but I cannot say that I regret drawing my sword. Open discussion between men of education is one thing; the peddling of pernicious &

*perfidious untruths quite another. Oh, how mankind corrupts itself &
takes as its innocent victims those whom suffering has been visited to
excess already. The very thought of it hastens my pulse & sets my quill
to shaking against the page. Will those of us who have all our lives been
forced to endure the burden of another's wickedness be once again the
innocent repository of man's hatred?*

Simpson is a rogue & a villain & I wish him every ill fortune.

X

Dawn came all the same, bound by a low rope of cloud. As soon as the first tasks of the day were complete and breakfast eaten, my mistress sought me out and required me to go directly to my master's room.

"But my duties—?" I stammered.

"They shall keep," Mrs. Black said crisply. "Now upstairs with you. It does not do to keep the master waiting."

Slowly I mounted the stairs. The day had grown sunny and the glass pane above the front door was a clear pale blue. Too bright a morning for ghosts or demons. There was nothing to be afraid of. I would glance at his face, I told myself, just so that I knew. There were, after all, much more important matters to consider. I forced myself to consider what the process might be, whether he would have me drink something or if it would be a plaister, how severe the pains would be, and how quickly they would come upon me. You might die, I told myself fiercely as I raised my hand to knock upon the closed door. What do you care for your master's face when you might die?

There was the scrape of a key in the lock, and the door swung open. My master was a black shape against the sunlight that filled the room. I blinked, dazzled, and allowed myself to be directed towards an upright chair that stood close to the table, encircled on all sides by towers of papers and pamphlets and cloth-bound books bristled with markers. This room looked out over the lane, affording a view only of the house opposite and, above its gabled roof, the cloudless blue of the sky. You could not see the dome from here. The low sun slanted through the chimney-pots and drew patterns on the grimy window-panes. When I blinked, the undersides of my eyelids were marked with golden discs.

84

The apothecary did not greet me. Nor did he invite me to sit. He said nothing at all. Instead, he pressed his hands together as if praying, his fingertips against his lips, as, very slowly, he walked round me, his eyes moving meticulously over every inch of me as though I were a horse he thought to purchase. Careful of my mistress's orders, I kept my eyes fixed upon the sky.

In front of me he stooped, considering the slope of my belly beneath the folds of my skirt. Hurriedly, queasily, I glanced at his face, clasping my hands together to stop them from trembling. That I had half-expected it did nothing to ease the shock of it. His disfigurement was so—so ordinary. The stain was sizeable, it was true, extending from his temple down into the folds of his neck-cloth, but, although unsightly, it was hardly grotesque. Had he not attempted to disguise it with wig powder, which clumped in the coarse grain of the damaged skin like mould, it would have looked less disagreeable still. As it was, the powder gave the purple mark an unhealthy greyish tinge that was reminiscent of decomposing meat.

"Move your hands."

Hastily I glanced away, unlacing my fingers so that my arms fell to my sides. The apothecary gazed at my abdomen, his lips pressed together as though resisting the urge to smile. I sucked the wall of my belly in, compressing the worm, daring it to protest. It made no movement. Soon it would be gone. As my master reached out and took my left wrist, pressing his first two fingers against its underside, a spike of elation pierced my throat. It left my mouth dry, metalled with fear.

I swallowed.

"Shall it soon be done with?" I asked, keeping my voice light.

My master frowned then, but he did not answer. Instead, he bid me hold my tongue while he completed his examination. For the next few minutes, I stared out of the window while he palpated my flesh and peered into my ears and mouth. Even when his face was only inches from mine, I kept my eyes averted from it.

For his part, my master said not a word but only jotted notes on a scrap of paper. He lifted my eyelids, pulling them out by the lashes so that he might study the hidden parts of the white. He had me state the habitual pattern of my monthlies, the approximate age I had been when they had begun. He pressed the point of a pin against my finger until a bead of blood appeared, examining the blood closely before licking my finger to consider the taste of it. The pin did not hurt, although when he pinched me, I yelped.

When at last his investigations were complete, he bid me sit in a chair turned away from his so that it faced the wall. For perhaps an hour or more, then, he required me to join with him in what I could only describe as idle chatter. He had me write out my letters and read a little from one of his books, a purposeless humiliation which caused me to flush hot with indignation, but otherwise he displayed more the sensibilities of a lady at the tea table than a man of learning. I might even have found such a conversation pleasant, or at the least preferable to the usual round of my household duties, had it not been for the apothecary's rapid and disquieting shifts of humour so that he was one moment amiable, even avuncular, and the next, as grim as a gaoler. On one occasion he even struck the table with a whip, marking the varnish and startling me so exceedingly that I cried out in surprise. It unnerved me greatly, for without sight of his face I had no way of predicting his fiercer gusts of rage. Nor did I have the least notion of what it was in my answers that provoked him so.

As the hour passed, I grew more tentative in my responses. At last the apothecary fell silent. His chair creaked. I could hear the faint whistle of his breathing, the rustle of papers being gathered together, the oyster slap of a man sucking at his teeth. I stared at the wall, my hands clasped in my lap, awaiting his prescription, my belly tumbled with eagerness and apprehension. He sighed, a long exhalation, and drummed his fingers upon the desk.

"I shall require you to come to me every other day at this time, with the exception of Sundays. Go now. Doubtless you have much to attend to."

I frowned, shaking my head at the wall.

"But, sir. I had thought—that is, I had hoped—I—I don't understand, sir."

My master did not reply immediately. There was a rustle, the chink of glass. A moment later I heard the scratch of his pen upon the paper.

"I do not imagine you do," he said at last. "I do not mean to take dinner today. Have Mary bring me tea."

I twisted round, catching sight of the top of his head as he bent over his work before I recalled myself and hurriedly turned away. He had not seen me, but all the same, I felt agitated, alarmed in equal measure by my master's indifference and my own recklessness.

"Is there not—I mean, surely sir, if I could only—?"

"Tea," he repeated coldly, placing the page to one side and beginning another.

I was dismissed.

EC—interview 1

Confinement advanced some four or five months, with noticeable swelling to the lower belly & some enlargement of the breasts. Born in the village of W— in the county of Northumberland of English parents. Father deceased [pleurisy]

General health of subject robust:

- *eats & drinks heartily—detail of daily diet attached*
- *faeces firm with good colour/odour; no sign of worms*
- *urine straw-coloured/copious, free from sediment/clouding; no discernible taste*
- *blood watery but sharp with fine colour—no clotting or phlegm*
- *spittle clear & well-digested—no knotting or toughness visible*
- *breath odour strong but not sour/noxious, indicating healthful lungs*
- *teeth almost complete—rear gums slightly swollen*
- *eyes clear, with unnaturally white surround*

Character & Physiognomy:

- *short of stature, standing no more than 5 feet & 3 inches*
- *strong physique with pronounced breasts & rear, advertising crude sexuality*
- *thick dark hair with large dark eyes & choleric complexion of Latin breed*
- *skull tapered with indentation above right ear & low brow, indicating limited intelligence*
- *reads & writes to elementary standard [unusual—effects on imagination?]*
- *but, despite education, credulous & of superstitious nature ["a broom left bristles down has all the strength run out of it"]*

→ *early impressions indicate subject likely to display strongly choleric temperament, fortified by the rough instincts of the rustic: quick-*

witted, bold, furious, hasty, quarrelsome, fraudulent, persuasive, <u>exceeding stout-hearted</u>

↓

CONCEALED TERRORS?

NB. coarse & resistant: <u>persistent reinforcement critical</u>

XI

It came as little surprise that Edgar lost no time in seizing upon my disquiet. The prentice's brain might be all in his breeches, but he had a nose for weakness that might have put a terrier to shame. He was quick to acquaint me with the master's particular fondness for young girls. Indeed, despite the old man's churchgoing and Sunday closing and all his other pretences at virtue, he was, in Edgar's assessment, little more than a salacious old rogue, much addicted to the comforts a pretty young maidservant might confer. Edgar himself had several times made use of an expedient crack in the door to observe the old lecher with his britches round his knees and his bare breech jerking up and down like a fish on a line. It was said that the previous girl, an impudent chit if ever there was one but with curves to make a grown man weep, had refused his advances and what had happened to her, on the streets without good character? Edgar regarded me consideringly before finally declaring me not so fetching as my predecessor but possessed of a homely kind of allure which the master would doubtless find satisfactory. Besides, a girl of my type was surely not in a position to act so recklessly. No, Edgar sighed contently as he bit into a muffin, he was certain it would not be long before it was my plump white thighs that he would have the pleasure of observing through that convenient imperfection in the grain.

Although I knew better than to swallow Edgar's assertions whole, his predictions left me uneasy. He told the truth about the hole in the door, for I saw it for myself. And if the master did mean for me to give him comfort, he would hardly have been the first. How many girls in my situation were required to endure in silence the burden of their master's attention or lose their position without reference? Even without Edgar's vigorous stirring of the pot, a sensible girl would have always to be wary.

Two weeks passed, then three. Days were brief twilit breaks in the relentless sooty darkness of winter. Even on the rare clear days, the pallid sun seemed barely to manage to crawl across the rim of the tight-packed roofs before it sank exhausted from sight. Even at mid-day, we were required to burn tallow candles so that we might see our way about. The shadows were slick and salty with the stink of melted grease.

Nothing more was said of my situation, nothing done. I grew anxious and then fretful. I knew that it was crucial to act with all possible haste, and, try as I might, I could not fathom the purpose of the apothecary's examinations nor the benefit of further delay. Each day, as I performed my duties, as I responded to his purpose-less questions, trying to draw from the blank plaster of the wall some clue as to the answer that would best please him, the worm swelled and strengthened in my belly. Thinking on it caused my palms to sweat and pimples to break out in a band round my brow. Had I not been sent to the apothecary's house for one purpose, and one purpose alone? Had the apothecary not been chosen specifi-cally, hand-picked, his instruction to remove me and to exterminate any evidence of impropriety or boyish bad judgement? There was no one in the world who wished the vile worm alive, least of all here in the house at Swan-street.

All the same, as the weeks passed, I found myself unable to shake the terrible and persistent dread that my condition had somehow been overlooked or forgotten. I began to suffer headaches, belly-aches, rough rashes that bloomed beneath my arms and round my neck. My master noted them all, making precise sketches of the in-flammations that crusted my skin, but he said nothing. Any attempts I made at questions were met with silence or, more frequently, a strike of his rule across my palm. It was not long before I stopped asking. I took instead to complaining whenever my mistress was nearby, praying that accounts of the nagging pains in my reins, the cramps in my belly, the vomiting, might provoke her to acknowledge me, to assist me. They did not. Mrs. Black only smiled her thin smile and advised a tonic of industriousness and forbearance. It was a woman's duty, she informed me, to suffer such discomforts patiently. I dug my fingernails into my palms and felt the not-knowing stiffening my arms and twisting my face into lines. When she harried me into the parlour to black the grate, the bray of the hawker crying cabbages and savoys in the lane grated upon me so insufferably, it was all I could do not to run into the street and shove the largest of his vegetables down his detestable throat.

It was the next Sunday, as she intoned the words of the Psalms, her hands clamped around the heavy book on her lap, that I came to a startling and fearful conclusion. Mrs. Black wished me to suffer. She might not be able to prevent what was to happen, but she could delay it, she could make quite certain that I was properly punished for my transgression. My hasty departure to London had saved me from the shame and the whipping I would surely have been forced to endure if my village neighbours had discovered my condition, but she had no intention of sparing me. On the contrary, she intended me to suffer, to pay for my sins.

The more I contemplated this possibility, the more certain it became. I tried not to listen, but it was impossible not to heed the frequent references to wickedness in her carefully chosen passages. My mistress was a godly woman, her very flesh desiccated with piety. It was as difficult to imagine her ripe with child as it was to expect juicy fruit to spring from curls of dried-up orange peel. And yet Edgar had informed me that she herself had borne five children, not one of whom had survived infancy and whose names were never permitted to be spoken in the house. Before Mary had come to Swan-street, her name had been Henrietta. On her very first day, however, Mrs. Black had informed her that such a name was unacceptable for a servant and that from henceforth she would be known as Mary. Henrietta had been her second child, her only daughter. Edgar could not recall the cause of her passing, though he was reasonably certain that at least one of them had succumbed to the influenza.

Mrs. Black cleared her throat, glaring at me and tapping her finger on the page.

"Attention! 'Let death seize upon them, and let them go down quick into Hell: for wickedness is in their dwellings and among them.'"

For the first time since arriving in London, I missed my mother. I missed the cottage with its stone chill and the low branches that tapped against the windows. I had a longing for the familiar must of our bed so profound that it made me dizzy. That night I had a fearsome headache. I longed to creep up to the laboratory for the master's willow oil, but I did not dare. Instead, I snapped at Mary as we laboured over the linen and kicked out at the cat, who yowled and retreated beneath the dresser, his yellow eyes bright with reproach. Even when the work was finally done, I could settle to nothing but picked at the splinters on the underside of the kitchen table, taking a kind of savage comfort in the needles of pain as they jabbed the raw wrinkled skin beneath my fingernails.

The next morning was not one of my master's mornings, and I dragged myself through my chores. It was a little before the midday meal when Mrs. Black beckoned me into the dining-room. The room was cold, the fire not yet lit, and I shivered as she closed the door behind us, folding her hands together and bowing her head a little. I breathed shallowly, my belly churning with impatience.

"I wished to inform you that, from henceforth, there shall be no further Bible classes on a Sunday. Nor shall you be expected to attend church."

She looked up at me abruptly, her face twisted with anger as though she granted such exemptions only under extreme duress. It was clear she meant to say more.

"As you wish, madam," I said, willing her on.

"That is not all. I wish you to tend to the carpet in here. You are to dampen the saved tea leaves from our breakfast and brush them over its length to restore the pile. Then I would have you paint out the worn spots with ink. Mary must be kept out of the room while you perform these duties. Last time she attempted to eat the mess of tea from the floor." She nodded at me and, pressing her lips together, reached for the handle of the door. I gaped at her, appalled.

"But what about—surely—"

Mrs. Black's mouth tightened.

"You understand the task, do you not? Well, then, lose no more time."

"I thought—I just thought—isn't there something you—we—should I not be given something? For the—" I floundered, gesturing helplessly towards my belly. Mrs. Black frowned, but I could not stop now. I was perilously close to tears. "I beg you, madam. I mean, the weeks are passing, and I—"

"Ah. Of course." Mrs. Black inclined her head, and I was certain her features softened a little. "I understand. And you are quite right to bring my attention to it. We have left things long enough. I shall speak with Mr. Black today."

All that day I toiled in a state of delicious fear and anticipation. Each time I passed the laboratory, I could not resist the temptation to glance in, but there was only Edgar there. Just before supper I went again, peering through the crack into the cramped room with its strange contraptions. Edgar was seated before the table, a book open before him. All about him upon the long counter lay dirty phials, bottles, and retorts, heaped together with unscrewed jars and lidless boxes. I recognised none of the contents. As I turned to go, Edgar looked up.

"Spying on me now, are you?" he called after me. "I must warn you, I have little patience with Peeping Toms."

I thought of Edgar peering through the door into his master's room, but I said nothing. I had no wish to make an enemy of him tonight. Instead I leaned against the doorframe and shrugged.

"My mistress said she means to give me something. I thought perhaps it might be ready."

Edgar smiled, picking his teeth with a scalpel.

"Well, I may be able to assist you there," he said, winking lasciviously. "Provided you were to offer me some manner of favour in return, of course."

My desperation for the medicine overcame my natural distaste.

"You will always have my friendship, Edgar," I managed to say.

"Friendship!" he mocked. "A harlot's friendship! Well, well. Doubtless you would have me converse with a sirloin of beef before I carve it?"

Before I could reply, the bell rang for supper. I ate little. Though Mrs. Black made much of the beef she permitted us, the meat was dry and tough and caught in my throat. It was only much later, when we were putting out the fire, that my mistress came to me. She held out a cup of Lambeth delft from which a curl of steam uncoiled in a kind of promise. My hand shook as I took it from her and lowered my head over the cup, inhaling the tea's flowery scent. It smelled strangely sweet for something so injurious.

"An infusion of honey and nutmeg with a little syrup of motherwort," Mrs. Black said. "It will provoke the urine and settle the womb."

I shrugged away her fictions, swallowing the hot liquid so quickly it blistered the inside of my mouth. I licked my gums afterwards, seeking out a bitter flavour, but I found none. My mother had pounded fern with the pink-flowering hyssop that some country folk called gladiola, which she sent me to gather in early summer on the boggy ground near the river. She claimed the tincture helped ease the inflammations of the dropsy and the gout, but I knew that most of the women to whom she gave it were swollen with a quite different condition.

What Mrs. Black's prescription might be I could not guess. The liquid mixed with the fear in my belly until I almost retched, tasting soured honey in the back of my throat. When I asked Mrs. Black, my voice trembling a little, if I might depend upon her coming to me when I called, she snorted a little through her nose and bid me cease my nonsense. I did not doubt that she would derive some considerable satisfaction from finding me drowned in my own blood.

Taking a bundle of rags that I had been meant to char for tinder, I took to my bed. Mary came and as usual fell instantly asleep. For several hours I lay still, listening to her breathing, waiting for the cramps to come. I could sense them moving at the edges of my belly, dark and silent, gathering their strength. Biding their time. In the lane two dogs bellowed and howled, locked in ferocious battle. Their baying scraped down my spine, sharp with teeth, splattering across my skin like hot saliva. I buried my face beneath the pillow but the snarls crept into the spaces between the feathers and twisted themselves into my hair. They mixed with the churnings in my belly, with the silent moaning of the worm as the liquid blistered and burned and tore its tiny fists away from my flesh. The fear in my mouth tasted strong and gristly, like tainted meat.

Perhaps I fell asleep. When I woke it was almost dawn. There had been no blood, no cramps, no pain. Between the brackets of my hips, the swell of my belly rose matter-of-factly, resolutely.

In the hall Mrs. Black frowned as I seized her hands. Coldly she detached my fingers.

"You look tired, child."

"But nothing happened!" I said frantically. "Nothing at all."

"I myself was kept awake by the fearful racket of a dog fight," Mrs. Black observed calmly, as though she had not heard me. "Edgar tells me you are frightened of dogs, is that right? I have to confess last night I was somewhat unsettled myself."

Another time I might have taken pleasure in the idea of Mrs. Black being unsettled. Now I cared only for myself.

"Bugger the dogs!" I wailed. "Do you not hear me? Nothing happened!"

Mrs. Black glared at me. For a moment I thought she would strike me for cursing. I tried to stand straighter, to return her gaze without flinching. Then, abruptly, she pressed her lips together and let out a sharp puff of breath.

"What on earth did you expect?" she snapped, turning away. "Your stools indicate that your bowel is moving adequately. It would hardly do to purge you at such a time. Now, I suggest you rest. You would not want to overtire yourself in your condition."

And that was the end of it. Nothing more was said.

Jewkes came today. He was in sickeningly high spirits, having come directly from the Cathedral, which he claimed magnificent. He had climbed to the gallery in the dome & had had his man carve his & his companion's initials upon the stone. "For Posterity," he said, as though his graffito was as great a gift to history as the works of Harvey & Sydenham together. I can only despair of such a patron. He insisted upon raising objections to my method, most of them dull & all of them unscientific. No man questions the virtue of anatomising felons, who have been hung from the neck for their crimes against their fellow men. Why, then, can he not see that the subject has, through her actions, placed herself beyond the bounds of civilised society? At least this way she may atone in some way for the sin she has committed. If the man is so damned keen on Posterity, why can he not permit me to make my mark upon it unencumbered, & in his name? Truly, he is a Philistine.

Still, he pays & his visits calm Mrs. Black, whose thoughts are all for the tedium of pounds & shillings. Would that they calmed me too. For all that he cannot rob from me the pleasure I continue to derive from my work here, vexation with the man takes its toll upon my health. My stomach, though not painful, is unsettled, my digestion erratic & plagued with wind. The tincture does not soothe me as it once did but rather inflames my blood, striking in my breast a strange agitated feeling, so that my legs jump & twitch. My skin itches ferociously, upon the surface & deep within itself, as though ants crawl in my veins. Sleep is no comfort. I dream of dark shadows, bright with eyes & teeth, & wake exhausted.

But I must not succumb. All will be well. I must think always, only, of the work. Complexity & confusion rendered simple, perfectly clear. No pyrotechnics, no manipulations. Just the living proof. Nullius in Verba. The mysteries of Creation laid bare, in their magnificent simplicity.

Jewkes informed me today that the dome of that Cathedral is not a single dome but rather three, one set inside the other like eggshells. The dome that may be seen from the inside is quite a different structure from the lead casing that encloses it, & there is another of brick, or wood, I do not recollect which, that forces the two together. Jewkes of course thought it brilliant, his builder's brain quite unfit to grasp the iniquitous cheat of it.

Wren is a charlatan. He may deceive the citizens of London, but only a man of his arrogance could presume to deceive God.

XII

I meant to escape. I dreamed of it, planned it, staring out of the window at the dome that was not afraid of anything. All I had to do was to go as far as the stand-pipe and keep on walking. I had the four guineas I had taken from my mother. I could find lodgings somewhere else in London, find someone willing to expel the worm. It was the part after that I could not imagine. Four guineas was a fine fortune until it was spent. I knew not a soul in London. I thought of the thieves that lurked in the dark courtyards along the Strand, the villains and the swindlers, the pimps and the drunks and the whores and the half-wild dogs. I thought of the fights that broke out like boils, the thundering carriages and rearing horses, the trampling crowds, the dark doorways of Cheap-side where the broken-down beggars clutched at your skirts, half-naked and famished for the want of bread, and I thought—tomorrow. Tomorrow, if still nothing is done tomorrow, then I shall go.

The day I overheard the conversation was one such day. It must have been mid-morning because the dome's clock had just struck ten times. My breakfast finished, I had heaved a bucket of water upstairs so that I might mop the parlour. Distressed as always by the onset of her monthlies, Mary had wept when I asked her to assist me, complaining of pains in her stomach, and I was in a poor temper. In the hallway I clattered the bucket down, slopping water. The door through to the shop stood open, and I could see Mrs. Black outlined in the street door, the alligator hanging down above her head so that, from where I stood, it resembled a vast and jaunty hat. She was conversing with someone, I could not see whom, and I stopped to listen. It was the unusual timbre of her voice that caught my attention. There was something almost confiding about it.

99

"Oh yes, indeed," I heard her murmur. "The girl's husband is a relative of my husband's, a very good family, of course. But he has interests in the Indies that require him there, and now there are fears of smallpox in the parish. Naturally we offered to have her stay with us for the duration of her confinement. It is a great relief to his mother. After all, here we may attend properly to her needs."

"You are a good woman," I heard a woman reply. She moved a little so that she might more easily peer into the shop, and I saw that it was the wife of the chandler, Mr. Dormer, whose shop faced ours. She was a whey-faced woman with a weakness for fancy lace, which she wore in a soapy lather round her neck, and a powerful interest in her neighbours' affairs. It was said she possessed an archbishop's instinct for a sinner.

My mistress shifted a little, obscuring her view.

"It is no more than my duty," Mrs. Black corrected smoothly. "Ah, Mr. Nicholls, good day to you. I have your prescription already prepared. Mrs. Dormer, will you excuse me? I should not wish to keep a customer waiting."

Stepping back, she ushered Mr. Nicholls into the shop. I caught a glimpse of Mrs. Dormer on tiptoes, squinting and stretching for a better view, before Mrs. Black closed the door. As for me, I barely had the presence of mind to hide myself. My head swam. Mrs. Dormer knew. But how? Though I was a sturdy girl, I was naturally narrow at the waist. My breasts were swollen, but as yet my belly protruded only a little way and I was still able to wear my usual stays, albeit more loosely laced than usual. Even a friend of long acquaintance might not yet be quite certain. Surely Mrs. Black would never have confided such information of her own accord. Such an indiscretion might prove ruinous, particularly for the wife of an apothecary. It would take only a neighbour with a grudge, perhaps someone whose expensive preparations had failed to cure them or who owed the Blacks money. A woman of my mistress's disposition would hardly make so elementary a mistake. It wasn't even as though she was fond of conversation. Most of the time her lips were cramped so tightly together the sharp lines around them might have been stitches, sewing them shut. And yet had I not just heard her speaking of it openly, without a trace of shame?

I leaned dizzily against the wall, my legs unsteady. My hands were perfectly cold as I placed them flat against my belly. The worm's features pressed outwards from their blank clay, making of the lump a nose, ears, two hands. A child. Until this moment I had never thought it a child.

That night Mrs. Black brought Mary a tincture to soothe her stomach.

"White Archangel," she said, and set a cup before me too. "It is to be hoped it may improve your temper somewhat. Come on now, drink."

She crossed her arms, waiting. I hesitated. Then, quickly, hardly caring what it was, I snatched up the cup, drained it, and handed it back to her. My mouth burned. Mrs. Black raised an eyebrow and said nothing, turning instead to Mary, who gazed into her tea, her eyes crossed in concentration. The steam made sparkles in her sparse eyebrows. By the time she was finished, my nerve-strings were stretched so tightly that my toes clenched in my boots.

That night I could not sleep. Questions that writhed in my skull, frenzied and senseless, packed so densely it was impossible to know where one ended and another began. Beside me Mary snored, her mouth slack. More than once I kicked her, but she slept so deeply that she did not even turn over. But though I twisted and thrashed, I could not get comfortable. The rugs wound themselves about my legs, tethering me to wakefulness. Beneath me the apothecary traced his perpetual circles, the low murmur of his voice licking up through the floor like the suck and rush of a tireless sea, and beyond the window the dome gleamed, closed tight. I turned away from the casement, squeezing my eyes shut, but still the questions pressed in, closing my nostrils, filling my mouth with their metalled tang. I buried my face in my hands, my fingers plaited into my hair as though I might tug the answers from my scalp.

All of a sudden there was a noise on the staircase, running feet, hardly human, and something of iron like a chain clanking against wood. I hardly had time to be alarmed before the door to the garret banged open. Light blazed on the narrow landing, so brilliant that for a moment I was certain the house was on fire. Immediately I started out of bed, my eyes dazzled, shaking frantically at Mary's shoulder. She grunted but she did not wake. I struck her with my fist.

"Wake up, you gowking—"

The words died on my lips. For, at that moment, with a most awful roar, a monster from the depths of Hell hurled its full weight into the room, its chest held out before it like a shield, its front legs aloft. Its teeth mauled the darkness, great streams of slaver looping from its jaws. Its eyes were bright with murderous rage. It roared again, the length of its fiendish body resonating with the noise. It was so close I could smell its foul breath, sulphurous with sin. My ears were full of a deafening clamour, but I could not move. I stared instead at the creature's collar, a dark circlet set with iron studs and an iron chain that shook and banged. I could feel the warm seep of piss down the inside of my thigh. My bowels melted.

It had come for me. It was not the house that burned. The fires of Hell licked up the stairs, crimson flames bloody with vengeance. The envoy of the Devil had come to claim me, to drag my wicked soul back down into Hell's perpetual inferno. Frantically I tried to think of something, a prayer, a curse, anything to keep the monster at bay, but my mind was blank, white with shock.

Help me. Oh sweet Jesus.

The words were meagre and weak as cobwebs. It was too late now to plead for mercy. The deal was already struck. The thin stuff of my nightdress clung to my shaking body, soaked with sweat and excrement. The ghastly beast strained ever closer towards me, its tongue Satan-red, the sinews standing out from its neck in hangman's ropes, its teeth bared in a ghastly voracious grimace.

I could do nothing. I could only wait for the suffocating bulk of its body pressing down on mine, for the meaty stink of its fur, the scream of its claws burying themselves in my neck as its teeth tore into the flesh of my stomach. The beast roared again and hurled itself forwards. I screamed, falling backwards and striking my head against the corner of the bed. For a moment the room was streaked with colour, scattered all over with a fine silver dust.

Then it went black.

UPON THE MATERNAL IMAGINATION
Notes for Section ix, revision xvii

The female imagination is a temptation sent by God, to test a woman's virtue & determine her fitness for the Kingdom of Heaven, just as a man must do battle with the grossness of his carnal appetites

A chaste & virtuous woman may be certain that her imagination, be it ever so strong, may find, in the purity of her soul, a mighty shield, an unassailable fortress that may protect the soft & blameless flesh of her unborn infant

But in the bosom of the sinful the soul is <u>weak</u>, a rusting armour, a crumbling buttress, defenceless against the dark forces of the imagination, which must then vanquish the citadel of the womb, just as the gout seizes an old man's foot

The imagination imprints itself only upon those women who are sinful, godless, corrupt, but she senses it not & suffers not. She feels no pain. It is the child who must wear always the bitter stain of her sin, the child whom the world judges as monstrous

THE BASE WOMAN FEELS NO PAIN

XIII

When I woke it was morning, cold grey light pressing flat the awkward angles of the room and illuminating the sounds of the new day: the clatter of horses and carriages, the heavy rumble of shop barrows, the calls of the criers. It was late. I tried to raise my head from the pillow, but it was heavy and stupid, stuffed with sleep. My eyes and mouth were gritty and dry. With an effort I turned my head. Beside me Mary lay sprawled on her back, her mouth open, her twisted bolster blotched with spittle stains. I felt a choppiness in my guts, like a premonition. Why had the mistress not roused us? Then, humping the mess of rugs over my head, I closed my eyes and sought to burrow back into sleep. One of my hands was prickled with numbness, as though I had lain upon it all night, and I flexed my fingers sleepily. Mary would wake me when it was time. For an addle-head, she was vexingly punctilious.

"Colly Molly Puff! Colly Molly Puff!"

Again the uneasy twist in my guts. Reluctantly I pushed the blankets away from my face and, with an effort, struggled to sit up. Colly Molly, the pastry-man, did not pass this way until after nine o'clock. My breath made smoke as I shook at Mary's shoulder. She grunted in her sleep, sucking upon her tongue, but she did not wake. On its nail my stomacher hung empty, slack without the shape of me, but still I could not summon urgency, only a chill and queasy dread. Ice glazed the inside of the casement window. It was bitterly cold.

There was the brisk tap of footsteps upon the stairs, the rap of the mistress's knuckles upon the door as the key scraped in the lock.

"We are all slept late today. Up now and quick about it," Mrs. Black instructed crisply, but there was no harshness in her voice.

Hurriedly I stumbled out of bed, gasping at the shock of the cold floor against my stockinged feet, but she did not open the door. Instead, her soles tap-tapped away down the stairs. I shivered and, thrusting my arms into my dress, shouted at Mary to shift her idle backside out of bed. She half-raised her head, her eyes slitted against the light, and let it fall.

"Go 'way," she muttered, already almost asleep again.

I yanked hard at the laces of my bodice, pulling the waist as tight as I could bear it. It steadied me somehow. Twisting my hair into my cap, I stepped into my boots and, with a great sweep of my arm, pulled the rugs from Mary's prone body. She cried out, her face contorting with befuddled indignation.

"Didn't you hear the mistress?" I muttered. "Get up. Don't think I shall do your work for you."

Chafing my arms with my cold hands, I stamped across the room. A mess of bells rang out the hour. In the rippling silence that followed, a dog barked fiercely. I stopped, the fear rising in my throat like vomit. I swallowed hard, shaking my clogged head to clear it. The cracked basin with the blue stripe contained an inch of icy water. Steeling myself, I thrust my hands into it and splashed some on my face.

The chill of it ached against my temples. I pressed my fingers into my eyes, waiting for the pain to disperse, and abruptly the dusty red-black of my closed eyes gaped in a ghastly roar, framed by glittering silver teeth. I managed only a shudder of remembered terror before the bitter nausea spiked my throat. Hauling the chamberpot from beneath the bed, I was violently sick.

Groggily Mary raised her head, her hands tugging at her wild hair, but I did not look at her. I had to get out of the garret. Snatching up my shawl, I stumbled towards the door. I refused to notice the fresh white marks scored in the floorboards by the door but stepped over them, my fists clenched for balance. In the kitchen everything would be ordinary, dull. I would see the cups lined up in their usual places on the dresser, hear the giddy peeps of the linnet as it hopped upon its perch, the rapt greed on the face of the yellow cat as it pretended not to watch. Mary would come down and smile at me in her squinting lopsided way and wipe her nose against the back of her hand, and another dreary day could begin.

The dog barked again, his snarls stretched into an undulating howl. I fled downstairs.

The apothecary was in his study. I could hear his footsteps on the floorboards as he paced to and fro. But before I had set my foot upon the landing, he opened his door, craning his head out. His face was uncovered. He wore neither cap nor wig, and his shaved head was hazy with grey stubble. I could not endure any of his questions. I tried to slip past him, but he caught me by the sleeve. His grip was tight. In his other hand, he held a glass bottle, quite empty. His lips were dry and cracked and coated with something white as though he had been sucking on a stick of chalk. The white gathered in thick scabs in the corners of his mouth, making the stain on his cheek look redder than ever, and behind his spectacles, his eyes were huge black holes ringed with a thread of pale blue.

"Good morning," he said, and the tip of his tongue flickered over his lips. "You slept well?"

Too late I realised that I looked him directly in the face. I twisted my gaze away, gripping the handrail. The lateness of the hour suggested surely that he meant the question sardonically, but there was something fervent in his tone that belied mockery. Although I had looked directly into his eyes, I had no idea what it was he wanted of me.

"Thank you, sir," I replied carefully, trying to steady the tremble in my voice. "Though I think I am not quite well."

The apothecary took a step closer to me. He smelled of stale wine and liquorice and something charred and foreign like burnt caramel. I closed my eyes, willing him to let me go.

"Feverish. I shall see you directly after I have taken breakfast. Or perhaps—yes. Before supper, I think. When the sun has set."

My legs fell heavily against the treads of the stairs as I stumbled downstairs. The kitchen was empty, although the kettle whistled to itself on the range. I took a rag and lifted it from the heat, pouring the water into the waiting teapot. Then I took cups from the dresser and set them upon the table, along with a loaf which I put to warm in the ashes of the fire. The cheese was flecked with weevils, so I cut out the black spots before placing it on a plate. I still felt nauseous, but the routine nature of the tasks calmed me a little. As for the dread, I swallowed it down with all my strength and would not look at it. Gradually my hands ceased their shaking. When I sat, I concentrated on the feet of the people hurrying through the high slice of window and tried to imagine the missing parts of their bodies. I had often amused myself this way, but on this particular morning I set about the task with uncharacteristic resolve. When Mrs. Black rapped my shoulder with her knuckles, I jumped as though I had been burned.

"I am most displeased with you," she admonished me. "You disturbed the entire household with your hollerings last night. You are fortunate the apothecary is in merciful humour this morning. He sleeps ill at the best of times without a thoughtless chit of a girl bellowing the house down."

I stared at her helplessly.

"Don't look at me that way, my girl. You should be falling over yourself to thank me. After all it was I who was roused, I who was obliged to change you when you had soiled your nightgown."

I rubbed my face.

"My nightgown—?" I managed. My mouth was dry.

"Ranting on and on like a Tom o' Bedlam when frankly it would have behoved you to show some gratitude," Mrs. Black continued. "Next time I shall surely leave you to rot in your own filth."

"I—thank you."

"Indeed. It is clear something has inflamed you. I have asked Edgar to make you up something to cool your liver. But let me say this. Your lurid inventions have no place in this house."

"Inventions!" The tears started in my eyes. "But—"

Mrs. Black held up her hand for silence. Her face was grim.

"If you are to remain under my roof, you shall endure the sufferings that God sees fit to send you with considerably more courage than you have displayed thus far. I shall not tolerate hysteric distempers in my house, Mrs. Campling."

She pressed her fingers hard into my neck, feeling for my pulse.

"I shall see your pot when you have opened your bowel," she ordered. "Now eat and be quick about it. And where is the other girl? You are already lamentably behind with your work."

The day passed with agonising slowness. I stumbled through my duties hardly noticing the movements of my hands. When at last the idiot troubled to drag her idle bones downstairs, she chattered on in her unintelligible way, but I heard not a word of it. My head was already frantic with its own manner of gibberish, all distressed flappings and squawks that bounced off my skull and skittered out of reach in the darkness. Despite the chill, I sweated into my stays. Again and again the dog's jaws gaped in the soft bruised space between my eyes, and I had to squeeze them shut, my fingertips pressed into the sockets, until the shifting yellow patterns behind my eyelids forced the image away. In their place were scratches, long pale scratches, dug with claws into the soft timber of a floorboard. Not inventions. Not inventions at all.

It had grown dark when the apothecary's bell sounded, the moon no more than a curved gash in the black sky. The bells in the apothecary's house were used so seldom that we never troubled to oil them, and this one scraped tentatively, as though it cleared its throat. Mary bounced up and down on the balls of her feet, tugging at her apron and pointing. The bell rang again.

"For pity's sake, enough!" I snarled. "Must you ring that damned thing off the wall?"

The anger was solid, consoling. Snatching up a tallow light, I stamped up the dark stairs with enough force to make kindling of them. When I reached the master's door, I did not tap it with the knuckle of my index finger as I had been taught. I beat upon it with my fist.

"Come."

My master sat at the heavy oak table, a quill held aloft in one hand. In the centre of the table stood two great heaps of papers, one secured by a coffee cup, another by the sugar bowl, and beside them a tarnished girandole bearing five dripping candles. The flames dipped as I entered, shifting the shadows so that the furniture itself seemed to move about the room. He had put on his wig, the old-fashioned one with the horns, and a suit of rusty black. He reached for the girandole, bringing it closer so that it illumined his face. Quickly I looked away.

"So," he said.

Even with my eyes averted, his restiveness was striking. He moved like a draught round his papers, lifting corners and letting them drop. Even when he sat, his legs twitched beneath the table, his toes dancing a precise and dogged jig, round and round, while his fingers drummed on the arm of his chair and his wig flicked about his shoulders like a horse's tail. Even the stuff of his plain black clothes seemed constantly to shift, like a nest of stinging ants arranged in the shape of a man. Crumbs swarmed about his feet.

"What is it you want?" I demanded.

I waited for him to reprimand my insolence, but although his fingers flexed dangerously, the apothecary said nothing. Instead, he gesticulated at my usual chair with his quill, sending an arc of black ink spots across the floor. His hat hung from the chair's back, its veil almost touching the floor. I sat stiffly on the edge of the seat, as far from it as I could manage.

"Hmm. My wife tells me you suffered a nightmare last night." The apothecary unglued his tongue from the roof of his mouth, but still the words came out stuck together. He took a sip from a glass at his elbow. "You may begin by relating to me all you can recollect of the apparition."

Immediately my anger deserted me, leaving nothing but the cold roil of sickness in my stomach. Around me the shadows seemed to darken and shift. My lips were numb and dry, making words impossible. Pleadingly I shook my head.

"From the beginning, if you please. You shall describe first the particulars of the dream itself. I will then have a number of questions I wish you to answer. I would press you to speak clearly and pause when I tell you. I shall wish to make notes."

He reached out to dip the quill into the inkwell, his hand shaking so violently that he was required to steady the wrist with the other hand. I stared down at my lap, my head still moving from side to side. In the silence a log shifted in the fire, sending a fan of sparks up the chimney.

"Damn it, girl, speak! I shall not tolerate defiance!"

His eyes were red with agitation, the stain on his face dark as a bruise, as he hurled the quill onto the table. Hot tears swelled in my eyes.

"Come, come now, my dear, so distressed?" the apothecary said with singsong gentleness, the rage so rapidly extinguished it seemed certain I had imagined it. With quiet deliberation, he picked up his quill and, turning away from me, studied the nib before taking a knife from his pocket and carefully sharpening it. I could see his reflection in the window-pane, the way his mouth smiled. The purple stain was a dark hole through which I could make out the flaking white paintwork of the chandler's window opposite. I sniffed, wiping my nose on my sleeve.

The apothecary took a slow, deep breath.

"You are quite undone, are you not? Shall I have Mary bring us chocolate?"

Mary kept her eyes on the floor as she rattled the tray onto a side table and scuttled from the room. I had only ever tasted chocolate before on those occasions when I was the first to the master's empty cup and could run my finger around its bottom to rescue the last gritty dregs. Now the warm creamy liquid coated my tongue with its silky sweetness. I rested the rim of my cup against my chin and inhaled, allowing the fragrant steam to soothe the queasiness in my belly.

"I would encourage you to begin," the apothecary said smoothly to the window as I took another slow sip. "I shall need to know everything. And I shall not permit you to leave this room until I am satisfied."

He smiled again and his fingers drummed impatiently against the arm of his chair. I swallowed and pressed my teeth into my lips so that the pain might restore me a little and lend me the composure to begin. In my hand the cup rattled in its saucer.

"You would not wish me to impel you to speak now, would you?"

Although the smile still curved his lips, all trace of it had vanished from his voice.

"I—I—"

"Yes?" The quill stabbed.

"I—I don't understand." The words rushed from my mouth. I hardly knew I was thinking them until they crowded into the space between us. "It is—I don't understand, sir. Why you wish to know."

I gazed at him helplessly, braced for the wooden rule to slice the air. Instead, the apothecary stared out of the window, his chin resting upon his hand.

"Why I wish to know," he said at last.

"Yes, sir," I whispered.

The apothecary blinked rapidly, several times. Then, laying down his quill, he turned his chair round so that he faced me. I quickly looked away. Pushing aside a pile of papers, my master leaned across the table and motioned to me to give him my hand. I hesitated. Then, keeping my eyes averted, I did as he asked.

"Look at me," he commanded.

"But—"

"I said, look at me."

Slowly I raised my eyes.

"Yes, that's right, look. Look hard."

He was breathing hard, as though he had been running. I looked. Unpowdered, his stained cheek was the muted purple of blackberry juice, its surface pocked and coarse. It faded out gradually on the upward slope of his nose, like a wine stain on a tablecloth, but across his brow where the mark was raised and puffy, it came to an abrupt stop, which contrasted starkly with the yellowing wax of his high forehead. Observing the direction of my gaze, he traced the raised border with the tips of his fingers, inviting me to study it. In its dull purple frame, the white of his right eye was a livid red, its black centre no more than a pinprick. I shifted unhappily, my gaze sliding away.

"Well? What is it you see?"

"I—"

"You are disgusted. Doubtless you think me grotesque, a fresh-faced young girl like you."

"No, sir, no—that is, I—"

"Well?"

"It is not so very bad," I whispered.

The apothecary expelled a strange, strangled snort of laughter. His brow sparkled with perspiration.

"Not so very bad. Is that so? Let me tell you something. All my life people have looked upon my face and seen only this, this mark upon my skin. To them I am not a good husband or a loyal friend nor even a fine and original mind. To them I am only this, this patch of ruined flesh! A disfigurement made man!"

He seized his wooden rule and brought it down hard upon the table. I bowed my head, squeezing my hands in my lap, stiffening myself against the blow. I could not imagine how this must end.

"All my life I have suffered fearsome dreams." Once again he spoke softly, cupping his stained cheek tenderly in his hand. I had to strain to hear him. My back ached, my stomach too. I wrapped my arms round my stomach, willing the interview to be over. "Apparitions that stalk the darkness and cause me to wake with sweat upon my skin and a scream in my mouth. You seem surprised. Perhaps you thought a man of science impervious to, or even dismissive of, such imagined horrors. But you are wrong, quite wrong. I have embarked upon a study of such things. Yes, indeed. A study for no less than the Royal Society itself. And I require your assistance. Even a humble maidservant may bear witness. A man of science cares more for truth than for distinctions of birth. Come, let us begin. We have already wasted enough time."

His cajolery had a hysteric edge, the desperate conviction of a prophet or a madman. The candles guttered. The wooden rule twitched in his hand, pleasuring itself against the edge of the table, as very carefully I lifted my chocolate cup to my lips. The liquid had grown cold and a sticky skin adhered to my lips. My throat pulled into a knot as I picked it off with my fingernails. In my lap the cup rattled in its saucer. I knew then that this would never end, that, unless I told him what it was he wanted to hear, I would remain here in this room forever.

"If you wish it, sir."

"Excellent."

The master's face clenched, his eyes blinking frantically. Then, clearing his throat as he pulled a pile of papers towards him, he set about his questions. What was the nature of the dream? Had I believed myself asleep or awake? How had it affected my pulse, my bowel? Had I sweated with fear, or had I been rendered cold? Had I feared death? Had I suffered cramps, bleeding? How had I felt upon waking?

At first my answers were brief, each hesitant phrase requiring a great effort of will, but, to my surprise, as the interview progressed, my tongue grew looser and more willing. The words came in sudden unexpected surges that scoured the inside of my chest. It felt good to be rid of them.

To my relief, it seemed that the responses I gave were the right ones. My master's head nodded in convulsive little jerks as he wrote and wrote, his mouth working furiously as he numbered each fresh page. Sometimes he even sighed and closed his eyes, smiling tenderly as though he, too, had suffered just as I had. When he grew tired, he raised a hand to silence me, putting down his pen and making patterns with his fingers to ease the cramps. It was easier when he bid me turn my chair so that I no longer faced him. The wall made for an easier confessor. When I admitted that I had been sure that the beast was the agent of the Devil, sent to claim me for Hell, I surprised even myself. Behind me my master drew in his breath sharply. I clenched my fists in my lap, horrified by my recklessness, but, to my astonishment, he said nothing. He only wrote faster, pressing so hard with his quill that he tore right through the paper.

Then, suddenly, he dismissed me. He did not trouble to raise his head from his paper as I left the room, so engrossed was he in the act of scribbling. I rose unsteadily from my chair. I had no idea how long I had been there.

"My studies show that the most alarming dreams have a propensity to recur," he mused. "I hope for your sake that you do not suffer the same miseries tonight."

I flinched.

"I fear that the more afraid of our dreams we are, the more they haunt us. And you, I think, are very afraid. Go now."

"Sir." It was barely more than a whisper, but all the same a strange compulsion drove me on. "Sir, about the—about my condition—"

The apothecary looked up.

"What do you think you are staring at?" he barked, suddenly enraged.

I shook my head helplessly.

"Nothing, sir."

"I should damned well hope not, if you do not wish a night in the cellar. Brash little strumpets, the lot of you. Now get out, before I thrash you!"

He snatched up the wooden rule. Whimpering, I staggered to the door, wrenching it open. On the dark landing, I leaned against the wall, my heart thumping. The taste of chocolate soured in my mouth. Suddenly a light loomed up the stairs.

"Been helping the apothecary with his studies, have we?"

Edgar stood before me, a rushlight flickering in his hand. A smirk tugged at his lips.

"I don't see what business it is of yours," I retorted, but Edgar knew a winged bird when he saw one.

"Make sure you lace your stomacher back up before the mistress sees you," he drawled, fumbling a key into the lock of his door. "I wouldn't like to think what would become of you if she was to discover any of your smutty little goings-on."

"You shut your scurvy mouth before I shut it for you," I spat. "What kind of a trollop do you take me for?"

"Ah, let me think," Edgar shot back. "The kind of trollop who needs to come to an apothecary's house to be relieved of her troubles?"

He blew me a contemptuous kiss and shut the door behind him. The landing went dark, but the echo of his laughter clung to the chilly air, acrid as smoke.

Mr. Johanssen
Apothecary at the sign of the Golden Hind at Cornhill

Dear Mr. Johanssen,

I received your letter by this morning's post.

I would like to think, sir, that we are both men of science, distrustful of long words & fancy metaphors. I know you would desire me therefore to express my opinions to you with the utmost candour.

Like you, I hold the institution of the Royal Society in the highest esteem. Unlike you, I have not been cowed by the disrespect in which apothecaries have always (& frequently without justification) been held by physicians & their kind. Unlike you, I do not consider my intellect deficient because I have not purchased myself a degree in France & have not a tame bishop who might be persuaded (for a price) to confer upon me the distinction of Doctor of Medicine. It would behove you to remember that there remains a difference between one skilled in the art of physick & one skilled in the art of promoting himself as a physician.

As for your criticisms of my treatise, I take issue with almost every one of your remarks. I stand upon the brink of a great discovery, the proof of which I hold in my hands, <u>in my hands</u>. How dare you then to direct me that "when & if you discern anything of note, it would be appropriate to submit your observations to the Society without the encumbrance of attempted analysis or interpretation," as though I were no more than a common witness? Are you so blinded by the reputation of your fellows that you do not see what it is they do, extracting from men such as myself the work of a lifetime so that they might claim it for their own? I may be a simple scholar, sir, but I for one am not a fool.

Mr. Johanssen, I have been frank & I intend to be franker still. I would not presume to question the agency by which you contrived your election to the Society. I would, however, regard it as no less than my duty to counsel you that there is a considerable danger, when a man enjoys a measure of success, either through his own merits or the patronage of others, that he will become vain & self-regarding. Far from reaching a hand to others so that they, too, may ascend to greater heights, he kicks the ladder away so that he might protect his position & defend against those who would challenge his position.

A man's conscience may over time, & for greater ease & comfort, grow deaf & blind. But let me say this. Remember that the Lord God, into whose hands we must all surrender ourselves at the Day of Judgement, looks ill upon such men, for all that they are Fellows of this society or that, or held in esteem by the powerful few to whom they take care to ingratiate themselves.

It is imprudent in this short life to make enemies on Earth. It is surely calamitous to make them in Heaven.

I am, sir, &c.,

GRAYSON BLACK

XIV

Mindful of my master's warning, I endeavoured not to be afraid, but I found only that fear feeds upon itself, raising an edifice of apprehension from which I could not escape. The first night I drank the infusion that Mrs. Black gave me to help me sleep, but still the ghastly apparition came, so real to me I could smell the stink of meat upon its breath. After that I did not drink, though I pretended to. Instead, I fought sleep with all my strength, terrified of the horrors that lurked within its dark walls. And every night, when at last it overtook me, those horrors returned, not the same every night but altered in their form so that I was never able even to seek that shred of comfort that may come from a nightmare's dreadful familiarity. I woke to the sound of my own screams and, on the third night, to the shrill scrape of Mary's cries as well. Mrs. Black was roused and came to the garret, her face creased with sleep and her grey hair plaited in a rough rope that hung stiffly from her unadorned nightcap. When she had struck me enough, she informed me that tonight would be the last night she would tolerate my disturbances. From henceforth, I was to sleep in the kitchen.

The following morning Mary wept as I gathered my few things and placed them in my box for removal to the kitchen. She clung to me with her chapped hands, shaking her head.

"Doan', doan'," she pleaded, her clumsy tongue flapping in her mouth like a fish. "Doan' go. Pliss. Pliss, Lize. Stay Mar'—"

She buried her face against my shoulder, smearing me with snot and tears. I stared down at the top of her head. The sight of the bald hairless patch made the tears spring in my eyes. I felt a powerful urge to strike her. Instead, I pushed her roughly away. When I took up my box, its sharp edge barked her shin.

"See how you've unsettled the child," Mrs. Black reproved me when she came down to the kitchen later. "You will take no more beef for the remainder of the month. Its melancholic vapours have quite corrupted you."

Mary herself refused to look at me. Her cheeks were marbled with scarlet, the back of her hands pinched and shiny with dried snot.

At night, when the small fire had died, the kitchen was fearful dark. From the window of the garret, it was possible to stretch one's neck and see not only the dome but the glow of Cheap-side, ablaze with light through the small hours of the night. Even in the lesser thoroughfares, the laws of the city required the residents, on those nights of the month when the moon was slight, to display lamps until midnight in the winter so that the circles of light came close to touching one another. But in the kitchen, one lay beneath the level of the street, and, besides, ours was too insignificant a lane to be bound by such a obligation. At night, when the few faint lights in the windows across the way had been extinguished, the kitchen was as black as a tomb. Somewhere beyond the window, the dome traversed the sky like a lead ship, impervious to my subterranean misery. It would not remember me.

My first night alone there was windy, thick with rain. Outside the shop signs creaked and groaned, and a cascade of water poured from a spout in the wall, splattering the kitchen window with mud. The water bubbled and dripped where the frame had rotted. From time to time, unseen feet hastened past the window, rattling the glass. I had overheard the chandler's wife tell of the thieves who had stolen from an open window a pair of new and valuable curtains from their pole. These days the picklocks were so bold, Mrs. Dormer had sighed, that they might enter a man's house in broad daylight and carry out every last stick of furniture before you could say, "Stop, thief!" One might know such brigands, she added firmly, by their white stockings. At night it was too dark to make out white stockings.

I shivered, pulling the thin blanket round me. Beneath my palliasse the stone floor exhaled a damp chill, its crumbling mortar lush with the stink of the cesspit in the cellar beneath. I missed the haphazard slopes of the garret roof, the yeasty smell of our bed, its affable sag. I missed Mary's bulk beside me, her warmth, even the exasperating sticky sound of her champing on her tongue. In the kitchen the noises of the street came so close. I could hear the suck of muddy boots tramping past the window. They slowed, stopped. A lantern glowed lemon against the low slice of window, transforming the raindrops on the glass into one thousand brilliant splinters. My heart squeezed.

"Past eleven o'clock and a rainy night," the jack-o'-lanthorn wheezed, and he stamped his feet in the mud before taking up his lantern and moving on. A buttery smear of light greased the window frame and was gone.

Sleep came suddenly, unexpectedly. That night the beast came at me through the window, forcing its hideous head through the narrow opening. The following night it leapt out from the doorway; on the next from the narrow recess we used as a pantry. Each time it was lit with a brilliant dazzle of fire that stamped my eyelids like a seal. Each time the fear closed its hands round my throat and pressed out the hairs from my skin until my body burned with it. Every morning, when I had drunk my tea, Mrs. Black ordered me to hold out my hands for the birch. When I wept, she sucked in her cheeks so hard that the bones above them threatened to pierce the skin. One morning she had me march out into the lane so that I might show her the prints of this beast I insisted upon. There were none, only churned mud and a single boot print, freshly made. I did not know whether to be comforted or terrified out of my wits.

I sickened. My head shrilled with exhaustion. There was an unceasing pain in my reins so that I had to grip my back tightly with my hands whenever I bent over. My eyes were red and sore, my eyelids lined with sand. A necklace of boils encircled my neck. My teeth ached in their gums. I ate little, unwilling to subject them to the rigours of the gristly mutton Mrs. Black insisted I took in place of beef. My lack of appetite angered the apothecary's wife, who snatched up my plate when I pushed it away, poking with her finger at the food I had left there. She gave me meat to build my strength, she told me sharply. The apothecary would be angered if I did not eat. It would look badly if one of his household sickened. People would talk.

I hardly heard her. Words rattled in my head like dice in a cup and were as quickly despatched. I performed my never-ending duties in a grey haze of misery and fatigue. I stopped thinking about the worm. I did not have the strength to care what became of me. I feared I might be going mad. At other times I despaired that I was not.

On the sixth day I bled. When I felt the first slippery wetness between my thighs, I hardly knew what had happened. It was only when I raised my skirts and saw the rusty stains on the flesh of my thighs, the smear on my cambric petticoat, that I understood. The pains followed quickly, bringing with them a wild exhilaration. At last, at last, it was to be over. The waiting was over. Triumphantly I dragged myself up towards the garret. The pains were stronger now. I clung to the handrail of the stairs as another spasm clamped my belly, pressing round from my back like a metal band, twisting and tightening as if it would tear me in two. I gave myself over to the agony, moaning aloud, urging it forwards, biting down hard on my bottom lip so that I might bear them better. I had nothing to fear from the pain. Each cramp brought me closer to my release, my salvation. I arched my back, the sweat greasing my face, tasting blood in my mouth. I no longer attempted to move. By the time Mrs. Black found me squatting on the stairs, my arms wrapped round my belly, I was already exhausted. As the paroxysm retreated, leaving me gasping for breath, I looked up at her and laughed, a racking breathless sound that caused her to stare at me in undisguised alarm.

Taking both my arms, she pulled me to my feet. Her touch was not unkind. Her starched voice wrinkled at the edges as she bid Mary bring me wine and a warming pan. Once she had me in the bed, she placed a pillow behind my back and charged me to sit as upright as I could manage. Through my half-closed eyes, I could see the curve of the dome, its outline categorical against the smudged grey sky. The pain came in great cramping swoops, as though the Devil pulled my stays. In the breaths in between, I stared upon the dome's burnished cross and ball. When the pain came again, I could see the shape of the cross behind my clenched eyelids, red as blood. I could feel my strength failing, exhilaration leaking away.

I knew I would die.

The light faded from the sky, twists of cloud scattered like potato peelings across the darkening blue. The apothecary came to the door of the garret and conversed in urgent whispers with my mistress. The golden cross mellowed to bronze and then to a dark velvety plum. By nightfall the cramps had eased a little, the respite between them longer. Mrs. Black bound a hot plaister about my belly. She would not let me sleep, although fatigue weighted my eyelids and fogged my head. Instead, she gave me warmed wine with herbs and rubbed my shoulders with a strong-smelling oil. She took no supper, although she bid Mary prepare some for her master, but remained with me, watching me closely. By the time the night-watchman called twelve o'clock, I had ceased to bleed. Mrs. Black had Mary take away the worst of the soiled linen for laundry. Then she blew out the candle and bid me good night. She took the pillow with her.

I laid myself down carefully, inhaling the stale bed frowsty of sweat and blood. It hurt to move. Beyond the window the half-moon lolled upon its back, wan and listless on a narrow bolster of cloud, but the sky was brisk with stars. When at last Mary came to bed, the mattress shifted, jolting my aching belly. I whimpered. Mary gave a strange animal grunt and humped her back against me. Her breathing was thick, lumpy as porridge, and she sucked at her tongue as though she meant to swallow it. Twisted in with the familiar twinge of vexation was something else, something that tugged at my throat so that I swallowed.

For several minutes I lay there, listening to her. I did not kick out at her legs as I usually did or poke a sharp finger in her back, muttering at her to be silent. Instead, very slowly, my hand reached out and laid itself lightly upon her back. I could feel the soft bumps of her spine beneath their wrapper of flesh. Mary stiffened. Abruptly I pulled away my hand and turned over. The pale moon gleaming through the casement etched a dusty cross of shadow on the floor. Mary sighed. Rolling over, she burrowed against me, her sticky child's hand reaching for mine. I hesitated but I did not push her away. Champing busily, she plaited her fingers through mine as her warm body shaped itself against my flank. She was hot as a bed-jar beneath her nightgown and hardly awake. When I was certain she slept, I pressed her hand to my cheek, feeling the soft curve of her knuckles against my temple. Her fingers smelled of salt and cinnamon.

Then I slept too. This time there were no dreams.

Too close, too close. My heart is still racing for I thought it lost, I thought we had lost it. See how my hand trembles. The fear is still upon me, the stink of blood in my nostrils though I stayed away, unable to trust myself to wait. <u>All care must be taken to still the foetus</u>; bed rest for several days mandatory, clarified juice of plantain three times a day to stay the bleeding

I have taken a little tincture & feel myself calmer, my heart slower, propelling my blood less violently to my extremities. Clearer too & caught suddenly by the evident desire of the subject to be rid of child

IS THAT A POSITIVE CONTRIBUTOR TOWARDS SUCCESS OF IMPRESSION??
I had not considered before the <u>effects of maternal ill will</u> upon the foetus, but now it occurs to me that surely the mother's abhorrence for the foetus <u>must</u> alter the impression of imagination

Consider the excessive incidence of monstrosity amongst the poor & <u>in particular in those depraved alliances unsanctioned by matrimony</u>. Of course such women suffer an increased exposure to ugliness & deformity & thus a higher risk of imprinting; also their imagination is untempered by the civilising effects either of pious faith or of reason & scholarship & therefore wilder & more savage in its effects

BUT THIS IS NOT THE SUM OF IT

For is it not undeniable that amongst the low ranks of women, many, perhaps most, pregnancies are <u>unwanted/unwelcome</u>, because such women lack the gentler maternal virtues & the means with which to support their offspring, & therefore the fear & passion that elicit impression may be roused not only by external factors but by the <u>fact of pregnancy itself</u>

RESULTING IN a violent antipathy to unborn child; aggressive nature of ill will exaggerated by ignorance & coarse instincts

⟶ *additional heat generated causing pronounced fermentation &*
consequently <u>*increased salt deposits*</u> *that settle over the solid parts of*
the body of the unborn foetus & contaminate them with their image

↓

ADVANCE SUBJECT'S ANTIPATHY TOWARDS FOETUS
WHEREVER POSSIBLE

XV

The worm survived.

After the bleeding, I suffered a fever that persisted for nearly a week, confining me to my bed, and which, inflamed by the bitter weather that gripped the city in the latter days of March, weakened me severely. When the writhings of the worm roused me at night, I thought of the cramps like iron rings round a barrel, the dark patch where my blood still stained the landing, and I was filled with a bleak terror that squeezed the piss from my bladder in hot brackish trickles. One thought preoccupied me to the exclusion of all others. Dead or alive, the vile creature would be required to come out. I did not think I had the strength to withstand either.

It was more than two weeks before I was able to resume my duties, and even then I grew quickly fatigued, exhaustion fogging my head and dulling any appetite but the craving for sleep. But, in spite of me, my waist thickened, my belly arching into a dome. The waiting was a scream buried in my lungs. I coughed and coughed until my throat was sore, but I could not shift the weight of it. As the days lengthened, the worm grew angles that jabbed my agitated bladder and pressed the curves of my belly into corners. At night it pounded upon my spine. My stays no longer laced. Even though Mrs. Black pronounced me much recovered, it was no longer considered appropriate that I assist in the shop. On the few occasions that the master received visitors, I was instructed to remain out of sight. I heard voices behind closed doors, caught the vague unfamiliar flavours of strangers on the stale dark air of the landings, but, beyond the occupants of Swan-street, I saw no one. When I caught sight of myself in the hall mirror, for all my bulk beneath my loose gown, I had the pallid insubstantial cast of a ghost.

I had the strange sense that if I was ever to venture out into the lane, I might find myself quite invisible.

As for the master, the tread of his feet paced through my nights. According to Edgar, he walked and wrote incessantly, covering sheet after sheet of paper with his close writing, which he kept in a locked wooden cabinet in his study. Every page was printed at the top with the motto of the Society of Apothecaries, *Opiferque per orbem dicor,* which he had Edgar write out in readiness onto countless fresh sheets each day before breakfast. Edgar grumbled that while his dreams had once given him considerable consolation, they were now reduced to those four mean words, chasing each other like dogs round the circle of his skull. I wondered uneasily if the apothecary had intended it so and meant to include Edgar's dreams as well as my own in his study of the subject.

"What do they mean, those words?" I asked Edgar once, when I needed to hear the sound of my own voice.

"Your ignorance never ceases to astonish me," he declared. "Damn this wretched pen, must it smudge every line?" He glared at the paper and crumpled it into a ball, which he tossed towards the fire. It bounced off the chimney-breast, skittering across the flagstones. I picked it up and smoothed it out. "Since you ask, it translates loosely as 'I am called throughout the bringer of aid.' Something of an irony, when you consider it. What aid could our esteemed Turk of a master possibly claim to bring anyone? If there is a soul in this house who deserves such a title, surely it is I. I am up and down to that study with 'aid' so frequently, it is a miracle that the soles of my shoes are not worn clean through. And burn that paper, for the love of peace, before the mistress delivers another of her lectures about household thrift."

Edgar exaggerated but it was true that Mr. Black had come to rely heavily upon an infusion of opium to ease his discomforts. He suffered from agonising stomach cramps, and when the pains seized him, he would swallow a preparation of his own devising, a mixture of opium, rhubarb, and camphor taken in a tumbler of Canary wine. The effect upon him was at the same time remarkable and deeply disquieting. In the midst of an attack, the apothecary might be bent double with the pain, unable to walk or even to speak. But when he had swallowed his laudanum, his eyes shone like two black pearls, bright with dark fire, and his breath came in shallow excitable gasps, his whole frame seized with a fevered energy that danced in his fingers and caused the muscles in his face to jerk and leap.

One morning as I scrubbed the floor in the hall, the master came up behind me. He wore his hat with the veil so that I could not see his face, but from his awkward gait I surmised it was one of his bad days. I shuffled back against the wall, afraid to rouse his displeasure, and kept my eyes upon the bubbled puddle of water before me. I prayed he did not step in it and soil his shoes. He stopped above me, stooping down so that the burnt caramel odour of him filled my nostrils. His fingers were bruised black with ink.

"Soon," he murmured, so quietly I almost did not hear him. "Soon."

He swept towards the door, flinging it open.

"Such a sky!" he marvelled. "Surely all the pearls of the Indies do not gleam with so rare a luminescence."

I hardly heard him. *Soon.* The word clung to me like a cobweb. *Soon.*

That night the worm writhed and thrashed. I was roused frequently by the overwhelming urge to piss. The dome rose above me as I squatted, a cold moon of lead. *Soon.* An unsatisfactory dribble trickled into the pot. Suddenly, without warning, the worm butted my chest with its head. I gasped, the breath knocked from my lungs, and it was as though an obstruction had been shaken from my gullet. I swallowed, blinking, and stared up at the dome, pulling my nightgown over my knees.

Soon. What had become of me? I felt as though I was waking from a long and fevered sleep. *Soon.* I had waited so long, with such blind conviction, that my condition was already far advanced. My belly was round, my breasts heavy. The worm was fat and growing fatter, and soon, very soon, it would come out. It would be real,

solid, ruin made flesh. And I had no possible idea of what would become of it, what would become of me. I had been in the apothecary's house for weeks and weeks and weeks, and in all that time I
had done nothing. I had allowed myself to be given over to the
household, had waited meekly for them to do with me as they
chose. These people, whom I hardly knew, held in their hands my
life, my good character, all of my future. I had done nothing.

My brain worked hectically. I might never have been shown the
particulars of such matters, not formally, but I was my mother's
daughter. It was as yet only May, too early for hyssop or yellow
bugle or most other of the flowering remedies notorious as dangerous to women with child. But not too early for gladwin. Gladwin
might be found at all times of the year where there were ponds and
rivers. My mother had pounded the roots and rolled them into pessaries which she had given to women in the earliest stages of pregnancy. I had only the haziest recollection of the ingredients and
their quantities, but I could not think of that, not now. Nor could I
think of my mother's face, the familiar walnut creases of her face as
she frowned at her mortar. There could be no distraction. *Soon.* It
could not be too late. It just could not.

It was a simple matter to find myself in the hallway when Mr.
Black came down after breakfast. I made sure to hand him his veiled
hat, his silver-topped stick. He nodded, settling the veil round his
shoulders.

"Forgive me, sir, for my boldness," I ventured. "It is only that I—
it is early in the year, I know. Too early for many things. But even now,
there are many roots and barks I might fetch you that might be worth
something. Mrs. Black always says the old woman's charges are extor-
tionate. So I thought I might go for you instead, if you wished it. I
used to collect for my mother and I know what to look for."

The apothecary said nothing but only tapped my belly with the
top of his stick. I shifted. His face was invisible behind the black
shadow of his veil.

"I—I should like to be more useful to you, sir. After all you have
done."

There was another long pause.

"How fearful you must be," he murmured. "How very fearful, indeed."

I was left staring after him, the saliva cooling in my open mouth.

Several days passed. Then, one morning as I polished the hall mirror, I overheard the master and mistress in heated discussion in the parlour. I paused outside the door and listened.

"Are you gone mad? Of course I must have the books! How else may I work?"

"But so many? Might it not be possible to curb your expenditure a little? Our creditors grow so impatient, sir. There are mutterings of Newgate and worse."

"Madam, I stand at the threshold of greatness and you threaten me with a debtors' gaol? I will not be goaded so, do you hear me? Was Mr. Sydenham assailed with petty concerns such as yours? Was Hippocrates? If you wish to make economies, send the girl herbarising. Her mother was a cunning woman, was she not? Then she knows the primary herbs. Next time, I would have you demonstrate similar resourcefulness before you come complaining to me about your difficulties."

The next afternoon, while Mary polished the pewter, Mrs. Black handed me a pottle. I was to go north, to Islington Spa, a village famed for its waters some two or three miles away. I was to gather what I could. The soles of my feet tingled. It was not yet too late. I nodded eagerly at Mrs. Black, but she was not finished. I was on no account to go alone, she informed me. Edgar would be my guide.

Edgar smiled. My heart sank.

"Be home by nightfall, I beg you," my mistress added softly to Edgar as we prepared to leave. "It is a favoured road for footpads."

It was a gloomy day but mild, the air syrupy with certain rain. Even the dull light made me blink. I stood on the step, breathing in, tasting smoke and soot and animal dung. It had been more than a month since I felt the sky against my skin. Outside the closed crate of the house, I felt dispersed somehow, vague as a cloud.

As soon as I stepped into the lane, however, my feet grew heavy, my borrowed pattens soled with sticky mud. Edgar walked briskly ahead, his hands thrust into his pockets. At the north end of the lane, where it tipped its contents into Cheap-side, he paused so that I might catch up with him. Like a river in flood, the great thorough-fare roared and coursed between its banks of bright-windowed shops. Edgar had to shout to be heard over the din.

"Follow this road as far as the Cathedral. And in case you wondered, you little savage, a cathedral is a church, only bigger. The road north from there will take you directly to Islington."

I frowned, bewildered and still a little out of breath.

"But, Mrs. Black—"

"Dear Mrs. Black. I should not wish to have to turn her against you." He squeezed my arm, digging his nails into the flesh. "You will meet me at the church of Mary-le-Bow when the watchman shouts eight of the clock. Ask someone if you do not know it. It would be most imprudent to be late."

He thrust his face close to mine. He smelled of sweat and Stilton cheese. All round us people pushed and shoved, or stopped and shouted, creating rapids and swirling pools in the traffic, while sedan chairs careened between amongst them like a crush of small boats. Then, abruptly, with one last pinch, he released me. I caught a glimpse of the crown of his hat before he was swept away by the current.

I stared after him uncertainly. The people whirled and eddied round me, each man as contained within his own importance as a sausage in its skin. Almost immediately a ragged chicken-seller swung round, almost knocking me off my feet with his baskets of moulting fowl suspended from a pole over his shoulder. Stiffening my legs and thrusting my basket before me like a shield, I pushed myself out into the stream. A clothes-trader pushed before me, a bent old man wearing his own hair and over it three hats, one on top of the other. His velveteen coat was worn through at the elbows and was fashionably short, not by design but because its hem was quite rotted away. He stumbled and almost fell. I had to step smartly round him so that he might not take me with him.

Snatching up my skirts, I lowered my head and began to walk, pushing roughly through the crowds, my eyes fixed upon the muddy tips of my boots. I had walked without stopping for perhaps a mile before the road began to rise steeply and I was forced to pause to catch my breath. Only then did I permit myself to look back. Behind me the dome floated gracefully away from the choppy mud of roofs and chimneys, untouched by the petty concerns that measured out the lives of men. I held my basket tightly against my stomach as I looked. Then I closed my eyes and spoke the words aloud.

"Forgive me, Lord. For what I am about to do, forgive me."

I was fortunate. Although the spring had been unseasonably wet, in the low woodland beyond the city's ashy boundaries, I quickly discovered many familiar and useful remedies; dragonwort, butter-bur, black alder bark for purging the spleen and liver, late primroses, even dandelion, which ignorant folk call piss-a-beds. And root of gladwin.

I waited for Edgar outside the church, my feet set carefully upon unconsecrated earth, but all the same I felt the eyes of the godly boring into me through the closed oak door. He was late. It was already dark as we walked silently home, the moon muffled by cloud, but the light that poured from the shops was extravagant, excessive. The liquid white light of lamps overflowed their glass globes while forests of candles flamed in sticks and sconces. It danced in glass windows and spilled lavishly out onto the thoroughfare until even the dung in the kennels glistened silver. Faces loomed towards us, white masks, inked with shadow, their expressions comical or grotesque. Where the light stopped at the end of our lane, the darkness was complete, as though no individual scrap of light would dare to venture there alone. There was never darkness so absolute in the country.

Safely in the fire-lit kitchen, I wrapped the gladwin in a clean cloth and buried it beneath the other linens in the dresser drawer. I might have brought some for the apothecary if I had not been afraid to draw attention to it. It had such a strong odour that where I came from folk called it Stinking Iris. Not my mother. She refused to set a curse against a plant with so many diverse and powerful properties. The roots and leaves, powdered and added to wine, eased the pains of the belly. A decoction of the roots purged corrupt phlegm and choler. Or you might boil the roots with wine and roll the resulting paste into short fat fingers which you wrapped in muslin. I was almost certain that that was all that was required. If you thrust them in as far as they would go, the pains would follow.

Perhaps I mixed the preparation wrongly. Perhaps there were additional ingredients of which I was ignorant. I think perhaps it was simply too late, the worm grown too resilient. Certainly there were cramps. There was bleeding too, a little. But despite the storms, the worm clung to the wall of my belly, as a sailor clings to the wreckage of his ship, and waited for the gales to blow themselves out.

For some days after that, the worm was quiet, its movements subdued. I had more gladwin. I might have tried again. But I did not. I could not explain it, even to myself. I only knew myself defeated. The optimism that had prickled my feet as they hurried towards Islington was gone, replaced by a grim acceptance. The worm was stronger than I, the dark forces that fortified it too inexorable. At night I pressed my fingers into my stomach, willing it to move, to strain towards my touch. When it did, I was not tender. I clenched my fists and pushed my knuckles into the angles of it, filled with rage and dread at the tenacity of the creature. But on those nights it did not come to me, I felt lost.

June blew in like a sneeze, hurling hard rain at the windows. Though the nights were short, there was no sign of approaching summer. Instead, patches of greyish light seeped into the house, furred with sooty dust. Often the master was absent during the day, returning late to work for the greater part of the night. He brought with him cold air and the tobacco smell of coffee-houses so that the house no longer felt so sealed up. As a result, he saw me less often than before and always late in the evening. Once he had examined me—his hands fluttering in their particular way over my belly like moths too skittish to settle—he had me sit facing the wall as he always had. But now the questions came rarely. Instead, he talked almost to himself.

At night, when I removed my petticoats, the skin stretched over the egg of my belly, taut and insistent, and the navel poked forwards, inquisitive as a nose. The size of it was startling. There was nothing of me about it, nothing of conventional human shape. It protruded from me like a wen, a sickness my body was determined to expel. Except that it did not. One afternoon Mrs. Black had me bring the baby linens down from the cedar-wood chest in her chamber. I turned away then, but she recalled me sharply, bidding me to pay attention. When she shook out a gown, its soapy lace yellowed with age, her brow twisted and her eyes seemed to slide back into her head. Slowly she put it to her face and inhaled. It was hardly bigger than a handkerchief. I could not bear to look at it. Instead, I tugged the remainder of the linen roughly from the chest, careless of the frail stuff. Then, from beneath a pile of musty napkins, I unfolded a large white stretch of cloth. A winding-sheet. I bundled it up, thrusting it back into the chest, but the stuff caught upon my skirt, tangling itself round my legs. The omen was unmistakable. Crying out, I fell to my knees, the sheet wrapped all about me.

Mrs. Black glared, her lips peeled back from her teeth.

"Cease that bleating, for pity's sake," she spat disgustedly. "Repentance shall avail you nothing now."

At first the stories were no more than noise to fill the nights. As the bells quarrelled over the quarter-hours, counting the hours off till my confinement, the words wove themselves into ropes that bound me to my past, to myself, so that I could not drift away. As the time of my confinement drew ever closer, the house at Swan-street closed in on me until I could hardly breathe.

The present was impossible, the future unimaginable. Only the past was safe, its pleasures certain, its privations softened by time and wistfulness. It did not matter that I had only the idiot for an audience. It was myself I sought to divert, to console. I fixed my eyes upon the hole in the garret ceiling where the lathes poked through like fingers and I talked. I talked of the village where I had grown up, the cottage, the school, the people. I unearthed old affections I had quite forgotten, Dilly the butcher's daughter who wove me necklaces of grass and daisies, the rough blacksmith with his missing finger who let me watch him as he twisted scarlet metal, the soldier with the strange accent who had stayed for the harvest and who had tasted of cider when he kissed me. But the man I spoke of most was my husband, away at sea.

At first he was thin, insubstantial, but little by little my words nourished him until I might have reached out and held his hand against my cheek. His hair and eyes were the glossy brown of horse chestnuts and, when he smiled, his mouth curved more in one corner than the other, dimpling his right cheek. His family had not wanted us wed, desiring him to find a wife with a good portion. But he had refused to heed them, proclaiming me rich not in coin but in beauty and in good humour. Indeed, if I was to accept him, he declared, he would consider himself the most fortunate man alive, for he loved me with all his heart. That part was Mary's favourite, and she had me repeat it many times.

Of course his family had relented. From that day until his father's business required him to sail to the Indies, I confessed dreamily, we had not been parted. I touched the ring Mrs. Black had given me, turning it round and round on my finger before lifting it to my lips, and I pictured him standing alone at the prow of a great ship, his shoulders thrown back and his legs braced against the swell of the sea.

Mary sighed, tugging at my nightdress.

"Nay?" she asked. "Wha' nay?"

The picture blurred and I frowned. I had quite forgotten her.

"Lize, pliss. Wha' he nay?" Mary asked again.

I hesitated, although I understood her perfectly.

"Daniel," I said at last, and through the darkness he smiled at me, etching a dimple in his right cheek, and tipped his hat.

It is nearly time. Perhaps a week now, surely not more than two. This will be it, I am certain of it. My heart jumps in my chest, so frantic with keen blood that I am certain it must burst. Infusions of dittany cannot calm it. On the contrary, my body is become like the plant itself, so that the faintest spark of an idea ignites a flash that illumines my whole self. &, like dittany too, there seems no end to its combustibility. The fire comes again & again, each time intensifying the light.

I shall not permit Jewkes here, for all his insistence, & have instead despatched an invitation to Mr. Halley & await his reply. He shall come, I know it, for we are Englishmen both & cannot fail to recognise our duty as instruments of God's holy will. Was it not an Englishman who first understood that the plain white light that illumines us contains within itself all the colours of the universe? There were those who claimed we could know no more, that God would allow us no more of the blessed secrets of His creation. & yet, here I stand, humble & a little afraid, ready to hold aloft the lantern of my understanding so that the world's dark corners might be bathed in light. How wrong, how very wrong they are proved!

The pain eases, & the opium flows through me, cool as water, its effects quite restored now that I have increased the dosage by three grains. Lemery was quite wrong to assert that the gummy resin of opium emulsifies & retards the spirits in the brain. On the contrary, it scours the channels of my mind so that the dust & rubble of human weakness & delusion is swept away & I see only Truth, plain & purposeful, which suffers no cheat of words, no obfuscation, but seeks only the simplest of expression—the <u>creature itself</u>, ignorance & godlessness made flesh, the living embodiment of darkness against which might be discerned the purity of the light.

The scent of my coffee lingers in the air, holding within the structure of its aroma all the odours of the Orient. I breathe in & the tiny hairs inside my nose tremble with perfect pleasure. I have never seen such colours. The fire burns with unmatched ardour, the red-gold of its centre trembling with a liquid brilliance. It imprints itself upon my skull, pouring its molten light into its darkest recesses, so that I understand everything. A bird hops upon the window ledge. Each one of its feathers is a perfect symphony of colour & grain & its eyes are fathomless. I could gaze at it for all Eternity. It raises its wings & I feel the tears start in my eyes, for I know I look upon the flawless beauty of an angel.

I am overcome.

XVI

Mrs. Black came quickly when I screamed.

Immediately she had Mary set a fire in the dusty grate. Unused for many years, the chimney was blocked and the fire smoked, sending bitter clouds into the room. Mrs. Black opened the window and had Mary fetch the rags we had prepared for the purpose while she instructed me to lie back with my knees raised. The contractions came fast, compressing my ribs. The sweat greased my hair. I cried out that I could not lie, that the pain was bearable only when I sat up, that if I lay down the agony would surely kill me, but Mrs. Black paid me no heed. She rubbed her hand with duck fat and, pushing me back against the pillows with a sharp shove, she forced my knees apart and thrust her hand up between my legs. I screamed again. Then the cramps seized at me, so that the scream died upon my lips. I could barely breathe. The tears rolled unchecked down my cheeks. The pain was intolerable. I would surely die. I clutched my hare's foot against my cheek. The fur stuck to my skin in dark lashes.

"Hush," she scolded, but she spoke gently. "I wish only to feel how the child lies."

I gasped as her fingers probed me. When, with a sharpening of her cheek-bones, she hooked her fingers and wrenched, I screamed. The room swam before me, its walls dissolving into a silvered dust of tiny stars.

"The neck of the womb must be stretched to allow for the baby's passage," she said briskly. "How else do you suppose it may be born?"

The pain that followed was more terrible than I could have imagined. For all that my mother had been a midwife, I had no experience of childbirth. In my village, confinements had taken place behind locked doors, closed shutters, guarded by the taut and secretive faces of the gossips who attended the labouring mother. Birth to me was whispers, anxious faces, glimpses of dark, hot rooms before I was bundled outside. Even after a successful delivery, the gossips stood sentinel at the door, warding off anyone who might attempt to enter for as long as it could be contrived. An infant was a week old or more, and its mother considerably recovered, before their vigil might be abandoned and the family permitted to enter.

Part of me was thankful I had not known what to expect, or I might have died of the dread of it. The room was stifling. Mary was kept busy with the tasks Mrs. Black assigned to her, hanging a thick rug over our window so that sunrise might not disturb the darkness of the room, bringing a caudle of warmed wine sweetened with sugar for me to sip when I was able, fetching water and rags and other necessaries, but between her duties she crouched next to me, stroking the sweat-sticky hair from my forehead and murmuring singsong strings of words beneath her breath, which I took for prayers. When the pain receded a little, I prayed with her, begging God for mercy and deliverance. Mrs. Black bid me sharply to be silent then, but I whispered the words anyway, far beyond the reach of her admonitions. I would do anything, I implored Him, I would submit to the cruellest of terms, if He might only deliver me from my terrible agony and let me live.

By the time the creature was finally expelled from me, I was so weak I could no longer raise my head to drink. Mary tried to pour a little cordial into my dry lips, but she was clumsy and most of it dribbled down my chin. Mrs. Black alone was brisk. She sliced through the cord that bound me to it and, snatching up the bloodied mess, took it to the window, holding the curtain back with the spike of one shoulder. I heard her draw in her breath sharply, mutter something under her breath. Then, letting the curtain fall again, she snapped angrily at Mary to go directly to the apothecary and tell him that the child was delivered, although she feared there was little cause for hope. It would of course be brought to him directly so that he might examine it himself.

Mary kissed my hand and placed it carefully back on the blanket. I did not have the strength to protest. I closed my eyes. The pain trembled expectantly between my legs, waiting for me to move. The bed beneath me was slick with blood. In a corner of the room, Mrs. Black busied herself with a basin of water. There was a dull splash and then a thin high shriek like the call of a bird. Mrs. Black crooned, singing softly under her breath. For all the pain, a kind of tingling peace spread through me. I closed my eyes as sleep pulled insistently at me, dragging me down, dark and blissful as drowning. I let myself be taken—

The slap on the cheek sent spasms of pain through my damaged body. I cried out.

"Do not sleep, you foolish girl," chided Mrs. Black. In one arm she cradled a tightly swaddled bundle. "Mary will fetch you a compress to ease the pain, but you must remain awake. Do you hear me?"

I nodded and at once my eyelids began again to droop.

"What did I just tell you?" Mrs. Black scolded, shaking my shoulder. "Would you die now, when we have come so far?"

As though she were two different people contained within a single skin, she laid the bundle with great tenderness upon the bed and, turning away, stamped furiously over to the corner of the room. Her impatience made her clumsy. When the basin of water smashed to the floor, she cursed and bawled for Mary. No one came. Cursing again, this time more violently, she slammed out of the room.

With the fire banked high, the room was hot as an oven and my eyelids too heavy to fight. I sank backwards, surrendering to sleep. Then something whimpered. The noise caught in the fissures of my ripped flesh, sending quivers of pain through my belly and between my legs. I clenched my fists, refusing it, pressing my eyes closed. The whimper came again, louder this time, plucking at me. It would not stop.

With considerable effort, I raised my head. The creature had rolled on the sagging mattress so that it lay almost beside me. It stared up at me. I stared back. Its squashed face was purple and wrinkled, but its eyes were the dark vast blue of a midnight sky and it blinked them slowly, sagely, as though it already understood everything that there was to know in the world. Its hands flailed at its sides, each tiny finger curled like the frond of a new fern. Its nails were soft and long and needed paring. When it opened its mouth, I caught a glimpse of a petal-pink tongue. Then it squeezed its eyes tightly shut, and with a great gulping breath that seemed to suck every last gasp of air from the stuffy room, it began to scream.

The scream tightened the strings of my nerves until they sang. I no longer thought of sleep or of the pain that turned the saliva in my mouth sour and thick. Instead, I reached over and placed my hand on the bundle. It was warm, almost hot, as though all the vigour it would have need of in a lifetime already thrummed in its tiny body. My palm tingled.

Very slowly my hand slid upwards, following the fragile rise of its chest, the slope of its shoulder. It paused then, the root of the thumb resting almost imperceptibly against the line of its delicate jaw. Then, one finger, more courageous than the rest, reached out and touched its face. The skin was thin and silky, expensive-feeling. The eyebrows were perfect twin curves of surprise, soft and fragile as shadows. My fingertip traced their shapes before moving downwards, memorising the tilt of the miniature nose, the downward curve of the open pink mouth, finding the folded corners of its lips.

Something about the mouth made my heart squeeze. The upper lip formed a perfect bow, as though outlined with ink, tipped by a tiny bead of flesh. In that moment I separated from the pain of my torn and bloody body. All I could feel, all I could be, was in the tip of my index finger, where the rough skin of that bead gently grazed against my skin. I touched it only for a moment. Against my uncurled palm, the infant scream was hot and insistent, vastly bigger than the body from which it came. Then, abruptly, greedily, the mouth seized upon my finger and closed round it. Immediately the screaming stopped. I could feel the soft rasp of the petal tongue against the blister where I had burned myself upon the kettle. The toothless gums clamped round the fingertip, pressing down into the flesh as though they feared to let it go. Every part of the creature seemed given over to the effort of it. The face creased with concentration, its eyes squeezing tighter shut with every pull of its mouth. Even on the top of the creature's downy head, a circle of flesh the size of a penny pulsed in and out in time with the sucking. I stared at it and my heart thundered in my throat, so that I, too, was caught in the precise metre of my baby's mouth.

Around me, the room faded and withdrew. There was no pain, no smoke, none of the childbed stinks of blood and shit. There was only finger, mouth, pulse. Everything was contained within them. We were complete.

All of a sudden, the door swung open. Mrs. Black stood on the threshold, a fresh basin of water in her arms. When she saw me, she slammed the basin down upon the stool and snatched the infant into her arms. Immediately it began to bawl.

"Mary!" she commanded. "Here now!"

I gazed at my curled finger, bereft on the blanket, the saliva drying to nothing round the nail. The pulse in my throat jumped hopelessly, its rhythm quite lost. The screaming filled my throat and tore at my belly, at my heart.

"No," I protested, but my tongue was dry and clumsy, and the word stuck to the roof of my mouth. I licked desperately at my lips. "No! Please!"

Mary's feet slapped at the stairs.

"No wake," she panted. "Mister Bla', can' wake. Eye close."

"For pity's sake, girl," Mrs. Black snapped. "Must I do everything myself?"

Pushing past Mary, she hustled down the stairs, my infant cradled in her arms. On the floor below, I heard her thundering on the door of the apothecary's study, demanding to be let in.

My heart stretched out after her, tight and sick with fear and longing. As I lay in my tangle of filthy sheets, my broken body weeping blood, a ravenousness began to open up between my ribs, pressing outwards with such ferocious certainty that I was sure the bones must shatter. Pushing away the agony that shrieked through me when I moved, I tried to stand up.

"Come back!" I pleaded.

The sweat stood out upon my forehead. Bent over in a half-crouch, my arms clutched round my belly, I lurched towards the door. My legs were treacherous. The room tilted dangerously, spangled with glittering dust, and the sloped corners twisted and dipped.

"Please! I beg you, please, bring me back my child!"

At least I think that is what I said. I remember I felt the hot rush down my thighs, for I looked down then and thought the blood on the floor unnaturally red. In the centre of the puddle, there was a thick slab like uncooked liver. It shone glossily against the rough boards. The silver dust in front of my eyes thickened to a blizzard. I could no longer see the door. I was quite cold. My hands floated up to my face, white and unfamiliar.

Then my legs failed me and I fell.

I remember little of the days that followed. I drifted in and out of wakefulness, lost in the bitter heat of fever and despair. It was only afterwards that I learned that the apothecary had disappeared. When I dredge my memory, I believe I can hear doors slamming and voices raised in argument, but the recollections are roughly sketched, unreliable.

In the two weeks before sitting up, when I would at last be permitted to be bathed and to have my soiled bed-linen changed, Mrs. Black had Mary nurse me, bringing up poultices and herbal washes to clean and soothe my privities. She brought broths and cordials, as well as sweetmeats to tempt my appetite. I turned my face from her, towards the wall. In my stained and stinking bed, I clutched my misery round me like a blanket. I could not look out of the window, out towards the dome. Its haughtiness was intolerable to me now.

Instead, I kept my gaze fixed upon the flaking hole in the plaster, the crumble of dust and damp, the rotting strips of wood that stuck out from it as my womb clenched and cramped, folding itself back into its old shape. I hugged the pain in, letting it take me, although I could see no purpose in it. It would surely have been better for it to have been expelled along with the child. The first time Mrs. Black came into the room and stood over me, she wore the black weeds of mourning. Her face was greyer than usual, and dark shadows pressed down into the skin beneath her eyes. She walked carefully, her neck tall, and her face was sharp as folded paper.

I knew before she told me. The infant was dead. The words were hands round my throat, squeezing down. I shook my head, backwards and forwards, and breathed in shallow sips. Mrs. Black's mouth was pressed so small, there was barely room for the words to come out. No one was to blame, she said. There was nothing she or any other midwife could have done. The labour had been too protracted, the ordeal too great. She had done all she could, giving the infant a little softened butter and sugar to purge him and clear its breathing, even squirting a little warm wine up the nostrils, but to no avail. The child, fatally weakened by the travails of delivery, had survived only an hour or two.

I screamed then and wrenched myself up to grab at her arm. It was not true! She was wrong, I cried out, my fingers pressing into her flesh. She was wrong. I myself had seen the child alive, had heard it cry, felt the warmth of its mouth around my finger. It had looked well, strong. She was wrong. The child was not dead. It slept. She must go to it without delay, bring it to me so that I might suckle it. It would be hungry, in need of sustenance, in need of its mother. She was to bring it to me immediately.

The tip of Mrs. Black's nose was white. She prised my fingers from her arm.

"No, girl," she hissed, sinking to her knees beside me and gripping my wrist. Her face was so close to mine, I could smell the gravy on her breath. "Do not say such things. It is a common deception that the mind plays upon the mother, to think that all is well with her infant. Your child was too weak, its pulse too soft. It would never have lived. Be grateful instead that there was time to baptise it. It is with the Lord now. Surely there is comfort in that. I gave it the name of Grayson, after Mr. Black."

A boy. He was a boy. I shook my head, my breath coming unevenly. I wanted to sink my teeth into her hand, to see her face crumple in pain, to taste the crimson of her blood upon my tongue.

"Where is he?" I demanded, and my voice soared high and tight, fierce with desperation. "Bring him to me now, do you hear me? I want my son!"

Mrs. Black grimaced. Her lips were twisted and bloodless.

"Listen to me," she hissed. "You are not the first mother to have lost a child, nor shall you be the last. Infants die. Many die unsaved, before they can be accepted into the kingdom of Heaven. You should thank God for His mercy. Your child has been taken from a world of suffering and sorrow to a place of inconceivable happiness. Cry if you must. It is a mother's fate to mourn the loss of a child. But it remains her duty to endure it."

I did not cry, not then. All the tears, every drop of juice in my body, massed instead in my hardening breasts, bloating them with salty senseless milk until the straining skin threatened to split. My eyes were dry, hot, and gritty. It hurt to keep them open, but it hurt more to close them. When I closed them, he was there. A child with eyes as dark and deep as a well, wrapped in his swaddling bands and sucking upon my finger as though he would pull the flesh from the bone. How I loathed that finger and its repugnant failure to nourish him, my own most precious child. No matter how much I studied it for signs that it had somehow changed, it remained no more than a finger, the oval nail ragged, the blistered burn at its tip hard now and flaking. No mark of my son was left upon it, not even the palest pink imprint of toothless gum on its underside. I crushed my hand between my thighs, the knuckles bent painfully inwards, so that I might be spared the sight of it. It did nothing to ease the pain.

As my breasts engorged with useless milk, I ground my knuckles into their bloated mass. My child had never set his forehead against their blue-veined swell, had never closed his mouth round the brown nipple that chafed, vigilant and futile, against the rough stuff of my nightdress. If I had only nursed him, allowed him to drink from me, who remained so resolutely, so brutally alive, my son would have lived. I knew it with bleak certainty. If I had not let him be taken from me, if I had somehow found the strength to drag myself downstairs, to close his dying mouth over my breast, he would have lived. Instead, I had surrendered to the weakness of my own body, the heedless demands of my own flesh. Other mothers clasped their infants to their breast as lightning cleaved the very ground beneath their feet, curving themselves over, around, their ribs spread like umbrellas so that they might shield them from harm. Not I. Too craven to defy my pain, I had opened my arms and watched him fall.

Worse still, it was I who had caused it, who had made it happen. I had done everything in my power to kill my own child. It was not only the gladwin. Night after night I had lain in this very bed and wished for the creature to vanish, to unexist. I had wished it with all my heart, my thumbs squeezed in my palms, my brow furrowed with longing.

I had not thought anyone was listening.

NOTES FOR ANATOMISING:

*Follow <u>order of Mondino</u>, beginning with the abdominal cavity, tho-
rax, head, brain & finally the extremities:*

1. *wax model to be made of specimen prior to dissection, representing
   <u>precise</u> damage to specimen's head & thorax*

2. *soft parts to be individually labelled with appropriate weights/
   measurement, each one set against their matching part in human infants of similar size & preserved by the injection of quicksilver—particular care to be exercised with brain, heart & lungs*

3. *skull & skeleton to be cleaned & assembled with hanging hook for
   display*

   <u>Critical dissimilarities</u> in canine & human anatomies:

   - *skull narrower & flatter in canines than humans—see
     comparative illustration in Vesalius Bk. II showing human skull
     resting upon that of dog*
   - *lower jaw of canines comprises <u>two</u> bones; humans <u>one</u>*
   - *certain foramina described by Galen occur only in the canine skull*
   - *do not stop now you do well think clearly look closer it will be there
     if you only look closer*
   - *tongue considerably longer in quadrupeds than humans YES*
   - *& in dogs, rectus abdominis extends considerably farther towards
     the neck*
   - *Eustachio's <u>Opuscula anatomica</u> (1564): comparative figures of ear
     ossicles & tensor timpani in humans & canines*
   - *analysis of structure/form of canine versus human kidney—
     Realdo Columbo?*

GOD BE IN MY EYES, & IN MY LOOKING

XVII

I do not know how many days passed before Mrs. Black returned. I turned away as she entered the room but not before I had seen that she carried something in her arms. Though my heart leapt, I closed my eyes, drawing my knees up to my milk-hard breasts. I would not be tricked into something as treacherous as hope.

"God in His mercy has sent us a child," Mrs. Black said briskly, holding the bundle out towards me. "Its mother is unable to care for it. It is sickly and shall not live long, but by nursing it, you may prolong its life a little and do yourself a service besides. It is unwholesome to permit milk to collect in your breast. It will grow sour and impede your recovery."

Hope died. Vultures both, loss and grief swooped and settled. I clamped my jaw, pressing my face hard against the pillow. Mrs. Black sat beside me and pushed the child into my arms.

"Take it," she instructed.

I shook my head again, more desperately, squeezing my eyes shut.

"No," I insisted, twisting my face away. "No. I—I can't."

"Oh, but you can," Mrs. Black said, and her tone was almost cheerful. "And you shall. If you are to remain here, you must earn your keep. An ailing servant is a considerable expense. If you cannot help us to meet that expense, we must put you out into the street. Today. It is hard to imagine how you would manage alone and without lodging so soon after your confinement. Mary!"

Mary peered through the door, her mouth open. Her gaze slid uneasily round the room.

"Mary, you will remain here with Mrs. Campling until she has fed the infant. Then you will return it to me. Is that understood?"

Mary lolled her head forwards in a reluctant nod as Mrs. Black deposited the child in her arms, touching its cheek very lightly with the back of her finger. Mary held it awkwardly, away from her body, as though it were hot from the oven.

"Call for me if there is any difficulty. As for you, Mrs. Campling, it is high time you banished this morbid disease. This infant has reason enough for melancholy spirits without you infecting it with your own distemper. It would go badly for you if you were found to have turned your own milk."

When Mrs. Black's footsteps had faded, Mary darted over to me and, balancing the bundle in her lap, placed a cautious hand upon my hair. Her skirts brushed my cheek, filling my nostrils with their cooking smells. My throat clenched so painfully that I could not swallow.

"Lize sad," she said sorrowfully. "Poor Lize."

"Go away."

"Poor Dan'l," she said. "Dan'l sad so."

I whimpered. If only she would stop, take the creature away. I could not breathe.

"Poor lil' bab'," crooned Mary. "Bad hur', see? Bad bad hur'."

With her tongue pressed between her gapped teeth, she began very carefully to unwrap the parcel on her lap. When it mewled, my breasts tingled, oozing milk, and a single tear slipped down the slope of my cheek.

"Look, Lize," Mary said softly. "Poor lil' bab'."

Miserably I opened my eyes.

"Oh my—no!"

When I pushed it away, the infant scrunched its face unhappily, but it did not cry. Its head was covered with a thinly woven cap of hair, and the skin on its cheeks was scaly and raw-looking. The ribs stood out on its chest like the cross-pieces of a half-finished boat. It was neither large nor small, fair nor dark. Its face was neither angelic nor brutish. It was merely an infant, indistinguishable from one hundred other infants. That was, until you saw that it had no hands. What it possessed by way of arms protruded from its trunk in two stumps that extended not quite to the elbow. Each stump bore an approximation of a thumb and a single flailing finger, blunt and stubby as the pollarded branches of a lime tree.

Carefully Mary reached out a chewed finger to touch one stump. Then she lowered her face and kissed the shiny twist of skin that sealed it. For a moment the child was silent. Then it began to wail, a thin high shriek like wind in a chimney.

"Hung'y," said Mary, stroking its head. She looked at me, her forehead creased with anxiety, and her eyes slid across one another until she seemed to be studying the tip of her own nose. With her other hand, she reached out to touch my hair, tucking loose strands behind my ear. "Poor Lize."

I said nothing. I wanted to shriek, to vomit, to throw the freakish thing across the room, but I could not move. My tongue was a wedge of wood in my mouth.

"Milk," Mary urged. "Wan' milk."

Violently I shook my head, pushing the child away with the flat of my hands.

"No," I whispered.

"Yes. Or bab' die. An' Lize go. Don' wan' Lize go."

"No," I whispered again, and I rocked back and forth, my arms wrapped round my breasts. "Please, Mary, no. Take it away. I—just take it away."

"Can'," Mary whispered back. "Mar' here. Mar' help."

Very gently she pulled back the blanket, loosening my arms. Frozen with misery, the tears spilling onto the thin cotton of my nightdress, I let her do it. I clenched my eyes closed as she unbuttoned my chemise and pulled it from my shoulder, exposing my swollen breast. When the child whimpered, the brown disc of my nipple clenched obligingly, a drop of milk budding at its tip. My shoulders shook at the betrayal.

Mary bent down beside me and kissed me awkwardly on the ear. Then she pressed the child against my belly, her hand behind its head, guiding its mouth towards my breast. I felt the whisper of its tiny lips upon my skin, tasting, searching. Then abruptly, ferociously, the creature seized my nipple between its jaws and clamped down hard. The shock of pain and intimacy thrust a blade between my ribs, so that I cried out. Cramps tore at my womb. I wanted to scream and scream until the house shook with the pain that consumed me. I wanted to rip it from my flesh, to hurl the creature across the room. I could not endure its warmth, the pulse at the crown of its head, its urgent sucking mouth. I wanted to stifle it, to smash it, to stamp the life from it. I raised my hand. Mary caught it in hers. She squeezed my fingers hard.

"Is good," she murmured. "Lize good."

The door opened. In that instant I saw plainly the grotesque tableau that we made, the desolate jilt, the idiot maid, the monstrous child, and the anguish tore through me like poison, shrivelling what was still soft inside me. I was lost. I placed my hand over the infant's nose and mouth and pressed.

"I'm right obliged to you, miss. For your kindness."

The voice was rough, unfamiliar. Mary tugged away my hand, clamping it in hers. The child began to howl. A young woman stood in the doorway, ragged and dirty, with a torn apron and a scrap of a cap that barely covered her hair. Her lips were scabbed with sores. As she bobbed a clumsy curtsy from the doorway, something clinked in her apron pocket.

"May the Lord bless you all," she rushed. "Yes, indeed."

Gathering up her skirts, she hastened into the room. She touched the screaming infant briefly upon the shoulder with one blackened finger and hurried out again, her hand clutched tightly around her pocket. The stairs clattered, the front door slammed. Gently Mary lifted the child and latched it to the other breast. This time, when its mouth closed around the nipple, I felt nothing at all.

My son, despise not the chastening of the LORD; neither be weary of his correction: For whom the LORD loveth he correcteth; even as a father the son in whom he delighteth. Happy is the man that findeth wisdom, & the man that getteth understanding. For the merchandise of it is better than the merchandise of silver, & the gain thereof than fine gold.

There is no such thing as a failed example, only
new information & fresh insight.
—*Thomas Sydenham*

ALL WICKEDNESS IS
BUT LITTLE TO THE
WICKEDNESS
OF A WOMAN

XVIII

I nursed the armless infant for close to a month before it died.

Although I never ceased to dread the first fierce tug of its mouth upon my breast, the treacherous surge of milk which sent a shock through my belly, there was all the same a sombreness in the child's round black eyes that eased my hostility towards it. It never smiled. Nor did it grow distressed when I wept, pushing it from my lap. Instead, it gazed at me without blinking, as though it knew already all the inexpressible horrors of the world. Its acceptance of the inevitability of anguish was a kind of sympathy. It knew it would not live long. And so I let it suckle, wrapping my misery about us both like a shawl.

The sultry weather did not break. A breathless glittering stillness shimmered like shallow water across the city. Mrs. Black burned perfume in the main rooms of the house and scattered lavender along the skirtings, but nothing could keep the stench out. Beneath its slate roof the garret stewed, releasing a foul odour of rats and drying mould. The lice rampaged through clothes and bedding. Mary lay on her back, her mouth open and her arms outstretched, her hair dark with sweat. The heat came off her like a warming bottle.

After several weeks, at the end of my lying-in, Mrs. Black had me rise. Short-tempered and sour herself in the heat, she was infuriated by my low spirits. She claimed I was sick from contrariness and insisted upon all kinds of violent purges to restore me to myself. If she discovered me seated, she would have me climb up and down the stairs to open the bowel and encourage my blood to circulate. She cupped me, drawing out the air until I thought the glasses would explode against my flesh, and scarifying the skin of my back with a sharp blade in a series of inch-long cuts like those made upon a loin of pork for roasting. I never cried out. Punishment or cure, the pain was the only part of me I was sure of.

It was after one such bleeding, as I pulled myself shakily up the stairs towards the garret, that I saw the ragged woman again. Seized by an attack of giddiness, I had paused, leaning against the wall, to catch my breath. She did not see me, for she never looked up. Instead, she backed out of the apothecary's study, her head lowered, her hand once more closed round her pocket. The ribbons of her cap were lank and stringy, as if she had chewed them. I thought of the infant then. It had been fretful that morning, unwilling to latch on. Mad with impatience, I had slapped it. It had stared at me then, its black eyes round and expressionless, but it had not cried. I had watched as a scarlet print bloomed upon its back, and the stab of grief had been so sharp and sudden, I had gasped out loud.

"Thank you, good sirs," she cringed. "Bless you both. May the Heavens smile upon you for your kindness."

The door to the study closed with a click. Immediately the woman dug into her pocket. I saw several coins glint upon her palm as she raised them to her lips and kissed them. She jumped when Mrs. Black called out from the hallway. Swiftly she raised her skirt and, pushing the money into a cloth bag she had hidden beneath it, she scuttled downstairs.

Before I might move, the study door opened once more. A gentleman I had never seen before stood on the landing, as glossy and sleek as a fine horse. His fashionable wig was plump and freshly powdered and lolled indolently against the richly decorated stuff of his coat. Under one arm he carried a velvety-edged hat from which a magnificent feather bloomed. His stockings were as white as a thief's.

The visitor extended a meaty hand and gave my master's hand a perfunctory shake before turning to leave. I caught a glimpse of snowy white neck-cloth secured with a pearl pin and, above it, the most commonplace face I had ever seen, as round and red and as marked with pocks as a strawberry. A butcher's face, perhaps, or a knife-grinder's, roughened by work and coarse suggestions and creased, at this moment, with ill temper.

"It is hardly your place, sir, to tell me to whom I may or may not extend my generosity," the butcher said tightly.

"On the contrary," my master muttered. "I consider it my duty to defend your purse against every last hard-luck story in the parish."

"What then of yours? You would not deem your case amongst that number?"

The mark on my master's cheek darkened.

"If you had even half so much wit as effrontery, sir," he hissed, "I might consider you a worthy patron. As it is—"

The butcher was silent for a moment, his mouth working.

"For God's sake, man," he said at last. "Let us not quarrel. But we must have results, do you not understand that? I have no intention of appearing a fool."

"With respect, sir, there may be little I can do in that particular. Only a fool could imagine that the meaning of God's mysteries may be plucked from a tree like an apple!" Mr. Black banged the door jamb with his fist. "I am a man of science, sir, not one of your plaguey mechanical monkeys. You cannot turn a key in my back and have me dance for the amusement of your damned associates."

"Is that so? But you would make a monkey of me, all the same? Good day to you, sir. I shall see myself out."

The butcher's footsteps echoed in the stairwell. The master remained where he was, his breathing forced and loud, his fist still clenched against the door jamb. Dizzy with standing, I tried to creep away. A board creaked. The master looked up. In the windowless gloom, his dark cheek was an absence, his eyes gleaming above half a face. I pressed myself into the wall, wrapping the shadows about me.

"Do not think you shall not be punished," he hissed. "Look at you, all impudence, careless of the injury you inflict. But, let me assure you, a handsome face is no more recompense for a treacherous soul than a cloth laid over a cesspit. You are still quite rotten. I can smell the stink on you from here."

His half-face loomed towards me, his hands clenched. I smelled his burnt breath. Ducking beneath his raised arm, I fled.

A little before dark that afternoon, the infant died. When they told me, I wept like a child. Mary lay next to me, her tears mingling with mine, her arms around my neck. I clung to her as an infant monkey clings to its mother, my fingers wound in her hair. They say that by nourishing a child with the milk of her breasts, a wet-nurse passes on the fundamentals of her nature to the infant she suckles. My mother had often advised those of her patients wealthy enough to have one that care should be taken to avoid a nurse of a crude or violent temperament. What then of a nurse mired in sin?

There was no coffin for the child when its body was fetched away. It was wrapped in waxed paper, like a dead fish. If it had had a name, I never knew it. Now, whenever I think of it, for all that it was assuredly a girl, I think of it as Daniel.

Hewlitt & Bain, Solicitors at Law, Newcastle

Dear Sir,

We acknowledge receipt of your letter, dated 11th July 1719, & have, as you asked, made your request of our client.

However, we regret to inform you that he is prepared to countenance no alteration to the contract currently in place. While he appreciates the difficulties presented to you by such an arrangement, he would wish to stress that his own situation is equally problematic, given the delicate negotiations surrounding the impending marriage of his son.

Since the announcement of said marriage, a number of threats to my client's reputation & property have already been received from the mother of the ward, Eliza Tally. While these are hardly lawful, my client would prefer that they be dealt with privately & with discretion & he asks that you may oblige him with your continued tact & good judgement in this matter. He has therefore required us to extend the terms of the existing agreement between yourselves for a further twenty-four months, with an option to prolong the term as necessary. Given the absolute necessity of preventing any attempt at return to the village of her birth, we would require in addition that you intercept any correspondence written by, or on behalf of, the mother & return it to our office, so that we may deal with it in the most appropriate manner.

My client recognises that these requirements run counter to your personal wishes &, in acknowledgement of his gratitude for your co-operation, has instructed me to inform you that a single payment of thirty guineas be despatched to you upon receipt by ourselves of the enclosed papers. We would therefore ask you to sign & return them to our offices at your earliest convenience.

I am, Sir, your humble Servant &c.,

NICHOLAS HEWLITT

XIX

It was the hottest summer anyone could remember, soupy nights spilling into thick breathless days. The city rotted in its skin. At Swan-street the windows swelled in their frames until they could no longer be opened, and the shut-up house was stifling, its air solid with cesspits and the reek of rotting food. The smell of it sickened me. When the mistress locked us into the garret at night, the scrape of the key turning in the lock screeched against my spine. The master remained in his room, seldom venturing out, but the malignity of him seeped into the breathless half-light, making shapes of every shadow. The darkness clung to me as I walked up and down the stairs, insinuating itself like tobacco smoke into my hair, my clothes, and down into the impossible void I buried in the still-slack skin of my belly. Each closed room sucked at me like a physician's cup, draining me of blood. I lashed out at Mary at the least provocation, inflamed by a rage that frightened us both. As for Mrs. Black, I could no longer stand to look at her. The sight of her sewed-up darn of a mouth was sufficient to flood me with an antipathy so strong that it clamped my jaws and clenched my hands into teeth-white fists.

I had to get out. When I pressed the grocer's boy, who was hardly a boy at all but a loquacious man of considerable years and very few teeth, he shrugged.

"There's several households 'tween here and Lombard-street asked me if I knows of anyone," he assured me. "There's footmen aplenty, but it seems there's a shortage of your kind, like, the maid-of-all-work not too proud to do the rough work. It's 'Change-alley, see. A hundred new schemes every day and more comin'. They say there's a better chance of winning a fortune at 'Change-alley than there is at the Guildhall."

"'Change-alley?"

"Stocks market. Look round yer. The Lottery's one thing. But now they's found out the secret of how to turn paper into money, a maid with a good character can make five, six pound a year."

Before he left the grocer's boy gave me the names of two families and promised to put in a word for me with both on his next delivery. All day long the soles of my feet itched. Several times as I stood at the sink, a pile of muddy potatoes before me, I dropped my knife and ran up into the lane, certain I had seen his lopsided gait in the tangle of feet that passed the window. Each time I returned to the kitchen disappointed, the dim room seemed darker and more stifling than before. When Mrs. Black came to the kitchen a little before supper to rebuke me for my extravagance with water, I could contain myself no longer. I knew myself imprudent, even foolish, but the promise of liberty intoxicated me. I wished, I informed her, to tender my notice. I thought a period of two weeks sufficient for Mrs. Black to find a replacement. Mrs. Black considered me for several moments, her white lips pressed together, before she replied.

"It is quite out of the question," she said, her voice clipped.

I gasped, a wild laugh of a cough that caught in my throat.

"Excuse me, but I don't think—"

"I have said it is out of the question. That is the end of it."

She turned to leave. I wanted to seize her by her vile white ears, to shake her until her eyes rolled from the white casket of her skull.

"You may think you can stop me, but you cannot!" I cried. "Yours is not the only household in London."

Very slowly Mrs. Black turned back. Her white nostrils stretched tight.

"Listen to me, girl, and hold your tongue. I have no more wish to keep you than you do to stay. But stay you shall. Blame your mother, if you wish, for it is her insistence that keeps you here. The deal is struck, and there can be no reversing it. We must endure each other for as long as is required."

"I don't believe you," I said defiantly, clasping my hands to keep them steady. "My mother would not wish me held prisoner."

"You waste my time with such foolishness. You are not free to leave, and that is the end of it. Should you be imprudent enough to attempt such a thing, be warned: We shall find you out. There is nowhere in this city you might hide from those who require you here. Besides, what employer would offer you a position when appraised by a well-wisher of your partiality to thievery and whoring? I fear, Mrs. Campling, that, though neither of us wish it, you shall remain here. And in the meantime, and so that something may be made of you, it is agreed that I shall withhold your pay until that time is complete. It is to be hoped that such a measure may prove effective in subduing your insolence."

"You cannot do that! That money is mine, by law!"

"I find the law seldom troubles itself with people of your sort." She leaned close to me, her eyes cold. "Know this: What you wish for is not of the least consequence. You are here because others will it. And you shall remain here until they will it no longer. There is no more to be said on the matter."

When she was gone, I leaned back against the wall, unclenching my hands and holding them out before me as though they belonged to somebody else. The nail beds gleamed yellow-white in the gloom.

Until they will it no longer.

They. But who were they, these others? My mother? *It is her insistence that keeps you here.* I pressed my fingers as hard as I could against my forehead, leaning into the powerful ache in my temples. What manner of a deal had my mother struck to keep me a prisoner here, against my will? And with whom? She had already sold me once and proven that she would do anything for money. But not this, surely? She had taken money from the Campling boy's father, it was true, but had she not believed it to be for my own good? Perhaps she thought that, by keeping me here, she guaranteed my safety. She might think that a girl without reputation would not find another position and, cast out onto the street, might easily starve. She could not know that London's appetite for servants had grown voracious. Nor could she have the slightest notion of the nature of this place. She could not know the malevolence that quivered and turned in the air of the house, as dust turns in a beam of sunlight. If only she knew, she would not want me held here, against my will. Surely she could not want that. She was my mother.

Upstairs the front door slammed. I swallowed a blade of dread so sharp that it seemed to pierce my gullet. I would never escape. I would grow old here, forced to submit, meekly and without protest, to the tyranny of murderers, until the shadows extinguished my spirits and shrivelled the hair in my scalp to dust. All my life, made to swallow the bitter bile of hatred that rose in my throat until it rotted me from the inside out.

I could not do it.

That afternoon the air in the kitchen was liquid with heat, and the floor sweated a fatty skin that tugged at the soles of my feet. Mary slumped in the bentwood chair, scratching at herself incessantly. I felt like I was drowning. Seizing the buckets, I shouted at her to rouse herself.

"We are going for water."

Mary shook her head, her fat fingertips tearing at the crevices of her armpits.

"No pipe."

She was right, of course. During the hot weather, the turn-cock had good as disappeared and what water there was came out at a dribble for less time than it took for the bells to sound out two quarter-hours.

"We aren't going to the stand-pipe. We're going to the river."

Mary gaped at me. In all the time I had been at Swan-street, I had never ventured as far as the river, though it was hardly four streets away. Truth to tell, I was afraid of it. It was said that unwary children were stolen from the wharfs and taken to foreign lands as slaves. Certainly the violent and blasphemous abuse of the water-men, known to city dwellers as water-language, was notorious. Edgar had even declared the stream cursed, claiming that no one who had ever fallen into its fiendish depths had ever been seen again. Though I knew better than to believe him, the river oozed black and oily through the cracks in my imagination, its sinuous churn shifting to expose a brief gleam of fleshless bones and teeth before it rolled them up and hastened them away to the sea.

"They say it's clean enough," I snapped. "Now let's go."

I pushed Mary in front of me as we hurried up the kitchen steps towards the lane. The urge to get out drove all other considerations from my head. In my haste I almost fell over a hog nosing lazily in amongst a heap of rotting rubbish. I kicked out at it, and it grunted irritably and ambled away. The lanes were narrow and dark with dust and shadow, the torn strip of white sky between the houses slung about with the rusting laundry of shop signs. The air barely stirred. As the slope steepened, there was a powerful sea-stink of mud and rotting fish.

There was a press of warehouses and then, beyond them, a shifting shimmer of light and movement. I pushed forwards, towards the quayside, until I stood at the edge of a narrow jetty, its grey planks curved and cracked by the sun. And yet even then, I could barely see the river beneath its burden of skiffs, wherries, sailing barges, and water taxis of every size and description, hacking at the hidden stream with a barrage of oars. It was a riotous mass of green and red and tarnished gilt. Barges were garlanded with swags and flowers. The noise rose up from it as relentlessly as the stench, the air crammed with scurrilities as putrid as the slicks of mud and black weed that greased the struts of every quay.

Along the length of the shore, for as far as I could see, passengers yelled and signalled conveyances to attend them at scores of stairs, landing-stages, and pontoons. Not twenty yards from where I stood, a swarm of men as black as ants unloaded a coal barge so heavily weighed down by its cargo that the scrolled lettering upon its flank was half-buried in the brown murk of the river water. A villainous-looking child, so black with dirt it might have been its own shadow, darted between the coalmen's legs, pouncing upon dropped lumps, which it wrapped in the tails of its ragged shirt.

I let the noise fill me, surrendering to its authority. Then someone behind me called and pointed. I turned, following their finger, to look downstream in the direction of the bridge. I blinked, hardly able to make sense of what I saw. For there, straddling the river as though it were no more than a muddy puddle, was not a simple crossing but a full and shameless street of houses, handsome elegant dwellings several stories high, their windows throwing back the fire of the sun in a glitter of light, the columns which supported them braced like mighty thighs against the brown roar of the tide.

London-bridge is broken down, broken down, broken down. London-bridge is broken down, my fair lady. Bricks and mortar will not stay . . .

The children in the alley sometimes chanted the song, tossing stones into the mud, so close, sometimes, that I feared for the window. I thought of my long-dead forebears who had for many centuries believed that the only way to placate an angry river, and to safeguard the bridge set across it in defiance of its will, was to offer up to it a child as a sacrifice. I had a sudden unwelcome memory of a tiny mouth, a bead of flesh at the bow of its upper lip, and my nipple stiffened, sending a jolt through my breast. Another year. My stomach flipped. Tightening my fingers around the handles of my pails, I turned away.

It was only then that I noticed Mary was gone. Hastily I jostled a path through the throng, calling out her name, scanning the crowd for her distinctive face. There were too many people. I could make out only a chaos of cloth, wigs and hats, and bundles shifting and changing shape, forming nothing. As I stretched onto my tiptoes, a man in a rusty coat thrust a handbill into my face. It was covered in close writing with some kind of woodcut at the bottom, smudgy with ink.

"Sign of the Fountain by Shoe-lane till Sat'dy," he hissed. "Make yer eyes pop, it will. Y'ain't niver seen nothin' like the Hedgehog Boy. Bristles hard as horn."

"Did you see a girl come past here, an idiot girl, brown stomacher—?"

"Only sixpence," he added encouragingly. "Be chargin' a shillin' for this anyplace else."

He waved the handbill in front of my face. I glimpsed a

smudged picture of a boy covered all over in spines before the man slid the handbill into my pail.

"For the love of God!" I snapped, and I banged my pails hard against his shins. He yelped like a dog as I pushed past him. The crowd was thicker now, more sluggish, as folk stopped to look about them or to exchange pleasantries. Their indolence infuriated me. My pails caught on legs, on barrows. I could barely move my arms.

And then I saw her. She stood amongst a cluster of people before a low stage decked out with banners and gay strings of bunting upon which a monkey and a clown gallivanted. While the clown was a regular Jack Pudding, sweating profusely in his heavy costume with its donkey's ears and sawing away at his fiddle, the monkey swaggered in a red velvet cloak and a hat with an elaborate plume, a clay pipe held aloft in one tiny hand. The joke was that each time the clown contrived to draw something resembling a tune from the instrument, the monkey would leap up and settle itself upon the strings, leaning back on the bridge like a gentleman in a coffee-house. Holding the pipe to its lips, it would blow out mouthfuls of smoke with great contentment. Mary gazed at it enchanted, her hands pressed over her mouth like a lid to keep the laughter in. I pushed my way through.

"How dare you bolt like that?" I rebuked her. "Do you want to be stolen?"

Mary nodded happily, intent upon the stage. A thread of spittle spooled from her mouth. I scowled at her. In her own idiot way, she would always be free.

"Monk'!" she exclaimed, nudging me in the ribs. "See, Lize? Monk'!"

On the stage the monkey leapt onto the clown's head, snatching the bow from his hand so that it might beat him about his ass's ears. The clown tried to swipe at the creature with his fiddle, but the monkey was too quick for him, and the clown succeeded only in delivering a sharp blow to his own forehead. Mary's eyes bulged with held-in delight as the crowd roared their approval.

"Mary!" I protested angrily, tugging at her sleeve, but she only nodded impatiently and strained towards the stage, where the clown was somersaulting in frantic circles, his arms over his head as he tried to escape the monkey's hailstorm of blows. It did him no good. Dropping the bow, the monkey darted over a rope to seize the clown by the ears, tying them neatly together so that his arms were imprisoned. The crowd shrieked with laughter, and Mary shivered, every inch of her stretched tight with pleasure. As she squeaked and craned for a better view, she slipped her arm through mine, and I felt my anger cool to a sort of exasperated tenderness. At least she did not want to go home.

Reluctantly I allowed my attention to be drawn to the stage, where the clown ran in circles, his arms still trapped above his head, begging the audience to come to his rescue in rhyming couplets of increasing coarseness. The audience cheered and stamped, but it served the clown no purpose. The monkey, matching Mr. Punch in his violent use of any weapon that might come to hand, trounced him roundly at every turn and finally chased him clean off the back of the stage. There was a cry, a crash, and then silence. The little creature straightened its cloak, smoothed its whiskers, and set the fiddle stick behind its ear. Then, sweeping off its plumed hat, it effected a deep bow. Mary squealed and clapped, her hands slapping together like fish. With my fingers in my mouth, I whistled.

As the audience applauded, an extravagantly dressed gentleman ascended the platform. Beneath a cape secured at the throat by a chain of large golden links, he wore a lace collar and breeches decorated with shiny buttons and a mass of silken tassels. His head was crowned with a wide soft-brimmed hat, and from his jewelled and buckled belt there hung a long sword, its hilt the head of an exotic bird. With all the authority of an admiral upon the prow of his ship, he strode to the front of the platform and gazed down upon his audience, his hands wide. Behind him the monkey clambered up the tightrope and proceeded to peg out a series of papers, most of them crusted with seals.

"Lords, ladies, and gentlemen," the gentleman sang out from beneath his curled moustache. "I, Aengus O'Reilly, favoured physician to the Grand Duke of Tuscany, declare myself your true and faithful servant."

There was a hum of chatter from the audience. Several observers, mostly fish-fags recalling their duties at the nearby market, began to drift away.

"Beautiful ladies!" O'Reilly called out. "Take heed of my Elixir Vitae. In no more than three doses, this unparalleled preparation restores in full the lost bloom of girlhood and stirs the womb again to fruitfulness. Not to mention fastening loose teeth to a miracle. Why, I have a certification here from the Tsarina of Muscovy herself to testify to its consummate efficacy."

The quack flung his arm behind him to gesture at one of the papers that the monkey had put up. The fishwives muttered and scoffed, but they paused all the same, their eyes narrow beneath their battered hats.

"As for you gentlemen, pray do not think this reason to abandon me. I have here also a sovereign remedy of extraordinary virtue, ground from no less than sixty ingredients and so powerful that it can in a single draught undo the damage of the Devil's own vice. If any here have anchored in strange harbour and fear themselves corrupted, let them come to me. And ladies, listen well, for it cherishes up the drooping spirits of a married man and does quicken them again just as a rose that receives the summer's dew."

At this the mountebank winked hugely, and a rumbling of laughter and muttering broke out over the crowd. The mountebank pressed home his advantage.

"Ladies and gentlemen," he gasped, and the tears seemed almost to stand in his eyes. "Contained in these two phials are medicines of such force and vigour that taken together they might revive the very Dead. Were that not a mystery set aside for God. Their true value is two guineas, but I seek profit in the next life, not this one. For you, a shilling each. May Heaven and all its angels smile upon you."

The audience pressed up against the rickety stage, watching as the first customers fumbled for coins. Mary tugged at my hand.

"Home," she mumbled, and she ran an anxious finger over her palm. It sparkled with sweat, the red welt across it fat as a lip. I shook my head. Not yet.

"Water," I said firmly.

As we turned round, Mary gave forth a yelp. A man stood before us, a startled smile upon his face. It was a moment before I recognised him as the butcher-faced visitor to Swan-street, Mr. Jewkes. To my astonishment, he seized Mary's hand.

"Mary!" he exclaimed. Seeds of sweat stood out upon his strawberry face. "There you are, Mary. Off for water, are you. Buckets'll be awful heavy in this weather, I don't wonder." He patted her hand awkwardly, his eyes upon the ground. "It's been some weeks, I know. Forgive me. It is only that—well, with things as they are—"

Snatching up her hand, he placed a kiss upon the tips of her fingers before thrusting his own deep into the pockets of his coat. Mary blinked at him, her mouth loose as, with the same rough haste, he took up her hand once more and pressed something into the palm, folding her fingers over it.

"A little something," he muttered with a shrug. His ears burned crimson. "Goodbye, my dear. I shall come again when I can. Till then be a good girl and obey your mistress."

He had hardly rounded the corner before I had seized upon her hand and opened her fingers. Inside there was a shiny half-crown.

"What in the name of the Devil is that for?" I cried, snatching the coin from her hand and biting upon it to see if it was real. Mary did not protest. Instead, she bent slowly over and took the smeared handbill from my pail, gaping at the picture upon it. I ripped the paper from her hand, throwing it to the ground. My lips tasted of money.

"Why, Mary?" I demanded, thrusting the coin in her face. "Why the money? Bewitched by the sheer loveliness of your face, is he?"

The cruel words were out of my mouth before I could stop them. There was something so infuriating about Mary's slowness, her half-witted incuriosity. It made you want to hurt her, to slap her cheek or take her soft wrist in your hands and twist the skin between them until she cried out. Mary said nothing. Instead, she squatted down to pick up the discarded bill, smoothing it out and staring at it. I wanted to shake her.

"Well?" I shouted.

"Like Mar'," she said simply. "Kiss Mar'. Kind."

"You stupid little bawd!" I screamed, seizing her by the shoulders. "You let him touch you?"

Mary blinked at me in astonishment and slid the bill into her apron pocket.

"Kind," she repeated, more hesitantly this time. "Kiss Mar'."

"You let him kiss you for money? You addle-headed trull, what else do you let him do? This is half a crown, for pity's sake! A man expects more than a few kisses for half a crown. So what does he do to you, Mary? Just what do you let him do?"

Mary shook her head, backing away from me.

"He like Mar'," she muttered again. "Kind."

"Are you so soft in the head that you think that a kindness? Is that what he tells you when he hoists your skirt, when he thrusts himself between your legs? That he is being kind? Mary, what the — are you such a moon-calf that you would let him make a whore of you and not even know it?"

Mary raised her head. The set of her jaw was mutinous, her pink eyes bright with tears and refusal.

"Kind," she whispered, and then, seizing up her buckets, she fled up the alley towards home.

"You stupid little —," I called after her. "Well, don't come crying to me when you find yourself Frenchified half to death with a hole where your nose should be!"

She was gone. My heart pounded, my skin liquid in the heat. I could not rid my head of the image of the butcher as he ripped at Mary's petticoats, at his own breeches. I stamped after her.

At the end of the lane, I saw the top of her cap as she ran down the kitchen steps. The house looked flat and ordinary from here, a house with a door and windows like any other, no different from its neighbours. A high note rang against the side of my pail, then another. Then a sharp sting like a wasp upon my elbow. I looked up. Across the lane two boys lurked at the entrance to a shadowed alley, their fists full of pebbles. When they saw me, they cackled and darted away. I bent down and lifted the pails. They were light and, apart from two tiny stones, quite empty.

I had forgotten all about the water.

Yet another conversation with the boorish Jewkes in which I am certain he had not the faintest notion of what it was I said. I could swear he has never even heard of Descartes, let alone grasped the fundamentals of his opinions. How such a dullard has contrived to become so very rich is both a mystery & a gross injustice.

All the same, the frustrations of our exchange have left me in a pensive mood & it occurs to me even as I write that, while the Cartesian assertion that neither brain nor soul are required to manage the "machine" or animate body cannot possibly be true of Christians, the same is not necessarily true of <u>savages</u> & <u>idiots</u>.

Surely since imagination & memory are organs with specific functions equivalent to heart & liver, an idiot whose body conforms to the involuntary facilities of breathing, heart beat, digestion &c. must also be subject to the involuntary functions of imagination & memory.

What is more, without the intercession of the rational mind (explaining away the causes of fear, passion &c.) or the godly soul (providing protection from the excesses of imagination) how significantly are the effects of imagination increased?

Oh God, oh my dear & merciful God.

In the idiot may be found <u>the most formidable imagination of all</u>.

XX

That night I dreamed of my mother. It was an uneasy dream, filled with objects I knew to be ordinary but which I was unable to identify. It was not the cottage I dreamed of but some other place, a place which, just as the other aspects of the dream, was at once familiar and quite foreign. In this place I reached out to my mother, trying to touch her, to strike her or embrace her or perhaps both, but however much I extended my hands, she was always beyond my reach. She wore upon her belt an iron key the size of a man's hand which she played with, stroking it tenderly like a cat, and, when she turned to smile at me, she had no face. When I woke, a spiteful headache smeared across the underside of my skull, I remembered that part, though the other particulars of the dream eluded me. I told myself it was her due punishment, that I could no longer remember what she looked like.

Until they will it no longer.

All that day, I toiled up and down the dark stairs, my shoulders screaming with the weight of water and of coal. In the relentless heat, the house was more oppressive than ever and, in each room I entered, the sashes of every window set bars against the white sky. I banged the mop against the floor until my palms blistered, defying Mrs. Black to punish me for making too much of a disturbance. Mary was with the apothecary again, the third time in a week. I had a sudden memory of Mr. Jewkes, his greedy butcher's face leering at her, the sticky coin forced into her hand. Could it be that—? I pushed the thought away, but it lingered, insinuating itself beneath my scalp until I was obliged to kick over the fire irons with a startling clatter.

We took our dinner in silence. Mary ate with a dogged determination, stuffing wads of bread into her mouth which she chewed in circular open-mouthed motions, like a cow. Again I saw the goatish Mr.

Jewkes, one hand clamped upon her shoulder, the other tugging at the buttons of his fly. Mary blinked when I slammed my fist upon the table and pressed another mass of bread into her mouth. So my mother had struck a deal. It mattered not at all whether she had intended it for her own advantage or mine. What mattered was that she unstrike it.

Pushing away my plate, I rose from the table, my legs suddenly restless. I would send my mother a letter. In that letter I would inform her that, although I understood she had sought to safeguard my position through the terms of her arrangement, I wanted no part of it. On the contrary, I now wished to take up employment elsewhere, with immediate effect. I trusted that she would therefore relinquish any further claims upon my future at Swan-street and return any outstanding monies owing to the requisite parties. In return I would pledge her a regular stipend from my own pay, a pension for my freedom. As much as I begrudged such an assurance, I was sage enough to know an appeal to her good nature would hardly be encouragement enough.

Mrs. Black's stringent government of household provisions extended even to the master's paper and ink powder, which she kept in the tea cabinet and gave out only in careful rations. It was fortunate for me that Edgar was a poor copyist and a worse shot. I had to wait only a matter of days before I was able to retrieve a balled-up piece of paper from the kitchen range, its edges only a little charred. After supper that night, as Mary dozed in the bentwood chair, I took the discarded paper from my pocket and smoothed it out on the table, folding Edgar's attempted calligraphy and slicing it away with the boning knife. A stub of pencil was kept in the drawer of the kitchen dresser so that Mrs. Black might make notes of provisions required or jot a new recipe in the book she kept on the shelf over the mantel. I took it out and licked it, my bottom lip caught between my teeth.

I had had little opportunity to practice my letters. Slowly and with considerable effort, I pressed my hand against the page. The rushlight burned down until it was no more than a greasy smear in the cup, more smoke than light, and still I pored over the paper. I was so intent upon my business that I did not hear Edgar until he slammed the door, filling the kitchen with the stale port and tobacco stink of taverns. Hurriedly I tried to smuggle the paper into my apron pocket, but Edgar was too quick for me. Seizing my arm, he twisted it behind my back, extracting the paper from between my fingers. The noise roused Mary, who startled up from her chair, her hands flapping like a frightened hen.

"Well, well," he slurred. "How interesting. A rustic attempting the rudiments of penmanship? With whom can she possibly be corresponding?"

I made a grab for the paper, but Edgar extended his arm upwards out of my reach and fluttered it above my head.

"Patience, you cunning little doxie, patience."

Turning his shoulders away from me, he tilted the paper towards the light of the fire and studied it. Again I snatched for it, but again he twisted out of reach. Mary whimpered.

"Give that back!" I cried.

Edgar did not reply. Instead, he considered the paper a little longer. Then he turned to face me, the page extended with a flourish between his fingers.

"Well, well," he said again, as I seized the paper and thrust it furiously into my pocket. He smirked. Taking hold of a chair with the careful precision of intoxication, he sat, patting the seat of mine in invitation. I glowered.

"Please yourself." He shrugged, regarding me. Then, to my confusion, he began to laugh, his hand over his mouth like a girl.

"What?" I demanded, crossing my arms. "What is it you find so droll?"

Edgar opened his mouth. Then he closed it again, shaking his head and clutching his soft belly with amusement. Beside me Mary reached out to squeeze my arm. I shook her off angrily.

"What?"

"It is—it is nothing. It is only that—well, you must confess it is amusing. The idea that your toothless crone of a mother of all people is responsible for your position here. It is—well, you must admit, it is something of an absurdity. I mean, where do you imagine she would get that kind of money?"

Edgar chuckled again. I hesitated.

"What the Devil do you know about it, anyway?" I asked sullenly.

"More than you, it would appear."

I said nothing but only stared at the floor.

"I happen to know, for example, that our esteemed master receives a stipend to keep you here. A considerable amount too. And that, unless she is recently married into the upper ranks of the gentry, it most certainly does not come from your mother."

"You expect me to believe that the master told you this himself? It is no more than hearsay, idle gossip."

"Doubtless there is all manner of that kind of talk about you, sluttish little jade that you are. But in this case, you are mistaken. An apprentice must keep a close eye on all aspects of his master's affairs, if he means to profit from the arrangement and have at least as firm a grasp of the finances of his business as the master does himself. For as long as his patron requires you here, it would appear that you, dear Eliza, are one of the master's few assets."

"His patron?"

"I use the term loosely. Your patron perhaps. The gentleman who pays to keep you here. And pay he does, handsomely. Why so shocked? A girl in your unhappy predicament should be grateful that Mr. Black is in no position to negotiate."

I stared at Edgar. My mouth was dry.

"They cannot make me stay," I protested. "There are many households in London that require servants. I can leave whenever I choose."

"Without a character? I hardly think so. And even if you found an employer fool enough to take you without recommendation, you think he would not find you? The apothecary is a dolt, it's true, but not so much of a dolt that he might readily surrender his golden goose. If you try to leave, he will put advertisements in every newspaper and coffee-house in town until he finds you. And should your patron come to hear of your exploits—well!" He chuckled, pinching my cheek hard. "Who knows what reward might be tendered then for your most unfortunate demise?"

The next day I was despatched once more to Islington. It was the first time the mistress had sent me there since ... certainly, it had been many weeks. Mrs. Black sat stiffly on the shop's high three-legged stool, the leather-bound ledger of accounts open on the counter before her, listing her requirements as she copied the details of the week's business into the great brown book. Her nails clicked insistently against the worn wooden beads of the abacus.

There was a knock at the door, two men in velveteen coats, one pushing a handcart lined with straw. Mrs. Black let them in, nodding towards the barometer that hung upon the wall opposite the hall mirror. As his companion lifted it from its nail, the smaller one appraised me with the cool efficiency of a coffin-maker.

"What the Devil are you staring at?" Mrs. Black snapped harshly. It was a moment before I understood that the rebuke was directed at me.

Muttering, I ducked my head and slouched downstairs. Mary was with the apothecary again, and the linnet hunched listlessly on its perch, its feathers dull and mothy. For some moments I stood motionless in the gloomy silence, staring into the earth-crumbed depths of my basket. Then, with a great effort of will, I snatched it up and flung open the door, taking the kitchen steps two at a time. For weeks now, pickled in the bricked-up stink of Swan-street, I had longed for such a task, longed to breathe in the vast bowl of the sky, to feel the jostle of the streets stretching my loose nerve-strings and quickening the flow of my blood. Now, as I toiled up the narrow lane, the heat pressed down on me, drawing the vigour from my body like a poultice. My legs dragged, heavy and disobliging. The house at Swan-street seemed to pull at me, sucking me back, its stale breath hot on my neck. Several times I stopped, twisting round abruptly to scan the crowd for someone who might be following me. *Unfortunate demise. Unfortunate demise.* The words clicked across my skull, precise as an abacus.

The wooded glades of Islington were lush and airless, their silence too conducive to reflection. I did not linger. Gathering the required plants as quickly as I could, I hastened back to the city. The sky was a hot white glare, as though the sun had infused every part of it, and the sweat greased my bodice and slicked my forehead, stinging my eyes. At Butcher-hall-lane the stink of the shambles was so powerful that the tumbling in my belly threatened to overwhelm me, and I was obliged to stop and cover my mouth with my apron.

I was still nauseous when I returned to Swan-street. The drapes were drawn, and the house wore the blind blank look of Fate itself. I could not endure to go back there, not yet. Instead, I turned, slipping down Artichoak-lane towards the river. There the sparkle of salt upon the air might pass for a breeze. I pushed my way through the press of warehouse-men loading barges with barrels of preserved fish. Beneath the white sky, the river had a densely metalled glint, as though the water were not liquid but a solid thoroughfare of mud, churned by countless striving oars.

Beyond the wharf the mountebank had returned. A crowd of people, most of them women come directly from their work at the fish market, strained to watch the monkey, who, having trounced its ass-eared opponent, rolled about on its back, its hands clutched over its mouth, convulsed by merriment. Then, leaping to its feet, it snatched up three phials of green glass and began frantically to juggle them, tossing them high into the air. The crowd roared and stamped as the mountebank solemnly ascended to the stage.

"Beloved women," he cried, "who are the admirablest creatures that ever God created under the canopy of Heaven, to the preservation of whose beauty, health, vigour, and strength I have dedicated my studies, nay, truly, my life itself!"

The monkey bowed its head and solemnly placed all three bottles in the mountebank's hand before slipping from the stage. The crowd of women nudged each other and grunted and pressed a little closer to the quack, whose voice carried easily on the windless air. Already several of them had their hands upon their purses.

Miserably I turned away.

I am resolved. There is no other way forwards. When I think of how He came to me, how He stood before me, the Light pouring from His divine countenance, & required me, in that voice at once so mellifluous & so dreadful, to do His will, the tears once more spring to my eyes. I am His instrument.

Oh sweet God, no. It is back, the dark figure that lurks in the corner of the room, eyeing me with its cold crocodile eyes, choking me with its sulphurous breath. It sees my fear & it laughs, a vile laugh containing all the evil sounds of the universe. I lower my head to my work, but the creature insinuates itself beneath my skin, torments me with its cancerous embrace, its abominable eyes besieging me in one thousand thousand repetitions that leer at me from outside & within. They twist in my belly writhing ripping my stomach torments me. More tincture. The opium shall open my eyes to the shadows & drive back the horrors to their loathsome brimstone lairs.

Work. The simple precision of thesis & proof.

These alone shall keep me steady, protect me from the evils of doubt & the purposeless ravings of the outside world. Listen not to the voices. It is they who corrupt you, not the work which must be done, which must always be done, whatever the cost, to the greater glory of the Lord.

Thy kingdom come, thy will be done, on Earth as it is in Heaven.

XXI

And so the days went on, marked out by the grinding repetition of household work. The stifling summer eased its garrotte, though the cooler air did not penetrate far into the house. I fell into a low distemper, my stomach disturbed, my bowels loose and stringy. Mrs. Black glared at my chamber-pot and warned me that any attempt to shirk my responsibilities would be punished. Each time the door to the house or the shop stood open, I imagined lifting my skirts and running, running, until I was nothing but a speck on the smudged Surrey hills, ant legs still running, never turning around. But when I turned around, I was still there, pale but definite in the speckled glass of the hall, my eyes smudged around with coal dust and fatigue.

I missed Mary. The sticky hiss of her breathing had always irked me, but it seemed I had grown used to it. Without the ballast of her bulk beside me, the room had an insubstantial feeling about it and the cries and shouts of passers-by sounded closer, more shrill. Long after they had ceased, the room quivered with the echo of them.

Mary had begged not to be moved to the kitchen, but Mr. Black had insisted, claiming himself driven close to distraction by her relentless snoring. The first night I watched as she pushed the table across the flags and rolled out her palliasse. She was crying but silently, her back turned towards me. I felt the twist of vexation that her misery always roused in me and, beneath it, something else, something more desolate. She pulled a mess of rugs from the dresser shelf. The trailing hem of a rug knocked a pewter plate from the dresser, so that it clattered noisily upon the floor.

"Why must you always be so clumsy?" I hissed angrily. "If the old sow hears you, she'll beat us both."

Mary said nothing. Instead, she wiped her nose on the back of her sleeve and crouched to pick up the plate. I wanted to kick her.

"Get a hold of yourself," I added sharply. "I have slept here myself, remember? It's not so bad."

Abruptly a spasm of memory clutched my belly. Turning away from the dark window, I stared hard at the dresser, examining with uncharacteristic attention the tea service on the top shelf. One of the cups was chipped at the lip, and the raw edge of the china had a yellow crust, like a cut gone bad.

Whimpering, Mary crept over to me and buried her wet face in my skirt. I pulled away, tugging the fabric roughly from her hands so that she fell forwards, catching her forehead upon the corner of the dresser. The wound gaped white, shocked as a mouth, before the blood leapt up into it, flooding it with crimson.

"For the love of God!"

Snatching a rag from the line above the fire, I thrust it at her. Her face was grey, the blood that cascaded over her brow startlingly red. Awkwardly, she turned her head, moving her arm in front of her face as if to conceal the wound.

"Mary, please!" I admonished her, seizing her head. "Would you bleed to death?"

Mary looked up at me as I pressed the rag to her brow.

"Mar' wan' stay wi' Lize," she said, her pink eyes pleading.

I said nothing. The wound was wide but not deep, and the bleeding seemed to be slowing a little, although Mary's face was fearfully pale. I closed her fingers round the rag, but she let it fall away. Blood seeped into the faint arc of her eyebrow, white stitches of hair against the scarlet.

"Mary!"

"'Fraid," she whispered.

"Don't be. It's not so deep. But you must staunch the bleeding. Come now, help me, at least. I can't do it by myself," I snapped, snatching up her hand more harshly than I intended.

"Lize—Lize, I—pliss—so 'fraid—"

Her voice split. Squeezing her eyes shut, Mary rocked herself back and forth. The tears gathered beneath her eyelids and issued down her cheeks, sending pinky tracks through the smeared blood and pasting strands of sticky hair to her face. Something broke open inside me. Without stopping to think, I dropped down beside her and took her in my arms. She clung to me like a monkey, her hands gripping the stuff of my dress.

"Oh, Mary," I murmured. "I'm sorry. I was—there's no need to be afraid."

The kitchen door slammed.

"How very charming. The idiot and the whore." The viciousness in Edgar's voice was only slightly softened by the slur of liquor. "A pietà worthy of Michelangelo. Of course, it would be more authentic if the moon-calf were indeed dead. All over, that is, rather than from the neck up."

"Go fuck with yourself," I hissed, tightening my arms around her.

"Ah, I would but, thanks to the close attentions of a spirited little creature upon London-bridge, the fucking is already done," Edgar sniggered. He collapsed into the bentwood chair and fumbled off his shoes. Then, stepping with exaggerated care in his stockinged feet, a finger against his lips, he helped himself to a bottle of the master's best wine from the top shelf of the pantry and tiptoed upstairs.

For a moment the kitchen was still. In the fire a charred lump of wood shifted a little, the ash sighing as it dropped. Mary was quiet in my lap now, her breathing gluey but even. Licking a corner of my apron, I wiped the streaked blood from her face, tucking her hair behind her ears. In sleep Mary's pink lips pressed together, closing the gap in her upper lip so that her mouth looked almost ordinary. It was not only her mouth. Sleep and candlelight smoothed the skewed mismatch of her features, neatening her face so that, rather than discerning its deficiencies, you noticed instead the pale creaminess of her skin, the sweet curve of her chin. Above the black gash upon her forehead, her hair glowed red-gold.

Tucking the blankets more tightly round her, I kissed her very gently upon her damp cheek and blew out the candle.

Now that the rains had come, the stand-pipe was open again. Several times each week Mary and I were required to fetch water, and each time she insisted upon circling by the river to see if the mountebank was there.

"Monk'," she said, and she rattled her empty buckets longingly. "Lil' monk'."

I obliged her, less to please her than because I felt too weary to protest. While she watched the monkey's antics, I watched her. Her hands flapped at her sides, and her tongue thrust from her loose mouth, frantic with pleasure. When she laughed, her head rolled giddily on the stem of her neck. Mr. Jewkes had not been to the house for weeks. I hoped the vile lecher was sick or injured or both. We never spoke of him. Indeed, she hardly spoke at all. Perhaps she feared the unpredictability of my humour, for it was true that I was often snappish and sometimes cruel. There was a native wisdom in Mary for all her idiocy.

As the mountebank took to the stage, the monkey streaked across the stage, flinging itself into the audience. Mary pushed forwards into the crowd, trying to get closer and trampling the foot of a sharp-faced knife-grinder.

"Watch yerself, you cussed rattle-head," he spat, raising his right fist to reveal a sleeve quite eaten away by his wheel.

"If there's a rattle-head round here, I'm looking right at him," I spat back.

"Is that right?" hissed the knife-grinder, and he pushed me hard so that I stumbled backwards.

"You all right, miss?"

I blinked. The mountebank's clown stood beside me, his ass-eared hood slack upon his shoulders. He was taller than he looked on stage. My head came only to his shoulder.

"You wouldn't be wanting any trouble now, would you?" he said flatly to the knife-grinder, who muttered under his breath and, spitting into the dust at my feet, stalked away.

"You didn't need to do that," I said to the clown. "I can take care of myself."

He shrugged, his toe scuffing the whorl of sputum into the dirt.

"Fighting ain't good for trade," he said.

"Bastards like that aren't good for anything."

His mouth twitched.

"Enjoy the show," he said, and, whistling, he ducked into the crowd.

I had to push through the throng to find Mary. She stood at the very front, bent almost double over the rough stage. On the boards before her, almost sitting upon her hands, was the monkey, its whiskery face held up towards hers.

"Come now," I hissed, tugging at her arm.

Mary twisted obstinately as the mountebank turned, throwing out a ring-heavy hand towards me.

"Now see here a girl with the complexion and humour particular to green-sickness. Miss, you are well-advised to come here today. In but three doses, the noble Syrop shall cure your poor skin colour, your listlessness, your want of appetite and digestion, and in every way necessary restore you to yourself."

"Mary," I hissed again. "Or do you want a beating?"

Reluctantly Mary bent to pick up her buckets. Even as we walked downriver towards the stand-pipe, I could hear the mountebank's voice carrying over the clamour.

"Proof enough that it is a matchless fool who takes an idiot as an advisor!"

"Pay no heed to him," I muttered to Mary. "It is those women who are the fools, parting with their shillings in droves for quack medicines that are no more than water and dye when the rightful cures to their ills grow wild a mile from here."

And so the idea began to grow. The city was crowded with fools who might part with their money upon the least provocation. What then was to prevent another elixir from luring the pennies from their pockets, an elixir of my own devising that mixed together all the most efficacious roots and herbs known to medicine? My mother had made little from her endeavours, but she had proved herself a poor businesswoman in all matters but the trading of her only daughter. Persuasively labelled and prettily bottled, my elixir might be taken up by any number of taverns and coffee-houses. One day it might become as famous as Stoughton's Grand Cordial or Anderson's Scots Pills. For did I not know as much of herbarising as any other?

As my arms ached with the effort of scrubbing the linens or hauling the coal or even the foul and headachy task of painting the bedsteads with mercury against the lice, my mind turned over the teachings of my childhood. Foxglove for dropsy. Laurel and white hellebore to destroy the tooth worm before it grew strong in the jaw. Cowslip flower and madder root to restore the skin to youth. I was not entirely displeasing to look at, when I was well. And a shrewd woman might use the impediment of her sex to her advantage. Now, when we went for water, it was I who insisted upon visiting the mountebank's pitch, I who listened attentively as he declaimed the wonders of his nostrums. And although I found myself daily altering the recipe, it was with considerable impatience that I waited for Mrs. Black to despatch me once again to the abundant fields and woods of Islington.

Edgar was there when she summoned me a week later. I turned my face from his. For all his flabby self-importance, his eyes were discomfortingly sharp.

"We must have marsh sow-thistle and Jack-by-the-Hedge in particular," Mrs. Black instructed as she spread a green-flecked paste upon a strip of leather. "And mugwort. I require quantities of the herb rather than the flowers. Wrap it in a wet rag to keep it fresh. It must not become dried out. And dove's-foot. I have had about all I can endure of your foul expulsions."

"Yes, madam."

"Do not turn away from me like that, girl," Mrs. Black snapped, frowning at the plaister. I lowered my eyes, my countenance studiedly blank. "You are also to collect a parcel from the bookseller Mr. Honfleur. The master is not well enough to venture out today." She cleared her throat sharply. "You will find the shop in St. Paul's Churchyard, close by the sign of the Hand and Scribe at the western end. Do you read?"

There was something in the way her hand protected the letter she drew from her pocket that made me think it might be important. I shook my head.

"As I thought. Very well, give this to Mr. Honfleur. Tell him I do not expect a reply. Mary, why are you loitering there? The floors shall not scrub themselves."

Mary startled, hastily thrusting a much-thumbed handbill into her apron pocket. She was too slow. Mrs. Black snatched it from her hand.

"Where did you get this? Have you been in the master's room? You know perfectly well that is quite forbidden. Well, have you?"

She fingered the birch at her belt, and Mary backed away, shaking her head.

"It is not the master's," I said quickly. "It's mine. A man gave it to me. At the stand-pipe."

Mrs. Black peered at me and then at it, narrowing her eyes.

"Nothing but cheap trickery," she said at last, crushing the paper into a ball. "The spines are surely fixed upon that child with glue."

Lifting the plaister with both hands, she left the room.

Edgar belched as Mary rubbed her face gratefully against mine, leaving a smear of spit across my cheek. I wiped it on my sleeve and tried not to think of Mr. Jewkes and his butcher's eye for flesh.

DOCTOR
JAMES
TILBURG

Now living at the Black Swan in St. Giles
in the fields, over against Drury-lane end,
where you shall see, at night, three Lanthorns
with candles burning in them upon the Balcony

FIRST, he cures the French Pox,
with all its dependents

SECONDLY, he takes away all pains in
the shoulders, arms, and bones, therefore all
ye that are troubled, come to him before
you are spoiled by others

THIRDLY, if any have anchored in a
strange harbour, fearing to have received
damage, let them come to him

LASTLY, he helps them that have lost their
Nature, and cherishes up the subdued spirits of a
marry'ed man, by what occasion soever they have
lost it, and does quicken them again as a Rose
that hath receiv'd the Summer's dew

XXII

I did not open the mistress's letter to the bookseller until I had gathered all I had come for. Though I was still unable to settle emphatically upon a single remedy, I had secreted beneath the wrapped parcels of shop herbs several I thought might serve me well, including sweet balm and mint, which my mother considered peerless in quickening the faculties of Nature and encouraging a cheerful heart. What untold hundreds of people must there be cloaked in the grimy folds of London, I thought, who yearned for a cheerful heart?

My head was full of Tally's Quickening Syrop as I unfolded the letter and studied it. The script was cramped, hard to decipher, and hardly merited the effort of it, being only to do with matters of accounts and payment. Disappointed, I folded it up again carefully, fitting the knotted twine over it like a bridle. Even Edgar would have struggled to profit from a letter of that kind.

The Churchyard was crowded with booksellers, each with tables of books spilling out in front of their premises and a doorway in which the shopkeepers leaned as though petrified, a pair of finger-smudged spectacles set low upon their noses. So motionless was their posture, their heads settled low between their rounded shoulders and their arms around their plump chests, that they resembled sleeping pigeons upon the roost.

Mr. Honfleur's shop, when I found it, was a quite different-looking place. For a start, the books on the table outside were not bundled together higgledy-piggledy and tied up with lengths of twine. There were no stacks of loose papers or dog-eared periodicals, all jumbled together with packets of sugar and tea. Instead, they were arranged in neat rows, the spines all facing outwards so that they might be easily inspected, and above them a broad awning of canvas had been stretched to prevent the sun from fading their bindings. A lanky boy of perhaps seven years sat upon a three-legged stool beside the table, his back stiff but his arms and legs wrapped round themselves in a series of complicated knots. As I approached, out of breath, he untangled himself and stood, peering at me with a severe expression. His brown hair was long in the front and fell over his eyes.

"I would show you in myself," he said. "But I cannot leave my post. You might think that, here, in the very shadow of the house of the Lord, you would be safe from the perils of thievery. But you would be mistaken."

The evening sun did not penetrate the shop, for thin calico drapes had been drawn across the windows, but the dim light had a pearly sheen, a quiet contemplativeness that was quite different from the sealed-up dark of Swan-street. I stood in the doorway, afraid to enter. I had never seen so many books in all my life. Not an inch of wall was visible. Even the slice of space above the window contained two narrow shelves, both crammed with volumes. As for the shop itself, it was a maze of bookshelves, all of them higher than my head and with barely enough room for a grown man to pass between them. Where there was a crack of space between the books there were piled neat sheaves of writing paper, quills, ledgers, letter cases, sealing wax, wafers, slates, pencils, ink powder, even on one shelf a box of spectacles. It was impossible to imagine that a proprietor might be accommodated in such a place unless he, too, were bound in leather and his name tooled upon his spine in letters of gold. As I stared about me, my mouth open, a mote of book dust caught in my throat and I coughed.

"Yes?"

The woman who stood before me wore a simple dress of plain dark stuff. Her face bore not the faintest trace of paint, not even a reddening of her pale lips, and her hair was hidden beneath a white cap that put me in mind of a nun's wimple. Even her features were neat and plain, answering impeccably to the requirements of a face without attempting the slightest embellishment. The only decoration she wore was a brooch at her bosom. It was in the shape of a flower, with shiny petals of a deep blood-red. A green enamelled stem curled from its underside, and upon one of the red petals, there rested a single tiny pearl like a bead of dew. I stared at it entranced, the letter in my outstretched hand forgotten.

"If you are possessed of a tongue, I would be obliged if you might use it," the woman said drily. "I have many other matters to attend to."

"Forgive me," I stammered. "I am sent by Mr. Black. To collect his books."

"Ah, the inestimable Mr. Black. The apothecary who seeks to be the next Mr. Harvey. 'But happy Thou, ta'en from this frantic age, / Where ignorance and hypocrisy does rage! / A fitter time for Heaven no soul e'er chose— / the place now only free from those.' But then it is reasonable, is it not, to assume your master is not a great admirer of the likes of Cowley, however wise their epitaphs?"

I shifted unhappily as she sighed, her fingers at her throat. If she thought I understood her, she was mistaken.

"I—I have this too," I managed, proffering the letter.

"Indeed. Doubtless my father will be greatly interested in the contents." She considered me. "Wait here. I shall fetch him down, in case there is to be an answer."

"The mistress said—"

She was already gone. The dying sun lit the calico windows like candle shades. The shop smelled of dust and beeswax and a warm brewery aroma that was, I think now, the moulder of old paper but which I took to be the smell of learning. I had not known that such a place could exist. I thrust my raw, red hands into the pocket of my apron, suddenly ashamed of them, and wished the discomfiting woman would come back. Without her as chaperone, I felt illicit as a thief.

Before me a sweep of books fanned the low table, the linings of their worn covers poking through like tongues. One stood open upon a stand of dark wood, a dark blue ribbon hung between its pages. It looked old. The ribbon was frayed, a pulled thread wrinkling the silk along one side, and the paper was thin and delicate, almost transparent, edged in a tarnished gold and covered all over in thick black words. So many words! They swarmed at you so that you could not see where one started and the next began. Not daring to step closer, I craned my neck towards it, screwing up my eyes. Perhaps if I concentrated all of my efforts on just one tiny part—

"You are fond of Marlowe?"

I startled upwards, my face burning.

"I beg your pardon, sir, I—," I stammered, my eyes on the floor. The bookseller's shoes were plain and narrow, his ankles trim as a girl's.

"Please, look all you wish. Books are like people. They do not bear loneliness well. Those that remain unnourished by another's touch wither and die. Here, hold it, read a little. So long as your hands are tolerably clean, that volume shall be grateful for your favour."

The bookseller spoke with an unfamiliar accent that buzzed upon his lips and set certain words to spinning at the back of his throat. His tone was gentle, but there was more than a little of the daughter's dryness in it. I watched his long fingers unfold my mistress's letter. As he read it, his lips twisted a little. Surreptitiously I wiped my hands upon my apron.

"Hmm," he murmured. "So that is why he sends you and does not come himself."

"My master is confined to bed, sir."

"If the man allowed himself more air and a great deal less self-satisfaction, he would enjoy considerably better health." A faint smile upon his lips, the bookseller re-folded the letter and pushed it between the covers of the large black ledger on the counter. "He might even find men like myself more inclined to extend him the terms he asks for."

Lifting a wrapped pile of books onto his counter, he proceeded to cut the string. From the pile he took two of the largest volumes and set them to one side. Then he pushed the smaller stack and their mess of paper and string towards his daughter, who sighed and set down her book.

"You shall take only these. Your master will understand me, I think."

"Very good, sir."

He considered me thoughtfully until I squirmed beneath his gaze.

"A fine face. But not a native of London, I think?" he mused, tapping a finger against his lips as his grim-faced daughter handed me the wrapped books.

"No, sir."

"A foreigner, then, like myself. It is better so. This great city blinds its citizens, with the dust of all its rush and bustle and its desperate grubbing about in the dirt in the hope of a little profit. We foreigners are more fortunate. We see things more clearly, I think, standing a little way off. *Alors. Bonsoir, mademoiselle.*"

The bookseller bowed and, stepping round me, held open the door. I hesitated, then, inclining my head, I walked through it with a rustling flourish of my skirts. It was the first time in my life anyone had opened a door for me.

her eyes in the darkness the gleam of the rag about her mouth but she does not cry out not any more it is not her screams that haunt me but her breathing the sticky choke of her breathing the way her hands clench the knuckles bright as bone sharp as bone rotten as

Steady now. Dear blessed laudanum. Perfume in my veins. Breathe. Better. Slowly now. The pen jumps upon the paper like a cricket. Pulse easing. Better.

notes

- *no knowledge/understanding of act of copulation nor process of conception*
- *physically mature: developed breasts & pubic hair*
- *sexual organs normal, although labia unusually large & pronounced*
- *menstruation regular*
- *passivity: imagination driven by passion; anger fear grief where are they where are they idiot insensate vacant dumb*
- *nerve-strings slack heart slack muscles slack blood slack*
- *imagination dormant dead mind dead*
- *plough her punish her rent her in two slap strike twist bite burn*
- *force her to fear to flinch to cower to weep*
- *to feel*

SEPTEMBER		OCTOBER		NOVEMBER	
1		1	†	1	[M due]
2		2		2	† no M
3		3		3	
4		4	M [conf.]	4	
5		5	M	5	†
6	†	6	M	6	†
7	†	7	M	7	
8		8	M?	8	
9	M [?]	9	†	9	
10	M [confirmed]	10		10	M? [spotting]
11	M	11	†	11	clear
12	M	12		12	clear
13		13	††	13	†
14		14		14	
15	†	15	†	15	
16	†	16		16	†
17	?	17	X	17	
18	†	18	†?	18	
19		19		19	
20	X	20	††	20	
21	††	21		21	
22		22		22	†
23		23	†	23	
24		24		24	
25	†	25	X	25	vomiting
26	†	26	†	26	
27	X [?]	27	†	27	vomiting
28	†	28		28	fatigue/vom.
29		29		29	fatigue/vom.
30		30		30	please God
		31	†		

XXIII

If proof were required of the efficacy of Tally's Quickening Syrop, it might have been found in the improvement to my spirits in the weeks that followed. In the kitchen I mixed a distilled water of the two herbs, which I sweetened with sugar I chipped from the sugar loaf, making sure to carve it where my pilferings might not be noticed. The dozen bottles I bought cheaply from a slippery-eyed druggist who occupied a small grimy crevice of a shop in an alley behind Newgate-street and brought back to the house wrapped in a rag. They clinked together quietly beneath the master's bundle of books, like coins.

Once I had corked and sealed them, I hid all the bottles of Syrop but one in the garret, tucked into the hole in the corner of the ceiling. At night I liked to reach up into the crumbling plaster and stroke their smooth skins. The remaining bottle I concealed in the bottom of my basket, beneath a scrap of sacking. Each time I was despatched upon an errand, to the bookseller or in search of herbs, I made sure to visit at least one tavern or coffee-house so that I might attempt to convince them of the wondrous properties of this extraordinary medicine.

And although I did not enjoy the manner of immediate success I had wished for, I refused to be discouraged by the repeated rounds of discourtesy and rebuttal, by the small anxious voice in my head that woke me before dawn with its peevish doubts, its ceaseless fretful worrying and prodding. I moved the bottle from the basket to new hiding places, fearful of discovery, and at night I slept with it concealed beneath my pillow. When I woke, I took it in my hand and told myself to be patient, to hold steady. The Syrop was my only chance. Did I not grow more fluent, more assured, and more mendacious with every petition? Surely, then, it would not be long before Tally's Quickening Syrop was as favoured a cure as Dr. James's Powders themselves.

As autumn shrivelled into winter, it was Mary's turn to sicken. Her condition alarmed me. When I suggested we sneak once more to the mountebank's show, she shook her head listlessly. Even my Syrop, which I fed her hurriedly and in secret, failed to restore her. Unless I roused her and dressed her and pushed her up the stairs, she only huddled in the kitchen, staring into the fire. Mrs. Black had taken to leaving the key of the kitchen door in the lock when she turned it at night, and most mornings I came downstairs to find the door still locked and Mary asleep upon her palliasse. She slept deeply. When I shook her shoulder, she jolted upright as though a strike of lightning had passed through her, her eyes wide with shock. Sometimes she screamed. When I placed my hand over her mouth to quiet her, she bit me. Then, as abruptly as it had come, the convulsion would pass. Her body would go slack and her eyes would close and she would fall back onto her pillow, hauling the blanket over her head. Some mornings it took all my strength to haul her upright.

Mrs. Black brewed her a tea of her own devising. The foul-smelling tisane had to be sweetened before Mary would drink it, and even then she sometimes dropped the cup, her hand slipping away from it as though their fibres had been cut. It effected no improvement. Her distemper proved so unyielding that after several weeks I went myself to Mrs. Black and begged that something more be done. Mrs. Black eyed me beadily and informed me that the master was doing all that was necessary. Mary suffered sluggish blood thickened by a poor digestion for which he had prescribed purgatives and regular clysters that he administered himself.

The purgatives made Mary vomit until she retched nothing but a thin yellow bile, but the clysters were worse. On those days Mary emerged from the apothecary's room glassy-eyed and trembling, her hands pressed between her thighs. When I tried to embrace her, she was stiff as a corpse.

She did not improve. I watched her anxiously, certain that the apothecary had mistaken her disease. But although she limped a little and complained of pain in her lower belly, Mary showed none of the usual symptoms of failing health. She had no fever, no coughing, no sores nor blisters. Thanks to the master's clysters, her evacuations were plentiful and of good colour. Even the frequent vomits resulted in no loss of appetite. On the contrary, she ate constantly, rapaciously, devouring mouthful after mouthful of barely chewed food as though the demands of her stomach would never be satisfied. Even when she was finally finished, she sneaked as much as she could manage into the pocket of her apron. When we rolled her bed away in the mornings, there were greasy fragments of cheese and buttered pastry caught amongst the blankets. She grew fatter. Her cheeks puffed and her belly, which had always been round as a child's, nudged out the skirts of her loose dresses. When she held my hand, her fingers were damp and spongy between mine, her knuckles a line of dimples in the doughy flesh.

But it was plain that she was far from well. She might have been one of the waxworks in Mrs. Salmon's museum, down to the yellow skin and glassy eyes. She stumbled through the days like a cow plodding to and from the milking shed, her head low between her shoulders. She chewed at her lips and her fingernails until they bled. Her duties went undone. She had taken to pulling out her hair so that the bald patch on her scalp, which had once been no bigger than a child's palm, now extended over almost to her ear. Amber hairs clung like cobwebs between her plump fingers.

In the evenings when our duties were finally finished, I took to dressing her hair. The rhythmic strokes of the brush were soothing to both of us, and with Mary seated at my feet, I was saved the burden of her eyes upon my face. We did not talk much. I spent hours with curling papers and rags to create heartbreakers, the two small curls at the nape of the neck that were supposed to set men's pulses racing, and confidantes, smaller curls near the ears. For all its fineness, Mary's hair held the ringlets well.

There was a glass in the kitchen, a cheap scrap of one with only the most cursory of frames, which Mrs. Black had put there so that I might ensure that my appearance was presentable before I went up to the shop. For some reason that had always irked me, the glass agitated Mary. Even when I took her over to examine my handiwork, she would look only when the reflection contained us both.

"Mar'?" she would say then, and despite the uncertainty in her voice, her mouth curved up slightly at the corners. Not a smile exactly, it looked as though it might permit itself to be coaxed into one. "Is Mar'?"

"Look at you!" I encouraged. "See here, how it curls over your shoulder. Don't you look handsome?"

Mary gazed and gazed, smiling and not smiling like an angel in a chapbook. She never dared lay a hand on her own head. Instead, she would reach out and touch her reflection in the glass with no more than the tip of one finger, as if the picture were wet and might smudge. Frowning with concentration, she would follow the elaborate crest of her scalp, the looping whorls of hair that framed her face. Then abruptly she would turn away, laying the glass face-down upon the table and crouching in front of the fire with her forehead resting upon her knees. She was quiet, but I never doubted that she liked it, in her own way. She never asked me to stop.

Then one evening, quite without warning, she snatched up the glass with both hands and slammed it down hard upon the kitchen table. Mercifully it did not break. Seven years is a very long time. Quickly I put the glass on the high dresser shelf where she could not reach it. It was a moment before I realised that she was tearing violently at her hair, ripping at its fixings so that pins skittered across the floor.

"Mary, stop!" I cried out, anxious but angry, too, at the ruin of my careful artistry. "For God's sake, you'll hurt yourself—"

I tried to pull her hands away from her head, but she was too strong for me. She glared at me stonily, a hank of hair tumbled over her face, her mouth making silent shapes. Then, pushing roughly past me, she fled from the kitchen. I shouted after her then that she could shave her head bald for all I cared about it, for I would never trouble to dress her hair again.

She must have hidden in the coal-hole, for when at last she came back, her dress was filthy. When she took my hands in hers and rubbed them against her cheek, I saw that her chewed nails were rimmed with black. I imagined her squatting in its chill blackness, the whites of her eyes swelling, and the thought of it vexed me unbearably. Mary was terrified of the coal cellar.

She did not let me comfort her. I tried kisses, I tried threats, often both at once, but nothing worked. She recoiled from my touch. It was as though the warm soft parts of her had been cut away, and all that was left between the slabs of cold flesh that shaped her was an empty, hungry hole. She ate and ate, pressing down handfuls of bread into the sack of her belly, but the hole could not be filled. When she looked at me, I could see the black depths of it in her glassy, desolate eyes.

To Grayson Black
Apothecary at the sign of the Unicorn, Swan-street

Black, sir,

 I do not think that it will surprise you greatly to receive this letter. In recent months I have made no secret of my dissatisfaction with both the nature of your work & the manner in which you choose to conduct it. On the several occasions that I have attempted to discuss my misgivings with you, I have gained the distinct impression that you regarded my intercessions as no more than a tiresome interruption to the business of your day.

 These difficulties would be of little consequence to me if I was assured that you were intent upon producing the paper which, when we met two years ago, you promised would make both of our names. I suffer no illusions about the extent of my usefulness to you. I was always content to provide the funds & leave the intricacies of science to you. However, your secrecy, your obdurate refusal to discuss your progress with me, always an impediment to our partnership, has of late become insufferable. I have no idea whether you have subjects for study &, if not, how else you mean to seek out your proofs. I understand from the girl that you rarely go out. You tell me nothing at all.

 Once I might have excused such silence as little more than your habitual ill manners. No longer. Time and considerable expenditure have, at last, made me wise. You are silent, sir, for the simplest of reasons, because there is nothing to tell. I can no longer deceive myself that a successful outcome to your work is certain, or even likely. I enclose a little money in conclusion of our arrangements.

 I shall of course continue to support the girl, as I have always done. I remain much troubled by the matter of her persistent ill health & would wish nothing in the world to impede her swiftest recovery. I trust that you are gentleman enough not to permit the hostility between us to affect your conduct towards her, who is quite without blame.

 I remain, sir, &c.,
 MAURICE JEWKES

2nd day of February 1720

XXIV

Her voice when she told me that the master wished to see me was barely audible. I set down the coal bucket with an awkward crash and turned away, crossing my arms tightly across my chest.

"Me?" My agitation made me harsh. "I don't think so. What would he want with me?"

Mary shrugged dully, her toe scuffing the edge of the ash pile.

"Don't do that!" I snapped. "Don't I have enough to do around here without you making me do everything twice?"

Mary's expression did not change, but her fingers tangled in her hair, twisting and tugging.

"Why must you do that?" I cried. "Damn it, Mary, do we all not suffer enough?"

I clenched my fist when I knocked, striking my knuckles painfully hard against the wood. When he instructed me to enter, I had to force myself to turn the handle, to step across the threshold. I felt dizzy and wild. The thought of his damaged face thrust towards mine, his importunate questions, gorged with his wheedling grasping inquisitiveness, scraped the skin from my spine. Taking a deep breath, I set my jaw. It was a matter of enduring. I would not look at him. I would stare at the wall, and I would seal myself up against him, answer him in monosyllables, endure until he grew weary of my obduracy and the blank, resistant wall of my dreamless nights. If that bastard thought he could rip anything more from me, he was grievously mistaken.

It was months since I had last entered his room. The shades were pulled, so that the room was filled with a dim light like liquid dust that smelled sickeningly of over-breathed air and aniseed. The master himself sat hunched over the table, a blanket around his shoulders. I could not see his face, for his wig hung in loose flaps on either side of his face, but his posture and smell were those of an old man. His bony hands were clasped on a pile of papers set before him. Blue veins ran like ink blots beneath the yellowed skin.

"Sir."

"Sit, girl, sit."

I sat, turning my chair so that it faced the wall.

"I wish to speak to you of Mary." His voice was metal on stone. "You cannot have failed to observe that she ails."

Mr. Black broke off, shaken by a fit of coughing. It was some minutes before he was able to resume, his voice thinner now but harsher too, tight as a fiddlestring.

"Mrs. Black says she is attached to you. What, then, is the nature of that attachment?"

I thought of Mary's fingers pulling out her hair, her hand in mine in the dark, and I stared harder at the wall.

"She is a half-wit, sir," I said tightly. "She depends upon me as a child might, because she cannot manage alone."

"And like a child, without the wit or reason of their elders, an idiot is given to foolish and powerful passions. You see her daily. Doubtless you understand her better than she understands herself. You may help me help her. Come now, what arouses her appetites, what causes her to laugh, to weep, to startle out of her skin?"

The question took me so much by surprise that I glanced sideways. His hands were clenched so hard that the knuckles shone white.

"I—I have never thought about it."

"Then do so now. Let us start with a simple one. What gives the girl pleasure?"

I paused. I thought of Mary laughing, her tongue loose as she clapped her hands together in clumsy delight, and my spine softened a little.

"The usual things," I muttered. "The things a child likes."

"Which are?"

I shrugged. Surely so innocuous a question could do no harm.

"Honey. Sweetmeats. Chocolate. She loves chocolate."

"Of course. What else?"

"Baked wardens."

"Nothing but food? Surely she is not so much of a savage."

I hesitated.

"She likes it when I make shadow puppets. With my hand."

"They do not frighten her?"

I shook my head.

"I do not make frightening shapes, sir."

"So what do you make?"

"Rabbits, birds, you know. The usual things."

"Mary is fond of animals?"

"Yes, sir."

"Any in particular?"

"Any she can find, so long as it is small and soft. The yellow cat. The linnet. Even mice, when she finds them."

The apothecary scribbled and looked up.

"She has a favourite?"

"Of those? The cat, perhaps. But it is the monkey she truly loves. The one that belongs to the mountebank's clown on—"

Immediately I tensed, clamping my lips closed. I knew quite well that the very mention of mountebanks sent the master into a rage. But he said nothing, only jotted something upon his paper and poured more cordial into his glass. After he had drunk, he held the glass for a long time in both hands, considering it. I waited, biting my lip.

"Mary has been with us for many years," he said at last. "Her mother succumbed to a fever when she was but an infant."

He paused again. Then, swallowing, he continued. Not long after, Mary's father had taken a second wife, a young woman, who had agreed to wed upon one condition. She would have nothing to do with the half-wit. The girl must be removed elsewhere.

The master's voice cracked and, coughing, he took another long draught from his glass. His hands trembled as he set it down. Before Mary had come to Swan-street, she had never spoken a word. Indeed, she had proved so slow to understanding that they had assumed her deaf. When distressed, she had not cried but had beaten her head rhythmically against a wall. Mr. Black was the first person to assume her capable of human sensibility. Her progress under his tuition had defied all probability.

"Not that there is any recognition of her exceptional recovery," he said bitterly, draining his glass. "Idiots, apparently, are worth nothing. How can they look at Mary and say that she is worth nothing? They are blind fools, the lot of them, blind bloody fools!"

He slammed his hand against the table, wrenching his chair round so that I could not see his face. It was a moment before I realised he was weeping.

"Damn those bastards," he rasped. "Damn them all!"

There was a long silence. Carefully he cleared his throat. Then he turned back towards me. His eyes were huge and black, and he extended his hand towards me, the fingers plucking at the air. I stared at the wall, my teeth hard against my lower lip, my hands clasped tight in my lap.

"Do not defy me," he said in a strangled voice. "If she were to die now, if she—oh God, it would finish me, I swear it. Finish me. I could not endure it. Shall you have that on your conscience? Shall you?"

Despite myself, I turned. I had thought myself the only person who cared for Mary at all. The master closed his hand round the phial of tincture, and my heart squeezed as though he gripped it instead. The neck of the bottle struck the glass so that it chimed.

"Help me," he whispered, raising the glass to his lips. "Help me to make her well."

The silence lasted a long time. Then, very slowly, forcing my throat open with a considerable effort, I began to speak. At first the words came unwillingly, painfully, in ones and twos that hooked in my throat. My chest ached. I was obliged to draw saliva into my mouth so that I might describe, stumblingly, how she loved to eat potatoes hot from the ashes of the kitchen fire, grabbing at them so rashly that she burned her fingers and had to cool them upon the glass of the kitchen window. I paused then, remembering the way she had blinked at me, her eyes round with surprise and outrage and a child's impatient greed, and tears sprang unbidden into my eyes.

"Go on."

I hesitated. The ache in my chest had moved downwards to my gut, and for a moment I hugged it silently, holding it in. Then, very quietly, I told him of the way Mary would jump up and down and clap her hands together in a frenzy of delight whenever the organ-grinder struck up at the end of Swan-street and how she would sometimes grow so excited that she would urinate upon the floor. I told him of how she ran her finger round the base of his chocolate cup when it was returned to the kitchen for washing and how, as she sucked the dregs of chocolate from it, her eyes would close in dreamy pleasure. I told him how she loved to knead the bread dough, moving her elbows with such ferocious energy that the flour billowed round her like smoke from a soap-boiler's chimney. I told him how, to amuse her, I sometimes shaped the leftover scraps of dough into mice or butterflies. Once I made a spider, with eight fat legs, which I set upon her plate. It made her shriek. Mary was terrified of spiders. She would not kill them, though. She would have made a lousy butcher's girl. The sight of any dead creature made her weep. I told him of how she liked to burrow into our bed like a badger and how I would often wake to find her toes against my cheek and, beneath the blankets, her heavy head upon my shins and her fingers tangled in the hem of my nightgown.

Behind me the apothecary coughed. I stopped abruptly. Caught up in my recollections, I had grown almost fluent. Immediately cold worms of compunction set to squirming in my sore belly.

"If you wish her well, sir," I hurried, "I think that if she were only allowed to return to the garret—she fears the dark, you see, and the kitchen—"

The master's quill, which had scratched tirelessly at the page, fell from his hand. He moaned, laying his head upon the table.

"Sir?"

"Why can you not leave me alone? I only wish to sleep. Just to sleep."

"Are you ill, sir?"

I scraped back my chair. Mr. Black's eyelids fluttered, his hands clenching and unclenching as if he meant to catch something. White scum chalked his mouth.

"Where is the boy?" he murmured. "He is a comfort, the boy, always a—oh, how my hand aches, it is an agony to me. Write for me, madam, as you used to. I always liked the neatness of your hand."

"Mrs. Black is not here, sir," I stammered. "It is only I, Eliza."

Suddenly Mr. Black snatched his head back up from the table. Clutching the arms of his chair, he cast round the room, as though he was searching for something, for someone. I stumbled stiff-legged towards the door.

"Mrs. Black! I shall fetch the mistress, sir, and she shall come directly—"

"You may not show yourselves, you are sly, so sly, but I can see you. Don't think I cannot see you!"

Snatching up his inkwell, he hurled it past my head. It struck the panelling with a dull thud, sending an arc of dark ink up across the wall. I fumbled behind me for the door handle as he reeled round, his head swaying like a snake's. His eyes were holes in his skull, black and red at the same time. Tearing open the door, I fell down the stairs, screaming for my mistress, for Edgar, for anyone.

The shop door opened and Edgar peered out, a small bottle in one hand.

"Cease in your hysterics, damn you," he hissed. "We have a customer."

"But the master," I sobbed. "That bastard, he—I think he means to kill me."

Edgar snorted and rolled his eyes.

"...my clumsiness." Mrs. Black backed into the hall, a box in her hand. "Permit me to fetch you another dose." She closed the door, and her shopkeeper's smile shrivelled on her lips. "What the Devil is going on here?"

"It is the master," Edgar drawled. "He has another of his tiresome fits."

"Then go to him, Edgar," she ordered. "Directly, I implore you! Mr. Jewkes is expected here shortly. Mr. Black must be ready for him."

"He asks for you, madam," I whispered.

"Does he, indeed?" she retorted, snatching a jar from the shelf. The pills rattled against the lip, scattering across the table. "Do you think food appears on the table by magic? Who will manage the business if I do not?"

She fumbled two pills into the box, leaving the remainder where they lay, and stalked back into the shop. I leaned unsteadily against the jamb of the door. I could not comprehend how I had failed to see it before.

Mrs. Black was more afraid of her husband than I was.

To Mrs. Grayson Black at the sign of the Unicorn at Swan-street

Dear Madam,

I received your letter by this morning's post & accept your gracious apologies for your husband's unfortunate letter.

In response I would seek to assure you that I bear no lasting grudge & have no desire to cast a shadow over what has been a long & mutually advantageous association with your husband's family. I know that during the long years of their acquaintance my late father regarded Daubeney Black as a friend as much as a customer. Like you, I would consider it most regrettable if hot words on either side were to bring an unhappy end to that fine tradition.

Nevertheless I regret that it remains impossible to extend to you the terms of credit you wish for, despite the considerably more courteous terms employed on this occasion. A woman of your business sensibilities cannot fail to appreciate that I must manage my business as I am certain you seek to manage your husband's, judiciously & with prudence. Such scruples are become quite rare in these reckless times— people of our kind are, I fear, a dying breed. Therefore as a gesture of good will, & given the urgency of your patient's requirement, I shall have my boy deliver with this letter some 100 grains of opium. In the same spirit, I would ask that I may depend upon your husband to settle his account with us <u>in full</u> before the end of the month.

I remain, madam, your humble & respectful servant &c.,

ISAAC THORNE
Thorne & Son, East India House, Leadenhall-street

18th day of February 1720

XXV

Through the darkest days of winter, Mary did not improve. Neither did Mr. Black, though he continued on occasion to receive visitors. Snow fell, a grimy grey veil, and the lanes froze in toothed ridges. But although the master's indisposition required him to keep a fire in his room at all times, we were no longer permitted to light one in the parlour, and after supper Mrs. Black had me pick the remaining coals off the grate in the kitchen so that they might not be wasted.

Her thrifts extended to every aspect of the household, and she punished the slightest of squanderings. There was no more Indies tea. I was no longer permitted vinegar to clean the windows, nor soap for the heavier linen. The sugar loaf was locked in the dresser, the level of the salt box examined closely. In the evenings when my other duties were complete, I made rushlights, as I had done as a girl, from reeds and bacon fat. I was required to rise a half-hour earlier than before so that Mrs. Black might get to the market ahead of the rest and secure the cheapest cuts of meat. They had to be boiled for hours before they were soft enough to swallow. But although the apothecary hardly slept and Mrs. Black's face grew thin and pinched, there was no abatement in his demand for books. Though such errands robbed me of any time to rest, I thanked God for such mercies. I clung to my visits to the bookseller as a sluggard clings to sleep, refusing the wearisome grind of his daily life. I willed that vile rogue to read faster, more widely, to recall volumes long forgotten or to find out a crucial new pamphlet that he could not manage without.

It was not only the shop itself that drew me. My thoughts as I hurried along Cheap-side, my thin cloak clutched against the wind, were all of money, of liberty. Out of the dark house, my Syrop in my basket, I might imagine myself free.

Even when the thaw came, the mercury barely rose. A spiteful wind shivered over the skins of the puddles as I hurried along Cheap-side, and the sky was a purple bruise, threatening more rain. Beneath my shawl my neck dragged at my aching shoulders. Mrs. Black had roused me at four so that I might clean and polish all the jars and bottles in the shop which she thought grimy and an affront to customers. I was already awake. The master had been shouting again, screaming at someone to stay away from him, to get their filthy hands off him. The first time I had lain paralysed with fear, certain an intruder had broken in. Now I had grown so accustomed to the nightly hollerings that, had Mrs. Black not thundered upon my door, I might have turned over and gone back to sleep. I could hear the master's screams as I stumbled down the night-choked stairs.

The early start had fatigued me. My hair was lank with dust and fragments of dried herb, my hands raw. In recent weeks I had ventured farther afield, seeking out establishments that I might persuade to take the Syrop. But still my efforts yielded little. It seemed that there were one hundred such nostrums jostling with one another for space upon their shelves every day, with every physician in the land promoting a powder or a pill named for them. A dark little chop-house with greasy windows took three bottles for sixpence and told me to come back in a month. Everywhere else I had been turned away.

This morning I had ventured farther than ever, seeking out a druggist who traded close by the Temple. He had hardly allowed me to open my mouth before bidding me leave him in peace. Smarting with disappointment, I walked doggedly, my hood pulled high and my head lowered against the miserable wind, so that when the monkey leapt onto my shoulder, I feared myself assailed by a thief and struck out with my basket. I pushed away my hood, basket still raised, as, with a frightened chirrup, it leapt away.

"So you are still hot for a fight, I see."

The mountebank's clown no longer wore his ass ears but a suit of clothes in a hairy brown cloth of the kind favoured by country tradesmen. The monkey cowered on his shoulder, clutching his ear for support.

"I—he frightened me," I muttered.

"And you him, so justice is done. I fear the poor creature's bored stiff. Time we got him some honest work."

I sighed and was silent.

"You are walking this way?" He pointed west towards the Strand. "I'd appreciate the company."

I shook my head.

"Well, perhaps I'll run into you again. I've taken lodgings with the laundress in Little-whalebone-court, off of Drury-lane. Do you know her? Face like a mangle."

My mouth twitched, despite itself.

"There, I knew you could do it. Take it from one who knows, you can forget your fancy elixirs and all that foreign rubbish. Fight less, laugh more. The only secret of a long and healthy life." He held out his palm. "That'll be a shilling, thank you kindly."

I turned so abruptly then that I almost overturned the buckets of the milk-seller behind me. By the time I reached the Churchyard, it was late and darkness had begun to fall. All around me windows flickered and swelled with light. I hurried through the throng, the first chips of hail stinging my face as I ducked through the low door and inhaled the now familiar smell of leather and old paper. I did not attempt to understand why it comforted me when it served as a persistent reminder of my own ignorance. It was enough to breathe it in and feel the way my shoulders eased and the clenched spaces between my ribs relented a little.

The bookseller's daughter glanced up as I entered. She held a small volume in her hand, and although she had half-closed it when she heard the jangle of the shop's bell, she had kept her finger between the pages to mark her place. When she saw it was me, she sighed and returned immediately to her reading. She did not take her eyes from the page as she reached down with her other hand and drew a single cloth-bound volume from a shelf beneath the counter. In my turn I took a parcel of books from my basket. In recent weeks it had been agreed that the books my master no longer needed might be returned to Monsieur Honfleur for resale.

"Tell your master that the other book he wants must be sent from Holland," she added sharply. "If he wants it, he must pay for it in full. And in advance. We shall not lend it, nor accept it for return."

I nodded, glancing shyly past her towards the open door behind her. My feet ached and I longed to sit down. The daughter crossed her arms. The brooch on her chest glowered.

"My father is gone out."

I shrugged, concealing my disappointment, but immediately the air in the shop felt chillier, thinner, like the air at the peak of a high mountain, and I hurried through the formalities of the exchange, eager to be gone. Without the Huguenot to admonish them, the books grew haughty, disdainful. They pulled in their bindings as I passed the shelves, the leather curled with fastidious contempt. The daughter encouraged them. But when he was there, they did not dare. For all his scholarship, he was quite without airs. At first I wondered if he did not know that I was nothing but a maidservant, for he was never curt nor condescending. He talked to me easily, familiarly, making no attempt to moderate his language. From the beginning he assumed I understood exactly what he said. It was not always so, but I was resolved that he should never know it. When he spoke to me, I had the same sense of solidity that I experienced when, by refusing to concede the wall, a gentleman was required to step round me in the street. I felt present, definite, as though by being there I changed things a little.

I found myself caught not only by what he said but the manner in which he spoke, the way the words buzzed and gurgled in his throat. Although he had lived in England for more than thirty years, he had adopted nothing of the London way of speaking. He was, he told me, sipping at his little cups of thick black coffee, a *réfugié* from France who had smuggled his family to England in the terrible times after the revocation of Nantes. I did not know what that was, but I nodded all the same. His own father had been burned at Nérac, accused of having irreverently received the Host. His house had been demolished, his woods seized. His family had been fortunate. They had managed to escape to England. Honfleur had purchased an illegal passage on a coal barge while his daughter, whose name was Annette and who had been no more than a babe in arms, had been smuggled in with her nurse onto a ship bound for Dover, concealed in a fish barrel. It was a thrilling tale. I could have heard it daily and never tired of it.

There were often other Frenchmen crammed into the shop, most of them refugees too, who spoke a pepper-and-salt mixture of English and their own language. They talked mostly of men of their acquaintance and several in particular whom they never tired of discussing: Mr. Wren, Mr. Boyle, Mr. Hooke, Mr. Pope. It was some time before I understood that these men were known to them by reputation only, for the Frenchmen talked of them as fathers talk of their sons, their affection marbled with exasperation. Except for Mr. Newton. They had nothing but respect for Mr. Newton.

When the Frenchmen went home, the Huguenot talked to Annette and to me too, when he remembered I was there. But unlike ordinary men, he did not tease us nor tell bawdy stories, though he laughed often. He talked instead of governments and laws, of the discoveries of science or the wonders of astronomy. Occasionally he would take up a volume and, raising a finger for silence, would read aloud from it in support of a point he wished to make. Often, too, he touched the books as he talked, his fingertips absently tracing the gold tooling of a binding or fanning the edges of the soft gold-dipped pages between his thumb and forefinger. Mostly, however, he sat in his shop much like a chandler sits amongst his soap and candles, steeped in their distinctive exhalations, at once an extension of the essence of his wares and aloof from them, as if they were already in his bones. He left the tending of them to his daughter, who was never without her nose in one. She even borrowed the words from them instead of using her own. Though I seldom understood them, it was not hard to tell when Annette was speaking other people's words, for her voice grew deeper and her fingers stretched into stars.

"'Come, let us go, while we are in our prime! We shall grow old apace,'" she would chide if her father dawdled.

Or, "'The glorious lamp of heaven, the sun, the higher he's a-getting, the sooner will his race be run, and nearer he's to setting.'"

"Take pity upon the inestimable Mr. Herrick, I implore you," her father would say with a sigh then, his slow smile starting to pull up the corners of his mouth, and he would wink at me, so that I blushed. "The man would turn in his grave to hear his verse pressed into such disreputable service."

The bookseller did it himself, mind, stealing the words from books, only it was harder to tell when he did it. There was neither the swollen voice nor the reverent spaces around the words. Instead, he spoke as he might observe the weather, easily and without the expectation of an audience. Maybe it was because I never saw him, as I so frequently saw his daughter, with his head bent over a book in study, but I fancied that, unlike Annette, who scribbled notes in a journal as she read, the words entered the bookseller by stealth, suspended like dust in the bookshop air that he drew into his lungs. I could not see otherwise how he might have swallowed so many.

I could hardly believe my ears when, after I had been coming for a few weeks, he asked if he might seek my assistance.

"Excuse my presumption, but you read, do you not? I am wrong, perhaps, but there is something in the way you look at the books that suggests you understand their secrets a little."

I blushed.

"I do not read well, sir. That is, I have learned my letters, but these books—"

Mr. Honfleur laughed.

"I do not mistake you for a scholar, my dear. You are far too young and pretty for that."

Behind me Annette released a sharp breath. My blush deepened. I dreaded that he would ask me to read something and that I would not be able to manage a word. He would be kind, of course, but he would never speak to me again in the same manner. As though we might almost be equals. Mr. Honfleur laughed again.

"Do not look so alarmed. I am embarked upon a new venture, books of stories particularly for children. There is quite a vogue for them, it would appear, and you are not so pickled in erudition that you would dismiss the lot of them as injurious to health." He rolled his eyes at Annette and winked at me. "I should like your opinion of them."

I need not have feared. I was accustomed to a hornbook, a flat piece of board with a handle upon which was tacked a paper printed with the alphabet and the Lord's Prayer. But though the gold-tooled volumes the Huguenot brought me bore no greater a resemblance to such a primer than a hog bears to an Arab stallion, they were simple enough, with easily deciphered script. I pretended that I attended to them only on Mr. Honfleur's account, but in truth I loved to look at them, to peel the words from the page and set them in my head, one upon another until the story formed its own special shape. There was a small chair in one corner of the shop tucked beneath a high shelf where I might read without being under anybody's feet, and I tried to arrange it so that I might manage a few minutes curled up there before I was required to head back to Swan-street. They forgot about me there. If I sat quietly enough, the dusty air of the shop stilled and I had the curious sense of knowing what it felt like when I was not there.

One evening, as I set down the book I had looked at, Mr. Honfleur came into the shop. He did not notice me. He stood behind his daughter, leaning down to place his arms round her neck. She did not close her book nor did the stiffness in her spine relent, but she tilted her head just a little, so that the back of it rested against his chin.

"I am a very foolish, fond old man," he murmured into her cap.

She smiled, her eyes on the page, and reached up a hand, which she placed gently against his cheek.

"And I your Cordelia? To deal plainly, I fear you are not in your perfect mind."

He laughed then but softly, closing his eyes and drawing her against his chest. I thought of my mother then, the press of her fingers upon my jaw when she rubbed her nose against mine, the way her sharp chin rested upon my shoulder when she slept, and the tug in my chest pulled tight as a stitch.

Quickly, while there is sense in me. I have increased the dose again &
again, but I cannot silence these infernal nightmares. I wander through
Hell itself with Death always on my heels, its eyes red with greed &
lesser men's blood, but I can find no exit. There is no exit.

I vow I shall not take it. But the pain, the agony takes me over until I
can think only of the poppy. I would crawl upon my belly & lick up the
dust from the floor with my tongue if I might be allowed one spoonful
of that precious liquid. I am an animal, a miserable howling beast, as
bereft of wit & reason as a maddened dog.

Oh Lord God, what am I become? This flower is become my God, the
altar before which I prostrate myself, the treacherous ease of the Devil.
I close my eyes & he looms from the red velvet of my lids, the poppy in
his black hand, his voice curling about me like smoke. Drink, he says,
& I drink. Feel nothing, he says, & I smile & feel nothing. Sleep, he
says, & I lay down my pen like a child. It is he who laughs then, when
the words stop, he who claps his hands in delight. Now, he says, I am
in you & of you. While your soul sleeps, I flow through your veins,
blackening your blood, & set up my shrine in your unfeeling heart.
Now you are mine.

I cannot succumb. Life is suffering. Did our Lord Jesus Christ not en-
dure agonies upon the Cross & call only for water to ease the dryness
of His throat? The Creation shall not surrender its mysteries to an in-
different observer. Only in the pain may we find the Truth. Oh God,
fortify my resolve & give me the courage to do Your will.

AMEN.

XXVI

On the first day of March, when the cold peeled the plaster from the walls and it seemed that spring would never come, the city was seized by violent gales. The wind howled in the chimneys and clattered at the windows, causing the shop signs to swing and groan ominously on their brackets. In his room beneath the garret, the master howled back, so that my nights reeled with the clamour of it. In the streets men clutched at their hats and the horses whinnied fretfully, startled by fierce spirals of dust or gusting cabbage leaves. A woman died in Paternoster-row, struck upon the head by a dislodged tile. But, though fleshy clouds fattened and bruised beyond the distant hills, it did not rain.

It was restless, reckless weather.

"The master refuses to take his medicine," Edgar announced on the third day of the storms. "What a fool he is! Any apothecary worth the name knows that a man is one hundred times more likely to die of the lack of opium than the taking of it. Mrs. Black shall be a widow within the week."

It was no longer possible to dismiss Edgar's pronouncements as the lazy exaggerations of a braggart. I had never seen my mistress so discomposed. She did not eat. Nor do I think she slept. Instead, at night as the wind raged about the house, rattling handles and locks, she crouched over ledgers in the parlour, clicking at the beads of the wooden abacus. The glow from the smoky rushlight made silver wires of her hair and scooped dark hollows in her cheeks. At her elbow a pile of letters was secured against the draught from the window by a heavy slab of flint, its rough husk broken open to reveal an interior of smooth grey cut with white like a frozen puddle.

"Five pounds, no more," Edgar urged her, his hand fluttering over her shoulder. "How can the business prosper if we do not invest? There can be no dividend for those who do not own shares."

"Five pounds? You may as well ask for five hundred."

"Come now, surely the situation is hardly so calamitous."

"Edgar, it is worse! He swore this work would be finished months ago. But if he should die now, his debts—how shall we live?"

The rising edge to my mistress's voice was interrupted by the shop bell and Mrs. Dormer's high-pitched wheedle. But I hugged myself, smouldering with a grim excitement. At last the time had come. Had I not seen it with my own eyes? For that very morning the mistress had insisted upon my bringing fresh water to the master's room. I had not seen him in weeks, and the lurch of disgust and exultation I had experienced still had the force to make my heart beat faster. I had not imagined a man could so resemble a corpse and still draw breath. His cheeks were yellow and sunken, the port stain on his cheek the used-up colour of dried blood. Beneath his nightgown his body was hardly more than an empty husk, its contents already plundered of anything wholesome or juicy. The moans seemed to seep from his skin like sweat, like the final cries of the animal spirits as they abandoned his body. There was hardly anything human about him. It was as if his layer of flesh had been no more than a disguise, allowing him to live amongst ordinary mortals undetected. Stripped of it he was revealed as he truly was, stinking and malign.

The master was dying, steadily and with great suffering. Each morning that week I rose quickly, eagerly, certain that before nightfall there would be black drapes at the window and hushed voices on the stairs. I was certain that they could not keep me here, surely, if he did not live. His agreements, whatever their nature, would expire with him. I would be free. But his endurance defied reason. Each day he clung to life, just warm enough, the breath no more than a shiver in his mouth. At night he screamed, tortured by his dreams and the rattling of the windows in their frames. I had stuffed the parlour window with rags to prevent it from breaking, but I did not trouble with his. Our neighbours protested angrily at the disturbance, and I suspected that many avoided the shop for fear of contamination, for there were few customers. Mrs. Black's fingers flicked and flicked at the abacus, sending the beads spinning along the frame.

The house held its breath. Only Edgar seemed blithe, impervious to the heightened atmosphere, the feverish silences. For Edgar, spendthrift proponent of one hundred failed schemes, in debt to a score of creditors across the city, had a new plan.

"This house belongs to the master, did you know that?" he announced to me one day, his feet upon the kitchen table as he cleaned his nails with the cheese knife. "Extraordinary, is it not? He has always allowed Mrs. Black to think it rented, doubtless as an inducement to frugality, but, blow me, if when I was arranging his papers, I did not turn up the deeds. It is his outright."

"What did she say, when you told her?"

"You foolish whelp. Tell her? Where would the profit be in that?"

He meant to marry her, and he wasted no time setting about it. All that week, as we waited for the master to fail, his attentiveness was grotesque. Edgar had no instinct for moderation, for the chessboard strategy of the long game, and no taste for it either. The appeal of subtlety, of quiet manipulation, evaded him. Besides, he was desperate. The mistress's slightest remark, even if it was no more than a tight observation that the rain was easing a little, was wont to elicit gasps of admiration. He hastened to open doors for her, to help her on with her cloak or to bring her a chair so that she might rest between customers. Almost every day he presented her a little trifle, a plum tart or a pretty length of ribbon.

I dismissed his ambitions as the outlandish manoeuvrings of a lunatic. The mistress was distrustful by nature, alert to the faintest whiff of a swindle. I was confident that Edgar's obsequiousness would, before long, provoke her ire. But it was clear that she, too, was hardly in her right mind. Although she repeatedly bid the prentice to hush, there was no severity in her reproaches. She had a way of saying his name, snapping the first syllable against the roof of her mouth and drawing out the second in something close to a sigh, that made the hairs upon my arms bristle. It was not unusual to walk into a room and see them together, Edgar's head bent over as he mixed or pounded something while Mrs. Black's gaze fluttered against his face like a moth.

One morning, at the end of that week as the mistress sat with Mr. Black and waited, he pressed himself against me, and I felt the stiff thrust of his yard on my thigh.

"Like that?" he whispered, and poked a finger into my ribs. "When I'm master here, you may have as much of it as you like."

The very next day, when I returned to the kitchen for water to bathe the master's sores, I discovered Edgar lolling in the bentwood chair, his feet on the chimney-piece above Mary.

"So you see," he was saying to Mary, who squatted before the fireplace. "Once the master is gone, I shall be your master. So it would be prudent to oblige me, do you not agree? After all, what chance do you have of employment elsewhere?"

Leaning down, he placed a hand upon her shoulder. Mary hung her head, but, although she shuddered, she did not shrug him off.

"Get your greasy hands off her!" I cried, slamming the door. Edgar blinked and snatched his hand away, but when he saw it was me, he let it drop once more.

"Good God!" he drawled, palpating Mary's flesh with his fat fingers. "Your mistress is right, the scarcity of good servants these days is a scandal."

And, even as I snorted in disgust, I saw our future. Edgar, our master. Edgar haggling with me, with us both, day after day like a fish-fag at Billingsgate, bodies for board. It was all the currency we had.

TO THE CUCKOLDE APOTHECARY,

YOU HAVE BEEN MADE A FOOL OF LONG ENOUGH.

I HAVE NO ARGUMENT WITH YOU. I PITY YOUR DIS-EASE AND KNOW YOU AS A GOOD AND HONEST MAN. BUT CAN YOU NOT SEE THAT YOUR OWN ABODE IS BECOME A CESSPIT OF LEWDNESS AND DEBAUCHERY?

OPEN YOUR EYES TO THE FALSE FORNICATING PRENTICE WHO TILLS YOUR WHORE WIFE WITH THE PLOUGH OF HIS PRICK & DELIVER TO THEM BOTH THEIR MOST DESERVED PUNISHMENT.

A CONCERNED FRIEND & NEIGHBOUR

XXVII

The master refused his tincture a full week. Then, on the eighth day, when it seemed impossible that he could contrive to cling to life for another day, he called for Mrs. Black and, declaiming her a murderous whore, asked for laudanum. And, in the days that followed, Mr. Black of Swan-street returned from the dead.

I can only guess at the manner of pact that bastard struck with the Devil, but if he surrendered what charred scraps remained of his soul, he regained, for the most part, the vigour of his spirits. Had I not seen it with my own eyes, I might not have believed it, so astonishing was his recovery. Although his body remained frail and perilously thin, the master exhibited a high-strung vigour that danced in his fingers and stretched his eyes wide open so that he appeared both unnaturally wakeful and quite astonished. Once he had swallowed his breakfast of opium, he rose from his bed to sit at his desk, where, with few exceptions, he remained for the rest of the day, covering sheet after sheet of paper with his frenzied script. He took more of the medicine at dinner time and often another draught at sunset, often as much as ten grains in a single day. Sometimes he found himself strong enough to venture downstairs or even for a short stroll in the lane. When in the afternoon he found his vigour flagging, he had Edgar apply leeches in clusters behind his ears so that he might rub opium directly into the puncture marks. While the leeches fixed and swelled, he lay upon the settle with a cloth upon his forehead, soaked in a mixture of opium and rosewater.

The Devil extracted his punishment all the same. The poppy-juice dried his mouth and bent his hands into hooks. If you stood outside his room, you could hear the whimpers of pain and frustration as he tried to write. Frequently he was obliged to put down his quill and part his fingers, rubbing life back into their whitened tips.

It closed his bowel too, causing the build-up of putrid matter which poisoned his blood. His rare stools were tiny black buttons, laced with blood.

His discomforts were something of a consolation. When my skin crawled with the thought of him and I longed to break something or someone, I took some solace from knowing that the Devil lurked in that villain's chamber-pot, his brimstone breath hot against that monster's scabbed and blistered buttocks. But it was hardly enough. Whenever I thought of what I had told him about Mary, I felt a spike of such pure loathing that I was sure I would vomit. It was not that I had lied or exaggerated. I had broken no promise, divulged no secret, said nothing that Mary would have denied or protested. But I had betrayed her all the same.

I intended to punish him for it.

He gave her a monkey. He told her it was to lift her spirits. It was a mothy little creature and clearly advanced in age, but though it had the mournful eyes and wizened complexion of a whiskery old man, it was possessed of a small boy's impish disposition. When she brought it down to the kitchen to show me, her words mangled with pleasure and her eyes stretched with disbelief at the extent of her good fortune. She could not put the creature down but kissed it over and over, cradling it in her arms, stroking its fur, her fingers seeking its infant grip. When at last the creature wriggled free and leapt across the room away from her embrace, her face crumpled. Gently I took her arm and pointed to the punch bowl upon the dresser, where it peeked over the blue-edged rim, its eyes bright and mischievous. Mary blinked, her mouth working. Then she laughed out loud, without covering her mouth. Mary had not laughed for months.

The change in her was close to miraculous. She was still weak and easily distracted, but her dull gaze quickened. Her cheeks grew less pale. She regained something of her old childish vigour. She no longer ate with the unthinking relentlessness of a starveling, and she lost something of the puffiness around her face, although her belly still protruded in the manner of a hungry infant, the weak curve of her spine exaggerating the shape of it. When I bid her stand straight, she only whispered in the monkey's ear and coiled its tail more tightly round her throat. At meals it sat on her lap, and she fed it the tastiest morsels from her plate. Across the table it eyed me suspiciously, curling against Mary as though it meant to protect her from me.

It was the master who insisted that Mary give the monkey a name of her own choosing. After much tongue-chewing deliberation, she settled upon Jinks, which suited the ill-behaved whelp very well. Each afternoon she was required to bring Jinks to see the apothecary, who claimed himself as much a beneficiary as Mary of its restorative powers. Certainly they laughed together a great deal over its antics and indulged the creature dreadfully, petting it and feeding it sweetmeats by hand.

If that was not enough, the master even had Edgar bring up an old cradle from the coal cellar in which the wretched thing might sleep. The sight of it stretched the skin across the back of my neck.

"Not here!" I snapped as she set it before the fire, and snatching up the poker, I stirred the coals fiercely, sending up a flurry of red sparks that stung my hands. "The way you indulge that louse-ridden beast! Do you wish to burn down the house?"

As for Mary, she spent precious hours laundering and pressing the tiny linens that fitted inside the crib. At night she lay curled up beside it, singing softly as she rocked the beast back and forth. She even attempted to cajole the wretched creature into donning a little bonnet and a shift which she had uncovered from somewhere. Mercifully Jinks would suffer no such indignity, and I was glad when she abandoned her efforts and put the garments away in a drawer. I had laundered them myself, a long time ago.

Wrapped up with the monkey, Mary hardly remembered I was there. Briskly, I bid myself to be thankful for it. All winter, as she had ailed, I had strained against the weight of her, her need of me an iron shackle that chained me to the house. Now she was recovered, I need concern myself with her welfare no longer. The master was fond of her, was he not? And she had managed quite well alone, before I came. Besides, she was not possessed of the finer sensibilities of ordinary people. If only I might find a way to contrive it, I was once more free to go.

The master's appetite for opium grew more voracious. Mrs. Black kept the resin locked in an iron cabinet with the other exotics, but every morning she unlocked it and, her jaw rigid with concentration, silently measured out the apothecary's daily requirements so that Edgar might mix it up. *Ten grains of opium with eight of rhubarb pounded with a little camphor & taken in a tumbler of Canary wine, blood warm.* Edgar claimed that he repeated it in his sleep, and even I, who was expressly forbidden to enter the laboratory, knew the recipe by heart.

It was late one evening as I took myself wearily to bed that I heard a whimpering noise coming from the laboratory. I peered through the hinge of the door. Several illicit candles burned as Edgar spooned opium into the glass beaker beside him and stirred the mixture with a long-handled spoon. It was a long time since I had seen so much light, and, moth-like, I found myself drawn to it. Edgar glanced about him, but he did not see me. Wiping his nose roughly against his sleeve, he quickly added another spoonful of opium and another, until the liquid in the beaker was black and syrupy. When he poured it into a bottle, it fell from the beaker in sluggish gobbets. Taking a paper package from his pocket, he tore it open and tipped its contents into the jar of opium grains, shaking it to blend them. Then he took the bottle and, pulling one of the master's old books from its place upon the high shelf, concealed the bottle behind it and pushed the book back into place. My face was pressed so close to the door that it swung a little, creaking on its hinges.

"Mrs. Black?" he called uncertainly. "Is that you?"

I darted away from the door, stumbling upstairs before I might be discovered. Edgar meant to be my master. I no longer doubted he would succeed.

That night I could not sleep. I stood in the window, peeling clumps of moss from the slates outside my window and hurling them as hard as I was able at the thick black hole that the dome stamped upon the night. But the moss was light and the night breeze fresh. The dome towered upwards, perfect and impervious. Mr. Honfleur had told me that its builder had thought being an architect a poor profession. "I should have been a physician," the old man had said. "At least I should have been rich."

RESURGAM.

The strange word came unbidden into my head, remnant of another of the bookseller's stories. When the architect of the Cathedral was first marking out the dimensions of his new dome upon the razed foundations of the old church, he had fixed upon the precise centre point and ordered a labourer to bring a flat stone to be laid there as a mark for the masons. The labourer quickly happened upon a broken gravestone of the appropriate dimensions and brought it to the spot that the architect had indicated. It was only when he laid it down in its allotted place that he saw that one word survived of its original inscription, carved in large capital letters at the centre of the slab. The labourer, unable to read, paid it no heed. But when the architect saw it, he fell to his knees, thanking God for His blessing upon the mighty endeavour. For the single word carved upon the stone read simply RESURGAM or, in English, "I shall rise again."

Ten grains of opium with eight of rhubarb pounded with a little camphor & taken in a tumbler of Canary wine, blood warm. Not the two-bit balsam of a country cunning woman but a miraculous remedy, capable of bringing a man back from the dead. The unsheathed sword of the murderer, pressed against his own neck. In Edgar's hidden bottle, there was dissolved enough opium for a dozen phials.

RESURGAM.

The boards of the stairs were chill against my bare feet, but they made no sound. I was almost at the master's landing when I saw him, his marked face a darker patch of shadow. Holding my breath, I pressed myself back against the wall, but he did not look up. Instead, he slipped silently into his room, closing the door with a click that echoed through the stairwell.

When my breathing was steadier, I stole past his door, every part of me alert to the slightest noise. When I took the chamber-stick from its nail on the wall, scraping the iron loop of its handle against the plaster, the hairs on my neck were sharp as pins. But no one came. I would light it from what remained of the kitchen fire and take it directly to the laboratory. Although the kitchen door was kept locked at night, my mistress had for months left the key in the lock when she turned it so that I might rouse Mary and begin our duties while she was still at market. When I slipped through the door, Mary turned over, expelling a noise halfway between a sigh and a snore. I stepped over her, squatting before the fire. Her face shone pale in the glow of the embers, the lump of her strangely swollen in the crimson light. Kicking at the fire, I held the wick of the candle to a red coal until it caught and held it up. The flame dipped and curtsied. Shivering, I looked over my shoulder. The door leading up to the lane stood ajar. Holding a hand around the candle to prevent it from going out, I hastened across the room to close it, glancing uneasily about me. Every customer to the shop had their own grim tale of thieves and vagabonds. I did not see the foot until I almost fell over it. I might have cried out, had I not recognised the shape of it. Instead, I seized the blanket and ripped it away. Mary moaned and turned, burying her face in the pillow. Crouched beside her, fully dressed, was Edgar. The stink of taverns rose from him like shit from a pigsty.

I kicked him. He groaned and blinked, his eyes swollen and un-focused, his nose crusted with dried slime.

"You poxy bastard! If you have laid so much as a finger on her—!"

"That thing? I'd rather *die*," Edgar slurred. Then his face con-torted and he began noisily to bawl, his face slack with wine and self-pity. "Oh, sweet Jesus, Eliza, help me, I beg you. Don't let me die. I don't want to die."

And so it was that he made his confession, clutching my skirts in desperate appeal as though I were the Madonna herself. Edgar had the French pox. He had discovered the first pustules a few days before and already was driven half to lunacy with the dread of it. He dared not consider the mercury cure. How would he explain away the loosened teeth, the black saliva, the endless spitting, the distinctive fetid smell? If Mrs. Black was so much as to sniff the stink of it upon him, he was finished. The only other cure of which he was certain was to fuck a virgin, the younger the better, but where was he to find one? The madam at the bawdy house had set the price for one at ten guineas, a sum entirely beyond his means.

"After all my years of patronage, how could she turn my misery to her own profit?" Edgar sobbed. "Oh, Eliza. They say the pain is unendurable."

He fell into a cataract of weeping. I said nothing but waited until his sobs subsided to hiccups and he rocked miserably, his arms round his knees. Then I made my own silent prayer, holding my thumbs for luck.

RESURGAM.

"My mother had her own treatment for the pox," I said slowly. "Without mercury. Often it worked."

Edgar sniffed.

"I am reduced to the defective poundings of a country witch?" he snivelled.

"My mother was no witch. But if you think yourself too high-up for such—"

"No, no!" Edgar pleaded. "Let us try it, I beg you. I beg you."

"Of course, if I am to make it up for you, I shall need your help. I would have to get into the laboratory."

"Of course."

"And it shall cost you. A shilling a bottle."

"A shilling a bottle? But—very well. Yes. Anything, anything, whatever you need."

When at last I crept back to bed, dawn was a ribbon of oyster silk threaded through the chimney-pots. In the pale light, the lead struts of the dome looked like fingers, pressing down on the still-dark skull of the Cathedral.

"*Resurgam*," I whispered to myself, gripping the iron catch of the window so tightly that it impressed its curled pattern upon my palm. "*Resurgam*."

in search of paracelsus
the father of modern medicine

the irony of it does not evade me
for did paracelsus himself not say that "what makes a man ill also
cures him"?
behind the books tucked out of sight a bottle of tincture
my opium
mrs. black tells me she locks the opium so that she may prevent its
misuse
& yet here it is
from the smell & thickness of it a concentrate 50 or 60 grains per pint,
perhaps more

intended as some manner of insurance for her?
now for me

i hold the precious bottle in my hand enough to kill a man & i have to
wonder:
does she mean to save me or to drown me?

XXVIII

I scrabbled behind the row of aged volumes, sending up clouds of thick dust, but my fingers closed only on cobwebs. Agitatedly I pulled one tome down, then another, peering into the shelf. I had hardly any time. Mrs. Black had gone for provisions, and Mary and the mothy monkey were once more secreted in conference with the master, but I could hear Edgar as he clattered bottles restlessly in the shop. Hurriedly I groped again, reaching as deep as I could. But though I ran my hand along the very back of the shelf, I found nothing.

The bottle of opium tincture was gone.

Hustling the books frantically back into position, I struggled to think calmly. The shop's supplies of opium were kept locked in an iron cabinet to which only Mrs. Black held a key. Even if I contrived to pocket a little when I made up the master's tincture, it would not be long before she grew suspicious.

There was an alternative. I might purchase it on my own account. Such a purchase would require guile and a large part of my mother's money, but as the days passed and the walls of Swan-street pressed inwards and downwards, snuffing out the first green flickers of spring, I knew it worth the difficulty and expense. What more fitting end that the money from my sale be used to purchase my freedom? Tally's Elixir. Powerful enough to bring a man back from the very brink of death. At night, straining out of the casement window, my thoughts were all of pestles and strainers, wine and herbs, bottles and seals of wax. When at last I slept, I dreamed of holding in my hand a delicate phial the dark red of Annette Honfleur's brooch. But when I pulled the cork, the liquid inside it dispersed in a coil of black smoke, leaving only the acrid, choking smell of burnt caramel.

———

It was a full three weeks before the apothecary required me once more to venture abroad to the bookseller. The waiting curdled my stomach. Though the weather grew warmer, the house was damp and chill. Pale sunlight caught in the veils of dust on the windows and fell away. Malign and triumphant, the shadows crept across the floor unchecked, and the master grew stronger, sustained by opium and malevolence. And by Mary and the monkey, whom he summoned every morning after breakfast. I laboured through the work alone, scrubbing and pounding and beating with a ferocity that banished thought. The only subject worthy of consideration was how soon I might get out.

It was a little after dinner when I saw the packet of books on the hall table. My hands were black from polishing pewter, but I tore open the front door without bothering even to untie my heavy canvas apron. My lungs and legs ached with the need to run. I flung myself down Cheap-side, barging and pushing, gulping down the fetid summer air as though it were beer until I reached Newgate-street and the druggist from whom I had bought my first dozen bottles. He had made it plain by the slip of his eyes that he would do what he could to favour me with a bargain.

When I emerged a few minutes later with the pound of opium concealed beneath the folds of my apron, I had parted with six shillings and a promise to walk out to Hockley-in-the-Hole with the druggist the next Sunday. I had forgotten the promise before I had closed the door behind me, but the opium bumped reassuringly against the books in the bottom of my basket. It was a tentatively warm afternoon, and I tipped my head backwards as I hastened southwards, relishing the stroke of the sun on my face. When at last I reached the Huguenot's shop, I paused on the threshold to remove my apron and stow it in my basket. I could taste the metal tang of nerves on my tongue. I was sure that the Frenchman would have forgotten me.

"Well, look who is here!" Mr. Honfleur cried delightedly as I tapped the door softly with my knuckles. "What a pleasant surprise!

We thought you surely dead—or, worse, married. Is that not so, Annette? You are not married, are you?"

I blushed and shook my head, my basket awkward against my thighs.

"'Coquette and coy at once her air, / Both studied, tho' both seem neglected; / Careless she is, with artful care, / affecting to seem unaffected,'" Annette said under her breath, lowering her head once more over her book.

Her father frowned at her.

"Pay her no heed," he whispered to me, loudly enough so that she might easily hear him. "Still, it is hardly any wonder that my daughter is unwilling to embrace what is new. No man has yet written the words to express them for her."

"And so you expose your folly," Annette replied tartly. "There is wisdom and prudence enough for your grandchildren's grandchildren in these volumes, were you to pay any heed to them."

"And I know of no grandchildren ever begotten by the reading of books."

Annette's mouth tightened.

"Besides," Mr. Honfleur continued more gently. "Did not Mr. Marvell himself remind us that ''tis time to leave the books in dust, and oil the unused armour's rust'? He understood that there was a time for study and another for action, for enterprise."

"You would take a man's paean to a moral war to defend your disgraceful bubbles? You should be ashamed of yourself, Father."

"We must seek our counsel where we can. A poet may claim the hidden secrets of a man's heart, but only a fool would take a bard for a financial advisor."

It was with a rush of pleasure that I realised, for all my absence, nothing whatsoever had changed. I smiled. Mr. Honfleur studied me thoughtfully.

"Take Eliza, for example. Ignorant of Shakespeare as a babe in arms. But in Paris a sensible girl like her would have begged, borrowed, or stolen the money to take a stake in the Mississippi

Company, and by now she would doubtless have her own equipage and a handsome comte of a husband, to boot."

Annette grunted and said nothing.

"So many investors from all walks of life that at night the troops are called to clear the crowds from the rue Quincampoix," Honfleur marvelled. "What kind of an alchemist is this man who has made paper more valuable than gold?"

"If that is so, you should consider yourself most fortunate, Father," mocked Annette. "Your hoards of paper would shame Croesus himself."

I tried to imagine Mr. Honfleur in a suit of gold brocade, his fingers heavy with rings, stepping from a gilt-flashed barge to the fanfare of liveried musicians.

"It is nothing but a confidence trick," insisted Annette. "Heed the words of the wise Lucretius: 'Nil posse creari de nilo.' Nothing can be created out of nothing."

Honfleur shrugged.

"Had Lucretius been fortunate enough to know the redoubtable Mr. Law, he might have come to a rather different conclusion. Doubtless he, too, would have begged the Englishman to favour him with the secret of his success, not to mention an allowance of shares."

"'Look round the habitable world! How few know their own good; or knowing it, pursue,'" scorned Annette, in the special voice she used for the words she copied from books. "Mr. Law is a charlatan. He means only to line his own pockets at the expense of ordinary men."

"On the contrary, ma petite, John Law is a visionary economist, and the ordinary men, as you call them, have a good deal to be grateful for. Thanks to his reforms, France is rich and there is no longer any tax on wine, bread, oats, oil, and one hundred other staples. Coal is half the price it was a year ago. So it is not just his stockholders but every Frenchman who profits. Every Frenchman in France, that is," he added, and he cuffed me gently on the arm. "Pity me, Eliza. For it is a poor time indeed to be a réfugié."

I blinked. I had been so occupied with my own thoughts, I had forgotten where I was. Annette watched me over the edge of her book, her eyes narrow.

"Does your mistress not require you home?" she said sharply.

"Annette," her father reproved her. "She does no harm."

"She does nothing at all," Annette retorted. "A fine life for a maidservant."

"I—she is right," I stammered, seizing my basket. "It is time I was going."

Annette's mouth twisted.

"Would it be too great a trouble to take the book your master ordered?"

I flushed unhappily as she dropped a volume into my basket, string tied in a cross over its bindings. Her nose wrinkled as if it smelled rotten.

"I have not wrapped it. Paper is an additional expense, after all. Tell him he may have the rest when he settles his account. It is already six months overdue."

Honfleur frowned at his daughter as I stumbled out of the shop and through the press of the Churchyard. A red sun rested briefly upon the low roofs and was gone. The clouds were rosy strips, their bellies polished to gleaming copper, and the evening was filled with the pale pink promise of spring.

The very next day I tipped away what remained of the Quickening Syrop. It had grown greenish and foul-smelling, and I had to rinse the bottles repeatedly to rid them of the slimy residue. An agitated Edgar unlocked the laboratory door and reluctantly handed me the key. His eyes twitched as I closed the door and locked it behind me. I could hear the squeak of the boards in the hallway as I hurriedly made up one bottle of the decoction of white love-lies-bleeding that was his weekly medicine and my first six bottles of Tally's Elixir. *Ten grains of opium with eight of rhubarb pounded with a little camphor & taken in a tumbler of Canary wine, blood warm.* As I bent over my mortar, I repeated it under my breath, over and over until it had the metre of a prayer.

tumour
advanced
no mistake

lower part of belly, close to right hip
size of small apple, hard/tender to touch
black in colour
skin yellowed in centre with reddish-purple outer area
network of black veins securing it to surrounding skin

second smaller lump in 2 parts, 2 inches above
small & purple, like small grapes
skin puckered all about

application of red lead plaisters to draw out infection
juice of ground-ivy boiled with honey & verdigris
cream of arsenic
opium provides temporary relief from pain

no other treatment known

XXIX

For all the apothecary's apparent improvement, no visitors came to Swan-street. Even the butcher-faced Mr. Jewkes did not come back, although letters from him were sporadically delivered by his boy, a pock-marked lad in a showy livery of silver-blue who always asked for a sip of small beer and sat in the kitchen, the cup untouched in front of him, staring at Mary across the table as if she were a long word he was determined to decipher. Mary blushed then and covered her face with her apron, dusting her hair with flour. Otherwise, we saw only the tradesmen and then only infrequently. As for the master, he remained closeted in his room, the door locked.

Tally's Elixir. The thought of it caused my toes to curl in my boots in anticipation. At the first chance I had, I took it directly to a coffee-house on London-bridge famous for its purveyance of patent medicines. At Swan-street Mrs. Black spat the name of the place from her mouth like a tainted oyster, for she blamed it bitterly for many of her difficulties. In the lane I breathed deeply, filling my chest with the ripe polluted stench of city air. Somehow it had become spring. The farmers' waggons were lush with green, and the peeping of birdsong seasoned the raucous city like the glint of salt over the Thames, ticklish and new.

At the coffee-house I was required to wait so long I knew I would be punished, but still I did not leave. When at last the proprietor received me, I knew immediately from his expression that my wait had been purposeless.

"Now Dr. James, he's a fine physician, that Dr. Daffy too. Even Mr. Ward I've the time of day for. But a chit of a maidservant, thinking she can mix up a soup of a nostrum in her kitchen and pass it off for physick? You must think me a perfect fool."

Outside the coffee-house I wept, though I knew the tears were wasted even before they had ceased to fall. That night I stared out at the dark shape of the dome, my hand smarting and my heart grim as lead. It would require better planning, I saw that now. Proofs, warranties, testimonials. I had not the faintest idea of how I might obtain them.

I was still turning over the same questions in my mind when I returned two days later to the bookseller and again several days after that. I was required to pass several coffee-houses on my way but on neither occasion did I take the Elixir with me. Although I pretended to myself that I had no choice, that there was not the time for any diversion, I knew myself simply too weary for refusal.

On those mornings, as he had before, Mr. Honfleur enquired after my master as he examined the books I returned to him for signs of wear or damage. I squirmed at the question, replying as briefly as propriety permitted. But the bookseller could not be so easily deflected. The second time he shook his head, flapping his hands as though clearing tobacco smoke.

"No, no, enough! When a man underwrites another's hopeless endeavour, with no prospect of reward in this world, he seeks more in recompense than dreary platitude," he protested. "He wishes to be amused. Now try again, my dear."

Annette frowned and declared her father nothing but a common gossipmonger, but the bookseller merely held out his hands to me, his face contorted in a parody of entreaty.

"I am certain life with your quack of a master brims with humorous incident. Come, sit by me and tell me all about it."

My tongue was wooden in my mouth.

"Sir, I do not think—"

"For pity's sake, Father, leave the child alone," Annette chided, but when I glanced at her in gratitude, she looked away. "Can you not see that you discomfit her?"

"This one? Surely she is not such a milksop. On the contrary, I would wager from the look of her that she has sharp eyes and a sharper tongue. Am I right?"

I hesitated, torn between discomposure and my eagerness to oblige him. Behind me Annette grunted scornfully. I had not noticed it before, but there was something of Mrs. Black's sharpness about her features. I felt a prick of dislike.

"I fear you may be, sir," I replied, and was rewarded with a smile of triumph.

"There, what did I tell you? Then I shall expect regular despatches."

After that the bookseller always demanded the latest news from the apothecary's house and was disappointed if I had no new morsels to impart. I did my best to satisfy him, for I was quick to discover the consolations of indiscretion. In rendering the details of my life at Swan-street as comic tales, I stripped them of their menace. It helped me endure it.

For instance, I told him of the night when, on my way to bed, I had encountered the apothecary on the stairs, bare-headed and with nothing to cover his nakedness but a small blanket, and how he had raved that the Devil had stolen his nightgown. I said nothing of how he had leaned close to me and spat full in my face or of how fright had made icicles of my bones. There was no amusement in that. I simply rolled my eyes in long-suffering ruefulness at the master's weak head for liquor. The bookseller's laughter wove a kind of armour of lightness about me that, if I husbanded it carefully, might last for hours or even days.

I plundered both my memory and my imagination for stories that might amuse him. I told him of Edgar, of his hopelessness in the laboratory and even, in a fit of audacity, of his plans to be my mistress's next husband, although I had the sagacity to make light of my master's illness, given what I guessed were the Frenchman's generous terms of credit. Instead, I elaborated upon Edgar's vanity and the implausibility of his ambitions. I told him of Mary and her monkey and how fat and alike they grew with every passing day. Mr. Honfleur laughed until his sides ached. It made me feel safe, at least as long as I was in his shop. But it grew harder and harder to return to the smothered shadows of Swan-street. At night I lay awake, picking over the carcass of our conversation till it was stripped bare. Above me the broken lathes poked like fingers from the hole in the ceiling, and the hidden bottles of opium made a dark bulge in the damp plaster.

As spring strengthened, something changed within me. It was as though my skin contained two of me. At Swan-street I was tentative, pale, silent. At supper I watched Mary fooling with the monkey, and the bread grew mould in my mouth. It was as if the shadows of the house had finally taken up occupancy inside me. I grew as jumpy as Edgar, as grim and grey as Mrs. Black, my skin stubbled with unrelenting goose-flesh.

But when I entered the Huguenot's shop, I was transformed. I grew bolder, less prudent. One day, when urged for the latest intelligence, I batted my eyelids a little at the bookseller, and then, in precisely the reverent tone Annette favoured for the regurgitation of books, I declared:

> "Cock-a-doodle-doo!
> My dame has lost her shoe;
> My master's lost his fiddling stick,
> And knows not what to do."

I meant only to amuse him, but before I had even finished speaking, I knew that my enthusiasm had overcome my reason. Annette was his daughter, after all. I stared at the counter, my mouth dry, and my armpits prickled with shame and apprehension.

"You are a sharp mimic," he observed at last.

I swallowed, not daring to meet his eyes.

"So sharp indeed that I would prefer my daughter to remain innocent of your skill. I do not think you would wish to cause her distress, *non?*"

After that I fell into the habit of rehearsing my stories as I made my way to the Churchyard. Most bore only a passing resemblance to the truth, but I did not think Mr. Honfleur the type of man who would favour bare fact over an amusing tale. Annette might prefer her stories on mouldy paper in strenuously small letters, but her father's learning, it seemed, had not hardened him against mirth.

I did not see the hand-barrow until I struck my shin against its strut and, with a cry that was as much surprise as pain, fell to the ground with such force that the contents of my basket tumbled out onto the road. The mackerel-seller, an ancient crone with a palsied face and puckered eye, spat curses at me as she rearranged the tarnished fish on their bed of straw. I swore back, groping for the master's book as a pair of soldiers in tattered uniforms stumbled past me, one almost setting his boot upon my hand. Sodden with gin, the men's eyes were as milky as newborn kittens'. They clutched at each other, their laughter fragile and desperate-sounding, before they reeled away again, their shoulders pressed together for support.

Leaning against the wall, I inspected the book anxiously for damage. Although the bindings looked unharmed, some of the pages were bent, revealing a pale gash in the smooth gold band of paper between the covers. Tugging loose the cross of string that secured it, I opened the covers so that I might smooth them flat.

There was only a little writing on the page, an unfamiliar curling script that looked like numbers. In place of words there was a large illustration, inked in colour so that it more resembled the chapbooks of my youth than a learned manuscript. But while the chapbooks contained pictures of fairy palaces and dragons, the woodcut in this book showed a freak-boy of the kind you paid to see at fairs, only this one did not have the usual horned head or excessively hairy body. Instead, it had stunted arms and legs, one hand having only two fingers and each leg reaching only as far as a knee might be. One of these half-legs ended in a foot, the other in a twisted stump that resembled the branch of a tree. On his head he wore a jaunty green hat with a feather. It came down almost over his eyes.

I turned the page. There was a plain sheet of paper so fine you could see your fingers through it and then, behind it, another tinted woodcut, this time of a man with a second head growing out from his belly. The next showed a boy with the beak of a bird, the next a man and a horse, conjoined at the shoulders; a third an adult woman with the head and tail of a monkey. There had been talk of things like this, when I was a girl. Of women who indulged their desires with animals and even with fish. Once at a fair, I had seen a grown woman only fourteen inches tall. The mother had been seduced by a fairy or perhaps terrified by one, I could not remember which. Either might have as powerful an effect.

I licked my finger, tasting the thick smell of parchment upon my skin, and turned first one page and then another. I had seen pictures like these before, but even such an amateur as I was could see that these were drawn with considerable skill. As I moved the pages, the eyes of the monsters seemed to follow me, as though they silently begged me to rescue them from their paper imprisonment. Something swelled in my chest, dark and knotted like a great clump of hair, but I could not stop looking. Faster and faster I tore through the pages until something stopped me, something that froze my fingers and set the blood singing dizzily in my ears.

A picture of a boy with the head of a dog.

I stared at the picture, and the clot of hair in my chest grew so thick that I could hardly breathe. The boy on the page was no more than an infant. The soft defencelessness of his pale naked body, the plump folded flesh of his wrists and ankles, his tender stub of a penis, contrasted violently with the head upon his shoulders. There was nothing charming about this head, nothing puppyish. It was the head of an adult dog, black as coal and with a murderous constriction to its eyes, which glared up at me with undisguised hostility. The artist had set the dog's jaws open in a snarl, exposing a curl of scarlet tongue between rows of pointed teeth, and it slavered a little, a loop of drool falling from its lips. I could almost hear the growl vibrating in its throat, the bellicose stink of its breath. The fur about its neck was matted and spiked. Its ears pricked forwards, intent upon weakness and fear, as it strained from the child's round innocent shoulders.

I closed my eyes, but it did not recede. The ghastly dread of lying there in the darkness of the kitchen. The explosion of terror as the monster burst through the open frame and roared until its lungs seemed sure to burst, its teeth a terrible bright white in the darkness, the saliva dripping from its jaws as it came closer, closer, closer—

"Well?"

Mr. Honfleur extended his hand to take back the book, an anthology of Greek myths. I had stared at its plates for a long time, but instead of the snake-haired Medusa or the maze-maddened Minotaur, I had seen only the dog-child, its slavering jaws sharp against the white infant flesh of its chest, the ghastly black pelt of its matted neck.

"Did you think it as agreeable as those stories of Ancient Rome?"

"Rome—yes." I blinked. "I—I am sure it is a fine book."

Honfleur frowned.

"Are you unwell? If so, you should go home. Fevers favour Frenchmen."

"I am quite well, sir."

"You are pale. Go home and get that quack of a master of yours to dose you with something suitably unscientific. Hurry now. And leave the door open when you go."

I stared at my lap.

"I wondered, sir, if I might—if I might ask you a question?"

Honfleur gestured towards the door. I stood reluctantly.

"I never make promises I might be obliged to break," he replied. "Now get along with you."

In the door of the shop, I paused.

"I wished to ask—what exactly is the nature of my master's work?"

"If he has not told you, perhaps he does not wish you to know."

I swallowed, biting my lip.

"With respect, sir," I murmured, "I think it likely there are things I have told you that he would not wish *you* to know."

Mr. Honfleur's mouth twitched.

"I was right, then, about the sharpness of your tongue," he observed drily. "But though you are pert, you are not without wit."

For a moment the shop was silent, dust turning on a treadle of sunlight between the shelves. Then Mr. Honfleur sighed, snapping the covers of the Greek book together with a clap.

"Ah, it is hardly a secret. Your esteemed master writes a treatise. Has been writing it, indeed, for a number of years, although not a word of it has yet been published."

"And his subject?" I whispered.

"The notion of maternal impression or something close. He declares himself always upon the verge of categorical proof of his singular theories, but so far we have seen only his ability to beg, steal, and borrow the ideas of other, wiser men than himself. Of which, I must confess, there is no shortage."

"Maternal impression?" I stammered.

"The effects of strong emotions, fear, desire, and such like, upon the physical form of a foetus. You have perhaps heard of the Dutch woman who saw a man broken upon the wheel and delivered a child whose bones were all broken in the exact same manner and could never be set? This and her ilk are the subject of his study."

I stared at him dizzily. The roaring in my ears made it difficult to make out exactly what he said, and I had a sharp pain in my side as though I had been running.

"Of course, as your master liked to remind me, the eminent gentlemen of the Royal Society have long been fascinated with monsters. It would be unreasonable of me, then, to draw a comparison between those who take a scientific interest in the subject and the rough hordes that ogle freaks for entertainment. You seem shocked. But what kind of living might a man make if he did business only with those of whom he approved? Your master's work may be profitless and injudicious, but at least it is harmless. In the meantime I live in the false but glorious hope that, one day, he shall sell his ramblings to one of my rivals at an inflated price and I shall be properly paid!"

Galen on cancer:

excess of black bile which causes cancerous tumours may be <u>stimulated</u>
<u>in any man, if he must endure a prolonged period of excessive cruelty</u>
<u>or low spirits</u>

tumour but the outward & visible sign
of his inner anguish

OF THE MALEVOLENCE & <u>PERFIDIOUS DECEIT</u>
OF MY TORMENTORS

XXX

I took great gulps of London air as I stumbled back to Swan-street, filling my lungs with its comforting stinks. The pain in my side had eased a little, but I trembled violently and several times I doubled over, certain I would vomit. *Maternal impression.* And then, like a chorus, in a harmony that danced and dipped round the principal melody, *My precious son.* Round and round they went, in their infernal a cappella, round and round, as insistent as the sawing fiddlers at the Covent-garden. *Maternal impression. My precious baby son. Maternal impression.* I squeezed my hands around my temples until my head ached. The clamour on Cheap-side sharpened itself on my spine. *Maternal impression. My son. My son.*

At Swan-street I crept undetected to the garret and pulled the rugs over my head, but still the words poured like spiders from the cracks and fissures of my brain until my head swarmed with them. Black and indisputable as print, they declaimed their vicious chorus: *maternal impression, maternal impression. Eliza Tally, you blind fool, how could you not have seen, not have known?* And then softer, more gleefully: *You might have saved him, if you had only seen. If you had chosen to see.*

I turned over, burying my face in the mattress, but my skull was alive with those words, and they spun their venomous webs around me, holding me captive. *Maternal impression, you dumb trull,* they gloated. I could not escape them. They gripped me by the ears and peeled back my eyelids so that I might be forced to bear witness to their irrefutable truth.

The apothecary had brought me here to make a monster of my child. He had done all he could to pervert and distort him, to rip apart the godly parts of him and to seed at their centre the brutish spirit of a beast so that from his innocent neck might thrust the vile neck and slavering jaws of a cur. The picture from the book pressed itself into the jelly of my eyeballs until I moaned out loud. Somehow, I did not know how, my child had thwarted him. I imagined him then, curled like a new fern in my belly, his fingers plugged into his ears as the taut strings of my nerves played their terrible music around him. He had held tight to his human form, and he had prevailed. When I had held him in my arms, there had been not the faintest trace of the brute about him.

Despite it all, he had been perfect. Despite the apothecary's worst endeavours. Despite my own.

My stalwart, unyielding, perfect son.

The supper bell rang, three brisk tolls. I did not move. I stared instead at the ceiling and wondered distantly how long I might remain here before someone was sent to find me. It would not be long. In the meantime if I was not present in the kitchen, Mrs. Black might punish Mary for it. She had done so before. I thought of Mary's sweet enduring face and heavily I dragged myself to standing. I could not bear to be the cause of more pain, more misery. My face felt swollen and stiff, my eyes puffy, and my hair and ears wet with tears. I had not even known I had been weeping.

Mary.

The thought caught in my throat. Her loose mouth, her divided lip, her child's sensibilities, were they, too, the results of his vile chemistry? Had the apothecary not managed things as he had, would Mary, too, have been perfect?

Leaning heavily on the banister, I made my way falteringly downstairs. As I passed the master's study, the door opened a crack and the apothecary thrust out his head. His face was withered and pale, the purple stain upon his cheek scummed with grey, his eyes dark holes into his skull.

"You may pursue me all you will," he whispered stickily. "I shall never succumb to you or your cancerous embraces. Never."

His voice caught in his throat, and he convulsed in a choked coughing.

"You bastard," I whispered. "You vile, vile—"

"Never!" he rasped, and he slammed the door shut. The dark landing trembled with the force of it.

"—bastard," I managed, and my ribs screamed with the effort of not weeping.

"Did you not hear the bell?"

Mrs. Black stood outside her chamber on the lower landing, her hands upon her hips. Her mouth was pinched into a knot.

"Answer me, girl! Did the master summon you?" she demanded. "No? Then what exactly do you think you are doing?"

"I—," I protested, hardly audibly. "Nothing."

"Nothing. You idle good-for-nothing puss, your consistency might be a credit to you, if you were ever to direct it towards your work. Now get yourself to the kitchen immediately before I whip you there myself."

Mary looked up as I entered the kitchen, and her face puckered a little, spilling her tongue onto her bottom lip. When she handed me the bread for the master's supper, she frowned.

"Quick, quick," she urged. I took the bread woodenly, dropping some upon the floor. Mary clucked her tongue and pushed me towards the fire, where a pot bubbled. I stared at it, my arms slack at my sides. I longed to scream, to weep, to hold Mary in my arms, to beg forgiveness for what I had done or not done, to her and to my beautiful flawless son, and at the same time I had no notion of how to be or what to do, no idea of what came next. The not-knowing lodged like a fish bone in my throat.

My legs trembled and I sank into the chair, my hands tight around its arms, my gaze lost somewhere in the dark hollow at the heart of the flames. Casting a nervous glance over my shoulder, Mary squeezed my wrist and laid her cheek briefly against my shoulder. The bone jabbed so that I could not swallow.

That evening Mary managed the chores alone. It grew late. I knew I should go upstairs, but I could not find the will to rouse myself from the chair. At last, when the lights in the houses opposite were all extinguished, Mary rolled out her palliasse upon the floor and, taking me by the arm, urged me into it. She was agitated but insistent, hustling me beneath the covers. I did not resist her. When Mrs. Black knocked upon the door, reminding Mary to douse all the lights before retiring, she did not see me, curled behind the kitchen table. As was her way, she left the door a little ajar, and the long thin shadow of her wriggled like an eel in the narrow stripe of light from her candle as she mounted the rough wood of the stairs. Then it was gone. Mary padded across the floor, snuffing out the last low light on the windowsill, and scrambled into bed beside me. I had forgotten how dark the kitchen was at night. I had a sudden longing to be somewhere else, anywhere else, and I struggled to sit up, my arms invisible in the thick darkness.

Very gently a hand reached out and coaxed me back towards the pillow. She murmured gently as she folded herself against my back, her arm heavy round my ribs, her lips against my shoulder. Reaching behind me, I took her hand and clasped it between my own. It was damp and slightly springy, like fresh bread dough.

Time crumples into unfamiliar shapes in the darkness, bunching and stretching so that you lose yourself in the dips and creases of it. When I next heard the night-lanthorn, he was calling three of the clock. The fire was almost out and it had grown cold, the stone floor exhaling its chill breath beneath the thin mattress. Mary had shifted round a little, so that she lay with her back to me, my right arm caught under her. When I eased it from beneath her, it was numb and I flexed my fingers, feeling the prickle of life returning to their tips. An answering prickle nudged in my chest. I sighed. Mary sighed back, turning round once more and snuggling up against my back. Squeezing my eyes shut, I pressed myself against her comforting warmth.

When I felt the first kick, I thought she had just twitched in her sleep. She had always suffered from poor digestion. I pulled my knees up to my chest, waiting for the familiar rumble of her fart. Then it came again, a distinct nudge against my spine. I opened my eyes. The kitchen flared with the light of a passing link-boy before returning to darkness, leaving his shrill shout lingering like smoke on the night air. Turning over, I placed the flat of my hand upon Mary's stomach.

Even in the pitch darkness, there was no mistaking it. Around her hips and across the surface of her belly, the flesh was soft and pliable as it had always been, but beneath it there was a curved bowl of muscle, pulled taut. As I rested my hand upon its slope, I felt again the pressure against my hand, a hard square shape there for a moment and then gone. I pressed down harder with the palm of my hand. There was a shifting, a larger, rounder mass briefly pushing against my fingers, a ripple of moving parts. Mary sighed and mumbled in her sleep as she humped herself over onto her back. The firelight made a dome of her stomach, its lantern the soft pastille of her protruding belly button. In the red glow, her skin had an alabaster fineness, the chapped areas around her mouth like the chipped edges of a china cup.

Of course I knew. For months I had seen it and not seen it. I had told myself it was not possible that an idiot might conceive a child. True, Mary had suffered from her monthlies, disconcerted and alarmed each month by the shock of blood, but in every other way she was barely more than an infant. I had observed her swelling and told myself only that she grew fat. In the cradle beside the bed, the monkey muttered in its sleep.

Sweet God above, the monkey. My hand trembled as it traced the arch of Mary's belly. The creature was still now beneath its canopy. Perhaps like my son it would be perfect, the strength of its virtue protecting it from the beastly impressions that would force themselves upon its waxy flesh. But even as I longed to believe it, I knew it could not be true. Mary herself was formed of unresistant clay, her passions fierce and free of the restraints of wit or discretion. She loved that monkey with all her heart. How then could it not be so, that it might be a child and not an ape-foetus that crouched in the liquid darkness of her child womb, its wildness tethered only by the choke of the birth-string?

Mary stirred and lifted her head. The crumpled rugs had left a dark red crease upon her cheek. She blinked at me in sleepy bemusement, clumsily smoothing away the tear that ran down my face.

"Poor Lize," she murmured, hardly awake. "Still sad."

The grief twisted my heart.

"Oh, Mary, sweet, sweet Mary."

I reached out and touched her creased cheek. Mary stroked my hand briefly, and then, closing her eyes, she curled up once more.

"Sleep." She yawned and held up the rugs so that I might cuddle down beside her. I lay down, my face towards hers, our noses almost touching. Her lashless eyelids were translucent, etched with lilac. She breathed deeply, already almost asleep.

"Oh, Mary," I whispered. "Forgive me. I can't bear that you have endured this all alone."

I squeezed her hand tightly under the covers. She murmured something and pulled away. I knew that I should let her alone, but I could not stop myself.

"Mary, you know, do you not, that—you know that you—that you shall—?" I broke off. Then, brusquely, I shook her shoulder. "Mary, this thing, this thing that is happening to you, that is growing inside you, in your belly, do you know what it is?"

Mary rolled over away from me, making a shield of her shoulders.

"Sleep," she insisted.

"I can't sleep. Not until you've told me everything. Oh, Mary, who has done this to you? Is it that Mr. Jewkes, is that who? That monster, I swear I could—"

Mary twisted round, her eyes suddenly wide awake and round with fear.

"No. No. Hush. No talk. Never. Secret. Big secret. Mus'n say."

"Who told you that, that dog Jewkes? Or our murderer of a master? Who, Mary?"

"Mus'n say," she said again, but her voice quavered and the chewed tips of her fingers pressed into my cheeks. "Prom's to Heav'n. Be punish. Mus'n say."

Her eyes pleaded with me, bright with fear. I took her into my

249

arms, wrapping my arms about her so tightly that the creature in her belly squirmed. I hugged her closer, swallowing my shudder.

"Oh, Mary, my dearest love, what is it they have done to you, to us both?"

There was a stirring amongst the knotted shadow of rugs beside her. The monkey pressed itself against Mary's side, tugging at her undress before skittering onto her shoulder and wrapping itself in her hair. It peeked out at me, its dark eyes bright with mischief, its ginger whiskers glinting. In the streaky rushlight, it was hard to see where one ended and the other began.

I stroked her hair until she slept again, her fingers plaited into the monkey's tail. I could neither bear to look at it nor bring myself to part them. From what I could tell, Mary was five months gone, possibly even six. Whatever the grim vitiations to be wreaked upon the child, they were likely already complete. And though I longed to rip the beast from her embrace, I could not deny her the consolation of it. Her situation was already bleak enough. All the same, I looked down upon the creature, nestled against her cheek, and I wished it dead. And the child inside her too. Wiped clean from memory, so that, somehow, in some way I could not quite imagine, we might be able to begin anew.

I did not sleep again. I stared at the kitchen ceiling, and I thought of the dome and the way it alchemised with the darkness to stamp a thick black hole upon the sky. Daily in its shadow, its people were falling sick, starving, grieving, facing ruin and miserable death, but it never looked down. Instead, it kept its gaze upon the horizon, impervious as God Himself to the agonies of the petty lives that surrounded it. Mr. Honfleur had once told me that it was the opinion of Mr. Wren, the Cathedral's architect, that every building should aim at eternity.

I stood quickly, pulling the blanket up over Mary's sleeping shoulders. She sighed in her sleep, sucking on her tongue. My head ached with unanswered questions. I knew only that we could not remain at Swan-street. Whatever the cost, we had to escape it. It might be too late for the doomed child, its waxy bones already distorted into the grotesque form conceived for it by our monster of a master. It was not yet too late for her.

It was still night when I slipped out of bed. I lit a rushlight from the embers of the fire and hurriedly dressed myself in its smoky light. We could leave before anyone might know we were gone. I had a little money to keep us from destitution, the remains of my mother's guineas. I would find employment for us both with someone kindly who might neglect to observe the swelling of Mary's belly. It could hardly be so very noticeable if I had failed to see it. I would—

I stopped, my bodice only half-laced, and my hands fell to my sides, heavy and palsied.

I would ruin us both. The ravaged beggars on Cheap-side plucked at my skirts as the fire that had lit my belly flickered and went out. There was no one I could go to for help. With neither commendation nor character, I would never find work, and without it I had barely enough money to keep us alive. Where would we lodge, what would we eat, how long before the filthy kennels of the city opened to swallow us whole? My entire fortune comprised a few shillings and several bottles of Elixir that no one wanted to buy. Mary had nothing but a swollen belly and an idiot's features. I was hardly more fortunate, a woman without relatives or reputation. What hope did either of us have of sympathy?

My knees buckled. I squatted on the side of the mattress, staring at nothing. I could feel the tiny movements of my ribs as I breathed in and out. Beside me Mary snored, one arm thrown out beside me upon the covers. Upstairs Grayson Black paced his room, making his endless figures of eight.

Grayson Black. Murderer, rapist, maker of monsters.

Master.

It was past dawn when the door banged open, setting what was left of the pewter clattering in the dresser. As I startled up blearily, Edgar flung himself down on the mattress, tugging at my arm.

"The medicine, you have to make it stronger," he begged me. "The sores—oh God, they—"

Beside me Mary stirred, kicking the mess of rugs away from her legs. I gasped as the memory struck me open-handed, Edgar sprawled where I lay now, his face crusted with tears and snot.

The only other proven cure was to fuck a virgin, the younger the better.

Edgar fell backwards as I clawed at his face, kicking with all my strength at his shins, grinding my knuckles into the soft slope of his nose. His blood spurted against my fist. Had he done it alone? Or had he offered himself for hire to Mr. Black, a duty performed for the advance of his master's great work? The discrepancies of dates and probabilities were a faint murmur, powerless against the blind frenzy of my fists. As sharply as I could, I brought my knee up into the slack of his groin. Edgar groaned, doubling up. I struck out with my boots, kicking him hard in the back of his knees as I slammed my fist once more into the mashed disorder of his nose. Perhaps he had even secured himself a payment for the unappetising task, two birds slain with a single stone. Had he congratulated himself for the perfect symmetry of his subterfuge, when he left Mary sprawled and weeping upon her mattress, his vile sediment sticky on her thighs? He groaned again, an agonised clutching at breath, before collapsing against the leg of the table, heavy as a felled tree.

Mrs. Black appeared in the doorway. Edgar hauled himself to stand, turning his head away so she could not see his bloodied nose.

"I want the two of you upstairs in five minutes. The master desires to see Mary later, and there are one hundred duties to be done before she can be spared."

The door slammed shut.

Edgar moaned and clutched at his face. Disgusted by us both, I threw a rag at him and snatched up a comb to tidy my hair. The teeth gouged my scalp, steadying me. Edgar suffered still. Was that not some small comfort? Edgar's condition was not yet obvious, with none of the crusted scabs and foul stinks of the advanced disease, but they would come, and then it would be he whom others regarded with revulsion, he who found himself alone and abandoned. What hope would he have then of gathering into his lap the last crumbs of the Blacks' fortune? He would die a dreadful death, his body decaying from the inside, his petty ambitions as rotted as his flesh.

It was then that I saw my chance. Edgar gaped at me as I outlined my terms, his mouth working furiously beneath his swollen nose, but although he was witless, he was endowed with sufficient of the worldly form of wisdom to recognise that he had no choice in the matter. My silence was perhaps of even greater necessity to him than my medicine. He appealed with pleas and threats in turn to my conscience, to my shame, to my instinct of self-preservation, but I informed him coolly that, of the trinity, I possessed only one and that it left me with no choice. My terms were fixed. Five shillings a week for my silence and another for the medicine, take it or leave it.

"You are a contemptible little bloodsucker," he hissed when he surrendered his first payment. "You shall not get away with this."

I curtsied, my face grim.

"Please come again, sir," I said. "We so appreciate your continued patronage."

That evening I sewed the coins Edgar gave me into the hem of my dress. The way it dragged a little to one side when I walked was my first presentiment of freedom.

The gladwin pessaries had dried to ancient chrysalises beneath the cloths in the kitchen dresser. When I picked them up, they crumbled in my hand, flecking my palms with brown. I threw them on the fire and watched them take. They burned fiercely, privately, rolled in orange flame.

I made no more. It was much too late for gladwin. Any attempt to expel an infant so much grown would require powerful and dangerous intercession and would most likely take the mother off with it. I might have taken such a risk on my own behalf. I could not countenance it on Mary's. What scandalous loss of reputation might be suffered by one who had never been permitted the privilege of claiming one? Besides, the spectre of her writhing upon her palliasse, her cheeks clay-grey, fatty sweat greasing her hair as she screamed, the puddle of scarlet blood spreading its stain beneath her—the image of it was intolerable. It would be safer for her now to carry the creature to term, whatever the horrors that awaited us then. It was the monster the master wanted, not Mary. Every day, he had her come to him. The hours she spent with him unspooled in slack loops that caught around my neck and made it hard to breathe. I began the same duties over and over again, completing none. At night I stared up at the ceiling, and I made lists in my head.

Lists of herbs that might bring down a child before its time: alkanet, anemone, barberry, brake, bryony, calamint, gladwin, hellebore, hyssop, sabine, wormseed.

Lists of the words I had mastered in my reading practice and must commit to memory: capital, constable, conscience, candour, cataract.

Lists of the perils of the maternal imagination taught to me in childhood: If an expectant mother urinated in a churchyard or crossed a water-filled ditch, her child would be a bed-wetter; if she peeped through a key-hole, he would squint; if she helped to shroud a corpse, he would be pale and sickly; if she spilled beer on her clothing, he would turn out a drunkard; if she ate speckled bird eggs, his skin would be thickly freckled.

Lists of the fates that faced a poor woman without employment: thief, whore, beggar, corpse.

Lists of remedies for the curse of the mother's imagination: If a hare should cross your path, tear your dress; think upon gods and heroes; baptise the unborn child with holy water. Avert your eyes from cripples and felons hanging from the neck.

Lists of infusions against the French pox: mezereon spurge; sarsaparilla; soapwort; spikenard with dandelion, burdock, and yellow dock; walnut.

Lists of the ways it was possible to kill a man: aconite; agaric and other toadstools; the flowers of the buttercup distilled in wine; the root of the daffodil, cooked in place of onions; dog's mercury; foxglove taken daily over the course of a month; juice extracted from the roots, leaves, and berries of belladonna.

To Mr. Grayson Black
Apothecary at the sign of the Unicorn in Swan-street

Mr. Black, sir,

I am of course glad to know that your health is a little restored and hope that each day that passes hastens your recovery.

I enclose for your attention once again the outstanding account of monies owed by yourself. As you can see, the sum is grown considerable. I was diverted by the contention in your last letter that my best chance of payment lies not in withdrawing my services but in permitting you the completion of your studies. How neat is your reasoning! In order to pay me, you must have me send you more books. I only hope you are half as good a scientist as you are a logician.

Still, harbouring no particular affection for the grim processes of English law, I therefore suggest the following. I shall continue to supply you with the books you require. I shall however increase the cost of each loan by 6d., which I shall set against your outstanding debt. As before I shall expect each one returned unmarked and within three weeks of receipt. In addition, I shall accept for resale any books you have already purchased from me, if they are in sufficiently good condition, and credit any monies accrued thus to your account. As for the balance, I shall take no action if the full amount is settled six months from today.

I believe my terms to be generous. If you wish to oblige me further, you should continue to send that charming maid of yours with your books. You are fortunate that her pretty face provides me something of a consolation.

I am, sir, your obedient—not to mention commendably patient—servant,

ÉTIENNE HONFLEUR
Bookseller at St. Paul's Churchyard, London

2nd day of June 1720

XXXI

Two weeks passed before I was sent to the bookseller's again. This time I took two bottles of the Elixir with me. It was a white weatherless day, the bandage of the sky wrapped tight around the sun, and the door to Mr. Honfleur's shop was propped open with a heavy iron weight. Just inside an artist's easel had been set up, and upon it were pinned a number of handbills, some covered thickly with words, others illustrated with woodcuts. The largest showed a man seated at a table, quill held aloft, as an angel descended from a cloud above his head, an open book in her hand and a banner covered all over in tiny words streaming from her mouth. I squeezed past it into the shop. In the bottom of my basket, the rag-wrapped bottles of opium sounded softly together.

"Ah, the prodigal is returned!" Mr. Honfleur declared. "And what do you think of our latest business venture?"

"You would be well advised to study the hearts of the men who trade so frenziedly at your beloved Exchange," Annette protested, as though I were not there. "I defy you to find anything but venality and greed and the determination to profit at the expense of one's associates."

"If you don't mind, I am in something of a hurry today," I murmured, taking the books from my basket. Beneath my skirts my legs jiggled impatiently. If I was quick, I might have time to visit two coffee-houses and not be missed.

"But all profit is at the expense of another," the bookseller declared, unwrapping the master's books and idly studying the bindings. "There is meat upon our table because our enterprise answers more readily to its customers' demands and at a better price than that of Mr. Roe's next door. This is all you have brought?"

"Yes, sir." I nodded, willing him to make haste. "And if I could—"

"And because you turn away from books," Annette interrupted. "Which may teach a man how to live, in favour of selling patent medicines and life insurance, which prey upon his basest fear of death!"

"Medicines?" I burst out, before I might stop myself.

"What nonsense, Annette! If a man chooses to purchase a packet of pills or a policy along with his Plato, it does not devalue the currency of print. Why might a man not leave our shop richer in both happiness and health?"

"While you, sir, grow richer in coin? How very convenient."

"Do not pretend naïveté, Annette. This is commerce, not coercion. A man may profit only by satisfying the needs of his customers."

"'Vain wisdom all, and false philosophy,'" pronounced Annette, pressing her lips together.

"It is declarations of that kind, daughter—" Mr. Honfleur threw his hands above his head and rolled his eyes at me. "Truly, she is impossible. Come, we shall pay her no more mind. She can busy herself with your master's order. As for you, sit here, beside me, and tell me what news you bring from the apothecary's house."

But I could not sit. I stared at the bookseller, excitement rising in my chest.

"Mr. Honfleur, do you truly sell patent medicines? I had—"

"*Mon Dieu!*" Mr. Honfleur cried. "No more! You women—I am quite tired of the subject. If you wish to stay, we will talk only of agreeable things. Annette! Here. I wish this seen to immediately."

I flushed. From behind her book, Annette considered me coolly, the faintest trace of a smile upon her lips. I ached to stamp down hard upon her smug little foot. Instead, summoning all the false gaiety I could muster, I launched into a wild tale of the monkey's latest antics. But even as my tongue tumbled over the words, my head resounded to a single rhythm. *Medicines. Here. Here. Medicines.* I gazed at Mr. Honfleur as he laughed, and my blood pounded until the pulse in my neck throbbed with it.

"If it is monkeys you are fond of," he chuckled, "I shall have to have you accompany me to 'Change-alley one day. The place is more awash with simians than the forests of the tropics themselves."

I managed a smile. My cheeks were flushed, and I could feel the sweat trickling between my breasts.

"And now I have an appointment. Good day, my dear. We will not wait so long to see you again, I hope."

Saluting us, he straightened his wig and was gone. I paused as Annette slowly lowered her book and sighed, reaching with limbs slow as treacle for the apothecary's books. Then, snatching up my bonnet, I ran from the shop, casting about me until I made out the sway of Mr. Honfleur's back, pushing through the throng towards Paternoster-row.

"Mr. Honfleur, sir, please stop," I shouted after him. He turned, frowning a little, and I seized his sleeve. "Excuse me, sir, but stop a moment, I beg you. I—"

"You forget yourself, child," Mr. Honfleur protested not un-kindly, detaching my fingers from his arm.

"Forgive me, sir," I pleaded. "It's—it's only that—there is—I mean, I have—well, you were speaking—with Annette—she talked of—you sell patent medicine, do you not? And, well, there is—that is, I have prepared—I call it Tally's Elixir. I have it here, in my bas-ket. The preparation is close to a miracle and may relieve the most agonising suffering. Look at Mr. Black. He has been so unwell and yet, and I—well, since you said—"

Mr. Honfleur studied me. Then very slowly he began to smile.

"You wish to sell me a remedy you have stolen from your master?"

Although his lips still smiled, his brow creased with incredulity. Immediately I understood the terrible extent of my misjudgement. The bookseller found me amusing, perhaps even charming. He was not so antique nor I so very plain. But my master was a customer and a fellow merchant. Beside the mutual obligations of London's respectable burghers, the frail amity of master and servant was no more than a loose thread, quickly brushed away, as quickly forgotten. It was the iron girders of shared citizenship, of common interest, that held the structure of the metropolis aloft.

"It isn't like that—," I whispered, staring at my boots, and my treachery quivered in the space between us.

"Well, then, I think I must see what it is you have to sell, do you not agree? Bring it to me tomorrow, and I shall consider it." Gently he placed a hand beneath my chin and raised my face till our eyes met. His mouth twitched. "Why so disconsolate? It is a fine idea. Together we may contrive to recoup a little of what your master owes me. Besides, how may I resist the chance to drive my dearest daughter perfectly to distraction?"

He was still laughing as he disappeared into the crowd.

The very next day I took my two bottles of the Elixir to Mr. Honfleur's shop. The bookseller took one of the phials and, uncorking it, sniffed at its contents. I watched him, my throat tight with hope.

"So this is Black's preparation," he murmured. "I hope, for his sake then, that it relieves that most disabling of human afflictions, false vanity."

Carefully I outlined my pitch as I had rehearsed, making my claims soberly and without excessive embellishment. When I was finished, Mr. Honfleur did not speak but lifted the bottle once more to his nose and inhaled. I waited, my hands in fists in my lap.

"You have copied the apothecary's recipe exactly? You are sure?"

"I have only added some herbs, sir, for a better flavour."

Mr. Honfleur placed the cork carefully back into the bottle.

"Very well," he said at last. "I shall consider it."

"Oh!" I gasped. "Oh, Mr. Honfleur, sir, thank you. Thank you! You shall not regret it, I promise."

The bookseller laughed and held up a hand to silence me.

"I shall need to satisfy myself as to its efficacy. For all my daughter's misgivings, I am not entirely without scruple. Send me a dozen more bottles, and I shall give you my opinion as soon as I am able."

"But how—?" I hesitated.

"How? You are the woman of business, my dear. You work it out."

I hesitated.

"I—I am sorry, sir," I blurted out, "but the Elixir is dear, and I have a pressing need for money. If I am to make more. You are a gentleman, I know, and honourable, but—"

My voice trailed away. Mr. Honfleur sat back in his chair, his arms crossed over his chest, and considered me, his head on one side. I stared back, my chin jutting out, biting my cheeks so that I would not cry. I could not read his expression.

"*Ma petite,*" he said, shaking his head, and a smile began to ripen round his mouth. "*Est-il possible que deux filles soient si différentes?*"

"I—I don't understand."

"No." Mr. Honfleur reached into his coat and plucked out a crown. "Shall this be sufficient? Until we are agreed?"

I stared at the coin and the tears sprang into my eyes.

"How long—how long until you shall know? It is only that—I cannot wait long."

Mr. Honfleur regarded me thoughtfully.

"How about this for now?" He held out his handkerchief and smiled as I took it and wiped my eyes. "As to the rest, I shall let you know as soon as I am able, I promise you that. You drive a hard bargain, *mademoiselle.*"

All the way back to Swan-street I kept my fingers curled, crossed over one another for luck. *He shall take it, he shall take it not.* As a child I had cheated when there were few enough petals to predict the way it would come out. I wished I could manage things so easily now.

I slipped across the hall. But as I reached the kitchen stairs, the laboratory door opened and Edgar emerged. His face was flushed and his eyes glittered.

"Not so fast, my little sluttikin," he hissed, grabbing my arm.

"Edgar, please," I muttered, alarmed. "Let go of me."

Edgar's grip tightened.

"But I have some good news for you, my little Hackney whore. Although I fear perhaps it shall not delight you wholly. At least not so much as it does me."

"Good news is always welcome."

"I wonder if you shall think that for long. It transpires that those blisters you were treating with such—such *dedication*—were not the French pox, after all, but only a local infection, quite common and happily now cleared. Which means I am no longer at your mercy, either as cunning woman or confidante."

The heat drained from beneath my skin.

"I am pleased for you," I said shakily. "It must come as quite a relief."

"Oh, it does. It does. For it is not only the burden of illness that I have contrived to escape. It defies belief, I know, but there are those out there, those so wanting in the slightest shred of humanity, so untrammelled by conscience or compassion, that they would not hesitate to extort blood money from a dying man."

I said nothing, but my skin tightened into goose-flesh.

"Shocking, is it not? I knew you would be sickened by such a thing." Edgar reached out dreamily and pinched my cheek hard between his thumb and forefinger. "Of course they shall return all they have taken. In full."

"But what—what if they have it no longer? If it is spent?"

Edgar snorted.

"You think a money-lender considers that adequate explanation for his losses? If it is spent, it must be found elsewhere. All of it. Not to mention the interest due upon the capital sum at a rate of two pence for each shilling taken."

"Two pence? But that is—?"

"To increase by a penny each month that the debt remains outstanding."

The self-satisfaction upon Edgar's face was intolerable. I crossed my arms.

"I only hope that you can prove what you claim," I declared. "Otherwise, I imagine you have little hope of recouping your losses."

Edgar seized my wrist.

"Don't you even try—"

"Edgar, I do not know what it is you talk of. Perhaps we should take this matter to the mistress to decide."

"There is no need of the mistress in this matter. For they shall pay. And if they do not, I shall seek my revenge upon such leeches. They will pay a heavier price in the end for their treachery." He thrust his face so close to mine that our noses grazed. His breath was sour and hot. "They would be advised to think on it, you know. I shall endeavour to exceed their worst imaginings."

the laughter of the neighbour woman it torments me she comes to me
in my dreams & she quivers her chins & licks her lips to whisper in my
ear & the telling arouses her & greases her fat white thighs

she fucks him here in my house my wife that cunt bitch fucks the
apprentice
i see it in her eyes in her scorn she scorns me & brings the stink of him
in on her cunt
she takes from me all of what is mine by law <u>mine</u>
my business my money my house my wife

is there no limit to the baseness of woman

then let them starve
& see if the poor-house is as fine a master as i

XXXII

Edgar proved as good as his word.

If I walked into a room where he was, he walked out. On more than one occasion, I found him in my garret, rummaging through my box. And whenever he could, he made a point of whispering with Mrs. Black, sending me significant glances that made me both angry and afraid. Each time my mistress summoned me, I was certain she knew of my extortions and meant to beat me or worse. The atmosphere was worsened by a feud of some kind between my mistress and her neighbour, Mrs. Dormer. Frequently I saw the chandler's wife standing in the window of her first-floor chamber, her arms crossed over her bosom, glaring like a gaoler across the lane. She seemed to be waiting for something.

When, a week later, Mr. Honfleur greeted me with the news that he would take the Elixir for three months, by way of a trial, I almost kissed him in my relief. He raised an eyebrow when I pressed him about how soon we might expect to see a return. What proceeds there were, he declared lightly, would be divided directly down the middle. I was to remain responsible for the Elixir's manufacture, which, in order to avoid difficulties at Swan-street, would from henceforth be undertaken in what had been a tiny storeroom at the rear of the Huguenot's shop. Mr. Honfleur in his turn would take charge of the Elixir's promotion.

The preparation, he informed me, would be sold under the appellation of Dr. Huppert's Febrifuge. Perhaps I was not aware that only last winter this miraculous nostrum had brought the King of France himself back from the brink of death. The grateful King had pressed ennoblement upon the doctor, but the good man had refused, asking instead for the freedom to practise his religion without concealment and the permission to share his medicine with his family in the Protestant faith. Unable to refuse the man to whom he owed his life, the King had agreed.

"He is a fine and pious man, is he not?" Mr. Honfleur declared happily. "A man to set every Pope-hating heart in London a-pounding. I have been acquainted with him for only a matter of days, and yet I myself am already exceedingly fond of the good *docteur*. It is a privilege indeed to act as his representative here in London!"

He pinned a notice to the easel extolling the virtues of the Elixir in French, scattered with dashes that gave the words quizzical eye-brows. He meant to print labels for the bottles to match it, each with the doctor's signature and seal. Though I feigned enthusiasm, in truth I could hardly control the impatience that twitched in my fin-gers. There was so little time. Such absurdly elaborate preparations only delayed the tincture's sales. The medicine was miraculous and that was the end of it. Surely we had only to tell the customers that and we would sell it by the waggon-load.

"Trust me," the bookseller reproached me. "The educated man does not purchase an item only because he requires it. He buys it be-cause every possession he acquires holds up a mirror to his imagin-ings and reflects a superior image of himself."

I sighed. Outside the bells of the Cathedral scrambled to sound out the hour. So little time. Honfleur frowned.

"But of course I am right," he protested, as if I had contradicted him. "A man purchases a trifle, a silk scarf from Persia, let us say. How much softer and more colourful, then, is the silk if he can be persuaded to imagine the cloth that he now holds in his hands was once entwined round the sweetly perfumed shoulders of a dusky princess? How much sweeter the sugar chipped from King George's own sugar loaf?"

I ached for money, strained towards it with an effort that pulled at my neck. But for the bookseller the pleasure was all in the schem-ing, and in irritating his daughter. He relished the thought of argu-ing with her on the subject and longed to provoke her ire.

"The flood of money undammed by the South Sea Company laps daily further into the provinces," he announced to her. "All over

England men have money to burn, and they yearn for long and healthy lives in which to burn it. Surely it is my duty then to offer them this Febrifuge. For only God may set the allowance of a man's life."

But to his perplexed vexation, she said nothing. She kept house as she always had, she saw that her father visited the barber and wore clothes of adequate cleanliness, she even assisted in the shop when required to, although she obstinately refused to take money for anything but books, but she did so without uttering a single word.

At first the bookseller considered her silence a great joke. He engaged in elaborate displays of dumb show, and when that failed to amuse her, he declared himself delighted with the unexpected peace of it. And though at first I had feared it as yet another reason for delay, I was soon to understand the advantage in it. For, to provoke her, the bookseller took the books from the front window and replaced them with an exhibition of the Febrifuge, whose merits he made a point of rehearsing to every customer who came in. As I gazed at the display, I prayed she would not relent.

She did not. Mr. Honfleur grew impatient. He criticised her publicly, rebuking her for her idleness, her lack of filial piety, and, when that appeared not to affect her, made much of my attentiveness, my humility, the readiness with which my opinions converged with his own. I was, he declared provokingly, the model of a dutiful daughter. He found simple books for me and encouraged me to read to him, to memorise lines of poetry which he had me recite, all the while pressing her for her opinion on my progress. Her eyes were chips of ice, but she said nothing.

In time he grew morose. The Frenchmen still came to talk at the shop, but Mr. Honfleur no longer led the discussions but wandered about the shop, picking up books and flicking at their pages in weary disgust.

"'But far more numerous was the herd of such, who think too little and who talk too much,'" he spat, slamming a volume with such ferocity that I imagined the poems crushed between its pages like flies. "Why the Devil must poets insist on such commonplaces?"

And then, one pale triumphant morning in May, Mr. Honfleur greeted me with a bow and handed me my first purse of coins.

"We are not yet rich, I fear," he said drily, "But, *alors,* it is begun."

I blinked at the bookseller, and I felt a rising in my chest like a great wave.

"Six shillings. Spend it wisely."

"Six shillings?"

"Every fortune begins with shillings." He raised his little cup of coffee. "To Dr. Huppert—and the future."

I did not trust myself to speak. Instead, I nodded and squeezed the bag of money in my hand, feeling the press of the coins hard against my palm.

"Why so glum?" He pulled a face. "It is a cause for celebration, is it not?"

Shaking his head at me, he seized me by the waist, spinning me round in a clownish dance. I ducked my head and blushed and begged him to stop, but he only laughed and stamped his feet like a rustic at harvest-time. Then, without warning, he stopped, snatching his hands away from me so abruptly that he almost pushed me away.

"My dear, to what do we owe the pleasure?"

I twisted round. Annette stood framed in the doorway, her outline stamped against the light.

"I hate to interrupt your celebrations," she hissed. "But —"

"She speaks!" Mr. Honfleur threw his hands up. "A miracle, indeed."

Annette's face tightened.

"I wished to inform you, Father, that I can no longer remain in this house while you make free with your whore."

The bookseller exploded like a firecracker.

"How dare you speak to me so! You are not too old, daughter, that I may not take you across my lap for such insolence!"

Annette's contempt might have turned a tree to ash.

"It would be my husband's place to strike me, Father, if such action should be necessary."

"Until you have such a husband, I—"

"Oh, did I not tell you? How foolish of me. Father, I am to be married."

The words seemed to strike the breath from Honfleur's belly.

"Why so aghast, Father?" Annette enquired sweetly. "He is a curate, a man who venerates God, not Mammon. It should comfort us all that, in these days of madness, such men survive. He shall make a fine husband."

Honfleur gaped at her, his mouth working like a fish.

"Do you not mean to extend us your blessing? Not that I require it, of course. We shall be married directly."

"But—?"

"But what about you? Dear Father, have you not already secured the services of an obliging little whore of a maidservant? Surely the slut is dexterous enough to keep one hand in your breeches as she empties your chamber-pot?"

Then, with a swish of her skirt, she was gone. As the door slammed behind her, Monsieur Honfleur sank against the table, his legs bowing beneath him.

"Sir, are you—?"

He looked up and his face was crumpled and purple as an infant's.

"Go!" he roared. "Get out! Take these damned books and get out!" Snatching up the books, he hurled them at me. "I said, go!"

I knelt and clumsily stacked the books into my basket.

"You should not suffer her to slander me so," I whispered, but if he heard me, he said nothing. Instead, he bowed over the table, his fingers pressed hard into the tight curls of his wig, and exhaled the strangled cry of a rabbit caught in a gin.

"We are still in business, are we not?" I asked in a tiny high voice. "The Febrifuge—?"

"Damn it, girl, did you not hear me? Get out!"

There was nothing else to be done. Picking up my basket, I walked stiffly away.

At Swan-street the kitchen was empty and supper not begun. There was no sign of Mary. Quickly I hid my bag of coins in the back of the dresser drawer. A painful lump lodged in my throat as I chopped vegetables, wielding the knife like an axe. It was some time before I heard Mary's heavy footfall and the chirruping voice she used with the monkey.

"Where the Devil have you been?" I rebuked her, my distress curdling to anger, and I hurled a handful of vegetables into the pot.

"Wi' mast'," Mary said in a faraway voice, holding the monkey against her cheek. It wore an infant's lace bonnet tied tightly over its whiskery face, and it tugged at the ribbons, shaking its head unhappily. "Jinks bab'."

"For pity's sake, Mary, it's an animal, not a child!" I cried, snatching at the bonnet. "Why can you not—?"

Mary swayed backwards and forwards as though intoxicated, cradling the monkey against her breast.

"Mar' nurse Jinks," she murmured. "Like Lize."

I frowned.

"Milk. Like Lize."

For a moment I did not understand her. Then the shock burst like a bag of soot in my chest, black and deadening.

"Mary, no! You did not do it, did you? Tell me you did not let him do it."

Mary cradled the monkey against her chest.

"Like Lize," she said again more softly, and a single tear fell upon the monkey's bonneted head and quivered there. I swallowed but the stone in my throat was not so easily dislodged.

"We are going to get away from here," I whispered, and the pain in my throat choked me. "We shall go where you shall be safe, where he will never find you. Just a few more weeks and it shall be over, I promise. All over. We shall be free."

"Is that so?"

Mrs. Black stood in the open doorway, the white blade of her nose slicing the shadows.

"This is how you would repay our kindnesses?" she enquired coldly. "With theft and cozenage?"

"And whose kindness swells Mary's belly?" I spat back. "Whom may we thank for that generous bequest?"

In the silence that followed, the fire hissed with dismay.

"We are not felons," I said shakily. "You cannot keep us here against our will."

"It would seem that you oblige me to do precisely that. Mary, come here."

She snapped her fingers. Her head bowed, Mary rose leadenly and went to stand beside her in the doorway. Without looking at me, Mrs. Black walked across the kitchen and locked the door to the outside steps, putting the key in her sleeve. Then, gripping my wrist, she turned my hand palm upwards and struck it six times as hard as she could with the birch at her belt. The pain was distinct but disconnected from suffering, like a memory of pain, and I made no sound. Only Mary whimpered, covering her face with her hands. When she was finished, Mrs. Black stalked back to the door and, taking Mary by the arm, pulled her out of the room. The door slammed. I heard the scrape of the key in the lock, then nothing. I did not rattle the door nor demand to be let out. I only stood there, immobile, as the fire sighed and the throb of my sore hand marked time, as regular and purposeless as the ticking of a gaoler's clock.

At dawn Mrs. Black unlocked the door. She looked as weary as I, her face white and pinched.

"You shall not see Mary again," she said, and the act of speaking seemed to cost her prodigiously. "She is to be kept apart from you and from anyone else who might seek to undo the master's work, under my close and constant supervision. Any attempt to see or speak with the idiot girl shall be severely punished. You shall not ruin us, do you hear me? I should see you dead before I let you ruin us."

At the door she paused, her hand at her throat.

"From today you shall perform her duties as well as your own. I can only hope that the burden of work shall teach you something of humility."

An hour later I crouched in the hall, scrubbing the floor. My hand moved the brush mechanically over the boards, backwards and forwards, backwards and forwards. The scraping of bristle against wood muffled the voice in my head. *List them*, it urged, *come now, Eliza, list them—*

"To the kitchen! Now!"

Mrs. Black stood over me, her boot against my ribs. Slowly I put down my brush and stood. Gripping my arm, she dragged me to the top of the kitchen stairs.

"Lize."

"Silence!"

I twisted round. Mary shuffled a little out of the shadows, her hands twisted into knots at her mouth. Her clothes were filthy, her face wan and streaked with soot. Smeary black shadows circled her eyes, and her cheeks were rucked with twists of dried and blackened snot. Her distended belly poked against her soiled skirts like a deformity. She blinked, squinting up at me as if the dim light hurt her eyes.

"Mary, dear one—," I pleaded. "Everything shall be all right, I promise."

Very slowly Mary raised her head. Her eyes were pink, raw with misery. As I held out my hand to her, Mrs. Black wrenched at my arm, twisting it painfully in its socket.

"Lize."

The anguish crumpled Mary's face, and she squeezed her eyes tight, rocking backwards and forwards on her heels, her hands wringing and twisting together.

"Oh God, Mary—"

Mrs. Black struck me so hard across the cheek that I bit my tongue. I choked, tasting blood.

"For every time you say her name, she'll have another night in the coal-hole. Is that what you wish her? Now get down those stairs before I throw you down!"

"Lize."

I half-fell down the stairs. My cheek smarted and my tongue swelled in my mouth. I thought of Mary crouched in the darkness, her arms hugging her shins, her forehead pressed hard against her knees, rocking back and forth to the shrill tuneless sound she made when she was distressed, and my throat ached so sharply that I could hardly breathe.

Mary feared the coal-hole more than any other place on earth.

I, Grayson Moses BLACK, Apothecary & Scholar of Swan-street in the Parish of Saint Martin-in-the-Fields in the County of Middlesex, being weak in body but of sound & disposing mind & memory, do make & ordain this my last Will & Testament in manner following so that all difficulties & controversies about the same may be prevented after my decease. That is to say,

Item: I commit my soul unto the hands of Almighty God, my Creator & Redeemer, & my body to Christian burial

Item: I give & bequeath to the Royal Society the full extent of my writings & other papers so that they may be preserved for the nation in the manner due to them

Item: I revoke the bequest sworn to in my previous testament to grant unto my wife Margaret BLACK the remains of my Estate & the full guardianship over any such direct dependents as shall exist at the time of my decease or afterwards. Margaret BLACK is an adulterer & a whore & it is my Will that she shall know the agonies of poverty & destitution due to the harlot who cuckolds her husband under his very roof.

Item: I declare as null & void the apprenticeship of Edgar Horatio PETTIGREW, who has, through his vile conduct while under my tutelage, so cruelly betrayed my trust that neither shall any part of the three hundred pounds of his indenture be considered due to him from the remains of my Estate nor shall he have consideration within his lifetime for admission to the Worshipful Company of Apothecaries.

Item: May it be noted that, instead, I give & bequeath all the rest & residue of the monies owing to me from any person or persons whomsoever & of all my money in the public stocks or funds & of all other my goods, chattels, & personal estate whatsoever that I shall be possessed of, interested in, or anyways entitled to at the time of my decease, together with the full & lawful guardianship of the sum of my dependents & any offspring thereof, unto my brother, John BLACK of Newcastle, to have benefit thereof during his natural life on condition of the construction of an <u>appropriate & public monument </u>to the name of BLACK & all that has been achieved in that name for the greater glory of God.

In witness whereof I have hereunto set my hand & Seal this eighteenth day of July in the year of our Lord one thousand seven hundred & twenty, <u>Grayson BLACK</u>

       in the presence of two witnesses as undersigned
     Silas PEEL   Sampson MATHER

XXXIII

I did not see Mary again. Mrs. Black made sure of that. I prepared her meals in the kitchen, and she took them up to her on a tray. On the second day, I placed a tiny feather from the linnet's breast beneath her soup bowl. When the tray came back, it was gone. After that I hid something beneath the plate every time. It was never much, only a curl of my hair or a scrap cut from the hem of my dress or even the paring of a fingernail. I prayed that she was safe and that she understood.

There were no errands. I kept Mr. Honfleur's handkerchief tucked in the pocket in my skirt, a knot tied in it to hold in the luck, and I took it out when I was alone to give me courage. And still the days passed and the time of Mary's confinement grew ever closer. The handkerchief grew limp and grey from handling. I tried not to think of the anger with which the Huguenot had ordered me from the shop. Instead, I brooded upon the ways in which I might once again secure his favour. I prayed that he did not remember my remonstrations, that we might pretend the whole episode forgotten. Desperation, after all, is no ally of dignity.

Mrs. Black did not speak to me, folding her lips closed whenever I encountered her. When she took Mary for her regular interview with the apothecary, she locked me into the kitchen so that I might not attempt to intercept her. She kept the front door to the house locked. Even the shop door was kept bolted and only opened when a customer rang the bell. I was as much a prisoner as Mary.

And then, after nine days, there was a book on the hall table. I touched it with one finger, barely able to believe in its solidity. When Mrs. Black unlocked the door for me, she withdrew the key from her belt like a knife. She said nothing, but the air around her smelled scorched like the air after a strike of lightning. In the lane I ran, simply to feel the stretching in my legs. All along Cheap-side I pushed and jostled, giddy with desperate liberty. It was only outside the shop that I hesitated, suddenly afraid to enter. When at last I forced myself to step across the threshold, the Huguenot looked up and smiled. Although he looked tired and not altogether clean, there was nothing in his manner to suggest we had parted on ill terms. Rather he greeted me as he always did, rubbing his hand over his unshaven chin.

"You have books for me?"

I nodded, staring at my feet. I thought of the sight we must have made, dancing together in the crowded shop. I did not know what to say.

"Annette is to be married," the bookseller said at last.

He wished it forgotten. Everything was going to be all right.

"She is?" I said, relief pinking my skin. "But that is fine news."

"Is it?" he asked. "It came as something of a shock to me." He sat heavily in his chair, tipping it back onto its hind legs. "I had become accustomed to her."

"She is already gone?"

"She tells me she will lodge with his aunt until he has enough set aside. I have offered to assist them, but naturally she will not hear of it. My coin is clipped with chicanery, you see."

"Surely not—"

"It is hardly unusual, of course," Honfleur continued bitterly. "Every daughter should use the institution of marriage to advance themselves in society. The only difference is that Annette wishes not to become the lady of the manor but the *principessa* of high principle. It makes no difference in the end. Either way, they consider themselves justified in despising you."

I shifted unhappily.

"She is a respectful daughter," I protested. "Surely she will soften."

The bookseller let forth a snort of mirthless laughter.

"How little you know her," he said.

We were both silent then. The clock ticked upon the wall.

"'Tell us, pray, what devil this melancholy is, which can transform men into monsters.'" Honfleur sighed to himself. Pressing the pads of his thumb and forefinger into his eyes, he pinched his nose hard. Then he raised his head. "So. You thrive, I hope? It has been some days since your last visit, if I am not mistaken."

"Yes. I—I was hoping for news of the Febrifuge. You see, I have an urgent need—that is, I wondered how it went. How profits are."

Honfleur shrugged.

"I do not recall. Still, the market rises daily, despite Paris. There they use bank notes to wipe their arses. But we pay no heed to them. In London every last man is turned stock-jobber. Most of their womenfolk too, for that matter."

"Except Annette," I said, attempting a joke.

Honfleur's mouth twisted.

"Except Annette. And her censorious sophist of a husband."

"Then our partnership flourishes?" I asked, despite myself. "There shall be more profits?"

Honfleur did not answer. Instead, a smile began to spread across his face.

"Why, of course!" he declared, slapping a palm to his forehead as his chair thudded forwards. "Of course! I cannot believe I did not think of it before!"

"I beg your pardon?"

He held his hands out, palms up.

"We shall be married!" he announced. "I shall take you as my wife. Such an arrangement would suit us both. We shall be married and live like kings on the proceeds of the Febrifuge!"

"Married?" I repeated dumbly.

"Married," Honfleur said, and a mist of impatience rose up from him. "I have the right word in English, do I not?"

"Your English is impeccable," I stammered.

"Then we are agreed," he said. "We shall marry. The sooner the better."

I stared at him as he leapt to his feet, my face slack and stupid.

"But—"

"But? Eliza, I wonder if you appreciate your good fortune. I should have thought 'Yes' a better answer."

The lightness of his tone did not quite balance the reproof. Still I could not answer. My heart raced, my mouth opening and closing in soundless disbelief. Monsieur Honfleur wished to marry me. It was the answer to everything. I would be free, Mary too. She would come to the bookseller's as my maid. We would leave Swan-street forever and we would never have to go back. We would live here together. We would be safe. I could hardly imagine it, the sheer unimaginable good fortune of it. The tears filled my eyes as I looked up at the bookseller, holding out both my hands to him in mute gratitude.

"Look at this—you are shaking, my dear."

I nodded helplessly, and the tears spilled over and fell unchecked down my cheeks.

"Why, you are overcome. Then I shall ask you again. Shall you be my wife?"

I opened my mouth, but my tongue was palsied and my lips trembled so violently I could not speak.

"Still no answer? Be careful, the market for marriage is come like the market for stocks—there is a grave shortage of profitable opportunity for those women without fortunes to trade." There was a peevish edge to his teasing. "Tomorrow I might wake a more prudent man."

Hastily I pressed my fingers to my foolish lips, working sense into them.

"Forgive me, sir," I whispered, and I bowed my head. "My answer is yes. Yes, yes, of course I shall marry you. I can think of no greater honour."

"I should hope so." He shook his head humorously, extending his hand towards me. "Look at you. How very simple you are, for all your boldness and bluster."

Taking my face between his hands, he kissed me very softly upon the mouth and wiped my tears away with his thumb, licking their salt from his skin. The taste of them stirred something within him, so that his mouth grew hot and greedy. Pulling me towards him, he pressed my body against his, kissing me hard upon the mouth. I clung to the stuff of his coat and parted my lips. When he thrust his tongue deep between them, he tasted not unpleasantly of bitter coffee and pipe tobacco. His hands closed round my breasts as he kissed me more insistently, his tongue quickening and his breath coming in gasps. I forced my own tongue to move, responding to the bookseller's own parries. I wished to please him, and it was not so difficult. Gratitude has much in common with affection.

The bookseller groaned, a long gluttonous grunt, and ran his wet mouth down my neck before burying his face between my breasts. His chin was gritty with stubble. I thought of my mother and her ambitions for her only daughter, and I suddenly felt very old.

"Be mindful of my virtue," I murmured, caressing his face gently with my fingertips. "We must wait till we are wed."

Honfleur looked up at me. He looked quite unlike his usual judicious self. His eyes were bright and feverish, his lips a deep crimson, their edges smeared against the surrounding skin like wet ink. Two circles of scarlet flared upon his cheeks. With powder and patches, he might have passed for a courtesan, an ancient and wanton courtesan. His hands circled my upper arms, and he pulled me to him once more, his hand reaching beneath my skirts. I pulled away, this time more firmly.

"Monsieur, come now, I beg you. I must go home."

Honfleur shook his head and sighed, rubbing his hands along his thighs.

"*Mon Dieu,* very well." His lips pouted into a smile. "But I will countenance no delay. We shall beat Annette and her whiffler to the altar, you may be sure of that."

I walked back to Swan-street in a dream, my heart darting and wheeling in my chest like a swallow. We were safe. Safe. Our future secured, mine and Mary's, by a deliverance of such miraculous fortuity that I should never have dared to have hoped for it. As I made my way along Cheap-side, the smile spread stupidly across my face and my feet danced. Mr. Honfleur the bookseller, a man I admired, a man who had shown me kindness, wished to take me, Eliza Tally, a maidservant without wealth or reputation, as his wife. What angels gazed down from the Heavens upon the grimy reaches of my soul and set upon my sinning head the light of their celestial blessing? What acts of goodness had I performed, asleep or unknowing, that now repaid me so?

I knew myself undeserving of such extraordinary good fortune. But now that, by whatever accident of Fate or seraphim, it was indeed mine, I would endeavour to merit it. I would permit no fissures, no cracks into which ill luck might creep and breed, but I would steep myself in those qualities that would preserve my undeserved good fortune as vinegar preserves onions, humility and obedience and the bowed kind of gratitude that knows it can never repay the debt owed to it.

Mrs. Eliza Honfleur.

Mrs. Eliza Honfleur and Mary.

We were saved.

formal invitations to hand-picked members of royal society to attend delivery

    Halley

    Sloane

    Tabor

    Cowper

archbishop of london?

wright? But he asks only for money & more money that exchange of his has a maw like a great whale

fine wine & roasted meats & pies & pudding

Conversion of parlour to exhibition hall

skeleton of monkey to be displayed alongside that of human infant

idiot in cage to underline simian association?

or formal lady's gown in order to emphasise transformation by impression?

everywhere apparatus of science finest microscopes & orreries those bastards shall not dare to deem me less of a scholar than they

10 shilling entrance charge—note well Mr. Wren how much more my creation is worth than that popish grotesquerie of yours out there

fecundation of the other whore girl debts must be settled if they insist upon keeping her here they must surely permit me to make use of her worthless harlot

begin again & again while there is still time

subsequent proofs categoric proofs proofs for all eternity

bring the whores to me & i shall make monsters of them all

OF THEM ALL

XXXIV

As the days passed and still the master had no books for me, my exhilaration faded. I grew distracted and then anxious. What if Annette had persuaded her father to change his mind? What if he had regretted his proposal? Or forgotten it altogether? There had been no witnesses, nothing to make the offer binding. What if, when I entered the shop, he acted as though nothing at all had happened? What would I do then?

When on the sixth day I came upstairs to find in the hall a small package of books tied with string, I rushed through my tasks, banging brushes and coughing dust, so that I might spend careful minutes before the scrap of glass in the kitchen, combing my hair and pinching my cheeks to give them a pink glow. A little bacon fat gave my lips a glossy fullness. I pinned on a clean cap, using a damp finger to set a pair of curls upon my temples, and laced my bodice as tight as I could bear, arranging my breasts so that they curved generously above the muslin trim. Outside the house I looked up to the window where Mary was imprisoned, hoping to catch a glimpse of her, but as usual the drapes were pulled and the panes were milky-blank with borrowed sky.

"Hold your thumbs, Mary," I whispered. "Hold your thumbs for luck."

Then, lifting my skirts, I ran so that I might be at the shop before she forgot the instruction and let the wish spill carelessly out onto the floor.

"Good day, sir," I called breathlessly as I pushed open the door, my pulse knocking in my throat. "I hope I do not come at an inconvenient time."

"My dear, come in, come in. Your mistress keeps you too close."

He smiled, half-raising himself from his chair and fumbling in his coat pocket with a forefinger. "Look, I have something for you."

He handed me a small roll of oyster-coloured silk and watched as I unwrapped it with clumsy fingers.

A ring.

"If you tremble so, you shall drop it," the Huguenot chided lightly. "And it was not cheap. Here, let me."

He slid the ring onto my finger. It was a tight fit, but the book-seller twisted it like a screw, forcing it over the knuckle.

"There," he announced. "It looks fine."

I gazed at my hand. The ring bit into my flesh, rigid and irrefutable.

"I can hardly believe it," I murmured.

"How young you look when you blush."

"We are truly contracted?"

"Unless you prove yourself in debt or quite insufferable, I be-lieve we are." Honfleur smiled, tapping my nose with his finger. "I would urge you to make me a loving and careful wife. I have borne enough shrewishness for several lifetimes."

I smiled, swallowing the lump in my throat, and stood on tiptoe so that I might kiss him upon the cheek.

"Oh, I shall, I shall," I assured him, and I knew that I had never before spoken with such sincerity. "Thank you, sir. You shall not re-gret this. I mean to make you as contented a husband as there ever was in history."

"Then we should set about satisfying that wish with all haste. I want nothing with the business of banns. Why declare one's busi-ness to all the world in a public place when the curé will do it snug and without to-do at Threadneedle-street? We shall have a couple of guests to serve as witnesses, eat a hearty dinner, and consider our-selves well satisfied."

My heart lurched. I thought of the Campling boy, of the cere-mony at the cottage.

"But, sir, it must be done properly, must it not—?"

"Dear God!" Honfleur frowned. "I did not have you for one of these foolish girls who craves luxury and extravagance. You shall have a new dress for the occasion, but you must not put on airs. Your humility has always become you."

"On the contrary, I desire no luxury," I insisted. "It is just that I—I wish it properly lawful, sir. That is all. I should not want it underhand."

"Underhand? Dear Eliza, do you mistake me for a Fleet man, all secrets and lies? I am a Frenchman, remember. It shall be done correctly, I assure you."

I had vexed him. Quickly I took his hand and pressed it to my lips.

"Then I shall be quite satisfied, sir. It is marriage I desire, sir, not ceremony."

Mollified, the bookseller studied me thoughtfully.

"I myself have always been a great admirer of the gentler virtues: modesty, courtesy, patience. Powerful enthusiasms are treacherous. When they cool, as all enthusiasms must, they curdle into bile and bitterness. My countrymen would do better to learn from your Earl of Dorset: 'Love is a calmer, gentler joy.' Do you know the poem? Dorinda's Cupid he declares 'a blackguard boy that runs his link full in your face.' A fine metaphor, *non*? The wise man has no desire to char his eyebrows."

"I am quite sure you are right, sir," I agreed.

"Do you mock me?" Honfleur grimaced. "Truly, Eliza, you are in a most trying temper."

I shook my head in distress. I did not know how I had contrived to provoke him when I was so intent upon the opposite.

"Forgive me, sir, if I displease you. It is only that I—I am overcome. Your kindness exceeds all expectation."

Again I took his hand and kissed it. Mr. Honfleur patted my cheek absently, his attention on the street outside. Then suddenly he stiffened. Turning to me, he seized me by the arms and pulled me towards him.

"Then favour me with a kiss," he declared, and covering my

mouth with his, he forced his tongue between my lips. There was a cold drip on the tip of his nose. The shop bell jangled. He kissed me again, more slowly, before raising his head, his hands clamped about my forearms.

"Annette, dear daughter," he cooed. "What a pleasant surprise. To what do we owe the pleasure of your company?"

Annette said nothing. The flower brooch flashed at her bosom.

"I—I should go home," I muttered, attempting to free myself.

"This shall be your home soon enough," Honfleur purred, and his fingers tightened upon my arms. "Annette, you will doubtless be delighted to learn that Eliza and I have agreed on a date for our marriage, St. Bartholomew's Day, five weeks hence." He thrust out my hand, displaying the ring. "We may depend upon you and your curate to act as witnesses, may we not?"

Annette drew herself up taller, gazing at her father down the length of her nose.

"St. Bartholomew's Day, but of course how perfect!" She clapped her hands, a disconcertingly coquettish gesture. "What other place for a girl of her quality to be married than at the Fair? Doubtless you have arranged for a dwarf to preside over the ceremony? Or perhaps a pair of Siamese twins? A grotesque of some kind would describe the character of the occasion so admirably."

"Is that so?" Honfleur replied icily. "To my mind, there is little more grotesque than religious fervour. There is no more certain way to leech the joy from this life than an excess of pious enthusiasm."

"And no more certain way of ensuring eternal damnation in the next than the patronage of sixpenny whores. '*Il connaît l'univers et ne se connaît pas.*' "

"You listen to me, you little—!"

But Annette was gone. Dust turned in anxious spirals in the sunlight, and above the door the bell shivered, breathless with shock.

"I'm sorry," I murmured, rubbing my bruised flesh. "It—"

"No, no, it is I who should apologise." Mr. Honfleur's voice was weary. "Excuse my daughter's intolerable rudeness. The curate has done nothing to temper her ill nature. She is—"

He broke off, his shoulders hunched. Tentatively I placed a hand upon his arm. He regarded it as a scientist might regard an unfamiliar specimen on the glass of his microscope. Then he clapped his hands, affecting briskness. I took my hand away.

"Since you are here, you must read," he said. "After all, we must begin work in earnest if you are to make sufficient progress before the wedding. A bookseller's wife must not be discomfited by her ignorance. Herrick shall do well, I think. His fondness for simple language favours the inexpert pupil."

He handed me a thick volume bound in leather. I opened it, though I knew that it grew late, for I dared not risk his displeasure.

"Where do you wish me to begin?"

The bookseller said nothing but only sighed, leaning upon his elbows and pressing his fingertips into the sockets of his eyes.

"Shall I begin with the first poem, sir?" I attempted again.

"'I dare not ask a kiss,'" he murmured into the twin shells of his palms. "'I dare not beg a smile, lest having that, or this, I might grow proud the while.'"

"Perhaps you might direct me to the verse?"

"'No, no, the utmost share of my desire shall be only to kiss that air that lately kissèd thee.'"

The words hung in the air, turning slowly like dust as I leafed through the book, hoping to find the poem. Honfleur sighed again. Then, slowly, he took his hands from his face and blinked at me, as though his eyes were not accustomed to the light. I smiled tentatively at him, unsure of what he wished me to do next. He did not smile back. Instead, he plucked the book of poems from my hand and tossed it onto the table.

"I have no appetite for the old fool. Let us talk of other matters."

I hesitated.

"Come," he said, somewhat roughly. "It would appear you are shortly to be my wife. Surely there are things you would wish to ask me?"

He leaned forwards, as though steeling himself against an onslaught of enquiry. It was plain that silence would only contrive to vex him further.

"Of course," I said cautiously. "How goes the Febrifuge?"

"No, no! I seek an affectionate wife, if you please, not a stock-jobber!"

I bit my lip.

"Forgive me. Then, if it pleases you, sir, I should like to know your name."

"My name?"

"Your given name, sir. I know you only as Mr. Honfleur."

The Huguenot frowned.

"I hope you do not hold with the new fashion for addressing a husband by his first name. I am an old man, I know, and so likely out of step with the world, but it does not sit comfortably with me."

I sighed, beset suddenly with weariness.

"No, sir. I should like to do as you wish in all particulars."

"But you are curious, of course," he conceded. "I was baptised with the name Étienne. In English you say Stephen. It was a family name. All the same, I do not think of it as mine. My mother disliked it and always called me by my second name. It is that name that truly belongs to me."

"And what is that name?"

"Daniel," the bookseller said. "I think of myself always as Daniel."

I did not take the ring off until I reached the top of Swan-street. It comforted me to look down upon it and know myself neither ridiculous nor mad. Five short weeks and I would be his wife. Twisting his ring upon my finger, I forced away my uncertainties. It was not only the ring I had but also his daughter, reluctant witness to his declared intent. Did the law not regard such a promise as binding? It would not be a simple matter for the Huguenot to break his word.

To steady myself, I gave myself over to imagining life at the Huguenot's house. I lit a fire in the grate and placed myself where

Annette liked to sit, behind the counter, arranging Mary in the chair I had always taken. She had a soft smile upon her lips and a chapbook in her hand, held before her so that I could see the curve of her brow and the twin peaks of her knees. As for what came between, I pushed it away. For now it was enough to imagine her quiet and content. It would take her time to trust another master, but she would grow to love Mr. Honfleur, for he would be kind to her. He might teach her to read, if she wished it. She would learn without being herself the subject of study, the various parts of her puzzled over and broken down into manageable syllables. She would make Mr. Honfleur coffee just as he liked it, and he would sip from his little cups, peering at her through the spectacles he balanced upon the end of his nose, and he would smile at her, for he would see beyond the shape of her, which bore witness only to the disfiguring tyrannies of science, but to her spirit, which lit her from within. When I thought of him then, I felt a tender gratitude towards the bookseller that was not so very different from love.

I was required to lick my finger before I could slide the ring from it. My knuckle throbbed red as I concealed the band in the hem of my sleeve. When I bent my arm, the circle of it pressed against the crook of my elbow. Five weeks. Reflexively I looked up at Mary's window before crossing the kennel. The face that gazed back at me was unmistakable, white and gaunt, the damaged cheek lost to shadow, lips peeling away from brown teeth in a grimace that was neither smile nor snarl as it raised two clawed fists and squeezed them together as though intent upon strangling the air between them. Then it was gone. All that remained was a cloudy patch upon the glass that faded as I watched. Slowly, the drapes began to move across the window.

"Mary!" I cried, as though I might throw myself through the narrowing gap. "Mary, can you hear me?"

Behind me Mrs. Dormer, the chandler's wife, opened her front door, her chins shivering like a pork jelly upon their dish of lace.

"Is all well?" she enquired. "I was just asking your girl here if all was well. I should not wish to think all is not well, Mrs. Black."

Mrs. Black stood in the doorway of the shop. Her expression was grim.

"All would be quite well," she said tightly. "If one could only get servants of the proper quality."

Mrs. Dormer sighed and her hands kneaded each other avidly.

"Although I understand you are more than content with Mr. Black's apprentice. They say that you would be lost without him, is that not right, Mrs. Black?"

"A dutiful wife does not permit her husband's business to suffer neglect, Mrs. Dormer, while she amuses herself. Now if you will excuse me?"

Seizing me by the nape of my neck, she pushed me into the shop.

"How much trouble must you make before you are satisfied?" she hissed, snatching up her birch. Twisting I tore myself free, knocking from the table a basin that fell to the floor and broke in two. Scarlet liquid spread across the wooden floor.

"What does he do to her?" I screamed. "That bastard—that bastard is killing her!"

"If you refer to my husband, he bleeds her, you stupid little drab," Mrs. Black said grimly. "He bleeds her as physicians across the country bleed their patients; for their health. Our neighbours would doubtless be aghast at the scandal. Now get downstairs before I whip you there, so help me."

She pushed me so hard that I stumbled, striking my elbow against the counter. I clasped it against my belly, feeling the ring in my sleeve.

"Mary," I whispered, bracing myself. It was worth the beating to ask it out loud. "Is she—is she well?"

Mrs. Black looked at me strangely, her pale lips working.

"She—she endures. It shall be a relief to us all when she is safely delivered." Then she stiffened, clearing her throat. "For pity's sake, girl, why do you gape so? Anyone would think idiocy contagious."

She sent me to the laboratory to assist Edgar with its cleaning. The scrubbed wooden table was littered with dirty jars and beakers.

I began slowly to gather them up, stacking them on a tray. In one corner Edgar hunched over a flame, watching a blackened glass tube in a metal frame.

"Where the Devil is my money?" he hissed without looking up. "You test my patience exceedingly with your postponements."

I opened my eyes wide.

"What money, Edgar? You know quite well I have none and never have had."

"You could get it if you wished to. You could borrow it from your friend, the bookseller. From what I hear, the old man is a perfect fool for you."

"Then you hear wrong."

Edgar turned slowly, eyes narrow.

"Or do I?"

My neck reddened. Frowning, I tossed my head, clattering bottles and phials.

"So it is true? You dirty little strumpet! I had heard whispers, of course, but thought them nothing but rumour. So the bookseller fucks you, the lewd old goat!"

"Spare me your filth. The bookseller is an honourable man. Unlike some."

"Which means what? That he intends to make an honest woman of you first?"

I was silent, my hands petrified before me.

Edgar stared and a smile spread slowly across his face.

"Well, well," he drawled. "This *is* interesting. I presume, then, that the honourable Mr. Honfleur knows that you are already married? And that there are some years still to pass before your husband might lawfully be declared lost?"

"You know quite well that that is not true!" I protested. "That my marriage was—that it meant nothing. In the eyes of the law. You know that."

"Oh, I'm sorry. So the child you bore, the child Mrs. Black delivered in this very house, that child was a bastard? Mr. Honfleur knows of the child, I take it?"

"It was not like that. You are twisting things—"

"I do not believe that in our past dealings you have concerned yourself unduly with the precise particulars of fact. You should be grateful that, in return, I mean to stick more closely to the truth as I see it. I am certain that your future husband would find the story most engrossing."

"Edgar—" I swallowed. "I shall repay what I owe you. I swear it. As soon as I am married, you shall get it all."

"Ah, if only it were that simple."

I gaped at him.

"But—what then? What is it you want from me?"

"Interest on my oh-so-generous loan. Ten pence for every penny."

"Ten pence? But that is extortion!"

"Then you shall be familiar with its conventions. Ten pence for every penny. Or I shall tell the Huguenot the truth about his sweet little blowzabella."

"But, Edgar, how many times have I've told you? I have no money."

"The Huguenot has money."

"Which I may make use of only once we are safely married."

Edgar frowned, his mouth working.

"Edgar, listen to me. If you go to Mr. Honfleur now, you shall have your revenge, it is true. But you shall also take away any chance I might have for setting things right. For you, for Mary—," I faltered. "Please, Edgar. I shall repay you. But I can only do it if you permit my marriage. It is all the hope there is. For any of us."

There was a sudden sharp crack, like a gun shot, as, over the flame, Edgar's tube exploded in a glitter of broken glass.

"That bastard," Edgar whispered, and he buried his face in his hands. "When is that poxy bastard going to *die*?"

XXXV

Upstairs, locked in her curtained solitude, Mary grew daily closer to the time of her delivery. And inside her, in its own liquid confinement, the tiny monstrous creation stretched and strengthened, thickening her blood with clots of its black primate hair, its simian skull pressing ever harder against the mouth of her womb. In perhaps two months it would be delivered. But in five weeks I would be married. Hold tight, I whispered when I passed her door, hold tight. I shall not fail you.

I was not fool enough to consider Edgar reliable. But when a week passed, and when still he did not go to the Huguenot, I permitted myself to breathe a little more easily. And though the days passed with painful slowness, little by little the wedding plans advanced. A mantua was chosen and brought to the shop so that it might be adjusted to fit me. It had a skirt of scarlet silk with a cream-coloured underskirt, the pale gold bodice tied across the stays with scarlet ribbons. When he confessed that he had paid £1 8s. for it, I gasped out loud. Such frugality became me, the bookseller commented approvingly, but there was something regretful in the way he smoothed the skirt down as I took the dress and hung it in the press.

"'It is a silly game where nobody wins,'" he murmured as I drew the curtain across it. "Though a sensible man pays little regard to the views of Mr. Thomas Fuller. It was he who claimed that 'learning hath gained most by those books which the printers have lost.' He would have done better to recognise that catchpenny drollery makes a fool of us all."

He paused, caught by his own thoughts. Then he smiled, patting my hand.

"Come, let us not be discouraged by such a dotard. Your books await you. A little Webster, perhaps, to sharpen our wits, 'And of all axioms this shall win the prize: 'Tis better to be fortunate than wise.' And so forth. You will find much in it with which to concur, I fancy. Now what is it you have memorised for me?"

I straightened up, my hand smoothing the skin of my throat.

" ' 'Tis just like a summer bird-cage in a garden: the birds that are without despair to get in, and the birds that are within despair and are in a consumption for fear they shall never get out.' "

"How quickly she learns."

Annette stood in the doorway, her face grave, her hands clasped loosely before her. Her voice was almost gentle, but her composure had a taut quality that set the sunlit shop dust to spinning more frantically upon its axis. She studied us both for a moment, seated side by side, the book on the table before us. When she opened her mouth, I thought she would say something more. But she only touched the tip of her tongue to her lip, then, with a tiny nod, turned and left, closing the door quietly behind her. Honfleur let out a breath, and his fingers flexed.

Lightly I placed my hand on his.

"Shall I fetch you some coffee?" I asked.

" 'There's nothing of so infinite vexation as man's own thoughts,' " the bookseller murmured to himself. Then he sighed, forcing his mouth into a smile. "Dear Eliza. But we have work to do. We shall make a scholar of you yet."

As soon as I turned the corner into Swan-street and saw the front door standing open, I knew that something was seriously amiss. I ran down the lane, my basket bumping against my thighs, and in through the open door. The screams came in keening waves, so vivid with grief and loss that it pierced the chest to hear them. They cut through the walls of the narrow house, burying themselves like knives in the crumbling plaster until the splinters bristled in the floorboards and the glass in the sashes issued a low rattling moan. The agony in them was a kind of madness.

It had happened at last. Mr. Black was dead.

The hall was deserted, occupied only by dust and shadows that pressed back against the walls, as though to accommodate the magnitude of anguish contained in the ghastly cries. There was none of the usual business of death, the gossips with their covered heads and expressions of assiduous piety. The doors to the laboratory and the shop stood open. Both were empty. Closing the front door behind me, I tiptoed up the stairs. I saw no one. The door to Mr. Black's chamber stood open. It seemed to tremble upon its hinges as the wailing traced its desperate arcs up and down, up and down, shrill and savage as the cries of a seagull.

Trembling myself and with my face averted, I pushed it wider and, fearfully, stole a glance inside. The angle offered only the end of the bed, where a white foot protruded from beneath the weight of bedclothes. The toenails were ridged and yellow and curled over the end of his toes. The skin too was yellowish, with a chill waxy sheen. I shivered as another scream began to swell. Steeling myself to enter, I snatched another look and what I saw stopped my heart in my chest. The foot moved. It twitched quite distinctly against the bedclothes, so that the blanket fell away from it a little. By now I was truly frightened. I had known the master capable of unutterable wickedness. I had not thought it possible that he might triumph over Death itself.

I backed away from the door. I longed only to flee, to run from this house and never return. The air tasted poisonous upon my tongue, and the shadows reached out to me like beggars, plucking at my skirts, sucking the spirits from me, and drawing me into their dust and darkness. My hand closed round the stair-rail, and I gripped it tightly so that I would not fall. For a moment the house was still, as though the scream itself drew in all the breath in the house, and then there was another wild howl that tore through my bones.

And then, quite suddenly, I knew. It was not Mrs. Black who screamed. It was Mary. All of her suffering, all of the raw and miserable incomprehension of her unformed soul, was contained in the anguish of those ghastly cries. I flung myself at the door so precipitately that I almost fell.

My master was not dead. On the contrary, his face, habitually grey and pinched, was lit by a strange pink glow. His hands trembled and jumped upon the paper he propped upon his lap as though unable to contain their vigour, and his lips moved in wordless spasms. Mary lay half across his legs, her head in his lap, her body wracked by sobs. In her arms she clutched a blood-soaked bundle which she pressed against her distended belly, rocking backwards and forwards as she was overtaken by yet another maddened howl of grief. The blood smeared the front of her bodice in thick rusty streaks and stained the fine hairs along her forearms. Her face was swollen, shapeless with grief.

In a moment I was beside her, taking her in my arms, holding her close. The smell of blood flooded my nostrils, hot and metallic and undercut with the reek of shit, the stink of a shambles on a summer afternoon. I stroked her head, crooning to her under my breath. She rocked back and forth against me, her nose buried in the bundle in her arms.

"Mary, Mary, I am here now. Sweet Mary, Eliza is here."

"Get out," the master said, and his voice was sticky and thin. "Why do you come here? This is none of your concern."

He laid a yellowed hand upon Mary's head. She did not resist him.

"Don't you touch her!" I cried, wrenching her away from him. "What the—oh, Mary, Mary, my sweet girl, what has he done to you? What has he done?"

Tugging her by the arm, I tried to pull her to her feet, but she fought me, twisting and biting at my hands like a savage.

"If it is your intention to aggravate the girl's distress, you do very well," the master observed, and his face jumped as, with a shaking hand, he made a mark upon the page before him. "You do very well, indeed."

"You—you are a monster!"

The master opened his mouth to speak, but suddenly he was convulsed with a spasm of such ferocity that his whole body jerked and his black hole eyes contracted in bewildered astonishment.

"Mary, dear Mary, please, come," I whispered desperately in her ear. "Let us leave now, while we can."

But Mary only buried her face in the blood-stained bundle and howled like a animal. I held her, wrapping myself about her as though my flesh might protect her from her anguish, murmuring reassurances and urging her to collect herself, to trust me, to try to stand, but she only surrendered more completely to her anguish, her cries drowning out my words.

The colour quite drained from his face, the master fumbled upon the table beside him until his fingers closed round a cup which he endeavoured to bring to his lips. Some of the liquid ran down his chin as his hand and the cup dropped away, the cup falling with a dull thud upon the floor. The skin on his face loosened and eased as he took a series of shuddering breaths. When once more he raised his head, his eyes burned with black fire. He licked his chalky lips.

"Come," he murmured to Mary, and with an effort that strained the ropes of muscle in his neck, he eased the bundle from her arms. Mary did not fight him but only moaned, her eyes squeezed shut, her fists clamped round two handfuls of her own hair which she tore at as though she would rip it from her head. He murmured soothingly to her as he unwrapped the bloody bundle.

"See, Mary, see well," he murmured. "The creature is dead. It is not sleeping nor can it ever be restored to life, however warmly you embrace it. It will do you no good to pretend otherwise. Come, look. I wish you to see this for yourself."

Uncovering the tiny corpse, he held it aloft. I gasped, the acid threat of vomit at the back of my throat. It was a dreadful sight. The monkey's head had been almost completely severed from its body. Worse almost than that, its arms had been hacked off just above the elbow joint, leaving only two stumps, black with congealed blood. Its narrow chest was a glistening plough of blood, flesh, and splintered bone. Behind the pale curve of its left ear, I could see the tiny nails that tipped its fingers. The monkey had been cradled in its own arms.

Mary's screams snagged and slowed as, with great gentleness, she extended one finger to caress the creature's blood-clotted cheek.

"It is altogether a most unpleasant incident," my master observed, and fumbling an uncorked bottle from the crowded side table, he took a long draught. He sighed, leaning back against his bolsters. "Mrs. Black was a fool to leave the window unlatched. London swarms with thieves. Besides this, they made off with the pewter."

"Thieves? You expect me to—what have you done?" My voice rose uncontrollably. "This—you know the grief shall kill her!"

"I sincerely hope you are mistaken. But certainly her passions are as violent as any I have ever observed," the apothecary agreed, and steadying his writing hand with the other, he picked up his quill and directed it towards the ink pot. "See how she can barely breathe. She is quite undone."

"You—you conscienceless dog!" I shrieked. "How much more must you have her suffer before you are satisfied? Oh, Mary, come, I beg you. You cannot stay here."

But Mary would not move. She clung to the bundle and to the bedclothes, writhing away from me, her elbows thrust out before her. The apothecary patted her hand, his eyes blinking at a point somewhere beyond her head. Then, leaning his head back upon the couch, he closed his eyes.

"See how your derangement distresses the creature," he observed serenely. "Her passions are inflamed beyond the bounds of human endurance."

I stared at him. Mary huddled on the floor, weeping silently into her hands.

"You dare stand here and blame me for her grief? A man who would corrupt the very essentials of Nature without the slightest conscience, who would destroy blameless lives, and for what? Money? Renown? Sweet God, you are the agent of the Devil himself!"

I swallowed, scrubbing roughly at my nose with my fist. Beside me Mary lifted the butchered monkey into her arms and tenderly pressed her cheek against its face.

"Why must women always prove themselves so lacking in the higher qualities of reason and intellect?" Mr. Black remarked. There was no anger in his voice. Rather it had a dreamy, singsong quality.

"It is truly observed that a woman is but a child of larger growth. It is little wonder such damage is done to so many."

"The damage is done by you, you bastard! By you!"

The apothecary did not reply but only lifted his quill and once more placed the point upon his paper. I strained to see what he wrote, but there was no sense to it, nothing but wild swoops and circles and black-edged holes where the pen had pierced the surface of the paper. When he raised his head, it swayed slightly from side to side, as though his neck was insufficiently strong to support it.

"Madam, I am tired and wish to rest. I shall say only as I have said on many previous occasions that, but for us, the child would have suffered the fate of all those unfortunates who serve society no useful purpose. Now she may repay us and make her own small mark upon the understanding of Man. You would deny her this comfort, a child to whom Providence has proved so unkind?"

"A comfort? That she be forced to part her legs for whatever stinking cock-stand you choose to thrust between them?"

"Madam, please, such lewdness does not become you. The advance of human learning will not falter before an onslaught of foul words or empty accusations. The hunger for earthly knowledge is a provision given to Man by God Himself. It is only through the precise and detailed understanding of its myriad complexities that we may see His creation clearly, in all its great glory. Long after we men of science are brought to dust, our discoveries will shine like beacons in the world, beacons illuminating the rough and rugged path towards enlightenment." His hands reached upwards and his voice strained after them, taut with awe and shortness of breath. "As I now trace the course set before me by my forebears and press forwards into the darkness that they could not penetrate, so, too, the scholars of the future will place their feet carefully in the footprints I shall leave behind me, advancing further and further towards the horizon of perfect understanding, their bright-burning flares of wisdom held aloft until the darkness of ignorance and superstition is quite expunged and we stand shoulder to shoulder with God, made whole by His truth."

His voice was faint and rasping, but each word shivered with certainty.

"And if the child is unmarked?" I cried. "What method of killing is it you favour? Stifling or burning, or crushing his tiny skull? It is clear from the monkey what kind of butcher you are. Is that how you killed my child, by carving him up like a chicken?"

Grief encircled my throat like hands. Mary whimpered at my feet, but I paid her no heed. With an effort the apothecary raised his head, blinking and frowning as if perplexed to see me there. The purple mark on his cheek glowered.

"How the Devil did you get in here? Mrs. Black! Where did that bitch go? How may a gentleman work with all these disturbances? Mrs. Black!"

"You murdered my son."

"For the love of God!" he rasped. "When you came here, you wished me to rid you of a bastard child. To perform an illegal act, an act against God, so that you might be spared the consequences of your immorality. And you have been duly spared, though you hardly deserve such good fortune. No harm has come to you. You have been well looked after. The child is no more. Most importantly, your reputation has suffered no stain, although, given your insolent and reckless nature, I can hardly believe such a situation shall continue so for long. I struggle to understand your lack of gratitude. Mrs. Black! Where are you?"

I stared at him. I wanted to plunge my fingernails into his face, to pull open the seams of his frown and score raw red lines in its pale implacability. I wanted him to shriek, to writhe, to bleed. I wanted his pain to last forever.

"You murdered my child," I whispered. "And now you kill Mary too. You destroy everything I have loved."

"On the contrary, I saved you from ruin and provided for you a second, and quite unmerited, prospect for a better life. As for Mary, through my work she has found a purpose and, in all likelihood, a fortune too. I trust that, unlike you, she shall display the good sense to be thankful."

Mr. Black broke off, his voice lost in a spasm of coughing. His fingers groped once more for the bottle beside him but this time they did not find it. With a swift chop of my hand, I knocked it over, sending a gush of liquid across the table. The apothecary howled, the coughs convulsing his thin frame as he struggled to raise himself from the bed. His hands clawed desperately at the sodden papers as I snatched the bundle from Mary's arms and ran with it from the room. With a wild cry, she flung herself after me.

It was only afterwards that I thought of the candles. A trio of them had stood in a stick upon his table, bubbles of wax oozing down their lengths like spittle. I might have set light to his coat if I'd only had the wit to. I imagined the flames devouring him, seizing upon his cuffs, his stock, his wig, engulfing the narrow chaise until their orange tongues glowed bright as petals in the empty darkness of his eyes.

There was peculiarly little comfort in it.

To Maurice Jewkes, Esq., at his house at Jermyn-street in the parish of St.-James's

Dear Mr. Jewkes,

My husband acknowledges receipt of your letter, the discourtesies of which he is prepared to overlook, & has asked me to reply to you, both to ease your anxieties & to remind you once again of the terms of our indenture. Your objections, sir, have no place in law.

As I have already informed you, the monkey purchased for the girl had begun to stimulate swift & startling improvements in her persistent ill health & we harboured strong hopes for a rapid recovery. The sudden demise of the creature is therefore greatly to be regretted. However, Mr. Black counsels strongly against purchase of a replacement as this will serve only to provoke the girl's habitually feeble memory & thereby deepen her malaise. He has instead prescribed bed rest & regular bleedings, supplemented with a nourishing diet & a restorative tonic of his own devising. As agreed, the bills for her treatment will be despatched to you monthly.

In order to speed the patient's recovery, you will appreciate that every effort will be taken to ensure that she suffer no undue excitement or agitation. Mr. Black would therefore have you desist from an attempt to visit her here at Swan-street until such time as we detect a manifest restoration of her health. Neither shall your boy be permitted entry. We shall of course continue to send word of her, as required by the terms of our agreement, & hope that we shall soon be able to inform you of considerable improvements in her condition.

Mr. Black has me acknowledge receipt of the monies as agreed & remains &c.,

MARGARET BLACK

27th day of July 1720

XXXVI

I did not stop running until we had crossed the sluggish brown stream of the New Canal. No one would find us in the tangle of lanes that criss-crossed the undergrowth of the wharves. The water of the canal was lumpy with dung and dead cats. On the western side, in the scale-silvered turmoil of fishwives and eel-sellers that bellowed their wares round the foot of the bridge, I turned and held the blood-stained bundle out to Mary. She snatched it from me and began to weep, her head bowed over the blanket. The swell of her distended belly was rusty with drying blood, and there were red-brown smears across her face and arms and around the chewed stumps of her nails. Her hair escaped her blood-streaked cap in whippy tails. Only in London could we have come so far unhindered.

It had begun to rain, a powdery drizzle comprised as much of soot as water.

"Mary, forgive me. There was no other—forgive me."

Mary did not answer but only held the dead monkey closer.

"I shall take you to a safe place. Somewhere far away from him, where we can be together."

I pushed Mary ahead of me. Beyond the makeshift market, the lanes were noisome and narrow and the stench of the river so thick that it left a greasy tallow-skin upon your tongue. Curses and rough laughter spilled from tavern doorways, propped open with rocks or slabs of splintered wood. From blind walls and ash-heaps, dogs and ragged children materialised like dark phantoms to swarm about our legs. On house after rotting house, pinned to warped door jambs or propped up behind cracked and grimy panes of glass, were faded signs depicting a man's hand joined with a woman's and the words MARRIAGES PERFORM'D WITHIN. Behind one I glimpsed a parson in a soiled surplice, his eyes empty and red-rimmed in his pale yellow face.

We skirted the high walls of the Temple and emerged onto the traffic-choked jostle of what I guessed was Fleet-street. I paused, holding Mary before me, so that I might judge where it was we were. Immediately a chairman bawled at us to clear the path before he walked right over the pair of us.

"Addle-headed numbskull," he jeered as I pulled Mary out of his way. Mary gaped. Then, as though her knees gave way, she slid down the brick wall to squat upon the rain-spotted ground, her knees clamping the bloody bundle against her chest.

"Come on," I urged her gently. "I have a friend who will help us."

"Home," muttered Mary, and she bowed her head over the blanket. "Home."

"What? You would go back to that bastard, after all he has done?"

"Mast' make med'cine," Mary said very quietly. "Mast' make Jinks better."

"Oh, sweet Mary." A knot tightened in my chest. "If only it were possible."

"Mar' take care. Make better." She gazed up at me longingly. "Soon better."

"Mary, don't. It's too late. There is nothing anyone can do for him now."

Mary shook her head.

"No. Mar' help. Mar' mama for Jinks. Mama."

"Yes." I swallowed hard, and trying to smile, I reached out and took her hand. "You were a fine mother to him. No one could have loved him better. I am so sorry."

Mary stared at our hands, at our fingers plaited together.

"Mama. Make better."

"No." My mouth tasted of ash. "No. Mary, please, listen to me. Jinks is dead."

Mary turned over the package of our hands, twisting our wrists together. Then, slowly, she looked up.

"Dead," she echoed.

I nodded, not trusting myself to speak and squeezed her fingers.

"Jinks dead," she said again.

"Yes."

"In Par'dise."

I thought of Jinks's furtive attempts on the sugar loaf, the curl of his mothy tail as he scaled the dresser with a penny or a stolen teaspoon.

"Imagine Jinks with wings," I murmured. "There'll be no catching him now."

"Wings."

Mary leaned against me, her hand still woven in mine, and placed her head upon my shoulder.

"White feathered wings," I said. "Like a dove. And sugar for dinner every day."

"Yes. Ever' day."

"Feather beds too. From the angel wings. And—"

Her sudden yelp of pain startled us both.

"Clear out the bloody way, can't you? This is a thoroughfare, you smuts, not a bloody pleasure garden!"

The porter thrust his face so close to mine I could smell the Geneva water on his breath. His skin was porridgy with pockmarks, his handcart piled high with wooden tea chests. A row of iron nails bled rust into the raw wood. I pressed myself against the wall so that he might pass. He thrust the barrow angrily ahead of him as though it were a cudgel, muttering under his breath.

"Bloody doxies, clutterin' up the streets like they owned 'em—" He hawked noisily, despatching a bubbled pellet of saliva into the mud.

"In Paradise the spit is made of sugar water," I murmured to Mary. "And the mud is the thickest, sweetest chocolate you could ever imagine."

Mary's hand twitched in mine.

"And the porters—the porters push little monkeys round all day, wherever they wish to go, when their wings grow too tired to carry them."

"In Par'dise?"

"In Paradise. It sounds fine, doesn't it?"

We left the dead monkey in an orange box upon the steps of a small church near the river. The doors were locked and the stained brickwork exhaled an air of weary disuse, but Mary stood quietly, her head bowed, as I murmured a few words about committing the monkey's soul to God. She made no difficulty about leaving then but only tore a fragment from the blanket that wrapped the mutilated creature which she held to her lips as we walked. Her quiet endurance was more painful to observe than all of her extravagant grief. I held her hand tightly, as we walked northwards towards the Churchyard. It was perilous to go directly to the bookshop, for I thought it one of the first places they would seek us, but I could think of no other possibility. Mary grew tired; before long she would be hungry. We had no money for board or lodgings. It occurred to me that I might manage the interview with Mr. Honfleur better alone, but I dared not leave Mary anywhere in case she was not there when I returned.

And so we made our way together, with me glancing over my shoulder every few steps to check we were not followed. At the pump close by Fleet prison, we stopped so that I might wash from Mary's face and clothes the worst of the blood. The rain had stopped. The late sun spilled into the blue summer evening, reddening the roofs and polishing the bellies of the lingering clouds to gleaming copper. Somewhere, carelessly, birds sang.

The door to the bookshop was closed when we reached it, the shade pulled down, but a light burned within. Swallowing my trepidation, I raised my hand to knock. Beside me Mary sidled up to the bow window and pressed her face and hands hard against the thick panes. Frowning and snapping my fingers at her to summon her back to my side, I knocked.

"Mr. Honfleur? Are you there? I am sorry to trouble you so late, but—well, it is I, Eliza. If you are there, please open up!"

I heard the sound of footsteps inside the shop. Again I hissed at Mary, but she paid me no heed. There was no time to concern myself with it now. Taking a deep breath, I composed my face into a smile. I heard a cough before the shade snapped up and Mr. Honfleur peered out. His chin was faintly stubbled with grey, and crumbs gathered in the corners of his mouth. A wire-rimmed pair of spectacles rested upon his forehead. They winked in the light as he fumbled to open the door.

"Eliza?" he said, frowning sleepily at me. "What brings you here so late? I have been closed a full hour at least."

"Mr. Honfleur, I'm sorry but I had to come."

"Did you, indeed?" He looked suspiciously at Mary. "And whom, may I ask, do you bring with you? I would prefer it if she did not lick my windows. It does nothing to improve their efficiency."

"No. Of course. Come here, Mary. This is Mary. She works— that is, she was maid to the apothecary. With me."

Mary turned to face him. I watched his face change as he took in her face and then the great curve of her belly.

"For God's sake, have you taken leave of your senses? You bring a pregnant whatever it is she is—there is no husband, I assume? You bring her here, at night, to a respectable establishment? *Mon Dieu,* what were you thinking of?"

"I beg your pardon, sir. I did not know where else I might go. Mr. Black, he tries—he means to make a monster of it. Of the child. To put into his book. He—I fear it is already done. Inside her. Growing inside her. The thought of it—oh, Mr. Honfleur, sir, please, I beg you, if you have but the slightest affection for me, take pity on her."

"Not yet wed and already you would come here with your— this creature—and haggle with me like a fishwife? Eliza, I have misjudged you calamitously."

I bowed my head.

"I have not come to haggle, sir, but to throw myself on your mercy. You are a good man, a just man. I know you shall direct me as to what is best to be done."

"I shall, indeed. You shall take that girl back to her master, where she belongs. The apothecary may be a philanderer as well as a fool, but what he elects to do or not to do in the privacy of his own house is a matter of concern only to his wife and to God."

"But what if he succeeds, if he has made a monkey of it?" I whispered. "What then? I—I have seen the pictures. It cannot be imagined."

"A monkey."

"She was ill and the master said he gave it to her to restore her spirits, but—oh God—she loved it like a child. And he urged her on, wants her only to—oh, sir, he did such terrible things, monstrous things, why, I have never told you, but when I—and then he killed it. He killed it. So that the grief might—might force itself upon the child. Look at her, sir. She is quite undone."

Honfleur regarded Mary as she breathed upon the glass and drew patterns with a wet fingertip. Sighing, he crossed his arms.

"So your master seeks to create his own monster?" Honfleur mused. "It is a fascinating idea, but I hardly think the old dog capable of such ingenuity. The man is a dullard, scarcely competent to render the ideas of others in intelligible prose."

"You are wrong, sir! I mean—there have been others."

Even as I clamped my mouth shut, the chasm opened before me, leaving me dizzy with the terrible proximity of it.

"Others?"

"I—I think so."

"But you have never seen them?"

Miserably I shook my head.

"But you saw him kill this—this monkey?"

"No, sir," I whispered. "He claimed it for thieves."

"So the sum of your proof is that he gave your idiot friend here a monkey as a plaything and that the poor creature died?"

I stared at the floor.

"And you consider *her* imagination unhealthily inflamed? You have built quite an edifice of presumption from an act of kindness, would you not agree?"

Still I said nothing. Mr. Honfleur sighed.

"Take the girl home," he commanded. "If the child she carries is indeed your master's, then let him disentangle himself from the fix as well as he is able. I am weary of obliging the cantankerous old bastard. His wife shall doubtless take the news ill. As for me, I shall, I fear, take some small pleasure in witnessing his mortification."

"But—please, might she not stay here, if only for a few days? With Annette gone, you surely require a servant, and she works hard—"

"Enough!"

Mr. Honfleur uncrossed his arms. His face was grim.

"For all your youth and inexperience, you are, I am sure, sufficiently artful to know what a fragile creature is fortuity. It is unwise for a woman whose dowry resides all in her amiability to prove perversely troublesome, Eliza. Now go home."

It must have been my fear for Mary that made me reckless. I ploughed on.

"Mr. Honfleur, sir, I do not mean to vex you, I swear it, but if I might only ask for a little money, against my share of the profit from the Febrifuge—"

"Eliza!" Anger slammed the word shut. "Hold your tongue! I have given you my decision. Now cease in your insolence this moment or, God help me, I shall silence you myself!"

I hung my head. There was nothing else to be done.

"I—forgive me, sir," I whispered, curtsying before him. "I—I have vexed you abominably. I never wished to—I—please, forgive me. I beg you. I beg you."

"Eliza," he said sadly. "Why do you seek to try me?"

I swallowed.

"Forgive me, sir," I whispered.

"There shall be no more of these—these fantasies, you hear? As for that poor creature, you shall return her to Swan-street directly. I desire no further quarrel with your master."

Honfleur pressed his fingers into his eyes. Then he sighed.

"Then the matter is complete. Doubtless your master shall punish you as he sees fit. Endure it without complaint for my sake, for it shall make a wiser woman of you. It is your good fortune that it is not in my nature to harbour resentments. In my turn, I trust that you have learned a valuable lesson. From henceforth I shall hope to see a great deal less impetuousness in you and considerably more discretion. Now since you are here, you may take a book to your master and leave me to my supper before it is grown quite cold. I shall expect you tomorrow at a more reputable time."

He smiled a little then, shaking his head in reproof, and ducked into the shop to fetch the book. When he held it out to me, I took his hand and pressed my lips against his fingers. The Huguenot did not press his advantage, although he squeezed my waist a little.

"Oh, I almost forgot. Your master's apprentice came to see me yesterday. Weak-looking fellow, is he not? But then your master was never much of a judge of a man's character. I fear he has wasted his time with that one."

"What—what was it he wanted?"

"He did not say. Only that he wished to make my acquaintance. Since I have rarely seen a man less interested in books, I can only hope he has been charged with the clearing up of your master's accounts. So. Off you go. Tomorrow then," he said, and his tone was almost gay.

"Tomorrow," I echoed.

When I led Mary away across the dusky Churchyard, her hand tight in mine, he had the delicacy to look away.

To Jewkes at Jermyn-street

listen to me, you bastard, you bring her back here do you understand me you have no claim upon her you signed her over, you & that ruthless wife of yours you could not be rid of her quick enough then, remember? well, do you remember?

she is my property mine alone you hear in the eyes of the law & in the sight of god her & all that is in her all of it I have it signed & witnessed damn you you vile & plaguey thief bring her back or like a common thief I shall see you hung i swear it be glad 'tis only theft I threaten when the king himself discovers your treachery you may be sure it shall be <u>treason</u>

i should have known you would betray me you pox-ridden parvenu it is all profit & loss with your kind no number of south sea millions could make gentlemen of any of you fine porcelain could never be fashioned from such vulgar clay

bring her back she is all I have left what use do you have for her except to spite me she has only ever been a source of shame to your family shame & mortification shall you now betray everything I have laboured for given my life for i shall not let you destroy my legacy i shall see you dead first dead, do you hear me BRING HER BACK SHE IS <u>MINE</u>

GB

XXXVII

Mr. Honfleur assisted us in one way, though he would have been dismayed to know it. Before it could grow warm in my hand, I sold the book he gave me for my master to a merchant in a courtyard at the dingy end of Paternoster-row whose grimy window resembled nothing so much as the press of a slovenly man, its curtain drawn back to reveal a discarded jumble of worn coats and cracked shoes and wigs with the locks all askew. In amongst the chipped shaving cups and threadbare neck-cloths, I could make out a handful of dog-eared volumes, but I chose it mainly because it seemed the kind of establishment that would be quite invisible to a man of the Hugue-not's education and sensibilities. At the end of the narrow yard, the low windows of a tavern spilled light and rough laughter into the deepening gloom. The raucous swagger in it put me in mind of Edgar. But I could not think of Edgar, not yet. One matter at a time, I told myself, or else I would go mad.

I sat Mary upon a doorstep in a shadowed corner as far from the tavern as I could contrive it and, kissing her, bid her not to move from her position upon any account but only to watch the shop. I would be back for her as soon as my business was complete. Dumb with fatigue, her shoulders slumped in piteous submission, she obeyed me. When, upon reaching the door, I turned to look at her, she was already almost asleep, her pale cheek propped against the crumbling brick. The proprietor—a man in a greasy velvet cap and the distrustful expression of a habitual swindler who, expecting al-ways to be swindled in return, is ready to be outraged by the men-dacity of his fellow man—glanced at the book's several plates with careful indifference and offered me a shilling for it. When I declared it was worth ten times that much, he only shrugged and declared his customers not greatly interested in book-learning. All the same, I observed how he kept his hands locked together beneath his chin and his index fingers against his lips, as though uneasy that, unconstrained, they might betray him, and though it was almost night and I was in no position to negotiate, I demanded two and held his gaze without blinking. The proprietor was the first to look away. With a half-hearted exhibition of indignation and much satisfied muttering about thieves and charlatans, he paid almost what I asked.

It was the taller of the two men I saw first, for he stood directly before Mary, his gait unsteady and both hands occupied in a drunken tussle with the front of his britches. His coarse laughter was a boast that rose vertiginously even as I ran across the yard, catching him off guard and sending him staggering into the wall.

"Poxy—whore!" he slurred, sliding unsteadily to a squat, and I saw, between his fingers, his slack member from which issued, down his leg, a steady stream of piss. In the doorway behind him, his associate issued a screaming bark of amusement. He held Mary's head in his lap and her jaw open, as an animal's jaw might be kept open, by exerting the pressure of his fingertips at its hinge, but Mary did not struggle. She did not even look afraid. Instead, though her eyes were opened, I almost thought she slept, so blank and sealed was her gaze. Only her tongue moved, its rigid tip circling her lips like the hand of a clock.

Pulling back my fist, I struck the seated man full in the face. He stared at me in perfect astonishment before expelling a kind of breathless whimper and falling backwards so that he struck his head with a dull thud against the door. Seizing Mary's hand, I dragged her upwards. The other man lunged at me as I passed, but gin dulled his instincts and weakened his grip, and he only sprawled upon the ground, expelling his slurred curses into the summer dust.

We passed that first night in a chop-house near the Strand that advertised itself by means of signs in the grimy windows as both cheap and late to close, and then, at the recommendation of a fellow diner when we were at last required to leave there, in a coffee-house that opened before dawn to serve the river trade. As we staggered through the grey early morning, our limbs strange with weariness, I glanced about me, fearful every minute of seeing Edgar or Mrs. Black coming towards us through the crowds. A girl of Mary's description might be easily identified, but at least here no one troubled to notice us. The wharves and landing-stages swarmed with people, stumbling beneath their bales and barrels like scuttling crustaceans. Chains and ropes clanked and shrieked as casks and crates and huge coarse sacks were sucked from the jetties into the dark narrow spaces between the warehouses. Porters shouted and swore. Amongst the frenzy of activity, the stores and mills seemed to press closer to the water, reaching out towards the scramble of boats as though they would swallow them whole.

At the coffee-house I bought bread and a cup each of small ale, though Mary looked longingly at the bacon, and we ate and drank in silence, watching the hurried comings and goings of the other occupants, heads bowed beneath the low ceiling. It was a busy-enough place, and its regulars too set in their habits, for our presence to elicit more than brief flickers of curiosity, but I sought out a small table at the back all the same, away from the fire, where we might attract little attention or animosity. In the doorway a pair of ragged chimney-sweeps, refused entry, waited as the girl brought them their breakfast, wrapped in grease-pearled paper. They twirled their brushes as they shambled away, rousing a burst of protests from the mob outside.

I think we slept a little, propped together as the wall exhaled its chill breath into our backs. Certainly when we emerged, day had taken hold and the dawn wharves had hardened into something more commonplace. I wrapped Mary's face in her shawl, so that her features might be obscured, and hunched my shoulders as we hurried north, staying away from the main thoroughfares.

We had spent as parsimoniously as I could contrive it, and already I had parted with almost a shilling. Along with the money in my dress, our savings might last us four or five days, a week if we were careful and did not care for hunger or a place to sit or to sleep. I thought of the man in the alley the night before, taking aim while his friend held Mary's mouth open in readiness, and I squeezed Mary's arm so that she turned and blinked at me.

"Home," she murmured, but it was no longer a question, and the word caught in the folds of her shawl, heavy and without hope.

It was the only other place I could think of to go.

Little-whalebone-court was a sliced-off corner of Drury-lane, tucked between a tavern with the sign of the Crossed Keys and a sag-roofed stable. I could hear the horses whinnying and thrashing in their stalls as we passed through the slit of an entranceway, navigating the mahogany-stained puddles and scattered hillocks of straw-bristled manure. Beyond the stable the courtyard opened to the sky, but you would never have known it. The yard was criss-crossed with ropes and ropes of wet laundry, rising up in layers like the drapery of an elaborate tent so that, for all the harsh brightness of the day, the light in the courtyard had a vaporous quality, as though we stood inside a cloud. Beside me, the crumbling brick wall echoed with the sharp hollow blows of horses' hooves striking wood, sending the taut-stretched sheets and cloths into a dance of shivers and jerks. Dark petals of water lay strewn across the dusty ground.

Pushing a sheet aside, I ducked beneath the line. The linen sweated the sour stink of lye.

"Hung'y," Mary muttered mulishly.

"Mary, you cannot be!" Anxiety had me speak more harshly than I intended. I sighed. "Come, let me get what I am come for. Then we shall find you something to eat. Although if we are to make do at all, you shall have to learn to manage on less. You have the appetite of an elephant."

I pushed aside another sheet, holding it up so that Mary might pass beneath it. There were beads of water caught in her coppery hair. I smoothed them out with my hand as she bent under my arm. The damp hair was darker and clung in sparse tendrils to the shape of her head, exposing the pale wax of her scalp.

"All is going to be well," I murmured, and hiding my hands in my armpits, I crossed all of my fingers.

The laundry occupied a narrow steam-filled room at the rear corner of the courtyard. Piles of dirty sheets and cloths drifted like city snow against the long wall, while all about the room were baskets and barrels of cambrics and muslins and Holland shirts and other small linens, both dry and damp. Two girls of perhaps six or seven years old stirred at coppers of linen with long wooden poles, their bare feet straining upwards from their three-legged stools so that they might keep from scalding their elbows on the hot metal. Another girl, a little older, rubbed with soap at a ruffled collar thrown over a low table. The wooden tub beside her, which reached to her waist at least, overflowed with soiled linens. Behind her a fourth girl, smaller and slighter than the others but with a feverish flush to her cheeks, pumped at a handle that passed wet pieces of cloth between two great wooden rollers, squeezing the water in a steady stream onto the puddled brick floor.

The laundress was a glint-eyed woman with a high forehead and a choleric complexion coarsened by steam and lye. She was young, though, and vain enough to dispense with an apron so that her neat waist might be displayed to advantage. Her perse petticoat was streaked with spattered stripes the colour of thrushes' eggs. When I asked if the mountebank's clown still lodged there, she wiped her nose on the back of her raw red hand and sucked at the gaps between her teeth as though they were sugar plums.

"You mean Petey Smart?" She looked me up and down disparagingly, as if I were a stained neck-cloth. "'E ain't 'ere."

"Will—will he be back?"

"What am I, 'is blinkin' keeper? Gawd almighty. As if I don't 'ave my fill of witless little doxies wastin' my time already." She clapped sharply at the girls. "What you gawpin' at? Heads down, unless you want to miss yer dinners."

"Dinners," echoed Mary longingly as she stalked away. "Wan' dinners."

The girl at the table tittered and ducked her head at her friends, damp strings of hair catching in her mouth.

"Thirst'," Mary muttered, tugging at my arm.

"I know, I know. Just one moment, while I—" I pressed my knuckles against my forehead, kneading my temples, but no thoughts came.

"Thirst'," she pleaded, and her face crumpled. "Thirst', Lize."

"Here."

I looked up. One of the laundry girls stood shyly before us, holding out a dipper of water. Before I could thank her, she had slipped away. I waited while Mary drank. Then I took the dipper back into the laundry. The steam clung to my hair as I thanked the girl for her kindness.

"Petey Smart, does he still lodge here? I—I'm trying to find him."

The girl nodded but jerked her head towards the door.

"Go, can't you?" she muttered. "Or she'll have us, just like she said. Since the last girl upped and went, she don't let up on us what's left, not even for a minute. There's more work than twice of us can do."

When I presented the two of us for hire, the laundress laughed derisively. She had only a position for one, she sneered, and she would take neither an idiot nor a strumpet neither, for she disliked the quick-witted impudence of the street girl just as much as she abhorred the slowness of the simple-minded.

I bore her insults without flinching. Instead, I suggested that we might share the position between us, each one offsetting the excesses and insufficiencies of the other. Two girls, paid the same as one, would work harder, I reasoned, being seldom fatigued. The laundress snorted, but as she watched Mary turn the handle of the mangle, her eyes were dark with calculation and her tongue worked busily between her teeth. She could not deny that we were strong and the work simple, mostly a matter of turning the handle and making up the lye.

It was fortunate for us that the laundry-woman was one of those kind of women who was quite incapable of refusing a bargain, however much its terms offended her. I was to bring the idiot to the wash-house at dawn to ensure her punctual arrival; tardiness would not be tolerated. I would then work from the two o'clock bells until the night's work was complete. The idiot would be required to make herself scarce at those times; she would not have her fooling around and distracting us from our work. I looked at Mary then and the thought of her fooling around leaked a warm patch of wistfulness against my chest.

The laundress saw my face and frowned. Plain meals would be provided, though, as two halves of a single worker, she would provide only one between us. There would be meat once a week and small beer to drink. There was no room for us to lodge at the laundry but we might find accommodation in a rooming-house known to the laundress in the lanes east of the Tower, close by the wharf they called Cole-harbour. It was a considerable walk away, but the rent was cheap and the landlord incurious. I hesitated. Lodgings at the Tower would require us to pass close by Swan-street every day. We could not risk it.

"Please, madam," I begged her. "Let us sleep here. We want for very little."

"Fink you can 'aggle wiv me, do yer? Go on, then. Go on and 'aggle yerself right out of a position an' all."

I was silent. The laundress narrowed her eyes, crossing her arms over her chest. The pay would just about cover the cost of our lodgings with a bit over for necessaries. I hesitated only for a moment. Then I accepted. Spitting on her hand, the laundress had me shake it to seal the agreement.

Nothing was said of Mary's condition, though it was impossible she had failed to notice it. Still, keen perception was a gift of little value to a washerwoman of no particular scruple who had secured herself a pair of good workers at negligible expense.

Hewlitt & Bain, Solicitors at Law, Newcastle

Dear Sir,

We are obliged by our client to communicate to you the extent of his displeasure at your extraordinary letter.

It is unclear from the raft of reckless accusations contained within that injudicious document whether you meant to issue an apology or to seek one. However, from a legal standpoint, the terms of the contract could hardly be clearer. Upon acceptance of our client's exceptionally generous terms, you undertook to guarantee that the girl might be retained in secure lodgings & on no account to be permitted to return to the parish of her birth. That you have in all likelihood failed in that undertaking is a matter for serious & immediate concern.

Our client has therefore required that it be made clear to you that it is <u>your full & lawful responsibility</u> to locate the girl at the first opportunity & effect her secure restoration at your establishment. Should you fail to do so, he shall not hesitate to seek reparation for any losses sustained due to the dereliction of the lawful duties detailed in the contract signed by both parties, by whatever means deemed necessary.

I am, Sir, yours &c.,

NICHOLAS HEWLITT

XXXVIII

We made sure to walk to Cole-harbour the long way, by way of Bed-lam and the stinking market at Smithfield. Even so I kept my head bowed as we hastened along, my skin prickling with the fear of discovery. When a harassed clerk pushed past me at London-wall, I was so convinced that he was Edgar that I cried out. It was only when we were past the Tower and lost in the maze of tiny alleys behind Radcliffe-highway that I considered us tolerably safe. It was impossible to imagine anyone respectable in a place like that.

The house itself was a ramshackle structure built of yellow brick, slimy to the touch. Towards noon, as the sun grew stronger, it exhaled a powerful smell of stale fish. Several of its windows were boarded up. The room we were offered was damp and dark, a narrow slice of the second storey that looked out directly onto the coal-stained wall of its taller neighbour, with only enough room between the two of them to accommodate the span of my hand and the mudflat reek of the river. It was furnished only with a straw-filled mattress and an ancient tea chest with a plank for a lid. Canvas was pinned across the window where once there had been glass. I took comfort in its gloominess. Matters might be managed here in a manner that could not be stomached in sunlight.

Once we had given the landlord what he asked to secure the room, we had no money left for food but we slept heavily, too bone-weary to be disturbed by the infestations of the palliasse. The next day, as agreed, I walked Mary to Little-whalebone-court some minutes after five in the morning. The houses were shuttered, breath-less with sleep. As we passed the Tower, we heard the fretful roar of the lions confined behind its thick stone walls.

I meant to walk a little, so that I might compose myself before going to the bookseller's. I knew what it was that I had to do. I would bow my head in shame and remorse, and along with a few tears and the humble admission that I did not deserve his clemency, I would beg his forgiveness. When he reprimanded me, as he most certainly would, I would hang my head and accept it all.

Mrs. Eliza Honfleur. Three weeks and five days.

Somehow, though, the hours skittered away. I walked west towards Westminster where everything was unfamiliar, scratching the bites on my arms and neck and watching the traffic. Around me on water and on land, boats and men and horses and waggons moved vigorously, purposefully, in no doubt of where it was they were going. When I grew tired, I sat on a wharf, my legs drifting like weeds from the damp wood, until a bargeman barked at me for blocking his mooring. I thought of Edgar pressing his fat hand into the Huguenot's long-fingered one, the smile pressing into his puffy cheeks and lighting up his sucked-bone eyes, and I hugged my knees against my chest and pressed the tips of my fingers into my eyes. Close by a group of ragged children played in the dust, their faces sunk with hunger. When I gave them half of the slice of bread I had bought for my breakfast, they fell upon it like rats.

When I returned to the laundry at two o'clock, the washerwoman hustled me into the laundry room, nodding at Mary's back, bent over the copper in the boiling room.

"She'll do," she conceded. "She's slow but she'll do."

"And today she will do no more. You shan't have both of us, not for the price of only one."

The laundress frowned. Then, snapping her fingers, she instructed Mary to give me her oiled apron. Mary blinked with fatigue as she fumbled with the strings. Her hair hung in dark tails about her face, and her hands were red and chapped from the lye. I took one in mine.

"Poor Mary. When there is time, I shall make up something to soothe the skin."

"Came?"

"Me? Of course I came. Wait for me where I can watch you. I shall be done before long."

"Came," Mary repeated, and her eyes filled with tears.

"Oh, Mary. You shall not have to do this much longer, I promise you. I promise you."

The work at the laundry was back-breaking and numbingly repetitive. It cracked and blistered our hands, shrivelling the skin to fish scales, and cramped our shoulders until we could barely lift our arms. The meals were plain, but there was enough bread, and I tried to sneak sufficient scraps into my apron to give Mary something of a supper when at last I was finished. We hardly talked, but I watched the way our feet struck the twilight roads in an unspoken rhythm and it consoled me. At night, on the lice-ridden mattress, her sticky breath stitched itself through my dreams. Sometimes she cried out in her sleep, and the creature in her belly writhed and jumped, but it did not come. I turned my back on it then and closed my eyes. I did not talk to her about the child or about the terrors of confinement or what we would do when the creature came. I had never attended any birth, except one, and had only the vaguest notion of how such a terrible miracle was managed. What did I know, whose only rehearsal for the delivering of an infant was a wrenching, drowning, blood-slippery scream of pain? There was no purpose in frightening her, in frightening myself. There was time enough for that, when things were more settled.

One matter at a time.

On the morning of the third day, I forced myself to go to the bookseller's. As I walked, I rehearsed my apologies: I wanted to come before, but my mistress had not permitted it. I had not dared to show my face, so ashamed was I of my disgraceful conduct. For three days I had wept inconsolably, terrified that, through my own thoughtlessness, I had put in jeopardy a marriage that meant more to me than life itself. And with each pace, I grew more certain that when I got there I would find Mrs. Black behind the counter, her hands crossed like blades over her lap.

I could feel the sting of the birch on my palms as I rattled the handle. The door did not open. When I looked closer, I saw that the window shade was pulled and a sign propped behind it declaring the shop temporarily closed. I gazed at my distorted reflection in the thick panes of the window and saw the rawness of my skin, the draggled dullness of my hair, the crumpled disorder of my cap robbed of starch by the ceaseless steam. My skirts were dusty and stained with dirty water, my hands red and itchy. There was nothing about me of a bookseller's wife, nothing at all. I did not look up at the Cathedral as I pushed my way out of the Churchyard, the lye stink of me hot in my nostrils, but fled to Drury-lane, where the hunched press of houses had a dirty and defeated look, and dirty and defeated people hunched as they hurried along the dusty alleys, unjudged and unnoticed.

It was a windless day, and the curtains of linen hung sullenly from their lines. I called out to Mary, who turned the handle of the mangle in laborious circles, her face shiny with sweat. When she saw me, she straightened up and, kneading at her sore shoulders, came out into the courtyard, blinking her welcome. Then, abruptly, she looked up, covering her mouth with one hand and pointing above my head. I turned. Behind me the sheets cracked and billowed, marked with faint shadow like spilled ash as, along the lines, the clown's monkey darted and swung. It wore its red velvet cloak, but instead of a hat, it wore around its head a lace handkerchief which it clasped beneath its chin with one hand. Then a hand sprang up and snatched the creature down.

"Bad boy," the clown chided. "Give me that."

The monkey clucked at him, tweaking his nose. Mary laughed, a spluttering snort behind her fingers. Both clown and monkey turned.

"Hello," I said shyly.

The clown's brow creased. Then he smiled. As for the monkey, it dropped the lace handkerchief upon its master's head and, leaping to Mary's shoulder, wrapped her coppery hair round its fingers and crooned in her ear. The clown clicked his tongue, calling for it to come, but it paid him no heed. Instead, very gently, the monkey rubbed its whiskery cheek against Mary's pale one. Mary squeezed her eyes shut, her fists opening and closing at her sides.

"Jinks," she breathed.

"His name is Jabba," the clown told her, looking sideways at me. "He likes you. I have never seen him so affectionate with a stranger. What is your name?"

She did not answer.

"This is Mary," I told him.

"Your sister?"

"No. Though I would think myself fortunate if she were. She is my friend."

The clown looked at Mary and smiled, holding out an apple. The monkey bounced eagerly, its hand extended, but still it did not go to its master.

"He does not wish to be parted from you, Mary. Shall you help me feed him?"

He skinned the apple expertly, a curl of peel spiralling from his knife. He held it out to the monkey, who, tearing it in two, offered one half to Mary.

"And you," he said, slicing the apple flesh into pieces. "I do not know your name either."

"I am Eliza."

"Eliza. And what brings you to Little-whalebone-court, Eliza?"

I shrugged, smiling slightly. The clown smiled back. He had a kind face.

"Fate," I said quietly. "And penury."

When at last my work was done, Mary and I walked together in silence down towards the river. The summer night was purple-dark, but on Bishopsgate-street we saw a pedlar selling birds in the light of an oil-lamp. They were a wretched lot, their feathers dull and patchy, but Mary crept towards them, pushing her fingers through the bars of the cage and chirruping softly. The birds shifted on their perches, sending up a miserable creaking. The pedlar frowned. Idiots were bad for business.

"Buy," Mary begged, and she pointed to a bird which cowered at the back of the cage, its abject demeanour quite at odds with the violent scarlet of its feathers.

"How can we?" I scorned. "We have barely enough money to eat."

Mary wriggled her finger. The bird buried its face in its wing.

"Buy," she said again, more urgently.

"Why, Mary, it is nothing but an ordinary pigeon coloured red and half-dead at that. Whatever could you want with it?"

Mary's hand tightened round the bars of the cage and her shoulders shook. I touched her gently on the arm, coaxing her away. When at last she relinquished the cage, the palm was striped pink.

"Hur'," she wept, and she rocked, pounding her fists against her chest. "Hur', Lize."

I held her tightly then, my cheek against her sticky one, and the desire for vengeance flushed my cheeks.

"I know," I murmured. "I know."

"Yer buyin' or not?" grumbled the pedlar.

Gently I took Mary's hand and pulled her away from the birdcage.

"Come, let us go home. And how about sausage for supper?" I said recklessly.

"Saus'? For me?"

"Yes, for you. Oh, Mary, I will set things right, I swear it."

Above me, beyond the shadowed jut of a roof, something flashed in the early evening sun. I did not have to look up to know it for the golden cross of the Cathedral. I had not seen it for weeks but it was always there, presiding over the metropolis with its ever-vigilant eye. There was no happening, however secretive or insignificant, to which it failed to bear witness. It saw everything, heard everything. Just as its creamy stone absorbed the city's foul air, assimilating its greasy soot into its bones, so, too, did that vast gilded cavern of an interior sop up all the fiendish vitality of the city, each foul thought or evil deed tarnishing a length of altar rail or flaking away at the angels that crowned its elegant colonnades.

Buildings should aim for eternity.

It would not bring the Cathedral down, the stench and corruption of a million lives ill-lived. On the contrary, it seemed to me that the Cathedral gained its strength from the squalor around it, each day sending its roots deeper into the tainted London soil, while above it, like a great lung, the dome filled magnificently with each and every foul-smelling exhalation, from the strident obscenities of the watermen and the shrieks of the robbed to the curses of murderers, the murmured whispers of confession, the rustles of bills and paper money. Sustained by the rich and abundant nourishment of London's sins, the Cathedral would surely outlive eternity itself.

I looked up at the cross without blinking, until the dazzle of it burned a hole in my skull. When at last I closed my eyes, it branded the darkness, two fiery unflinching bars of red.

"Now come," I said briskly, taking Mary by the hand. "I am ravenous."

she is gone quite gone no trace of her left

it is over

a single tide shall wipe my footprints from the sand
no mark no shadow
no one to remember
the tide comes i can see the foam of it upon the horizon
then nothing

it is in the striving that we find salvation not in the success
the grand task of life is preparing for death a life well lived in the
service of the lord
he does not judge us by our worldly triumphs but by our fitness for
heaven

oh god how may it be borne

XXXIX

The next day I went again to the Churchyard. Outside the west front of the Cathedral, I paused to smooth the chopped ends of my hair into my cap and taking the ring from the hem of my sleeve, forced it back over the knuckle of my finger. It shone unnaturally yellow in the flat grey light. Before the western entrance, a group of prosperous-looking gentlemen conversed in an unfamiliar guttural tongue, their complacent expressions at odds with the harshness of their language. Above them St. Paul gazed down from his pediment, holding aloft the sword that would be the instrument of his own execution, the dome swelling self-importantly behind him.

On the other side of the Churchyard, a woman in a dark mantua stopped, turning to look in my direction. Her profile was sharp, the pinch of her waist narrow as a girl's. For a moment I stood frozen, unable to move. Placing her basket upon the ground, the woman lifted her hands, tipping her head backwards so that she might adjust her hat. Not Mrs. Black but a young woman, perhaps twenty years old.

My stomach twisted, my bladder seized with an urgent need to piss. My knees trembled as I squatted in the shadow of a buttress, the books balanced in my lap. The urine mapped a brisk path through the mud, splattering warm droplets against my calves. Smoothing down my skirts, I pinched my cheeks to lend them a little colour, and adopting an expression I hoped both modest and blithe, I strolled through the Churchyard and pushed open the door to Mr. Honfleur's shop.

As soon as I saw him, I knew that something was terribly wrong. I smiled with stiff cheeks, my heart pressed up against my ribs.

"I am glad to see you," I gabbled. "I want to beg your pardon for what happened. I was wrong to ask you, to bring her here—I would have come before, but Mrs. Black is grown most suspicious. She suspects us, I think, though I do not know how. But then I should not be surprised if she were possessed of some dark power of prophesy. She has a great deal of the witch about her, don't you think?"

The words withered upon my tongue, desiccated by Mr. Honfleur's grim face. I swallowed, bowing my head.

"I—I have come to beseech your forgiveness," I said quietly.

"So I see."

The shop looked dusty and unkempt, piles of books stacked higgledy-piggledy upon the floor. The table bore traces of several meals, dirty cups and dishes stacked together with old crusts of bread and yellowing bacon rind, the wood grained with sticky marks.

"Mrs. Black visited me yesterday," he said.

I said nothing but clutched at the table, suddenly dizzy.

"She was considerably distressed," he went on in the same flat voice. "She wished to know if I had seen you. When I said I had not, she informed me that you had been missing since Thursday last. That you had stolen from them irreplaceable property of prodigious value and vanished. That you were nothing but a common criminal and that they meant to see you hanged."

"If it is the book—"

"She made no mention of any book."

I said nothing but stared at the table, tracing with one finger the pale circle of a cup mark. The gold ring flashed.

"I fail to understand what it is you intend, Eliza. Perhaps you would be kind enough to enlighten me." He crossed his arms. "No? Very well, then, let me tell you something instead. You shall return the apothecary's property to him today. Today, *vous comprenez*? This nonsense must end. Then we shall decide how best to deal with you."

"But—"

"My terms are plain. If you fail to observe them, our contract is broken. Is that what you wish for?"

Still I did not speak. I could think of nothing to say.

"Come, Eliza, surely you can do better than that. You have acted unlawfully and against my express command. You are fortunate I do not throw you out this instant. The very least you can do is to fall to your knees and plead mercy."

"Forgive me," I whispered, not looking at him.

"Mrs. Black made it clear to me that it is the idiot they want. Only the idiot. Should you return her unharmed, the matter shall end there. They shall take no further action. I trust you concede the generosity of such an offer."

"Yes, sir."

"You are fortunate, too, that I consider it time that my business arrangement with the apothecary be terminated and that another condition of the girl's return is the payment in full of their outstanding account. As it is, I blame that man for most of this madness. It would appear that, not content with taking leave of his own senses with the idiot girl, he has taken those of all his household with him. The sooner you are removed from Swan-street the better." His lips curved. "A wiser man would doubtless turn you out and congratulate himself upon a narrow escape. I trust that you appreciate the extent of my generosity. My affection for you renders me foolish."

I managed a nod.

"Good. Now if you would be so kind, I will have that ring." He gestured at my finger. "You shall have it back when I receive assurance that the idiot girl has been returned to her rightful place."

I swallowed.

"Please, Mr. Honfleur. I beg you, have pity on her. On us both."

"What did you say?"

His voice was low, the blade of his anger still half-sheathed as he leaned over the table towards me. I raised my head and looked at him. My eyes felt hot. This was my chance. Surely, so long as I took care to describe everything exactly, the Frenchman could not help but feel sympathy. He was a good man, a just man. More than that, he was an educated man, steeped in the wisdom and compassion of the greatest writers of all civilisation. He knew the obligations placed upon humankind by the requisites of morality, of humanity, of the simple absolutes of love. He of all men would understand that I could never leave her. It was simply a matter of explaining it properly.

I took a deep breath, my hands clasped before me, aware that of all the words I had ever uttered in my life, these were the only ones that truly mattered.

The bookseller's face tightened ominously.

"Well?"

"Nothing, sir," I muttered. "I said nothing."

To John Black at the sign of the Scroll & Feather, Newcastle

Dear John,

I fear that this is hardly the letter you hoped for. Your brother is dying. He has battled ferociously with his illness for many months, but it would seem that, in recent days, he has lost the will to continue his fight & he weakens with every passing day. It is therefore my duty to request of you that you make the journey to London with all haste. It would give him great comfort to bid you a final farewell.

Your letters have made no attempt to conceal the extent of your rage & bitterness towards your brother. A man is fortunate if, at the close of his life, he may seek the forgiveness of those he has wronged. But though there are others against whom he has sinned most grievously, your brother has not done so with you. It is not towards Grayson that you should direct your invective but towards myself. So that he might be spared the burden of your financial difficulties, given the extremities of our own, I have burned your letters before he might see them. Blame me. All his life my husband could deny you nothing.

I do not regret my decisions for myself. It is some time since Grayson's health permitted the judicious consideration of matters pertaining to money & business. However, aware as I am of his particular fondness for you, I cannot allow for him to pass from this world in the shadow of your undeserved censure. My conscience is burden enough already.

I can send no money for your journey, but I would ask you to come to London all the same, for your brother's sake. If this is impossible, a loving letter would suffice.

I am &c.,

MARGARET BLACK

XL

One matter at a time.

After that I kept Mary close, hurrying her through the streets before sun-up or after dark, when we might not be seen. I told myself that Mrs. Black would never find us, either at Cole-harbour or at the laundry, hidden in its secret courtyard, but I was careful all the same. I had Mary remain in the room when I went for food, my shawl over my head despite the summer heat. In the afternoons she stayed where I could see her, playing with Petey's monkey while he went in search of work. Her belly had grown suddenly enormous, its bulk pulling her off balance. I watched her as I worked, and I knew it would not be much longer.

I did not go to the Churchyard again. When I thought of my marriage and the graze of the bookseller's ring over my knuckle, it was without regret but rather with a kind of incurious bewilderment. My recollections had the elusive half-remembered flavour of a dream, the Huguenot's face at once close to mine and at the same time blurring and becoming, with the ease and logic of dreams, the face of Edgar or of the dead monkey.

One matter at a time.

It was five days before the festival of St. Bartholomew, a little before three in the morning, that Mary was seized with violent contractions. It was a warm night, the shadows rendered harsh by the glare of a round white moon, and in bed beside me, Mary gave off more heat than a bread oven. For hours I had drifted in and out of sleep, my dreams restless with a woman I knew to be Annette, though she had the face of Mrs. Dormer, dressed in a mantua with a skirt of scarlet silk and a pale gold bodice tied with scarlet ribbons. As soon as I heard her cry out, I knew that it was time. Reaching beneath the mattress, I fastened my hare's foot around her neck. She sat bolt upright, her arms clutched around her belly.

Holding tightly to her hand, encouraging her to breathe, I struggled to keep my face steady. The preparations had all been made. We would manage perfectly well. The laundress, for all that she remained resolutely blind to Mary's condition, had, little by little, allowed us to accumulate a small collection of scraps and rags that she had no use for. These we had boiled and dried and wrapped in a piece of muslin so that they might remain clean. We were fortunate, too, that the clown, lonely without Aengus, had become a regular visitor to Cole-harbour, bringing food for supper and sometimes even wine too, the dregs of which I saved so that I might have something to give Mary after her delivery. Without his kindness, we would have been more frequently hungry. Beside the door I set at the ready a pail of water from the river. The bucket's muddy exhalations flavoured the air, intimating themselves into the lye smell of our hair.

When the first pains began, it was terrible to witness her distress. She clutched at me, certain she was dying. As her labour progressed and the contractions came harder and more closely together, she clawed at her belly as an animal caught in a trap may bite at its own leg, as though she might tear the source of her agony directly from her body.

I could do little but wipe the perspiration from her brow and urge her to greater endurance, all the time praying that the birth be straightforward. I dared not call a midwife. She would require the identity of the father, so that the child might not become a burden on the parish. The more officious of the breed might even demand that the father be summoned and brought to the room during labour to confess his misconduct. As for the child itself—

No, I could have no witnesses. I thought of Cain, of Herod, of the Pharaohs of Egypt, all twisting in Hell like chickens on a spit, and I was grateful for the wall that stood outside the window of our room at Cole-harbour, obscuring any glimpse of the dome. Sometimes I felt God's hot breath upon my neck, thicker and saltier still than the smell of the river, but though it made me shiver, I did not doubt what I must do. A monster-child would make a monster of its mother, a brace of curiosities to be chained up and carved open and cackled over by boy-men disguised as scholars, their fingers greased with duck fat so that they might thrust them in more easily. Moon-calf mother and monkey boy. Fairground freaks, the pair of them, to be stared at for a sixpence. For a shilling you might jab at them with a stick and marvel as they moaned, weeping tears so lifelike they were almost human.

It happened in a great rush of slither and blood. The crown of the infant's head was dark, streaked with hair. I dared not look at it. Instead, I gripped Mary's hand, urging her to push. She screamed and writhed and begged God and all His angels to let her die, and then, with a tearing moan, she set her teeth together and drove the child out. I had only to place my hands beneath its arms and pull, and it was free. Its tiny body hung like a root from the bulb of its great head, the birth-string pulsating, blue and fatty. Without looking at the infant, I took up my knife and cut through it. It was resistant, muscular, like the scrag end of lamb. The child opened its mouth and its eyes as wide as it was able, convulsed with outrage. Then it screamed.

Mary whimpered, pressing her hands over her ears. I murmured comfortingly to her as I washed the child. Morning was already advanced, and the sun struck the smeared windows, filling the room with greasy light. Setting the child on the floor upon the clean square of muslin, I knelt and forced myself to examine it with detachment.

The creature had no eyelashes or brows or any of the human arrangement of hair. Instead, its entire body was covered in a fine pelt, not black as I had feared, but pale and downy, like the fluff of a dandelion clock. Its face was creased, its features squashed close together, and its limbs were unnaturally long, the knuckles of its hands curved in the way of larger apes who use them for walking. Its testicles, which I could hardly bear to look upon, were grotesquely enlarged and a dark red-purple.

And so it was. There could be no denying it.

The apothecary had made his monster.

Quickly I wrapped the thing up. In my arms the monkey-child fussed, its searching mouth open and quivering, nudging my breast. I swallowed my agitation, holding it away from me and tugging at the cloth until its face was obscured. The bundle was so light, it might have been only an armful of laundry.

On the pallet Mary sighed and closed her eyes. Anxiety stabbed my numbness.

"No, Mary, no. You must not sleep," I cried. "I have some wine I have kept by. It will restore your strength a little."

Setting the bundle on the floor, I rummaged in the wooden tea chest for the bottle. Behind me the bundle began to wail.

"For pity's sake, hush!" I muttered. "Do you want us discovered? Here, drink."

I knelt beside her, holding the bottle to her lips, but Mary turned her head away, clamping her lips. Her hands over her ears, she rocked back and forth, her own moans drowning out those of the bundle.

"Make stop," she wept, over and over. "Make stop."

On the floor the creature screamed steadily, its feet kicking against the tight swaddling, its knees pushing the stuff into corners. I crouched beside it, my hand on its chest, as though I might press the screams back into its lungs. It did not quiet. Beyond me, in my basket, I could see my shawl. It would take nothing to place it over the bundle and press down, press down, until at last—

My hand shook. I felt the creature move beneath me and the sudden strength of its jaws as it took the tip of my finger into its mouth. Immediately it fell silent. I closed my eyes, a blade of memory sharp between my ribs. Hardly considering what it was I was doing, I snatched up the bundle and dragged Mary upwards by the arm until she was half-sitting. Mary fought me, but the efforts of labour had exhausted her. She had no strength left. Forcing her knees flat, I thrust the infant into her arms.

Mary gave a strangulated cry, twisting away from me.

335

"No!" she gasped, and her face was grey and scooped out with an adult anguish that made no sense of her childish features. Afterwards I thought it was likely the pain in her womb that twisted her so. But then, at that moment, I looked at her and I saw myself. Then I knew that it was loss and longing that hollowed out her face and which would soon spread into the heart of her, eating away at the soft parts. I knew that she would carry with her always the sense of something absent, something amputated, without which she would never be complete.

Pulling back the blanket, I pushed the creature's head towards her breast. It nosed at the skin for a moment, blindly searching, before it seized upon the nipple, clamping it hard in its mouth. Mary flinched and closed her eyes. Her face was slammed shut, her jaw set and twisted away from her body, refusing complicity. But she did not push the child away. Perhaps it did not occur to her that such a thing would be possible.

Several times that day I put the creature to her breast. When I grew tired of holding it, I fashioned a kind of sling in which the creature might be cradled. Mary never once looked inside the sling.

For four days we remained concealed in my room, the three of us. I slipped out for food when it grew dark. I tried not to think of how little money we had left. It was easier than I might have expected not to dwell unduly upon the gravity of our predicament. The powdery twilight of my nightly incursions bleached the colours from things, softened their sharp edges. Even in daylight, there was an insubstantial quality to the world beyond the covered window, its muffled clamour no more urgent than the gurglings of our own stomachs. Concealed in this place, we might stop the hands of time. Without time, there could be no consequences.

The creature fed well and slept much of the time, as did Mary. As they dozed, I prowled about the darkened room, my limbs fraught and effervescent. I could not stand to look at the creature, but at the same time I could hardly tear my eyes away from it, interrogating every one of its movements for betrayals of its simian nature. When it slept, it made tiny muttering noises with its tongue that raised the hair upon my neck. As for the moment when its fist first closed around a hank of Mary's hair and clung to it, I felt a spasm of such disgust that it made me dizzy. But I could not kill it. With every day that passed, I knew more certainly that I could not kill it.

I was watching them both sleep when the knock came. As soon as I heard it, I knew that I had expected it. I had known that they would find us. Sooner or later they were bound to find us. Now that they were here, I realised that I had not the first notion of what to do. Frantically, my heart hammering, I snatched up the child and cast about for a place to hide it.

"Mary, Eliza, are you there?"

Not Edgar. Petey.

My head swam dizzily as I struggled to straighten my thoughts. Then, lifting the plank lid from the tea chest, I carefully set the child inside and covered it with my grey shawl. I could only hope that I could get rid of Petey before it woke and began to cry. The plank I set back at an angle so that it might have air to breathe.

"Why, good day," I said, opening the door a crack. "We had not expected a visitor."

Jabba sat upon the clown's shoulder, intent upon grooming his hair. Shivering, I looked away.

"The laundress said you had not come to work. So I presumed—the child. It's come?"

"Yes, it came," I said hurriedly. "But it—it died. It was too early, I think."

"I see," Petey said gravely. His kind eyes regarded me. I jutted my chin.

"Mary does well enough, though she sleeps now. She has a slight fever today."

"Then perhaps when she is better I can bring Jabba to see her? She is so fond of him, he might cheer her a little."

I shrugged awkwardly as the monkey bounced and chattered on the clown's shoulder. Then, without warning, it leapt to the ground and, streaking through the narrow opening, disappeared inside the room. I started.

"Come back, come back here, you little—"

"He has little respect for the opinions of others, that one," the clown said drily. "Here, let me fetch him out."

I hesitated. Then, biting my lip, I pushed open the door.

"But quickly. I don't want Mary woken."

With its curtained window, the room was dim, its grey light like liquid dust. Petey moved tentatively, chirruping in the monkey's own whistling inflection.

"Come, Jabba, Jabba. Come, Jabba, Jabba."

Swiftly I crossed the room so that I stood in front of the chest. Mary slept on, her fist nestled into her cheek. Suddenly the monkey startled out from behind me and streaked across the room. It trailed something behind it, soft and grey in the soft grey light.

"Jabba, come now, give that to me," Petey reproved it gently.

Behind me in the box, the creature began to scream.

It was Petey who insisted on taking the sailcloth down from the window so that what little light there was might be allowed in. While I had Mary nurse, he went for food and brought soup and bacon, which, despite her fever, Mary ate ravenously, splashing the sling with spots of grease. I could not eat. I sipped only at water, trying to calm my stomach as I watched Petey take the creature gently from its sling and into his lap. He stroked its simian head with one finger. I closed my eyes, burying my face in my cup. The water tasted stale, brackish with the sealed smell of sleep.

"I had thought you might—," Petey murmured. "But you have done well. The child thrives."

I said nothing.

"I had thought she must surely bear another one. Like her. But this one seems quite ordinary."

I choked.

"How can you—?" I spluttered. "Look at it. Look at it!"

Petey blinked.

"But—"

"Are you quite blind, or have you simply spent too long leering at the freaks at the Bartholomew Fair? Can you not see that the—the thing—that it is—"

"He is come a little before his natural time, but he has suffered little for it. He is a bonny little bugger."

I stared at him.

"Bonny? It is covered all over in hair. And the—the—"

"The balls?" The clown guffawed at my clumsy gesturing. "Grand, ain't they? God's way of making sure even the dullards can tell the difference."

"I suppose you are an authority on infants?"

"Aye. Well, me ma was a wet-nurse, so I seen 'em all and some right sickly little scraps of flesh, I can tell you. Not this one. He's blooming."

"But—you are certain? Nothing is amiss?"

"Don't look like it."

"It's not—he does not strike you as—" I took a breath and forced my unwilling lips to form the words. "As resembling a monkey?"

The clown chuckled.

"All the scraggy ones look like monkeys, 'specially if they come before their proper time, which is what likely happened with this one. The fat ones, they resemble boiled puddings. There's only the two kinds."

"So—?"

"So he'll fill out. And grow up to be a worry to his mother, same as any other infant."

I gazed at the child. It scrunched its face, twitching its nose.

"But I thought—"

"What?"

"You are certain? That there is nothing at all wrong with it?"

"With him," Petey corrected me. "Yes, course I am. Quite certain."

Slowly I reached out a hand to stroke the child's face. My face felt starched, resistant to the crease of it, but I could feel the smile on it continuing to widen, forcing the flesh to give. In the cage of my ribs, my heart twisted like a landed fish.

"What do you mean to do next?" Petey asked later. "The father, he can be found?"

I pressed my lips together.

"Oh, he can be found. But I do not mean to let him anywhere near us."

The clown frowned.

"But how will you manage? You must have him pay his dues."

I stared across the room. Beyond the window the damp wall bloomed with coal-stain flowers. I had given no consideration to the future, of what came next. For the first time in days, I thought of Mr. Honfleur, and I was startled to see how very far away he was, his features tiny and blurred, his voice hardly audible. There was a river of ceaseless time and circumstance rushing through the gully beyond the window. In this room we might be safe, for now, but we were marooned all the same, stranded as the city swirled and rushed around us. It would always be the same, the secrecy, the fear, the swift furtive forays for food, the way my belly twisted every time I glimpsed a woman's sharp profile or heard voices in the stairwell. We might have escaped Swan-street, but without the funds to flee the city forever, that bastard still held us prisoner. He always would, until he ceased to search for us. Until he knew himself defeated.

A sudden hot rush of saliva leapt from beneath my tongue.

"Petey!" I exclaimed. "Do you know how to write?"

TO MISTER BLACK THE APOTHECARIE OF SWAN-STREET

MAIRIE IS WITH ME OF HER OWEN CHOOSING CONSIDER THIS LETTER AS HER NOTIS PROPLY GIVEN

SHE IS BEGUN IN HER LABOR

IF YOU WISHE TO SEE HER AND THE CHILDE IT WILL COSTE YOU 10 POWNDS IN GOLD COIN NO BANK BILL I SHALL COM ALONE TOMOROW HAVE THE FULL SUM READY

IF YOU FAIL TO PAY OR IF YOU DO ME ANY NATUR OF HARM YOU SHALL NEVER SEE MAIRIE OR THE CHILD AGAYNE

I MENE IT BE IN NO DOWTE

ELIZA

XLI

It was plain, from the first, that Petey was uneasy about the arrangements. He considered the sedative unsafe, the scheme for the creature's retrieval risky and ill-considered, the likelihood of mishap considerably too great. He was, frankly, loath to oblige me. When, unsure how else to persuade him, I offered him money, the expression on his face convinced me that I had blundered irretrievably.

It was his affection for Mary that decided him, in the end. Petey might have struggled to claim for himself an immaculate reputation for honesty and candour in all of his business dealings, but, at bottom, the clown was a decent and kind-hearted man, more honourable than most so-called gentlemen. Once he understood how grievously Mary had been misused, he could not stand aside.

And so it was, two nights later, a little after the bells had struck one o'clock, that we made our way west towards Swan-street. Mary's fever had finally abated a little and she slept, a light gasping sleep that made it hard to leave her. It was a dark night, the waning moon blotted by cloud, and Petey carried a small torch of the kind carried by link-boys. At the top of the lane we parted, as agreed. He took up a position in a doorway, his light aloft. As for me, I gathered up my skirts and ran to my master's house. I did not have to pretend to gasp for breath as I thundered with all my strength upon the front door.

"Mr. Black, Mr. Black! It is I, Eliza, come with urgent news. Wake up!"

I kept banging at the door until I heard the clatter of shoes on the stairs. The door opened a crack and a face peered sleepily out.

"Edgar, in God's name, let me in!" I shouted. "I must see your master."

A door slammed upstairs.

"What the Devil—"

"She is here?" Mr. Black's voice cut across his wife's. "That venomous little bitch is here?"

Grimacing at me uncomprehendingly, Edgar opened the door. I shook my head.

"I shall not come in. We shall speak down here or not at all. I have asked the lanthorn-man to wait." I gestured towards Petey's torch. "For my own safety."

The apothecary had grown so weak that Edgar was obliged to put down his candle and carry him down the final flight of stairs, his arms crossed before him to make a seat. He had barely to strain to lift him. Mrs. Black followed behind them, her white undress drifting down the stairs like ash. I could see the pale yellow gleam of her clenched knuckles upon the banister rail.

Edgar settled the apothecary in an upright chair upon the threshold. His cadaverous face was grey as he leaned forwards, his roped hands gripping the arms.

"Where is she, you cunt-bitch?"

"Such civility. Very well, if you do not wish to speak to me—"

"Come back here, you stinking trollop. How dare you?"

"How dare I?" I replied smoothly. "Mr. Black, if you wish to see Mary again, it would behove you to address me with a little more courtesy."

"She is mine," he muttered, his breath painfully short. "You have taken what is mine. You are a whore and a thief."

"She is gone into labour," I said conversationally.

Mr. Black stared up at me, the dark centres of his eyes spreading like ink blots. Behind him Mrs. Black gave a little gasp.

"She—"

"The child should come by morning."

"Morning," he breathed.

"It shall be yours. Upon payment of my terms."

"It is blackmail!"

"Blackmail? No, sir. There are accounts to be settled. The laws of the parish make it clear that all such expenses should be paid by the child's blood father."

"You—"

"Of course, if you refuse me, I shall find a benefactor for the child elsewhere. You are surely not the only man in London with an interest in freaks."

The apothecary's eyes stretched as he battled for breath and composure.

"No! I shall not be blackmailed...by a common slut..."

Again his words were lost in a paroxysm of coughing. He twisted, gasping, in his chair. The knobs of his spine made shadows down the back of his nightdress.

"As you wish," I conceded. "Good night, Mr. Black."

Raising my hand, I gestured towards the clown's light. The torch dipped in response. I kept my steps slow and deliberate, praying that I had not misjudged him.

"No!" Mr. Black called after me. "No. Come back."

I paused but did not turn.

"Come back," he said again. This time the sigh of defeat was unmistakable.

The agreement was much as I had hoped it would be. Mr. Black would give me two guineas immediately, by way of a bond. I would get the remainder when I brought back Mary and the child. The apothecary instructed his wife to unlock the safe box where the money was kept. She counted it out and handed it to me, dropping each coin into my palm as though it were poisoned.

"You foul leech, how can you come here to demand money while she labours? What if she should die while you are gone? Have you not the faintest trace of compassion?"

"Mrs. Black!" the apothecary croaked sharply. "You shall be silent."

Mrs. Black closed her mouth. As I looked up at her, she fixed me upon the points of her eyes, grinding her disgust into my face. I had a strange, fleeting compulsion to confess the truth. Then I looked once more at the apothecary's straining face and I closed my heart.

"And a good night to you too, madam," I murmured, and nodding at the apothecary, I hurried away.

I returned the following evening, a wrapped bundle in my arms. When I banged at the door, Mrs. Black opened it almost immediately. I pushed past her, clutching my bundle, and before she could stop me, I ran up the stairs. I did not stop until I reached the apothecary's study. There I banged once on the door before flinging it open.

The apothecary was lying upon his couch. He could hardly lift his head as I entered the room, but his eyes flickered and his hands fluttered in front of his face.

"It is come?" he breathed, the words catching roughly in his chest. "And is it, is it—?"

I knelt before him, holding out the bundle, my face twisted.

"Truly, you are the instrument of Satan," I said quietly.

Mr. Black's hands shook violently as he fumbled with the cloth. "Closer."

Behind me I heard the door open and the deliberate footsteps as Mrs. Black crossed the room to stand beside me. She said nothing. Taking a step towards the apothecary, I pulled the cloth away from the creature's face. Mrs. Black gasped, a tight choking quickly covered by one hand. As for the apothecary, the muscles in his neck pulled tight, stretching the yellow skin taut over the elbow-sharp points of his cheeks. For a moment one might have hoped him dead. Then something in his face worked loose, and his mouth spread in a slack and awful smile.

"It—it is a monster," I said.

"Yes," he murmured, and his eyes closed over in a kind of rapture. "Yes. It is come at last."

Unsteadily, he tried to tug away the rest of the cloth, but he had not the strength for it and instead broke off into a fit of coughing that caused his arms to jerk at his sides. Quickly Mrs. Black crossed to the other side of the bed and, leaning down, lifted a cup to his lips. He drank clumsily, his brow creased with the effort of it.

"Open it," he rasped at me as Mrs. Black wiped the dribbles of liquid from his chin. "Let me see it."

Edging forwards I placed the bundle on his lap. It was Mrs. Black, who, with trembling hands, unwrapped the cloth. Jabba lay upon his back, his hands tucked beneath his chin. The Febrifuge had worked. He slept soundly, making little snoring sounds in his throat, as the two of them gazed. The corners of the apothecary's mouth worked.

"Perfect. It is perfect." He sighed, the breath rattling in his chest, and a tear ran slowly down his nose. "Where is the idiot? She must be brought."

"That is not possible," I said. "She is not yet well enough to be moved."

"Of course she is. The afterbirth, the proofs—I require her here within the hour."

"No. The exertion would surely kill her."

The apothecary reached out and gripped my skirts, twisting them in his hand.

"Bring her, I tell you. Or I shall—"

"You shall what?" The apothecary was weak, and I detached my skirts without difficulty. "Do not threaten me."

On the other side of the bed, Mrs. Black bristled.

"If you care for the girl at all," she hissed, "you shall bring her here where she may be properly cared for."

"Cared for? Is that what you call it? To be stabbed at and scrutinized like a felon's cadaver? I should rather die first."

"And Mary? You would wish her death also, in service of your own petty extortions?"

"No, madam. I wish only to save her the misery of ever setting eyes upon the pair of you again. You have the—the creature. Surely that is all the proof you require. And you have me, who may bear witness to the birth. Why is that not sufficient?"

"You?"

"I shall give an account to whatever audience you choose. Mr. Black has always declared the gentlemen of the Royal Society superior stuck-ups, has he not? Then summon them, to bear witness to his triumph."

Mrs. Black's eyes narrowed. Her lips pressed together, she looked at me and then at her husband. He nodded, his head awkward upon its stalk of a neck.

"Call that bastard Jewkes," he whispered. "Have him bring those doubters here. And fetch me up another draught. Thirty grains, do you hear me? I must be steady now and clear."

Mrs. Black hesitated. Then, with swift light steps, she crossed the room. In the doorway she stopped and turned. Her face was half in shadow and impossible to read. Then she was gone.

"So," I said. "Let the show begin."

There was a pertness to my tone that I regretted the moment it was out of my mouth for, to my ear, it spoke far too plainly of my intent. It was fortunate for me that the hubris of prideful men swells about them like a rising sea and fills their ears with nothing but the roaring of the ovations that await them. I might have told the apothecary every detail of the plot then, I think, and he would have heard nothing. If he had observed the opening and closing of my lips, doubtless he would have taken it for applause.

"Great is Truth," Mr. Black rasped triumphantly as two tears fell from his eyes and quivered expectantly upon the sleeping monkey's chest. "And mighty above all things. Praise be to God."

blacks law
grayson black fellow chairman newton sloane black

the pen is steady
the opium curls like a vine round my feverish mind green & fresh &
juicy it smells
like summer
the beginning of it
how clear it is how perfectly sweet

opium & joy what perfect salve for agony what unusual power
I am weeping & my tears taste salt & sweet so sweet

it is done sublime joy
& i am at peace
thanks be to god

XLII

I was put to wait in the room Mary had occupied in her last weeks at Swan-street. As the key turned in the door behind me, I crossed the room and looked out of the window to the other side of the street. The scraping caw of crows caused me to look up. The angle of the roofs obscured them, but I could just make out a cluster of the black birds settling upon the chimney-pots.

It seemed that no one had been in this room since Mary left it. The bed was a tangle of rugs, and on a low table beside it, a plate stubbled with crumbs bore the dried-out crusts of a half-eaten slice of bread. I lay upon the bed, burying my face in the pillow. It no longer smelled of Mary but only, faintly, of mildew. The table bore a single small drawer, without a handle. The front of it was warped so that it did not quite close. Idly, I inserted a finger and pulled it out. It was so light, I thought it empty, but when I glanced inside, I saw instead a mess of tiny scraps of fabric, small feathers, clippings of yellow fur from the cat. I stared at them without touching them, and their inadequacy tightened something in my chest. The poor furtive remnants I had sent up on her trays so that she might know that I did not forget her. She had kept every one.

When Mrs. Black unlocked the door, I was lying on the bed, staring at the ceiling. I longed now to be finished with it, for the whole ghastly circus to be over. Without speaking, I followed her to the apothecary's chamber and waited as she knocked crisply at the door.

"Mr. Black? May I enter? We expect Mr. Jewkes and his associates directly."

When there was no answer, she pushed the door open. The room was still and perfectly quiet, filled with gently turning spirals of dust, solid in the sunlight. In the centre of the room in a pool of

349

melted light was a crib of dark wood with high carved sides. In its shadowed centre lay the monkey, wrapped tightly in its swaddling bands. It slept, its face twitching with dreams.

Beside it, folded over in the prostrate posture of an Eastern mystic, was the apothecary. His hands were spread out wide upon the floor, the bony fingers splayed and their tips pressed against the boards and his shoulders shook in silent spasms. He wore neither hat nor wig. His stubbled head shone silver in the sunlight, while his worn black coat had the green gleam of beetle wings. He was surrounded by drifts of paper. A little beyond his reach a quill lay abandoned, a drop of black ink quivering upon its nib. There were holes in the upturned soles of his boots.

Mrs. Black pushed past me and into the room.

"Sir, are you taken ill?"

Very slowly the apothecary raised his head. His face was a startling ghostly white, the purple of his stained cheek muddied to a dark brownish-grey. Even his lips were white. Only his eyes were red, the lids swollen round the great dark holes of his pupils. The tears ran down his cheeks, falling onto his coat and clinging there for a brief shining moment before surrendering to the weave of the fabric. In one hand he held an empty bottle, in the other a quill, its blackened nib crushed and split.

"We—we are vindicated," he rasped weakly. "The name of Black shall…"

His voice failed him. As he held his arms upwards, his expression was of exultation, of almost beatific ecstasy. In the crib the monkey chirruped softly to itself and was silent.

"Mr. Black, the—the creature, it wakes," Mrs. Black said with uncommon gentleness. "There, there, do not fret. Perhaps you should entrust it to me until you are strong enough to examine it. I shall ensure it is fed and cleaned. When you are ready to resume your examination, inform Edgar here and I shall have it brought up to you. You look a little recovered already."

With a clatter Edgar put down his tray. The apothecary gazed up at him with his punched-out eyes. The smile still curved his lips, but his mouth had collapsed somehow into his face, peeling the flesh away from his teeth. Raising his hand with great effort, he brought the bottle down upon the table as though making a toast.

"Edgar," Mrs. Black instructed. "The brandy if you will."

Briskly she extended her hand, but Edgar did not move. His eyes were fixed upon his master. Mr. Black gave a hollow rattling snort, lifting his head a little as though with great effort. His eyes bulged in their sockets, then rolled backwards, and his head fell forwards with as much force as though it had been cut from his neck, his nose striking the table with a pulpy thud. A spasm of vigour jumped through his limbs as a puppet's limbs jerk when the strings are pulled. Then he was still. The bottle fell to the floor with a dull thud. It did not break but rolled idly across the floor, coming to a stop against the iron grate of the empty fireplace.

"Edgar," Mrs. Black said again, more sharply. "Must I ask you again? The brandy, if you please."

She did not look at her husband. Instead, she stooped to lift the monkey from its crib, clasping the bundle tightly to her chest. It stirred and, with a soft surprised gurgle, she took a step backwards, raising the creature's face to hers until their noses brushed. Her movement dislodged the apothecary's arm from the edge of his desk. It fell, the elbow twisted outwards at an unnatural angle, the fingers of the pale hand uncurling. Purple stains marked the yellow skin. Mrs. Black did not turn. Instead, she cradled the monkey in her arms, swaying a little backwards and forwards, her eyes half-closed.

"Be still, my little one," she crooned into the bundle. "My misbegotten little savage one. Be still. I am here."

Again the monkey stirred, its tiny fists balled against its cheeks. Mrs. Black clasped it against her chest and rocked it backwards and forwards, crooning a lullaby under her breath. It whimpered, wriggling in her embrace. With great deliberation Mrs. Black walked upon stiff, straight legs, across the room and away down the stairs. Edgar stared at me, his face creased with bewilderment. Then, with the air of a man walking to the gallows, he followed her.

I remained where I was, suspended in silence. It was over. Dust stirred itself in slow circles into the white glare of the window, thickening the air, and a pair of fat flies buzzed, drawing zigzags across the room. One settled upon the apothecary's coat, the other on his head, insinuating itself into the details of his ear.

From downstairs came the muffled sound of raised voices, then the thud of feet taking the stairs two at a time. The butcher-faced Jewkes pushed me aside.

"That bastard! Where is he, that damned bastard!"

He stopped, frozen, staring at the apothecary slumped over the desk.

"He is dead," I observed, and I brushed reflexively at my ear. "Already dead."

Mr. Jewkes hardly looked at the dead man. Instead, he wheeled round, seizing me by the shoulders.

"Then where is she? Where is my little girl?" He thrust me away from him, covering his face with his hands. "Oh, Henrietta, my sweet child, what have I done, what in the name of the Devil have I done?"

He pressed his fingers against his brow. His hands were pale and freckled, gilded with pale hairs, and I had a sudden startling picture of one of them moving down Mary's neck and over her breasts, as the other fumbled with the front of his breeches.

"You shall burn in fiery Hell for all eternity," I said, and my quiet, steady voice seemed to come from somewhere very far away. "For it is not the child you have made a monster of but yourself. Now if you will excuse me—"

Mr. Jewkes caught me by the arm. His grip was gentle, almost apologetic.

"Where is she?" he whispered. "Is she here?"

"You disgust me," I said, and I swallowed back the tears that clenched my throat. "You think I would bring her back here, to him, after all that has happened? You are as much a monster as he is."

"So where is she? Please, tell me, I beg you."

His voice was pleading, wretched. I wanted to rip the hair from his scalp, his eyes from their sockets, anything to make him feel something of her pain, the pain he had devised for her.

"Somewhere you and your scalpel-sharpening cronies shall never find her. Somewhere safe."

Mr. Jewkes dropped his hand.

"Thank God. Does she require a physician, money, anything? I—I should like to help her, if I can."

"As you have helped her already? Trust me, you have done enough."

Jewkes lifted his head. He held my gaze steadily, humbly, as if he had forgotten I was only a servant.

"I have betrayed her most grievously," he said quietly. "I shall regret it always."

The abruptness of his confession caught me off guard.

"So you acknowledge it? That you—that you are the father of Mary's child?"

The shadow of a frown passed over Mr. Jewkes's face.

"You mistake me. I am her father."

"Her father? But I—I don't understand."

"No. No, I hardly understand it myself. But I am her father all the same."

I stared at him stupidly.

"You are Mary's father?"

"Yes. May God forgive me, her father. And she is not Mary. She has never been Mary. Her name is Henrietta. Henrietta Sarah Jewkes. My second wife did not—she wished to be rid of her. And I let her. I let them take her away."

I shook my head, but still it would not clear.

"You are her father?"

"I am. Though I may hardly be considered worthy of the name." He sighed miserably, staring at his hands. "How is she? Does she do well?"

I thought of all the curses I had heaped upon his head, the images that had tormented my imagination. I thought of Mary's white face, greasy with sweat, the low pained murmurs as she turned in her sleep. He was her father. I could hardly look at him.

"Well enough," I whispered at last. "Though her ordeal has been considerable."

"Might you permit me to send my physician, just to see her? It—it would give me some comfort. To know her in good hands."

Immediately I knew myself tricked.

"If you think all your manipulations shall have me tell you where she is, you are quite mistaken. In all this time you have been nothing of a father to her. Why should I trust you now, when so much is at stake?"

Mr. Jewkes swallowed and his shoulders slumped.

"I—I do not know," he said very quietly. He stared at the floor. Then, fumbling in his coat, he drew out a fat leather purse. Without opening it, he thrust it into my hands. "Here. Gold keeps its own counsel and betrays no one. Take care of her."

I weighed the purse in my hand. It was heavy. After the birth Mary had seemed to improve. But when I had helped her up from the pot last evening, she had moaned, half-falling, and I had wiped away the gush of dark blood that rushed down her thigh. In the pot, I had found more blood and a glossy wine-red slab like pig's liver. It was then that the fever had returned.

"Go," he urged softly. "There is nothing more for you here. And if you will, tell my daughter when she is well enough that I shall never forgive myself. That I have always loved her, though I served her so ill."

From downstairs there came a scuffle of voices, the sound of a door slamming. Jewkes sighed and, rubbing his chin, stared impassively at the apothecary.

"Have my boy come up. The priest must be sent for and the undertaker. The sexton too, so that the bells may be rung and the cause of death properly reported. The weather is warm and we should not delay. As for that—that creature downstairs—"

He broke off as Edgar stumbled up the stairs. His wig was askew, his cheek scored with what looked like scratch marks.

354

"I require your assistance, sir. With the mistress. The master's death has dealt her a severe blow. She—well, she is most discomposed. Agitated."

"Surely—"

"Please, sir," Edgar urged unhappily. "Perhaps if you saw for yourself—"

"For the love of God!" Jewkes growled, but feeling my gaze upon him, he bit his lip. "Very well. Take me to her."

Almost pushing the man before him, Edgar hustled him downstairs. Holding the heavy purse in my hands, I looked around the apothecary's room one last time. It smelled of ink powder and old wigs. The surprise about death, in the end, was the ordinariness of it. In the lilac light of evening, the iron dome beyond the window was tinted with lavender. It looked gaudy, foolish, a stout matron coiffed and rouged like a girl.

Closing the door, I walked slowly down the stairs. The house was shadowed, the doors off the stairway all closed. Like a skeleton, I thought before I could stop myself, the stairs like the knobs of a spine down through its hollow centre, and I crossed my fingers to drive away the ill fortune. I had only to retrieve the monkey and I might walk away from this house forever. In the hallway two slim cloth-bound volumes waited on the table, fastened together with string, and angry voices set the parlour door trembling against the jamb.

"You have no claim upon the child," I heard Mrs. Black howl with a violence that rattled the door upon its hinges. "The child is ours, do you hear me? Ours."

"Child?" Mr. Jewkes's tone was quieter but no less savage for all that. "You call that—that *thing* a child?"

"It is ours. Ours alone. You shall not profit from it, you hear me? You relinquished any blood claim when you gave her up to us. It makes no difference that he is dead. You understand me? You have no claim. No claim whatsoever. It is ours."

"You think I would want anything to do with that monster? You think I am not already so crushed by the burden of shame and guilt

355

that I wish now to profit from my misdeeds? That creature is an atrocity, an act against God. It revolts me that I have been complicit in its creation. I have betrayed my own conscience. Worse, much worse, I have betrayed my daughter. You may have made an abomination of her child, but you shall never make one of her. I would die first."

"You defy all reasonable civility, sir," spat Mrs. Black. "Mr. Black has always thought you the coarsest of men. Give me back the child this instant and get out, or I shall have him throw you out. Have we not told you? You are not welcome here."

Suddenly the door flew open, and Mrs. Black stood swaying in the doorway. Though I stood directly before her, she showed no signs of seeing me. Her eyes had a glassy unfocused look.

"Edgar!" she cried shrilly. "Edgar, are you there? Mr. Jewkes threatens me."

Mr. Jewkes pushed past her into the hall. He held the monkey aloft, his hands tight round its narrow throat. Jabba wriggled frantically.

"If you think I shall permit this—this freak to live—!"

"No!" I cried. Startled, Jewkes turned, and before he could stop me, I seized the monkey from him. "Please. The monkey has done no harm."

"Thank you, Eliza," Mrs. Black said smoothly. "Now return the child to me if you will. It requires feeding and then my husband must see it."

"Your husband is dead, madam!" Jewkes roared, and he tore roughly at my arm. "Give me that—that beast. I shall not stand by and let it live."

"No, sir," I begged. "Listen to me, I implore you. This is not Mary's child. I fear I have—do not hurt him, I beg you. He is nothing but a monkey."

"I shall not—"

"A clown's monkey," I said again. "Of the kind one sees in the city daily. I borrowed him. So that I might—I borrowed him."

"The girl is gone mad!" Mrs. Black declared hectically. "Do you hear her? She is quite mad. Where is Mr. Black? Edgar, fetch my husband so that he may finally put an end to these absurdities!"

"He entertains the crowds as part of a mountebank's show, sir," I said quietly to Mr. Jewkes. "His name is Jabba."

At the sound of its name, the monkey wriggled a little in my arms and opened its eyes. It gazed blearily at me. I kissed the top of its head.

Jewkes stared.

"I do not—"

"Mary has a son. He thrives."

"A human—an ordinary infant?"

I nodded.

"The child is with her?"

"Yes, sir."

"And this—?"

"Is a trick, sir. A hoax." I stared at my feet. "Mr. Black—well, I thought—"

I did not see Mrs. Black until she was upon me, pushing me backwards with such force that my legs folded beneath me. The monkey gave a little shriek and, leaping out of reach, fled up the stairs.

"You lying little slut!" Mrs. Black screamed, seizing me by the hair. "You bitch! You filthy foul-mouthed harlot! Edgar! You are lying! I know you are lying! Where is the child? Where is it? Edgar!"

Jewkes seized the old woman's arms and hauled her backwards as Edgar peered from the door of the laboratory, his face rucked with fear and dismay.

"Fetch me something to calm her nerves," Jewkes ordered the apprentice as Mrs. Black kicked out at me savagely, her teeth displayed like an animal's. "Quickly, I implore you. As for you, Eliza, take the monkey and go. Its presence here will only inflame her further."

Mrs. Black twisted and writhed.

"Get the child," she hissed at Edgar. "It went upstairs. I must have the child."

Edgar hesitated. Then he drew himself tall.

"Jewkes, what in God's name is happening here?" he managed, though his voice squeaked.

"Edgar, for pity's sake!" Mrs. Black shrieked. "We must have the child. The papers too. All the papers. Fetch them from his study. Edgar, I beg you. Think what will become of us. We cannot let this villain steal what is rightfully ours."

"Believe me," Jewkes said grimly. "I want nothing from you."

Edgar hesitated again, his eyes flitting anxiously from Mrs. Black to Jewkes and back again. Then slowly he stepped forwards and took hold of his mistress's legs. Together he and Jewkes began to carry her into the dining-room.

"Mr. Black!" Mrs. Black's cry was piteous now, the mewl of a kitten in a sack. "Mr. Black, why do you let them treat me so? Why will you not help me?"

The door closed. Like dark water, the shadows quivered and settled. Suddenly there was a scampering on the stairs. Swift as a rat, the monkey streaked across the floor and into the laboratory. I followed it, calling it, but it did not come. In the dim room I could not see it, though I heard a scuffling amongst the bottle-crowded shelves on the far wall.

"Goodbye, Eliza."

I turned to see Mr. Jewkes standing behind me in the doorway, his shoulders hunched and his hands thrust deep into his pockets.

"And thank you."

I nodded. Suddenly a clamp fell with a great clatter to the floor, so that both of us startled. The monkey sat upon the table, something in its hands. The napkin round its waist glowed white in the dusty light. Bowing, the monkey held its hands out towards us. They contained a small pill box. Prising open the lid, the beast took from the box a dark-coloured pastille of which it proceeded to make a thorough study. Mr. Jewkes and I glanced at each other, and something in his eyes loosed the cords round my chest a little. On the table the monkey held the pastille up to its mouth and pretended to take a bite, rubbing its little stomach with its free hand. The napkin round its waist slipped. Mr. Jewkes's mouth twitched. The monkey frowned and tugged at it before picking up the pill box and, jumping up and down, pointing a finger helpfully at its lid.

"I only hope your physician, when you summon him, is not such a charlatan," I murmured.

Mr. Jewkes squeezed my arm, his lips clamped in a swallowed smile.

"Thank you," he muttered. "For everything. Take care of her for me."

I hesitated. Then I looked up.

"Is your carriage outside?"

"Yes. Yes, it is."

"Then let us take it. Mary will be wondering where we are."

Mr. Jewkes sent his boy for the doctor and, calling up his equipage, required his coachman to take us with all speed to Cole-harbour.

"You are sure, sir?" the coachman asked doubtfully. "It is a wretched place and hardly safe, even in daylight."

"I am perfectly certain. Now hurry."

Shrugging his shoulders, the coachman whipped up the horses and the coach lurched forwards. I perched on the edge of the seat, feet braced against the rattle and jolt. But close by the Exchange, the narrow streets became choked with traffic, and we slowed almost to a standstill. Mr. Jewkes lowered the window and called up to the coachman.

"It's the Alley," the coachman called. "Been pandemonium there since dawn."

"Try the river."

The coach tipped as it turned, its wheel passing so close to a chair that the chairman dropped the struts to shake his fist at the coachman.

"You poxy dog!" he shouted. "May your filthy mother be cursed with the warts of a toad!"

"Ah, take pity on the poor rogue," sneered his associate. "By tomorrow the sinking of the South Sea'll have taken him and his master's fancy conveyance with it, and he'll be in the gutter where he belongs!"

Beyond the Tower the equipage elicited considerable curiosity. When at last we reached the wharf and the footman had put down the steps, the coachman looked ill at ease.

"Shall I wait here, sir?" he asked.

Jewkes nodded. The coachman and footman exchanged a glance as he gestured me forwards into the lodging-house, the monkey in my arms.

"Send Dr. Kingdom up when he comes," he instructed.

"Very good, sir."

The room was quiet when I pushed open the door. Petey half-stood, his finger to his lips. On the palliasse Mary slept.

"How does she do?" I whispered.

"Not so well," Petey replied, holding his arms out to the monkey. "The fever is stronger, and she cries out in her sleep."

Quietly I crossed the room and knelt down beside her. Her closed eyelids sketched a delicate tracery of blue and purple across their pale curves. Her tongue lolled a little from between her parted lips. I stroked her cheek, taking her hand in mine. Both were burning hot. Jewkes stood in the doorway, his arms crossed over his chest, as though restraining himself from entry.

"The doctor shall be here soon," I whispered. "He shall make you well again."

Jewkes turned to Petey.

"What have you need of here? Wine, water, soft food? Tell me and I shall send my man for them."

The two men conferred quietly.

"We shall be back directly," Jewkes said to me. He looked at Mary and his face twisted. "Directly."

Mary and I were alone. Dipping a rag in the basin of water beside the bed, I wiped Mary's face with it. Her eyelids fluttered.

"No cry, Lize," she breathed, and her hand fluttered in mine. "No cry."

Rubbing my nose hard with the back of my hand, I forced myself to smile.

"I am not crying," I rebuked her softly. "Why should I cry when you are almost well? Mr. Jewkes means to take care of you, you know. You were right, he is a good man. We shall be safe now, quite safe."

Mary murmured something inaudible and closed her eyes. Settling myself beside her on the palliasse, I took her in my arms. At some point, when it was almost dark, Mr. Jewkes entered but he said nothing, only stood with his back against the wall, watching and listening. I did not stop in my singing, not until the door opened again to reveal a fat little man with a kindly face, considerably out of breath. Mr. Jewkes turned and extended his hand.

"How goes it, Kingdom?"

"Excellent, excellent," the physician said, bowing as best he could over his globe of a belly. "Though I hardly would have expected to find you in a place of this kind. For a moment there, I thought myself certain to be robbed and never seen again!"

"It is an insalubrious spot, I grant you. I thank you for coming."

The physician nodded.

"We shall need light, of course. There are candles?"

"In my carriage. I shall have Watkin bring some up."

"Very good, very good. And you are well, Jewkes? Not caught up in all this nasty business with the markets, I trust?"

"There shall be no difficulty with your bill, Doctor."

"Goodness, man, what a cynic you are! A courteous enquiry, no more. And here is our patient. Good, good. Now, missy, excuse me if you will."

Very reluctantly I loosened my embrace. A pained flicker passed over Mary's sleeping face as the physician felt for her pulse.

"You shall make her better, shan't you?" I said, unable to help myself.

"That is why I am here," he replied, his hands working circles upon his belly as he surveyed her, pushing aside her skirts to peer more closely at the blood-stained sheet beneath her. At the door the coachman handed Jewkes a lit candelabra. Shadows jumped, startled, against the walls as he brought it to the bed and set it down close to Mary's head.

"Thank you, Jewkes," the doctor said thoughtfully, tapping his teeth with a gold pencil. "Perhaps the girl could stay, in case I should require anything. Otherwise, if you would wait downstairs—?"

Though there was nowhere downstairs to wait, Mr. Jewkes murmured his consent, closing the door. The physician considered Mary for a few long minutes, his head on one side as he moved round the low bed, then asked me for the details of her confinement. I gave them shakily, hardly able to remember.

"Hmm," he said at last. "I shall require some tea. Let it steep awhile."

"Mary prefers it weak, sir."

The physician frowned at me.

"Does she, indeed? Now make haste. I cannot think well on a parched throat."

It was an agony to leave Mary, even for a few minutes. I pressed my lips to her hand, squeezing her fingers between mine.

"Be brave," I whispered. "I shall be back directly."

The physician gestured impatiently.

"Tea."

I waited in the lane as the footman went with exaggerated apprehension to purchase the physician's tea at a small tavern near the water. The shouts of the sailors carried over the low hiss of the advancing tide. When the footman returned, carrying a cup of ale, his face was stretched with affront.

"The physician may have this and consider himself fortunate," he snapped. "I shall not risk my life for tea."

Hurriedly I carried it upstairs. The physician had pushed Mary's knees up and tented them with a cloth which covered his head and shoulders. As the cloth jerked, Mary gave a strangulated scream and her eyes startled open. Clattering down the ale, I crouched beside and gripped her hand. I felt the twitch of her fingers as she squeezed back. Beneath the cloth the physician pushed her knees wider. She gazed at me wildly, hardly seeing me. The sweat stood out on her forehead and darkened her hair. Her breath came in ragged strips. Her grip tightened.

The physician lowered the cloth. His right hand was dark with blood, a metal hook protruding from his palm like a terrible sixth finger. A smudge of red rouged his cheek.

"It would appear I am become a man-midwife," he observed, taking up a clean cloth and wiping his face fastidiously. "You have my tea?"

"Only porter, sir."

Dr. Kingdom sighed.

"How does she do?" I asked, afraid of the answer.

"We shall not know for some hours. She is very weak. The afterbirth is corrupted and obstinate, but I trust we shall do better with the proper instruments. Please do not concern yourself unduly. Such a process is not uncommon and is usually successful. Permit her to rest for now. She must conserve her strength for what is to come. I must talk with Mr. Jewkes downstairs." He paused in the doorway, nodding at me kindly. "Keep her warm and have her drink as much as she can. I shall return directly."

When he was gone, I lay down beside Mary as she dozed, her nose close to mine, her hands hot between my cool ones.

"How does the patient do?"

I turned my head. Mr. Jewkes stood in the doorway, his hand extended towards me. I did not know if he intended to offer support or to seek it.

"I—I should never have left her," I whispered. "Forgive me."

"It is not you who should seek forgiveness but I," he replied softly. "You have never abandoned her, never closed your eyes to her plight as I did, as I have always done. You have protected her. You have showed her affection. I, her blood father, was never a father to her, but in you, who owed her nothing, she found a sister. I shall always be grateful to you for that."

"I have never loved anyone as I love her," I murmured, and it was only as I said it that I knew it to be true.

"Then she is fortunate, indeed." He paused, gazing at the bundle asleep in the tea chest. "And this is the child?"

"Yes, sir. Your grandson."

Jewkes squatted, pressing his fingers against his lips.

"He is a fine boy," he said at last.

"Yes, sir. He is."

We were silent for a moment, watching Mary sleep. Jewkes's fingers played absently with the end of the infant's blanket.

"Kingdom should be back soon," he murmured. "Then, when he considers her fit enough to be moved, I shall take her home. Mrs. Jewkes shall simply have to endure it."

I blinked at him. In its chest the infant began to cry. I had brought Jewkes here, had accepted his kindness, his help. I had never thought that he might claim her.

"She shall not miss the laundry," I managed, though my mouth was dry.

There was a knock on the door and Petey looked in. Jabba the monkey rode on his shoulder, its fingers around the clown's ears.

"The physician is returned," he said.

"Show him up. And have the footman bring fresh candles. These ones burn low."

"Yes, sir."

Petey made to withdraw, but the monkey, spying Mary upon the palliasse, leapt down from its perch and skittered across the room to curl upon her pillow. Mary stirred and opened her eyes.

"Jab Jab," she said dreamily, and she smiled, her face ivory-smooth in the guttering candlelight. "Ev'rythin' fine now, Jab. Ev'rythin' gon' be fine."

Peel Mather, Solicitors at Law, Poultry, London

For the attention of John Black, Esquire, at the Sign of the Scroll &
Feather, Newcastle

Dear Mr. Black,

We regret to have to inform you of the death two days since, that is, the
4th of September of this year of grace one thousand seven hundred and
twenty, of Mr. Grayson Black of Swan-street, London.

Since you, his brother, are the primary beneficiary of Mr. Grayson
Black's last Will and Testament, we would beg your attendance at our
Offices at the earliest convenience so that the terms of said Will might
be fully and expeditiously executed. Given the circumstances of the be-
quest, such funds as may be required for such a journey may be ad-
vanced from the amount due to you if necessary.

We hope you will accept our most heartfelt condolences for this, your
sad loss.

We remain, sir, your humble servants &c.,

    SILAS PEEL   SAMPSON MATHER

    6th day of September, the year of our Lord 1720

XLIII

Mary died.

Years have passed, but still my hand trembles when I write those words and a stitch of loss tugs at my heart. Mary died. Not that day, nor for several of the days that followed, but a week later. The physician first bled her from the feet in an attempt to bring forth the corrupted afterbirth and afterwards, when that yielded nothing, endeavoured to remove it with a scalpel, but it was a more difficult process than he had predicted, demanding several hours of cutting and scraping. Mary had scarce been able to tolerate the pain of his endeavours, frequently falling into a faint from the agony. At last he had sighed and requested Mr. Jewkes's permission to cease in his surgery. There was a chance that Mary's womb would expel the remaining fragments of tissue of its own accord. If he persisted, however, he feared that she would not have the strength for it.

And yet, perhaps if we had pressed him to continue, he might yet have saved her life. He was a fine doctor and a decent man and would have done what we asked, even at the cost to his reputation, had we insisted upon it. As it was, we conceded, grateful to spare Mary further pain. The puerperal fever took hold two days later, and she succumbed to it quickly, without a struggle. The memory of it still plagues me. If I had only had more courage on her behalf, she might be sitting with me now before the fire, the flames warming her cheeks and lighting sparks in her copper hair. It might be her hand, and not mine, that strokes the child's head as he sleeps, his dark eyelashes quivering against the ripe swell of his cheek. She might look up at me, with that sweet slack smile upon her face, and call my name. Lize. No one but Mary ever called me Lize.

I miss her. At first I think I imagined that there would come a time when I would not miss her, when the skin of the passing years would close over the wound of her, but that time has never come. It is true that the raw grief has softened into a tender bruise that is tolerable if I do not press it too hard, but even now I still find myself talking to her as I always have. I never stopped talking to her, not even in those bleak months immediately after her death when my heart stopped and my limbs withered and there were no words in the world for the ripped-out anguish of it.

I was hardly alone in my desolation that autumn. The great edifice of the South Sea Company had at last collapsed, bringing down with it the swarms of investors who clung to its crumbling brickwork. The year of soaring prices and reckless abandon was brought to a shuddering end, and the wreckage was everywhere. All of London was convulsed with the groans of the afflicted. Exchange-alley, which had echoed with such noise and excitement to the call of the stock-jobbers, sprawled, winded, alongside the Bank of England, shocked and silent. Overnight, vast fortunes were obliterated while men who had purchased shares against future profits and believed their fortunes assured reeled at the mountainous extent of their debt. Paper money was suddenly worthless. Houses were left half-built; orders for ships cancelled; newspapers filled with advertisements for pictures, china, and glasses. Long-lane and Regent-fair were full of rich liveries to be sold, and on every street corner there was to be found a stall hawking gold watches and jewelry for a fraction of their true value.

Thousands of families were ruined. Even the bookseller's favourite, the brilliant Mr. Newton, had proved himself greedier than he was astute and was rumoured to have lost more than £20,000 of his own fortune in the collapse. The disaster drove many to madness and more to put an end to their misfortunes through the taking of their own lives. The metropolis lurched and staggered with scandal and distress as, one after another, gentlemen and merchants of previously good reputation hung themselves by the neck or drowned themselves in the muddy waters of the Thames, leaving behind wives and children and the ruins of their estates. There were rumours of a gentleman who threw himself from the Whispering

Gallery of the Cathedral, smashing his head open like a pumpkin upon the marble floor beneath.

Monsieur Honfleur was one of those who fled. It was Edgar who brought me the news when he came to say goodbye. Like Mr. Newton, the bookseller had extricated himself once from his commitments in Exchange-alley only to be tempted to return for a final gamble. According to Edgar, he had pledged to purchase shares on an instalment plan, which meant that, even before the worst of the crash, he had owed significantly more than his stock was worth. It seemed that he had slipped away in the hope that, in the great blizzard of paperwork that had snowed down upon Exchange-alley in the previous months, his promise might somehow be lost or forgotten.

"It is to be hoped, for his sake, he is not gone back to France," Edgar remarked, watching my expression. "They say the plague is at Marseilles."

"And Annette, is she gone also?" I asked, but Edgar only sighed.

"How careless you are, Eliza, to let yet another husband wriggle from your hook," he said instead, and a flicker of his old spirit lit his face for a moment. "You see, it is proof that we were indeed intended for each other."

"Or perhaps we were neither of us meant for marriage at all."

"But you have your Mr. Jewkes, at least. A mistress may manage at least as well as a wife, if she is canny."

I only shook my head.

Edgar looked sallow and ill. His face had grown thin, and as if his head had shrunk beneath it, his wig tilted oddly, slipping over one eye. When I asked him what it was he meant to do next, he shrugged.

"There is the possibility of a passage to Virginia," he said. "They say the Thirteen Colonies are a positive Arcadia. Unlimited land and Negro slaves as far as the eye can see. Cheaper than a wife and much more obliging. You may imagine me upon my plantation, a piccaninny girl on each knee and at least one of your erstwhile husbands to raise a glass with. What more could a gentleman wish for?"

He said nothing of his debts nor of Mrs. Black. His plans, like the plans of so many adventurers in London, lay in ruins, snatched from his hands just at the moment he had thought them secure. He could surely never have imagined that Mrs. Black, whose mind appeared shut as tight as a trap, could have permitted herself to have become so deranged by the death of her husband. He knew nothing before their precipitate arrival of the family of Mr. Black's brother, who arranged her removal to an unwilling cousin and as swiftly took control of the shop and all of its contents. Edgar had had time only to bundle up the apothecary's papers, which he supposed might have some value and which he now lodged with me for safe-keeping. Naturally, being Edgar, he had also had sufficient wit to offer to the brother's oldest daughter his hand in marriage. Doubtless it had not escaped his attention that she was not only much younger than her aunt but also possessed of a considerably more ample bosom.

Naturally she had refused him. Edgar appeared resigned to the failure of his efforts. Something of Edgar, it seemed, had been despatched along with Mrs. Black, and it was a smaller, quieter creature who took his leave from me that dark afternoon. I knew that I would never see him again. I felt a tinge of affection for the apprentice but no regret. When he stepped away from the threshold, he would carry away with him the final traces of Swan-street and of what I had become there.

"Nursemaid and whore," he murmured softly and quite without spite. "A secure future indeed and better than most in London have managed."

I said nothing but hugged my arms around myself as I gazed down into the crib. The sleeping infant yawned, showing the soft pink of its mouth, and his nose twitched like a rabbit's.

"He will leave soon," I said silently to Mary. "And we shall be peaceful once more. The three of us, as we like it."

"You are not too solitary, here alone?" Edgar asked.

"I am not alone," I replied.

"And when he tires of you?"

I bent down and took the child into my arms. He was waking up now, and his eyes peered blurrily at me from beneath their heavy lids. I kissed him very gently upon the button of his nose.

"A boy does not tire of his mother."

"You know I did not mean—"

"Goodbye, Edgar. And may good fortune go with you."

When Edgar had left, I took the sleepy child upstairs to the room occupied by the wet-nurse. The boy would be weaned soon, and then she too would leave. She was a pleasant Scottish woman with an even-tempered demeanour, but I would be glad to be rid of her. She was obliging in her own way and almost tender with the child she called the poor orphan bairn, but, for all that, it remained difficult living at close quarters with someone who had never known Mary. The cottage was a small one, and her idle chatter seemed to fill the spaces where Mary might settle, forcing her out. When she nudged me and winked and muttered gleefully that we had surely fallen on our feet in such hard times to have found ourselves so spendthrift an employer, I found myself frowning and charging her to be silent. It did not feel right to speak of Mary's father that way where she might so easily hear it.

I talked to Mary as I set Edgar's cup in the sink. The winter would have to be endured. But when the spring came, I would begin once more to collect plants. The cottage was on the edge of a small hamlet that reached out hopeful fingers in the direction of the larger village of Hampstead. There were many herbs that grew here and many more that might be cultivated in the scrap of garden behind the house. I wanted no more to do with opium or its other foreign relatives, but I had conceived of an idea to produce potions to enhance the beauty of women, complexion waters for the face and creams to augment the swell of the breast or the whiteness of a lady's hands. With my preparations, a woman might triumph over the vagaries of nature and find herself always young and beautiful. Mary, who had grown more ironic in death, thought the idea perfect.

I did not mean to tell Mr. Jewkes of my plans just yet. He had insisted that he would always provide for me and the child and had

had lawyers draw up the necessary papers so that his wife might find no way to overturn his intentions. The money would, he assured me, last for as long as I required it. Unlike most of London, Mr. Jewkes had emerged from the financial disasters of the summer unscathed and had contrived to purchase an estate in Norfolk at a price that would have been thought laughable only weeks previously. As he himself observed, he was in a position to be generous.

Besides, he was exceptionally fond of the child. Whenever he could, he visited us and dandled the little boy upon his knee, singing snatches of nonsense and contorting his butcher's face into humorous expressions to make the child chuckle. Our cottage, he said to me once, as he flung himself contentedly into the chair by the fire, was not unlike the one he had lived in as a boy, a place where he might loosen his collar and his proprieties a little. I had the impression that in the Norfolk house he was careful as a caller, anxious not to dirty the fine carpets or break the porcelain. From what he said of his wife, it was easy to imagine her wincing as he set his feet upon the silk-upholstered chaises or blew his nose upon the lace-embroidered napkins. He never complained of her, but there was a softness that came over his features, an easiness in his sigh of pleasure when I brought him muffins hot from the oven upon a battered tin plate, that assured me he was happy with the arrangements he had made.

I had no need to concern myself with the business of making money. But all the same I wished to. It occurred to me that when I had made a little I might send for my mother, if she was still alive. The idea pleased Mary considerably. I would continue with my studies, improving my reading and writing so that our son might know what it meant to know the joys of scholarship. That way, too, I told Mary, I might be able to set down our story, so that one day, when he was old enough to be told it, he might know how, despite all the attempts to deprave him, he had held firm and come into the world in his own fine form, untouched by the perversions of a fiendish imagination, truly himself and truly loved, as completely as any boy in history or fable.

Now it is done. Mary's headstone is mossy and the humped blanket of earth that covers her is thick with the juicy bright grass of May. Henry and I visited the grave yesterday and left flowers, handfuls of bluebells that Henry had picked himself. Clods of earth clung to their startled roots. His hands are plump with dimples for knuckles, not yet the hands of a youth, but they are strong and know nothing of hesitancy. I watched the child as we made our way back to the cottage and marvelled at the eagerness that springs in his limbs, as if he can hardly wait for the next minute of his life to begin. I do not know yet how much of this account I shall share with him, or which of the papers that Edgar left in my care I should permit him to see. I am not yet ready for him to learn that there are people in this world who may not be trusted.

As we closed the wych-gate behind us, Henry spied a cat lurking beneath a hawthorn hedge and, dropping to his knees, crawled in beside it and set about engaging it in serious discourse. As I waited for him to finish, a lady in a dress of fine blue silk came up the path. She carried a flat basket filled with white and yellow flowers and looked for all the world like one of those shiny shepherdess figurines whose porcelain hands and glazed features owe nothing to ordinary work. Her expression stiffened a little when I did not immediately step out of her way, but when she saw Henry's bottom protruding from beneath the hedge, she permitted herself a small smile.

"How engaging," she said graciously, inclining her head towards me. "Chattering away like a veritable monkey."

The cat uncurled itself from Henry's embrace and, stretching, disappeared into the dark reaches of the hedge. Henry wriggled backwards, his hair stiff with twigs. His bottom lip protruded as he frowned up at me, ready to blame me for the cat's precipitate removal. Smiling, I shook my head at him and held out my hand.

"Oh, no, madam," I said firmly as I pulled Henry to his feet. His hand was warm and slightly sticky. "There is nothing of the monkey about this boy. Nothing at all."

AUTHOR'S NOTE

At about the time that I was finishing my first novel, an old friend of mine from university who is now one of a tiny and elite group of Courtauld Institute–trained wall-painting conservators called me and asked if I would be interested in coming to visit her latest project. She and her partner had just won for their company what was arguably the most exciting contract in London for a decade: to clean the eight frescoed panels in the dome of St. Paul's Cathedral, painted by Sir James Thornhill between 1715 and 1719.

Her working conditions were by any standards spectacular. Suspended from a central pillar (a distance from the tip of the dome's cross to the floor of 365 feet, a deliberate one for every day of the year), the scaffold covered one-quarter of the dome at a time. Between the wooden planks one could glimpse the black and white marble of the floor hundreds of feet below, a precarious-enough feeling. But the men who had painted these enormous and elaborate scenes from St. Paul's life had worked at this height on rickety wooden platforms, held aloft by ropes and pulleys. The thought of it filled me with a kind of queasy awe.

St. Paul's Cathedral, at the same time a monument to God and to the wealth and might of England's first city, had always seemed to me to embody the contradictions that defined the early eighteenth century. Its design, for example, took much of its inspiration from St. Peter's Basilica in Rome, and yet it was the centrepiece of a faith that held tight to a profound distrust of Catholicism (Grayson Black's distaste for the structure was by no means a rarity). It was a source of civic pride, and yet the tax on coal that paid for its construction was widely resented. Its architect, Sir Christopher Wren— esteemed architect of more than fifty London churches in the thirty years after the Great Fire of London in 1666 and knighted by King

Charles II in 1673—was all the same in 1710 accused by Parliament of corruption and had his salary suspended. Indeed, he was to provide £2,000 of his own money towards his cathedral's completion, a small fortune at that time. And when, after thirty-five years, the magnificent edifice was finally finished, the voices of its bishops were frequently drowned out by the racket of picnicking families and petty traders. Even the dome itself was an illusion, not one but three domes, one inside the other, to support its massive weight and to create the perfect proportions Wren sought, both inside and out. That day in the dome, I knew before I was back at ground level that my next story might be found somewhere in the shadow of this remarkable building.

Georgian society was, if far from secular, a time of practical and moderate Anglicanism. There was a widespread distrust of fanatics and their religious "enthusiasm." England, after all, had, some seventy years earlier, been embroiled in a bloody civil war in which religious differences had played a major part; throughout the first decades of the new century, papist Jacobites plotted to topple the state. Small wonder then that, in a sermon delivered in 1715, the Bishop of Gloucester accused zealots of wreaking "more cruelty, wars, massacres, burnings, more hatred, animosity, perverseness and peevishness" than almost anyone else. England, by contrast with Catholic Europe—where heretics were still routinely persecuted, even burned—was a place of tolerance, its religious freedoms enshrined in law.

And yet religious urges remained deep and strong. Samuel Johnson wrote often of his terror of damnation, of being "sent to Hell, Sir, and punished everlastingly." Away from the metropolis, much of religious belief might be rooted in magic and superstition, but Johnson was right when he said that "there are in reality very few infidels." Moreover, religious divides ran deep; the old spectre of popery remained alive and well.

There were other fundamental contradictions. The first decades of the eighteenth century were economically capitalist, materialist, and market-oriented; enterprising small businessmen found rich rewards in the ebullient commercial climate. A national lottery, designed to raise funds for the Exchequer, had been introduced in 1694, and a number of winners rocketed to riches in this way. The newly established Bank of England had made credit secure, and the South Sea Company, with the king as governor, spearheaded a feverish interest in investment. In the course of a single year, its stock rose from £100 a share to over £1,000. It mattered little that its economic foundations were a chimera.

For more than a year, England was in the grip of speculation madness. Among the many companies to go public in 1720, one famously advertised itself as "a company for carrying out an undertaking of great advantage, but nobody is to know what it is." Spoof or not, it attracted considerable interest from would-be investors. But by the late summer of 1720, the fragile edifice could support itself no longer. It crashed spectacularly. Some vast fortunes had been made; many more were lost.

Those who had made money moved comfortably into the gentlemen classes. It was a time of easy mobility between classes, so that the Swiss lexicographer Guy Miège was able to claim that "the title of gentleman is commonly given in England to all that distinguish themselves from the common sort of people by good garb, genteel air or good education, wealth or learning." Even Daniel Defoe, the novelist and commentator—himself a native of England—agreed that "our tradesmen are not as in other countries the meanest of our people. Some of the greatest and best and most flourishing families, among not the gentry only but even the nobility, have been raised from trade." It was a remarkably fluid society, with rapidly fluctuating prosperity and impoverishment, depending upon application, astuteness, and the luck of marriages and health. Success was precarious, and every wealthy family was forever keeping poor relations at bay.

It is revealing, however, that at the same time Defoe fretted over what he considered shopkeepers' "ostentation of plate." For all its culture of enterprise, politically England remained hierarchical, hereditary, and privileged. Upward mobility was individual rather than collective, and while it was easy enough to slip quietly between the ranks of the gentry, rare was the humble man who penetrated the very highest levels of society. It was easier to marry a peer than to acquire a peerage. Professional bodies such as the College of Physicians and the Inns of Court operated as closed monopolies that guarded their privileges jealously and made sure that the pecking order was carefully maintained. Physicians looked down upon surgeons, who were in turn snooty about apothecaries, who themselves derided druggists.

The practice of medicine was bedevilled with similar contradictions. Newton's massively influential *Principia*, published in 1687, presented a new mechanical and mathematical interpretation of the natural world. The medical experiment was central to the generation of new medical knowledge; the discovery by William Harvey of the circulation of the blood was a direct result of his detailed study of the heart and its valves. By the second decade of the eighteenth century, systematic experimentation and clinical trials were recognised procedures for the validation of medical theories. Several cadavers of criminals were made available to the College of Surgeons every year for anatomisation; dogs were cut open alive before an audience in pursuit of a finer understanding of the specific functions of their organs. There was much disagreement over the meaning of what was found, and interpretations of the body were put forward that were variously mechanical, corpuscular, experimental, or anatomical (although interestingly almost no consideration was given at all to the ethics of practice).

And still the College of Physicians clung tenaciously to the medieval principles of Galenism, which explained the workings of the body in terms of its four humours, even if they were forced to accommodate them rather uncomfortably within the framework of newer philosophies. They argued, not altogether unconvincingly, that the practice of traditional medicine worked better than any medicine based on the new philosophy. Certainly Roy Porter has shown that hardly any eighteenth-century advance helped to cure the sick directly. Physicians continued to avoid the physical examination of ailing patients, considering such an approach a breach of so-cial etiquette and sexual propriety. Instead, they based their diag-noses upon their interpretations of a patient's "history." The medieval palliatives of blood-letting and emetics remained the staple treatment. As Matthew Prior quipped in 1714, "Cur'd yester-day of my Disease, I died last Night of my Physician."

And always the advance of rational scientific knowledge came up against the resistance of deep-seated religious belief. At all levels of society, illness was still regarded by many as a matter of trial or punishment and death as divine retribution. Life was precarious and recovery a matter of God's will. All the same, there was a seemingly inexhaustible appetite for patent medicines, preferably with as many "active" ingredients as could be crammed into the bottle, and they continued to be sold not only by travelling mountebanks but by many reputable shops and establishments. A significant number contained active ingredients such as opium that were not only poi-sonous in large doses but also highly addictive; one, Anderson's Scots Pills, first introduced in 1635, were still being sold in 1876. It is interesting to note that while there was an awareness of opium's ad-dictive properties, opium addicts were considered less shameful than quaint or eccentric, an object of curiosity rather than censure or alarm. Assumptions that we find bizarre today, such as the theory of maternal impression, central to this novel, remained for the most part conventional orthodoxies, with reports on monstrous births and extraordinary pregnancies read frequently at the meetings of the Royal Society and published in their *Philosophical Transactions*.

And what of the spirit of England, of London? What were they like, these people who would breathe life into my story? As the late historian Roy Porter succinctly described it, "The House of Hanover inherited a hard-working, hard-living, plain-speaking na-tion which only gradually became more preoccupied with refine-ment." Londoners had an ingrained tolerance of drunkenness and squalor and were notably unsqueamish in their habits (the diarist Samuel Pepys once nonchalantly defecated in a fireplace, leaving it for the servants to clean up). Emotions were near the surface; the stiff upper lip that has since come to define the English had not yet been invented. Life was noisy and violent, compensated by the aggressive pursuit of pleasures and passions. Foreigners were astonished at the licence permitted to the people and found the English extraordinarily politically well-informed and assertive. The lifeblood of popular politics ran through the torrent of newspapers, handbills, ballads, posters, and cartoons that flooded the ubiquitous coffee-houses and taverns and spilled out onto the streets.

Public life was a men's-only club. The prevailing opinion was that men were intended to excel in reason, in business, and in action; women, by contrast, should always be submissive, obedient, virtuous, and modest. As Lord Chesterfield opined, "Women are children of a larger growth....[A] man of sense only trifles with them." Indeed, once a woman was married, she had as little right under the law as a child; everything she owned, down to her undergarments, became the property of her husband. He maintained, moreover, the legal right to beat his wife so long as the stick was no thicker than a man's thumb. At the beginning of the century, it was still common for a father to arrange his daughter's marriage, giving her at best a veto over his choice, and the law clearly stated that while a woman's adultery was grounds for divorce, this rule did not apply to her husband. There are in the records examples of independent women who ran chop-houses, taverns, shops, and brothels, most of them widows or daughters who had inherited their businesses from their fathers. But for the majority of women, such freedoms remained out of reach. For those without private means, marriage or servitude were the only alternatives to destitution and, for both, proof of "good character" was a prerequisite. Those like Defoe's Moll Flanders or indeed Eliza Tally—rash, wilful, headstrong, and denied the protection afforded by either money or good birth—could all too easily destroy their lives almost before they had begun.

Early eighteenth-century London affected me as it affected so many of its occupants, leaving me breathless and exhilarated. So much bustle and noise, so many distractions and diversions, so many

ACKNOWLEDGMENTS

There is insufficient space here to acknowledge each one of the many historians and writers whose work has helped to illuminate my understanding of eighteenth-century London but there are some without whom I most certainly would not have been able to begin this book.

Eighteenth-century London boasted social commentators of matchless wit and acuity and I have shamelessly plundered the writings of Samuels Johnson and Pepys, Jonathan Swift, Joseph Addison, and the German visitor and chronicler Zacharias Conrad van Uffenbach, who in 1710 famously had his man carve his initials into the stone of the lantern of St. Paul's Cathedral. My favourite among all of these, however, remains the diary of an ordinary visitor to London in 1704, one Ned Ward, who chronicled his innumerable adventures in the capital with laugh-out-loud wit and gusto in *The London Spy*.

As for more contemporary analysts, I am particularly indebted to the late Roy Porter who was as mind-bogglingly prolific as he was brilliant. *English Society in the Eighteenth Century, London: A Social History,* and *Enlightenment* were all invaluable resources in understanding the society and sentiments of the period. The more colloquial perspective of the ordinary man was admirably provided by Peter Earle's *A City Full of People: Men and Women of London 1650–1750* and *The World of Defoe. Manners and Customs of London in the Eighteenth Century* by J. P. Malcolm, and Maureen Waller's *1700: Scenes from London Life* were equally evocative, while *The Monster City* by Jack Lindsay provided wonderfully vivid pictures of the seamier sides of London life. *The Criers and Hawkers of London* by Sean Shesgreen provided the double treat of his perceptive commentary and the wonderful drawings by Marcellus Laroon that brought the street sellers of late seventeenth-century London vividly to life on the page. I am also obliged to Peter Ackroyd, whose *London: A Biography* proved, yet again, an inexhaustible source of anecdote and inspiration. A special mention should also go to Dennis Severs, sadly now dead, whose painstaking restoration of a Huguenot silk weaver's house at 18 Folgate Street in Spitalfields, London, allows the visitor an extraordinary insight into the living conditions of the time.

In my quest to understand the medical structures and sensibilities of the early Enlightenment I am in debt once more to the indefatigable Roy Porter, whose *Quacks: Fakers and Charlatans in English Medicine* proved endlessly useful. A number of the works he wrote in partnership with Dorothy Porter, particularly *Patients' Progress* and *In Sickness and In Health*, were equally critical to my understanding of contemporary medical theory, as was the collection of essays he edited, *Patients and Practitioners*. On the subject of maternal imagination, Jan Bondeson's *A Cabinet of Medical Curiosities* and Dennis Todd's *Imagining Monsters* provided excellent starting points, while I relied heavily for the detail upon the several tracts published by two doctors in the 1720s, James Blondel and Daniel Turner, whose views on the subject were radically opposed to one another. Ulisse Aldrovandi's extraordinary collections of drawings of "monstrous" humans, *Monstrorum Historia*, first published in 1642, directly inspired the book examined with such horror by Eliza in the novel. I would also like to thank the staff of the library at the Royal Society who allowed me access to their remarkable archive of original documents and who, on discovering my particular interests, went out of their way to dig out for me far more and better material than I had thought to request.

Two lively and informative studies of the causes and effects of the South Sea Bubble also proved useful in researching this book, *The Moneymaker* by Janet Gleeson and Malcolm Balen's *A Very English Deceit*.

Finally, thanks must go to Mary Mount and her team at Viking, to Clare Alexander, to Sophie and Stephen Paine whose invitation to visit their restoration of the dome at St. Paul's Cathedral provided the inspiration for this novel, and to Chris for his never-ending support and enthusiasm.

DATE DUE

LIVING MARINE MOLLUSCS

LIVING MARINE
MOLLUSCS

C. M. Yonge and T. E. Thompson

COLLINS
ST JAMES'S PLACE, LONDON

William Collins Sons & Co Ltd
London · Glasgow · Sydney · Auckland
Toronto · Johannesburg

TO
FELLOW MALACOLOGISTS
WHOSE
OBSERVATIONS HAVE MADE THIS
BOOK POSSIBLE

Distributed in the United States by
american malacologists
P. O. Box 4208
Greenville, Delaware
19807, U. S. A.

First published 1976
© C. M. Yonge and T. E. Thompson 1976
ISBN 0 00 219099 0

Made and Printed in Great Britain by
William Collins Sons & Co Ltd Glasgow

Contents

*

Photographs

*

7

Introduction

*

'So, that alone is worthy to be called *Natural History*, which investigates and records the condition of living things, of things in a state of nature; if animals, of *living* animals . . . . this would indeed be *zoology*, *i.e.* the science of *living* creatures.'

Philip Henry Gosse, *A Naturalist's Sojourn in Jamaica*, 1851

THIS book, initially planned as a single-handed account of British marine molluscs has emerged as a work of wider scope and with a second author whose expert knowledge has greatly increased its value. Each author is, however, solely responsible for the chapters he has written. The original restriction to the British fauna has been widened to cover marine molluscs in general and with necessary concentration on a limited number of animals. There are a number of excellent books about British molluscs most of them largely, if not exclusively, concerned with their shells. It would be pointless to produce just another such survey. It is a general account of living molluscs, of their extraordinary diversity of form and habit, which is lacking and which this book attempts to supply.

The British molluscan fauna, although extensive, is that of the north temperate Atlantic and inevitably lacking in representatives of many groups that live in warmer, or colder, latitudes, in other oceans or in open waters far from land or in profound depths. Such animals appear in these pages but in the majority of cases these have all been personally encountered and studied as living animals during widely ranging visits in many seas.

The author of a faunistic book rightly endeavours to describe the shell or outward appearance – if it be a shell-less sea slug or a squid or octopus – of every mollusc likely to be encountered in that area by the most assiduous collector. Concern with the living animal, on the other hand, involves describing them in some detail and saying a good deal about a selected number of representative molluscs. Those chosen are either extremely common – such as the limpets, winkles, cockles and mussels of the shore – or are of outstanding interest as revealing the bewildering ramifications of molluscan evolution. The dramatis personae are therefore limited, consisting on the one hand of the common and successful and, on the other, of molluscs usually adapted for life under unusual circumstances or that have chosen unusual means to achieve their ends. Instances are the camouflaged carrier shells and also the tridacnid bivalves of Indo-Pacific coral reefs that 'farm' plant cells in widely exposed and richly pigmented tissues (Fig. 1). Only to the sea-slugs, the particular concern of one of us, does this contrast between the commonplace and the spectacular not apply. Little noted in standard conchologies (after all few have more than the vestige of a shell), they are among the most beautiful of marine animals (Plates 8, 9, 10), and almost every one a *prima donna* with its own colour pattern and its individual food and method of feeding.

Understanding of living animals demands some knowledge of structure. But most emphatically this is *not* a work on comparative anatomy. Little more is mentioned about structure than is normally exposed by the active animal or, in the bivalves, by removal of one valve to expose the mantle cavity with contained gills and foot. Starting with the first, far-remote molluscs, the structure and life pattern of which can only be surmised, evolutionary pathways are traced to their present, often so completely unpredictable, end points (and this excludes freshwaters and the land where we do not follow them). Vertebrate evolution would seem – at least to man – to attain one culmination but in the molluscs it leads to a bewildering diversity of form and to the conquest, by so many routes, of innumerable environments.

Concern here is with molluscan activity, how these animals crawl, swim, burrow or bore into rock or timber, how they feed and respire, how they reproduce, with significant facts about development including larval forms. There is less concern about internal organs although constant preoccupation with behaviour which involves sense organs and muscles – often acting by moving fluid in the extensive molluscan blood spaces – and so bringing in the nervous system. But technicalities are rigidly avoided.

So much of the value of a book like this depends on illustration and here collaboration has had the great added advantage of involving that of G. H. Brown who is entirely responsible for the drawings of sea-slugs in Chapters 10 and 11 and also for redrawing, arranging and lettering the bulk of the other figures. It is a pleasure that half of the colour plates are from photographs by Dr D. P. Wilson. C.M.Y. wishes to record his gratitude to Mrs Ellen Thorson for her kind permission to reproduce several of the late Professor Gunnar Thorson's Christmas cards, famous to all fellow marine biologists and providing such ideal illustrations here because depicting such very vigorously living molluscs. Other figures were originally drawn by Miss Jan Campbell and Mrs Vera Warrender as illustrations for research papers and thanks are renewed for the skill and care they represent. Thanks are added to Mr Dennis Cremer for expert photographic assistance and to Christopher Yonge for copying figures. We unite in gratitude to Vera Fretter and Alastair Graham whose *British Prosobranch Molluscs* has been a rich source of illustrations, and this gives an opportunity of mentioning this wonderfully erudite and comprehensively illustrated book hardly, it is true, for the general reader but representing a supreme achievement of British malacology.

Where the source of a drawing is not acknowledged, it represents either original drawings by G. H. Brown or else the reproduction (sometimes with the addition of lettering) of illustrations that have appeared in previous publications by the authors.

On the subject of shells there is here neither space, nor indeed need, for more than the briefest reference. Of recent years the molluscan shell has been

Introduction

the subject matter of a series of magnificently illustrated volumes, revelations of beauty in both form and colour. The colour plates of many have been produced in Japan which has also been responsible for books on the shells of the world as well as those from Japanese waters. All such books are listed at the end of this volume.

Happily we are equally fortunate with descriptions of the British molluscan fauna. All British shells likely to be encountered are covered in *British Shells* by Nora F. McMillan and in the *Identification of the British Mollusca* by Gordon Beedham while, each confined to one major group, are *British Prosobranchs* (marine snails) by Alastair Graham and *British Bivalve Seashells* by Norman Tebble. Both are admirably illustrated and these two provide probably the best accompaniments to this book. To them will be added (about the time this book is published) Volume I of the *Biology of Opisthobranch Molluscs* (sea-slugs) by T. E. Thompson and the synoptic *British Opisthobranch Mollusca* (corresponding to Alastair Graham's *British Prosobranchs*) by T. E. Thompson and G. H. Brown.

Molluscs are further described in the context of the shore – where most of them will be encountered – in *The Littoral Fauna of the British Isles* by Nellie B. Eales and in *Collins Pocket Guide to the Sea Shore* by John Barrett and C. M. Yonge. Mention might also be made of the New Naturalist volume on *The Sea Shore* which, apart from general descriptions of common shore molluscs, contains more colour plates including, in particular, two showing the file shell, *Lima hians*, with extended orange-coloured tentacles and justifying the claim that this is the most beautiful of British bivalves.

Literature about molluscs is endless. Beginning in the fourth century BC with Aristotle – a magnificent marine biologist whom we shall have reason

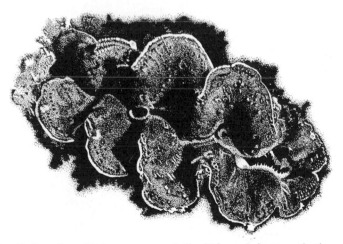

FIG. 1.   Boring clam, *Tridacna crocea*: shell within rock but mantle tissues containing symbiotic plant cells fully expanded exposing these plants to the light. (By permission of the Geological Society of America)

11

to mention particularly when dealing with octopods and squids – book after book and ever increasing floods of research papers have been written about them. Generally speaking these dealt first with the shell (although this does not apply to Aristotle) and only later first with the structure and then with the functioning of the entire animal, with its development and the sometimes unexpected course of its life history. Most recently interest has broadened to include ecology and behaviour. There are, at the time of writing this, no less than eighteen journals produced in ten countries together with a further two which are internationally published, all exclusively devoted to the publication of papers on molluscs which also appear in a large number of journals of general zoological content. What should be chosen for description and comment out of this ever growing wealth of knowledge? No two writers who attempted a book of this type would choose the same animals or approach the subject matter from the same standpoint. Each would write about the animals he knew best and this is precisely what we have done, hoping that this bias will be justified by the greater authority with which we write and the greater freedom for comment it confers. We shall be satisfied if it confirms and extends the interests of those who read what we have written.

Chapter 1

Historical

*

A BOOK dealing with the nature and habits of marine molluscs calls for some brief introductory words about the growth of interest in these animals. Long before the dawn of history man was keenly interested in intertidal and shallow water molluscs as a source of food, to an extent that is indicated by the vast mounds of shells in prehistoric kitchen middens. The larger shells were used as drinking vessels, lamps or trumpets, smaller ones for decoration while fish hooks and other objects were made from shells. In classic times the scallop was to become a motif in decoration and later the badge worn by pilgrims to the shrine of St James at Santiago de Compostela.

Science emerges out of the first stirring of curiosity about the surrounding world which accompanies the birth of civilization. In the western world it takes shape in Greece where Aristotle, a supreme marine biologist, sought to arrange in orderly manner the Mediterranean animals known to him. His subdivisions of the animal kingdom included 'Ostracoderma' which comprised snails, slugs and bivalves, and the more elaborately organized 'Malacia' of octopods, cuttlefish and squids which he placed higher in his static ladder of life, the highest rung of which was occupied by man, the sole possessor of a 'rational' soul. He also collected much information about the habits, including reproduction, of molluscs.

So knowledge long remained, more debased by additions of credulity than increased by critical observations. The gradual removal of the dead hand of authority at the time of the Renaissance led to a reassessment of the then state of knowledge at the hands of a group of encyclopedic naturalists of whom the Swiss, Conrad Gesner, who lived from 1516 to 1565, is the most famous. The great advance in science in the seventeenth century, the age of Harvey, Boyle and Newton in this country, sees the beginning of the scientific study of molluscs. The first book devoted entirely to them, by the Jesuit, Filippo Buonanni, entitled *Ricreatione dell'Occhio e delle Mente nell'Osseruation' delle Chiocciole*, was published in Rome in 1681 and consists largely of conchological information with numerous figures of shells. One of the three title pages is reproduced in Figure 2.

Meanwhile a more significant figure was appearing in this country in the person of Martin Lister, a medical man who practised first in York and then in London, shortly before his death in 1711, where he was to be appointed physician in ordinary to Queen Anne. In zoology he links the pre-Linnean John Ray, whom he befriended over a difficult period, with the eighteenth-century Hans Sloane whom he proposed for election to the Royal Society and whose widely ranging natural history collections were to form the basis of those of the British Museum.

FIG. 2. Title page of *Ricreatione dell'Occhio e della Mente nell' Osseruation delle Chiocciole, Proposta a' Curiosi delle Opere della Natura*, by Filippo Buonanni 1681.

Lister's first work, *Historia Animalium Angliae*, published in 1678, is an attempt to describe the British fauna although only dealing with spiders, land, freshwater shells and sea shells together with 'stones figured like them'. These were fossils, the true nature of which he failed to realize, unlike a few more far-seeing contemporaries. Far more significant is his second book, published in sections between 1685 and 1692, which aimed at a comprehensive description of all known shells. This *Historiae sive Synopsis Conchyliorum*, to be described by Linnaeus as the most thorough account available of any group of animals, consists of 1057 engravings of shells made by his daughter Susannah and his wife (just possibly second daughter Anna) and mounted on 486 pages. There is no text apart from what is engraved on the plates and many figures are not even named although the great majority are recognizable. These are useful comments about localities and, most significantly, the plates are grouped in sections based on similarities some of which remain valid.

In Paris around this time, Lister visited the King's Library where he was cordially welcomed by the Deputy Library Keeper who, in his own words (*A Journey to Paris in the year 1668*), 'made me in particular a very great Compliment, as a considerable Benefactor to that place, showing me most of the Books, and the Names of the rest, I had publisht in *Latin*; and shewed a great satisfaction, that he had got the *Synopsis Conchyliorum*, which he had caused to be Bound very elegantly, I told him, that I was sorry to see it there, and wondered how he came by it; for it was, I assured him, but a very imperfect trial of the Plates, which I had disposed of to some few Friends only, till I should be able to close and finish the Design; which I now had done to my

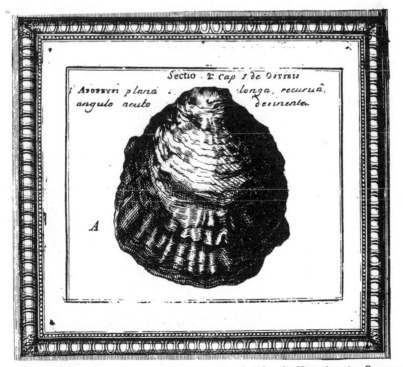

FIG. 3. Native oyster, *Ostrea edulis*, from Martin Lister's *Historiae sive Synopsis Conchyliorum*, 1685.

power, and would redeem that Book with a better Copy at my return into *England*: The same Promise I renewed to the Abbé *Louvois*, the Library Keeper, at his own instance, when I had the Honour to Dine with him.' Adding that 'The Reader will pardon me the Vanity, if I tell him, that this Book was no inconsiderable Present, even for so great a Prince, as the King of *France*; for that besides the time that it took me up (Ten years at least) at leisure hours, to dispose, methodise and figure this part of Natural History, it could not have been performed by any Person else for less than 2000*l*. *Sterling*; of which Sum yet a great share it stood me in, out of my Private Purse.'

He would have been happy had he known he was to be later designated the 'father of British Testacology'. Overwhelmed by the wealth of shells coming from all over the world, he realized that adequate classification must be preceded by a general survey of all known types and so, in the words of Peter Dance (*Shell Collecting*, 1966), 'the first of the major shell iconographies was born'. There were indeed many to follow, some magnificently illustrated in colour, over the following two centuries as voyages of scientific exploration brought back an ever-increasing diversity of shells. And new species continue to be found to this day.

Lister's final contributions reveal his interest in the animal itself. In three *Exercitationes* produced between 1694 and 1696 he examined and figured the organs of the body and speculated on their function in land snails and slugs, in the snail *Viviparus* and the bivalve *Anodonta*, both from freshwater, and, of more significance here, in the squid *Loligo* and three common intertidal bivalves, species of *Cardium*, *Tellina* and *Tapes* (now *Venerupis*). Finally, in a paper contributed to the 19th volume of the *Philosophical Transactions* of the Royal Society, he deals with the structure of the scallop, *Pecten*.

Linnaeus is important because in his *Systema Naturae*, where he attempted to reveal the plan of creation, he adopted (although he did not originate) binomial nomenclature – one name for the genus, a second for the species. By so doing he established what came to be universally accepted names for every species of plant and animal, including of course the molluscs. In other respects he made little advance. He divided the invertebrates into two classes, Insecta and Vermes, characterized by the supposed general presence of antennae and tentacles respectively. The latter included an order he named Testacea which comprised the shelled molluscs but also barnacles and worms in calcareous shells; he divided all these into multivalves, bivalves and univalves, the last with or without a regular spire to the shell. He was no anatomist and followed earlier customs in largely disregarding the animals or 'testaceous bodies' which he grouped – with minimal reference to the shells – into ten 'genera', *Limax*, *Doris*, *Spio*, *Amphitrite*, *Terebella*, *Nereis*, *Ascidia*, *Tethys*, *Triton* and *Sepia*. Later conchologists who employed the Linnean system would describe the shell in detail merely referring 'its animal' to one of these genera of which only the two first and the last three are even molluscan. The shell-less 'naked tribes' Linnaeus did designate Mollusca this also embracing in 'admired disorder' all manner of worms and zoophytes with starfish, sea urchins and other echinoderms.

Historical

This division of interest between the shell and the enclosed animal raises problems unique to molluscs – one never, for instance, distinguishes between the shell and animal in lobsters or in sea urchins. But from very early times molluscan shells, often brought from distant countries with the animal unknown, have been regarded as objects of beauty or utility in their own right and without consideration of the animal which originally formed them. Indeed the connection between the two was often far from clear and malacology as distinct from conchology only slowly appeared. Conchologists and malacologists persist to this day, the former primarily interested in shells which are often of prime consideration in classification as well as eminently collectable, how much so the reader can discover by reference to the modern books on *Shells* listed at the end of this volume, many of them containing coloured plates showing shells of striking beauty both in form and colour.

The old-fashioned conchologists were apt to take the first opportunity of getting rid of the unwanted 'soft parts'; the animal was regarded as of negligible importance, a mere inhabitant of a much more significant shell, a wide assemblage of which were thought to house similar occupants. But to the malacologist it is the animal that matters and the shell, which may be lost in the adult – as it is in marine and terrestrial slugs and in octopods – is a calcareous structure which, however elaborate and beautiful, is a protective covering formed by living tissues and to which muscles are attached. It differs from the shells of other invertebrates because formed by a 'mantle' instead of by the whole body to only a certain region of which does it therefore conform. Moreover its growth may be accompanied by the formation of spines or other protuberances which have no counterpart on the surface of the body. Certain regions of the animal may extend outside the protective covering of the shell to be withdrawn by contraction of the attaching muscles. Many modern conchologists are, of course, keenly interested in the animals and, although there are some differences in approach, it is largely historical development which is perpetuated in the names of the two British societies concerned with the study of molluscs, the Conchological Society of Great Britain and Ireland and the Malacological Society of London.

Returning to history, two contemporaries of Linnaeus wrote about British molluscs. In the fourth volume of his *British Zoology* published in 1777, Thomas Pennant (or just possibly his son of the same name) dealt with Vermes in which he included both naked 'Mollusca' and shelled 'Testacea'. His classification was Linnean but something was recorded about habits and distribution and he quoted local records such as those of William Borlase, antiquarian and natural historian of Cornwall (Fig. 3). Also devoted solely to British species is the *Historia Naturalis Testaceorum Britanniae* or *The British Conchology* published in the following year by Emanuel Mendes da Costa who was the son of a Portuguese doctor resident in London. This is a handsome volume, written in English and French in parallel columns and very well illustrated. It contains, incidentally, what appears to be the first use of the word conchology. The current attitudes to patrons – whose prior subscriptions alone made publication possible – and to the subject matter are revealed in the dedication to Sir Ashton Lever in acknowledgement of 'The

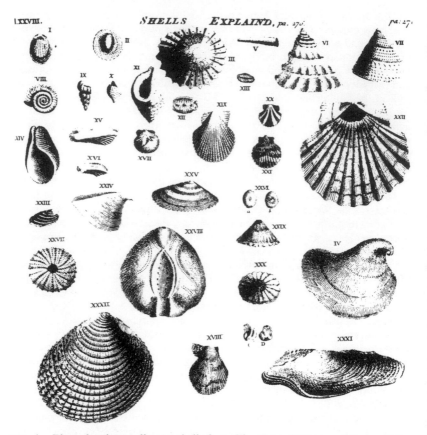

FIG. 4. Plate showing molluscan shells from *The Natural History of Cornwall*, by
William Borlase, A.M., F.R.S., published in Oxford, 1758.

noble, magnificent, and curious Museum you have collected at Leicester-
House, for the inspection of the Public . . . A glorious study! that leads the
human mind into a truly religious contemplation of the numberless, and incomprehensible Works of the Awful and Eternal Divinity'. There is more information here than in Pennant but unfortunately da Costa had his own,
non-Linnean, method of nomenclature. A distinguished conchologist and a
man of wide interests, his career ended in poverty and disgrace. Elected to the
Royal Society, he resigned the fellowship in 1763 when appointed Clerk to
the Society but four years later he was dismissed and enquiry revealed large
deficiencies in the funds for which he was responsible. His collections and
library were sold and he was sentenced to five years imprisonment.

Two French zoologists now demand attention. Following Linnaeus, the
classification of shells was greatly improved by Lamarck, probably the most

18

prolific namer of molluscan species especially in his *Histoire Naturelle des Animaux sans Vertèbres* (1812–22). Even more significant are the contributions of his fellow countryman, Cuvier, a supreme comparative anatomist who revealed the basic organization of the Mollusca which he regarded as comprising one of the four systems within which the structure of all animals was comprehended. In the later words of George Johnston, the author of *An Introduction to Conchology: or, Elements of the Natural History of Molluscous Animals* (1850), a leading naturalist of his time and the founder of the Ray Society which publishes books on the British Fauna and Flora, including molluscs, 'He has lifted the subject (Conchology) above raillery and ridicule, and placed, in its due rank, a large class of animals, than which none other more deservedly claim the attentions of the naturalist, the physiologist, and the geologist.' Cuvier was a supreme malacologist although failing to realize that, despite the shell plates that surround them and give a superficial molluscan appearance, barnacles are really crustaceans. This fact was to be demonstrated in 1830 by an obscure but, as one now realizes, outstandingly perceptive amateur marine biologist, John Vaughan Thompson. Born in Berwick upon Tweed, he became an army surgeon and in due course found himself stationed at Cork in the south of Ireland. There he proceeded to collect the minute animals of the plankton in what were possibly the first nets ever used for that purpose. It was by that means that he discovered the early, freely swimming stages of barnacles with the general appearance and jointed segmental limbs of crustaceans. Their change at settlement into immobile animals encased in calcareous plates is one of the most remarkable metamorphoses in the Animal Kingdom.

A further reduction of Cuvier's Mollusca was later made by the discovery that in the bivalved lamp shells, where the two valves are disposed above and below instead of laterally as in bivalve molluscs, the internal structure is totally different. They now constitute the Phylum Brachiopoda and are unlikely to be encountered although deep water species can be dredged in numbers from the Norwegian fjords and great populations of the stalked lamp shell, *Lingula*, collected from mud flats in tropical seas.

From the early years of the nineteenth century books on molluscs appear in ever increasing numbers, many deal with the shells of the entire world, sometimes consisting of plates showing, as far as possible, every known species so that collectors who must have numbered many thousands were able to arrange their 'cabinets'. Many of these books are magnificently illustrated but the reader is best referred to Peter Dance's *Shell Collecting* and *Rare Shells* for an account of these and of the great shell collectors of whom the Englishman, Hugh Cuming, a sailmaker who settled for a time in South America and later made a series of extensive collecting expeditions, is the most striking figure.

He owed much to Colonel George Montagu (1753–1815) a Devonshire squire and a naturalist of rare gifts, ornithologist as well as conchologist, of whom it was later written that 'he spoke of every creature as if one exceeding like it, yet different from it, would be washed up by the waves next tide. Consequently his descriptions are permanent.' His three-volume *Testacea*

Britannica or *Natural History of British Shells* remains of value; although his classification is Linnean it contains a wealth of personal observation.

A modest single volume *Conchological Dictionary of the British Islands* appeared in 1819 under the authorship of William Turton. He was an eccentric physician who, we are told, almost abandoned his profession so overwhelming was his desire to study British shells. His name is perpetuated in that of the small bivalve, *Turtonia minuta*. Although, unlike the massive tomes produced by earlier conchologists, his book was of pocket size indicating the rising popular interest in shell collecting, the colour plates are crude; his classification remained Linnean although in a subsequent larger and better illustrated work he accepted Lamarckian genera. There are numerous early nineteenth-century conchologies many of them of little scientific merit but their numbers and the frequent editions into which they ran do emphasize the extraordinary interest then taken in shells and their supposed high educational value, largely it would seem by the emphasis given to the diversity and beauty of the works of the Creator.

There may be instanced, *Lessons on Shells, as given to children between the ages of eight and ten in a Pestalozzian School, at Cheam, Surrey* published in 1832 with ten well chosen lithographic plates. Here the tone is set in Lesson V which begins,

> *Teacher.* Let us consider in what situation the mollusca are placed. They are, as you know, exposed to the dashing of the waves, borne by the violence of storms against rocks; and carried down rapid rivers. You can readily imagine the consequences of their being situated amidst such perils.
>
> *Child.* Yes. The shells must frequently be broken, and the poor animals perish.
>
> *Teacher.* Your first conclusion is true. The shells are often broken or injured; but God always makes a suitable provision for the circumstances under which he places his creatures. . . . This providential care is very evident in the history of the mollusca. We find that the construction of the shell varies according to the situation in which it is placed. . . . Some of the mollusca by adding to the weight of their little bark, are enabled to descend and seek a shelter in the deep of the ocean; some, you learnt, anchor themselves to rocks and thus bid defiance to dangers. But in spite of all these, and many more equally beautiful contrivances a breach is often effected in the habitation of the mollusca.
>
> *Child.* And then the poor animals must perish?
>
> *Teacher.* This is by no means inevitably the case, for they are gifted with the power of repairing their shells.

One wonders what interest in the molluscs was generated by such means but, no such criticism can be levelled at Mary Roberts's *The Conchologist's Companion* (1834) with a charming Baxter colour print as frontispiece and consisting of a series of letters 'written amid scenes of tranquillity and beauty. . . designed to exhibit the rich materials afforded by the science of Conchology for reflection and amusement. . .' A more scientific approach is made in the *Conchologist's Text-Book embracing the Arrangement of Lamarck and Linnæus, with a Glossary of Technical Terms* first published in 1831 by another military figure, Captain Thomas Brown, a voluminous writer on conchological and other matters who was to become curator of the Manchester Museum. This ran into many editions, the later ones corrected and enlarged by William MacGillivray, Professor of Natural History at Aberdeen. An early edition of this book had the unusual distinction of being plagiarized by no less a person than Edgar Allan Poe as *The Conchologist's First Book. . . .* published in Philadelphia in 1839. This is hardly a subject that would attract the pen of an impecunious author in these days but does indicate the then popularity of conchology in the United States, the contemporary and later scene of so very much distinguished work on molluscs.

These popular works, for moral edification and for the accurate arrangement of the shell cabinet were to be superseded in the middle of the century by works of a very different character. The inspiring figure was that of Edward Forbes, a Manxman educated at the University of Edinburgh who from childhood had collected shells and indeed all manner of creatures from the seas around his island home. Under his guidance dredging expeditions were carried out around British shores and the molluscs of offshore waters brought to the surface. This is a memorable period in British malacology celebrated at the annual meetings of the British Association by ditties such as Forbes's 'Song of the Dredge' which celebrated the success of dredging off the Shetlands in 1839, the first verse of which runs,

> Hurrah for the dredge, with its iron edge,
> And its mystical triangle.
> And its hided net with meshes set
> Odd fishes to entangle!
> The ship may move thro' the waves above,
> 'Mid scenes exciting wonder,
> But braver sights the dredge delights
> As it roves the waters under.

The results of his collecting and dredgings were published in some of the most charming, as well as the most erudite, books ever published on marine animals, on medusae, on starfishes and above all on molluscs. Here he collaborated with the like-minded Sylvanus Hanley of Oxford in the production of their four-volume *History of British Mollusca and their Shells*. This is one of the great works of British (indeed European) natural history, treating every species then known and as much concerned with the animal as with the shell it inhabited. As the authors note in their introduction, 'whilst the shelly portion of the body of the Mollusk was carefully inspected, treasured and delineated, the more perishable parts were sadly neglected, and although some of our earlier English naturalists, especially the illustrious Lister, attended to the organization of the entire creature, the shell alone occupied the attention of the majority of observers, even from the time of Linnaeus until within comparatively few years ago'. They were fortunate also in the artists who executed the long series of plates, illustrating the animals as well as their shells, both of them members of the Sowerby family, a dynasty of natural history artists and authors responsible for the illustration of many conchological and other natural history works over a period of some 150 years.

Living Marine Molluscs

Within ten years of the publication of 'Forbes and Hanley' – as it is always known – appeared the no less valuable *British Conchology* of Gwyn Jeffreys, another enthusiastic dredger who had been a companion of Wyville Thompson in the deep sea expeditions that led up to the great oceanographic circumnavigation of the world by HMS *Challenger* in 1872–76. He explained its production so soon after the other volumes as due to the need for a less expensive work and it was indeed produced by the same publisher. But even earlier than these two books, over a period of ten years starting in 1845, there had appeared the impressive seven parts of the Ray Society's *Monograph of the British Nudibranchiate Mollusca*, 'with appropriate coloured plates and figures showing anatomical details'. This beautifully illustrated account of British sea-slugs was the work of Joshua Alder and Albany Hancock and the originals of their plates may still be viewed at the Hancock Museum at Newcastle upon Tyne where they worked. A supplementary volume by Sir Charles Eliot (at one time British ambassador to Japan) appeared in 1910. The British marine molluscan fauna was thus finally covered only recently to be extended and the subject matter approached from more functional and ecological standpoints in the books mentioned in the Introduction. Nevertheless 'Forbes and Hanley', 'Jeffreys' and 'Alder and Hancock' will always repay consultation.

Going briefly back in time, it was with the information provided in such books that the growing volume of Victorian shore biologists, followers of Philip Henry Gosse – the 'Father' in his son's *Father and Son* – and of his numerous disciples including Charles Kingsley and George Henry Lewes, sought and identified the molluscs exposed on rocky shores and in tide pools left by the retreating tide, dug out of similarly exposed sandy beaches and mud flats or dredged in shallow offshore waters. Scores of popular shore books stimulated and guided their activities.

This interest lapsed, in part owing to the destruction of the shore populations over which these enthusiasts had searched and all too successfully collected. This century has seen the growth of a more scientific interest in the adaptations and life history of shore animals and plants and in zonation and other ecological aspects of intertidal life which one of us has attempted to describe in *The Sea Shore* volume of the *New Naturalist* Series. Such interest has embraced the molluscs which are among the most important and often the most conspicuous animals on rocky shores while digging reveals the wealth of burrowing bivalves and predatory snails beneath the surface of sandy beaches.

Today, as evidenced by the array of books about them, there is a worldwide increase of interest in shells, most marked, perhaps, in the United States which has the advantage of being washed by the waters of the two major oceans and so the home of both Atlantic and Indo-Pacific molluscs. Added to this is the realization that the molluscan animal is every bit as interesting as the shell it forms (and that many of the most beautiful do not form a shell at all) and that with the fascinating array of different forms goes an equivalent diversity of habits and adaptations. It is this growing interest in living molluscs which this book aims to foster.

Chapter 2

The nature of molluscs

*

IF we are to appreciate the full fascination of molluscs we must realize that they represent the end products of widely diverging evolutionary paths. On first, or indeed often detailed, examination, who would imagine that snails, oysters and cuttlefish represented variations on a common theme? Those outwardly so very different animals are constructed on a common ground plan and constitute one of the major subdivisions or phyla of the animal kingdom. Members of most phyla have obvious external similarities. The crustacean shrimps and crabs are clearly related to the insects, spiders and centipedes, all comprised within the Phylum Arthropoda; the radially symmetrical starfish, brittle stars, sea cucumbers and sea urchins no less obviously constitute the Phylum Echinodermata.

But the molluscs are very different. Their external appearance tells us little, may indeed be very misleading, and even the shell can vary widely in form or become enclosed within the tissues and finally lost. To understand these animals some initial knowledge of the basic structure is essential. And this is easy to convey because it is so simple, a simplicity, moreover, that lies at the root of success. It is the accompanying plasticity of the molluscan ground plan which has permitted its members to evolve in all manner of directions and to exploit almost every environment in the sea and in freshwaters and many of those on land. Within the sea molluscs occur both on and within the sea bed, in mid waters and again in wide and successful diversity in the illuminated surface waters where they form important sections of the plankton. There is even a flying squid which glides for short distances by means of enlarged lateral fins! Molluscs extend from the uppermost regions of the intertidal to the greatest depths of over 35,000 feet and from polar to tropical seas. There are probably somewhat over 50,000 species of marine molluscs.

The basic plan differs from that of all other phyla because, as we shall shortly see, it involves two symmetries, a basal one which is bilateral (like that of worms or arthropods, or vertebrates) on which is imposed another symmetry which is radial like that of the coelenterate jellyfish or sea anemones. This is a major cause of a diversity of form and habit exemplified by limpets which crawl over and adhere to rocks; snails which may crawl or burrow or, with reduced transparent shells, live in surface waters; bivalves which burrow into sand, bore into rock or timber or by various means attach themselves to hard surfaces; coat-of-mail shells (chitons) which crawl over irregular surfaces; soft-bodied octopods which inhabit crevices in rocks, cuttlefish which seek shelter in sand, and the stream-lined squids of mid and surface waters which, over short distances, are the speediest of all marine animals. These cephalopods also include the largest invertebrate animals, the giant squids,

23

species of *Architeuthis*, the food and the worthy antagonist of sperm whales. All these animals are molluscs and the gradual tracing of common structural features was a major triumph of comparative anatomy. The excitement of studying molluscs comes both from examining what they are and what they do but also tracing how they became what they now are.

A major event in evolutionary history occurred when primitive elongated, multicellular animals began to crawl on the one surface with one end normally in front. They now possessed an upper, or dorsal, and an under, or ventral, surface with anterior and posterior ends. Because the one end was constantly encountering new surroundings the sense organs needed for exploration developed there and with them nerves that carried information so received into the first beginnings of a co-ordinating 'brain'.

Increase in size raised problems solved in a variety of ways. In creatures such as the marine bristle worms (annelids) the elongated body became divided into segments each in some measure independent although all under control of the anterior brain. But the molluscs did things differently. They accumulated all the viscera, i.e. gut, heart and circulatory system, excretory and reproductive organs, in a 'hump' on the dorsal surface with the muscular system largely concentrated in a ventral 'foot' which from very early times could well have enabled the animal to crawl in much the same manner as modern snails. The animal became more compact but with an accompanying exposure of the most vital parts of the body. For this reason it is hard to envisage even the most primitive mollusc without a protective shell to cover this visceral hump.

This shell was formed by a sheet of tissue known as the mantle. This exclusively molluscan structure is almost infinitely plastic and of overwhelming significance in the extraordinary series of evolutionary changes which have resulted in the appearance of the modern array of molluscs. With its appearance (Fig. 5) over the viscera, the animal became divisible into two regions, the underlying foot with the head in front and above this the visceral mass with the covering mantle (or pallium). While initially the animal could be cut down the middle line into symmetrical right and left halves (i.e. was bilaterally symmetrical), yet the manner of growth was different in the two regions. In the former, increase was in length with the head dominating, but the mantle grew marginally, like additions to the skirt of a bell-tent. The mantle, therefore, has a radial symmetry which in some molluscs it imposes on the entire animal. By changes in growth around its margin it becomes responsible for the elaborate and varied coilings of snail shells and the various asymmetries of many bivalve shells.

Much of the evolutionary history of the molluscs is a consequence of the interplay of these two major regions of the body with their different modes of growth. Bilateral symmetry may never be lost or, after being lost, it may be reacquired – at least externally – and, where the constraining shell is reduced or lost, such animals may become highly active like squids. At the other extreme are molluscs in which radial symmetry is largely or completely imposed, the animals becoming sedentary or permanently attached.

Although molluscan shells are calcareous, the crystals of calcium carbonate

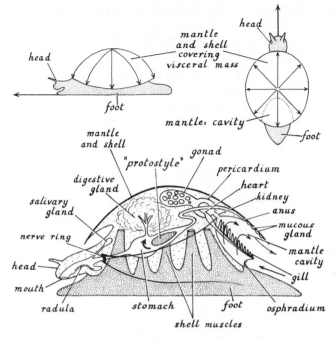

FIG. 5. Diagrammatic drawings indicating the basic molluscan characters: over-arching of head and foot by radially symmetrical mantle (and shell), posterior respiratory (mantle) cavity with gills and probable course of primitive water currents. Other details in text.

are laid down within a protein framework known as conchiolin. This non-calcareous matrix appears first in development and also most probably in evolution. In the earliest fossil-bearing rocks molluscs are already present; all the major existing groups occur together with a variety of enigmatic shells which probably represent all we shall ever know about extinct molluscan classes, the anatomy and habits of which we can only surmise. And behind all these extend millions of years of evolutionary history about which we know effectively nothing. Moreover non-calcareous shells leave little or no impression in sedimentary rocks. The early protective covering of toughened protein was probably relatively soon impregnated with crystals of calcium carbonate, a necessity as predatory animals became larger and protection against them became increasingly important. A series of alternative possibilities of profound future portent must early have presented themselves. The protein shell could be impregnated from one, two or several centres of calcification so giving rise to univalve, bivalve or multivalve shells.

When describing the evolutionary history of the vertebrates, we proceed in the series, fish – amphibia – reptiles – birds or mammals, and there are abundant fossils indicating when these major groups arose and how the later classes evolved from the earlier ones. But with the molluscs the position is totally different. Of the original mollusc from which all others evolved there is now no trace; we can but deduce its structure from that of its modern descendants, no group of which is descended from any other; we are dealing with the results of radiating evolution. To understand the relationships of modern molluscs, how they have diverged from one another and how not infrequently they have *converged*, we must indicate the probable structure of this hypothetical common ancestor (Fig. 5).

We noted its general form, the elongated muscular foot with the head in front and over this the humped complex of organs protected by a dome-like shell formed by a radially growing mantle. The simplest molluscs doubtless explored their surroundings by touch or chemically by way of sense endings on the head tentacles, some of which were stimulated by light and later evolved into increasingly complex eyes. Messages passed to the simple brain, the paired cerebral ganglia, from which nerve cords extended into the foot (so controlling movement) and also into the mantle and viscera. This is more or less the condition in the simplest modern molluscs although most of these possess paired accumulations of nerve cells in each of the four distinct regions of the body – head, foot, mantle and viscera. These ganglia vary in importance according to the relative significance of these regions in different molluscs because in these uniquely constructed animals, while the viscera must always be retained, the head, the foot or the mantle may each be lost, indeed in some both head *and* foot are lost.

The other attribute of the head is the presence of the mouth and within it the uniquely molluscan structure of the lingual ribbon or radula* (Plate 4). This horny tooth-bearing ribbon works in conjunction with a pair of biting jaws, sometimes united into a single structure on the upper surface. For the moment we merely note that the ribbon can be protruded through the mouth opening and its rows of teeth, acting as a rope on a pulley, scraped hard against the substrate, passing back, as on a conveyor belt, food material largely consisting of encrusting plants. As teeth are worn away new rows are continuously being added at the base. The numbers and form of the teeth vary greatly fitting their owners for dealing with all manner of different food materials. The evolution of the radular apparatus is one of the reasons for the supreme success of the molluscs, yet in one major group – the bivalves – it has been lost!

The mouth leads into a gut (Fig. 5) which opens at an anus situated at the hind end of the visceral mass, *not* at the end of foot which, when moving, represents the hind end of the animal. (The anus actually opens into the respiratory chamber raising problems we discuss later.) The form of the gut varies enormously throughout the molluscs in relation to the food which varies from plant to animal and from microscopic organisms to living prey little smaller than the molluscan predator. The stomach is an extraordinary organ initially concerned with sorting rather than digestion which proceeds largely within extensive digestive tubules, the long intestine being largely con-

---

* Beautifully described in Alan Solem's *The Shell Makers*.

cerned with packaging the waste into pellets before discharge through the anus.

Here we must stress the supreme importance in molluscs of cilia – minute vibratile hair-like projections from the free surface of cells – and of mucus. Ciliated surfaces are also mucus producing surfaces and molluscs have exploited their joint possibilities to a unique extent. In the gut cilia ensure movement and material is aggregated in mucus. In primitive molluscs the gut is dilated where it leaves the stomach and here mucus with entangled waste is moulded into a cylindrical mass or 'protostyle', the probable precursor of the unique tapering gelatinous rod, the crystalline style which is present in the gut of all bivalves and of many primitive snails and is probably the best instance of a truly revolving structure in the animal kingdom. Although to become an organ of digestion and also of mixing, it must have begun as a means of consolidating waste particles, a matter of supreme importance to animals that, however surprisingly, defecate into a respiratory chamber housing delicate gills that must on no account be fouled.

This brings us to the subject of respiration. Simple animals like sea anemones have no respiratory organs. Oxygen is taken in and carbon dioxide released through the delicate surface tissues. In more complex animals where the surface becomes increasingly impermeable localized gills with delicate, much-folded surfaces appear. Something of this sort had probably occurred in molluscs (or their immediate ancestors) when the mantle and shell first appeared. The presence of gills and the water currents they created may well have been the reason why in certain areas the over-growing mantle did not adhere to the underlying body-surface. This space – the mantle cavity or respiratory chamber (names respectively indicating its nature and its function) – has enormous significance.

While never losing its respiratory function, it becomes a supremely efficient feeding chamber in the bivalves and a uniquely powerful organ of jet propulsion in the squids and cuttlefish. In the land snails it loses the contained gills to become a no less efficient air-breathing lung, although here the anus and the excretory pore migrate to open outside it. Only in a few cases, including the sea-slugs which acquire new gills, is it lost. There is controversy about the shape of the original mantle cavity and the number of paired gills which it contained. Until recently the mantle cavity was usually regarded as having originated at the posterior end and to have contained a single pair of gills. From such a condition could be derived those existing in all the then known molluscs. But, and the point of this digression will soon become apparent, we are still exploring the natural world and in 1952 the Danish Deep-Sea *Galathea* Expedition, which was working its way around the globe sampling the life in the deepest ocean basins, dredged a number of 'limpets' from depths of around 5000 metres off the Pacific coast of Mexico. Later examination of these at Copenhagen revealed that they were unlike any other limpets (and of how many distinct groups of these exist we shall learn later) but were living representatives of the Monoplacophora, a class of molluscs only recently erected by palaeontologists to include a group of fossil shells from

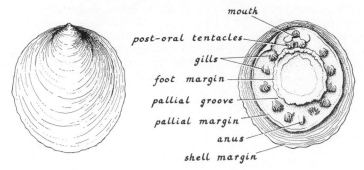

FIG. 6.   Monoplacophoran, *Neopilina galatheae*: *left*, limpet shell seen from above, apex near the front; *right*, under view showing central foot with pairs of gills in surrounding pallial groove, mouth at front, anus in rear. (After Lemche & Wingstrand)

the early Palaeozoic and thought to have been extinct for some 500 million years.

The discovery of *Neopilina galatheae* was the most exciting molluscan event of this century. Here surely would primitive structure in all its basic simplicity be revealed. But the facts were quite otherwise. The animal is almost embarrassingly complex with features that have been interpreted as evidence for segmentation, that serial repetition of similar parts so obvious in annelid worms and in arthropods such as caterpillars or centipedes but always regarded as absent in molluscs. This is no place to pursue somewhat abstruse arguments; it is probably enough to say that *Neopilina* may well have failed to compete with other molluscs because it was *too* complicated, the race going to the simpler with their greater potential for successful evolution. While so many monoplacophorans became extinct the ancestors of *Neopilina* survived by descending into the less competitive abyssal world – and there in succeeding millennia evolved along lines of their own.

Neopilina is mentioned at this juncture because the mantle cavity there consists of a groove encircling the larger rounded foot and housing six pairs of small gills. It is uncertain, and may so remain until living specimens are examined, whether these are true molluscan gills, the very characteristic nature of which is described below. If they are then their multiplication, which some have regarded as evidence of segmentation, may be the consequence of the confined space in which they function. This, as we see in Chapter 4, is certainly true in the chitons where the undoubted true molluscan gills have been multiplied up to as many as eighty pairs in certain species.

The molluscan gill is so characteristic as to have received the distinctive name of ctenidium, indicating its comb-like appearance. Originally and in most existing molluscs it is paired arising, although opinions differ, probably from a single pair in a restricted mantle cavity at the hind end. It is a most beautiful structure fitted to perfection for its role as an organ of respiration but at the same time of such adaptability that, while continuing to serve its primary function, it becomes in the bivalve molluscs the most efficient ciliary feeding organ in the animal kingdom. It represents a further factor in the supreme success of the molluscan plan.

Each ctenidium consists of a longitudinally extending axis with alternating rows of filaments on each side (Fig. 7). Within the axis run nerves, strands of

FIG. 7. Molluscan gill (ctenidium) showing section of axis with four alternating filaments on sides. Large arrows indicate direction of respiratory current, broken arrows of cleansing currents, dotted arrows of blood flow within filaments.

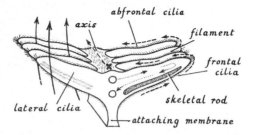

muscle and blood vessels. All surfaces are ciliated but the cilia are arranged in tracts with a consistent direction of beat and serving different functions. The most significant tracts are those that occupy opposing surfaces on the filaments. These *lateral* cilia produce the current of water from which oxygen is taken. With a gill on either side, water is drawn in below each of them into an *inhalant* chamber and then upwards between the parallel filaments into an *exhalant* chamber, leaving as a single stream posteriorly. It carries with it the faecal pellets and the excretory (renal) and reproductive products, all discharged from openings *above* the gills.

Respiratory currents are created in diverse ways in different groups of animals but where, as here, by ciliary beat into a confined space, there is supreme danger that the delicate meshwork of the gills will be clogged with suspended sediment. Elaborate means, involving sense organs, cilia and mucus, exist for dealing with this problem. As water enters below each gill it impinges on a sensory swelling, the osphradium, on the hind end of the membrane attaching the gill to the floor of the cavity. Its surface is covered with cilia and with sensory hairs and originally (though *not* always in modern molluscs) it probably estimated the density of suspended matter in the respiratory current. If this rose too high the shell muscles would contract and the respiratory chamber close.

As water currents enter the cavity the largest particles drop out of suspension to be removed by cilia on the floor, all others being carried upward to encounter the under, technically 'frontal' surfaces of the gill filaments which form a sieve between the two chambers. Their impact causes mucus production and the cilia on these surfaces which, unlike the lateral cilia, have a solely cleansing function carry particles and mucus to the tips of the filaments. They pass round these and, now under control of 'abfrontal' cilia, are conveyed to the axis. There a third set of cleansing cilia carry these mucus-laden strings to the tip of the gills and so away in the outflowing current.

However the sieve is not complete – we see later how it is perfected in the bivalves – and many particles are carried between and around the filaments to strike the roof of the cavity and the surface of large, 'hypobranchial', mucous glands. These ensure a final accumulation of sediment in mucus which is carried rapidly away.

The relatively powerful upward flow of water might be expected to buckle up filaments delicate enough to allow free passage of oxygen through their surfaces. This problem is solved by a system of fine horny rods which extend along each side of the filament below the zone of lateral cilia where upward pressure is greatest. These rods are connected with strengthening bars running along the axis. In this also run two blood vessels. From the one along the upper side, blood flows into each filament through the delicate walls of which it is exposed to high concentrations of oxygen in the upward flowing water currents. The now oxygenated blood is recollected in a vessel running along the under side of the axis. Thus within the filaments blood flows in the opposite direction to that of the water outside, an arrangement that makes for maximum efficiency.

The axis and the filaments are not completely rigid; muscles run along the former so that it can bend and so, by way of more delicate strands, can the filaments. The skeletal rods are flexible. These muscles are under the control of nerves which extend the length of the axis. In all, the molluscan ctenidium is a structure of high elaboration and precise efficiency.

There remain the viscera, the organs concerned with circulation of the blood, with excretion and with reproduction. Here we encounter another molluscan feature, reduction of the body cavity with enlargement (for important functional reasons) of the cavities containing blood. The former, so large in many other animals, is reduced to a space, the pericardium (Fig. 8), which encloses the heart and into which open the paired reproductive organs (or gonads, a name which covers both ovaries and testes) and out of which pass the paired tubes which form the excretory organs or kidneys. In the more primitive molluscs the reproductive products (egg or sperm) are ex-

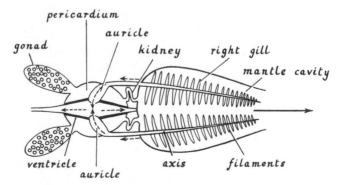

FIG. 8. Diagrammatic drawing showing, from above, the pericardium with its associated organs, gonads opening into it, kidneys (shown much reduced) opening out of it, blood from gills into auricles and so ventricle.

pelled through the kidneys but most modern molluscs possess separate reproductive ducts.

The heart is a very simple organ consisting of a single, muscular ventricle with a thin-walled auricle entering on either side. Blood comes from the gills into the auricles and then into the ventricle which contracts to drive it into the major anterior and posterior blood vessels, back-flow being prevented by valves. So it reaches all parts of the body although soon leaving these vessels to enter extensive spaces or sinuses, the various organs being bathed in blood. This is not an efficient method for transfer of oxygen and collection of waste products but then, apart from the cephalopod squids and octopods where other mechanisms have been evolved, molluscs are sluggish animals and it is adequate for their needs. What is significant is the quantity of blood accommodated in these spaces.

When the animal is protruded from the shell, spaces in the head and especially the foot are dilated with blood. Withdrawal involves contraction of the shell muscles and accompanying transference of blood into spaces deep within the viscera. When expansion occurs again these muscles relax while others contract to force blood out of these inner spaces into the head and the foot where, as we shall see, hydrostatic pressure plays a fundamental part in movement.

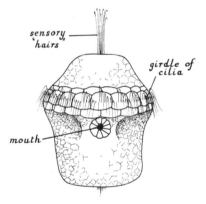

FIG. 9. Trochophore larva of the common limpet, *Patella vulgata*, showing typical appearance. (After Smith)

Now comes the supremely significant matter of reproduction. Initially molluscs appear to have been of separate sexes (unlike modern land snails) with eggs or sperm (collectively gametes) liberated through the kidney openings into the mantle cavity and so, primitively, always into the sea where eggs and sperm from different individuals would unite in the process of fertilization. We can never know how development then proceeded, but in the most primitive existing molluscs fertilization is followed by formation of a larval stage known as a trochophore (Fig. 9) which the molluscs have in common with segmented worms, indicating some degree of remote relationship. This is top-shaped with a girdle of cilia but is soon converted into the more elaborate and exclusively molluscan veliger larva which carries a densely ciliated sail or velum of one, two or four lobes (Plate 6), used for both loco-motion and feeding and which can be withdrawn within the shelter of a shell which the enveloping mantle now forms over the surface. Food consists of microscopic members of the plant plankton, diatoms and dinoflagellates.

For variable periods – depending on temperature and on the species – the veliger remains a member of the varied planktonic life of surface waters. Then behaviour changes: it avoids, instead of seeking, light and sinks to the bottom where it is faced with the crucial problem of settlement which involves funda-mental changes in structure and habit. Moreover the often dramatic meta-morphosis which is involved demands the stimulating presence of the appro-priate substrate of rock, sand, gravel, mud or even wood on or in which the adult will live. Should this not be immediately available, should the larva fall on metaphorically stony ground, metamorphosis may be delayed while the larva is carried to and fro on the sea bed with the chance that the suitable environment will be encountered during this 'latent' period. Nevertheless a high proportion of these larvae must die; it is only their vast numbers which ensure survival of the species.

We are left with general comments about the mantle and the shell it forms which becomes large enough to enclose the entire animal. The shell is three-layered. The outermost periostracum is of toughened protein, sometimes obvious – like the brown layer on mussel shells – but often inconspicuous or worn away. Beneath are two calcareous layers, an outer one of prismatic crystals, an inner of thin crystalline sheets which may be nacreous forming iridescent 'mother-of-pearl'. The crystals are deposited within an organic matrix of conchiolin.

The three layers have different origins; the innermost, which is added to throughout life and so thickest in older regions of the shell, is formed by the general surface of the mantle. The two other layers are added at the growing edge of the shell. The prismatic layer is formed by a region around its outer margin while the periostracum is produced by glands on the *inner* side of this largely within a 'periostracal groove' so that there is a limited peripheral

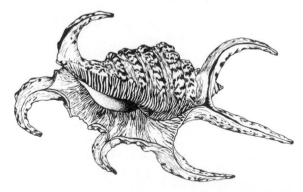

FIG. 10. *Pterocera chiragra* var. *arthritica*, Indo-Pacific spider shell: under surface with apex at top and long aperture fringed with finger-like projections.

region where only this transparent and flexible layer is present. Marginal increase of the shell proceeds by bursts of activity which die down in the winter (at least in temperate regions). Apart from shell formation, the mantle margins may be concerned with control of water flow into the mantle cavity and with sensory perception; we shall encounter these developments in the bivalves.

Attachment to the shell is primarily by way of the shell muscles, initially paired and numerous (as in *Neopilina*) and by their successive contractions responsible for movement. These have become reduced to usually two pairs in the bivalves and in the vast majority of snails to the single columellar muscle attached to the central pillar of the twisted asymmetrical shell the contraction of which draws the snail back within its protection.

Chapter 3

Classification

*

MOST phyla divide rather obviously into a series of major sub-groups known as classes. There are inevitable differences of opinion about the relative significance of some of these – for instance, should they be considered classes or merely subclasses? – which are the result of attempting to fit into a rigid framework the present consequences of millions of years of evolutionary change, a process, moreover, that still proceeds.

Recent estimates indicate a total molluscan population of around 50,000 species which fall naturally into seven major groups each of which we will accept as a class. A few introductory words – of dismissal in two cases – about each appears necessary at this stage.

Class 1. MONOPLACOPHORA.   The salient features of the deep-sea representatives of this very archaic class have been described on pages 27–28.

Class 2. APLACOPHORA (or Solenogastres).   Probably comprising two completely distinct groups, the animals usually very small and worm-like. An occasional British specimen may be taken in the dredge. Although all are undoubtedly molluscan, radula and ctenidia are not always present. They are primitive in some respects but very specialized in others, with a pedal groove instead of a foot and the shell sometimes consisting of spicules that may represent a primitive condition. There could be about two hundred and fifty species but none calls for further mention.

Class 3. POLYPLACOPHORA (or Loricata).   These chitons or coat-of-mail shells are an important class but very poorly represented in British waters. They are elongated but also flattened with a very broad and long foot over-hung by a girdle in which the eight shell plates are embedded. They are *par excellence* crawlers on irregular hard surfaces and, in suitable places, enormously abundant on exposed rocky shores although some species occur in abyssal depths. In some respects they are primitive, in others highly specialized but largely for only the one type of life. There are around 600 species.

Class 4. GASTROPODA.   These univalves or snails (or slugs if, as in a variety of unrelated cases, the shell is lost) are the most numerous, diversified and ubiquitous of molluscs of which they are the one class to have spread both into freshwaters and on to land. With total numbers of something under 40,000 species they represent some 80% of living molluscs. Extraordinary things have happened during their evolution; first a symmetrical coiling of the shell, then a swinging round of the visceral mass with covering mantle and shell so that the mantle cavity comes to face forwards, opening above the head. Coiling becomes asymmetrical, although it may be lost. These changes pose problems that have been most ingeniously solved and the gastropods evolved in all manner of directions revealing perhaps the most impressive display of adaptive radiation in the entire animal kingdom. Although the more striking species are tropical, there is a wide range of British species.

Some further subdivision of the gastropods is necessary. With minor uncertainties the class divides into three **sub-classes**: (1) the **Prosobranchia** (largely marine snails) obviously asymmetrical (a snail cannot be divided into similar right and left halves) with the mantle cavity and its contained gills in front; (2) the **Opisthobranchia** (largely sea-slugs) where the shell and mantle cavity are reduced or lost and where the animal is reorganized to assume an external bilateral symmetry; (3) the **Pulmonata** (land snails and slugs) where the mantle cavity becomes a lung. The majority of pulmonates are terrestrial and do not concern us but we shall encounter certain dubiously related marine pulmonates.

Proceeding one stage further, the *Prosobranchia* are here divided into three **orders**: (A) the **Archaeogastropoda** with primitively elaborate gill and with the reproductive system opening by way of a functional kidney; (B) the **Mesogastropoda** where the gill and mantle circulation are simplified and the reproductive system is emancipated from dependence on the excretory system; and (C) the **Neogastropoda** consisting of the most highly specialized, exclusively carnivorous, prosobranchs.

Class 5. BIVALVIA (or Lamellibranchia, Pelecypoda or Acephala). Despite an impression to the contrary, the shell is a single structure but consisting of three parts, two valves and a connecting elastic ligament. Bivalves are the second largest class comprising some 7500 species found in all depths of the sea and also abundant in freshwaters. They are laterally compressed with mantle and shell entirely enclosing the body. The head and the otherwise ubiquitous radula are absent, the mantle margins taking over sensory functions and the enormously enlarged gills (ctenidia) forming the most efficient mechanism of ciliary feeding (on microscopic organisms) in the animal kingdom. Initially adapted for life within and progression through soft substrates, many have become attached to hard surfaces into which others bore. A supremely successful class with populations of some species attaining astronomical numbers. Many British representatives.

Class 6. SCAPHOPODA. A very small, purely marine, group possessing the characteristic 'elephant's tusk' shell, usually slightly curved and always tapering and open at both ends. Their 350 odd species inhabit soft substrates with only the tip of the thinner end of the shell projecting. Some of their characters are rather intermediate between those of gastropods and bivalves but others are unique. They always live below tidal levels (some in profound depths) but the distinctively solid shells of the few British species may be dredged (usually empty) or be found washed up.

Class 7. CEPHALOPODA. These are the unmistakable octopods, cuttlefish and squids which represent the summit of molluscan – indeed of invertebrate – evolution. Far less numerous than formerly, many of the existing 600 or so species are animals of highly impressive efficiency. Their characters are too complex to summarize but the immediately obvious ones are the ring of tentacles armed with suckers around the head, the immense eyes (as elaborate as those of vertebrates) and the siphon leading out of the mantle cavity on the underside. All are marine and are predacious carnivores with powers of accurately controlled movement involving elaborate sense organs, a highly developed nervous system and a high rate of metabolism involving much more elaborate and efficient digestive, respiratory and circulatory systems than in other molluscs. Only the tropical *Nautilus* has an external shell. British species are few but representative.

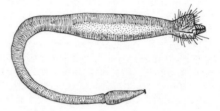

FIG. 11. British Aplacophoran, *Chaetoderma nitidulum*. (After Wirén)

Chapter 4

Chitons

*

THESE are usually obscure molluscs needing careful search on or under stones on the middle or lower levels of an exposed rocky shore, but unmistakable when encountered. Of a world population of perhaps 600 species only twelve are British and these are small, seldom over 20 mm long and usually drab-coloured. The largest chiton is the massive *Cryptochiton stelleri* of north Pacific coasts which may be up to 30 cm long with the shell plates entirely enclosed within the extremely tough dark red-brown mantle. But many of the well over a hundred species living along the coast of California are sizeable animals over 5 cm long with an impressive range of vivid colours and colour patterns. These are much sought by collectors who mount them immediately on boards to prevent their curling up. Large although dull-coloured chitons are extremely numerous on the irregular, often honeycombed surface of dead coral rock both in the Atlantic and the Indo-Pacific (Plate 14). Some species occur in profound ocean depths.

Chitons are unmistakable because of the linear series of eight shell plates (Fig. 12) inserted in the tough mantle and bounded by a broad girdle which is strengthened marginally by calcareous spicules or scales which sometimes form conspicuously projecting tufts. These animals have taken the basic molluscan form to its further extent in terms of flattened length allowing the

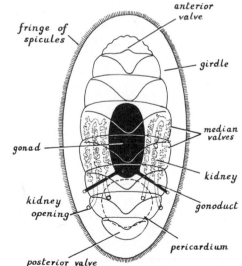

FIG. 12. Diagrammatic view of a chiton from above, showing eight shell plates with surrounding girdle, fused gonads with ducts, pericardium and U-shaped kidneys.

anterior valve

fringe of spicules

girdle

median valves

gonad

kidney

kidney opening

gonoduct

pericardium

posterior valve

37

most intimate adherence to a hard substrate. The mantle and shell clearly dominate form with neither foot nor head ever projecting beyond the confines of the surrounding girdle. The plates articulate so that the animals conform to uneven surfaces which they grip with the broad foot and the flat under surface of the overlapping girdle. When detached they curl up like the very similarly constituted woodlouse or pill bug.

If placed on glass under water they soon adhere and can then be viewed from below (Fig. 14) when the head, devoid of tentacles, is seen to point downwards, with the mouth from time to time opening to expose a radula consisting of successive rows of seventeen teeth – one central tooth with eight laterals on each side. Owing to a high concentration of iron these are particularly hard and scrape the closely encrusting vegetation together with appreciable amounts of the rock on which this grows. Using a hand lens the scraping tooth marks may be seen. Chitons detect the presence of vegetation by means of a subradular 'tasting' organ which is protruded from the mouth between successive actions of the radula.

The spacious posterior mantle cavity we have presumed present in the ancestral mollusc is here drawn out into narrow pallial grooves running between foot and broad girdle on each side. The anus opens at the hind end and the gills, which although very small are true molluscan ctenidia with axis and alternating rows of filaments and the usual ciliation, hang down from the roof of the grooves (Fig. 14). Apart from increasing in number with growth,

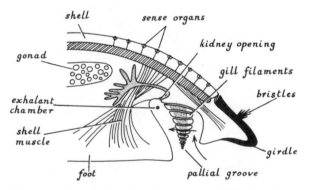

FIG. 13. Diagrammatic cross section through right half of the body of a chiton where kidney duct opens showing shell muscles, one gill, shell with sense organs and girdle with bristles. (After Morton & Yonge)

the gills vary very greatly in numbers in different species. In one group they are confined to a few on either side of the anus but in the shore chitons they start further forward and are more numerous. They extend along the grooves which in some exotic species they may completely occupy with over eighty pairs in all. But in all chitons successive gills are in close functional contact by way of interlocking cilia – a not infrequent device in such structures as we shall find when dealing with the bivalves – so that all work as a unit. This, incidentally, is what the gills of *Neopilina*, judging by their appearance after preservation, do *not* appear capable of doing which makes it difficult to accept them as ctenidia.

The action of the lateral cilia creates an inflowing current which enters the pallial grooves (the respiratory chambers) at no predetermined place but wherever, on either or both sides, there is a local raising of the broad flanking girdle (Fig. 12). Water then flows between the gill filaments into a space along the edge of the foot passing back within this exhalant chamber. The excretory pores open into this and so do the separate reproductive pores, the products of both being carried out together with the faeces in a combined exhalant current in the mid-line at the extreme hind end. This is just what we have taken to be the primitive state of affairs appropriately altered to fit the modified structure of chitons. The gills have been multiplied in relation to the very reduced space available for any one of them in the narrow pallial grooves (Fig. 13). But each is a true ctenidium with its elaborate structure of ciliated tracts, blood spaces, skeletal supporting rods, nerves and muscles, all solely concerned with the vital matter of respiration. The total area of respiratory surface – represented by that of the lateral faces of the filaments – is just about the same as that of a marine snail with only a single gill.

Internal anatomy need not long detain us. Vessels from the numerous gills carry blood into the ventricle by way of more than one pair of auricular openings; the reproductive organs are united forming a single gonad (Fig. 12) in front of the pericardium but opening not through this but by way of a gonoduct on each side directly into the pallial groove just in front of the kidney openings. These are modifications associated with the elongated and

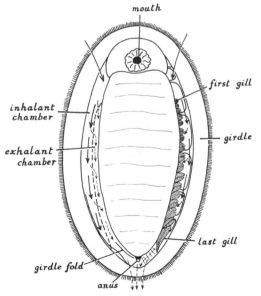

FIG. 14. Common chiton, *Lepidochitona cinereus*, viewed from under surface showing central elongated foot surrounded by narrow pallial grooves containing series of gills (ctenidia) on right, currents created by them on left, exhalent current emerging at hind end.

39

flattened form. Sexes are almost always separate with egg and sperm expelled through the gonoducts, the former sometimes in gelatinous strings, so that fertilization usually occurs in the sea although in a few exotic species this takes place in the pallial grooves. The trochophore larva elongates and the first six plates appear before settlement and change into the adult form.

In animals of such habit there is clear need for a common act of spawning and in some tropical species this occurs month after month at certain phases of the moon. Such lunar periodicity in spawning is not uncommon among marine invertebrates – it occurs in various other molluscs – and while the precise nature of the stimulus, probably by way of the tides, remains obscure, there is obvious advantage when an external agency causes simultaneous release of egg and sperm by the widely scattered members of an effectively immobile species.

A surprisingly elaborate digestive system, without trace of a crystalline style, deals with the largely vegetable food scraped by the radular teeth. Starch is digested by means of quaintly termed 'sugar glands' and there are most elaborate means of compacting faecal pellets in an exceptionally long intestine, the involved coils of which occupy the greater part of the visceral mass. An almost complete monotony of feeding habit is broken only by members of the exotic, largely Pacific, family Mopaliidae. In the Californian *Placiphorella velata* (Fig. 16) the flattened girdle is extended forward as a wide head flap which is held aloft while behind it a tentacular lobe grips the surface. The animal remains motionless in this posture until a small crustacean or worm ventures beneath when the flap suddenly descends and the prey is passed to the mouth. This appears as the sole departure of shallow water chitons from an exclusively plant scraping existence. But chitons which live in abyssal depths where no plants exist must find nourishment in the remains of dead animals or in organic debris.

Because the head is enclosed it should not be supposed that chitons are completely out of touch with their surroundings other than the rock surface below. Sense organs (Fig. 13) known as aesthetes penetrate the shell plates and are probably sensitive to light, indeed in some chitons they possess a focusing lens and a receptive retina. Shore-dwelling chitons have a general pattern of behaviour which involves sensitivity to light, to gravity and to humidity, all well displayed in the common British species, *Lepidochitona cinereus*. This is a true intertidal animal, commonest in the middle shore where, when the tide is out, it will be found aggregated on the under side of stones, in greatest numbers where these lie in pools.

Simple experiments reveal that these animals move into regions of low light intensity and also move downward in response to gravity (Fig. 15). Movement largely ceases when they pass into shade or into water but the response has then achieved its purpose and the animals withdrawn from exposure which in sunshine on a windy day will cause death within the hour. With the return of the tide they tend to move-upward into more illuminated but now submerged regions where there is greater plant growth. As in effectively all mobile intertidal animals, the pattern of behaviour is fundamental ensuring survival in a constantly changing environment.

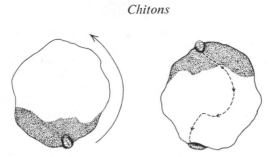

FIG. 15. Drawings illustrating behaviour of *Lepidochitona cinereus* following over-turning of stone (indicated by arrow on left). Moist surfaces stippled. (After Evans)

The Class Polyplacophora (the chitons) is divided into two orders, the Lepidopleurida, species of which live offshore, some indeed in profound depths, and Chitonida which, like the species just mentioned, are largely intertidal. The major structural difference between the two is the presence in the latter of 'insertion plates' which can be detected when the shell plates are removed from the girdle in which they are marginally embedded. There is also the difference in the arrangement of the gills mentioned earlier. Because the plates are found in fossil deposits it is known that the Lepidopleurida is the older group. The characteristic chiton form represents an obvious adaptation for life on uneven surfaces in turbulent seas, light and aerated water providing perfect conditions for the growth of encrusting algae on which the animals browse. This must be the conclusion of all who view them in their multitudes on the irregular surface of dead coral rock exposed to oceanic surf (Plate 14).

It could well be that they evolved under much these conditions hundreds of millions of years ago in the Palaeozoic and were never exposed to the hazards of intertidal life so that the less efficient gill arrangements and the less intimate association between the shell plates and the girdle would not matter. But such things were better arranged in the later-evolved Chitonida which ousted the original population and were able to extend upward and exploit the rich food supplies between tide marks, at the same time acquiring appropriate behaviour patterns. Meanwhile, as so often in evolutionary history, the less efficient moved down into the less exacting conditions of sublittoral or even abyssal existence – but with their body form giving clear evidence of the environment where this had been evolved.

Four species of lepidopleuran chitons occur in the British fauna, none, except possibly during extremely low tides, ever likely to be encountered except in dredge hauls. Of these *Lepidopleurus asellus*, from 13 to 19 mm long and somewhat yellowish in colour with narrow girdle and keeled plates is much the commonest with *L. cancellatus*, less than half that length and relatively narrower, not uncommon. Of the other two, *L. scabridus* is confined to the Channel Isles and extreme south-west of England, and *Hanleya hanleyi* (which does have an insertion plate on the first valve) occurs in the north. Both are rather rare.

Of the Chitonida, *Lepidochitona cinereus* is almost universally present, largely under stones, on rocky shores. Again from 12–19 mm long, it has a broader girdle and the valves have a shagreen-like surface of varied colour, red, brown and green. *Tonicella marmorea* is the largest British Chiton, sometimes attaining a length of 40 mm, and is very smooth. It occurs only in the north. The smaller *T. rubra* is generally distributed and is distinguished by the red and white chequered girdle. *Callochiton achatinus* is another smooth chiton with a broad girdle and of general reddish-brown colour variegated with white or green. It is usually around 20 mm long and 10 mm wide. Never common, it is seldom exposed except at very low tides. *Ischnochiton albus* is a rare species occurring only in the north and distinguished by its yellowish-white colour. It is small and lives very low on the shore.

The last three species, all of *Acanthochitona*, are easily separated from the others owing to the tufts of bristles on the girdle. Far and away the most likely to be encountered is *A. crinitus* of medium size, very variable colour and bearing eighteen tufts of bristles. Of the others, the slightly larger *A. discrepans* has nineteen to twenty such tufts but is confined to the Channel Isles and the south-west of England running up into the Irish Sea. The still larger *A. communis*, again with eighteen tufts, only comes into the British fauna because it occurs in the Channel Isles at the northern end of a southern distribution.

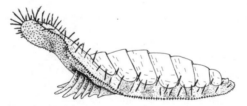

FIG. 16. Californian chiton, *Placiphorella velata*: lateral view showing large head-flap raised in preparation for seizing animal prey. (After McLean)

Chapter 5

The first gastropods

*

WE have briefly described what could possibly have been the form of the earliest molluscs (there can be nothihg approaching certainty in such matters) and then shown how, if this were flattened and pulled out and the shell sub-divided, chitons could have evolved admirably fitted for exploiting the possibilities of life closely applied to irregular surfaces. But, while retaining their crawling habit, these early molluscs were to evolve in other and potentially far more rewarding directions. Possibly with dramatic suddenness, the gastropods appeared.

This was likely to have been heralded by an increasing concentration of the viscera – the furtherance of a process so fundamentally molluscan – which, with the enclosing mantle and shell, accumulated in a peak on the back. The shell aperture was diminished in diameter and the number of shell muscles reduced to a single pair. The most efficient manner in which the increased height could be carried was by coiling, brought about by suitable changes in the growth gradients around the mantle margin where new shell is added. If this takes place evenly all round then a conical (limpet-like) shell will be formed but if there is greater growth in any part of the margin then the shell will bend over in the opposite direction. In the process of genetic variation such local increase might occur anywhere but if it occurred on either side the shell would incline on the other side and become unstable. Natural selection would soon obliterate all such variations. Only coiling in the longitudinal

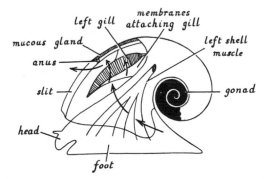

FIG. 17. Diagram showing possible appearance of an early 'bellerophont' gastropod with shell coiled in the plane of the paper, mantle cavity anterior with exhalant current expelled upward through slit in mantle and shell. (After Morton & Yonge)

vertical plane would produce a shell that would be stable but with another proviso, namely that there should be no obstruction of the opening into the mantle cavity with its all-important gills.

This is precisely what would occur if the curvature were directed backward, but if directed forward, with the weight of the coil carried on the 'neck', this opening would tend if anything to be enlarged. Variations leading in that direction would be selected and a bilaterally symmetrical plano-spiral shell – like that of a modern Nautilus (Fig. 146) – be gradually evolved. The visceral organs were inevitably further extended with those concerned with reproduction at the apex reduced to a single structure. This could have been due to fusion (which occurred in the unrestricted chitons (Fig. 14)) or by loss of one gonad which is the more probable because only one duct, on the later (gastropod) right side, persists.

Such animals were the fossil bellerophonts. Some of these have numerous muscle scars like *Neopilina*; they fade out in the middle of the Palaeozoic. But others with only a single pair of muscle scars and with a depression or 'emargination' in the centre of the free margin, may well have been among the first gastropods (Fig. 17).

Evolutionary changes must often have been sudden but possibly never more so than those that produced these animals in which the mantle cavity has moved to the front, immediately behind and above the head. This must have involved a 180° movement in an anticlockwise direction of the visceral mass with the covering mantle and shell in relation to the head and foot. Such profound change in the relations between major regions of the body is unique in the animal kingdom and only possible because of their separation into distinct entities in these molluscs. The soft 'neck' between head and viscera, probably associated with the development of the elaborate odontophore containing the radula, can be twisted – with impunity – to produce this extraordinary and yet viable result. The consequences are momentous, no less than the production of one of the supremely successful groups of animals comprising the great majority of molluscan species inhabiting sea, freshwaters and land.

This turning movement is known as torsion. Its occurrence was originally postulated by a German zoologist in the 1880s as providing the only possible explanation of striking anatomical facts, in particular the looping back on itself of the gut, the anus opening anteriorly still within the mantle cavity, and the twisting into a figure of eight of the major nerve cords connecting the nerve ganglia in the head with those in the viscera, now above instead of behind them. However, as later discovered, the whole process continues to be enacted during the development of the simpler existing gastropods where eggs are fertilized in the sea to hatch out as trochophore larvae. During subsequent development of the later veliger stage the shell muscles running from head and foot to the shell develop asymmetrically, with the result that at a certain stage their contraction causes the shell and enclosed viscera to twist round in an anticlockwise direction in relation to these other regions (Fig. 18). The process takes place in two stages: an initial rapid one through 90° followed by a slower final stage when, by a process of differential growth,

44

complete turning round is achieved with the mantle cavity now in front and above the developing head.

There is no question about the sequence of events; what *does* arouse controversy is how and why this remarkable process originally took place and thereby brought this most successful group of molluscs into existence. Without wishing to enter into the intricacies of a problem which is unlikely ever to be solved, something must be said. Beyond all question altogether new possibilities opened up when the mantle cavity moved to the front. The gills now drew in clear water free from the sediment raised by the passage of the animal. This also made it possible to test what lay ahead, a capacity which becomes highly developed in the higher carnivorous gastropods which can 'smell' their prey by means of the sensory osphradia originally, in this writer's opinion, developed in a posterior mantle cavity to estimate the content of sediment in the inhalant water current. It would certainly not be the only sense organ to change its function in the course of evolution. Moreover, the left-hand side of the cavity may now be prolonged into a siphonal tube so that clear water can be drawn in while the animal burrows within sand or mud. This would have been impossible had the respiratory cavity remained at the hind end.

However the first gastropods were hardly likely to appreciate the wide evolutionary prospects now opening ahead; indeed they were faced with initial problems of sanitation due to the uniquely molluscan feature of defecating and excreting into the respiratory chamber! This raised no serious problems when this chamber was at the hind end but presented major ones when these operations took place immediately over the head. These difficulties were to be successfully overcome as we shall shortly see, but the immediate problems must have been considerable.

However the larva, living a very different life in surface waters before settling to change into the form of the bottom-living adult, has also to be considered. The immediate advantage of the change could be to this stage; natural selection could be acting here rather than on the adult. Following torsion, the head and delicate ciliated velum – the larval organ of both locomotion and feeding – would be withdrawn into the shelter of the mantle cavity followed by the foot with the early operculum acting as a plug. It would then, it has been suggested, have better chances of survival than before when the velum could not be withdrawn. The larva could sink into the shelter of deeper water or in this condition pass undamaged through the gut of other animals.

Such possibilities were first advanced in 1928 by the late Professor Walter Garstang. He had a happy facility for presenting such problems and their possible explanations in verse and developed his theme in *The Ballad of the Veliger* or *How the Gastropod got its Twist*, which begins

> The Veliger's a lively tar, the liveliest afloat,
> A whirling wheel on either side propels his little boat;
> But when the danger signal warns his bustling submarine,
> He stops the engine, shuts the port, and drops below unseen.

Succeeding verses note how the original veligers were an easy prey until by fortunate chance, namely an appropriate genetic change or mutation in-

volving asymmetry of the shell muscles, torsion occurred, the final verse
recording that

> . . . when the first new Veligers came home again to shore,
> And settled down as Gastropods with mantle-sac afore,
> The Archi-mollusk sought a cleft his shame and grief to hide,
> Crunched horribly his horny teeth, gave up the ghost, and died.

However, as we now know, a few of these 'Archi-Mollusks', ancestors of
Neopilina, did find refuge and achieve survival, with just how much subsequent
change we cannot know, in abyssal depths.

By no means all modern malacologists accept the view that torsion was of
such advantage to the larva; they prefer to think in terms of the undoubted
eventual advantage to the adult. Possibly the correct interpretation is contained
in recent views that while the first 90° of torsion was of value to the larva, the
second stage which takes place more slowly was to the advantage of the young
crawling adult. Viewed in any of the three ways the problem of torsion is
fascinating. All to be related in the remainder of this chapter and in those that
immediately follow it deal with the evolutionary consequences of torsion.

Meanwhile the adult was faced with this problem of sanitation. This was
solved – and surprisingly in certain gastropods is still solved – by local withdrawal of the mantle margin to form a slit or emargination in the middle of
the roof of the mantle cavity (Fig. 17). Water continued to be drawn in below

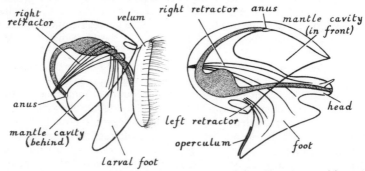

FIG. 18.   Process of torsion during development: *left,* veliger larva with posterior
mantle cavity and asymmetrical right velar retractor (shell muscle); *right,* by
straightening this muscle, the mantle and shell are swung round through 180° in
relation to the foot, with the mantle cavity now anterior. (After Morton & Yonge)

the gills, now on either side of the head, and then to flow upward between the
filaments and so out through the slit. The anus opened at the base of this so
that faeces with the urine from the kidneys, also egg and sperm during
spawning, were all carried out in this powerful upward flow of water. The
shell can be envisaged as that of a bellerophont with a marginal slit (this end
now pointing forward) but still a plano-spiral.

Probably at about this stage another event of profound significance occurred.
The shell became asymmetrical. The centre of the plano-spiral was pulled out

laterally, usually to the right to form a right-handed or dextrally coiled shell, although there are some sinistrally coiled species (Fig. 47) and this condition may occasionally occur in a normally dextral species. This had the advantage of allowing the shell (and enclosed viscera) to be drawn out still further and yet form a compact mass. A periwinkle or a garden snail is a very rounded object. This represented the culmination of the molluscan tendency to concentrate the viscera. But if unaccompanied by other changes the shell would become unstable, liable to topple over to right or left. Adjustments involved rearrangement of the shell with the opening pointing to the right and the spire of the shell directed obliquely upward. This is well shown in the figure of *Lacuna* (Fig. 29). After these changes the now helicoid shell became stably balanced on the foot below but this new twisting to the right (or left) had an important effect on the internal organs, still more on those in the mantle cavity. The right side was restricted with consequent reduction of the gill, mucus gland and osphradium on that side while the organs on the left side, now bearing the major responsibility for respiration, enlarged.

With this change in the functional mid-line, the slit and the anus also moved over to the right. Internally the right auricle (taking blood from the now reduced right gill) became smaller with accompanying reduction of *either* one *or* other kidney. Which of the two was reduced (and finally lost) had far-reaching consequences – a notable instance of structure affecting the future

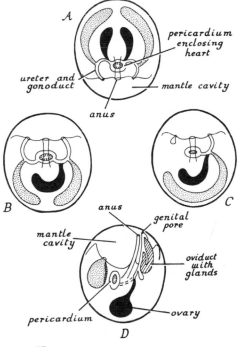

FIG. 19. Diagrams showing inter-relationships of anus, gonad, pericardium, kidney and mantle cavity: A, before torsion, with the mantle cavity posterior and both gonads and kidneys paired with common opening into cavity; B, after torsion (initial hypothetical state), gonad reduced to one organ opening on post-torsional right side, both kidneys functional; C, condition in archaeogastropods with left kidney reduced and gonad opening through functional kidney duct; D, condition in higher prosobranchs with functional kidney on left and ducts of the right kidney now exclusively concerned with reproduction, with extension along mantle wall. (After Fretter & Graham)

course of evolution. In the animals of immediate concern (more precisely their modern descendants) the right kidney remained functional, with only vestiges of the left one (Fig. 19). We have already surmised that the gonads had previously been reduced to one which opened, after torsion, on the right side, i.e. egg and sperm were discharged through the outlet duct of the *functional* kidney.

This had notable effects. With very minor exceptions (to be noted later) the fact that the duct is also a ureter prevents its modification to form an extended penis in the male or an enlarged glandular oviduct in the female, and so makes internal fertilization impossible with all we shall see that this implies. Eggs and sperm must have passed freely into the sea where fertilization occurred with formation of free swimming trochophore and later veliger larvae.

A variety of living gastropods possess the primitive slit or some modification of this, including a variety of British species. But we should take the story farther before describing these. By further enlargement of the left at the expense of the right side of the mantle cavity, the right gill and associated organs finally disappear and so does the slit, the anus moving forward to open near the margin on the extreme right, where the outgoing current emerges (Fig. 20). Now, with the appearance of a left-right circulation through the mantle cavity, the problems of sanitation become a matter of the past. The left side of the mantle cavity can now be pushed forward to take in clean water while it comes to vie with the head in sensory exploration of what lies ahead. However the major potential of this change, the development of a long respiratory siphon enabling the animal to move below the surface while drawing in clear water from above, is not realized in these archaeogastropods and again there is a reason.

This resides in the nature of the persisting, now more elongate left gill. This retains the alternating rows of filaments (it is an 'aspidobranch' gill) and is maintained in a functional position secured to the roof and floor of the cavity by way of upper and lower membranes attached to the axis (Fig. 20). This, however, involves the presence of an enclosed pocket between the gill and the wall of the cavity and represents a major hazard if much sediment is drawn in with the inflowing current when this pocket will become choked and the respiration impeded. For this reason – their very limited ability to live in water carrying much sediment – *all* archaeogastropods live on hard surfaces. It was left to the mesogastropods to make the further changes in the gill structure needed for exploitation of life on or in sand or mud (Fig. 20).

Archaeogastropods, then, are epifaunal animals living on hard surfaces and so particularly common on rocky shores. Almost all are exclusively vegetarian, scraping encrusting algae which may well have been the primitive molluscan habit. This raises the question of the means employed, namely the radula. This exclusively molluscan structure, the perfect feeding organ for a slowly moving animal intent on scraping the closest of encrusting vegetation, was probably a prime reason for their original success and certainly for that of the modern chitons and gastropods. In the latter it is capable of extreme and finally positively dramatic modifications.

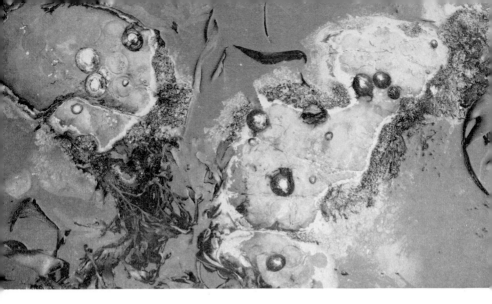

PLATE 1. *Above*, common limpet, *Patella vulgata*, on flat rocks showing area cleared by grazing, and also 'home scars'. *Below*, shore at Port St Mary, Isle of Man; dark strip caused by the removal of all limpets within this area, with resultant increase in algal growth because no longer grazed.

PLATE 2. Scanning electron micrographs of radulae: *above, Patella vulgata* (× 1900), docoglossan type; specimen of shell length 2cm; from the shore at Dale, Pembrokeshire. *Below, Monodonta lineata* (× 43), rhipidoglossan type; specimen of shell length 22mm; same locality.

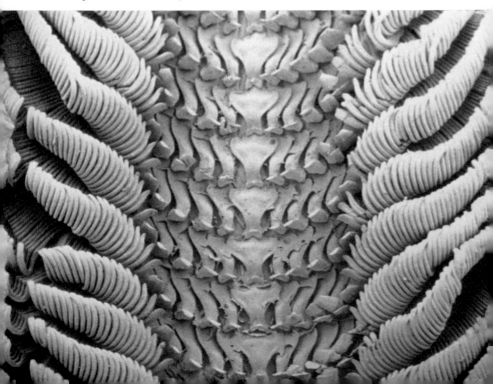

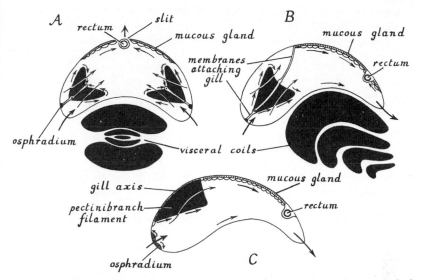

FIG. 20. Diagrammatic sections through mantle cavity in A, bilaterally symmetrical bellerophont (see Fig. 17); B asymmetrically coiled top shell (archaeogastropod); C, typical mesogastropod. Symmetrical and asymmetrical coiled viscera also shown in A and B. In A water enters on either side of head, passes between gill filaments to issue through slit above. In B only left gill retained and anus moved to right; water current now flows from left to right but single gill is attached to roof as well as floor (for stability), creating chamber between it and the mantle wall. In C gill is reduced to a single row of filaments with the axis fused to the mantle wall – completely efficient system. (After Morton & Yonge)

The radula consists of a continuous 'lingual ribbon' bearing successive rows of teeth (Plates 2 and 3) constantly being added to in the radular sac at one end and as constantly worn away at the other. It forms the operative part of the massive odontophore, an extremely elaborate structure, adequate description of which lies beyond the scope of this book and should be sought in the pages and unequalled figures of Vera Fretter and Alastair Graham's *British Prosobranch Molluscs* and in Alan Solem's *The Shell Makers*. When the odontophore protrudes, the radula is exposed and by a to and fro movement, which involves alternate exposure and infolding of the teeth, food is scraped and, as by a conveyor belt, transported into the gut along which it is passed by ciliary or muscular means. There is an accompanying production of saliva, initially for lubrication but in the more elaborate carnivorous snails also concerned with digestion.

The adaptability of the entire radular apparatus is one of the keys to the outstanding success of the gastropod molluscs. It can be used for so many purposes, to grasp and bite or grasp and suck, to gouge or to brush; extended at the end of proboscis it can seek out food within cavities or bore through shells to tear the flesh within; it can, as we shall see, become a highly efficient harpoon; or it can be dispensed with and feeding proceed by other means. And yet, although so adaptable, the radula does have a standardized pattern within the major groups and so is valuable in classification. Each row has a central or rachidian tooth with a series of laterals on either side and beyond these possibly further marginal teeth. The simplest condition with most numerous teeth occurs in the archaeogastropods where, on either side of the rachidian tooth, the fan-like rhipidoglossan radula (Plate 2) has five, strong, cusped laterals, bordered by many fine marginals. Such a radula can rasp and at the same time sweep a wide surface; it represents an ideal feeding instrument for animals restricted to scraping encrusting vegetation and is possessed by two out of the three groups of archaeogastropods, namely the zeugobranchs (coiled with *two gills*) and the top shells (coiled with *one gill*). In the ubiquitous and more highly adapted common limpets (patellids with or without a single true gill) the radula is more specialized, reduced to thirteen teeth without marginals and the central tooth diminished or even absent with one of the laterals on each side enlarged. This spear-like docoglossan radula (Plate 2) is impressively efficient.

We can now begin to review the archaeogastropods, confining ourselves in this chapter to their most primitive members which form the superfamily Zeugobranchia where the early condition of two gills and associated slit has surprisingly persisted. The most primitive of all, the pleurotomarian slit-shells (Fig. 22) occur only in deepish water, 400 metres and more, off the West Indies in the Atlantic and off Japan and Indonesia in the Pacific. Once thought to have been extinct since the Palaeozoic, the first indication of their survival was the discovery in 1855 in the Caribbean of an empty shell which was brought up in a deeply laid fish trap into which it had been carried by its occupant, a hermit crab. The first accounts of anatomy appeared about the end of the century and today seventeen species of these pleurotomarians are known. Living in regions too deep for significant plant growth, they appear to feed largely on sponges. The radula has a remarkable number of teeth, in some species exceeding a hundred on either side.

The nearest relative to these exotic shells in northern waters is *Scissurella crispata** also from some depth off the continental shelf from which it can be collected in dredge hauls from mud bottoms. It is minute, only some 2 mm in diameter, and must move about on the surface of small stones or empty shells on the surface of mud, it certainly cannot live *within* this. Viewed under low magnification, the flattened shell consists of no more than five whorls with an almost centrally placed slit from the base of which a tentacle extends when the animal expands. There are also a pair of head tentacles and a series of foot or epipodial tentacles. On withdrawal the shell opening is closed by a horny operculum. In contrast to the much more asymmetrically coiled pleuro-tomarian slit-shells, the gills and other organs in the mantle cavity are almost symmetrical, a condition leading on to the complete symmetry in other zeugobranchs.

We have still to mention the most successful of all such two-gilled gastro-pods, the greatly flattened ear-shells of the family Haliotidae. One of these

* The animal shown in Fig. 21 is the very similar *S. costata*.

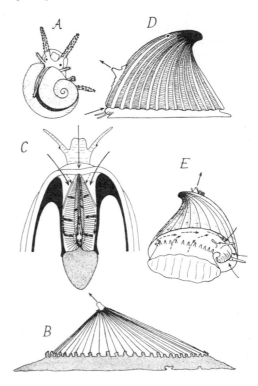

FIG. 21. Archaeogastropods: A, slit-shell *Scissurella costata*, from above; B, keyhole limpet, *Diodora apertura*, from right side; C, mantle cavity of *Diodora nubecula* viewed from above; paired symmetrical gills draw in water on either side of the head, expelling it apically; D, *Emarginula reticulata*, from left side; siphon protruding through top of slit; E, *Puncturella noachina*, turned to show epipodial tentacles round foot and head with tentacles bearing eyes.

the Mediterranean *Haliotis tuberculata*, just qualifies as a British species because it extends as far north as the Channel Isles where it is known as the ormer and so much prized as food that stocks have to be carefully conserved. Although up to 10 cm long this is but a small representative of a genus which includes the red, pink, green, black, flat, pinto, white and threaded abalones of the Californian coast some of which are up to three times that length. Other species occur off Japan and also around Australia and New Zealand. The shells are unmistakable with the curved line of some seven separate openings and the iridescent inner surface of the shell. This is vividly displayed in the New Zealand paua, long used by the Maoris in decorative work and described as having a 'lustre of opalescent greens and blues, with occasional fiery flashes.'

These animals are great limpets, a name which indicates a form and accompanying habit, *not* any particular group of gastropods. The primitive mollusc, like the archaic *Neopilina*, was probably a limpet; then from the coiled tubular gastropod shell the limpet form has been evolved time after time in the course of later evolution. This involves a rapid widening of the coiled shell so that the animal is entirely accommodated in the final whorl. Usually all trace of the initial coiling is lost in the adult shell (as in species of our common limpet, *Patella*) although these are plainly apparent in *Haliotis*. Enlargement of the shell opening involves a rounded enlargement of the foot and the loss of the now useless operculum. All limpets live on rock surfaces over which they very slowly move, relying for protection against the forces of the sea and the attacks of predators by gripping tightly with the foot and pulling the shell firmly down by contraction of the enlarged shell muscles. Once detached, limpets are utterly vulnerable.

All this has been most successfully accomplished in *Haliotis*. The gills are paired, those on the right somewhat the smaller, water being drawn in on either side of the head to emerge through the shell apertures, below the penultimate one of which the anus opens. These openings represent the slit; during growth new ones successively appear as marginal indentations which are then closed off. As the mantle grows forward beneath them, the oldest ones are filled in below although remaining apparent. The massive oval-shaped foot holds on with a tenacity that only the greatest oceanic storms can overcome.

Wherever man has not collected them almost or completely to extinction, these animals are enormously abundant. In areas where they are protected along the coast of California they occupy every cranny within the irregular rock surface often touching, even overlapping, one another. Typical archaeogastropods, and therefore herbivorous, they are confined to intertidal and shallow offshore waters from which they are now largely sought by diving, an ancient practice in Japan where a common theme of colour prints depicts diving by women for 'awabi'. The Mediterranean ormer was noted by Aristotle and it was first illustrated in the Renaissance works of the French naturalists, Belon and Rondelet, to appear a century later in the first conchologies of Buonanni and of Lister. There are probably no other bivalves which combine beauty of shell with such high edible qualities. After suitable beating to break up the muscle fibres, thin slices of the foot are admirable when fried.

The remainder of these two-gilled gastropods comprise a most interesting assemblage of true limpets, i.e. without a trace of spiral coiling in the adult shell, in which complete bilateral symmetry has been regained as far as the shell and the gills and associated organs in the mantle cavity are concerned. But, of course, internal asymmetry persists, the gut turning round to open in front, the principal nerve cords twisted into the figure of eight and both gonad and kidney opening on the right. British species are small and need careful search in rock pools or under stones at low water of spring tides.

Such search could be rewarded by discovery of the widely distributed keyhole limpet, *Diodora* (*Fissurella*) *apertura* (Fig. 21), only up to 4 cm long but unmistakable because of the somewhat dumb-bell shaped apical opening. If allowed to settle down in a bowl of water containing fine sediment (a jet of milk will do admirably) currents will be seen entering on either side of the head to emerge as a single upward-directed jet through a short siphon that projects through the apical opening. Here the numerous apertures in *Haliotis* have been replaced by a single and permanently functioning opening. The anus has retreated to the summit of the mantle cavity which occupies the frontal slope of the animal. The gills are a perfectly symmetrical pair with

52

extended filaments which create the powerful jet. This symmetry is not, however, that of the original bellerophont gastropod but a resumption of this condition following loss of the asymmetrical coiling present in the slit-shells and in *Haliotis*. This resumption of symmetry is possible where coiling is lost with the right gill still persisting. Later we shall see what happens when this reversion to bilateral symmetry of the shell occurs *after* the right gill and all traces of the slit have been lost.

The mantle tissues, edged with short blunt tentacles, curl upward around the margin of the shell, a first indication of the tendency for enclosure and eventual loss of the adult shell which reaches its culmination in the sea-slugs. Indeed the process goes much further in exotic keyhole limpets than it does in our solitary species. The shell of the impressive *Megathura crenulata* of the southern Californian coast may be over 20 cm long and is almost completely obscured by the thick mantle which, in striking contrast to the yellow colour of the underside of the foot, is jet-black. There is no reduction of the shell as there is in the almost equally large and similarly black 'ducksbill limpet', *Scutus breviculus* of New Zealand shores where the shell is reduced to an oblong plate which roofs over the anterior mantle cavity. In such animals, as in the sea-slugs (p. 116), protection is provided by defensive glands in the mantle which increasingly extends over the shell with the slow deliberate approach of their prime enemies, starfish. These limpets are all herbivores, *Scutus* feeding on the green sea lettuce, *Ulva*.

More difficult to find because less than half as big but no less common in the same localities is *Emarginula reticulata* (Fig. 21). The apex of the ribbed shell is pointed with a pronounced backward curve (the shell is unmistakable despite its small size), while, as its generic name indicates, there is a short anterior marginal slit. A short siphon projects through this leading out of a relatively short mantle cavity which contains a symmetrical pair of gills, the inner filaments, unlike those of *Diodora*, greatly extended and creating an impressively powerful current. The mantle never spreads over the shell but sensory tentacles occur around the pedal margin as in *Scissurella*. Other species occur offshore to be collected only in dredgings which may also bring

FIG. 22.   Pleurotomarid slit-shell, *Mikadotrochus hirasei*.

in specimens of the closely related *Puncturella noachina* (Fig. 21). Here the emargination has become an apical opening, although not actually at the tip of the backwardly directed summit of the shell. Shell characters are otherwise identical with those in *Emarginula* while the gills have the same specialized features. Unquestionably the change from marginal slit to apical opening has evolved separately in the keyhole limpets and in these animals, the first example to be noted of convergent evolution of which the molluscs provide so many striking instances.

Chapter 6

Limpets and top shells

*

THE abalones are by far the most successful of the gastropods that retain the two gills and this is undoubtedly 'due to their limpet form and habit, the extensive rounded foot achieving such secure attachment and the flattened shell offering the minimum of resistance to water movements. This mode of life is so suited to animals that feed on encrusting vegetation which grows most abundantly in shallow, and particularly intertidal, waters that the limpet form has been independently evolved time and time again in the evolutionary history of the gastropods; there are no better instances of convergence. Nowhere has greater success been attained than in the second superfamily of the archaeogastropods, the widely distributed limpets which comprise the Patellacea or, taking an alternative name from the form of the radula, the Docoglossa.

These include all the common intertidal limpets of the north Atlantic and Pacific. In warmer waters, those nearest being probably around Bermuda, they may be replaced by the externally very similar siphonarid limpets only to be distinguished by the presence of a slight bulge on the right side of the shell. These are pulmonate limpets with a mantle cavity that opens on the right side. The ctenidia were lost when the ancestral animal moved on to the margin of the land and the mantle cavity became an air-breathing lung; with later movement back to the shore these limpets acquired a semicircle of secondary gills that hang down from the roof of the cavity.

The Patellacea comprise three very distinct families, the Acmaeidae, the Patellidae and the Lepetidae. The first possess a solitary ctenidium in the forward directed nuchal cavity which with the pallial groove that encircles the foot forms the mantle cavity in these animals (Fig. 23). In the Patellidae this is replaced by a series of secondary gills in the pallial groove between the foot and the mantle margin (Fig. 23). The Lepetidae, a small group of blind limpets (the others have simple eyes at the base of the head tentacles), which always live at some depth, obtain such oxygen as they need through the surface of the mantle and have no gills.

We start with the Acmaeidae because they are the most primitive. They represent the result of assuming the limpet form *after* loss of the right ctenidium so that although external symmetry is regained and, of course, without the presence of a slit, the small anterior mantle cavity contains only a single, although conspicuously large, gill. This arises from the left side and, when fully extended, may project beyond the margin of the shell. It is free except basally with alternating rows of filaments on the two sides and creates a powerful inflowing current on the left side. Faeces from the anus and reproductive products during the breeding season are all carried into the sur-

55

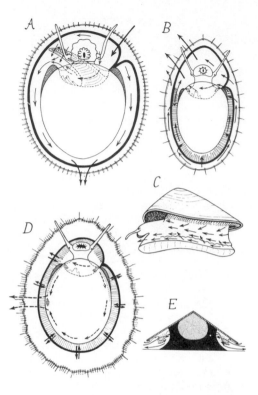

FIG. 23. Archaeogastropod limpets: A, *Acmaea tessulata* viewed from below through glass, showing single ctenidium in mantle cavity, inhalant current on left (when viewed from above), exhalant current and waste expelled at hind end; B, *Patina pellucida*, from below; ctenidium replaced by secondary gills in pallial groove round foot; exhalant current and waste to right anteriorly; C, *P. pellucida* from left side showing ciliary currents and fringe of gills; D, *Patella vulgata* from below; secondary gills also round head, cleansing currents (broken arrows) in pallial grooves carry waste to right side where expelled by muscular contraction; E, *P. vulgata*, section showing circulation between gills in pallial grooves.

rounding pallial grooves where they are conveyed back to be passed out at the hind end. It adds up to a simple and efficient system with the apparent disadvantage that the delicate gill could easily be damaged if such limpets were exposed to desiccation high on an exposed shore. This would indeed appear to be the case around British coasts where our two species, the white or pinkish *Acmaea virginica* and the tortoise-shell *A. tessulata*, each around a centimetre long, are confined to the lowest areas of the shore and down to depths of a few metres. Obviously they are less well adapted for shore life than the larger and more robust species of *Patella* everywhere common between tide-marks on all our rocky shores.

However it is otherwise elsewhere. On the shores of California no less than seventeen species of *Acmaea* (with the much larger owl limpet, *Lottia gigantea*) compete for attention from the highest to the lowest levels of the shore, some confined to well defined zones, two indeed to particular marine plants, one on a brown seaweed the other, much modified, on the thin strap-like leaves of the sea grass *Phyllospadix*. No species of *Patella* occurs on those shores and, despite invariable possession of a ctenidium, appropriately adapted species of *Acmaea* can resist long periods of desiccation high on the rocks.

The other features to be seen in a living *Acmaea* (Fig. 23) are the pair of head tentacles, each with an eye near the base, the downward-reaching limpet mouth and the fringe of mantle tentacles which project slightly beyond the shell when the animal moves. The various orifices open on the right side of the shallow mantle (or nuchal) cavity while a large blood vessel (which may be seen in the intact animal) runs around the margin of the mantle to pass into the heart on the left side. The two shell muscles so dissimilar in size in the abalones are here symmetrical, grown back and united to form a single horse-shoe shaped muscle. This faces forward arching around the nuchal cavity. The low conical visceral mass is occupied apically by the gonad and beneath by the much coiled gut and other organs.

Here we may leave these animals, noting that the white *Acmaea* is widely distributed but the tortoise-shell species occurs only round northern shores from north Wales round to the Humber. Like all such animals they can best be observed living by inducing them to attach to a small area of glass and viewing them through this upside down in water, as they appear in the figure (Fig. 23).

The dominant north Atlantic limpets are species of *Patella* (Fig. 23) which abound on every rocky shore. Apart from acorn barnacles and winkles, with which they are usually associated, no shore animal is commoner. The shell is larger, rougher and more conical than in *Acmaea* where the apex is further forward. Until fairly recently all were regarded as belonging to the one species, *Patella vulgata*, the common limpet. This is indeed everywhere much the commonest species. However, doubts crept into the minds of those who observed them and eventually it became clear that there are really two other species. *P. aspera*, the China limpet, lives low down on exposed shores although occasionally higher up in pools encrusted with calcareous weeds. It is absent in the south-east of England, between the Humber and the Isle of Wight. The black-footed limpet, *P. intermedia*, is a southern species con-fined to the south-west, to Wales and the west of Ireland; also an inhabitant of exposed shores, it never reaches so high as *P. vulgata*.

Bearing in mind that the two last occur in restricted areas, the three species are distinguished by characters of both shell and body. *P. vulgata* is the biggest, up to 10 cm in diameter, and, although very variable, is also the tallest as well as being the sole limpet on the highest shore levels. In *P. intermedia* and the still flatter *P. aspera* the surrounding mantle tentacles are white; they are colourless, indeed virtually invisible, in *P. vulgata*. The foot is olive green in this species, cream coloured in *P. aspera* and, as the common name signifies, dark in *P. intermedia*. After removal of the body, the interior of the shell is a pale greyish green with the scar over the head silvery in the common limpet; the interior is dark with the margins brightly coloured in *P. intermedia* whereas in *P. aspera* the interior is white and the head scar cream. But these differences are not always as clear as these statements imply.

The common limpet is familiar to everyone who has ever walked over a rocky shore and it is difficult to imagine any animal that is more perfectly adapted to its environment. Looking at the under surface through glass (Fig. 23) as we did with *Acmaea*, the shallow nuchal cavity is seen to contain no ctenidium. This organ is functionally replaced by a ring of thin-walled ciliated flaps of tissue which, in association with a conspicuous encircling blood vessel, hang down from the roof of the pallial grooves completely surrounding both the foot and the head. These secondary gills take over the function of current production. When the shell margins are raised they create a gentle inflow above and outflow below, respiratory exchange taking place in the process.

Meanwhile cilia on the walls of the nuchal cavity and around the margin of the foot carry sediment together with faeces and other discharged products not, as in *Acmaea*, to the hind end but to the right side where all accumulates to be expelled from time to time by sudden contractions of the shell muscle. This may be an adaptation to the somewhat more sedentary life, sometimes on mud-covered rocks. However, conditions are different in the Californian species of *Acmaea*. Those highest on the shore rely on water movement (so very powerful on exposed Pacific shores) to remove all sediment while other species which live in sheltered subtidal areas eject such waste from the right side as in *Patella*. The large Californian owl limpet which lives fully exposed and has *both* a ctenidium *and* secondary gills like *Patella* with both types of respiratory current relies entirely on water movements for cleansing. This problem of cleansing is one of prime importance to molluscs which rely for oxygen on easily blocked ciliary mechanisms.

Patella received its name initially from Martin Lister although this did not become universally valid until accepted by Linnaeus in his *Systema Naturae* in the middle of the eighteenth century. No shore animal has excited greater interest. So many questions present themselves to the enquiring mind. How does it maintain itself under what are often such precarious conditions of storm and exposure? How does it subsist on what often appear the barest rocks? How, indeed, does it obtain food and over what range can it forage? How does it resist the wide range of temperature experienced not merely over the year but often during the course of a single day? How, again, does it reproduce and maintain its frequently vast populations?

Such matters have exercised the minds of man from the days of Aristotle who, in his *Historia Animalium*, writes of the close attachment of limpets to rocks from which they only detach themselves to go in quest of food. Borelli, the great seventeenth-century physiologist, denied such movements but Aristotle's observations were supported in the following century by Réamur, primarily an entomologist but with widely ranging interests, who was possibly the first to conduct experiments on *Patella*. He suspended weights from limpets attached to the under surface of rock and found that it took one of 30 pounds to detach them. Many have been impressed by the easily demonstrated fact that a sudden kick at an unsuspecting limpet will send it flying but if such attempt be preceded by even a slight warning tap, the shell may often be broken before the animals can be detached. The foot is clearly more than just a suction pad held on by atmospheric pressure; even when cut radially it retains its hold. The area of attachment, viewed through glass, can be seen to increase in response to efforts of dislodgement. All the evidence indicates that some adhesive is produced by the sole of the foot and that this is responsible for the exceptionally secure attachment.

This serves the double function of maintaining the animal against mechanical shock – and if dislodged limpets may be turned over never to regain attachment – and, when the tide is out, of retaining water in the pallial grooves and nuchal cavity. Respiration can then continue while the evaporation of this water during long periods of summer exposure lowers the temperature. Clearly it is essential that the margins of the shell should make perfect contact with the rock below or water will be lost. Such contact may be achieved by the shell conforming to the underlying rock while, by continual contraction of the shell, softer rocks may be ground away so that the animals come perfectly to fit a shallow depression or 'home scar' (Plate 1). But in either case the limpet comes to rest at a place where shell and rock make perfect contact, deliberately turning round until this is achieved. Limpets also move about, particularly where the rock is smooth and offers a variety of suitable sites. Observations in such areas on the Isle of Man revealed that only nine out of 182 limpets occupied their original positions after six months, most had not moved far, the most enterprising only some 30 metres.

It is none too certain precisely how the home journey is made. If moved beyond their normal feeding range, limpets usually fail to return but within it they must rely on some vague capacity for 'memory' or, more likely, on following the mucus trail left on the outward journey, which could be identified by the mantle tentacles. Already encountered in chitons, these problems of behaviour are as significant to shore-dwelling animals as are the more obvious structural and functional adaptations but are usually more difficult to interpret.

Movement then is purposeful, taking the animal to its feeding area or back to the home. Limpets may be active when exposed so long as the rock remains damp and cool and so most frequently by night. Movement is produced by contractions of muscles in the foot operating against the blood which, confined within spaces between the muscles, forms what is termed a 'fluid skeleton'. Viewed through glass, as the animal moves forward 'ditaxic' waves of muscular contraction are seen to pass backward alternately on the two sides; when turning a tight corner one half of the foot goes forward, the other half back. Each wave begins with the front margin lifting clear and stretching forward then to be re-applied, the process followed by a backward running sequence of such movements.

These limpets feed on closely growing vegetation, often algal sporelings, and on detritus containing diatoms and organic remains which collects on the rock surface. They do so by means of the characteristic docoglossan radula (Plate 2). Here the central rachidian tooth found in the rhipidoglossan radula present in all other archaeogastropods (including the top shells) is reduced or absent. On each side there are three lateral teeth with especially hardened black tips bounded by three smaller colourless marginals. This is a finely tempered instrument for scraping the hardest rock surfaces on which its marks may often be detected. Not surprisingly the buccal mass which supports and operates the complex odontophore is the most elaborate organ in the body. During feeding several rows of radular teeth are simultaneously pressed against the rock surface by muscles red with the haemoglobin needed for adequate oxygen supply. The normal blood pigment in molluscs which possess one, is the far less efficient copper-containing haemocyanin. The results of radular activity are passed back into a gut well supplied with carbo-hydrate-splitting digestive enzymes suitable for chemical conversion of the plant food.

The continual feeding activities of the great limpet populations have an inevitable effect on the seaweed cover on the shore and so on all animals which live on or under this. This effect was dramatically displayed following a major experiment in nature carried out at Port St Mary, I.O.M. by members of staff of the marine station at Port Erin. In October 1946 a strip of rocky shore 10 metres wide running up from the lowest tidal level over a series of lime-stone ledges for a distance of 115 metres was completely cleared of limpets and with them all the larger seaweeds. The entire operation occupied some six months. The immediate effect was the appearance on the ledges of a fine 'felt' of green weeds so that the strip stood out vividly against the surrounding area kept largely bare by browsing limpets (Plate 1). During the following winter the sporelings of species of brown fucoids began to appear and the green weeds diminished. Then from the early summer of 1948 the algal growth started to decline as limpets began to move in from the margins to forage on the rich growth of weed. They had the further advantage that the thick covering of weed had prevented settlement of barnacles, elsewhere extremely common, the presence of which inhibits limpet movements. Only gradually over succeeding years did the limpets resume their domination, eating down the existing vegetation and destroying the newly settled spore-lings.

Precisely the same thing was to happen following the *Torrey Canyon* disaster in 1967 when areas of the Cornish coast were polluted with crude oil and then hosed with highly poisonous detergents. In some of the most heavily treated areas the limpets were killed and these areas later appeared bright green due to growth of sporelings normally removed by limpets. Again the normal balance was only slowly re-established.

There are notable differences between limpets living high and those living low on the shore. The former are taller, a probable consequence of greater exposure and so more continuous contraction of the horse-shoe shaped shell muscle which will restrict outward shell growth. This has been proved by transferring marked high level limpets into rock pools where they are never exposed; further shell growth formed an outward extending ledge around the margin of the high conical shell. Less obvious differences concern radula length. In *P. vulgata* this tends to be about twice the length of the shell in high living individuals but only about half this in animals lower down where opportunities for feeding with resultant radular wear are so much greater. The position is more complex with the two species living lower down. *P. aspera* has a radula on average about the length of the shell but *P. intermedia* has one more than twice the length of this. But this animal lives under conditions of greatest exposure which may have as great an inhibiting effect on movement and feeding as high level exposure.

There are many obvious difficulties in life high on the shore where the population is occasionally devastated by extreme and prolonged winter frosts and will annually be affected by exposure on hot summer days. Animals such as limpets will then absorb radiant energy and encounter the full effects of desiccation. High level limpets have a lower metabolic rate and are able both to resist water loss and to survive greater loss than those lower down the shore. These functional differences also prevail for other limpets living within the far closer limits of the almost tideless Mediterranean.

The three species differ in the breeding seasons: *P. vulgata* spawns between October and December, *P. aspera* in the summer (it is a more southern species as its distribution indicates) and *P. intermedia* throughout the year although most actively in the summer. Change of sex – a not uncommon phenomenon in molluscs – occurs in certainly the majority of common limpets, from an earlier male to a later female phase, the gonad changing from one producing sperm to one producing eggs. In a few cases, actually just 30 out of 64,576 specimens examined, the animals had functional gonads producing both eggs and sperm, this hermaphrodite condition being some ten times commoner in *P. aspera* than in either of the other species. When, after suitable months of preparation, the gonads are ripe the act of spawning appears to result from physical shock induced by rough seas and onshore winds. Former ideas that it is initiated by the direct effects of temperature, tidal conditions or, as once strongly held, position in the lunar cycle, must all be abandoned.

Once begun, spawning spreads throughout a local population. As in all archaeogastropods so far mentioned, eggs and sperm are discharged into the sea where fertilization occurs and veliger larvae develop feeding on microscopic plant life. When ready to change into the adult form, the larvae settle on rock, probably below tide level and quickly metamorphose. The adult shell appears and the velum is lost while buccal mass and radula develop and feeding begins on bottom diatoms and more delicate weeds. Gradual movement is made upshore to heights that vary according to the species but with *P. vulgata* always reaching the highest levels, indeed sometimes attaining such a degree of exposure that it may be endangered by high summer temperatures. But such marginal fluctuations do not influence the underlying stability of limpet distribution.

Although we have but three species of *Patella*, other shores are as rich in these limpets as the shores of California are in species of *Acmaea*. Along the extensive coasts of S. Africa live no less than eleven species of *Patella* with five species of allied genera but only two of *Acmaea*. *Patella cochlear* is of unusual interest. It lives very low on the shore in regions of moderate to strong exposure on rock surfaces covered with encrusting growths of the calcareous red seaweed, *Lithothamnion*. It grows in communities or 'mosaics' so dense that 1400 have been counted in a square metre. Except where the population is sparse all the young ones live on the algal-infested shells of the larger ones to an observed maximum of forty on a single shell. These mosaics are often fringed by algal 'gardens' on which the limpets do not appear significantly to feed but do apparently maintain, possibly by way of spores which pass unharmed through the gut. Certainly when the limpets are removed the 'gardens' tend to diminish and finally disappear.

The solitary remaining intertidal limpet on our coasts is the common and very widely distributed little blue-rayed limpet, *Patina pellucida*. This is only about 1 cm long, smooth and usually marked with rays of brilliant blue. Viewed from below (Fig. 23) it resembles *Patella* but the ring of secondary gills is discontinued around the head and ciliary currents carry sediment to the right side of the head; there is no muscular discharge as in the more specialized *Patella*.

This limpet is rarely found anywhere but on the fronds, or within cavities in the massive holdfasts, of species of the large oarweeds, *Laminaria*, and so is rarely exposed except at low water of spring tides although it can easily be collected by wading. It is of particular interest because occurring in two forms, *P. p. pellucida* on the surface of fronds and *P. p. laevis*, which has an irregular pale shell with blue rays, confined to the cavities in the holdfasts. Breeding occurs largely in winter and spring with young, some 2 mm long, settling in May on the wide surfaces provided by the extended fronds. There many feed and grow, becoming sexually mature when about 5 mm long to die at the end of a year still all *P. p. pellucida*. But during the summer a proportion migrate down the stalk or stipe to the holdfast there finding and enlarging a suitable recess. In the process they become irregular and, probably due to absence of light, marginal formation of blue rays ceases. Some of these animals, all now *laevis*, survive into a second year of life. This downward migration is particularly significant in *Laminaria digitata* which casts its fronds and with them any adherent *Patina*. So what appear, in form and habitat, as distinct species are really varieties, their differences the consequence of exposure of the growing animals to different environments.

We are left finally with a few obscure limpets living at moderate depths largely to the north-west of the British Isles. These are *Propilidium exiguum*, *Lepeta caeca* and *L. fulva*. They belong to the family Lepetidae and so are devoid of both ctenidium *and* secondary gills while the lateral radular teeth are fused. Personal observations on the Pacific species, *Lepeta concentrica*, dredged from depths of around 45 metres in Puget Sound, showed that these limpets browse on isolated stones lying half embedded in mud. Their food at this depth can only be organic detritus. Oxygen needed for so simple an existence is obtained by diffusion through the soft tissues of the pallial grooves into which water is drawn by cilia on their surfaces. Here all waste is carried to the hind end and voided by ciliary means.

Limpets and top shells

Turning from these ubiquitous limpets to the top shells, or Trochacea, that form the next group of archaeogastropods is to return to the primitive gastropod form with asymmetrically coiled shell. Like that of the pleurotomariid slit-shells, this is a broadly based pyramid, like an inverted spinning top (Fig. 24). But here the slit with the right gill and associated organs have been lost

FIG. 24. Top shell, *Calliostoma zizyphinum*, left side in life, showing operculum. (After Fischer)

while the anus has moved over to the right (Fig. 19). Water now enters on the left, passes between the gill filaments and emerges on the right taking with it all waste products and, when ripe, the eggs or sperm. A notable advance has been made with the problems of sanitation solved by creation of a left/right (instead of a below/upward) circulation through the respiratory cavity. Moreover to some extent here, and to an even greater extent in the higher gastropods, the entrance into the cavity is extended forward on the left and the exit moved back on the right so that the flow of water becomes increasingly in an anterior/posterior direction.

But, as we saw, owing to the primitive nature of the gill, danger from sediment remains. Thus although top shells are amongst the commonest animals in shallow water environments the world over, they are largely restricted to rocky bottoms where the water is normally free of sediment and rarely if ever within sand or mud (this demands modifications yet to be encountered). Some, usually small, species dredged from soft bottoms possibly live on isolated stones like the blind limpets. But along rocky shores top shells are usually extremely common and probably because such conditions are most extensive on coral reefs it is there that the largest species occur.

Like the limpets, all are herbivorous feeding on encrusting vegetation by means of the many-toothed rhipidoglossan radula (Plate 2). They are obviously much concerned with the nature of the surfaces over which they crawl and, as in all two-gilled gastropods, carry around the upper margin of the foot a series of 'epipodial' tentacles which must aid the head tentacles in tactile and chemical exploration. Top shells appear less adapted for intertidal life than limpets; certainly the smaller foot has no such powers of sustained adhesion although attachment is aided by sticky secretions. If knocked off by wave action, the foot is withdrawn, the shell opening closed by the horny operculum and the animal rolled about with considerable impunity, often to be deposited in a crevice from which it later emerges. Top shells are not, however, as common as limpets on steep slopes but tend to be restricted to flat rocky shores with broken surfaces. Young animals often concentrate in pools or in damp areas under stones or weed.

Compared with warm temperate and especially tropical seas, the British population of top shells is small, only some fifteen species, largely confined to southern and western shores. Much the commonest intertidal species are *Gibbula cineraria*, *G. umbilicalis* and *Monodonta lineata* and only the first of these, the grey top shell, is generally distributed. About 10 mm in basal diameter, the somewhat flattened shell has deep depressions (sutures) between successive whorls and is light grey with dark grey stripes. Usually associated with brown fucoid weeds, on which, with algal debris, it feeds, it is common from the level of high water of neap tides to below tidal levels. It is thus never exposed for more than one tidal period. Except on the east coast where this second species does not occur, it may easily be confused with *G. umbilicalis*, the flat or purple top shell. This is the same size but distinguished by purplish markings and by the presence on the underside of a conspicuous central opening, the umbilicus, which extends upwards through the centre of the ascending spiral of the shell whorls. In *G. cineraria* this opening is smaller and oval in outline. In older shells of both species the underlying silvery layers are frequently exposed especially around the apex. *G. umbilicalis* extends somewhat higher on the shore than the grey top shell and does not occur below the lowest tidal levels.

Monodonta (sometimes referred to as *Osilinus* or *Gibbula*) *lineata* is one of the larger shore gastropods. It has a much higher spire with a basal diameter of up to 25 cm, the shell sutures are less deep and the umbilicus small. The shell is marked with zigzag streaks of dark purple with the apex frequently eroded. This shell is really unmistakable when encountered, often in considerable numbers, on southern and western shores. It could only – and that very initially – be confused with the common periwinkle, *Littorina littorea*, which is about the same size but with a more rounded final whorl and smaller spire. *M. lineata* extends fairly high on the shore in summer, being then commonest in the upper region of the barnacle zone which is so characteristic a feature of all rocky shores. It is usually encountered on bare areas with scattered fucoid weeds. Of British top shells it is certainly the best adapted to intertidal life. Starting about March all but the smallest individuals, which congregate under stones or in gravel, start to move upshore, the largest ones marking greatest progress but all coming finally to occupy a restricted upper zone during the summer. In November the reverse movement begins so that winter is spent at lower levels and therefore for long periods under water which is then warmer than the air. However cold so lowers activity that a long spell of intense frost such as was suffered in 1962–3 may kill off great numbers of exposed animals, unable to crawl down into the security of the relatively warmer water.

Another south-western species, *Gibbula magus*, although almost as large is easily distinguished because so much flatter, with rounded tubercles on the upper surface of each whorl. It is only to be collected at the lowest levels of tidal exposure and is very dubiously a shore species. Another, but this time

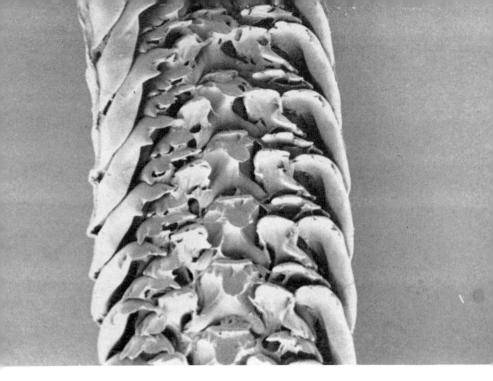

PLATE 3. Scanning electron micrographs of radulae: *above*, *Melarapha scabra* (× 250), taenioglossan type; specimen of shell height 18mm; from the upper shore at North Stradbroke Island, Queensland. *Below, Buccinum undatum* (× 67), stenoglossan type; specimen of shell height 6cm; dredged near Plymouth.

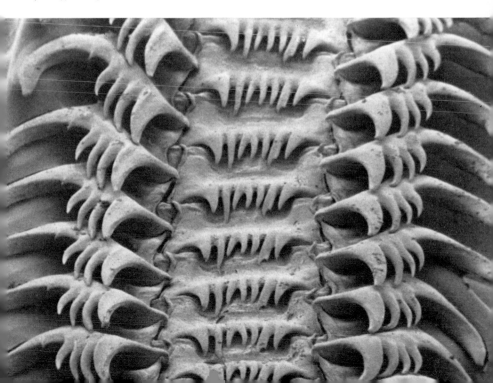

PLATE 4.
Camouflaged
carrier shells: *right*,
*Xenophora
conchyliophora*,
shown from above
with rubble
attached to upper
whorls, and
succession of valves
of dog cockles
(*Glycymeris* sp.) to
final whorls; from
Caribbean.
Below, X. pallidula,
shown from below
with radiating
series of high-spired
gastropod shells
attached around
the margin of the
final whorl. The
upper surface has
smaller such shells,
with valves of
bivalves and rubble.
From Central
Pacific.

quite unmistakable, species occurs below tidal levels and on to the lower shores, to be found usually under stones. This is the painted top shell, *Calliostoma zizyphinum* (Fig. 24), which is composed of ten to twelve tightly wound whorls without sutures. It is a straight-sided pyramid with a flat base, some 25 cm in both height and basal diameter. Certainly in colour this is our most beautiful gastropod shell, usually yellow or pink with red streaks although there are colour varieties, notably white and purple. The slightly larger *C. papillosum* obtained by dredging has a more ridged pink shell with a more rounded opening. The remaining top shells are small, down to 4 mm in diameter, some rare and others only to be obtained by dredging. This applies to *Cantharidus striatus*, the grooved top shell, another south-western species which may, however, be found on eel grass.

All of the above are trochids, species belonging to the family Trochidae. There is a solitary British example of the Turbinidae or turban shells, the pheasant shell *Tricolia pullus*. Taken alive, this is unmistakable because the operculum is white, rounded and calcareous instead of brown, flat and horny. About 8 mm high, the shell is taller than broad and composed of only a few whorls. It is usually yellow with reddish markings and is found, often in pools, at the lowest tidal levels and frequently on the red seaweed, *Chondrus crispus* (Irish moss or carrageen). It is the most northern representative of its family in the Atlantic and restricted to the south-west where it is not uncommon.

These are the common top shells, an interesting but not extensive and, apart from the painted top shell, only a moderately attractive group of shells. They could be considered as no more than the interesting remnants of a relatively primitive group of gastropods handicapped by a too-elaborate gill and by notable reproductive restrictions, but this would totally disregard their great abundance in warm and especially tropical seas. There conditions favour them – temperature is higher with usually limited tidal exposure and abundant algal food. Particularly over coral reefs, water is singularly free of sediment. Here live a wealth of top shells, many of great beauty and some of impressive size. A glance through one of the recent Japanese books on shells illustrated in colour reveals pages of species of both trochids and turbans, the majority from their southern, semi-tropical waters. The largest top shells are tropical, notably the great top shell, *Trochus niloticus*, mottled in red, straight-sided like *Calliostoma* but up to 12 cm in height and basal diameter. So numerous on the Great Barrier Reef of Australia and elsewhere in the tropical Pacific these formed, and in places may still form, the object of extensive fisheries. Below the thin superficial coloured layer, the thick shell is nacreous and a source of pearl buttons. The even larger green snail, *Turbo marmoratus*, with fewer and very rounded whorls is (or was) particularly common in the Indian Ocean notably off Kenya. This is the largest top shell attaining 20 cm in both dimensions. It is mottled green in colour and has long been known in Europe where large specimens may frequently be encountered in curio shops, also likely sources of the brilliant green and orange 'cat's eye' operculum which comes from *Turbo petholatus* which has a polished shell resembling marble. The pheasant shells (*Phasianella* spp.), so named because in colour and pattern they resemble the plumage of a pheasant, are equally beautiful. Reference should finally be made to the well-named Imperial sun trochus, *Astraea heliotropium* (Fig. 25), originally collected by Captain Cook in the temperate waters of Cook Strait between North and South Island, New Zealand.

To the restriction of top shells to a hard substrate must be added further limitations imposed by the reproductive system. In all archaeogastropods the functional kidney is on the right side so that the reproductive organ (in gastropods always on the right) can only open by way of the excretory or renal duct. The left kidney in these animals is small and largely functionless (see Fig. 19). Hence in the female there can be no elaboration of the pouches and glands where sperm may be received and, after fertilization, albumen and protective capsules be successively added, while in the male the genital tract cannot be prolonged into a penis for inserting sperm into the oviduct. Internal fertilization is impossible and egg and sperm must be extruded for fertilization and development in the sea. We shall see how differently these matters are dealt with in the higher gastropods and what major advantages are conferred by their capacity for internal fertilization.

In all British top shells, other than *Calliostoma*, eggs and sperm are liberated just as they are in limpets. In *Gibbula umbilicalis* and in *Monodonta* this occurs in the summer indicating that both are southern species at the northern end of their range. *G. cineraria*, on the other hand, spawns in much colder water in the spring, indeed in some years the water may never be cold enough for spawning to occur on the south coast. This is a northern species present in Iceland and growing noticeably larger in the north than in the south of Great Britain. It is the most northern intertidal top shell.

After fertilization a swimming larva is formed to be followed by what has been described in *G. cineraria* as a 'swimming-attempted-creeping' stage which lasts until the eighth or ninth day after fertilization when the young animal is capable of crawling on a hard surface on which it has apparently been indiscriminately deposited by the waves. This is in contrast to other molluscs which, as already noted, *must* settle on some particular surface if they are to change into the adult form and assume the adult habit.

Some attempt to protect the eggs after laying and fertilization is made in a few top shells; this is even true for some species of *Acmaea*. A small top shell of northern shores, *Margarites helicinus* which has a greenish globular shell some 4 mm across, deposits clusters of around a hundred eggs on the under sides of stones or on weeds by means of the foot. The process is taken farthest in *Calliostoma* which produces a ribbon containing relatively large eggs which hatch late in development so that some hazards of planktonic life are avoided. There is even a degree of difference here between the sexes, at least within the mantle cavity where the female aperture, on the right side, is extended further forward than in the male owing to incorporation of a section of the mantle wall. This probably includes part of the hypobranchial mucus gland because it is concerned with the formation of the substance of the egg ribbon. Sperm must be available at the time that eggs are discharged and this involves the proximity of males although actual copulation is impossible in any of these animals. At least here, as in *Margarites* and very possibly in other

66

species, the larger eggs stand a greater chance of survival. We now proceed to see how much better these matters are dealt with in the higher gastropods.

FIG. 25. Imperial sun trochus, *Astraea heliotropium*. (After Wilkins)

Chapter 7

Mesogastropods

*

WE have surveyed the simplest living gastropods, the coiled slit-shells with the various types of limpets, some supremely successful, and the sometimes impressively large top shells. We have noted, also, their restrictions largely to hard surfaces, to a herbivorous diet and, owing to reproductive limitations, to the marine environment.

Wider possibilities, however, present themselves to the mesogastropods we now encounter. Although they must have arisen from archaeogastropods – and there are a variety of views as to precisely from which of these – the fundamental differences are in a reproductive system which is completely separated from the kidneys (Fig. 19) and, in the gills, a simplification leading to greater efficiency. These two changes are not always, although almost always, associated. There are a few mesogastropods with an archaeogastropod gill such as the valve snails (*Valvata*) and the nerite (*Theodoxus fluviatilis*) both inhabitants of British freshwaters into which they have been able to penetrate because of the lifting of reproductive restrictions. The latter animal is worthy of note because the only northern representative of a major group of snails, the Neritacea, with many marine, freshwater and also terrestrial representatives all largely confined to the tropics.

In mesogastropods the functional kidney is on the left side so that the outlet ducts on the right are available for the sole and unrestricted use of the reproductive organs. No longer concerned with the outward passage of urine, these ducts can now be enlarged and extended (Fig. 19). In the male a groove from the reproductive opening leads sperm into the base of a conspicuous penis which grows out from the right side of the head, shown in *Littorina* in Fig. 28. Usually held tucked back within the mantle cavity, at the breeding season it is extended and introduced into the cavity of the female transferring sperm into the female genital aperture.

In the female the reproductive duct is enlarged and extended – to a much greater extent than in *Calliostoma* – by a local overarching of the walls of the cavity. This thickened oviduct reaches forward to open near the mantle margin, just to the right of the anus. It also distends internally to form cavities where sperm received at copulation are stored and where fertilization occurs while glandular areas produce albumen and a protective coat so that, after internal fertilization, the egg receives food and a measure of protection during development. Sea water is no longer an essential medium for fertilization or as a source of planktonic food in the form of microscopic plants for the developing larvae. Hence it is that we find mesogastropods, such as the European river-snail, *Viviparus viviparus*, in freshwaters and others like the round-mouthed apple snail, *Pomatias elegans*, in very limey areas on land.

These non-marine mesogastropods are easily distinguished from the commoner pulmonate snails because they retain the operculum.

The sexes are now easy to distinguish (cf. male and female *Littorina* in Fig. 28) while the tendency towards dual sexuality, already apparent in the archaeogastropod *Patella*, is emphasized; an early male phase may give place to a later female phase. This leads, in the largely naked opisthobranch sea slugs and in the terrestrial and freshwater pulmonate snails and slugs, to the establishment of complete hermaphroditism, organs of both sexes present and fully functional.

Simplification of gill structure comes with loss of the filaments on the left side and consequent fusion of the gill axis with the mantle wall. The now comb-like (pectinibranch) gill with its single row of individually larger filaments replaces the more elaborate, yet unquestionably more primitive, aspidobranch ctenidium. The simpler condition confers far greater efficiency as a comparison of **B** and **C** in Fig. 20 will reveal. A powerful respiratory current created by the broad rows of lateral cilia enters on the left to pass initially over an elongate sensory osphradium now sited along the base of the gill (see also Fig. 28). Certainly in the higher, carnivorous prosobranchs this is an organ for detecting prey, it is a chemoreceptor, but this does not cut out the possibility that it was originally, and possibly in more primitive gastropods still is, a means of detecting the sediment that is certainly carried over its surface.

Certainly every means is employed to collect and remove these suspended particles. The heavier ones are carried over the floor of the cavity, lighter ones are intercepted by the frontal cilia on the filaments or else pass between these to be entrapped in mucus from the massive gland on the roof of the mantle cavity, but all to be carried out with the exhalant current on the right side as indicated by the arrows in Fig. 20. No pockets remain between gill and mantle wall where sediment may collect and gastropods so equipped were able to leave rocky surfaces and begin to explore the wider possibilities of life within the mud, gravel and sand which cover by far the greater part of the sea floor. From being members of the surface dwelling *epifauna*, they become members of the sheltered *infauna*, animals that move through and feed within soft bottom deposits.

The mesogastropods have other general characters including loss of the right auricle of the heart, no longer needed when the right gill has been lost. Indeed these snails are often termed 'Monotocardia' in distinction to the diotocardiate archaeogastropods which all retain this second auricle. The mesogastropod radula is also distinctive, the teeth reduced to seven in each row, two marginals and a lateral on either side of a central tooth. This is a taenioglossan or ribbon-like radula (Plate 3).

While, as observed earlier, details of shell form must be sought elsewhere, a few general remarks are needed here. In consequence of their exposed positions on rock surfaces, archaeogastropods have broad-based, low-spired shells which are stable owing to the low centre of gravity. The very much greater range of environments inhabited by mesogastropods is accompanied by the appearance of shells of many forms such as the very high-spired screw shells, species of *Turritella* (Fig. 36), which invariably burrow.

Of the three layers of the shell, the inner and middle ones contain crystals of calcium carbonate within the organic conchiolin. There are complexities here but the middle layer (outer calcareous layer) is composed of vertically arranged crystals of aragonite and the inner layer usually of thin sheets of calcite more or less parallel to the surface, in some forming the iridescent nacre known as mother-of-pearl we have found so well developed in many top shells. This inner layer increases in thickness with age but the superficial periostracum and the outer calcareous layer, which are formed marginally, cease to extend when the animal becomes adult (i.e. sexually mature). The mantle margin represents the growing edge of all shelled molluscs and is entirely responsible for shell form which may alter during growth, as, for instance, in the spider shells (Fig. 10) which only acquire the spider-like projections at maturity.

The drawn out viscera of a snail are contained within an initially extending and widening tube which we have seen to become coiled owing to greater formation of shell on one side of the mantle margin – if this does not occur then a straight tube is produced as in the worm-like vermetids (Fig. 35) where coiling is unnecessary because the shell is cemented to a rock surface. The change, probably after torsion, from the original plano-spiral shell (as in *Nautilus* (Fig. 147)) into an asymmetrical and usually dextrally coiled turbinate shell or helicone has already been described. The vitally important

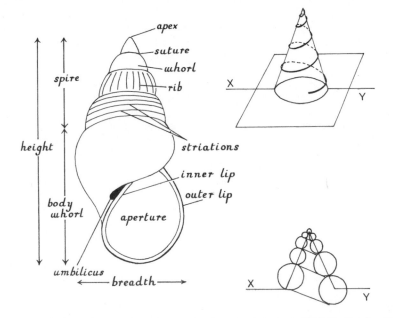

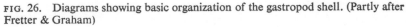

FIG. 26. Diagrams showing basic organization of the gastropod shell. (Partly after Fretter & Graham)

visceral organs could not be more effectively organized and protected than they are in snails. At the same time the elongate symmetrical foot can be extended during movement and feeding and then withdrawn within the coiled shell for protection, the operculum on its hind upper surface closing the opening.

The formation of the helicone shell can most simply be represented by the two diagrams on the right side of Fig. 26. For the sake of simplicity the tubular shell is shown as a thick line growing round a central cone, equivalent to the umbilicus so well developed in the pleurotomarids and persisting in some top shells and mesogastropods. If this simple, spirally wound tube enlarges its coils so that they meet, as shown in vertical section in the lower figure, then the coils unite so finally producing first a hollow and finally a solid central pillar like the central post of a spiral staircase although here diminishing in diameter as it ascends. This is the columella to which the massive columellar muscle is attached (Fig. 28), now the sole survivor of the many original pairs of shell muscles which were probably possessed by the primitive mollusc (Fig. 5) and are certainly present in the living *Neopilina* (Fig. 6). This muscle is the sole attachment of the gastropod to the enclosing shell (a very different state of affairs will be encountered in the bivalves) and by its contraction the head and foot are withdrawn into the shelter of the final or body whorl of the shell (Fig. 26).

The internal capacity of this whorl is indicated in the semi-diagrammatic figure of an unmodified mesogastropod shown on the left in Fig. 26. Viewed facing the aperture (on the right, so dextral) the shell is seen to be made up of body whorl below and ascending spire above composed of earlier whorls which house the viscera culminating in the single gonad which occupies the apex. When the animal withdraws, the aperture is closed by the operculum attached to the hinder upper surface of the foot (Fig. 31). Depending on the secretory activities around the generative curve of the mantle margin which forms the outer lip of the aperture, striations may be formed parallel to the lip and ribs be produced at right angles to this (both indicated in the figure). In addition, conspicuous spines may project from the surface in certain shells. These are produced at the end of a period of growth when areas of the mantle margin project outward to form them. They are usually calcareous although in the hairy snail, to be mentioned later (Fig. 31), they are composed of horny periostracum. The striking array of shell forms in the mesogastropods and the more specialized neogastropods (Chapter 9) which may be viewed in the many beautifully illustrated books on shells or in museum collections, are all consequences of the vagaries in the shell forming activities of the generating curve of the mantle margin. These widely differing shapes have all been tested by natural selection and been accepted because, sometimes for obvious and sometimes for obscure reasons, they increased the chances of survival in a particular environment or enabled their possessors to assume some new mode of life.

The growth activities of the mantle margin around the outer lip may produce only a slow increase in the diameter of successive whorls with final formation of a finely tapering shell. In other shells the diameter of the spirally wound tube increases very rapidly so that the final or body whorl is far greater in capacity than the sum of all the preceding ones. While this is hardly true of the shell illustrated (Fig. 26) we shall encounter many examples of such shells, initially in the winkles (Fig. 27). In limpets this increase in the diameter of the whorl is so pronounced that the entire animal is housed within the body whorl, the minute initial whorl breaking away to leave no trace. Overgrowth of earlier by later whorls may also occur, best displayed in the cowries (Fig. 34) where the adult shell shows no trace of the contained early whorls. These are only revealed when the shell is cut open (Fig. 33).

In temperate seas growth is not continuous throughout the year, dying down in winter to be intensified during the warmer months. But in all climates it proceeds in a series of bursts which the examination of most shells will reveal. This is most obvious when each burst ends with the production of a new row of spines. As new whorls grow over the lower surface of older ones any projections on these must be removed or the mouth of the shell would be restricted. The mantle margins are able to dissolve these at the same time as they proceed to extend the margin of the new whorl. This is but one instance of the capacity of molluscan tissues to remove as well as to form calcium carbonate; the growth of any shell is a process of remodelling.

All gastropods, indeed all molluscs, grow to a more or less predictable size after which the shell may continue to thicken by further addition of material to the general surface of the mantle, but there is no further marginal increase. Stoppage in growth is associated with development of the reproductive organs which increasingly demand all available material. In cases of heavy parasitism, usually by the intermediate stages in the life histories of trematodes (flukes) which destroy the gonads, parasitic castration occurs and growth continues with formation of abnormally large shells.

In certain mesogastropods the outer lip flares out often with formation of digitate extensions during the final stages in growth as we noted above in the case of the spider shells (Fig. 10). This final form has to do with the habits of the animal later described in the case of *Aporrhais*, the pelican's foot shell (Fig. 37). In other cases, coiling is lost, at least after early growth, so that the shell continues as a somewhat irregular tube which is cemented, like those of the common serpulid tube-worms, to a rocky surface. These vermetids (Fig. 35) are common in warm and tropical seas, also in temperate water in the southern hemisphere. Loss of coiling is accompanied by lengthening, the animal from time to time withdrawing from the end of the tube and forming a calcareous partition at the hind end of the rounded, worm-like body. There are, unfortunately, no British vermetids with their peculiar habit of extruding long mucus threads produced by pedal glands no longer needed to lubricate movement. With entangled planktonic food these threads are later drawn in and swallowed.

Withdrawal of a gastropod is concluded by closure of the aperture by the operculum. This structure, already encountered, is universally present in late larvae although subsequently lost in limpets, in parasitic and planktonic species and in the naked sea-slugs. Its origin presumably goes back to a period, possibly following torsion, when the primitive limpet form became drawn out

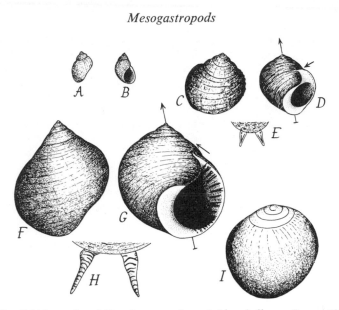

FIG. 27. British species of *Littorina*: A, B, *L. neritoides*, shell; C-E, *L. saxatilis*, shell and head tentacles; F-H, *L. littorea*, shell and tentacles; I, *L. littoralis*. (After G. E. Newell)

into a coiled tube with a restricted aperture. A means of closing this would give clear advantage to its possessors.

The operculum is formed by a disc on the upper surface of the back of the foot. Because they grow to a greater extent on the one side than on the other, opercula become spirally wound, in an anticlockwise direction when viewed from above. Archaeogastropod opercula are circular with a central 'nucleus' of growth; in higher gastropods this nucleus becomes marginally placed. However the operculum must have the same outlines as the shell aperture which it closes. Apart from the calcareous opercula of the turbinid top shells, they are formed of horny conchiolin with an added 'varnish' of uncertain nature. The edges are flexible so that the operculum fits closely within the shell aperture.

Consideration of mesogastropods inevitably begins with winkles, species of *Littorina* (Fig. 27), which occur the world over on rocky shores, the highest areas of which are known as the littorine zone although species occur at all levels. These are typical marine snails, their adaptations those of function and behaviour rather than of form, and in Great Britain there are four species all widely distributed. The largest is the periwinkle, *L. littorea*, up to 25 mm high and almost as broad, and so abundant that the collection of vast numbers to be boiled and eaten has no apparent effect on the population. It is an inhabitant of the middle and lower shore and so is seldom exposed for more than one consecutive low tide; it occurs on rocks, on stones and also on flat shores of mud-covered stones. It is clearly less restricted than are the top

73

shells from which it can easily be distinguished by the much more rounded shell, with the much enlarged terminal whorl and smaller spire and inconspicuous sutures. The only other gastropods with which it might initially be confused are the dog whelks which live on clean rocks in the barnacle zone but have an obvious siphonal extension at the base of the shell aperture. It is easy to crack open the periwinkle shell and, cutting through the columellar muscle, remove the contracted animal. Cutting down the mid-line of the roof of the mantle cavity will reveal (Fig. 28) the pectinibranch gill and osphradium on the left with, on the right, the rectum and beyond this the opening of the reproductive system, forming in the one sex a thickened oviduct which opens just short of the anus, and in the other a basal opening connected by a groove with the massive penis turned back into the mantle cavity except when in use. More care may be needed to pick out the right kidney opening on the

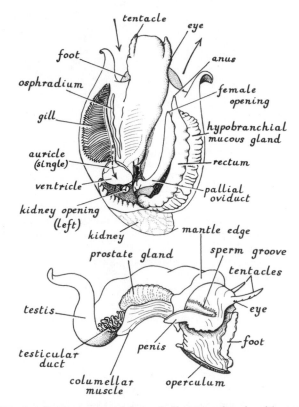

FIG. 28. *Littorina littorea*, removed from shell: *upper*, female with mantle cavity opened showing details of genital system; arrows show direction of respiratory currents, broken arrows course of blood from gill to heart; *lower*, male viewed from right side, mantle cavity intact, showing details of reproductive system including large bent penis, also columellar muscle. (After Fretter & Graham)

left side at the base of the mantle cavity. Here for easy inspection is the pattern of structure in the mesogastropod respiratory chamber with problems of indrawn sediment and of reproduction both admirably solved.

These littorines are herbivorous – change to the more specialized carnivorous diet comes later – making effective use of the taenioglossid radula for scraping encrusting vegetation or rasping the surface of the larger seaweeds. Work on one American species indicates that the gut contents may be completely renewed up to eight times daily. Where rock is scraped these contents include a proportion of fine fragments representing a perceptible rate of erosion, up to a centimetre in sixteen years.

The other species of *Littorina* consist of *L. saxatilis*, the rough winkle, *L. littoralis*, the flat winkle, and the much smaller *L. neritoides* (Fig. 27). Only the first is likely to be confused with *L. littorea* and then only with smaller specimens because it only grows to half the height of that species. But the shell is more rounded with a clear difference in the aperture: in *L. saxatilis* the upper lip meets the axis of the spire almost at right angles, in *L. littorea* it extends almost parallel to this. Further, when observed expanded, the tentacles in the former have longitudinal dark stripes; in the latter they are transversely banded. *L. littoralis* is slightly larger but almost globular with a smooth, often brightly yellow shell. *L. neritoides* does not exceed 5 mm in height, but is relatively taller than the others.

Each has its characteristic distribution on the shore. *L. neritoides* has the role, played by a variety of littorine species throughout the world, of delimiting the highest levels of the shore – the uppermost point to which marine animals, however supremely adapted for intertidal life, can extend. It lives in pools normally only filled by spray or in narrow cracks where spring tides reach occasionally. It has remarkable powers of resisting the effects of desiccation involving extremes of heat and cold, of widely varying salinity (these high pools may be flooded with fresh water or lose water by evaporation to become excessively saline). The one structural adaptation is a reduction in the size of the gill, the mantle cavity assuming the functions of a lung with blood vessels ramifying below the moist surface through which oxygen may enter from the air. It feeds by scraping fine vegetation from the rock surface.

L. saxatilis lives lower down, mingling with *L. littorea* but not descending so far down the shore. It is a particularly interesting species because very variable. It has been subdivided into four subspecies (which some regard as full species) *L. saxatilis*, subsp. *rudis*, subsp. *jugosa*, subsp. *tenebrosa* and subsp. *saxatilis*. Each has distinctive shell characters including thickness, sculpture and shape (colour is altogether too variable to be significant); anatomical features involving differences in radula, tentacles and penis; and range of exposure and of vertical distribution that it can withstand. All, however, extend highest under sheltered conditions. They are very possibly similarly distinct in their breeding cycles, their behaviour and even perhaps in the species of infecting trematode parasites. We are here viewing the process of species formation.

There is, moreover, a range of variation in all of these characters within ach subspecies but although always two, sometimes three and occasionally all four subspecies, co-exist on the same shore, there is no intergradation between them, at any rate not in *all* such characters and the experienced eye can always separate them. The inference is that the subspecies do not inter-breed and that we are viewing an early, but fundamental, stage in the process of speciation, in the subdivision of a single species into a number of distinct breeding populations each of which tend increasingly to separate from the parent stock and from each other. We are observing an evolutionary process.

The unmistakable flat winkle, *L. littoralis* occupies a somewhat wider zone from about average high tide level to extreme low water of spring tides but is almost always on brown fucoid weeds. The globular shell is strikingly similar to the rounded bladders which dot the fronds of the bladder wracks, *Fucus vesiculosus* and *Ascophyllum nodosum*.

Each of the winkles (and the subspecies of *L. saxatilis* or separate species) has its particular breeding season, varying somewhat with latitude, when the eggs become internally fertilized. What happens subsequently depends on the species. In both *L. littorea* and *L. neritoides*, lens-shaped egg capsules are liberated into the sea. The former, almost a millimetre in diameter contain up to nine eggs, the latter, only a fifth of this diameter, contain but one. These capsules float in the surface waters while veliger larvae develop within them. In *L. littorea*, they hatch out about the sixth day to swell the plankton for some two weeks before settling, probably below tidal levels. There they meta-morphose into the adult form and begin the slow crawl upwards. The adult zonation is attained about the end of the first year. Less is known about the smaller *L. neritoides* but this has further to go so will have to move faster if it is to reach its final destination at the same time.

The flat winkle goes about matters differently; it lays gelatinous egg masses often containing over 200 fertilized eggs usually on the surface of the fucoid weeds on which it lives. Here the element of chance is reduced, there is better protection during development which proceeds to the stage when, with a reduced velum but not as a swimming larva, the young hatch out. Already they can crawl and, finding themselves in the adult environment, all they have to do is to move about, feed and grow.

L. saxatilis takes matters further; the fertilized eggs, each in a cocoon, remain in the oviduct occupying a 'breeding-room' that may contain several hundred embryos at very different stages in development because the results of successive copulations are laid in successive batches. The liberated young are miniatures of the adult and in this instance also find themselves in the adult environment for life in which, equipped as they are with the adult be-haviour pattern, they are fitted from the start. With little doubt it is this manner of reproduction which has been responsible for the appearance of the subspecific (or specific) population. This would be impossible if all the young developed in the common medium of the sea to settle indiscriminately on the shore. Such isolation of populations is also impossible where the young mingle freely on weed and rock as do those of the flat winkle.

Maintenance on a particular zone on the shore is determined largely by the pattern of behaviour. The animal makes suitable muscular responses to external influences such as that of light which is received by the well-developed eyes and of gravity detected by the organs of balance or statocysts which are situated in the foot. Should the animal be carried by wave action above or below its normal levels of distribution its reaction to light and to gravity (the nature of which may be reversed according to whether the animal is submerged or exposed) will cause it to move back within these limits after which it becomes quiescent.

Periwinkles are more or less stationary except when the tide recedes from them or on the arrival of a flowing tide. If the shore be level they proceed to move towards the sun (i.e. are photopositive), later, when adequate food has been scraped, the reaction to light changes and each animal returns more or less to the point of departure. On a vertical surface movement is first downward (i.e. positively geotactic) again to be reversed so that the animal retraces its path. In both cases the end result is that the animals maintain the position on the shore for which they are adapted. Where such conditions are extreme as they are in *L. neritoides*, the animals are so adapted that they can survive exposure to a wide range of temperature, desiccation and salinity. In view of the rare contact with the sea, it was long believed that this small winkle was viviparous, the possibility of releasing fertilized eggs into the sea appeared so

FIG. 29.   *Lacuna parva* on red algae, showing crawling individuals, lens-shaped egg capsules and hatched out young. (By permission of Mrs Ellen Thorson)

slight. But in the event it is the lower living *L. saxatilis* which has proved to be viviparous. During the breeding season *L. neritoides* liberates egg capsules every two weeks at the periods of highest tides.

We have had a good deal to say about these common winkles for the simple reason that they are so extremely successful and therefore have a very great deal to tell us. Their nearest relatives are the common but inconspicuous Lacunidae or chink-shells of which there are four British species. All have very similar habits to the flat winkle but are smaller, no more than 8 mm across, and live lower on the shore and in the fringe zone of laminarian oarweeds. They can be distinguished when crawling by the presence of a pair of tentacles near the hind end of the foot, one on each side of the operculum. They live largely on delicate red weeds; for instance *Lacuna parva* occurs on species of *Delesseria* and *Phyllophora* on which it lays transparent flattened capsules containing some ten eggs from which, as shown in Fig. 29, young individuals emerge much as in the flat winkle.

Although so common, the numbers of littorinids fade into insignificance compared with those of the minute *Hydrobia* (or *Peringia*) *ulvae* which appear not so much as individuals but as a surface granulation over mid-tidal expanses of usually estuarine mud. This environment of soft mud with fluctuating salinity is not easily exploited but it offers rich rewards of food to those animals, of which *Hydrobia* is the most successful, able to do so. *Hydrobia* may occur in almost 'pure culture' reaching densities of over 30,000 per square metre in areas such as the Tamar, the Firth of Forth or the Clyde estuary. Double this density has been recorded in Denmark; an area of less than 2·5 square miles (about 6 square kilometres) in the Clyde contains an

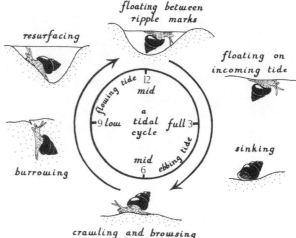

FIG. 30.   *Hydrobia (Peringia) ulvae*: behaviour during tidal cycle. (After R. Newell)

78

estimated population of over 30,000 *millions*. Few animals can occur in such densities in any environment.

Their success is explained by the manner in which during every tidal cycle they exploit two food sources (Fig. 30). The falling tide leaves them exposed on the mud over which – with diminishing activity as it starts to dry – they crawl and into which they burrow. Soon the surface is bare of animals, all lying with head up-ended and only the minute tentacles eventually exposed. All this time they feed on the rich supplies of microscopic diatoms and organic debris in the surface layers. When the tide returns they surface and launch themselves on to the surface film aided in buoyancy by formation of a mucous raft which also serves as a net to collect the inshore plant plankton. As the tide falls the animals drop back on to the mud surface and the cycle recommences, over the greater part of which food is taken from one or other of these sources. No wonder this species exists in astronomical numbers! Reproduction occurs during the summer when, in default of other hard surfaces, small capsules each containing a few eggs are deposited on the surface of the shell (Fig. 52). Although these hatch as veligers, larval life is very short with quick settlement on to the mud surface.

The hydrobiids like some other mesogastropods tend to lose dependence on sea water. *H. ventrosa* occurs in brackish water creeks and lagoons while the closely related *Potamopyrgus jenkinsi* is a freshwater animal. First observed here as recently as 1859, this species has spread all over Great Britain. Although a freshwater animal of such brief standing, like many such animals it has become parthenogenetic producing eggs that develop without fertilization. Only a single male specimen has ever been found.

These hydrobiids reveal the potentialities of the mesogastropods. Unlike archaeogastropods, they can penetrate mud and exploit its rich supplies of food. Because of internal fertilization the young can be retained within the localized adult environment – without it the larvae would be widely dispersed with rare chances of regaining it. And life need no longer be restricted to a marine environment.

There are many small shore-dwelling snails, some very similar in shell form to winkles and hydrobiids. They belong to a diversity of families the most important of which is the Rissoidae or spire-shells in which there are several genera containing some 26 British species. Search, especially low on the shore or in pools, is certain to reveal a number of these usually on weed, on sea grass, *Zostera*, or under stones. They crawl up and down mucous strings produced from a gland opening in the middle of the hinder region of the foot. No species is over 7 mm tall. There are many other such small mesogastropods, down to no more than 1 mm in any dimension, where size imposes an interesting simplicity of structure.

The so-called needle whelks with high-spired shells, mainly species of *Bittium* and *Cerithiopsis* include *Triphora perversa*, the sole sinistral species in the British fauna and so unmistakable if encountered, which will only be on south-western shores and at very low water or below. It is about 7 mm high and the first carnivorous mesogastropod to be noted; it feeds on sponges by inserting a proboscis into the oscular opening and scraping out the soft tissues

79

with the narrow radula. The more widely distributed common wentletrap, *Clathrus clathrus*, has a beautiful, many-whorled shell bearing prominent longitudinal ribs. It is only to be found at very low water of spring tides and usually in the spring when it comes inshore to attach strings of small triangular egg capsules (Fig. 52) to rocky surfaces. It also is carnivorous, feeding on sea anemones.

Animals of widely diverse form and habit now present themselves and, disregarding the classification which must be adhered to when describing shells, these are better considered in relation to a common habit of life which may have been reached by diverse evolutionary routes. Retaining concern with a rocky substrate, this chapter will conclude with descriptions of mesogastropod limpets and of our two cowries.

To the slit limpets and the patelliform limpets must now be added members of the mesogastropod superfamily Calyptraeacea the majority of which have conical limpet shells without opercula and are often completely immobile. But they have the gill, the radula and the reproductive facilities of the mesogastropods. Of the three families – Trichotropidae, Calyptraeidae, Capulidae – the first are not limpets but their study indicates how this form and habit evolved.

The solitary British species, *Trichotropis borealis*, the hairy snail, can only be obtained by dredging on hard bottoms off northern coasts. Like all related species it is covered with almost a soft 'fur' of periostracal hairs. The north Pacific species, *T. cancellatus* (Fig. 31), on the other hand, is both common and

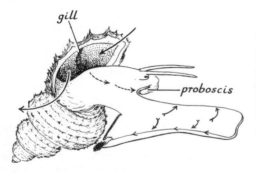

FIG. 31. *Trichotropis cancellatus*, viewed from right side, showing passage of material collected by the gills to the proboscis. Arrows on foot indicate ciliary currents carrying sediment to hind end where it collects below operculum.

easily obtained in Puget Sound where it was examined and what follows concerns this species, unlikely to differ significantly from *T. borealis*. The rather high-spired coiled shell is usual enough but not the mode of life. This is the first of a number of mesogastropods to be mentioned in which the cleansing currents on the gills are used to collect food. We have seen how the cilia on the frontal and abfrontal edges of each gill filament carry away sediment that is held in suspension in the respiratory current. All that is needed to convert this into a filter feeding mechanism is to extend the length of the single row of mesogastropod filaments so as to increase both the current-producing and the particle-collecting surfaces and deflect the passage of the outgoing mucus-laden streams around the right side of the head to the mouth. This lies at the base of a short grooved proboscis up which cilia move the food streams to be grasped by the radula and swallowed. The gut is adapted for dealing with such food notably by possession of a rotating gelatinous rod, the crystalline style, the significance of which is discussed when dealing with the bivalves where it is always present.

Ciliary feeding is a highly efficient means of obtaining food where plant plankton is abundant but it demands immobility or mud and debris will be raised and foul the inflowing current. Here the habits of *T. cancellatus* (and probably of *T. borealis*) come into the picture. This animal lives on an irregular, unstable bottom largely composed of dead shells. Placed on such a substrate in aquaria, each animal climbs as high as it can then, with mantle cavity widely open to collect food, it remains immobile, only resuming activity should it be displaced when again it seeks to attain the highest available eminence. Judging by their numbers, sometimes hundreds in a single dredge haul, this is a highly successful mode of life.

Another matter now arises. Hitherto animals have usually been of one sex or the other although with evidence that in *Patella* some individuals do change from male to female, not a matter involving much structural change in archaeogastropods. Now, in the hairy snail, we encounter protandrous hermaphrodites where a preliminary male phase is followed by a female phase. Apart from the change of the gonad from testis to ovary, the former state requires the presence of a large penis and the latter of elaborate glands to produce albumen and egg capsules. Such changes involve major structural alterations, presumably under the control of hormones produced by the gonad.

T. cancellatus spawns from mid February until May producing flat capsules about 4·5 mm across. These are attached to rock and laid in a close spiral to form a compact, rounded mass. The young develop into males, with an obvious penis, which are functional at the end of the first year. They are then about 25 mm high but reach 40 mm by the end of the second year when the gonad has become an ovary and a large capsule gland has developed on what is now the oviduct. Although still appearing to be males because retaining the penis, they are now, at two years old, functional females fertilized by the one-year-old males. Then the bulk die with a few persisting to spawn again when three years old. The same succession of events occurs in related animals but this species appears to be unique in retaining the now functionless penis throughout the female phase.

In terms of habit it is an easy transference to species of the next family, the Calyptraeidae, all of them limpets but easy to distinguish from others owing to the presence of a characteristic shelf within the shell. There are two British species, the little Chinaman's hat, *Calyptraea chinensis* and the introduced but now all too abundant slipper limpet, *Crepidula fornicata*. Even externally the former is easily recognized, the shell a smooth circular cone up to 15 mm in diameter. It occurs on stones in shallow water off western shores but is seldom found between tide marks except in sheltered areas in the south-west.

The Chinaman's hat is a ciliary feeder and a protandrous hermaphrodite. Spawning is in the summer and year-old individuals are all males which move on to the shells of the larger and completely immobile females, all two years old or over. The egg capsules laid after fertilization are attached to the rock under the head region and so protected by the shell. Change to the female phase occurs, as in the hairy snail, during the second year but in this case involves complete absorption of the penis with loss of mobility. To a ciliary feeder such loss is of no consequence; *Trichotropis* appears to move only when this is necessary to regain height. The limpet form has the advantage for these animals of enlarging the mantle cavity so that the gill filaments become longer and the feeding current is increased.

The slipper limpet is an American species first introduced into this country around 1880 with blue point oysters which were then relaid for growth and

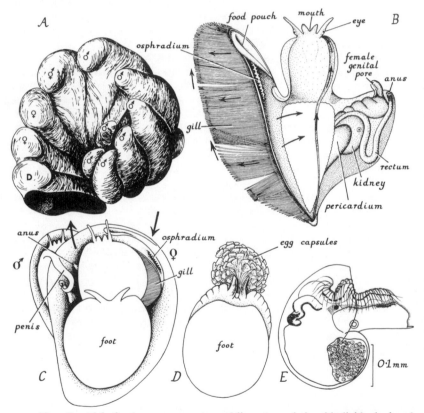

FIG. 32. *Crepidula fornicata*, mesogastropod limpet: A, chain of individuals, basal one (D) dead, above this females with males highest; B, mantle cavity opened to expose, on left, gill with elongated, food-collecting filaments, arrows showing route of food to mouth, on right visceral organs including female opening; C, under view of two members of chain showing penis of male entering genital pore of female; D, egg capsules retained *in situ*; E, newly hatched planktonic larva. (A, after Coe; B, after Werner & Grell; C, D, after Werner; E, after Thorson)

fattening on east coast beds. It has become a major pest on British beds not because it attacks, but because it competes with and, actually smothers, the oysters.

It is a fascinating animal (Fig. 32). Immobile at *all* stages of life, it grows in chains. Younger individuals attach to the shells of older ones to form curved masses consisting of up to a dozen individuals, although side chains may also develop when numbers rise to over thirty; the whole forming more than fist-sized masses. The animals are well named, the large internal shelf giving the empty shell just the appearance of a slipper some 40 mm long and 28 mm broad with a low posterior coiling.

Internal fertilization would seem to demand movement at least in the male but not in *Crepidula*. Emerging from the egg capsules the young have a brief planktonic life before settling permanently, with some initial mobility, on any clean surface. This includes the shells of other slipper limpets to which they are chemically attracted. Those young individuals which settle on shells develop into males with a long tapering penis with which they fertilize females lower in the chain. In those which settle elsewhere, however, the male phase – useless under these circumstances – tends to be aborted and the animal passes quickly into the female phase. Another animal now settling upon this one *will* become a male and when ripe proceed to fertilize the animal beneath it. In due course this second one, with another on *its* shell, will change into a female as shown externally by gradual loss of the penis. Thus the chain (Fig. 32) finally consists of a number of basal females, above them animals in process of changing sex and then the apical animals which are functional males. So has internal fertilization been reconciled with immobility.

Up to seventy balloon-shaped egg capsules are laid and secured, by the aid of the foot, to the underlying surface, namely the stone to which the basal animal is attached or, more usually, to the shell of the animal lower in the chain. There they remain – incubated in a sense but the immobile parent can, of course, place them nowhere else – until hatching.

The gill filaments extend as a series of long parallel ciliated rods across the broad mantle cavity and create a powerful inflowing current, the accumulation of food particles aided by the production of great quantities of entangling mucus from a glandular strip that runs along the base of the enlarged gill (Fig. 32). The entire gut with a large rotating crystalline style in the stomach is that of a highly specialized filter feeder collecting microscopic plant plankton – just the kind of gut we shall find in most bivalves.

It is not surprising that the slipper limpet is so successful. A five-mile stretch of the River Crouch, once famous for its oysters, was estimated some years ago to have a population of around 165 million slipper limpets weighing in all some 129 tons, a far higher population than that of the oysters which seek to collect the same food. From the east coast of England the slipper limpet has spread along the south coast and was carried across the North Sea to Holland in 1942 where it achieved some value as food during the later months of the last war. It has also reached north to Germany and Denmark and south to Belgium. It is now very much a member of the European marine fauna.

In animals of the third family of these increasingly immobile snails, the

Capulidae, this tendency culminates in what, in the molluscs, is the unusual condition of parasitism. The sole British species, *Capulus ungaricus*, with backward curved apex like a cap of liberty, was very adequately illustrated by Borlase in 1758 (Fig. 3). The shell, some 12 mm long, is covered with thick periostracum as in the hairy snail but here consisting of a series of projecting ridges, the most recently formed fringing the shell opening. There is no internal ledge and the shell muscle is horse-shoe-shaped as in the common limpets. It is not an intertidal animal but common enough in shallow water dredgings, frequently attached to bivalve shells and especially on those of the large scallop, *Pecten maximus*. It has extended gill filaments but also a proboscis like the hairy snail. Although it must obviously move around during the young male phase when it has to fertilize the females, when it reaches that phase the animal becomes almost stationary attaching its eggs to the underlying surface like the Chinaman's hat shell. Unlike that animal, however, the young hatch out as freely swimming larvae. This is necessary because they would have obvious difficulty in crawling to another shell. Doubtless at the end of the swimming phase the larvae are chemically attracted to the females and will tend to settle on bivalve shells occupied by them. But little is known about this.

The mode of feeding is a particular interest because the activities of the gills are supplemented by inserting the long proboscis between the valves of the bivalve and there pulling in food strings from the collecting gills. While hardly parasitism this certainly amounts to taking food that another animal has collected. True parasitism is also found. The bright blue *Linckia* is among the commonest of Indo-Pacific starfish and occasionally a small, similarly, and very beautifully coloured, limpet will be found attached to the groove on the underside of the arms. This is a capulid named *Thyca*. It is firmly attached not by the reduced foot but by the proboscis which penetrates deeply into the tissues which are sucked up and digested. There is no radula. This is a fascinating instance of external parasitism without any serious drain on the host animal. An early free-living male phase has to be presumed.

The manner of life in this very interesting group varies from that of the freely moving hairy snails with coiled shell to that of the two families of limpets, each beginning life free-living but ending it immobile. They have

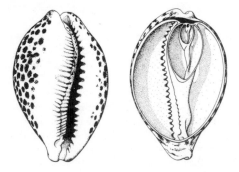

FIG. 33. Cowrie, *Cypraea tigris*: *left*, under view; *right*, interior of lower half of shell cut open horizontally and viewed from above, showing earlier whorls at hind end.

assumed a mode of feeding which draws food to them rendering movement unnecessary while they overcome problems of reproduction by dividing the life history into early male and later, invariably immobile, female phases. The final result, a consequence of settlement on the living surface, not just on the shell, of another animal, is the external parasitism found in *Thyca*.

Cowries are perhaps the best known of all shells (Fig. 33). The larger ones, mottled or spotted in all manner of colour patterns like the well-known tiger cowrie of the tropical Indo-Pacific, are amongst the most striking and most avidly collected of all shells. The golden cowrie, *Cypraea aurantium*, until recently worn as a symbol of royalty in Melanesian islands, can be claimed as the most beautiful of shells. The smaller yellow money cowrie was long used as currency in parts of Africa. The fancied resemblance of the opening to the female genital orifice was responsible for the association of this '*Concha Veneria*' with fertility and the worship of Venus.

The smooth rounded shell formed by the complete enclosure of early coiling within the final body whorl is unmistakable. This final enclosure involves the lengthways extension of the shell opening, the original left and right sides of which are now respectively in front and behind. In consequence water enters in front and is expelled behind. Thus the effects of torsion have been most neatly overcome with the advantage of a particularly massive shell and further protection from glands producing sulphuric acid within the exposed mantle tissues.

There is no operculum to close the narrow aperture out of which the mantle lobes extend. These envelop, one on the left the other on the right, the entire shell surface hence constantly resurfaced during life. At first sight a living cowrie may reveal no trace of shell. This is particularly striking in the large pure white *Ovula ovum*, the poached egg shell, which lives and feeds on the massive growths (like fleshy brown seaweeds) of soft Alcyonarian corals on Indo-Pacific reefs. The first impression is of a rounded black mass; touch it, however, and a line of white appears along the mid-line of the shell which quickly widens to reveal the pure white oval shell as the mantle lobes are progressively withdrawn.* Finally these disappear completely within the aperture, the head and elongate foot also withdrawn.

The true cowries (Cypraeidae), so abundant in tropical seas, are poorly represented in temperate waters: the very small *Simnia patula* is the sole British species. This can be dredged off south-western coasts to be invariably found on the surface of colonies of dead-man's fingers (the common soft coral, *Alcyonium digitatum*) on which it feeds and lays egg capsules. Other species, none more than about 10 mm long, are members of the closely related Eratoidae distinguished by various characters, notably the type of larva. The commonest, abundant about low water level and above or under stones, is *Trivia monacha*. The white shell with three purple-brown spots (not very obvious in Plate 5) is covered when expanded by the yellow mantle lobes. As shown in the Plate, this animal lives on compound ascidians (small sea squirts

---

* This and a variety of other expanded tropical cowries and other marine gastropods are to be seen in the magnificent colour photographs in *Australian Shells* by B. R. Wilson and K. Gillett.

which form brightly coloured encrusting growths). It probes into the colonies with a proboscis which carries mouth and radula at the tip, rasping out the tissues. At the same time a respiratory current is drawn in from a little distance above the bottom by way of an upward-pointing siphon which represents the extended left-hand wall of the mantle here situated in front. This is the first time we have encountered this structure, of so much importance to animals that live an infaunal life below the surface. These cowries lay vase-shaped egg capsules within cavities excavated in the ascidian colony. Essentially the same habit is possessed by *T. arctica*, a little smaller and without spots on the shell, and in the more harp-shaped *Erato voluta* (Fig. 34) both dredged offshore

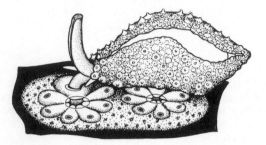

FIG. 34. British cypraeid, *Erato voluta*, feeding on the colonial sea squirt, *Botryllus schlosseri*; mantle covering most of shell, siphon pointing upward. (After Fretter)

although the former may occasionally be found on oarweeds at the lowest tidal levels.

Around Great Britain cowries are at about the limit of their northern range and seem to have shrunk to the minimal size! Even the Mediterranean possesses only four somewhat larger species, but farther south-east in the Indian Ocean species become larger and far more numerous. To the extent that we know about tropical species, all appear carnivorous each rigidly confined to a particular sedentary animal, a sea squirt or a soft coral on which it feeds and lays eggs. The elongate spindle cowries, species of *Volva*, live upon horny gorgonic corals which form much-branched, fan-like colonies. It could be the much greater abundance of suitable food organisms, especially on and around coral reefs, that accounts for the great tropical abundance of cowries.

FIG. 35. Bermudan vermetid, *Vermicularia spirata*, showing various shapes assumed by individuals cemented to corals of different growth forms. (After Gould)

Chapter 8

Mesogastropods – burrowers and drifters

*

WE have already, in *Hydrobia*, encountered a mesogastropod burrower which, alternating this habit with that of surface drifting, has attained success in both with surprisingly little structural modification. Next we come to three other British mesogastropods, all representative of world-wide populations, each of which in its own highly characteristic manner exploits the possibilities of life within soft bottom deposits. These are the screw-shell, *Turritella communis*, the pelican's foot shell, *Aporrhais pes-pelecani*, and species of moon or necklace-shells, *Natica*.

Only the third of these may be encountered living below exposed sandy beaches but the others may be so common offshore that their dead shells are often washed up. *Turritella* (Fig. 36) is the largest of British high-spired shells, about 5 cm long with up to twenty whorls; the Indo-Pacific *T. terebra* is twice that length while *T. duplicata* from India may be 18 cm long. All have the same habits, burrowing into muddy gravel bottoms at moderate depths.

When placed on its natural substrate, *T. communis* protrudes the small foot and then by a series of laborious jerks, in the course of which it turns from side to side, it works its way into the mud at an angle of around 10°. Finally it disappears from sight and burrowing movements cease. The foot then pushes forward to create a depression in the mud surface on the left side, consolidating the piled up mud in front with mucus from the pedal glands to prevent it falling in. Water can now enter the mantle cavity to emerge on the right. This it does by way of a tubular extension of the mantle margins which (in contrast to what we have just described in the cowries) forms an *exhalant* siphon which directs the outflowing current clear of the mud surface leaving this undisturbed. And there the animal remains passively for indefinite periods. It is feeding on suspended matter because a ciliary feeder although unrelated to the hairy snails and the mesogastropod limpets. They all live on hard surfaces and so in clear water but these screw-shells are exposed to the danger of drawing mud into the respiratory (and feeding) chamber, a danger guarded against by a screen of branched tentacles which fringe the entrance (Fig. 36).

Reproductive habits are also very different. *Turritella* does not change sex nor do the males have to attempt crawling through mud to reach and fertilize females; instead sperm are liberated into the water to reach the females in their inhalant currents. Populations are sufficiently numerous to ensure high local concentration of sperm, one spawning male doubtless setting off many others. The fertilized, developing eggs are deposited within balloon-shaped capsules attached by strings to the mud surface.

This is a very different mode of life from that of a winkle but certainly no

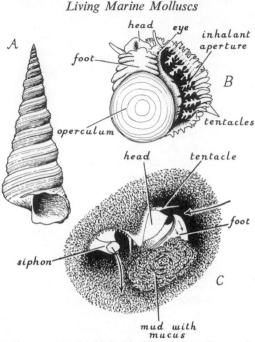

FIG. 36. *Turritella communis*: A, high-spired (empty) shell; B, animal viewed from in front showing branched tentacles screening entrance into the mantle cavity; C, animal *in situ* in muddy gravel, water expelled through siphon on left. (After Graham, and after Yonge)

less successful. The high-spired shell screws itself into the protection of the mud and then proceeds to avail itself of a constantly renewed source of microscopic plant food in the water above. There is no reason why it should ever move even for reproduction. Throughout the world, wherever coasts are bounded by a shallow shelf with areas of muddy gravel on the bottom, species of *Turritella* are conspicuous members of the infauna. Wherever they are dredged their presence is a sure indication of the nature of the bottom.

Aporrhais pes-pelecani, one of the most suitably named of shells, is unmistakable owing to the wide extension of the outer lip of the shell opening which is drawn out into a series of finger-like processes or 'digitations' very obviously resembling the webbed foot of a pelican. It lives in very much the same type of gravelly mud bottom as do the screw-shells and often in almost equal abundance. But *Aporrhais* is a north Atlantic genus extending into the Mediterranean and no further. The shells may be dredged in great numbers over suitable areas and may also be cast up empty on the shore where they were widely collected in Victorian days for gluing, overlapping each other, around framed pictures of marine scenes. These animals are much more obviously adapted for life in muddy gravel than are the screw-shells. They feed in a totally different way on a completely different type of food, so that

88

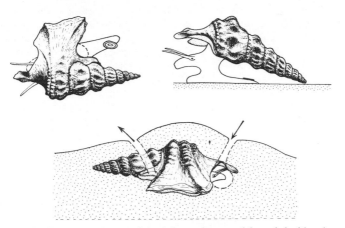

FIG. 37. *Aporrhais pes-pelecani*, viewed from above and from left side when reared up during movement on surface; also animal *in situ* in substrate showing direction of the respiratory currents; animal feeding with proboscis.

although the two often live in great numbers together they do not compete.

The pelican's foot shell (Fig. 37) is also the sole north Atlantic representative of an extremely interesting group, the Strombacea. These are largely tropical snails with many impressively large species including the queen conch, *Strombus gigas*, extensively eaten and collected for decoration in the Caribbean. Very many other species occur in the Indo-Pacific with the even more impressive spider shells, species of *Pterocera* (*Lambis*) (Fig. 5), the largest of which is over 35 cm (exceeding one foot) in length, the extended lip of the shell fringed with 'spider-like' processes covering a wide area.

All these animals are slow-moving, relying for protection on the particularly massive shell and, despite contrary statements, all herbivores, the great tropical species feeding delicately on the very fragile red weeds that grow as epiphytic tufts on the fronds of the larger brown weeds. All have a characteristic mode of progression, by a series of lurches. In a characteristic prosobranch, movement is by way of waves of muscular contraction passing along the under surface of the foot, in some cases affecting the whole surface, in others by alternate contraction – a kind of shuffling bipedal movement – on the two sides. In some the waves of contraction pass forwards, in others back, but both result in a gliding forward movement. This is not so in the Strombidae. Conditions are simplest in *Aporrhais* where the foot initially moves forward *without* affecting the shell. Having reached as far forward as possible the animal rears up, and the cumbersome shell (Fig. 37) is heaved forward in a single convulsive contraction of the columellar muscle.

However, surface progression is probably exceptional in these normally buried animals but the tropical strombids and spider shells always live on the surface of sand and progress with the aid of the long, spur-like operculum which on withdrawal closes the slit-like aperture (Fig. 43). This digs into the sand at the end of each forward movement so providing purchase for the powerful muscular contraction that heaves forward the often extremely massive shell. If turned over – when they might appear to be permanently immobilized like an overturned turtle – the extended foot is curled around the shell and the operculum jabbed into the sand below. A sudden contraction of the columellar muscle and the heavy flattened shell is righted. The same result is achieved by the pelican's foot shell, by twisting head and foot under the blade-like terminal projection followed by a similar muscular contraction.

When burrowing begins this terminal blade or 'digitation' is pushed at first obliquely down and then horizontally just below the surface, movement proceeding by a series of jerks at each one of which surface movements of the mud reveal that the shell is raised just as it is when moving on the surface. So far the only opening to the surface is one behind the expanded lip of the shell formed by ejection of water at each movement but as soon as the animal settles down the highly mobile proboscis pushes up to create a new one in front of this lip and to the right of the terminal blade. The proboscis twists and turns to excavate a rounded opening some 2 mm across. The sides of this tubular opening are consolidated with mucus. The proboscis then turns back to excavate and consolidate a similar opening above the hind margin of the lip. So the animal may remain, motionless, for days on end while the proboscis forages at will in the surrounding area collecting organic debris by means of the protruded radula. A continuous stream of water created by the gills enters by the anterior, inhalant, opening and leaves by the posterior, exhalant opening (see arrows in Fig. 37). When after a few days food is exhausted, the animal moves a short distance and re-establishes itself. *Aporrhais* possesses the usual secondary sexual characters so that, unlike the screwshell, internal fertilization occurs involving deliberate movement of males to females before spawning. Eggs, each surrounded by a thick yellowish membrane, are laid singly or a few together on the mud surface, hatching as early veligers.

This is a very different mode of life from that of *Turritella*, the animal feeding on what is *in* the substrate instead of what is carried in suspension in the water above. It was surprising to discover (in the Bergen Fjord in 1936) that *Aporrhais* is not a ciliary feeder. Later, in New Zealand, John Morton found that the related *Struthiolaria* which has similar burrowing habits has taken matters a stage further and uses the gills for feeding. There, also, numbers of eggs are contained in one capsule to hatch at a late larval stage, while in the still more advanced genus of those regions, *Pelicaria*, there is no free larva, the young already crawling when liberated.

A. pes-pelecani with its blade-like anterior digitation is confined to a medium of muddy gravel; it flounders in soft mud, the respiratory cavity quickly fouled. The allied, also British, *A. serresiana* has a more delicate shell with a more extensive outer lip and a finely-pointed anterior finger (Fig. 38). It lives only in softer mud; it cannot force its way through denser media. Species, as well as genera, have their distinctive needs for food or grade of substrate.

To this general group belong the carrier shells (Xenophoridae) among the

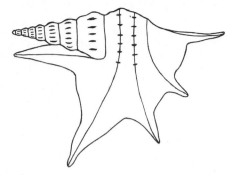

FIG. 38.   *Aporrhais serresiana.*

most remarkable of all gastropods because able 'deliberately' (as it would appear to the observer) to camouflage themselves. The shell resembles that of a flattened, very broad-based top shell to the growing margins of which the mantle attaches initially fine fragments or shells and then larger ones to the extending whorls. Every species of carrier shell acquires a characteristic covering (Plate 4) – some with closely arranged, slightly overlapping shells of bivalves, all with the inner surface uppermost, in others with the margins extended by stilt-like additions of high-spired gastropod shells up to 3 cm long so that a basal diameter of perhaps 6 cm is increased to one of 10 cm. In other cases, the attached objects are small coral skeletons, others again are always pebbles or rubble particles. Carrier shells that collect other shells have become known as 'conchologists' in contrast to the 'geologists' which collect pebbles.*

These animals are usually inhabitants of moderate to considerable depths, down to three or four hundred metres (which explains why some of them pick up the skeletons of small, deep-water species of corals) only to be obtained in the occasional tropical dredge haul. Fortunately one species, *Xenophora conchyliophora* lives in shallow water off Florida and has been maintained and observed in aquaria. Feeding appears to be very similar to what we have just described for *Aporrhais*. The animal lives a very sedentary life under the shelter of the extended, tent-like shell, the proboscis exploring the substrate in search of largely microscopic plant food (in the deep-water species this is more likely to be organic debris). It appears to have the unusual habit of burying the faeces, the foot making the hole and the proboscis later covering it over. It has been suggested that this is a device to prevent the animal being detected by smell; it could equally, in this writer's opinion, be a means of keeping the area clean during the apparently long periods that these animals remain stationary. From time to time they do move, by the same sudden convulsive process that occurs in *Aporrhais* and in the strombids generally. Despite the appreciable weight of all the added material, the shell is lifted clear of the bottom by the action of the powerful, pillar-like foot. Of how far

*There are four very beautiful colour plates in *The Shell* of carrier shells, one covered with coral skeletons and gastropod shells, another with little else but the latter, another with bivalve shells and, apically, some barnacles, the fourth just carrying rubble.

it may then move, in a series of lurches, to a new feeding area we have no knowledge.

In this Florida carrier shell, the process of attaching foreign objects to the shell involves their manipulation by both the head and the foot. Continuing in the words of the observer, Paul Shank, 'After rubble is finally jockeyed into a suitable position the job is still not finished. The *Xenophora* then carefully cleans all the area coming in contact with the mantle to insure a tight joint during the process of cementing it fast. Gaps are checked between the mantle and rubble and filled in by sticking pieces of sand and tiny pieces of debris to the mantle edge by cleaning them and placing them there with the proboscis, one piece at a time. Occasionally, it sticks its head and proboscis under rubble for support and very gently rocks the shell to and fro, evidently checking rubble for security of attachment. With the larger pieces of rubble the mollusc remains stationary for over ten hours to assure a tight bond before resuming its food hunting.'

The mode of attachment appears to be different in the deeper water New Zealand species, *Xenophora neozelanica*. There the head and foot turn upside down beneath the tent-like shell, the foot searching as widely as possible outside this for objects of suitable size and nature for attachment, a process performed in complete privacy. It must, however, involve (as in the other species) the firm pressing of the object against the margin of the mantle while this is the process – discontinuous as we have already seen – of producing an initially semi-fluid addition to the shell aperture.

There seems no reason to doubt that these gastropods do disguise themselves by the addition of spirally arranged objects. Certainly it must be excessively difficult for any predator depending on sight to distinguish these carrier shells from a surrounding area similarly covered with dead shells, coral skeletons, pebbles and rubble of all kinds. The long periods that are apparently spent in quiescent feeding while not, as in *Aporrhais*, actually buried below the surface, probably demand some such effective method of camouflage. What is remarkable is that this is produced by the *behaviour* of the animal.

Species of the family Naticidae, the moon or necklace shells, are no less infaunal in habit but in a very different way. There are three British species, *Natica montagui*, *N. catena* (Fig. 39) and *N. alderi* and, like their relatives the world over, they inhabit relatively clean sand. The two first may be dug in sandy bays at low tidal levels but all are commonest in shallow water offshore. The globular polished shell with a large umbilicus and an ear-shaped operculum is unmistakable. The largest species, *N. catena*, is some 3 cm in diameter but the giants of this family are species of *Polinices* which occur off both coasts of North America and include *P. lewisi*, with a diameter of up to 12 cm which is common on muddy sand flats from Alaska to Mexico. These animals are concerned neither with suspended plankton nor with organic detritus but are carnivores feeding on other infaunal animals, chiefly bivalves. To this end they must be able to move actively under the surface to secure their prey, penetrate the shell and consume the contents.

A globular shell appears particularly unsuitable for effective passage through

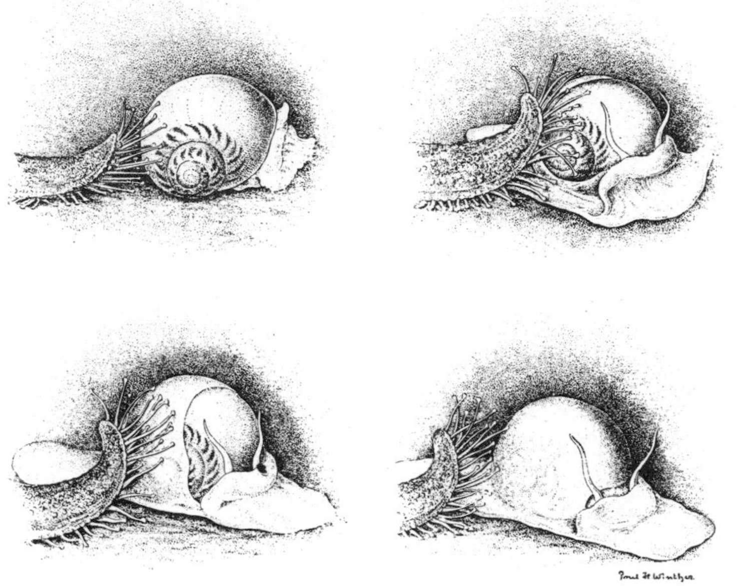

FIG. 39.   Moon snail, *Natica catena*: behaviour wnen approached by a starfish (see text). (By permission of Mrs Ellen Thorson)

sand but form is completely changed when the animal is fully expanded. What then emerges is literally much larger than the capacity of the shell. Alone among molluscs, the foot in these animals is inflated not only by internal blood pressure but by intake of water into a series of 'aquiferous' canals. Originally discovered almost a century ago, their existence was then denied until recent work on the American *Polinices dupliatus* revealed that a fully expanded animal weighs three times what it does when fully withdrawn. The difference is due to passage of water into these canals. This takes time so that full expansion takes from 3–8 minutes whereas retraction – the result of con-traction of the columellar muscle – takes only a few seconds. But the animals remain expanded for days on end, indeed they cannot survive prolonged retraction.

With the foot fully extended the animal becomes wedge-shaped and obviously fitted for penetration through sand (Fig. 40). The large frontal region of the foot, or propodium, is shaped like a ploughshare, its hind portion raised above the shell so covering the entrance into the mantle cavity. Behind this is the mesopodium which forms the greater part of the sole and at the rear end is the metapodium carrying the operculum and covering the hind end of the shell. Although the foot is distended by sea water, its move-ments are controlled by blood pressure governed by appropriate muscular contraction. Whereas burrowing in *Turritella* and in *Aporrhais* probably represents no more than the continuance of surface movements, aimed at

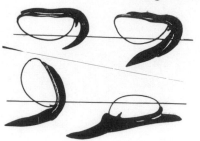

FIG. 40. Burrowing action of the foot in *Natica*. (From Morton & Yonge)

bringing the animal to rest under the substrate, in the moon shells it is a continuous process only interrupted while the animal is feeding. Burrowing movements consist of a series of digging cycles each consisting of an initial extension and then dilatation of the propodium which anchors the animal, the shell being pulled forward by contraction of the columellar muscle. Blood then dilates the mesopodium which in turn acts as an anchor while the propodium probes its way forward in a series of locomotory waves again to form an anchor when blood is transferred into it from the mesopodium. A number of shelled opisthobranchs, such as *Bulla*, *Philine* and *Scaphander* (Chapter 10), all burrow in the same manner. The bivalves possess an even greater burrowing efficiency.

The foot also serves to envelop and immobilize the prey. As in *Aporrhais* there is a protrusible proboscis bearing a radula with the sharply-pointed teeth of a carnivore (Fig. 41). If flesh is exposed this comes immediately into

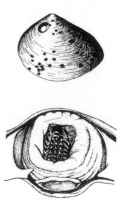

FIG. 41. *Natica millepunctata*, mouth with exposed radular teeth: the accessory (chemical) boring organ beneath; *above*, shell of bivalve, *Macoma balthica*, bored by *Natica catena*. (After Ankel)

play but usually the bivalve shell has first to be penetrated and this involves initial softening by means of an accessory boring organ in the form of a pad-shaped gland on the underside of the proboscis. Boring – at any rate of the bivalve *Venus striatula* by *Natica alderi* – is around the lower margins of the shell and young bivalves are most frequently attacked. First the area is cleared of encrustations and of horny periostracum by the radula, then the pad is applied, from time to time replaced by the radula which scrapes out the softened layer of shell, these alternating processes continuing until the shell is penetrated and the radula able to rasp out the contained flesh. These naticid borings can be distinguished because always bevelled on the outer side (Fig. 41).

Natica may itself be prey as well as predator. In his comments on the drawings reproduced in Fig. 39, Professor Gunnar Thorson wrote of how *N. catena* makes immediate response to 'a touch of the starfish *Asterias rubens*, even when withdrawn in its shell.' The tissues start to expand, the foot taking in water and swelling up with a transverse fold of skin appearing at the hind end of the shell. This proceeds to spread upward and forward forming a hood which finally covers 'the shell like a closed helmet'. Within one minute the process is complete, the shell covered with a protective mucous skin which provides no hold for the extended, groping tube feet of the starfish. The moon snail crawls away undamaged.

The collar-shaped egg capsules of these animals (Fig. 52), deposited unattached on sandy beaches the world over always arouse curiosity. Those of the large Pacific species have been described as looking 'like nothing so much as discarded rubber plungers of the type plumbers use to open clogged drains.' Their formation, seldom observed, is an elaborate process during which clusters of fertilized eggs are embedded in a jelly-like matrix full of sand grains. The mass is finally shaped and the surface smoothed by the foot, the animal moving around it as it does so. In the course of development of the enclosed embryos the matrix breaks down usually releasing veliger larvae. However, in some of the more northern moon shells, development proceeds farther, a minority of the embryos feeding on the others to complete development within the matrix and finally emerge as crawling individuals.

From burrowers we now pass briefly to consider mesogastropods that live pelagically, near to the surface of the sea and often at a considerable distance from land. Although rarely seen, the British fauna does include one of the transparent carnivorous heteropods, *Carinaria mediterranea* (Fig. 42) which,

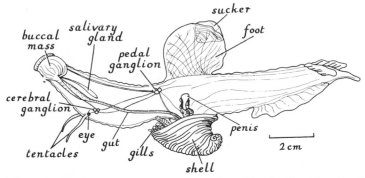

FIG. 42. Heteropod, *Carinaria mediterranea*: disposition in life with reduced shell below and longitudinally flattened foot forming a fin on the upper surface. A predaceous carnivore with a massive buccal mass. (From Fretter & Graham)

mingled with trailing siphonophores and salps, sea butterflies (pteropods) and ctenophores, such as the ribbon-like venus girdle, are the glories of the Mediterranean planktonic fauna in the spring. In the heteropods the foot is converted into a laterally compressed fin, the shell becoming first transparent, then reduced (as in *Carinaria*) and finally lost, an unnecessary encumbrance when life is spent in the active pursuit of living prey. These animals swim upside down, have enlarged eyes for detecting their prey and a massive proboscis for seizing it.

A very different kind of pelagic mesogastropod, the violet snail, *Ianthina janthina* (Plate 5) may be cast up along south-western shores after continued south-westerly winds. These surface-dwelling oceanic animals have a large float consisting of mucus-coated bubbles of air formed by the propodium which is raised, spoon-shaped, above the water surface to entrap an air bubble which, enclosed in mucus, is added to the base of the float below. The process takes under a minute and is repeated some ten times before a rest is taken. The compacted float is described as 'springy and dry'. The globular, rather flattened shell is very delicate and seldom found intact but is always to be recognized by the vivid blue colour.

Although at the mercy of water movements and devoid of eyes, *Ianthina* is carnivorous like the actively ranging heteropods. It has a short proboscis with a unique type of radula possessing incurved teeth while the prey may be anaesthetized by a purple secretion. This prey consists largely of the similarly drifting *Velella* or 'By-the-wind-sailor' frequently cast up with it. This is a colonial raft-like jellyfish with triangular blue sail above and a central mouth below surrounded by stinging tentacles and reproductive individuals. This in turn devours larval fish or small crustaceans which in turn feed largely on plant plankton. So *Ianthina*, although encountering its prey by chance contact, is high in the food chain. It is doubtless itself devoured by certain fishes. Like *Turritella* in this respect, the male has no penis. Sperm are discharged in packets in sufficient numbers to ensure fertilization. *Ianthina janthina* is viviparous in the sense that active veliger larvae are liberated from the oviduct but in two other species, *I. exigua* and *I. pallida*, which also occasionally reach British coasts, egg capsules are laid and attached to the underside of the float.

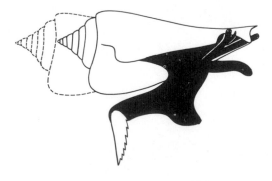

FIG. 43. Conch, *Strombus gibberalus*, showing movement achieved in a single 'leap', the foot with the elongate, spur-like operculum moving forward preliminary to next movement. (From Morton & Yonge)

PLATE 5. *Above*, British cowrie, *Trivia monacha;* mantle partly extended, orange-coloured siphon and tentacles at head end. *Below*, violet snail, *Ianthina janthina*, showing float and extended head.

PLATE 6. *Above*, dog whelk, *Nassarius incrassatus*, crawling over sea mat with siphon fully extended. *Below*, veliger larva of *N. incrassatus*, with four-lobed ciliated velum fully expanded.

Chapter 9

Neogastropods – scavengers and predators

*

EVOLUTION within the gastropods culminates in three uneven peaks of achievement, outside the prosobranchs by the terrestrial pulmonates which are not our concern and by the largely shell-less opisthobranchs and sea-slugs with powers of adaptive radiation as impressive as those of the mesogastropods and which are described in the two following chapters. Then within the prosobranchs, although coming not from the mesogastropods but from uncertain archaeogastropod ancestry, are the neogastropods or – taking the name from the radula of never more than three teeth to the row – the stenoglossids. These teeth (Plate 3) are large and curved, for seizing instead of scraping and with no accompanying jaws. Here evolution has proceeded in a restricted although highly successful path. The possibilities of a carnivorous habit are exploited, at their simplest involving feeding on dead or moribund prey but culminating in dramatic powers of sudden seizure and poisoning of active prey as large as, or even larger than, the predator.

These capabilities have been developed without significant change in the foot which remains an organ of deliberately slow propulsion. The ability to pounce and seize comes instead from frontal regions of the gut. These telescope when quiescent to be suddenly shot out well in advance of the head (Fig. 54). In all neogastropods the mouth and radula are situated at the summit of a flexible extensile proboscis able to probe deeply into cavities, in the case of the borers or 'drills', previously excavated by the animal. The simple snout of less complex prosobranchs has been modified to a greater degree than in the mesogastropod cowries and moon shells. As with the foot, the proboscis is extruded by blood pressure and withdrawn by muscular contraction, to such an extent that the mouth with the radular apparatus is finally pulled back completely within the head. What then appears to be the mouth is actually a 'false mouth' giving entrance to the cavity into which the proboscis has been withdrawn (Fig. 44).

In certain mesogastropods including the moon snails the retractor muscles are attached to the tip of the proboscis so that withdrawal has aptly been compared to 'turning a stocking outside in by putting one's hand in and pulling the toe towards the top.' But in all neogastropods, as indicated in Fig. 44, these muscles are attached farther back so that mouth and radular mass remain facing forward when retracted. Within this extensile proboscis lies the rachiglossan radula (Plate 3) with recurved teeth ready for seizing and tearing flesh. In these animals the salivary secretion is concerned with the first stages in the digestion of flesh as well as with the primitive task of lubrication.

Their food consists usually of isolated objects of prey each of which has to

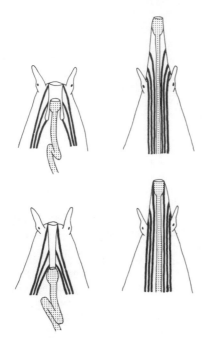

FIG. 44. Neogastropods: two types of proboscis, *left*, withdrawn by muscular contraction; *right*, extended by blood pressure. *Above*, 'pleurembolic' type where the retractor muscles are inserted near the base of the proboscis, true mouth (and radula) not withdrawn far within 'false' mouth; *below*, 'acrembolic' type where retractors attached nearer tip and true mouth correspondingly further withdrawn. Gut stippled. (Modified after Fretter & Graham)

be sought. This is done by way of the mobile siphon which is pointed first in one direction then in another. The water drawn in containing the 'scent' of possible prey is carried over the extensive surface of the elaborate sensory osphradium which here resembles a small gill with rows of filaments on either side of a flattened axis. There is no doubt whatever that in the neogastropods the osphradium is a 'chemoreceptor' able to detect the presence of extremely minute quantities of chemical substances in solution. If emanating from a prey animal, the whelk or other neogastropod moves immediately in the direction from which the 'scent' comes. The siphon is just as important as the

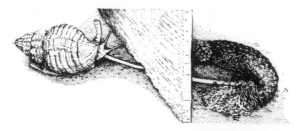

FIG. 45. Common whelk, *Buccinum undatum*, extending proboscis through a wooden partition so as to feed on moribund holothurian (sea cucumber). (By permission of Dr V. Fretter & Professor A. Graham)

proboscis to these animals; its invariable presence is indicated by that of a siphonal canal on the left (inhalant) side of the aperture in all neogastropod shells – on the right, of course, in a sinistral shell as shown in the figure (46) of *Busycon*.

Two relatively large neogastropods occur in British and north Atlantic waters generally. The common whelk or buckie, *Buccinum undatum* (Fig. 45), up to about 8 cm in height, has a greyish-white shell with undulating ivory ribs crossed with spiral ridges. It is everywhere common and conspicuous. The more northern *Neptunea antiqua*, the spindle shell, is somewhat larger with a completely smooth shell. The shells of both are symmetrically tapered with large apertures and conspicuously extending siphonal channels. These are the familiar shells of the shore that children hold to their ears to hear the sound of the sea within them and which were so frequently copied, arranged horizontally or vertically, in Victorian china ornaments. Shells picked up on the shore will usually be empty although living ones, especially of the common whelk, are common enough in low shore pools, in the laminarian zone and farther offshore. The animals wander freely over rocky and mixed sand and rocky shores, highly successful because nothing of animal origin, moribund or dead, comes amiss. These whelks were, and in some localities still are, a notable source of food and of bait.

Like a number of other northern European gastropods including the common periwinkle, *Buccinum* also occurs on the American side of the Atlantic where its inability to survive more than brief intertidal exposure has been dramatically revealed in the Bay of Fundy. Left stranded for long periods during full retreat of those impressive tides, the whelks fail to take the 'obvious' precaution either of withdrawing and then closing the aperture

FIG. 46. Northern whelk, *Neptunea despecta*: animal with egg capsules attached to back of shell; others, with emerging young, attached to rock (By permission of Mrs Ellen Thorson)

with the horny operculum or, by some suitable pattern of behaviour, moving into shelter. Instead they continue to move about, only by chance re-entering the sea but usually dying of desiccation during the long period of tidal exposure, a loss of no biological significance to a species the bulk of whose members live below tide level.

These scavenging whelks also include the obviously related but smaller *Chauvetia brunnea*, *Colus gracilis* and *C. jeffreysianus*, the first and last being southern and the other a northern species. But a global presence of some 2000 species of such animals, more of them in temperate and colder than in warmer seas, reveals the success of this mode of life, dead or moribund prey being sought with the aid of the mobile siphon and the flesh sought and torn out by the stenoglossid radula at the summit of a distended proboscis. They are unable either to penetrate the protected bodies of immobile animals or to seize active animals. Whelks are easily caught in wicker or wire 'pots' baited with offal. The great numbers of individual whelks and of different species indicate the abundance of the food they seek. Like scavengers the world over, in the sea particularly the hermit crabs, they play an essential role in the economy of life.

These animals are of separate sexes, the male carrying an impressively large penis. Horny egg capsules, each in the common whelk about 5 mm across but united into irregular clusters resembling sponges known in places as 'sea-wash balls', are frequently encountered among the flotsam on the strand line. Each female lays up to 2000 capsules over a period of some days and on occasion several individuals may form a common cluster containing up to 15,000 capsules. In the arctic species, *Neptunea despecta* (Fig. 46) the capsules may be carried on the shell. In the common British whelk each capsule contains about 1000 eggs of which only some 30 develop; the remainder form food for these few which, however, later turn on one another so that about ten win through to emerge as young individuals. At this stage the shell, of about $2\frac{1}{2}$ whorls, is 1 mm high and so these animals are well fitted for immediate entry into a competitive world – for life in which they have already displayed greater aptitude than their siblings.

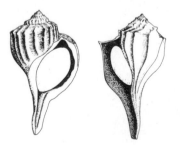

FIG. 47. American Atlantic coast whelks: dextral *Busycon carica* on *left* and sinistral *B. contrarium* on *right*; apertures closed by opercula. (After photographs in Magalhaes)

Other whelks are more frankly predatory including those of the genus *Busycon*, with shorter spire and elongated siphonal canal, which are common along the Atlantic coast of North America and include one species, well named *contrarium*, which is sinistral (Fig. 47). These animals feed largely on bivalves, where necessary first inserting the outer lip of the shell between the valves to force these apart, or where this proves impossible, making entry by chipping their edges.

The less considered trifles passed over by the larger whelks are quickly perceived and eaten by the smaller 'dog whelks' of the ubiquitous family Nassidae. Both the netted and the thick-lipped species, *Nassarius reticulatus* (Fig. 48)

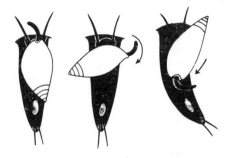

FIG. 48. *Nassarius reticulatus*: stages in shock reaction to the approach of starfish, shell and body swinging through 180° on the foot (shown black). (From Morton & Yonge)

and *N. incrassatus* (Plate 6), like miniatures of the larger whelks but respectively about 2½ and 1 cm long, are extremely common low down on rocky beaches especially in silty sand. These are certainly the most active movers of all crawling neogastropods. Often a little distance below the surface, the highly mobile siphon projects above this, continually testing the incoming water for evidence of carrion. Once detected the animal moves immediately in that direction. In the laboratory which he founded at Elsinore in Denmark, the late Dr Gunnar Thorson used to organize races between these animals.

Quick reaction and speed are no less important in avoiding enemies notably starfish which, with insidious approach, will wrap round them with tube feet, the stomach then everted to digest the prey no matter how far withdrawn into the shell. Unlike the moon shells (p. 92), the immediate reaction here is one of speed. Appropriate contraction of the columellar muscle swings the shell with contained mantle cavity and projecting siphon through 180° temporarily back to the pre-torsional position (Fig. 48). More slowly the head and foot turn to follow the lead of the siphon and away from danger.

Not all such animals are scavengers. Some congregate for feeding around immobile living prey such as the egg masses of polychaete worms which they consume by a process of suction. The common American mud snail, *Nassarius obsoletus*, which abounds on intertidal sandy mud flats, has the very different habit of feeding on the rich deposits of microscopic plant life, largely consisting of diatoms. (But it has also been observed to consume animal matter.) It has a shorter, less mobile, siphon than *N. reticulatus* while the gut contains the rotating gelatinous style already noted as characteristic of many herbivorous gastropods.

There is a notable family of whelks, the Muricidae, which comprises spectacular species with extremely long siphonal canals, the shell covered with row upon row of long finely-pointed spines. In others the canal is shorter and the spines replaced by undulating foliacious extensions. Both these and the spines are formed, as discussed earlier, by outward extensions of the mantle bordering the outer lip of the shell during periodic stoppage of extended growth. All muricids are active carnivores usually perforating the shell of the prey and frequently also having a poisonous secretion named purpurin. This was the origin of imperial or Tyrian purple for the preparation of which vast numbers of *Murex brandaris* and *Thais haemastoma* were once collected in the eastern Mediterranean.

While the spectacular species are largely tropical, there are no commoner intertidal gastropods on mid levels of rocky shores than the common dog whelk, *Nucella* (formerly *Purpura*, often *Thais*) *lapillus*. About the size of the largest winkle, it is easily distinguished by the characteristic siphonal canal and the higher spired and thicker shell capable of being rolled about with impunity by stormy seas. This is important because it lives on exposed shores with its prey of barnacles, mussels and to a lesser extent limpets.

This is an impressively efficient animal tending to feed on whichever of its prey is the more numerous and then switch over to another when supplies of the first are exhausted. Although it can force its way between the valves of young mussels it usually bores and by a similar combination of mechanical radula and accessory boring organ that we saw in the unrelated moon snails. The borings can be distinguished by their smaller degree of bevelling. It takes a dog whelk about two days to penetrate the shell of a mussel or a limpet after which the proboscis eats out the contained flesh. But their commonest food is acorn barnacles which are the commonest of all shore animals, reaching estimated populations of a thousand million along one kilometre of exposed rocky shore. The procedure there is different. The closely fitting opercular plates of the retracted barnacles are forced open, possibly with the aid of extruded purpurin which may kill the barnacle before the proboscis enters.

Nucella lapillus occurs in a wide range of colours not too easy to relate to habit or environment although yellow ones are commonest on more exposed shores while bands of brown pigment are associated with a diet of mussels; after change to another diet new shell growth is white. The closely related *Thais lamellosa* of north Pacific American shores displays an altogether bewildering diversity in both shell colour and sculpture with no apparent relation to conditions of life.

Breeding in these dense populations, closely congregated around their food, begins by pairing in crevices followed by the laying of straw-coloured capsules (Fig. 49) each resembling a grain of corn, which are attached in numbers together usually in crevices or under boulders. The process lasts about an hour and two or three hundred capsules may be produced. The majority of the several hundred eggs in each are not fertilized, serving only as food to the ten or twelve that eventually emerge as fully shelled crawling individuals after about four months of slow development (Fig. 49). These immediately swell the local population which can only be dispersed by crawling or by transport on floating timber or the like. Nevertheless *Nucella* extends not only along the coasts of Europe but, apparently by way of Iceland

102

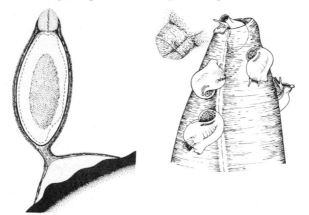

FIG. 49. Dog whelk, *Nucella lapillus*: *left*, intact egg capsule; *right*, young emerging after forcing off cap at apex. (After Ankel)

and Labrador, has made its way across the Atlantic where it reaches as far south as New York.

Allied animals are the drills of which we have two species, the native rough tingle, *Ocenebra (Murex) erinacea*, and the American oyster drill, *Urosalpinx cinerea*. These live lower down and feed exclusively by boring through the shells of bivalves (Fig. 50), particularly when available those of young oysters.

FIG. 50. Oyster drills, A, *Urosalpinx cinerea*; B, *Ocenebra erinacea*.

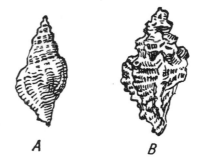

A   **B**

The former is slightly the larger, about 4 cm high with a more pointed shell of 8–10 whorls compared with the 6 or 7 of the rougher-shelled American drill. This, like the slipper limpet, came into Great Britain with imported American oysters probably much sooner than when it was first noticed in 1920. The native oyster drill was largely wiped out on the east coast during the very cold winters of 1939/40 and 1946/7 since when *Urosalpinx* has become the major oyster pest in England as it has long been in the United States. Whereas the slipper limpet smothers and competes for food with oysters, this animal drills through the shell and destroys a high proportion of young 'spat, oysters. An impressive volume of research has been conducted on these drills especially on the method of penetrating the shell, by a combination of chemical and mechanical action (Fig. 51), and also on methods of control.

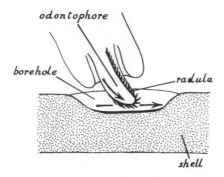

FIG. 51. *Urosalpinx*: mode of action of the radula during boring. (After Carriker & Van Zandt)

Both species come inshore to spawn during spring and early summer. The egg capsules of *Urosalpinx* are flask-shaped although triangular in section, those of the British species more flattened with an apical point. Like those of the dog whelk (Fig. 49) they are deposited separately on hard surfaces. *Urosalpinx* in particular deposits its capsules on the highest available site and these can be collected in quantity from the tops of short stakes purposely driven into oyster beds. In both species the young hatch out in the crawling stage which accounts for the more gradual dispersal of this drill after its introduction compared with that of the slipper limpet with its veliger larvae carried widely in the sea.

After emergence the immediate reaction of the young is to move upshore but with increasing exposure to light, behaviour changes leading them into shelter under the shade of stones or weed or under floating objects which may aid in their distribution. But, as in all neogastropods, the overwhelming urge is towards a source of animal food which can be detected from afar and to which they will return no matter how many times they are displaced. Growing animals can consume up to twenty spat oysters or other small bivalves a day. Such drills (often while still in egg capsules) have been carried all over the world with the animals they consume. *Urosalpinx* has been carried to the Pacific coast of North America as well as to Great Britain, the impressive Japanese drill, *Rapana thomasiana* with shell about 9 cm tall has been introduced with the Japanese oysters into the Black Sea. While this has had devastating effects on the populations of oysters and mussels, the free-swimming larvae of this drill provide food for shoals of sand eels that enter from the Mediterranean. Moreover the introduction of shells so much larger than those originally present enables the hermit crabs to attain a much greater size than formerly!

Limpets, this time carnivorous ones, reappear in the impressive form of the South American *Concholepas peruviana* (actually ranging along much of the extensive coast of Chile), the apex of the heavy shell inclined to the left over a greatly enlarged body whorl reaching 12 cm and more in diameter. The operculum, although present, is totally inadequate and the animal clings with the flattened foot to rocks in the surf zone. It has long been sought as food, the muscle first pounded like that of abalones; the shell is also used as a capacious drinking cup.

From the muricids one would pass, in any world survey, to the largely tropical Volutacea. Here come the appropriately termed olive shells (which do extend into temperate waters on American but not on European shores), of about the size of olives with polished shells like cowries and which hunt their prey within sand, the mitre shells of similar habit but without operculum and with a strikingly long proboscis that cannot be retracted, and the more spherical, extremely handsome harp shells, also usually under sand. The vase shells and the magnificent volutes, every one a carnivore, also inhabit sand, very often of coral origin, from low tide levels to some depth offshore. The largest of all are the melon shells or balers, species of *Melo*, up to 40 cm long, the final whorl forming a capacious bowl formerly used by Australian aboriginals for baling and many domestic purposes. The gelatinous egg cases

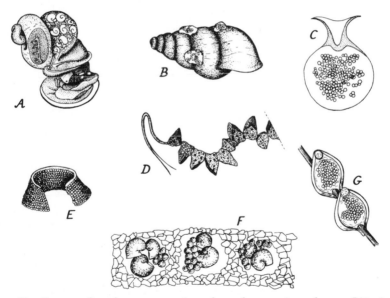

FIG. 52. Spawn of various mesogastropods and neogastropods: A, *Littorina saxatilis*, var. *tenebrosa*; animal removed from shell showing embryos in brood pouch; B, *Hydrobia ulvae*, female with three egg masses on shell; C, cowrie, *Trivia monacha*; egg capsule, laid within compound ascidians; D, wentletrap, *Scala turtonis*; part of egg mass, capsules attached to slimy strings; E, part of egg collar of *Natica* sp.; F, *Natica catena*, section through egg mass showing three egg spaces with large embryos and nurse eggs; G, *Nassarius reticulatus*; egg capsules attached to stalk of red alga. (A, B, D, F, G, after Thorson; C, after Lebour)

built up in spiral fashion to form a hollow translucent mass the size of a pineapple are the most striking productions of their kind.

Finally come the Toxoglossa where the radula is reduced to a series of separate darts which become charged with poison formed in a modified salivary gland. Temperate water representatives are few and only an occasional specimen of *Mangelia nebula* is ever likely to be collected at the lowest tidal levels around British shores. It is like a small whelk, a little over 1 cm tall, but distinguished, like all its relatives, by the absence of an operculum. Other species of this genus and of *Lora* and *Philbertia* can be obtained by dredging, for the first in muddy gravel for the other two in sand or sandy gravel. Information about their shells is available in any suitable conchological book, but beyond the fact that they are highly specialized carnivores we know singularly little about their mode of life. One point of great interest has, however, arisen in connection with *Philbertia leufroyi boothi* where almost identical shells are occupied some by animals with the typical poison equipment but others without this so that they must feed suctorially. There are also differences in the reproductive system. Two new species have been erected and although slight differences can be detected between the shells it is apparent that, as with the American mud snail *Nassarius obsoletus* and British species of this genus, very similar shells may be inhabited by animals of very different structure and habits. Although so convenient for this purpose, the shell alone may not always supply the final criterion of a species.

Tropical toxoglossids comprise the numerous auger shells (Terebridae) and the cone shells (Conidae). The former have long, finely-pointed shells and live in sand, burrowing, however, in a very different way from the passive screw-shells (p. 88). They have a terminally dilated foot like that of a bivalve (Fig. 53). They usually possess a poison apparatus. The cones*, of which

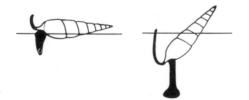

FIG. 53. *Terebro tristis*, burrowing in sand: the foot dilates terminally to form an anchor (as in bivalves); the columellar muscle then contracts pulling the shell down, the siphon retaining contact with the surface. (From Morton & Yonge)

around 500 are known, have been prized by collectors since first brought from the Far East and from Pacific islands. The unmistakable shell (Fig. 54) is apically broad where the initial whorls form a low central spire then tapers to a narrow base where the rounded siphonal canal forms the frontal end of the long and narrow aperture. Only a few species have a very small operculum. Colour and particularly colour pattern, often only fully revealed after removal of the thick periostracum, is nowhere more strikingly displayed. Many of the large tropical cones are objects of the greatest beauty and this combined with their scarcity – now reduced with the increased numbers collected by scuba

---

* Again both shells and living animals (one engaged in swallowing a fish) strikingly illustrated by Wilson and Gillett.

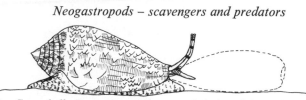

FIG. 54. Cone shell, *Dariconus textile*, expanded viewed from right side showing upward pointed siphon and proboscis; broken outline indicates the extent to which the proboscis can, very suddenly, be extruded. (After Sarramégna)

diving and the discovery of precise habitats – rendered them the most prized objects in conchological collections. The most famous of shells is the legendary *Conus gloriamaris*, the Glory of the Sea, of which it has been stated that 'In the entire animal kingdom perhaps only the Great Auk and its eggs have achieved comparable notoriety.'

But these beautiful shells are those of predacious carnivores some of which have killed men. Unable to move quickly, they kill and secure active prey by a violent extension of the proboscis up to a length equal to that of the shell (Fig. 54). With others held in readiness in the radular sac, a hollow radular tooth, barbed like a harpoon and bathed in poison, is held in readiness at the tip of the proboscis and shot into the body of the prey (Fig. 55). The wide

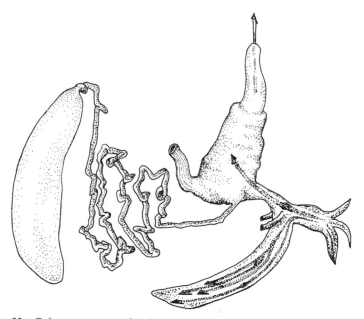

FIG. 55. Poison apparatus of typical cone, muscular venom bulb on left connected by coiled venom gland with the pharynx, below which is the radular sac containing long, barbed teeth, and above this is the proboscis with a radular tooth projecting from the mouth. (After Wilson & Gillett)

107

base is retained within the mouth so that both tooth and prey can be pulled back within its widely distended opening.

Cones are of three types: those that feed on worms, those that consume other snails such as strombids – which react to their approach by violent escape movements – and those that catch fish. These feeding differences are reflected in the form of the harpoon-like teeth and in the toxic and paralytic properties of the venoms. The prey, particularly where it is a soft-bodied fish, may be as large as the predator. It is rapidly broken down by powerful digestive enzymes after which the cone withdraws into its shell. Translucent flask-shaped egg capsules are laid, often by groups of animals. In some species the capsules are solitary, in others they are arranged in clusters or in trailing ribbons. They are attached under stones or corals with the young emerging sometimes as swimming veligers, sometimes as crawling individuals.

Two species of fish-eating cone, *C. geographus* and *C. textile*, appear to be responsible for the sixteen or so human fatalities the first recorded, by the Dutch naturalist Rumphius in 1705, being of a woman in the Moluccas. These are the only gastropods – possibly indeed the only molluscs because the cephalopods have a largely undeserved reputation in this respect and giant clams do so only as an incidental consequence of sudden closure of the large valves – certainly capable of actively killing human beings. Starting with the archaeogastropods, slowly scraping encrusting vegetation, we have come a long way to reach this apotheosis of evolution within the prosobranch gastropods.

Chapter 10

Opisthobranch sea-snails

*

W E have seen in how many different groups of prosobranchs (and incidentally in the pulmonate siphonariids) the limpet form and accompanying habit have independently been assumed, the animal completely sheltered beneath the stout conical or dome-like shell. This innate plasticity of the molluscan form finds further and very much more diverse expression in the evolution of animals, a few of them prosobranchs but the great majority opisthobranchs, in which the protection of a stout external shell with an opercular door is lost. It is replaced by what are, certainly to the writer of these two chapters, most exciting defensive adaptations. Dynamic chemical and biological methods of defence against sharp-toothed predators take over from the negative, passive method represented by the shell. Once liberated from the necessity to retreat into a calcareous shell each time an alarm sounded in the prosobranch central nervous system, these emancipated gastropods have been able to evolve more vivid ornamentation, extravagant epidermal colour patterns, and more varied patterns of locomotor behaviour.

No doubt some of the early evolutionary experiments along these lines ended in failure, but many were partially or totally successful and we are fortunate in that modern oceans contain about three thousand species of gastropods which show intermediate stages in the general trend outlined above. Some of these still retain the shell, in others this has become greatly reduced and may be partially or wholly internal (covered by the mantle), but in the majority the shell is lost at the end of larval life in each generation, and the adult is a sea-slug and not a sea-snail.

This extraordinarily fascinating group of gastropods constitutes the sub-class Opisthobranchia. These animals are among the most interesting and visually exciting of invertebrates; they are to the molluscs what the butterflies are to the arthropods, or the orchids to other flowering plants.

We are very ignorant about the precise antiquity of most of the evolutionary lines that lead up to the existing opisthobranchs, largely because these animals, with their inherent tendency towards the reduction and eventual loss of the shell, were unlikely to be preserved as fossils. So we must accept them for what they are, a large group of gastropods of doubtful evolutionary age, some of which are bottom living or benthic, others water borne or pelagic, some infaunal, others epifaunal, some herbivorous, others carnivorous, some minute, others weighing up to 2 kg, some drab, others as brilliant as jewels, some harmless, others potentially dangerous; in short, an array of animals showing a dazzling variety of form and function (Fig. 56).

We are fortunate in possessing many representative opisthobranchs al-though, as in preceding chapters, descriptions of these will be filled out by

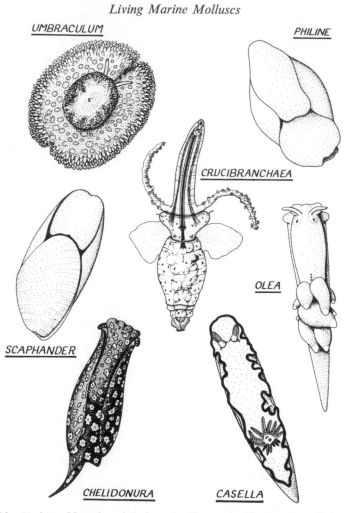

FIG. 56. Variety of form in opisthobranchs. The species illustrated are *Umbraculum sinicum* from Australia, *Philine aperta* from England, *Scaphander lignarius* from England, *Crucibranchaea macrochira* from the northeast Pacific, *Chelidonura sandrana* (after Rudman) from Zanzibar, *Olea hansineensis* from the San Juan Islands, Puget Sound, and *Casella atromarginata* from Australia.

reference to exotic species. In British waters there are about fifty valid species of opisthobranchs which have retained the shell, while the remaining ninety or so species are completely naked as adults. We shall deal in the present chapter with some of the shelled species, leaving the naked forms, chiefly the Sacoglossa and Nudibranchia, until the next chapter. It is important to note, however, that there is an intricate mosaic of inter-relationships within the opisthobranchs, and many of the shell-less forms are more closely related to some shelled species than they are to each other.

The shells of opisthobranchs are usually more frail than those of typical prosobranchs and an operculum exists in only a small number of the most primitive species. A British representative of such a primitive stock is *Acteon tornatilis* (Fig. 57) which may be found by digging in the sand near low water

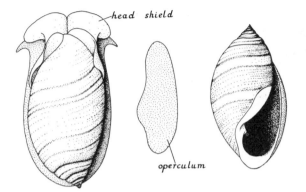

FIG. 57. *Acteon tornatilis*, a primitive shelled opisthobranch from the Gower Peninsular, S. Wales.

mark on a good spring tide in a clean bay. Beaches on the Gower Peninsula have yielded many specimens in recent years. The animal burrows, using its flattened, spade-like head, through the top few centimetres of the sand, hunting for its prey which consists principally of small polychaete worms. The overall length of the cream-white body can be up to 3 cm. *Acteon* shows us an ancient opisthobranch type of shell, solid, opaque and glossy, consisting of up to eight whorls, with an amber-coloured, elongated operculum which can fit against a conspicuous peg or tooth inside the shell aperture and close the door against attack. Acteonids are the most primitive living opisthobranchs and it is fortunate that *Acteon* is freely available for study. It exhibits many residual prosobranch characteristics. Not only the shell but also many of the anatomical features resemble fairly closely the corresponding structures in a mesogastropod. But its possession of a hermaphrodite reproductive system (with both sets of sexual organs functioning at one and the same time), the plicate gill deceptively resembling the prosobranch ctenidium in the mantle cavity, and several microscopic features, show us that *Acteon* is a genuine 'living fossil' representative of a very early opisthobranch stock.

Later shelled opisthobranchs evolved principally in the direction of more complete devotion to a burrowing, infaunal, mode of life. In most of these, the operculum is lost in early life and, in several British genera, the shell becomes wholly internal and even partially resorbed during later life. Fig. 58 shows some details of this trend using as examples various British opisthobranch genera. It has involved more complete commitment to burrowing in

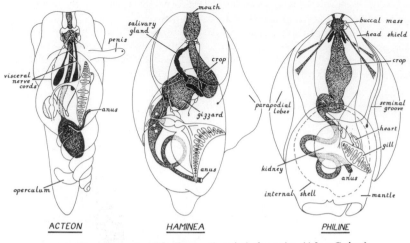

FIG. 58.   Anatomy of bullomorph opisthobranchs. (After Guiart)

soft substrates like sand or mud with several consequential changes. For instance, the mantle cavity and its contained respiratory and other organs have been displaced backward, probably to avoid clogging of the mantle opening by sand and mud during burrowing. This also alters the orientation of the chambers of the heart. In *Acteon* the auricle is still anterior to the ventricle, as in a typical prosobranch, whereas in higher opisthobranchs the ventricle has become the more anterior chamber. Another change consequent upon this reduction and then loss of the shell combined with the rearward displacement of the mantle cavity, is that the ancestral crossing of the major nerve connectives (streptoneury), which was inherited from the prosobranch forebears of the early opisthobranchs, is cancelled and in most higher opisthobranchs the nervous system shows only slight traces of the twisting produced by torsion when the first gastropods appeared.

There are several British species of *Retusa*, the most familiar being *R. obtusa* (Fig. 59). This is found burrowing in mud or muddy sand and may attain an overall body length of 15 mm. The flattened head-shield leads the way during the burrowing movements, and is produced posteriorly on each side into a flattened ear-shaped tentacle. The shell is extremely fragile, translucent and white, with a very long aperture through which the body extends. An operculum has only been found in some exotic species of *Retusa*. *R. obtusa* occurs in the west of Great Britain where these delicately beautiful animals live in the uppermost layers of muddy substrates. The typical form (such as may be found in the sand at Weston-super-Mare) has a distinct tapering spire to the shell, whereas the flat-topped variety *pertenuis*, which occurs in finer deposits (like the mud at Barry, Glamorgan) lacks such a spire.

Spawning occurs chiefly during the spring and the tiny egg masses are attached to the outside of the parent shell, an unusual occurrence in opistho-

PLATE 7. *Left*, thecasomatous (shelled) pteropod, *Spiratella retroversa*, showing transparent coiled shell. *Below*, marine 'pulmonate' snail, *Onchidella celtica*, on rocks in Cornwall.

PLATE 8. *Above*, nudibranch, *Polycera tricolor* (Pacific Ocean), showing spiky mantle processes loaded with defensive glands. *Below*, eastern Australian nudibranch, *Chromodoris splendida*, with vivid warning colouration.

branchs. After some weeks microscopic young – miniatures of the parents – hatch out. There is no free-swimming larval stage, an unusual omission for the opisthobranchs some of whose attractive whirling larvae will be described later.

Perhaps the most remarkable feature of the life of this species is that, even though it lacks speed or organs like the radula for catching prey, it feeds, apparently quite successfully, on one of the most rapidly moving British prosobranchs, the previously described *Hydrobia ulvae*. No one has yet described the manner in which this is accomplished, but a completely convincing photograph by Dr S. T. Smith shows an apparently intact *Hydrobia* inside the stomach of one of the Barry specimens of *R. obtusa*. Perhaps the little opisthobranch lurks just under the surface of the mud and sucks a *Hydrobia* into its pharynx as that animal passes overhead. Once inside the stomach the prey is crushed to pieces by the gizzard plates and then digested.

Another shelled opisthobranch found in muddy inlets and estuaries, perhaps more commonly on the French Atlantic coast (the Bassin d'Arcachon, for example) than in the British Isles, is *Haminea navicula* (Fig. 59). Another,

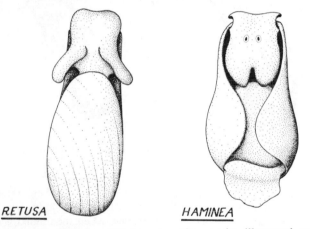

RETUSA   HAMINEA

FIG. 59. European shelled opisthobranchs. The species illustrated are *Retusa obtusa* from S. Wales and *Haminea navicula* from Arcachon, France.

closely related species, *H. hydatis*, also occurs in similar areas, and separating these two can be difficult even for the specialist. *H. navicula* is, however, maximally twice as large (up to 70 mm in overall body length) as *H. hydatis* and so is probably more likely to be encountered in the *Zostera*-covered mud flats where both may occur. These animals are adapted for ploughing along the surface of the fine mud rather than for burrowing in it. Wide flaps at the sides of the foot, the parapodial lobes, act during creeping like the well-designed runners of a toboggan. These lobes, acting with the edges of the head-shield, serve also to deflect mud-particles away from the entrance of the mantle cavity, with its delicate gill. There is some doubt about the diet of the

British species of *Haminea*, but many exotic species are known to be herbivorous and there is therefore a strong inference that this is also the case here.

Haminea is fairly closely related to the abundant species of *Bulla*, familiar in tropical seas. But another common herbivorous British opisthobranch, *Akera bullata* (Fig. 60) is more distantly connected and, indeed, some authorities consider that it is more closely related to the sea hares (*Aplysia*) to be mentioned later. Be that as it may, *Akera* is one of our most interesting opisthobranchs, and no one can possibly see it and forget it. This is because the shell has become so very fragile and light that vigorous swimming is possible. The

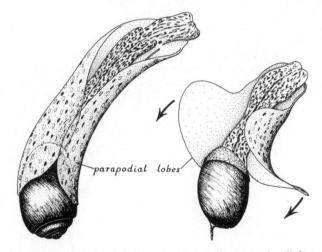

FIG. 60. The British shelled opisthobranch *Akera bullata*, creeping (*left*) and swimming (*right*).

shell has become a mere vestige so that the body cannot be completely accommodated during defensive contraction. The whole body may measure 5–6 cm in length and the aspect is rather dark when the animal is creeping among filamentous green algae on a muddy bottom. But, if alarmed, the parapodial lobes (noted earlier in *Haminea*) are extended and begin vigorous, graceful, rhythmic movements. The two sides act synchronously. During each effective (downward) stroke, the animal accelerates upwards, but loses some of this gain during the recovery stroke. The shape of the swimming animal has been compared to a small bell (the parapodia) containing a passive clapper (the shell and visceral mass). Its movements have also been likened to those of a delicate butterfly. Of course, feeding can occur only when the animals are creeping, and swimming must be considered here to be simply an escape response. While creeping, *Akera* ingests fragments of *Zostera* stems which are scraped off by the radula, swallowed, and then fragmented by spines in the stomach.

The method of swimming described for *Akera* is similar to that of species

114

of *Gastropteron* of warmer seas, but the parapodia in, for instance, the North American Pacific species, *G. pacificum*, meet above or below the body at the conclusion of each stroke. Somewhat similar movements can be seen during flight take-off in a pigeon.

The most perfect opisthobranch swimmers are the naked (gymnosome) and shelled (thecosome) pteropods; these 'sea butterflies' spend their entire lives swimming near the surface of the ocean. Thecosomes are said to rise to the surface near dusk, beginning to descend around midnight; it is difficult to catch thecosomes with a surface net during the day. Gymnosomes do not appear to undergo such diurnal migrations and remain near the surface throughout the day and the night. In pteropods the pedal sole has degenerated and the foot is represented chiefly 'by expanded, muscular parapodia, which beat continuously.

Thecosomes such as the tiny *Spiratella retroversa* (Plate 7), swim with the aperture of the shell uppermost, i.e. ventral side up (Fig. 61). The distal parts

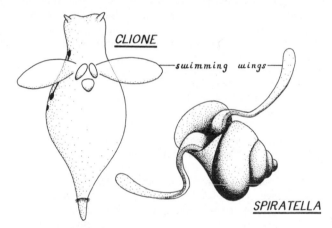

FIG. 61. Swimming pteropods. The species illustrated are *Spiratella retroversa* and *Clione limacina* from the N. Atlantic. (After Morton)

of the expanded parapodia are said to be non-muscular, the contractile proximal regions being responsible for movements of the whole. These parapodia, also known as wings or fins, undergo repeated cycles of active downward flapping, followed by passive flaccid recovery. Such a highly dis-continuous swimming mechanism can be effective only in an animal near to neutral buoyancy, and many thecosomes are able to stay afloat with the parapodia extended, without displaying any muscular activity. Feeding is on plant plankton by way of ciliated 'fields' on the wings. Some of the large Mediterranean thecosomes, which are among the most impressive of all planktonic organisms, have lost the delicate shell and form a gelatinous boat, or pseudoconch, in which they live.

The carnivorous gymnosomes – the only molluscs other than cephalopods to possess tentacles armed with suckers – are a totally distinct group. If locomotion in the thecosomes is like rowing a small boat, then the movements performed by the parapodia of gymnosome pteropods like *Clione limacina* are more like sculling. In *Clione* the body is stream-lined in shape and the parapodia rather small (Fig. 61). The co-ordination of parapodial movements in *Clione* is delicately governed so that both upward and downward strokes have a strongly effective component, directed rearwards, thus encouraging a hovering forward movement of the light, small body. Locomotion is more rapid and more controlled than in the thecosomes. Indeed, were this not so, these gymnosomes would be unable to catch the thecosomes upon which they customarily feed.

We return to the ocean bottom to consider two common British opisthobranchs that burrow through sand and muddy sand, searching for infaunal bivalves which are swallowed intact. The largest of these carnivores is the amber-coloured *Scaphander lignarius* (Fig. 56) which may reach an overall length of 6 cm (greater in Mediterranean specimens). The swollen, pale body is much too large to be accommodated within the shell, and these rather coarse-looking animals are commonly dredged in sublittoral sand; it is often difficult to be sure whether a specimen is alive or dead, they are so relatively helpless when removed from the sandy substrate. But in nature it is a different story, and a *Scaphander* can consume, rapidly and efficiently, many kinds of bivalves, as well as some polychaete worms, echinoderms and gastropods. It is itself said to be eaten by haddock, one of the few authenticated reports of any opisthobranch being taken as food by a fish, or, for that matter, by any predator.

The common white *Philine aperta* (Fig. 56) has similar habits but differs structurally in that the shell becomes wholly internal in adult life. It is strange that this effete organ has not been fully discarded, but it is generally true that in the evolution of various types of molluscs where the shell has become reduced in importance, it is never immediately discarded, but always passes through an internal phase before eventual disappearance. *P. aperta* occurs in sublittoral sand all around the British Isles. Its length may reach 7 cm and, like *Scaphander*, it feeds upon other infaunal invertebrates.

The skin of *Philine* contains many tiny crypts, each lined by cells which can produce and store relatively strong sulphuric acid. If an inquisitive fish nibbles a philinid, it gets a taste of this acid and usually retires in disgust. It is a remarkable fact, established by W. Bateson at the Plymouth Laboratory late in the last century, that fish abhor any food that tastes acidic, so natural selection has equipped *Philine* with a highly appropriate defensive mechanism. Such a chemical mechanism is plainly necessary because these naked molluscs can neither fight nor run away.

The shells in all species of *Aplysia* (Fig. 62) are similarly reduced and roofed over by the mantle. Unlike philinids, however, the aplysiids are herbivorous, feeding upon sublittoral algae, and their defensive fluids are rather complex biochemically, consisting of a whitish foul-tasting slime from the opaline gland in the mantle, and a vivid purple fluid (which also tastes badly to the human tongue) from other glands in the same area. These secretions, together

APLYSIA   PLEUROBRANCHUS

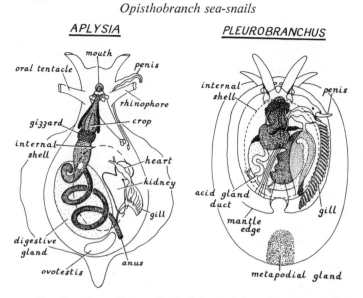

FIG. 62.   Anatomy of internally shelled opisthobranchs. (After Guiart)

with the rather sinister aspect these animals have been considered to possess, have no doubt been responsible for the folk-lore surrounding aplysiids. They have been considered beasts of ill-omen in Europe and it was believed that handling an *Aplysia* could be fatal. On the other hand, on the coast of China, dried bodies of *Aplysia* are employed medicinally in treating certain human optical defects. Their effectiveness has never been scientifically evaluated.

Young *Aplysia punctata*, our most common species, are usually pinkish brown in colour but, as they grow older and larger, they alter to a darker brown or olive colour. This may be associated with their changing diet as they move towards the shallower regions in which they are said to congregate to mate and lay their eggs. Aplysiids frequently copulate in chains. They are hermaphrodite, like other opisthobranchs, so each individual in the chain (except for those at the free ends) acts as a male for the one in front and a female for the one behind. These chains of aplysiids often curve to the right when viewed from above, because of the lateral positioning of the genital apertures.

The overall length of the adult body may be up to 20 cm in *A. punctata*. The diet consists mainly of algae, although adherent organisms are often taken. Spawning (principally during the night) has been recorded through most of the warmer months of the year in British waters, from February to November, but in most years the breeding season is in the spring. The tangled egg strings are yellow-orange, sometimes pinkish. A medium-sized string may contain about 140,000 eggs each of which can hatch after three weeks as a tiny swimming larva.

Two much larger species, *Aplysia depilans* and *A. fasciata,* have occurred on rare occasions on our south-western shores. These have numerous anatomical differences from *A. punctata* and, in addition, have the added capacity to swim if disturbed. These large species are relatively abundant in the Bassin d'Arcachon and in the Mediterranean Sea.

Another opisthobranch group with graceful stream-lined bodies and a reduced, internal shell, are the pleurobranchs, exemplified by one of our most attractive species, *Pleurobranchus membranaceus* (Fig. 62). This may reach 10 or 12 cm in length, with the widely-open flimsy shell measuring about the half of this. The mantle is pale brown with patches of dark brown between the retractile, soft, conical tubercles and on the foot. Slightly elevated ridges anastomose between the tubercles and the brown pigment is darkest alongside these ridges. In the pleurobranchids the mantle cavity is widely open on the right side of the body and a well developed bipectinate gill (totally distinct from the molluscan ctenidium) is a very conspicuous feature. The mantle edge is often crimped at front and rear to allow better access to the respiratory stream induced by ciliary action. Most of the epithelial cells over the whole of the body can produce sulphuric acid, which we also saw in *Philine*, but in pleurobranchs the cells must actually be burst open by an attack (perhaps from a sharp-toothed fish) for the acid to be freed. At the rear of the foot in mature individuals is a well-developed metapodial gland, which probably produces a sexual attractant during the breeding season.

The light-bodied *P. membranaceus* is a swimmer of some efficiency, but this serves more to buoy up the body for a while than to cause significant movements. In other words, this pleurobranch is better described as a passively 'planktonic', than as an actively moving 'pelagic' animal. To the malacologist the most interesting feature of swimming in such pleurobranchs is that the two sides of the foot are not synchronous in action; that of one side undergoes its recovery stroke at the precise time when the other is in the phase of effective beat. Swimming is invariably initiated by undulating movements of the foot. The edges of this become flattened, very thin, and greatly expanded, compared with their normal (creeping) state. Then the animal turns over on to its back, and may flutter over the bottom for some seconds before rising gently on a shallow climb to the surface. There is a high degree of instability in progression; the roll to either side is approximately 45°, and so a movement through about 90° occurs between each pair of strokes. There are about 55–60 strokes per minute.

Pleurobranchus feeds mainly upon solitary ascidian sea-squirts. It drills through the tough skin of the prey, using its radula and fine-toothed jaws, and then sucks out the soft organs inside. So it is usually found on the sea bottom in clean rocky areas, except during the occasional winters when huge populations reach plague proportions and undertake swimming behaviour, sometimes for days on end. Such plagues have been seen only three times in the last hundred years, once (the winter of 1873–4) in Torbay, once (in 1892) in Plymouth Sound, and once (the winter of 1958–9) in Port Erin Bay. We do not understand fully the adaptive significance of this rather rare phenomenon. Perhaps winter swarming results in aggregation in preparation for the spring burst of reproductive activity.

The other two British pleurobranch species are both smooth and yellow in colour, secrete sulphuric acid if disturbed abruptly, and can at present be distinguished from one another only by examination of internal anatomy (shell, radula and jaws). They are *Berthellina citrina* and *Berthella plumula*. Like *Pleurobranchus*, they feed upon ascidians, but they are unable to swim. In warmer waters there are many species of pleurobranchs but few of these can also swim so that we are fortunate in having *P. membranaceus* available in British waters. Perhaps the most bizarre tropical relatives of the pleuro-branchs of our coasts are the 'umbrella shells' (Fig. 56) of the Mediterranean and the Indo-Pacific basin. These may reach the size of a saucer and their shells are cap-like and external, not roofed over by the mantle like our more typical forms. They represent yet another – this time opisthobranch – type of limpet.

The last group of shelled opisthobranchs to be considered is the strong-shelled Pyramidellomorpha (Fig. 63). These are small and resemble proso-

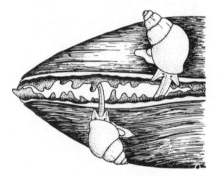

FIG. 63. The pyramidellid *Odostomia rissoides*, ectoparasitic on the common mussel, *Mytilus edulis*. (After Rasmussen)

branchs in many of their shell-features, but they are an ancient group of opisthobranchs. They exhibit many primitive features; thus the shell is external and multi-whorled and an operculum is present. But they have be-come specialized for ectoparasitic life and the alimentary canal is especially modified, with a long proboscis which may bear on its tip a piercing stylet (Fig. 64). The radula is absent and so is the gill.

There are about thirty British species of pyramidellids, but many of these are rare or imperfectly understood. Their hosts are always tubicolous poly-chaete worms or slow-moving molluscs. Each species of pyramidellid has rather restricted preferences and some species are considered to attack only one kind of host. Thus the proboscis of *Odostomia unidentata* may be delicately inserted through the skin of *Pomatoceros* (a common tube worm) so that a semi-fluid meal may be sucked out of the unfortunate host. Despite the im-mediate urge to think of the pyramidellids as an unimportant if fascinating offshoot of the early opisthobranchs, it is important to remember that they

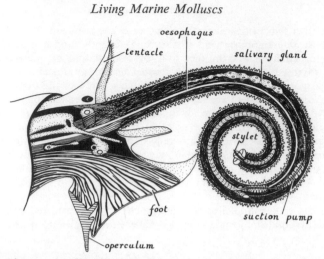

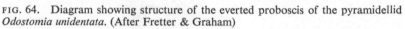

FIG. 64. Diagram showing structure of the everted proboscis of the pyramidellid *Odostomia unidentata*. (After Fretter & Graham)

are numerically extremely abundant and, with the acteonids, have been found in older fossil deposits than any other opisthobranchs. Their mode of life has proved extremely durable.

Chapter 11

Sea-slugs

*

IT is an intriguing paradox that, although the calcareous coiled shell, the strongly developed operculum, the anterior mantle cavity and the crawling habit were the hall marks of success in the prosobranch molluscs of the early Palaeozoic, many groups of the opisthobranchs (as well as, independently, many of the pulmonates) later achieved success by their gradual, but eventually radical, abolition of these traits. The summit of evolutionary progress in these animals is a slug-like body shape in which one must often search hard to find evidence of the shell (first covered, then resorbed by the mantle), gills and the bilateral asymmetry of their ancestors. The gill if present has moved posteriorly so that in the heart the auricle is behind the ventricle, and many of the most obvious features of the visceral torsion of the early prosobranchs, such as the twisting of certain of the ganglionic connectives, have been lost.

Such a slug-like level of organization has widened the evolutionary horizons of the stocks possessing it. They are no longer restricted in their range of locomotor activities, they are better able to employ tricks of epidermal coloration and ornamentation for defensive means, and they are able to pursue prey (or seek shelter from their own enemies) in a multitude of crannies on the sea bottom which few hard-shelled molluscs could enter. So it is perhaps not surprising that the slug-like body form has been independently attained by descendants of numerous distinct stocks of gastropods.

The common sea-slugs of temperate waters belong to five groups, all of course, gastropods, but not otherwise closely related. Of these, the first are air-breathing pulmonates, the second, the Lamellariidae, are prosobranchs, while the others are major opisthobranch groups consisting of the minute sand-dwelling Acochlidiacea, the shallow-water herbivorous Sacoglossa, and the ubiquitous carnivorous Nudibranchia.

Onchidiids are air-breathing pulmonates which possess a posteriorly situated lung and move about over rocky shores when the tide is low, searching for encrusting algae to eat. There is one British species, the rare *Onchidella celtica* (Plate 7) found only on our south-western shores (although the same species is abundant on the coasts of, for example, Portugal). These shy, pulmonate sea slugs live in crevices when the weather is too dry and also, paradoxically, when the tide rises to cover them. They come out to feed when the air is moist and the tide low. Only very few zoologists, even specialists in the Mollusca, have ever seen living *Onchidella* in Britain.

The Lamellariidae (with two British representatives, *Lamellaria perspicua* and *L. latens*) are mesogastropods and retain a large, internal, spirally-coiled shell, like that of their near relatives the cowries, and a mantle cavity containing a well-developed ctenidial gill, so they should not be confused with

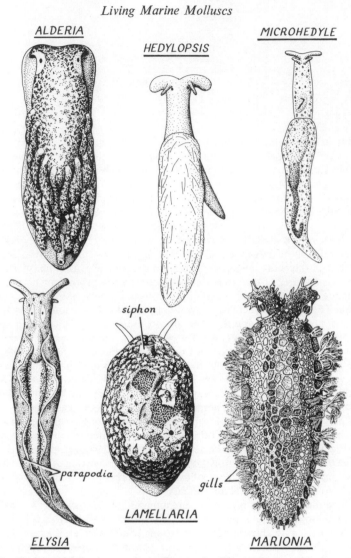

FIG. 65.   Variety of form in sea slugs. The species illustrated are *Alderia modesta* from S. Wales, *Hedylopsis suecica* and *Microhedyle lactea* from northern Europe (after Odhner & Swedmark), *Elysia viridis* and *Lamellaria perspicua* from Cornwall and *Marionia pustulosa* from Australia.

the opisthobranchs. Moreover, the sexes are separate in *Lamellaria*, whereas all the opisthobranchs are hermaphrodite.

   Lamellaria perspicua (Fig. 65) is found commonly in shallow waters around the British Isles, usually on hard substrata where its prey, consisting of encrusting compound ascidian sea-squirts, abounds. The slug moves about little so long as food remains available and it has been noted that the upper surface of the mantle may be modified, in colour and in texture, so as closely to resemble the ascidian colony. The slug may actually eat its way into the prey in an attempt further to conceal itself. The mantle epithelium is equipped with acid glands like those described in the last chapter and this will presumably function to dissuade an inquisitive fish which has been sharp-eyed enough to penetrate the visual disguise. As a matter of fact, the blood of many ascidians (including some of our commonest species) is also strongly acidic and may be defensive, but that is another story.

The eggs of *Lamellaria* are embedded in a 'nest' which it bites out of the tissues of the ascidian prey. From these will hatch in due course the Echinospira larvae, which are among the most exotic members of the temporary zooplankton (Fig. 66). After some time living and feeding on tiny drifting

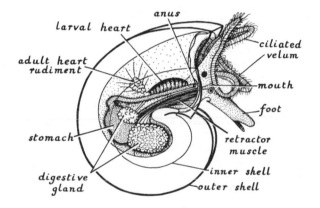

FIG. 66. The microscopic 'Echinospira' larva of *Lamellaria perspicua*. (After Fretter & Graham)

algal cells in the surface layers of the sea, these larvae settle on the sea-bottom and are transformed into adult form. The colour patterns of the dorsal mantle are extremely variable. As earlier mentioned, some individuals resemble closely the adult prey, but others merely exhibit a generalized mottled pattern. Perhaps the most interesting individuals are those not uncommon specimens in which the mantle bears concealment adaptations clearly designed to frustrate recognition. One such way is for the mantle to bear patches of red which resemble small colonies of red sponges, but the most remarkable case that has come to attention was the presence in two specimens from the Cornish sea-shore of mantle excrescences coloured and shaped exactly like intertidal barnacles (Fig. 65). It can be assumed that such perfect resemblances to their surroundings significantly benefit these individuals, but no experiments have been carried out using lamellariids and such potential predators as fish. Nor has it yet been established that such mantle patterns are inheritable.

The remaining sea-slugs are all opisthobranchs and (with rare exotic exceptions) they lack the shell as adults, have no restricted mantle cavity (although gills of various kinds are often evident) and are hermaphrodite with an invaginable penis. Probably the least understood group of these shell-less opisthobranchs is the Acochlidiacea, with which we can well begin.

Most members of the Acochlidiacea are less than 4 mm in length as adults, and are found in the interstices of marine sand and gravel, sometimes under water of low salinity. They presumably feed upon the micro-organisms living in that environment; they often have chitinous jaws and always possess a narrow but strong radula. They are often very abundant and the numerous species (of which four are at present known from the British coast) have in common a slender body with two pairs of head tentacles, conspicuous eye-spots (absent only in *Hedylopsis brambelli*), and calcareous spicules in the skin. We know very little about the breeding of these animals and few authors have reported finding the larval stages. (Fig. 65 shows the adults of two British species, *Microhedyle lactea* and *Hedylopsis suecica*.)

In terms of basic structure the Sacoglossa constitutes a compact group although paradoxically displaying a greater range of superficial body-form than occurs in any other group of the opisthobranchs. What renders them easily recognizable is a combination of two attributes, their herbivorous habit and their possession of a narrow radula (consisting of a single row of teeth) from which worn obsolete teeth do not drop away and pass back to be discharged ultimately in the faeces, but instead remain to give a more or less complete dental history of each individual. Sometimes these worn teeth remain attached to the radular membrane, but more often they drop into a special tooth-sac or ascus, from which they may be recovered for microscopic examination. The scalpel-like teeth (Fig. 67) slit open algal cells from which

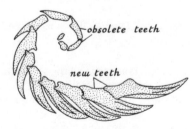

FIG. 67. Part of the radula of the British sacoglossan *Hermaea bifida*, greatly enlarged.

the nutrient juices are sucked. These are the plant suckers among gastropods

But outside this rigid nutritional uniformity, many other aspects of body-form are extraordinarily diverse, more so than in any other comparable group of molluscs. Nowhere else but in the Sacoglossa can one find representatives with bivalve shells, with univalve shells and with no shells at all; with a body-form varying from smooth in some species to papillose in others; and with species living in habitats ranging from temperate salt marshes to tropical coral reefs. While most sacoglossans are herbivores, two temperate species, *Stiliger vesiculosus* and *Olea hansineensis*, are semi-parasitic on the spawn-masses of other opisthobranchs, while others such as *Elysia viridis* and various related tropical species appear to supplement their diet by a symbiotic relationship, not with unicellular plants such as we shall find associated with the bivalve Tridacnidae, but with cell organs from within plants. These chloroplasts are sucked in with the other contents of the plant cells and are maintained intact within the cells of the digestive gland. In them is contained the chlorophyll which enables plants to form starch and other organic matter and their presence bestows a similar capacity on these animals. All in all it becomes apparent that the sacoglossans merit the closest study. The shelled sacoglossans do not occur around Britain, unfortunately, but we do have in our shallow waters several naked species, exhibiting a considerable range of body-form. One common species is *Elysia viridis*, which occurs associated with green algae in fully saline locations, in contrast to three British species of *Limapontia*, which are found on salt marshes or in intertidal pools subject to considerable fluctuations in salt content.

Elysia viridis (Fig. 65) may reach a length of 45 mm and has a smooth, flattened body, rendered somewhat leaf-like by the development in the adults of wide parapodial lobes. These lobes contain ramifying tributaries of the digestive gland which may be seen through the skin. This spreading or decentralization of the digestive gland is a trend which we shall see again in many of the true nudibranchs.

Despite its graceful form with wide and mobile parapodial lobes, *Elysia* has never been observed to swim. It lives out its life closely attached to green algae, species of *Cladophora*, *Ulva*, *Enteromorpha* and *Codium*, slitting open the plant cells by means of the scalpel-like radular teeth so that the turgid juices can be sucked out by the pumping pharynx. The body-colour is governed by the diet and may vary from green (most usual) to reddish. A green specimen can be induced to change to red within eighteen days, by feeding it upon red algae. Relatively constant features are, however, tiny glistening red, blue and green spots; white patches may also be found, particularly at the edges of the parapodial 'wings', and black markings are sometimes seen on the head and elsewhere. These markings are visible only with a hand lens or a microscope and, to the unaided eye, these animals usually appear somewhat drab.

The three British species of *Limapontia* are all less than 10 mm in extended length and are smooth, dark-coloured and slug-like, lacking parapodial lobes. As in *Elysia*, the digestive gland is divided, but to a lesser extent.

Limapontia depressa (Fig. 65) is the most accessible species because it may be found on salt marsh flats above all but the most extreme high tides. It feeds upon the filamentous green alga *Vaucheria*; it is rarely found in pools, but usually on damp mud. Under exceptional circumstances, such as drought or heavy rainfall, the slugs burrow into the mud, where they may remain for weeks at a time. In the laboratory vessels, this is the only species of *Limapontia* which habitually crawls out of the water. The body-colour is usually dark brown to black, often bearing tiny pale spots on the back; in the variety *pellucida* the colour is bright yellow, with the lobes of the digestive gland showing green through the skin. These colour patterns fade if the animals are starved for a few days.

While *Limapontia depressa* has a smooth head lacking any trace of tentacles, the other two species, occurring in clear coralline rockpools on the sea-shore, possess ear-shaped or finger-like head tentacles.Both of these rockpool species, *L. capitata* and *L. senestra*, are dark-coloured and feed upon species of green *Cladophora* and brown *Bryopsis*. *Limapontia senestra* is, in the adult, the easiest of the species to recognize at sight, because the head bears a pair of finger-like tentacles, quite different from the ear-like head-lobes of *L. capitata* or the smooth head of *L. depressa*.

The last British sacoglossan to be mentioned here is, perhaps, the most interesting of all because it shows some remarkable adaptations to its salt-marsh life as well as introducing to us a body-form which we shall encounter time and again in the nudibranchs. The body of the sacoglossan *Alderia modesta* contains numerous separate lobes of the digestive gland, each encased in a finger-shaped external process. Clusters of these processes, called cerata, cover much of the back of the slug. In *Alderia* they have a special function quite apart from their essential role in the digestion of the algal food material. They may be seen in life to undergo repeated cycles of slow muscular contraction, 20–60 per minute causing movement of blood in the sinuses. Heart and pericardium are absent in this genus, a deficiency found in no other mollusc. *Alderia modesta* is remarkable also for the great breadth of its geographical range, extending from the British Isles as far as the coast of California, always on salt marshes. It feeds like *Limapontia depressa* (with which it is often taken) upon filaments of the alga *Vaucheria*; unlike that species, however, it can tolerate a wide range of salinities, from 5 to 36 parts per thousand.

Finally we come to the largest order of the opisthobranchs, the nudibranchs, not all of which sprang from the same ancestors. In all existing nudibranchs the shell and operculum have been discarded in the adult. In several groups, independently, the back has become covered with finger-like extensions. Sometimes these dorsal papillae or 'cerata' contain tributaries of the digestive gland as in the sacoglossan, *Alderia*, but sometimes they simply harbour prickly bundles of calcareous spicules or batteries of defensive glands. At least twice, independently, these cerata have acquired the capacity to nurture *for their own defence* sting cells (nematocysts) derived from coelenterate prey such as sea anemones. So pervasive are the tendrils of the converging lines of evolution that the precise interrelationships between the dendronotacean, arminacean, aeolidacean and doridacean suborders (Fig. 68) may never be fully understood.

In the Nudibranchia can be clearly seen the great advantages acquired by gastropods which have exploited to the full the evolutionary loss of the constraints of passive mechanical defence represented by a shell-operculum system, and have replaced this by active dynamic biological and chemical defensive adaptations.

Nudibranchs are found in all the world's oceans and major sea areas; they feed on every kind of epifaunal animal material, as well as playing a significant

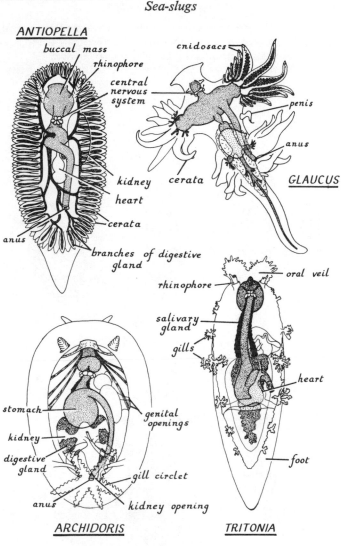

FIG. 68. Anatomy of nudibranchs.

part in some planktonic communities. They owe their success to their unique maintenance, during their evolutionary history, of a delicate balance between the shell and the skin as defensive attributes. They have remained viable during the long transition from the primitive condition, much as in the modern *Acteon tornatilis*, to the present-day naked carnivorous species. These have agile, soft bodies, perfectly adapted chemosensory tentacles (rhinophores) and buccal apparatus, virtual immunity to attack by fish and many other predators, while the searching nudibranch veliger larvae have extraordinary ability to recognize and then metamorphose upon the adult diet. Let us look more closely at these remarkable characteristics.

The most obvious feature of a nudibranch is its soft pliability (with certain

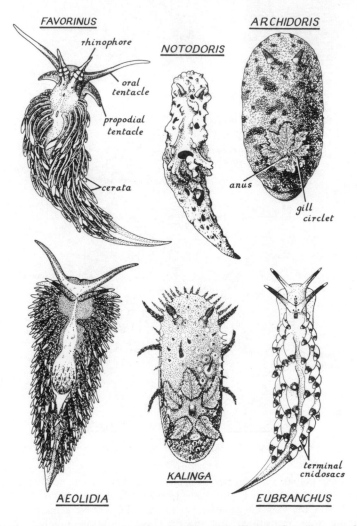

FIG. 69. Variety of form in nudibranchs. The species illustrated are *Favorinus blianus* from S. Wales, *Notodoris gardineri* from the Australian Great Barrier Reef, *Archidoris pseudoargus* from Cornwall, *Aeolidia papillosa* from Cornwall, *Kalinga ornata* from Australia and *Eubranchus farrani* from S. Wales.

tropical exceptions like the rock-hard *Notodoris gardineri*, Fig. 69). This in turn permits swimming, a capacity only possible in those opisthobranchs in which the shell has become flimsy, internal or, as in the nudibranchs, lost.

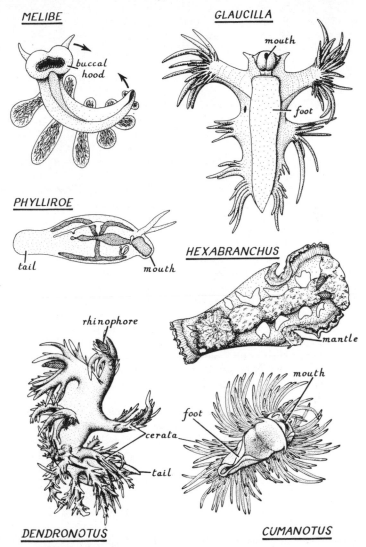

FIG. 70. Swimming nudibranchs. The species illustrated are *Melibe leonina* from the San Juan Islands, Puget Sound, *Glaucilla marginata* from Australia, *Phylliroe bucephala* from tropical waters around the world, *Dendronotus iris* from the San Juan Islands, *Hexabranchus sanguineus* from the Australian Great Barrier Reef and *Cumanotus beaumonti* from the San Juan Islands.

It seems probable that the pressure which led to the adoption of swimming in so many opisthobranchs was the need to escape from slow-moving, bottom-living, predatory carnivores. Many starfish and some crustaceans, for example, will eat virtually any motionless animal matter. A number of species of opisthobranchs possess swimming escape reactions which may have evolved so as to escape just such dangers (Fig. 70). The swimming mechanism may involve convulsive dorso-ventral muscular contractions of the whole body (as in *Tritonia*), lateral undulations of the flattened body (as in *Dendronotus* and *Melibe*) sometimes in an upside-down attitude (as in *Scyllaea*), or it may be accomplished by the movement of certain parts of the body especially modified for the task. The aeolidacean, *Cumanotus beaumonti*, possesses dorsal cerata which can in unison perform up and down movements not unlike those of a pigeon's wings, pivoting at their bases. The arrangement of the muscles which bring this about has not been investigated. When the animal is abruptly disturbed, repeated downward sweeps of the cerata propel the body away from the bottom for some minutes at a time.

The splendidly marked coral reef dorid nudibranch *Hexabranchus sanguineus* swims in a fashion that is unique among the gastropod molluscs, and paralleled only by certain cephalopods. When at rest, the margins of the mantle skirt are dorsally enrolled, and slow locomotion occurs by creeping on the broad pedal sole. But in swimming, the mantle skirt is spread out, dilated, and strong locomotor waves are propagated rearwards from the anterior margin. At the same time, the whole body undergoes great dorso-ventral flexions. Swimming may continue for many minutes, and probably this is more than a simple escape reaction. Certainly, a brilliant flash of colour accompanies the unrolling of the mantle edge, and swimming may be the behavioural component of an 'aposematic' or warning display.

The aeolidacean nudibranchs, *Glaucus atlanticus* and *Glaucilla marginata*, contrive to stay all their adult lives in the surface layers of the ocean (where, like *Ianthina*, they feed upon the planktonic coelenterates *Velella* and *Porpita*, but especially on the Portuguese man o'war, *Physalia*). They do so by a novel behavioural modification. Each aeolid gulps in air from above the water surface, and holds a bubble inside the stomach. These glaucid nudibranchs are thus passively planktonic. Movements of the cerata have been reported, but these do not appear to result in swimming. It is interesting that strong sphincter muscles guard the points of exit from the stomach, so that the ingested air bubble does not escape but remains to buoy up the sea-slug in an upside-down posture. The skin of the body is delicately countershaded by blue and white pigment so as to afford camouflage, but, because of the head-over-heels posture, it is the foot which is darkest blue, and the 'back' or dorsum which is silvery.

All nudibranchs are carnivorous and each family usually contains species which feed on broadly similar types of prey. For example, the Coryphellidae, Dendronotidae, Dotoidae, Eubranchidae, Facelinidae, Heroidae, Hancockiidae and Lomanotidae contain species which feed upon the small hydroid coelenterates. Most species of the Aeolidiidae feed upon sea-anemones (Actiniaria). Members of the Tritoniidae all feed upon soft alcyonarian corals.

The Proctonotidae, Polyceridae and Onchidorididae contain species which attack sea mats or polyzoans (although *Onchidoris bilamellata* feeds on sessile barnacles). The dorid families Cadlinidae, Chromodorididae, Rostangidae, Archidorididae and Kentrodorididae (and perhaps many more) all subsist on a diet of sponges. One or two nudibranch species feed apparently exclusively on the eggs of other organisms. We saw a similar habit in some Sacoglossa, and among the nudibranchs it is known to occur in the aeolids *Favorinus* and *Calma*. These are often very pale in colour and so pass unnoticed among cream-coloured or white eggs. Whereas *Calma* feeds upon the eggs of teleost fish, however, *Favorinus* takes the eggs of other opisthobranchs. In *Calma glaucoides* the anal opening is closed off early in development, presumably because there is little solid waste material remaining after digestion of the yolky food. *Favorinus* is less firmly committed to a diet of eggs and embryos and in this genus the anus remains functional throughout free life.

In particular groups of nudibranchs body shape is often related to the nature of the passive food material on which they prey. For instance, many doridacean nudibranchs are adapted for feeding upon encrusting marine sponges, and possess dorso-ventrally flattened bodies, a more or less oval outline, and a broad, flattened foot. Similar body-forms occur in other nudibranchs which browse upon flattish encrustations (like barnacle-aggregations, polyzoan and ascidian colonies, or the soft coral *Alcyonium*). The radula, moreover, is usually broad and jaws are often lacking. In nature, they are frequently well camouflaged through their shape, coloration and behaviour. Of course there are exceptions to these rules but they may serve as a guide in trying to assess the functions of the parts of the nudibranch body.

Similarly, those of them that feed upon arborescent, more erect organisms (for example, hydroids, sea-anemones, some polyzoans) are usually smaller and more elongate, with a long narrow foot adapted for clinging to this type of prey. They are active, voracious animals which in aquaria often exhibit cannibalism. Jaws are often well developed and the radula is narrower. In extreme cases (*Aeolidia*, *Facelina*) the radula may possess only one (central) tooth in each row.

In many nudibranchs, for instance, *Archidoris pseudoargus* and *Tritonia hombergi* (which are incidentally, two of the largest European species), the prey consists of a single species in each case. Observations on *A. pseudoargus* in the Isle of Man showed it fed on nothing but the sponge *Halichondria panicea*. These dorids were nearly always found on an encrustation of this sponge, often partially embedded in it. Such a close dependence upon a single prey-species has also been recorded in the Mediterranean dorid *Peltodoris atromaculata* which feeds only on the sponge *Petrosia dura*.

Tritonia hombergi is almost invariably found in association with deadman's fingers, the soft coral *Alcyonium digitatum*, which, as established by a series of dredge samples from the Irish Sea, is its sole natural diet. The related *T. plebeia*, however, feeds on *Alcyonium* and also on the sea fan, *Eunicella verrucosa*. Another example of high specificity of diet is provided by *Catriona aurantia*, an aeolidacean which feeds mainly on two species of tubularian hydroids, *T. indivisa* and *T. larynx*, on which it is commonly found around

British shores. According to some recent laboratory work, adult stages of *Catriona* can recognize these hydroids at a distance and are preferentially attracted to them in tests with other species.

Most nudibranchs, however, are known to take a variety of prey. *Doto fragilis* and *Eubranchus farrani*, for example, feed on several species of calyptoblastic hydroids; *Acanthodoris pilosa* consumes a number of encrusting intertidal polyzoans. *Doto coronata* attacks more than twenty species of hydroids. Only occasionally have preferences been revealed. One such case is the small dorid *Adalaria proxima*, which is common intertidally around the British coast. If given a choice between various encrusting polyzoans, these dorids almost invariably attack colonies of *Electra pilosa*. On British shores they are usually found on this widespread intertidal polyzoan, although other related species near by are ignored. But it has been established that adult *Adalaria* will feed in the laboratory on several other polyzoans if *Electra* is absent. *Aeolidia papillosa*, a nudibranch that preys upon sea anemones, has been found in the Isle of Man to prefer *Actinia equina* to other anemones, while in Holland, young *Aeolidia* have been reared on a diet of *Actinia* or of *Metridium senile*, but not on any other anemone. Nevertheless, these anemones and many more, are known to be eaten by *Aeolidia* from time to time. Clearly these may not be equally palatable and have equal nutritive content.

So much for the feeding activities of the nudibranchs; but what are their enemies, animals which may prey upon them? Experiments carried out in the Port Erin (Isle of Man) Aquarium showed that nudibranchs were almost invariably refused as food by a variety of hungry fish. Occasionally a fish would take a nudibranch into its mouth, but nearly always rejected it violently and immediately. In a tank containing several healthy, hungry fish such as pollack (*Pollachius pollachius*) a single nudibranch tossed on to the surface may be inspected, taken into the mouth, and then rejected, by every fish present before it reached the bottom.

We are beginning to understand the detailed functioning of some of the chemical and biological defensive mechanisms employed by these naked gastropods. First of all, it is important to recognize that any individual species may include in its repertory several different defensive adaptations. For instance, *Discodoris planata* spends most of its life on sponge-encrusted sublittoral boulders, on which it may be almost impossible to distinguish it. But if nosed out by a hungry fish, it can in a crisis expel quantities of sulphuric acid from multicellular acid-glands in the mantle. Now it has been known for many years that teleost fishes have an intense dislike of anything tasting acidic, and many species of opisthobranchs (like *Lamellaria*, the mesogastropod mentioned earlier) have capitalized upon this.

It happens that sulphuric acid secretions are easy to detect and characterize, so we know a good deal about this phenomenon of acid-secretion in gastropods. But other naked forms produce different defensive fluids, the chemistry of which has not so far been investigated. In all nudibranchs adequately studied, skin glands have been found, the position and function of which indicates that they must be defensive. These glands are usually commonest in those areas of the skin which would first be encountered by an inquisitive predator.

In species like *Polycera quadrilineata*, where dorsal papillae are present, these glands are usually concentrated there. Papillae of this kind are usually non-retractile unlike gills and rhinophores and can be rapidly regenerated if damaged. These defensive glands vary greatly in structure; they may be superficial or below the skin; unicellular or multicellular; their secretion may be exclusively fluid or may contain hyaline or other concretions. The secretion may be drab or colourful and it may or may not taste unpleasant to the human tongue. And, of course, more than one type of gland may be present in a single species.

Although the chemical make-up of the majority of nudibranch defensive secretions is almost completely unknown, it seems likely that they will be shown to be proteins. Some of them have proved in laboratory tests to be intensely poisonous to other animals.

A dramatic biological defensive mechanism is found in the aeolidacean nudibranchs (of which *Aeolidia papillosa* is a familiar British example), where the nematocysts of the anemone or other coelenterate prey are utilized for defence of the predator. Cuvier was the first naturalist to draw attention to the presence, near the tips of the dorsal cerata of aeolid nudibranchs, of internal sacs (Fig. 77) which in 1881 the Italian malacologist Trinchese illustrated rather sketchily. It was the Frenchman Vayssière who established in 1888 that these sacs normally contained nematocysts like those of Coelenterates. We now know that the nematocysts are separated in the aeolidacean alimentary canal from the nutritive parts of the meal and passed by a rather mysterious means to the cnidosacs of the mollusc, which are situated below external pores at the tips of the cerata (Fig. 71). If one of the cerata is nipped, the nematocysts burst from the ceratal pore. Immediately they reach the sea-water medium they discharge with the probable consequence that the hungry fish abandons the attack.

FIG. 71. Enlarged section through one of the cerata of an aeolid nudibranch (*Catriona aurantia*) showing the terminal cnidosac with its armoury of sting-cells derived from its prey, the hydroid *Tubularia*. (After Edmunds)

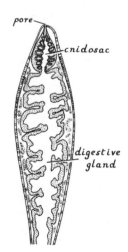

133

Furthermore, a process of nematocyst-selection in the aeolidacean alimentary canal has been described in the surface dwelling planktonic aeolids *Glaucus atlanticus* and *Glaucilla marginata*, which may eat *Physalia*, *Velella* or *Porpita*, but retain for their own defence only the exceptionally potent nematocysts of *Physalia*, and, moreover, only the largest of these stinging cells. Other types of nematocysts are broken down in the digestive gland. Glaucid nudibranchs are, in fact, somewhat dangerous for human beings to handle without protection, and painful stingings by *Glaucus* have been reported by bathers in Australia.

The utilization of these coelenterate nematocysts for defence occurs throughout the aeolidacean nudibranchs, with the exceptions of *Calma glaucoides* and *Favorinus* species, which (as was mentioned earlier) do not habitually feed upon coelenterates, and of *Phestilla* species, which feed upon zoantharian corals that have extremely small nematocysts, useless for molluscan defence.

A similar biological defensive mechanism occurs independently in the dendronotacean family Hancockiidae, but here the cnidosacs are found not only in the projecting cerata but also beneath the skin of the flanks of the body. The relationship of these cnidosacs with the digestive gland on the one hand, and the outside world on the other, appears to be the same as in the true aeolids, but their origin remains to be discovered.

When attacked, an aeolidacean nudibranch usually holds the cerata out erect and may muster them together aimed towards the enemy. In other words, attacks are invited towards the ceratal tips and directed away from the vital head and body. These defensive adaptations may not be infallible, but seem to function adequately.

There has been much argument about the significance of coloration in nudibranchs. The cerata of aeolids and the dorsal papillae of many dorids or dendronotaceans are frequently patterned in such flamboyant ways as to foster the theory that in nature these serve to attract the attention of a predator away from the less conspicuous (but more precious and fragile) head and visceral mass.

In many other cryptically marked nudibranchs (as well as in some sacoglossans and sea-hares) the resemblance in colour pattern to the normal substratum is so perfect that it would appear to protect these molluscs against attack by visually searching predators. But against this it can be argued that opisthobranchs appear to live predominantly in situations where there is little light (for instance, in deep waters or under boulders), and their colour patterns cannot therefore readily be perceived by potential enemies.

The truth is that we still have very little accurate information about the method of selection of food by predatory fish in different kinds of marine habitats.

The life cycles of surprisingly few species of opisthobranchs have been worked out in detail. In the British species of nudibranchs which have received close study, the maximal life-span has proved to be one year or less. Some of these species have annual life cycles, with one breeding period per year, while others may pass through numerous generations in a year. The purely annual species, such as *Archidoris pseudoargus* or *Tritonia hombergi*, tend to feed on organisms which have one conspicuous quality in common: their extreme abundance and stability in certain types of habitat at all seasons of the year. Those nudibranchs which are known to pass through a number of generations in a year, such as *Eubranchus exiguus* or *Tergipes tergipes*, are all species that feed upon more or less transitory prey, such as hydroids, which may spring up seasonally on submarine surfaces and be cropped to extinction within a few days. Nudibranchs which attack such organisms possess certain attributes in common. They often grow to sexual maturity very rapidly, reducing the risk of dying without progeny. They are active and voracious and many of them are known to attack a wide variety of food-organisms. Juveniles and adults are often found side by side, and spawning tends to occur through much of the year, contrary to the orderly, rather synchronous sexual development of the sponge, soft coral, and polyzoan feeding nudibranchs, many of which are tied to a single prey-organism throughout adult life.

There is a great deal of evidence that new populations of nudibranchs are commonly established in favourable situations by exercise of the ability of the searching veliger larva (Fig. 73) to recognize and then metamorphose to the adult form upon some component of the final diet. The searching phase may be as short as one or two weeks in *Adalaria proxima*, but may be prolonged for some months in *Archidoris pseudoargus*.

The veliger larvae hatch from a jelly-bound spawn mass that may be globular or ribbon-like, of various shapes, sizes and colours in different species (Fig. 72). The total embryonic period varies from 5–50 days in different species and the larvae may exhibit a great deal of individuality (Fig. 73). Unlike the prosobranchs, most opisthobranchs are true hermaphrodites, that is to say that each individual has both an ovary and testis and

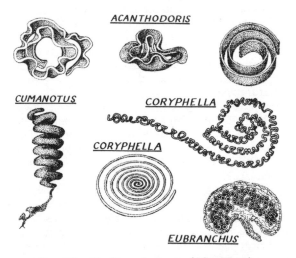

FIG. 72.   Nudibranch spawn. (After Hurst)

135

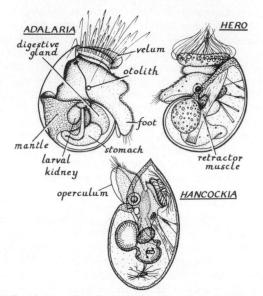

FIG. 73. The veliger larvae of nudibranchs (greatly enlarged). The species illustrated are *Adalaria proxima* from N. Wales, *Hero formosa* from the Isle of Man and *Hancockia burni* from Australia.

functions as both male and female (often simultaneously) so that fecundity is high. Some larger nudibranchs may procreate up to a million larvae, but the record is held by an individual *Aplysia californica*, shown to produce over 400 million eggs during its four-month breeding season.

The order Nudibranchia is divided into four suborders (Fig. 68), the Dendronotacea, Doridacea, Arminacea and Aeolidacea. Representatives of all of these may be found on British shores. Unlike so many molluscan groups, there are fewer representatives of the Aeolidacea in tropical waters than in temperate and polar latitudes. The other suborders appear to be equally common all over the world.

The Dendronotacea contains ten families of nudibranchs all possessing a mid-lateral anal papilla and distinct, and often elaborate, sheaths for the rhinophoral tentacles to be pulled into after an alarm. They feed upon coelenterates as varied as medusae, in the case of the Mediterranean *Phylliroe bucephala* (Fig. 70), hydroids, in British species of *Lomanotus*, *Hancockia*, *Dendronotus* and *Doto*, or soft corals, preferred by tritoniid nudibranchs such as the British *Tritonia hombergi* (Fig. 74). Horny mandibles may or may not be present and the radula shows a great deal of variation in the different families, from broad and multiseriate (Tritoniidae) to uniseriate (*Doto*) resembling the radula of true aeolidaceans. The pallial edge, forming a dorso-lateral ridge on each side of the body, frequently bears arborescent processes which function as gills. Sometimes these processes contain tributaries of the

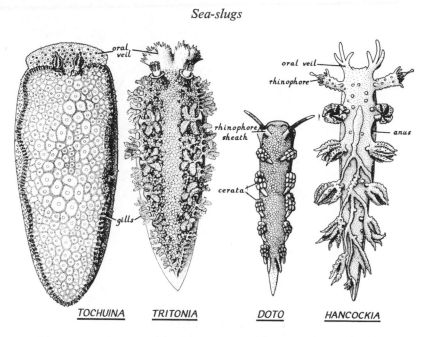

FIG. 74.   External features of dendronotacean nudibranchs. The species illustrated are *Tochuina tetraquetra* from the San Juan Islands (the world's largest nudibranch), *Tritonia hombergi* from S. Wales, *Doto yongei* from Australia and *Hancockia burni* from Australia.

digestive gland and a dendronotacean such as *Doto* can be mistaken for a true aeolid by the unwary student. Mention must finally be made of the family Tethyidae, which contains several species of *Tethys* and *Melibe* (Fig. 70) that lack radula or jaws and feed by casting about in muddy eel-grass and other rich areas for small crustaceans which are captured with the aid of a greatly dilated fimbriated buccal hood, and swallowed whole. Unfortunately none of these fascinating animals occurs on British shores.

The Doridacea (Fig. 75) with about twenty-five families, is the largest nudibranch suborder. These dorids often have rhinophoral cavities into which the tentacles may be retracted, but only rarely possess external sheaths surrounding their bases. The anal papilla is nearly always situated mid-posteriorly, under the mantle rim in *Corambe* and *Corambella* (and, incidentally, in all dorids at an early ontogenetic stage), but situated dorsally in all the typical forms, such as *Doris, Archidoris, Polycera, Adalaria, Hexabranchus*, and many others. A variable number of retractile foliaceous gill plumes emerges from the mantle surface close to the anal papilla. In typical dorids the gill plumes are arranged in a circlet and they may be retracted in a co-ordinated way into a sub-pallial pocket on alarm in *Archidoris, Discodoris, Jorunna, Chromodoris* and *Asteronotus* (and many other dorid genera). This pocket may in *Asteronotus cespitosus*, from tropical waters, be distinctly crenulate so that

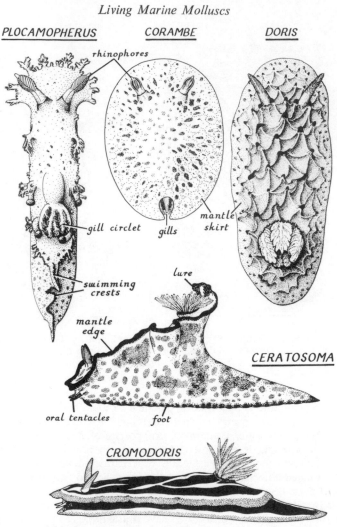

PLOCAMOPHERUS   CORAMBE   DORIS

rhinophores

gill circlet   gills   mantle skirt

swimming crests

lure

mantle edge

CERATOSOMA

oral tentacles   foot

CROMODORIS

FIG. 75. External features of doridacean nudibranchs. The species illustrated are *Plocamopherus ceylonicus* from Australia, *Corambe pacifica* from California (after MacFarland), *Doris maculata* from S. Wales, *Ceratosoma cornigerum* from Australia and *Chromodoris quadricolor* from Aldabra.

the margins interlock and give greater resistance to an inquisitive fish. In less advanced dorids, such as *Polycera, Crimora, Adalaria, Hexabranchus* and *Laila,* no such pocket is present, and each gill can be contracted separately down to the mantle surface. Sometimes large spiculose pallial papillae give extra protection to the gills and rhinophores, often containing elaborate defensive glands and luminescent or coloured lures to draw the attention of a predator away from the fragile vital parts. Such papillae never contain lobes of the digestive gland in the Doridacea, and the liver usually forms a more or less solid single mass close to the stomach. The radula is usually rather broad and certainly never uniseriate. But one successful family of dorids, the Dendrodorididae, contains species which lack the radula and jaws and ingest sponges by an ingenious sucking modification of the muscular buccal mass. Sponges, polyzoans, acorn barnacles, compound sea squirts or tube dwelling polychaete worms form the diet of most dorid nudibranchs.

The third suborder of the Nudibranchia, the Arminacea (Fig. 76), is rather more difficult to define, and certainly much more difficult to recognize from external features alone. The nine families currently contained here will certainly not fit into any other suborder, and (to a certain extent) this explains our conviction that a separate suborder is needed for them. *Armina loveni,* a

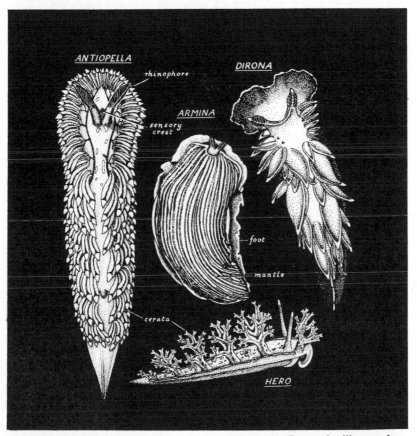

FIG. 76. External features of arminacean nudibranchs. The species illustrated are *Antiopella cristata* from S. Wales, *Armina californica* and *Dirona albolineata* from the San Juan Islands, and *Hero formosa* (after Alder & Hancock) from Britain.

139

not uncommon species of the sublittoral around British shores, has, externally, some of the features of a primitive dorid such as *Corambe* or *Phyllidia*, with external pallial leaflets forming a series beneath the mantle edge, but internally *Armina* proves to be very unlike a doridacean, for it has a much-divided digestive gland, a laterally placed anal papilla and strong mandibles.

Similarly, *Hero formosa*, *Antiopella hyalina*, and the Pacific Ocean *Dirona albolineata*, have a strong resemblance to the aeolidacean nudibranchs which will be dealt with shortly. But their dorsal ceratal processes lack cnidosacs with contained nematocysts, a fact which instantly separates them from the aeolids.

But our classification is not really as unnatural as we have perhaps implied, because the arminaceans *do* have certain important features in common. Their rhinophoral tentacles do not possess external protective pallial sheaths. The anal papilla is usually situated rather far forward either dorsally or laterally, on the right side. The radula may be narrow, but it is never uni-seriate (with a single tooth in each row). Oral tentacles are usually lacking.

The diets of the arminaceans are varied. *Hero formosa* certainly feeds upon

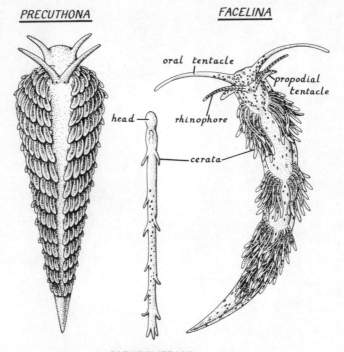

FIG. 77. External features of aeolidacean nudibranchs. The species illustrated are *Precuthona peachi* from Cornwall, *Pseudovermis mortoni* from the Solomon Islands (after Challis) and *Facelina annulicornis* from S. Wales.

naked or gymnoblastic hydroids, and *Armina*, too, is said to attack coelenterates (the alcyonarian sea-pansies in the case of the best-known species *Armina californica*). But *Antiopella* and *Proctonotus* feed upon encrusting polyzoans, while *Dirona albolineata* is known to devour a wide variety of shelled molluscs and other benthic invertebrates.

The final suborder of the Nudibranchia is the Aeolidacea, a very compact group containing twenty families of delicate, beautifully formed and patterned species (Fig. 77). They all bear clusters, groups or rows of elongated, finger-like smooth dorsal ceratal processes. These cerata contain the much-divided lobes of the digestive gland, together with, at their tips, the defensive cnido-sacs. The cerata are usually vividly marked in a characteristic way in each species. These cerata are extremely short in the sand-burrowing aeolid *Pseudovermis* but are in the majority of the species, the most conspicuous feature of the body. The rhinophoral tentacles are never retracted into pallial sheaths, while the oral tentacles are often very long and graceful and the propodial extremities are sometimes extended so as to form a third pair of anteriorly placed sensory processes (Fig. 77). Mandibles are usually well developed but the radula is reduced to a very narrow ribbon and sometimes bears only a single file of teeth (the uniseriate condition). Aeolidaceans (such as *Aeolidia, Facelina, Eubranchus and Catriona*) are usually active hunters feeding upon coelenterates. *Glaucus* or *Glaucilla* are planktonic aeolids preying upon siphonophores and chondrophores. The Pacific species *Phidiana pugnax*, however, attacks other opisthobranchs, even some aeolids, as its normal prey, while *Calma* and *Favorinus* devour only the eggs of their molluscan and fish prey. *Fiona pinnata* is a very unusual aeolid of wide distribution which occurs occasionally in British waters and attacks stalked goose-barnacles such as *Lepas*.

We are fortunate in Britain to have an especially rich fauna of aeolidacean nudibranchs, including perhaps the most beautiful of all aeolids, *Facelina auriculata coronata*, which can be found commonly wherever the 'organ-pipes' hydroid *Tubularia* flourishes. Let us study these dazzling creatures while we can, before unchecked industrial effluents pollute and destroy their sub-littoral habitats. At least as far as Northern Europe is concerned, this is a simple statement of fact, not an intemperate prophecy of doom.

Chapter 12

Origin and nature of bivalves

*

ANIMALS such as mussels, oysters, cockles and clams of all kinds, completely encased in a hinged bivalve shell, are among the best known of marine inhabitants, in part doubtless because so many of them are edible. Here the molluscan form differs greatly from that of the gastropods although with no less measure of success. It is obviously important to explain the extent to which these bivalves resemble and the extent to which they differ from other molluscs and how such apparently rigidly confined animals have become supremely adapted for life in the many aquatic environments they occupy. A major difficulty arises in that whereas an expanded gastropod, even a chiton and far more an octopus, is obviously a living animal, with bivalves this is often far less easy to realize. Many of them, oysters for instance, cannot even move and those that can usually do so within the obscurity of a medium of sand or mud. Only in rare instances is there any external indication of the presence of the elaborate feeding mechanism. A few bivalves, such as cockles or razor shells, show immediate activity when exposed but the majority have to be opened if we are to know anything about the contained animal – then alone can we learn anything about how they feed and respire.

Although in number of species second to the gastropods, in the economy of marine, and also in places of freshwater, life, the bivalves are the more important. Dense mussel or cockle beds are familiar to many but their populations are insignificant in comparison with the beds of trough shells, species of *Mactra* and *Spisula*, on the Dogger Bank where they cover up to 1000 square miles at densities reaching 8000 per square metre! Success is due first to the enclosing shell, still more to the unparalleled efficiency of the ciliary mechanisms in collecting the primary production of plant plankton. In turn bivalves are a major food of bottom living fish. But their mode of feeding and of locomotion confines all bivalves to aquatic existence; they accompany gastropods into freshwaters but not on to land.

Bivalves occur early in the fossil record and we can only postulate how they may have arisen from the no less hypothetical molluscs from which we earlier derived chitons and gastropods. Clearly lateral compression was involved and this was probably preceded by, and certainly accompanied by, extensions of the mantle that formed lateral lobes completely enclosing the body and the foot. This process must, one feels, at least have begun before the original tough protein shell became calcified. Later – and this is precisely what happens during development – separate centres of calcification appeared on each side with formation of the first shell valves.

Between these centres, along the mid-line, the shell remained uncalcified forming the elastic ligament which serves as a hinge for the valves. It also

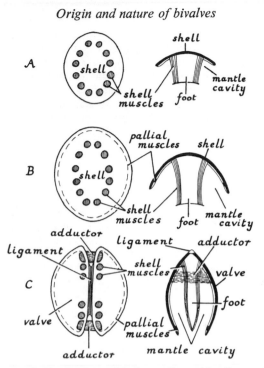

FIG. 78. Diagrams indicating how a bivalve mollusc with a ligament separating the valves and adductor muscles closing them could have evolved: A, Dome-like shell with attaching shell muscles; B, shell extending and mantle attached marginally by pallial muscles; C, bivalve shell formed by calcification on each side and an uncalcified ligament between; pallial muscles cross-connected at each end forming adductors; foot laterally compressed and shell muscles separated into anterior and posterior pedal retractors.

serves to open them when the adducting muscles relax. Valves 'gape' after death of the animal. As shown in Fig. 78, the extension of the mantle into the two lobes must have been accompanied by marginal attachment to the valves by way of a line of pallial muscles. Because each valve is not D-shaped but rounded, the line of attachment represented by the ligament is short with deep concavities at each end (Fig. 78). As lateral compression increased, the pallial muscles in the depths of these embayments would eventually cross-connect to form the characteristic anterior and posterior adductor muscles which, on contraction, compress the ligament and close the shell. Thus the means of opening and the means of closing the valves would appear to have evolved *pari passu*, a functional necessity.

These pallial and adductor muscles are peculiar to the bivalves and must not be confused with the original shell muscles which here persist as paired pedal muscles responsible for pulling the laterally flattened foot back within the closing valves. In some cases up to four pairs of these muscles persist (as in

Fig. 78) but most bivalves have only the two pairs inserted on each valve just within the anterior and posterior adductors. Together with the foot, they are absent in oysters and a few other bivalves. Scars on the inner surface of the valves reveal the position of the various pedal and pallial muscles and provided significant evidence about structure and habit in extinct bivalves.

There is nothing equivalent to torsion so that initially bivalves remain bilaterally symmetrical with paired ctenidia associated with paired auricles and with two kidneys and two gonads (Fig. 79). There is none of that intimate

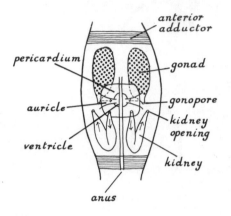

FIG. 79. Diagram looking down on bivalve showing central pericardium with contained ventricle and lateral auricles, paired kidneys opening out of pericardium but paired gonads now opening direct into mantle cavity. Rectum passes through ventricle, anus opening on posterior face of posterior adductor.

association between reproductive and excretory systems which plays so significant a role in the evolution of the gastropods. However there are notable instances of asymmetry in bivalves involving both the anterior and posterior regions, the animal remaining bilaterally symmetrical, but also (usually after bivalves have come like oysters to lie on one side) involving bilateral asymmetry. In many ways we shall find that bivalves are even more plastic in structure than are gastropods.

Eventual enclosure within the shell valves and so to a large extent within an enlarged, completely surrounding, mantle cavity, involved withdrawal and reduction of the head. While it is not suggested that the ancestral molluscs had anything like so elaborate a head as even the most primitive existing gastropod with its complex radular apparatus and sensory equipment of tentacles and eyes, the mouth must originally have been in direct contact with the substrate from which it obtained food. A simple radula may have acted as a conveyor belt before it developed into the elaborate scraping and finally predating organ it became in the gastropods.

But whatever its former size, there is no head in any existing bivalve, only the site of the mouth opening behind the anterior adductor muscle at the front end of the mantle cavity. How, then, was food obtained during the period when the mouth was being enclosed within the valves? This is clearly all-important; at every stage in evolution animals must be able to feed and to

PLATE 9. *Above*, young sea-hare, *Aplysia punctata*, in an alert, hungry attitude. The food usually consists of green and red algae. *Below*, prosobranch gastropod, *Lamellaria perspicua*, showing barnacle-like camouflage patterns on the mantle.

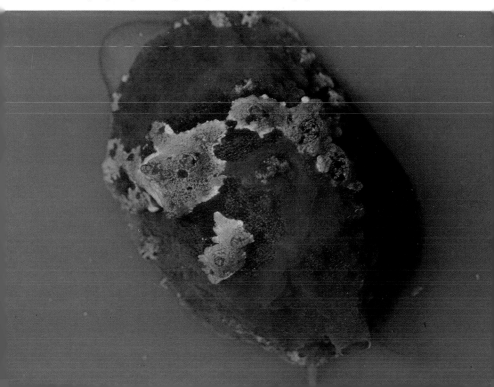

PLATE 10. Largest British nudibranch, *Tritonia hombergi*, attacking its prey, the soft coral *Alcyonium*.

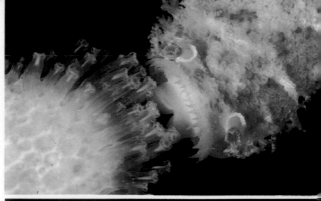

Common shore nudibranch, *Acanthodoris pilosa*.

Rare arminacean, *Antiopella cristatus*.

Voracious *Facelina auriculata coronata*, attacking the 'organ-pipes' hydroid *Tubularia*.

respire, a fact sometimes overlooked by those who construct evolutionary trees.

Lips such as those present in *Neopilina* (p. 28) could have elongated as the mouth was withdrawn. That can, however, be no more than a suggestion, there is no certainty that bivalves evolved from a creature having such structures. What is vastly more to the point is the highly successful survival of a group of bivalves which feed in precisely this manner, namely by way of enormously developed lips known as labial palps which are exclusively bivalve structures. Later we shall see how these organs work and how they are first supplemented by and later superseded by the gills as feeding organs.

Leaving for the moment this all-important matter of feeding, we now view an animal completely encased in a hinged shell, with two similar sides. It is therefore *equivalve*, but, owing to the absence of the dominating influence of a head with its auxiliary structures, the front and hind regions, including adductors and pedal muscles, are also almost equal in size. The shell is thus also *equilateral*. The dog cockle, *Glycymeris* (Fig. 80A) provides an excellent example of this double symmetry. Each valve originates in a rounded beak or umbo (plural umbones) situated on either side of the ligament (Fig. 80B) which they tend to overarch. A section passing from the umbones to the middle of the free edge of the valves has the form of two plano-spirals describing an ever widening, i.e. logarithmic, curve (Fig. 80).

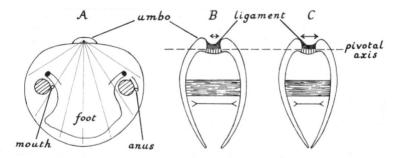

FIG. 80. Diagrams showing A, outline of a symmetrical (equilateral) valve, lines radiating from umbo indicating the radial component in shell growth; B, C, sections through valves: B, valves separated with adductor relaxed and upper half of ligament (above pivotal axis) compressed, lower half extended; C, valves closed with shortened adductor, ligament compressed below and extended above.

As in gastropods, shell growth takes place around the margin of the mantle which in bivalves is divided into two similar lobes each representing a generative curve. It is obviously essential that growth around these should be identical or the margins of the valves would not meet as they must do when the adductors contract. Growth in any shell can be resolved into a radial component which can be represented by lines radiating from the umbones (see Fig. 80) and a transverse component acting at right angles to this and responsible for the extent to which the two valves are separated (Fig. 80). Another component which acts tangentially to, and on the same plane as, the generative curve is present in a few bivalves with remarkable consequence in certain cases (p. 191).

The outline of any shell depends on the degree of marginal increase around the generative circle. If this is symmetrical at both ends, then an equilateral shell either round as in the dog cockle or, more usually, oval, will be formed. Much more frequently shell increment is not symmetrical so producing all manner of inequilateral shells, most usually with the hinder regions enlarged, in extreme cases pulled out into the linear form of razor shells with the hinge at the extreme front end (Fig. 81). Where there is no constraint (in the next

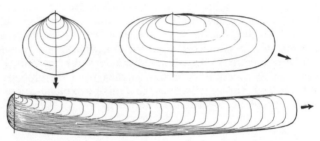

FIG. 81.   Outline of left valves showing the effect of changes in growth gradients around the mantle margin, vertical lines from umbones separating anterior and posterior 'territories' of mantle and shell (but *not* anterior and posterior halves of enclosed animal – see Fig. 113), arrows indicate major growth centres. Equilateral shell of dog cockle (*Glycymeris*); posteriorly extended shell of butter clam (*Siliqua*) leading to long drawn out razor shell (*Ensis*).

chapter we see what happens when there *is*) then the outline of the shells is entirely dependent on variations in secretion around the generative curve. Control is exercised by natural selection which retains only those forms which give their possessors some advantage over others living under similar conditions or else fit them for life in some new environment, in bivalves most often some previously unoccupied grade of bottom material into which it can now effectively burrow.

The transverse component is no less important. The external convexity of the valves depends on the magnitude of this component with the result that bivalves range from the excessively flattened tellinids (p. 198) to the almost globular cockles (p. 192). Where the magnitude of the component differs on the two sides, then bivalves such as the common scallop (p. 174) are produced with dissimilar valves, the upper one flat, the lower one deeply cupped. Such inequivalve asymmetry is usually, although not invariably, associated with the habit of lying on the one side, either free like scallops or attached like oysters. The great majority of unattached bivalves are equivalve like cockles.

Owing to the complete enclosure of the animal within the shell, the mantle

FIG. 82. Section through the margin of mantle and shell to show the nature and origin of the three shell layers and appearance of the three marginal mantle folds.

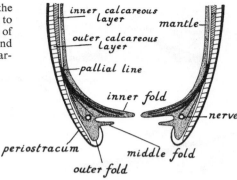

margins assume far greater significance than in the gastropods. They are invariably thrown into three parallel folds (Fig. 82) each with a distinctive and highly important function. The outer one is concerned (as in the gastropods) with shell formation; the middle one has assumed many of the sensory functions served in gastropods by the head; the inner one is muscular and controls the often powerful flow of water which enters the enlarged mantle cavity under the influence of the lateral cilia on the much lengthened and vastly more numerous gill filaments.

Putting the two last aside for the moment, all aspects of shell formation should first be discussed. As in gastropods, it consists of three layers – an outermost horny periostracum (in technical terms a quinone-tanned protein) with outer and inner calcareous layers. The outer mantle fold produces the two first. A glandular strip along the groove on its inner side forms the periostracum which extends as a flexible sheet over the edge of this fold to cover the surface of the shell. The outer surface of this outer fold is responsible for secretion of the outer calcareous layer. This is composed of prisms of calcium carbonate (in either the calcitic or aragonitic forms, laid down within a lace-like network of protein conchiolin on the inner surface of the periostracum. The inner calcareous layer (or layers), also within a protein matrix, is produced by the general inner surface of the mantle, usually only within the pallial line (Fig. 82). This is the only region of the shell which can be repaired following damage. Pallial fluid separates the mantle tissues from the shell except in the regions of muscle attachment where the characteristic scars are formed. During growth these inevitably alter in position as attachment extends over new areas while on the other side inner shell layer, formed through the agency of the pallial fluid, covers regions from which the muscle has moved. This inner calcareous layer is usually either porcellanous and dull or else nacreous when it forms the iridescent mother-of-pearl so conspicuously developed in pearl oyster shells (*Pinctada* and *Pteria*) and already noted in top shells such as *Trochus*.

The ligament (Fig. 83) is formed by the same agencies as the rest of the shell. Periostracum (unless worn away) covers it. Outer ligament layers are

Living Marine Molluscs

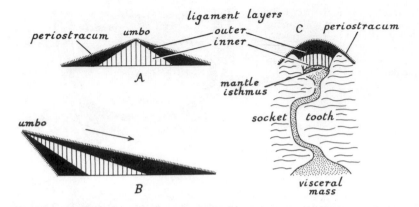

FIG. 83. Diagrams showing A, the structure (lengthways) of a symmetrical (technically amphidetic) ligament; B, of a posteriorly extended (opisthodetic) ligament; C, cross section through ligament, below a tooth in one valve fitting into a socket on the other, between them the secreting (and absorbing) tissue of the mantle crest.

formed by the outer surface of the outer mantle fold at each end, the inner ligament layer by the strip of mantle surface, the mantle isthmus, that extends between the lobes that form the valves. These ligament layers consist of largely uncalcified protein. Contraction of the adductor muscles produce stress in the ligament, the outer layers above the 'pivotal axis' (Fig. 80) being stretched and the inner, usually more fibrous, ones compressed. Like the valves, the simplest form of ligament (Fig. 83) is symmetrical at the two ends but in the more usual condition of posterior enlargement the hind region of the ligament is extended, becoming 'opisthodetic' (Fig. 83) instead of 'amphidetic'. In the much less frequent event of forward extension the anterior outer layer becomes the larger. Inequality of the valves profoundly influences the ligament which can assume surprising forms. In some bivalves it lies deep between the umbones in others it protrudes as a rounded crest forming what are known respectively as inner and outer ligaments (*not* to be confused with inner and outer *layers*). Many other things may happen, the ligament may be extended by fusion of the periostracal layers at one or both ends; it may be reduced, changed in orientation from longitudinal to transverse or vertical or even be lost, as in the shipworms (p. 214), its function assumed by other agencies.

Hinge teeth are usually obvious and are highly significant in classification including that of fossil shells in which, unlike the ligament which decays, they are retained indefinitely. They represent a series of ridges and grooves facing each other on either side of and below the ligament. Each tooth fits into a corresponding socket in the opposing valve, one the mirror image of the other (Fig. 83). Although so intimately fitting when the valves close, it has to be remembered that the shell surfaces on the two sides are *never* in contact:

there is always an undulating crest of mantle tissue (crowned above by the mantle isthmus that forms the inner ligament layer) between them. This mantle crest is responsible for the formation on one side of a continuously enlarging tooth and on the other of an increasingly deepening and widening socket into which the tooth must always fit. Secretion and absorption of shell must always balance, the two equally essential if calcareous structures are to maintain the same relationship as they grow.

Teeth ensure that the valves interlock, that there is no danger of the one slipping on the other. This is essential for the security of the enclosed animal, against the attacks of predators or the dangers of intertidal desiccation. Having little rigidity, the unaided ligament cannot ensure this.

The arrangement of teeth varies widely and is important in classification, for this reason fully described in books on shells. In the simplest (taxodont) condition there are numerous similar interlocking teeth on either side of and below the ligament but in the many 'heterodont' bivalves the teeth can be divided into central or cardinal members and a variable number of laterals, all diverging from a point below the umbones. In many deep burrowers teeth are reduced but the ligament is attached to broad downward-projecting chondrophores. But teeth are lost, and for a variety of reasons, in a variety of groups although sometimes replaced by secondary structures.

We can now return to the middle and inner folds of the mantle margins. Bivalves receive most of their information about the world they inhabit by way of the former which carries one or more rows of tentacles which are probably capable of detecting changes in temperature and salinity, and possibly also the presence of substances in solution in the water that enters the mantle cavity. As we shall later see, certain bivalves also carry eyes on this fold. Both tentacles and eyes are connected with the pallial nerve that runs along the base of the mantle folds (Fig. 82). The muscular inner fold is concerned with regulating the flow of water into the mantle cavity. It is therefore of particular significance in the lamellibranch bivalves where a great water flow is generated. These are discussed in the next chapter.

We now leave mantle and shell to view what they enclose – the much enlarged mantle cavity which, in addition to enlarged gills and other organs present in the gastropods, contains mouth, palps and foot and is bounded at each end by the adductor muscles. We are fortunate in being able to view this first in the nut shells, species of the archaic genus *Nucula* which happily have not to be sought, like *Neopilina*, in profound oceanic depths, but are abundant the world over in shallow water. Around Great Britain alone there are no less than six species, averaging around 1 cm long and varying in details of form and shell sculpture. Each is adapted for life in some particular grade of bottom deposit ranging from coarse shell gravel to flocculent mud, those inhabiting the last found in the greater depths where such deposits tend to accumulate. The texture of the substrate is a most significant feature in the life of bivalves, they must be capable of penetrating through it and also anchoring within it. Differences in shell form and sculpture, so useful in classification, are of prime importance in the life of the animal.

Removal of one valve and mantle lobe in *Nucula* (Fig. 84) reveals the

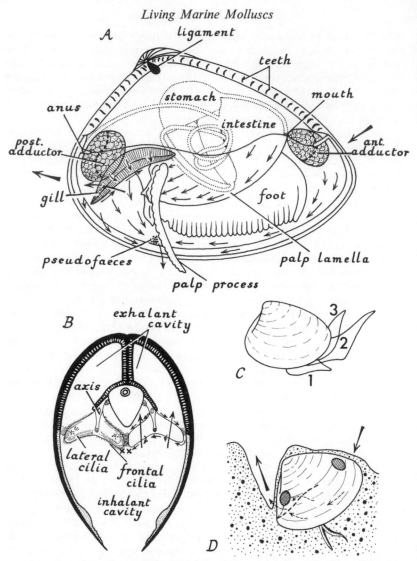

FIG. 84. Protobranch nut shell, *Nucula nucleus*. A, mantle cavity from right side, arrows without indicate positions of inhalant and exhalant currents, arrows within (apart from those on gill) ciliary currents collecting waste, B, cross section through region of gills showing how these divide the mantle cavity; C, stages in protrusion of foot; D, animal *in situ*, palp processes extended in feeding, broken arrows indicating passage of water through the mantle cavity and gills (broken line).

ligament with the numerous (taxodont) teeth on either side, also the two similar adductor muscles and the massive compressed foot drawn back by contraction of four pairs (not shown) of retractor (shell) muscles. The protobranch gills occupy little more space than do those of the simpler archaeo-gastropods which they closely resemble, consisting of an axis with alternating rows of horizontally extending filaments now, however, owing to the downward enclosing growth of the mantle lobes, attached to the roof of the cavity. There are the same lateral, current-producing cilia on the sides of the filaments and the same frontal and abfrontal cilia on their lower and upper surfaces (Fig. 84). The respiratory current created by the former enters the cavity anteriorly, flows back and then upward between the filaments to emerge as an outflowing, exhalant current at the hind end just below the adductor (and where the anus opens). This through-flow of water is a primitive bivalve condition; we shall see how it is altered and with what fundamental consequences.

But these gills show significant changes from those of gastropods. In the first place the filaments are more numerous, they are also attached to one another if only by interlocking groups of coarse cilia; projecting cilia on the outer and inner margins also connect the filaments respectively with the mantle surface and, in the mid line, with each other (Fig. 84). So a simply-maintained meshwork is created between lower inhalant and upper exhalant chambers. Moreover the space between the filaments through which the water passes is now guarded on each side by a row of large, complex 'latero-frontal' cilia. These act as strainers, eventually so efficiently in the higher bivalves as to retain particles down to one micron (1/1000th mm) in diameter. They certainly have no such efficiency in *Nucula* because the hypobranchial mucous glands present in all prosobranch gastropods are retained and this can only be for aggregation of particles that pass between the filaments. There is seldom such passage in other bivalves and these mucous glands are only retained in the most primitive of these animals.

Although possibly larger than is necessary for the respiratory needs of such relatively sluggish animals, these protobranch gills are primarily concerned with obtaining oxygen. Yet the pattern of things in bivalves with more complex gills already begins to be revealed. As in ciliary feeding gastropods, such as *Crepidula* (p. 82), the originally cleansing frontal and abfrontal cilia acquire a food collecting function. Intercepted particles are carried to the mid-line where the two gills are in contact and then, instead of being carried away as waste, the united stream (Fig. 84, B, ×) is passed forward towards the mouth but first passing between the palps.

These are impressive structures occupying much of the mantle cavity and consisting on each side of a pair of large flaps or lamellae with a long process attached to the hind end of the outer member of each pair. These processes are the actual feeding organs. They are extremely extensile with a groove lined with cilia and containing mucus glands running along the inner side. In life these processes extend well beyond the confines of the shell, actively groping within the substrate and collecting fine detrital particles which, inevitably mixed with inedible matter, are carried up the grooves and so between the lamellae. The inner surfaces of these are thrown into a series of alternate ridges and grooves, the surfaces of which are covered with a most elaborate succession of ciliated tracts. These are selective in function, the result of their activity being the separation of finer particles or mucus-laden

151

masses from larger ones, the former being carried across the ridges and into the simple mouth opening and the latter, mainly by way of the grooves, being conveyed on to the outer surface and so to that of the mantle. What little comes from the gills is added to what is collected by the appendages.

The rejected matter, with similar waste from all over the mantle surfaces, collects in the middle of the under surface in the form of 'pseudofaeces'. These accumulations are from time to time expelled by sudden contractions of the adductor muscles and this from the *inhalant* chamber; true faeces voided from the anus pass out in the exhalant stream. These cleansing activities, about which much will later be written, are vitally important to bivalves. We saw with what care the gastropods guard the respiratory chamber; in the bivalves where this also becomes a feeding chamber the problem is not to prevent particles from entering but the no less pressing one of removing the surplus of what is deliberately drawn in. This becomes a more pressing problem in the great majority of bivalves that feed directly with the gills than it does in *Nucula*.

A tubular œsophagus leads into a somewhat top-shaped stomach (Fig. 84) the upper region of which is largely lined with cuticle forming a kind of gizzard which squeezes edible matter into a complex of digestive tubules. What remains, largely mineral particles, passes into the lower, tapering region where it is mixed with mucus. In the great majority of bivalves this 'protostyle' is replaced by a firm revolving gelatinous rod, the crystalline style, already noted (p. 83) as present in the ciliary feeding slipper limpet, *Crepidula*. The nature and functions of the style are described in the next chapter. In *Nucula* the mucus prevents the sharp mineral particles in the faeces from damaging the intestinal wall and also provides the substance for the characteristic faecal pellets that are finally discharged through the anus. If these faeces were extruded in a loose flocculent condition they might well foul the elaborate ciliary mechanisms in the mantle cavity. They are usually so very firmly compacted as long to resist decay and so characteristically sculptured that it is often possible to determine the genus or even the species of the bivalves that produced pellets identified in sediments dredged from the sea bed. This 'biodeposition' can be highly significant.

A few words about other internal organs in bivalves (Fig. 79); these are typically molluscan, an auricle connected with each gill running inwards to open into a central ventricle which lies in a pericardium out of which kidneys extend forward and then turn back to open above the gills so that all excrement is removed in the outflowing current. The paired gonads open by way of the kidneys in *Nucula* and other simpler bivalves, but in the greater majority they open directly into the exhalant cavity. Withdrawal from their fellow bivalves within a completely enclosing shell removes any possibility of internal fertilization (a further reason why bivalves cannot pass on to land) so that sperm are always discharged freely into the sea, occasionally to fertilize eggs retained in the mantle cavity where they are then incubated. Finally, most bivalves are always of the one sex, a few are hermaphrodite while some have the unusual capacity of alternating, being first of one sex then of the other.

Bivalves maintain what contact they have with the environment by way of the mantle margins. For this reason the functions of the head (cerebral) nerve ganglia are largely taken over by the pleural ganglia which receive nerve impulses from the mantle. Only in a few bivalves, including the archaic *Nucula*, do separate cerebral ganglia persist (possibly due to the need for controlling the activities of the large palps); in almost all bivalves there are single composite cerebro-pleural ganglia.

Taking *Nucula nucleus*, which inhabits deposits of thick muddy sand mixed with gravel, as our example (Fig. 84), we can now view these animals in life. Laid upon its particular substrate, the animal quickly protrudes the foot, the retractors relaxed and blood is forced terminally by contraction of the appropriate muscles. The foot which is characteristically cleft on the under side probes down and then forward and upward (Fig. 84) the two halves opening out so that they grip the substrate. This type of foot is unique to these proto-branchs; in other bivalves the foot bulges terminally. It was this feature which gave the early malacologists the mistaken impression that *Nucula* crawls by what they described as a 'creeping sole'. After separation, the halves come together as the foot withdraws and only after a few of such probing movements does the foot proceed first to penetrate and then to grip the substrate with the retractors contracting and so first erecting the animal and then, in successive movements, pulling it gradually down. But it only penetrates until the front end is thinly covered (Fig. 84). Movement then ceases while sudden ejections of water from the hind end create a cavity in the substrate. The animal can now both respire and feed. With the valves adequately apart, the lateral cilia on the gill filaments draw in a stream of water through the thin covering of mud (no more than a millimetre thick) above the uppermost surface of the shell, water being expelled into the depression behind (Fig. 84). At the same time the palp processes protrude and search through the substrate passing a stream of material along the grooves to be sorted between the palp lamellae. How much discrimination these processes exercise, taking what is organic and edible and not what is inorganic, is difficult to determine. The animals may remain in the same position for days on end, the mound of accumulated faeces at the hind end from time to time driven clear by sudden contractions of the adductors which also maintain the cavity of the pit.

Such a state of affairs may well resemble the initial bivalve habit. Personal views are that the earliest molluscs lived on a hard surface for the further exploitation of which both the chitons and the earlier gastropods were concerned. Only some of the latter, such as the long-spired *Turritella* and the bulbous *Natica* with its distensible foot, subsequently became adapted for penetrating soft substrates and exploiting their rich supplies of food and possibilities for protection. But the whole form of the bivalves, with laterally-compressed hinged shell, similarly compressed foot, regression of head, with the palps and later the gills taking over food collection, unite in fitting the entire class for infaunal life in soft substrates. Later, it is true, many, such as common mussels and the oysters, become surface dwelling or epifaunal. But this is a secondary mode of life attained in ways to be described in the next chapter. At this stage we have outlined the basic structure of bivalves, postulated how this may have arisen and noted, in *Nucula*, the manner in which very early bivalves may well have lived.

Chapter 13

Evolution and adaptation of bivalves

*

STARTING far back in the Palaeozoic with bivalves having very similar shells and possibly very similar habits to those of living nuculid protobranchs, the aim of this chapter is to indicate the changes that produced the modern bivalves. First, however, we should mention independent developments within the protobranchs because they had by no means shot all evolutionary bolts with production of the nuculids. They began, like the remaining bivalves, by moving the site of water intake to the hind end below the exhalant opening. This is a basic bivalve character and one of the keys to their immense success. They can then penetrate sand or mud 'head first' with the hind end in free communication with the water above, in these protobranchs for oxygen, in other bivalves also for food. By extensions of the mantle at this end, siphons were formed which enabled the animals to live deeper and deeper under the surface.

Although they never live far below the surface, this second, nuculanid, group of protobranchs develop siphons as shown in the figure of *Malletia* (Fig. 85). But their unique feature resides in the gills which evolve in an

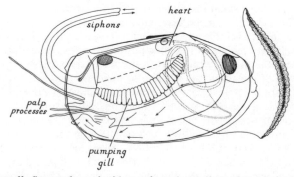

FIG. 85. Laterally flattened nuculanid protobranch, *Malletia obtusata*, foot extended and siphons projecting above, with elongated palps and backward extending processes and enlarged 'pumping' gill. The broken line indicates the position of the axis when drawn up.

extraordinary fashion. The filaments do not increase in number, as do those of the lamellibranchs we shall shortly be describing, but each one dilates so that the total length increases. Each such filament makes intimate contact, by ciliary means, with those on either side of it, with the inner side of the

154

corresponding filament on the other gill and on the outside with the mantle surface. The result is a membrane that separates the inhalant and exhalant chambers far more effectively than in *Nucula* because only pierced by a series of small openings each lined with upward beating lateral cilia. About every half minute the entire membranous gill is drawn up by contraction of muscles in the axes and suspending membranes to produce a sudden inrush of water through the inhalant, and a corresponding expulsion through the exhalant, opening. This flow is for respiration; these gills have minimal concern with feeding which remains the business of the palps with their long groping processes and selective grooved processes (Fig. 85).

This highly modified gill is common to all species of these nuculanid protobranchs. These are typically members of cold and even abyssal seas although the largest species occur in shallow water. The only one that is common in British waters, *Nuculana* (*Leda*) *minuta*, which has a characteristically elongated shell occurs off Scotland in depths of from 20 to 200 metres usually in gravelly mud. The Norwegian fjords are the best source of such animals which include the flattened *Malletia obtusata* we have just mentioned (Fig. 85). It is a little over 1 cm long and almost as deep and is one of the most beautiful of bivalvès. Composed largely of periostracum, the shell is translucent so that all that goes on within the mantle cavity including the up and down movements of the gills can be observed in the intact animal. *Malletia* has long siphons which arch forward as the animal moves forward a little below and parallel with the surface. As in all related animals, there is a single, presumably, sensory tentacle which projects from the hind end between the siphons above and the palp processes below (Fig. 85).

The most significant and largest of such bivalves are the various species of *Yoldia*, up to 8 cm long, which are common in shallow water especially in the north Pacific. They burrow vertically with the siphons and palp appendages projecting clear of the bottom (Fig. 86). With more organic debris available

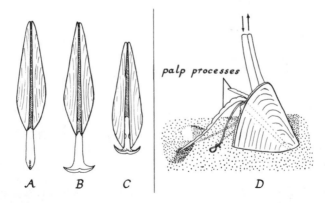

FIG. 86. Nuculanid protobranch ,*Yoldia limatula*: A, B, C, stages in protrusion of the foot during burrowing; D, animal *in situ* with siphons, palp processes and sensory tentacle extended above surface. (After Drew)

here than in deeper water, these animals are more stationary than the constantly moving *Malletia*. What movements there are tend to be vertical. These are the most successful of nuculanid protobranchs and are able, like the nuculids, to compete adequately with other shallow water bivalves, at least where there are adequate supplies of organic matter with the bacteria and other microscopic life that lives on it. Species of *Yoldia* are also among the commonest of recent fossils, giving their name to a stage in the formation of the Baltic Sea. There can only be mentioned in passing the existence of totally different protobranchs, species of *Solemya* occurring commonly in the Mediterranean, off the east coast of North America and in the Pacific. Here the gills are very large and the palps excessively small, the former certainly the means of feeding. These bivalves have many unique features including an intucking of the lower and uncalcified margins of the shell when the valves close.

We now come to the far and away more numerous lamellibranch bivalves, the most successful exploiters of the primary plant produce of plankton in the animal kingdom. As shown in the accompanying figure (Fig. 87), the gills are out of all proportion larger than those of *Nucula* (Fig. 84) forming four deep lamellae (hence lamellibranch) which stretch between the adductors and occupy almost the entire depth within the large mantle cavity. Collecting suspended planktonic food, they replace the palp processes as the feeding or-

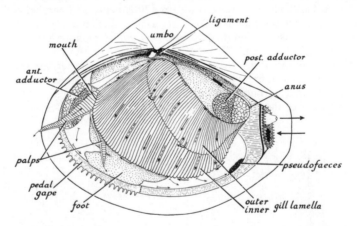

FIG. 87. Basket-shell, *Corbula gibba*: lateral view after removal of left valve and mantle lobe showing general structure of a lamellibranch bivalve. Plain arrows indicate direction of frontal currents on the upper surface of the gill lamellae, broken arrows those on under surfaces, feathered arrows the direction of cleansing currents on the mantle surface collecting pseudofaeces.

gans. The filaments increase greatly in numbers while each is many times the length of the short horizontal protobranch filament. As shown in the explanatory figure (Fig. 88) each one stretches down and then bends back forming 'descending' and 'ascending' arms so that the former straight

156

horizontal partition between lower, inhalant and upper, exhalant chambers now becomes a deep 'W' on each side.

This impressive linear extension of the filaments, each supported internally by a corresponding extension of the skeletal rods, involves increase in the current-producing lateral cilia and the originally cleansing frontal cilia. Much more water is now drawn into the mantle cavity than is needed for respiratory purposes, particularly low in any case in a group of at best very slowly moving and often completely immobile animals. The appearance of the complex multiple latero-frontal cilia (Fig. 89), noted earlier as distinguishing the filaments of *Nucula* from those of gastropods, gives to this elaborate and extensive sieving surface a selective capacity down to particles of about one micron (1/1000th of a millimetre) in diameter. So very little material can now pass between the filaments that, with a very few exceptions among the most primitive lamellibranch bivalves, none of these animals has mucus glands in the exhalant chamber as there are in *Nucula* (Fig. 84). Suspended particles, above all microscopic members of the plant plankton, are thrown by the latero-frontal cilia on to the frontal surfaces of the filaments (Figs. 89 and 90). (The upper, abfrontal, surfaces now face one another between the arms of the filament losing their cilia and ceasing to be significant). The long tracts of originally cleansing frontal cilia thus take over complete responsibility for

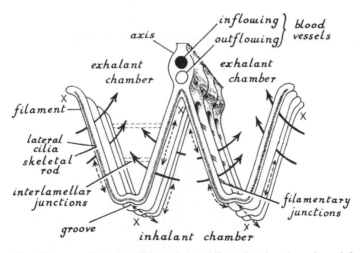

FIG. 88. Diagram of the lamellibranch ctenidium showing the axis and four filaments on each side. For greater clarity the descending and ascendng arms of each lamella have been separated. Positions of interlamellar junctions which unite these arms and of interfilamentary junctions which unite filaments into coherent lamellae are indicated. Water currents created by the lateral cilia shown by solid arrows, possible directions of frontal currents by broken arrows. Crosses indicate regions where currents carrying material longitudinally (i.e. to or from mouth) *may* occur. Primitive (filibranch) condition of blood vessels in the axis shown; nerves and muscles not shown.

food collection. They convey particles, aggregated in the mucus produced when these impinge on the frontal surface, either upward to the gill axis between the rows of filaments and to the upper ends of the ascending filaments at either side, or else downward to the lower margin of the lamellae (i.e. all regions marked with an 'x' in Fig. 88). Conducting grooves develop along one or both of these margins. Although conditions vary very widely in different groups of lamellibranch bivalves, anteriorly directed currents which will carry material to the mouth may exist on all five or on at least three of these marginal tracts. Currents in the opposite direction carry particles to join other waste for expulsion as pseudofaeces.

This is the general picture of the lamellibranch ctenidium. It exists in various stages of consolidation. The descending and ascending arms of the filaments which together constitute a lamella are attached by way of 'inter-lamellar' tissue bridges (Fig. 88). Adjacent filaments are most simply attached, like those of *Nucula*, by 'interfilamentary' junctions consisting of interlocking cilia. Such filaments are easily separated but as readily re-attach to form a coherent membrane. This type of union occurs in the gills of the more primitive lamellibranchs and is termed *filibranch*. It is replaced in the majority of bivalves by a more coherent structure, the filaments firmly united by fusion of their tissues, to be separated only by irrevocable tearing. Such is the *eulamellibranch* gill. Blood enters from the axis to flow through the cavities within the filaments (Fig. 88) and be recollected in vessels also in the axis in the filibranchs but duplicated and running along the fused margins of the ascending lamellae in the eulamellibranchs.

In the simpler lamellibranch gills (and in all filibranchs) the filaments are all similar but in the more complex gills larger 'principal' filaments appear at

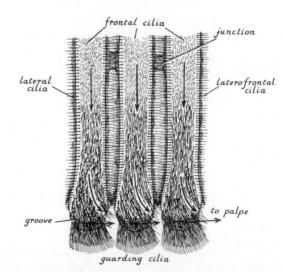

FIG. 89.   *Corbula gibba*, lateral view of the margin of a gill lamella.

158

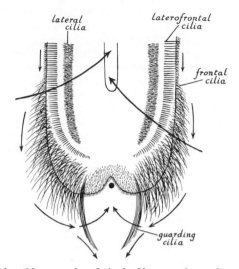

FIG. 90. *Corbula gibba*, margin of single filament shown in section with groove and major tracts of cilia.

regular intervals their two arms very intimately united. Such a gill appears as a series of low crests represented by some twenty or thirty ordinary filaments separated by depressions occupied by principal filaments. Frontal ciliation is often different on the two types of filament. Such a gill is termed plicate.

We have noted the differences in the direction of ciliary streams on the frontal surfaces, in some there are actually *two* sets of frontal cilia, longer ones that carry larger particles for eventual rejection in the pseudofaeces (Fig. 87) and rows of smaller ones that convey smaller particles in the opposite direction towards palps and mouth. But there is always some initial sorting on the gills often assisted by muscular contractions largely within the gill axis which 'blow' material off the surface of the gills. The free margin of some or all of the lamellae is often grooved (Figs. 88 and 90), the depression over-arched by guarding, sometimes impressively fan-like, cilia (Figs. 89 and 90). Outer filaments are attached to the mantle surface and inner ones to the body initially by ciliary junctions and later by tissue fusion.

The finally elaborated eulamellibranch gill, coming let it again be empha-sized from the relatively simple and purely respiratory organ we described in the gastropods, is a highly elaborate and most intimately united ciliated meshwork through which water is drawn in relatively enormous quantities. This flow is controlled in part by way of the muscular inner folds of the mantle margin (Fig. 82) and in part by restriction of the space between the filaments by contraction of contained muscle. Thus in an adult American oyster the water flow may vary between 10 and over 24 litres per hour. There is wide variation in gill form; some bivalves have only the one lamella (or demi-branch as they are usually termed) on each side, or the outer one may be reflected upward. There is even, as we shall see in Chapter 16, change from a ciliated gill to a muscular septum with ciliated pores and functioning somewhat like the pumping gill of *Malletia* (Fig. 85) and other nuculanid protobranchs, but the lamellibranchs so equipped are carnivores.

Although the palps are no longer feeding organs they retain the equally vital role of selection. Everything that is collected on the surface of the gills passes between their ridged inner surfaces exposed to the action of a complexity of ciliary currents. The end result of their action, aided in some degree by muscular exposure or closure of the intervening grooves, is that smaller particles or mucus-laden masses are passed over the crests of the ridges to the mouth and larger ones are passed into the grooves. From there they pass to the margin of the palps and so on to the mantle surface for later extrusion in the pseudofaeces. The palps are supremely efficient in their selective activities.

Although much else, if small enough, enters the small mouth, it is the plant plankton of diatoms, peridinians and the still smaller green flagellates – the true meadows of the sea – which are the food of the great majority of bivalves although a number, like the protobranchs, very successfully feed on finely divided bottom deposits. Drawn in by the gills, selected there and on the palps, food passes into the mouth and so into the impressively complicated cavity of the stomach, the precise working of which it has taken the labours of many malacologists fully to interpret. The protostyle we saw in *Nucula* (it is the same in the nuculanids) now becomes a firm gelatinous rod lying initially in a groove of the intestine which may become completely cut off to form a separate 'style-sac'. The style is formed by a ridge of cells along one side and is moulded into shape by the action of a covering of unusually stout cilia on the general surface. Beating transverse to their length, these cilia cause the style to rotate (in an anticlockwise direction when viewed from the stomach end). This is one of the very few structures in the animal kingdom that revolves; it is also the supreme product of this interaction between cilia and mucus production that is so characteristic of the molluscs (bar the cephalopods).

The head of the style beats against a cuticular structure known as the gastric shield which occupies varying areas of the stomach wall. The shield is also, surprisingly, a source of digestive enzymes. Other such enzymes, largely concerned with breakdown of carbohydrates within the plant food, are contained in the substance of the style and are liberated when the head of this dissolves in the stomach. This loss is made good by formation of new material in the style-sac, the style being continuously pushed forward. As it revolves it helps to draw in, like rope over a capstan, the mucus-laden streams of food selected by the palps. These are then mixed with the other contents of the stomach, including these liberated enzymes – altogether a unique and very efficient mechanism. In those species in which the style lies in a groove alongside the intestine (oysters are included in them) it dissolves when the bivalve is out of water. Formation but not dissolution then ceases. Where it lies in a separate sac it can resist unfavourable conditions (such as starvation if kept in filtered sea water) indefinitely, only the head end becoming semi-fluid. As

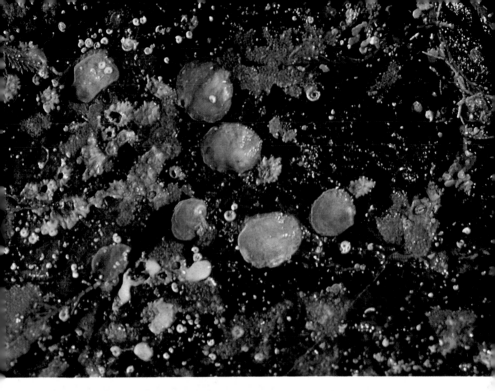

PLATE 11. *Above*, saddle oysters, *Anomia ephippium*, closely adherent to rock surface. *Below*, scallop, *Pecten maximus;* mantle margins showing eyes and tentacles on middle fold; pigmented inner folds behind.

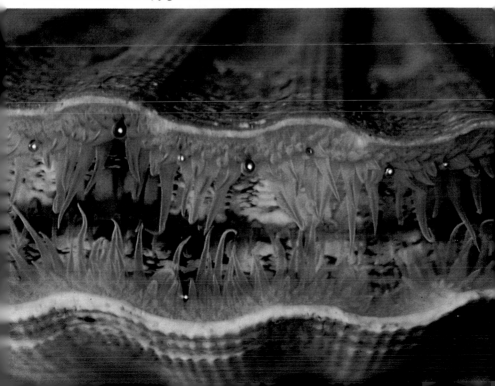

PLATE 12. *Above*, lesser octopus, *Eledone cirrhosa*, shown crawling on rocks. *Below*, side view of squid, *Illex coindeti;* stream-lined body with terminal fin; funnel facing forward below eye.

noted earlier, a style – with a gastric shield – occurs in certain gastropods, but only in those that also feed, usually although not always by ciliary means, on plant plankton or else on very finely divided vegetable matter, as do the strombid conchs and the spider shells (p. 89).

During this mixing and digestion, the stomach contents come under the influence of ciliary tracts that cover all areas of the stomach wall except those occupied by the shield. There is an extraordinary complexity of outpouchings and of sorting areas, of parallel ridges and grooves, acting on much the same principles as the grooved faces of the palps. Large particles are carried over the crests and smaller ones at right angles along the intervening grooves. Complexity is such that a suggested classification of the bivalves has been based on major differences between different stomach patterns. It is impossible to describe these; one can only indicate the ends achieved. Finer particles and digested matter are drawn into ducts leading into the brown mass of digestive tubules (the digestive gland or 'liver') which surrounds the stomach. What is dissolved is there absorbed and fine particles are taken into the cells for digestion. All indigestible matter is later returned into the stomach where it joins material too coarse to enter the ducts, all passing into a deep groove that leads into the intestine. This is long and coiled (as in *Nucula*), its major function the consolidation of its contents into the characteristic faecal pellets that leave the anus to be swept away in the outgoing current.

The original bivalve must have resembled *Nucula* in the freedom of the two mantle lobes. This is true of some modern bivalves including the scallops but in the great majority (including the nuculanid protobranchs) some degree of marginal fusion occurs leading to conditions where the animal becomes almost completely enclosed even when the valves are open. Fusion of the mantle margins is a prime factor in bivalve evolution.

Fusion proceeds in stages, the same in both the development of the individual and in evolutionary history. It is initially confined to the inner (muscular) folds (Fig. 82), then the middle (sensory) folds become involved and finally fusion extends to the inner surface of the outer folds so including the regions that form the superficial periostracum. If the *outer* surfaces also united this would involve fusion of the outer calcareous layers of the valves rendering them immovable. Fusion first occurs at the hind end between the upper region of outflow and the under (ventral) region where water is drawn in. Such separation became essential when this region of intake was transferred from the anterior end. It occurs, as we saw, in the nuculanids, first by ciliary attachment, then by tissue fusion, but always by the latter method in the lamellibranchs. Fusion next occurs at the base of the inhalant opening separating this from the pedal gape further forward where the foot is protruded and which varies in size according to that of the foot. There are normally these three apertures, increased for various reasons to four in a few bivalves.

Many bivalves possess siphons that protrude at the hind end so that, to a depth controlled by their length, they can penetrate deep into the substrate while still drawing in and expelling water at the surface. The siphon in the neogastropods enabled water to be drawn in for respiration while the carnivorous animal sought its food below the surface. In bivalves both food and oxygen are contained in the powerful inhalant current and penetration is purely for protection. The siphons represent posterior extensions of the mantle margins and are formed in one of the three ways just described. If composed solely of the inner (muscular) mantle folds they are active and are free from one another. If the middle (sensory) mantle folds are also involved then the two tubes are united and their openings fringed with an outer ring of tentacles (occasionally also with eyes). The inner mantle fold forms a ring of sieving tentacles around the inhalant opening and a membrane which concentrates and directs the outflowing current around the exhalant opening. Where the inner surface of the outer fold is incorporated, then the siphon is covered with stout periostracum. This is true in all the larger deep burrowing bivalves, coming from several different groups. It was the presence of this protective coat that enabled them to become deep burrowers. Enlargement of the mantle margins to form siphons involves increase in the pallial muscles at the hind end. These siphonal muscles are attached around an embayment or sinus into which the siphons can be withdrawn and the presence of such a sinus in a fossil shell reveals that this possibly long extinct bivalve had siphons and so must have burrowed. Siphons are extended by pressure of water in the mantle cavity, their openings closed during the process.

Cleansing is all-important; the elaborate ciliary mechanisms *must* be kept free of sediment if they are to function. Ciliated tracts on the surface of the body and of the mantle carry away material that falls on to them out of suspension or is passed on to them from the gills and palps to accumulate at the entrance into the *inhalant* chamber; at the base of the inhalant siphon if the animal has one. These accumulations of aptly-named false or pseudo-faeces are from time to time expelled by sudden contractions of the adductor muscles. These are composed of distinct groups of fibres, inner ones of quickly contracting striated fibres and outer ones of smooth fibres which contract more slowly but can maintain contraction over long periods with minimal expenditure of energy. These 'quick' and 'catch' muscles provide respectively for the sudden cleansing contractions and for the sustained closure needed for protection against enemies and, in animals which may be exposed on the shore, against the effects of exposure.

The bivalve foot consists of layers of circular, longitudinal and cross muscles surrounding a capacious blood space. Movement is produced by blood pressure created by appropriate muscular contractions. Although it comes to assume other highly important functions, the foot is primarily concerned with penetration through soft substrates by a series of movements constituting a digging cycle. Placed on a suitable substrate, E. R. Trueman has shown that a bivalve proceeds to burrow into this in a series of stages. As shown in Fig. 91, with adductors relaxed (a) the foot probes downward, the siphons closing and the foot extending to its maximum length (b). It begins to dilate terminally so forcing the now unanchored shell slightly upward. The adductors suddenly contract (c) forcing water from the mantle cavity through the pedal gape and assisting penetration. Meanwhile blood pressure has completed the terminal dilation of the foot which forms a *pedal anchorage*. Contraction of the anterior pedal retractor muscles (d) begins to pull the

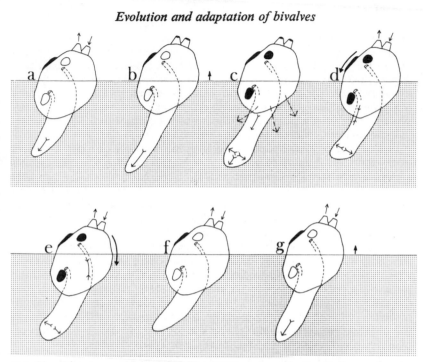

FIG. 91. Diagrams, explained in text, showing stages in the digging cycle of a typical bivalve. (Modified after Trueman, Brand & Davies)

animal forward on this anchor while the shell rotates in the direction indicated by the large arrow. After this the siphons reopen. Contraction of the posterior retractors follows (e) causing the shell to rotate in the opposite direction, further working its way down to complete the cycle. The adductors now relax (f) and, under the action of the ligament, the valves separate, pressing against the substrate to form a *shell or penetration anchorage*. This is released when the adductors contract. Anchorage is often aided, especially during the characteristic rocking movements with which each cycle usually ends, by the surface sculpture of ridges or projections on the valves. A stationary period (g) follows when the foot probes prior to starting a new digging cycle. Some bivalves are constantly active, others find a suitable place and there, if nothing happens to disturb them, they remain for long periods. The form of the foot varies according to the form of the shell and the nature of the substrate, the distinctive outward spread of the cleft foot in *Nucula* and other protobranchs which is under muscular control appears as a substitute for blood pressure which may there be too low.

More has to be added about the foot but only after some description of development. In the great majority of bivalves the eggs are fertilized and develop in the sea, first into trochophore larvae and then into bivalved veliger larvae (Fig. 101). The major exceptions are polar species where the season

163

may be too short for larvae to develop in the sea and in abyssal bivalves where there is no plant plankton and the journey to surface and back is impossible. In such animals yolk is stored within enlarged eggs which then develop, like those of higher gastropods but here in the mantle cavity, into the adult form. The unusual conditions in oysters are mentioned later. In a few bivalves of temperate shallow waters, change to the adult form occurs actually within the gills while development in the major freshwater bivalves (not our concern) involves parasitic stages on fishes.

In a typical bivalve, however, the fertilized egg develops into a ciliated trochophore on the surface of which, as in other molluscs, a 'shell gland' appears which forms a somewhat saddle-shaped cuticular shell which later calcifies in two symmetrical areas right and left of the mid-line where the ligament develops. As shown in Fig. 101, the veliger larva has now formed, the large velum protruding between the valves. This temporary structure pushes the mouth backward and, beyond it, the rudiments of the foot. This is ciliated and removes surplus matter passed to the mouth by the collecting cilia around the base of the velum. The anus opens into the mantle cavity which will spread all round the under surface when the velum is lost. At this stage the valves are D-shaped with a long line of attachment, only later does this reduce when the ligament and hinge assume the adult form. The rapidly revolving style can be seen through the still transparent valves, also the developing nervous system and often an eye, of importance while the larva is planktonic and responding to the influence of light.

Structure gradually changes until, after a period depending ᴜn the species and the prevailing temperature, behaviour alters: the larvae shun light, are attracted by gravity and drop to the bottom. They are now due to metamorphose into the very different adult form. This involves enlargement of the foot (even though it may soon after be lost) which now assumes the locomotory functions of the disappearing velum. The swimming veliger has become a crawling pediveliger. A gland, possibly of similar origin to the pedal mucus glands in gastropods, now appears at the base of the foot. This highly significant byssus gland produces a fluid protein which is directed by way of a groove along the under side of the foot to set, as a result of 'tanning', as tough attaching threads. Such byssal attachment which occurs in the common mussel as well as in a wide variety of other bivalves is an admirable form of attachment to rocks or stones. Initially, however, it has nothing whatever to do with the adult but only with the settling larvae. Whatever their adult habit may be, bivalve larvae need a brief period of attachment during the complex process of metamorphosis. This takes place when, sinking from the surface waters, the larvae seek their particular adult substrate which may be widespread or, if it be wood, for instance, or some other localized habitat, be very restricted. The larva may happen to fall directly on to 'fertile' ground but often must drift for some time dependent on chance to bring it there; failure to do so within this 'latent' period means death.

But when 'ecologically satisfied', the byssus gland comes into action, the thread or threads it forms holding the minute animal during the complex process when the velum goes, gills and palps appear, the shell changes in form and the foot assumes its definitive form. After this the byssus gland often disappears In other cases, involving bivalves from widely different groups, it persists to become an organ concerned with the permanent attachment of the adult animal. Such retention of a larval structure into adult life, a process known as neoteny, has occurred in many animal groups with major effects on the course of evolution. In these bivalves it has involved abandonment of the primitive burrowing infaunal habit to exploit the possibilities of surface, or epifaunal, life. This has had major effects on body form and so on habit.

In an unattached bivalve we saw how form depends on the vagaries of secretion of calcium carbonate around the curve of the mantle margins to produce shells which may be rounded, elongate or oval in outline, also be asymmetrical if the transverse component in growth differs on the two sides. Such changes in the form of the shell have, however, only secondary effects on the enclosed body although this has to conform to them. This is very clearly shown in the razor shells as we see later. But when the animal becomes permanently attached by byssus threads – and we are now thinking in terms of the immense periods of time involved in evolutionary change – the position is very different.

This is a matter requiring a little explanation. The simplest case of byssal attachment is that provided by the Noah's ark shell, *Arca tetragona* (Fig. 93). Here the animal is attached by a broad byssus issuing along the under surface of the shell which, although somewhat flattened, remains equivalve, with front and hind ends about the same size. But shell form can alter just as much in byssally attached as in free bivalves, and by the chances of genetic variation either end can enlarge at the expense of the other. In byssally attached bivalves anterior enlargement is unknown; it would not be viable because it would reduce the all-important inhalant and exhalant openings at the hind end. No such variation would stand any chance of being selected. It is just the opposite where the hind end is enlarged; this represents a major improvement over the original condition. When, as in *Arca*, the shell is pressed so firmly down that the inhalant opening is reduced then some water has to be drawn in anteriorly (Fig. 93), but when the hind end is enlarged both inhalant and exhalant openings are increased in size and raised well clear of the bottom with reduced danger from sediment.

As we shall see in the next chapter, the triangular mussel form so achieved is one of the supreme successes in bivalve evolution. In contrast with what happens in free bivalves, attachment (during the evolutionary process) involves constraint and the anterior regions of the enclosed body are just as much reduced as are those of the mantle and shell. This is particularly true of the muscles. From the original condition with two adductor muscles of about the same size (isomyarian) change is made to a dissimilar muscle (heteromyarian) condition which is characteristic of all mussels (Fig. 93).

This is far from the end of the story; the posterior muscle continues to enlarge and the anterior one to diminish until it disappears. The bivalve has now become single muscled or monomyarian which involves radical changes with this enlarged muscle assuming a central position and viscera and gills reorganized in a semicircle around it. Byssal attachment persists but with an ncreasing tendency to fall over on the one side with many, such as oysters and scallops, coming to lie horizontally. A new symmetry now appears the implications of which we explore in the next chapter.

Bivalves, then, are initially fitted for life within the various grades of soft deposits that cover much of the ocean floor and elaboration of the organs of respiration has enabled them to exploit plant plankton with supreme success. By retaining the means of larval attachment they have also successfully returned to epifaunal life on hard surfaces while others evolved siphons and penetrated deeply into soft substrates, some to bore into stone or timber. What about classification? This raises problems. Gastropods divide up into subclasses with ascending degrees of complexity. In bivalves there are major differences between protobranchs (composed, however, of two very different groups) and lamellibranchs. But filibranchs, eulamellibranchs and septibranchs tend to merge the one into the other. There are certainly differences in shell structure and in dentition which are equally valid for fossils but differences in the form of the stomach, like that of the gills, are obviously only valuable for classifying living bivalves. An early attempt was made at dividing the bivalves into three divisions according to habit, namely those that live in shallow water and are motile, those that are attached and those that burrow deeply or bore into rock. But this breaks down completely because bivalves reach the same end point of habit (and similarity of appearance) by all manner of different routes. In no animal group is such 'convergence' so common. The five deepest burrowers, superficially very similar, belong to dissimilar groups while members of no less than seven different groups have become specialized as rock borers.

The bivalves divide up satisfactorily into a number of superfamilies each with a convincing assemblage of basic characteristics which are unaffected by diversity in habit. The problem is the extent to which these can be grouped into orders and these into subclasses. The two first superfamilies, although widely separate, can be grouped under the subclass Protobranchia, the remainder under the Lamellibranchia. For the purposes of this book, concerned with living animals, we have to deal with lamellibranch superfamilies in very arbitrary fashion, partly keeping to accepted classification but more often grouping together animals with similar habits, such as borers. The result is apparent in the chapters that follow where we proceed from the primitive ark shells to the familiar mussels, scallops and oysters, all influenced by byssal attachment or cementation, then to the host of shallow burrowers and to the deep burrowers and the borers, both so diverse in membership. We conclude with the suitably named anomalous bivalves (Anomalodesmata) which lead up to the carnivorous septibranchs and the extraordinary watering-pot shells with minute valves embedded in a massive calcareous tube. Bivalves will be revealed as hardly less varied in form and habit than the more immediately arresting gastropods.

Chapter 14

Ark shells, mussels, fan and file shells, scallops and oysters

*

ALTHOUGH early lamellibranch bivalves probably burrowed superficially much as does *Nucula*, the immediately obvious bivalves on exposed shores the world over are the byssally attached or else cemented mussels, scallops and 'oysters' of one kind or another. Such animals, largely inter-related, appearing early in the fossil record and many of them supremely successful, are largely a story to themselves which is most suitably related now before proceeding to animals of more primitive habit, the unattached burrowers and the bivalves that evolved from them.

The first group is one of world importance although very poorly represented in British waters, namely the ark shells (Arcacea). They are unmistakable owing to the wide separation of the umbones with a broad 'deck' between them giving the appearance of a boat when viewed from either end (Fig. 92). The long hinge line bears a series of many similar teeth; the arks are taxodont like *Nucula* a character which distinguishes them from all other lamellibranchs. Unlike any of the other bivalves described in this chapter, although some, including British, species are byssally attached, the most numerous are superficial burrowers. The Noah's ark shell, *Arca tetragona*, found along southern coasts is the sole example found intertidally in Great Britain. No animal is attached by more massive byssus. This emerges from the under side of the long foot, extending for almost the entire length of the flattened under surface of the shell which runs parallel to the hinge line above (Fig. 93). The shell, up to 4·5 cm long, is broad and is usually to be found within rock crevices where it is both difficult to see and even more difficult to tear off.

FIG. 92.   Ark shell, *Anadara senilis*, viewed from hind end showing 'boat' shape with separated overarching umbones. (Drawing V. Warrender)

167

Apart from flattening of the under surface, byssal attachment has had little effect on general form, the two adductors remaining very similar in size. But restricted space at the hind end has made it necessary to draw in some water in front of the foot whereas in the unattached tropical arcids the inflowing current is entirely at the hind end.

Although ark shells of similar attached habit occur in warm and tropical seas they are greatly outnumbered (in individuals if not in species) by un-attached 'cockles' as they are often locally termed and which they generally resemble in both form and habit, burrowing superficially in muddy sand. The largest of these, the almost globular 'bloody cockle',* *Anadara senilis* (Fig. 92), up to 14 cm in general diameter occurs in estuaries along the shores of tropical West Africa where it has been a major food since prehistoric times. It moves very slowly by means of a purely locomotory foot coming frequently to rest with the inhalant and exhalant openings at the posterior end just flush with the surface. Smaller species about the same size as our common cockle, are equally abundant in the Indo-Pacific and are collected as food along the mangrove-lined shores of the Straits of Malacca and similar regions.

Wherever the sea bottom has a coarse covering of shell gravel (denoting considerable water movement) there are species of the dog cockle, *Glycymeris* (Fig. 93), immediately recognizable as arcids by the taxodont dentition and the characteristic 'chevron' ligament although the umbones are not widely separated. These animals have been noted as the most symmetrical of bivalves – fore and aft as well as from side to side – and they are perfectly adapted for life in shell gravel. They lie usually on their sides and, like *Nucula*, draw in water through the open substrate but here at the hind as well as at the front end and, of course, as a source of suspended food as well as oxygen. The common British species, *G. glycymeris*, thick shelled and about 5 cm in diameter with characteristic brown markings, may be found washed up.

Front and hind ends of arcids are usually not dissimilar but conditions are very different in the invariably attached mussels (Mytilacea) (cf. Fig. 93, A, C). No shell is better known than that of the common mussel, *Mytilus edulis*, pointed anteriorly and high and rounded behind. The umbo is anterior and the ligament extends backward from it at an acute angle to the flat under surface. There are no true teeth. A very small anterior adductor contrasts with a massive rounded muscle at the other end. This triangular mussel form attained, here and in unrelated groups of bivalves, as a consequence of byssal attachment has been a major success. Secured by byssus threads planted by the elongated foot like the guy ropes of a tent, the animal can align itself to the forces of the sea while the raised hind end allows ample entrance for an inflowing current created by gills that curl upward around the base of the large adductor. The outgoing current issues above and well clear of this (see arrows in Fig. 93, C). The widely attached pedal muscles are largely concerned with pulling against the opposing attachment of the byssal threads.

On rocky substrates no bivalves are commoner. The larvae settle and meta-morphose and then move upward before attaching semi-permanently in some

---

* So called on account of the presence, unusual in any mollusc, of the red blood pigment haemoglobin.

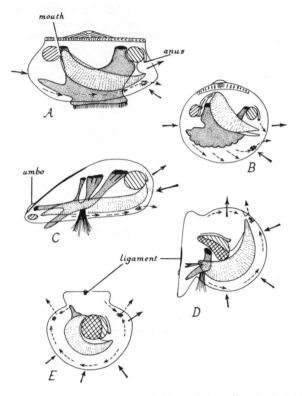

FIG. 93. Semi-diagrammatic side views (left) of A, byssally attached Noah's ark shell, *Arca tetragona*; B, free living dog cockle, *Glycymeris glycymeris* (both with adductor muscles of similar size); C. common mussel, *Mytilus edulis*, showing unequal sized adductors (heteromyarian condition); D, byssally attached pearl oyster, *Pinctada*, body reorganized around solitary (posterior) adductor; E, free living scallop, *Pecten maximus*, with horizontally disposed valves (both monomyarian).

depression or between adult mussels; if detached they again become motile before new threads are planted. Young individuals climb the vertical face of an aquarium tank by extending the foot, planting byssus threads and pulling upward on these, the animal parting from them when the next higher series has been planted.

Few bivalves are so widely distributed as the common mussel which has been carried from Europe all over the northern hemisphere attached to the bottoms of ships. Along the Californian coast it co-exists with the larger, rougher shelled *M. californianus*. Both occur in dense masses, layers of animals united by interwoven byssal threads, the latter on fully exposed rocks, the European species in more sheltered water. There it may extend over and consolidate gravel beaches as it does in the Conway estuary in N.

Wales where a mussel fishery has long existed. Elsewhere mussels are cultivated, in France on stakes interwoven with brushwood in the shallow muddy
Anse de l'Aiguillon north of La Rochelle. The methods derive from those
initially devised by a Welshman named Walton who was wrecked in that
vicinity in 1235. The Dutch cultivate mussels by transplanting young ones to
richer feeding grounds while a most impressive industry has recently developed
in the sheltered fjords or rias of NW Spain where mussels are collected and
grown on ropes suspended from pontoons or catamarans. Different species
of mussels are eaten the world over.

The horse-mussel, *Modiolus modiolus*, is our largest mytilid, attaining
lengths of over 12 cm; it occurs low on the shore and in shallow water. In this
genus the umbo is not quite at the tip of the shell while the thick yellow-brown
periostracum is extended into marginal filaments, more impressively so in the
smaller *M. barbatus* of southern and western shores. Small, shore-living
species of *Musculus* are distinguished by their rhomboidal shape, the umbones
raised higher than in *Modiolus*. The most interesting is the greenish *M.
marmoratus* which occupies a byssally-formed nest within shells or in the hollow
holdfasts of brown seaweeds or lives embedded within the nest of simple
ascidians (sea-squirts).

Not all mussels live on the surface; species of *Modiolus* occur on peaty
substrates in estuaries while some tropical mytilids live hind end uppermost
in the soft mud of mangrove swamps within a cocoon of byssal threads. In
such 'endobyssate' animals the under surface is rounded instead of flat as it
is in *Mytilus* (and still more so in the totally unrelated freshwater mussel,

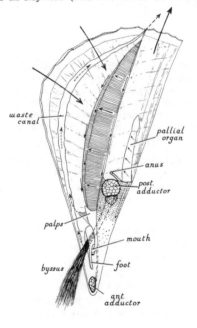

FIG. 94. Fan shell, *Pinna carnea*,
viewed from right side after removal
of valve and mantle lobe, showing
major structures with arrows indicating direction of major currents –
dotted arrows those on under surfaces of gill, broken arrows direction
of waste currents.

Dreissena). It has been claimed, partly on fossil evidence, that it was in this way that the mussel form evolved. But certainly in other groups this could not have been so, the heteromyarian condition there following attachment to a hard surface.

We face the same problem when considering the impressive fan shells (Pinnidae) comprising the genera *Pinna* (Fig. 94) and *Atrina* found the world over in shallow water. These are the largest heteromyarians and among the most impressive bivalves with many unique features. The British *P. fragilis*, once dug at low water of spring tides in the Salcombe inlet in south Devon, has now to be dredged. It is up to 30 cm long and about half that breadth; *P. carnea*, the 'Spanish oyster', common in very shallow water at Bermuda is slightly larger, while the Mediterranean *P. nobilis* initially described by Aristotle, is twice that length and some tropical species are still larger. In the form of a half opened fan, these animals live vertically embedded in sandy mud or gravel attached by long byssus threads to stones, the rounded posterior margins projecting above the surface. Underwater photographs reveal the existence of vast populations of these bivalves off the Hawaiian Islands.

Removal of one valve and mantle lobe is anticlimactic: there seems so little within because the tissues contract back to the level of the posterior adductor, only a third of the distance from the pointed anterior end (Fig. 94). Only gradually does the mantle re-extend to cover the major surface of the remaining valve, revealing the wide inhalant chamber with the long gills and parallel to them a gutter-like waste canal (also present on the removed mantle lobe) along which pseudofaeces which cannot be allowed to accumulate in a bivalve of such a shape are rapidly conveyed upward for expulsion. The anus opens at the base of an extended exhalant chamber alongside a massive and unique 'pallial organ' which, distended with blood, is undoubtedly concerned with clearing away shell fragments when the projecting margins are broken. These immobile bivalves face a major threat from any agency, notably fish such as rays, which break the shell.

All of the shell behind (when *in situ* above) the posterior adductor is formed by the mantle margin and consists exclusively of the outer prismatic layer with an exceptionally high proportion of flexible organic conchiolin. The margins bend inwards to make contact when the adductors contract; more important the shell can be rapidly repaired with up to a centimetre added overnight. Almost every fan shell shows obvious signs of extensive repair. As shown in Fig. 95, when damaged the broad extent of the mantle is withdrawn by contraction of muscles radiating within it while the pallial organ dilates and pushes out the crushed shell fragments. Under the further influence of blood pressure the mantle lobes with attached gills cautiously extend and the shell is quickly repaired. The fan shells are wonderfully adapted for immobile vertical existence with the waste canals removing waste from below, the pallial organ clearing the mantle cavity following damage from above and the extraordinary speed of shell repair. They represent a spectacular achievement of bivalve evolution.

The long golden-yellow byssal threads of the Mediterranean species were long collected to be spun and woven. Fishermen from Taranto in south Italy

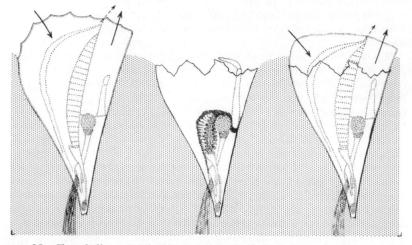

FIG. 95. Fan shell *in situ* showing immediate effect of damage, resultant withdrawal of mantle and probable function of the pallial organ. Later extension of mantle and very rapid regeneration of shell.

sought fan shells over wide areas originally by means of an apparatus known as a pernonico which consisted of two semicircular iron bars fastened at each end but separated in the middle. This was dropped over a projecting *Pinna* which was then twisted to detach the byssus and pulled up. The process is described and illustrated by Charles Ulysses in his *Travels through various Provinces of the Kingdom of Naples in 1789*. Today such woven objects are produced as curios.

Next come groups of bivalves with largely circular shells where all trace of the anterior adductor is lost and the body has been reorganized around the enlarged and more or less centrally placed posterior muscle. The original pallial line of attachment between the two adductors has gone and, as in *Pinna*, the mantle can be extensively withdrawn although always retaining contact with the shell margin by way of an excessively thin but elastic sheet of periostracum.

The first group to be mentioned, the Pteriacea, comprises the pearl oysters (*Pinctada* and *Pteria*) just represented in the British fauna on the strength of a few specimens of *Pteria hirundo* (common in the Mediterranean) found attached to gorgonic sea fans in the English Channel off Plymouth. But in the warmer and tropical seas, these are amongst the commonest bivalves. *Pteria* is distinguished by a much longer hinge line than the rounded *Pinctada* (Fig. 93) familiar owing to its frequent display, often with a contained pearl, in the windows of jewellers' shops. All are attached by a bunch of byssal threads that emerge through a small embayment on the right valve at the anterior end just below the hinge line. It is here that the foot has been finally displaced in the process leading from the two-muscle to the final single-muscle condition.

The flattened shell is usually secured almost at right angles to the surface but always inclined somewhat to the right. The valves are slightly asymmetrical and so is the foot and its attaching muscles which are better developed on the left.

These bivalves are also notable on account of the thickness and quality of the inner, nacreous layer of the shell. They are the source of mother-of-pearl and of pearls, the former chiefly from the impressively large gold-lip, *Pinctada maxima*, the latter from smaller species.

Pearls are formed by inpushings of the mantle tissues due to the presence of foreign bodies, often parasites. Layers of nacre are laid down around this 'nucleus'. For centuries pearl shells were collected by diving throughout the tropical Indo-Pacific, notably the Red Sea, Persian Gulf, off Ceylon and in the South Seas. A small proportion of the oysters contained pearls, the occasional one of outstanding size and lustre. The only competitors were artificial pearls made by coating glass beads with a suspension of 'pearl essence' prepared from the silvery crystals of guanin deposited in the scales of fishes. But today, following the discoveries of the Japanese, Mikimotu, oysters are induced to produce 'natural' pearls and a great industry has been established. Beads actually made from the shells of freshwater 'pigtoe mussels' imported from the United States, are enclosed in bags of mantle tissue taken from oysters sacrificed for this purpose. By a neat operation, these bags are inserted into the reproductive organs of intact oysters. The graft almost invariably takes and formation of mother-of-pearl proceeds around this artificial nucleus. The oysters are suspended in trays from rafts anchored in sheltered waters along the southern half of the east coast of Japan. To take full advantage of the spring increase in plant plankton, rafts are then towed farther north to be returned south before the winter. According to the size required, pearl formation takes from three to five years and something in the order of 500 million cultured pearls are produced annually.

Allied to the pearl oysters are the tropical 'hammer oysters', species of *Malleus* in which the bulk of the shell forms a long handle and the greatly extended hinge region the hammer head. They live, in a manner resembling the fan shells, almost completely embedded, usually in coral sands, one species byssally attached to stones well below the surface, another free, held in position by the elongated 'head'.

From these exotic Pteriaceans, the body reorganized around a central adductor and valves and body showing first signs of bilateral asymmetry, we pass to the supremely successful scallops found in all seas and in the most profound depths. This rayed shell, often beautifully coloured, has been used as a design from the earliest time, it was the badge of medieval pilgrims to the shrine of St James at Santiago de Compostela in NW Spain and formed the boat on which Botticelli depicted Venus arising from the waves. There are some dozen British species ranging from the large *Pecten maximus*, up to 12 cm in diameter, and the queen scallop, *Chlamys opercularis*, about half that diameter, to smaller, often brightly coloured species such as *C. tigerina*, the tiger-scallop, under 2 cm in greatest diameter.

What the pearl oysters took so far, the scallops have taken to the ultimate conclusion of horizontal rounded symmetry (Fig. 93). The shell is almost circular and the hinge line, though extended into terminal auricles is relatively shorter and with a secondarily symmetrical ligament, the inner layer forming a central rubbery pad. Superficially the scallops appear as symmetrically primitive as the isomyarian dog-cockles but with a byssal notch on the under valves just below the anterior auricle. All scallops begin life attached by byssus although resting on the right valve; with growth many species, including the two largest British species and all species of the deep water *Amusium*, become free. They always lie on the right valve and turn themselves over if placed the other way up. This has to do with the arrangement of the organ of balance. In species of *Pecten*, which comprises all the largest scallops, the under valve is deeply cupped and the upper one flat. They lie normally on a sandy bottom into which they work themselves, 'blowing' out sand to create a suitable depression. In *Chlamys*, *Amusium* and other genera, the two valves have much the same shape. A few scallops swim freely in early life and then become cemented (attached by way of the shell *not* by the byssus). The small British *Hinnites distorta* has this habit and so has the impressive 'rock oyster', *H. multirugosus* (Fig. 96), of the Californian coast which may attain a diameter of 25 cm with a very massive, irregular shell.

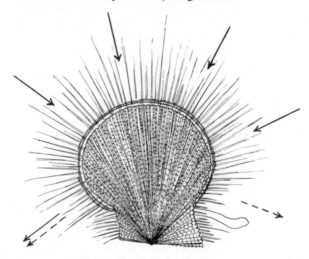

FIG. 96. Young rock scallop, *Hinnites multirugosus*, about 2 cm across, free swimming prior to cementation by right valve, foot and pallial tentacles extended. Arrows show direction of inhalant and exhalant currents, broken arrows sites of pseudofaecal discharge and of jet propulsive streams.

The interior of a scallop is as beautiful as the exterior. The widely-open gape of *P. maximus* is fringed with sensory tentacles interspersed with glistening eyes (Plate 11). Within these are the deep inner mantle folds also fringed with guarding tentacles and constantly parting and closing to permit or deny entrance of water into the mantle cavity over all but the posterior regions where the exhalant current emerges (Fig. 96). When ripe the eye is caught by the hermaphrodite gonad in the crescentric visceral mass, the terminal ovarian portion a beautiful vermilion pink, the upper testicular area cream coloured. The giant American scallop, *P. tenuicostatus*, is unisexual, the gonad either all pink or all cream. Food is collected by the ciliated but constantly mobile four-folded crescent of the gills (Fig. 93), the mouth guarded by palps and then by elaborately frilled lips. Waste accumulates at the two extremities of the mantle cavity to be rejected diagonally backward following contractions of the 'quick' muscle which forms the greater part of the adductor. The small foot, briefly an organ of locomotion, then one of byssal attachment (as it remains in many species) finally assumes a cleansing role, the funnel-like tip collecting waste from the depth of the cupped side. Cleansing is as important in these horizontally disposed bivalves as it is in the vertically erect fan shells.

The free scallops swim by jet propulsion (Fig. 97). They are stream-lined, especially species of *Chlamys*, such as the queen, and the flattened smooth-shelled species of *Amusium* that live in deep water. The big species of *Pecten* are more cumbersome but readily turn over if displaced and retreat when attacked. The mechanisms involved in swimming are those developed in relation to cleansing, namely repeated rapid closures of the widely-open valves by contractions of the 'quick' muscle of the adductor, and 'backward' ejection

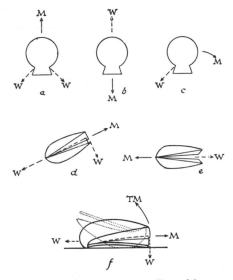

FIG. 97.   Movements of scallops: *a-e*, queen scallop; *f*, large scallop. Solid arrows (M) indicate direction of movement, broken arrows (w) direction of jet stream. *a*, swimming movement from above; *b*, escape movement; *c*, twisting movement; *d*, swimming movement from side, downward expulsion by overlapping mantle margins; *e*, escape movement from side; *f*, turning movement (TM) from side, final position shown by dotted outline. (After Buddenbrock)

of water of either side of the hinge, the animal moving by taking 'bites' out of the water ahead. To counter the pull of gravity the inner mantle folds on the upper valve overlap those of the lower valve to direct a stream of water downward. The animal proceeds forward and upward in a series of jerks, falling back a little between each propulsive jet. In the 'escape' reaction, provoked by an approaching predator such as a starfish, movement in the opposite direction is achieved by approximating the inner mantle folds except along the free margin where water is expelled to drive the animal suddenly 'backward' with hinge foremost.

Swimming efficiency has certainly been improved by greater stream-lining, by a more oblique and so more efficient disposition of the 'quick' as opposed to the 'catch' component of the adductor. The gape may also have enlarged to produce a greater jet but the fundamentals of the system reside in the cleansing mechanisms.

The numerous and elaborate eyes have been claimed as essential for swimming but they are just as well developed in byssally attached and cemented scallops. Every scallop, free or attached, has equal need for immediate reaction to the approach of predators attracted by the crescent of brightly coloured tissue exposed between the widely open valves (Plate 11). The shadow is perceived by the eyes and the result is immediate closure in attached, and a 'backward' escape movement in free, scallops.

As we noted earlier, attachment in rock scallops (*Hinnites*) is delayed, the young animals remaining free and actively swimming with periods of temporary byssal attachment until, in the Californian species, they are about 2 cm in diameter (Fig. 96). Only then do they cement themselves after which new additions to the shell are irregular, conforming to the rock surface. The tropical 'thorny oysters' (species of *Spondylus* and related to scallops) cement themselves early after brief byssal attachment. The under valve is irregular but the upper one is often covered with long spines; the shells a pure white or beautifully coloured. These are typical inhabitants of coral reefs. Like the similarly cemented *Hinnites*, the mantle margins are fringed with eyes.

The file shells (Limidae) have a characteristically oval shell ridged with fine spines. They are monomyarian like scallops but retain the vertical posture of mussels. In habit they fall into two groups, free and byssally attached and examples of both, the latter usually small, occur in the British fauna although these animals occur the world over. Byssally attached species may be very large like the impressive *Lima excavata*, up to 10 cm long, which lives deep on the scoured walls of Norwegian fjords. The free *Lima hians*, extremely common in shallow water amongst oarweeds or beds of horse-mussels, is the most beautiful of British bivalves. Here the fringing orange-coloured tentacles, retractable in attached species, are always fully displayed. These animals occupy any available cavity, lining this with interwoven byssal threads and extending it outward as they grow. The tentacles direct the water currents. Placed in an aquarium tank, they swim 'forward' by jet propulsion (Fig. 98) aided by languid oar-like movements of the tentacles rendered turgid by blood pressure. Such movements are doubtless made in nature when animals are forced out of the byssal-lined burrows where they otherwise remain. The

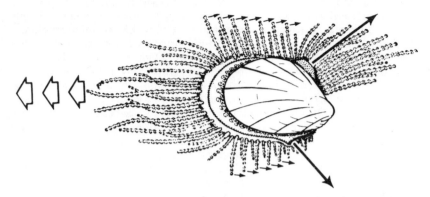

FIG. 98. File shell, *Lima hians*, swimming movements. Unlike scallops, the animal is vertically disposed. Large arrows indicate directions in which water expelled, arrows on left direction of movement, assisted by backward 'oaring' of tentacles (small arrows). (From Gilmour, by permission of the Marine Biological Association of the United Kingdom)

tentacles are most elaborate, highly muscular and internally partitioned. Predators are immediately repelled by copious discharge of a viscous acid secretion, any tentacles that may be severed being quickly regenerated from any level. Both the burrowing and the swimming movements appear to be escape reactions.

Here again swimming movements arise from cleansing reactions although *Lima* 'takes off' by the aid of a particularly powerful jet stream from the under surface (Fig. 98). Eyes only occur in some attached, never in swimming, species. The foot, used above all for planting the byssal threads, is reversed so that to the extent that they crawl the animals do so with hinge foremost.

These fascinating animals are somewhat of a diversion from the main theme now resumed by consideration of the saddle oysters or jingle shells (Anomiacea) of which there are three, usually inconspicuous, British species (Plate 11). Byssal attachment here reaches a culmination. The notch in the right (under)

FIG. 99. Saddle - oyster, *Anomia*: general appearance from above, showing embayment in under (right) valve through which byssus emerges *downward* to cement to rock. Large byssal muscle acts as main adductor. Broken arrows indicate cleansing currents.

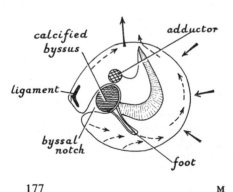

valve (Fig. 99) becomes a deep rounded embayment extending almost to the middle of the shell. Through this passes a massive byssus impregnated with lime and literally cemented to the rock surface to which the animal is closely adpressed. The two valves are widely dissimilar and the right half of the body is distorted by the byssus here extended at right angles to its original direction, namely to the right although topographically downward. It issues through a large round opening at the base of the foot which extends beyond it to form a long, highly mobile cleansing organ. The large byssal muscle takes over the closing function of the adductor which, reduced and almost entirely of 'quick' muscle, is concerned with cleansing. Anomiids are common enough but largely inconspicuous, although the largest may be confused with oysters. All British species occur from low tidal levels downward; the largest and commonest is *Anomia ephippium* (Plate 11), up to 6 cm across. There are also two species of *Monia* and one of *Heteranomia*, distinguished by the pattern of muscle attachment on the upper valve.

So specialized a bivalve, so far derived from the original bilaterally symmetrical ancestor with two adductors, might well be considered the culmination of its particular line of evolutionary change. But no! – in Malaysia and Indonesia an extremely thin oval-shaped bivalve occurs on the stems and lower leaves of mangrove trees, where it can only be submerged at high water of spring tides. This is an anomid, aptly named *Enigmonia* (Fig. 160), which, lying on the right side, moves about like a limpet. The enlarged foot emerging through the cavity on the underside has resumed a locomotory role, the byssus providing temporary attachment. These animals are certainly derived from permanently attached anomiids and this is equally true of the windowpane shells, species of *Placuna*, which occur widely in the tropical Indian and West Pacific Oceans. These lie, free but immobile, either valve uppermost, on the surface of mud flats. The excessively flat translucent valves, almost circular and up to 15 cm in diameter, have been used as window panes for centuries and, particularly in the Philippines, continue to be made into objects such as lampshades and trays.

We come now to the true oysters (Ostreacea), cemented but always by the *left* valve with complete loss of the foot except in the late larva where it plays an essential role. In pristine seas, unaffected by man, few bivalves could have been commoner than oysters forming extensive reefs in shallow water or covering rocks or the emerging roots of mangrove trees. Their edible qualities were soon detected as the mounds of their shells, with occasional crude oyster knives, in prehistoric kitchen middens bear witness. These qualities have been equally acclaimed by modern man although native reefs have now been almost universally destroyed and stocks are only maintained by increasingly complicated methods of cultivation.

There is an enormous literature on oysters, as fascinating in the diverse forms they have assumed in a long evolutionary history as their modern representatives are in life. They have been the object, first with the Romans, of increasingly elaborate culture methods, they have been the theme of gourmets and the subject matter of art from the Dutch painters of still life to the French Impressionists. The only general account, this writer's *Oysters*, is unhappily out of print and only the briefest account of these animals can be given here accompanied by some illustrations from that book.

The British 'native', *Ostrea edulis* (Fig. 4), ranges from the Black Sea through the Mediterranean to Scandinavia except for the coasts of Portugal where it is replaced by the more deeply-cupped Portuguese oyster, *Crassostrea angulata*. Species of these genera occur the world over, those of *Ostrea* extending farther into colder seas. The much larger and mainly tropical species of *Pycnodonta* are solitary and of no economic value. The valves of oysters, even when unattached, are not stream-lined like those of scallops, but frequently very irregular; the ligament, the upper surface of which rots away (permitting better insertion of the oyster knife), is totally different. Viewed after removal of the upper (right) valve and mantle lobe (Fig. 100), *O. edulis* resembles the mirror image of a scallop but is obviously completely static. There is the same central adductor, although with a relatively smaller 'quick' area, the mantle margins are simpler, with smaller tentacles and narrower inner mantle folds, the valves gaping less widely. Oysters are without eyes; few predators are tempted by the narrow band of exposed tissues although

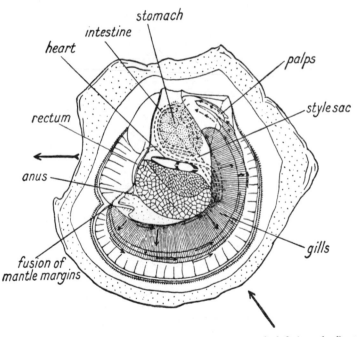

FIG. 100. Native oyster, *Ostrea edulis*: general appearance in left (attached) valve. Heart exposed and course of gut shown by broken lines. Large arrows indicate inhalant and exhalant currents, smaller arrows feeding currents on gills and palps. Pseudofaeces collect widely within inner mantle fold. (Hinge and ligament not shown)

young oysters are attacked by a wide range of predators. The smaller gape permits the union of mantle lobes between the inhalant and exhalant regions (Fig. 100). The gills are more coherent than in mussels or scallops with the filaments united by tissue; they are eulamellibranch instead of filibranch.

Water is drawn in widely and food selected by the same combined action of gills and palps but waste collects along the lower half of the inhalant chamber (totally unlike scallops) from time to time ejected when the 'quick' muscle contracts. The more turbid the water the more frequently this happens. No longer needed for locomotion or byssal production or for cleansing, the foot disappears.

The cupped oysters are very similar although longer (hinge to free margin); they have an additional pathway on the hinge side of the adductor for water passing through the gills from inhalant to exhalant chamber. This increases efficiency in turbid waters. The major differences concern reproduction. Oysters alternate in sex, usually starting life as males, then changing to female and so on. Such change is possible in bivalves where the reproductive ducts

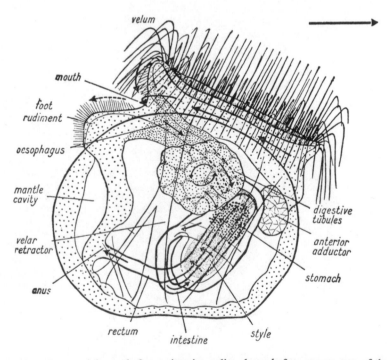

FIG. 101.   *Ostrea edulis*: early free swimming veliger larva before appearance of the posterior adductor (which alone will persist). Large arrow above shows direction of movement (mouth behind), smaller arrows direction of feeding currents around the base of the velum and into the gut, broken arrow rejection of excess particles by cilia on rudiment of foot.

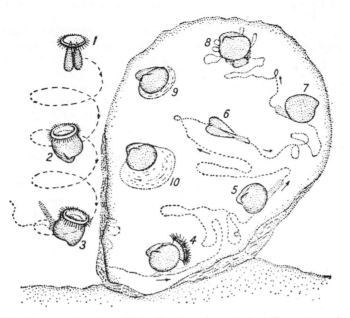

FIG. 102. Process of settlement in the American oyster, *Crassostrea virginica*, (essentially similar in *O. edulis*). 1, 2, swimming larvae with protruded velum; 3, 4, 'searching' phase with foot also protruded; 8, fixation; 9, 10, spat one and two days old with beginning of adult shell. (After Prytherch)

carry none of the complex glands found in all but the simplest gastropods. Spawning occurs when the temperature reaches a certain minimum, as low as 10°c in some species of *Ostrea* (*O. edulis* at about 15°c) but no *Crassostrea* spawns at under 20°c. In the latter both egg and sperm are discharged through the exhalant opening (involving different patterns of contraction for egg and for sperm) with fertilization in the sea. Over 100 million eggs may be liberated by the American, *C. virginica*. But in *Ostrea* only sperm is so discharged, the eggs, though larger because containing more yolk, pass through the minute, but temporarily distended, passages through the gills (i.e. *against* the normal water flow) to accumulate within the *inhalant* chamber into which sperm is drawn when adjacent males (i.e. individuals in the male phase) spawn. Spawning activity in one individual sets off spawning in others so that all ripe oysters in any area spawn about the same time. Nourished by the contained yolk, the fertilized eggs develop in this incubation chamber forming initially a whitish and then, as pigment accumulates, an increasingly darker mass, stages known to oystermen as 'white sick', 'grey sick' and 'black sick'. Species of *Ostrea* are not edible at this time hence the ban against catching them in the summer when there is an 'r' in the month. When *c.* 0.2 mm long, the veliger larvae (Fig. 101) are liberated into the sea and begin, at a later stage than those of *Crassostrea* which are not incubated, to feed on the most minute members of the plant plankton.

Some two weeks are spent as larvae growing and preparing for the elaborate metamorphosis. At the end of this period sense organs briefly appear, eyes permitting a negative response to light, statocysts a positive reaction to gravity, with an apical sense organ of dubious function. As the larvae settle, the foot develops and projects alongside the velum so that as the larvae drift close to the bottom it can grip any hard surface that may be encountered (Fig. 102). After exploratory crawling, this 'pediveliger' either settles or the velum re-extends and it swims on in search of a more suitable place. When this is found, movement stops, the foot attaches by the tip and the larva, hinge uppermost, rocks from side to side. Cement is produced by the foot and the shell secured by the left valve. The process of attachment is extremely elaborate involving a series of pedal glands as well as the mantle edge. When completed, the foot degenerates. Meanwhile the velum has been lost, contributing to the structure of the palps, and gill filaments appear and take over the function of feeding.

These settled or 'spat' oysters (Fig. 103) tend to aggregate; where one has settled others are more likely to do so, behaviour which, given ample time and no human or other interference, will produce massive reefs, new layers of oysters settling on the surface of the cemented masses of their predecessors.

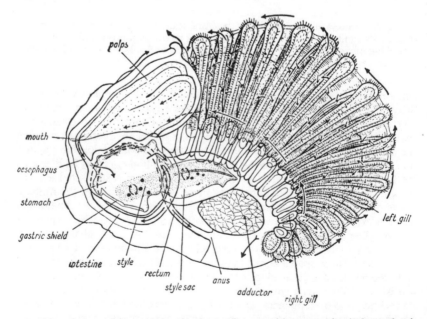

FIG. 103.   *Ostrea edulis*: spat shortly after settlement with upper valve (1·2 mm deep) removed. Arrows show direction of currents on gills (left develops before right), on large palps and throughout gut including rotation of style.

Until about the middle of the last century the European beds of *O. edulis* were enormously productive, then increasing human population and the development of rapid transport to industrial towns led to over-exploitation. Energetic measures were taken in the France of Napoleon III where methods were developed both for collecting spat and for rearing those in sheltered regions rich in plankton, such as the Bay of Arcachon, south of Bordeaux, around Marennes near Rochfort and along the south of Brittany farther north. In the southern beds *O. edulis* was later, and accidentally, replaced by the less valuable but hardier Portuguese oyster, *C. angulata*. Similar attempts at cultivation failed in Great Britain where decline in stocks was speeded by the import of pests such as *Crepidula* (p. 82) and oyster drills (*Urosalpinx*) (p. 103) introduced with American *C. virginica* ('blue points') which were 'relaid' for growth on British beds. In the United States and Canada, this species continued abundant until relatively recently but has been overfished in some areas and decimated by diseases elsewhere so that populations are much lower than formerly. The supremely successful oyster had been the Japanese, *C. gigas*. For some centuries cultivated on bamboo palisades, this is now done largely by suspension from rafts (Fig. 104) or attached to stakes in shallower water. Apart from local consumption, young oysters are 'hardened' for export as seed to the Pacific coast of North America, to Australia and increasingly to Europe where stocks of the related Portuguese oyster on French beds have recently been almost wiped out by a disease which destroys the gills.

Oysters are now cultivated in hatcheries where spawning is induced by brief exposure to higher than normal temperatures, the resultant larvae fed on rich

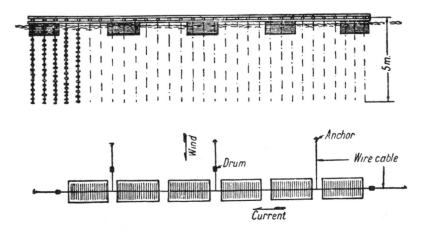

FIG. 104. Raft method of oyster culture as practised in the Inland Sea, Japan. *Above*, side view of rafts showing concrete floats with oysters, settled on large scallop shells, suspended on wires with 'spacers' between. *Below*, arrangement of the rafts in series and their disposition in relation to the current is shown. (After Cahn)

cultures of minute green flagellates and diatoms in mixtures and at concentrations experimentally determined and rigidly maintained. The small seed oysters, about 1 cm across, are planted out on suitable beds. Here again the Japanese species, though like all species of *Crassostrea* inferior to the native *O. edulis*, proves the easier to rear although the species is unlikely to establish itself in British waters because sea temperatures are too low for spawning.

Chapter 15

Shallow and deep burrowing bivalves

*

ALTHOUGH the most obvious bivalves on the shore are those described in the foregoing chapter yet it is those that retain the primitive burrowing habit and extend its possibilities that are the most numerous both in numbers of species and, in some of these, in numbers of individuals. Their presence is immediately revealed by digging low on a tidally exposed beach or by dredging on suitable soft bottoms. These bivalves have solved the problem of movement through bottom deposits while collecting the basic foodstuff of plant plankton from the water above. We have already noted (p. 142) the truly astronomical populations of trough shells on the Dogger Bank and beds of similar size and content occur widely on sandy bottoms where turbulence brings down endless supplies of plankton from surface waters.

A survey of such burrowers – the basket-shell, *Corbula gibba*, already illustrated (Fig. 87) is a good example – reveals that all possess the compacted eulamellibranch gill, have various patterns of hinge teeth and are diversely adapted in shell form and sculpture for life within every grade of bottom material. They have an enormous potential for evolutionary change. While exploiting the possibilities of shallow burrowing, members of different groups come, each by its particular route, to the similar destination of deep burrowing, others to a more superficial mode of life while both may lead to the final highly specialized condition of boring described in the next chapter.

Most of the groups awaiting discussion are adequately represented in the north Atlantic fauna. The simplest burrowers are the astartes (Astartacea) with simple rounded shells, equivalve and equilateral like dog-cockles and equally devoid of siphons. Even for bivalves these animals live particularly sluggish lives; placed on the surface they burrow with apparent reluctance to become barely covered with the inhalant and exhalant openings just flush with the surface. There are five British species, the largest, *Astarte borealis*, up to 4·5 cm across, all with solid shells, concentrically ridged and covered with thick brown periostracum. They are unmistakable, never departing from the one basic form and habit. This is not true of the related false cockles (Carditacea) of which the nearest species lives in the Mediterranean but which are common in the Pacific.

Some have much the same form and habit as the astartes but there is a small Californian species, *Cardita* (*Glans*) *carpenteri*, about the size of a crystal of granite which lives intertidally attached by a single byssal thread to boulders of that rock while another, the large and very laterally flattened 'mussel', *C.* (*Beguina*) *suborbicularis*, is secured by a massive byssus within crevices in coral reefs. Following the same evolutionary path, this has become almost

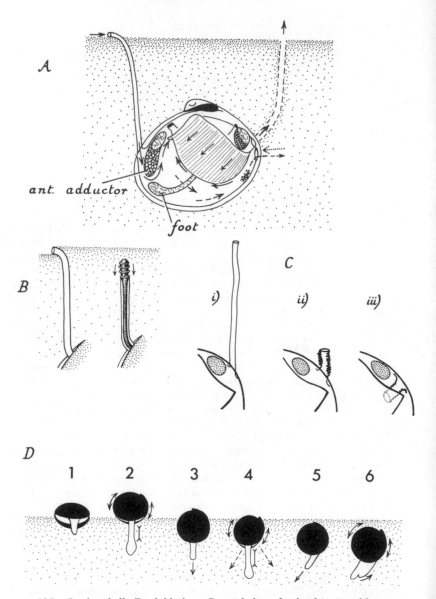

FIG. 105.   Lucine shells (Lucinidae): A, General view of animal *in situ* with *anterior*, mucus-lined, inhalant tube formed by the foot (tube and constructing foot shown in B), and posterior, mucus-lined, exhalant tube formed by siphon. C, (i-iii, Stages in extrusion and introversion of siphon). Usual inhalant opening largely for ejection of pseudofaeces (broken arrows). D, 1-6, Stages in burrowing. (Largely after Allen)

triangular in shell form and as heteromyarian as the common *Mytilus edulis* described in the last chapter.

The lucines or hatchet-shells (Lucinacea) are a widely distributed group of bivalves of which nine species of the genera *Diplodonta, Thyasira, Myrea, Divaricella, Loripes* and *Lucinoma* are members of the British fauna. All have colourless rounded shells with forwardly directed umbones, the largest about 2·5 cm in diameter, the smallest minute. They are biologically fascinating. Placed on the appropriate substrate they rapidly burrow down by way of a particularly long and characteristically bulbous-ended foot (Fig. 105, D). When below the surface the heel takes over propelling the animal forward until it comes to rest without contact with the surface. The foot now assumes the function we noted in the proboscis of the pelican's foot shell, *Aporrhais* (p. 88). It pushes out anteriorly and upward, extending and contracting to form a mucus-lined tube to the surface. Mucus is produced by glands at the bulbous end which is ciliated so that entangled particles are carried back to add to the tube (Fig. 105, B). On reaching the surface the tube runs briefly along this; the foot is extended from time to time to keep the cavity open.

Although these bivalves possess the usual posterior inhalant and exhalant openings, obviously very little can be drawn in from within the substrate. Water and food, which consists largely of organic debris with associated bacteria, enter through the anterior mucus-lined tube (Fig. 105, A). The lucines appear to be able to live where conditions are extreme and oxygen and food limited, although they certainly dominate the fauna in certain areas such as shallow sand patches within West Indian coral reefs where the eel grass *Thalassia* is abundant.

The gills are primarily concerned with producing the water current, the sizeable food masses entering with it being carried to the mouth by cilia on the inner surface of the enlarged anterior adductor. The palps are reduced and the stomach modified for dealing with this type of food. The posterior (true) inhalant opening must be mainly concerned with ejecting the waste which collects just within it. The outflowing stream emerges through the exhalant opening into the substrate except in the family Lucinidae (i.e. all British species except those of *Diplodonta* and *Thyasira*) where there is a solitary exhalant siphon formed from the inner mantle fold. This may extend to the surface but on withdrawal turns in on itself (Fig. 105, C) which no other bivalve siphon does. This anterior/posterior water flow has been claimed as primitive (as it certainly is in *Nucula*) and as indicating descent from primitive molluscs such as *Neopilina* (p. 28). However, far from this being so, the lucinids are strikingly adapted with this remarkable tube-constructing foot and a far from primitive means of dealing with relatively large particles of organic detritus.

The one other group of lamellibranchs with an anterior inhalant current, although entering through a permanent siphon, are the coin-shells or Erycinacea. There are twelve British species of these very interesting bivalves, with small symmetrical shells, all epifaunal and frequently attached by a single byssal thread, a habit which explains the extent to which they have become commensally associated with other invertebrates – echinoderms, crustaceans and worms. In many the shell is enclosed by an overgrowing mantle representing extensions of the middle mantle fold and so bearing sensory tentacles. The living animals, with transparent white tissues over the delicate shell, are amongst the most beautiful of bivalves, rivalling sea-slugs in all save colour.

Search in cavities, empty shells or rock borings, should occasionally reveal an almost globular white shell up to 1 cm in diameter. This unmistakable shell is *Kellia suborbicularis*, common along southern and western shores and to some depth. Water is drawn in anteriorly through a long projecting siphon, discharged through a squat siphon behind. In the larger *K. laperousii* (Fig. 106) of Californian coasts the shell is largely covered by the mantle and the

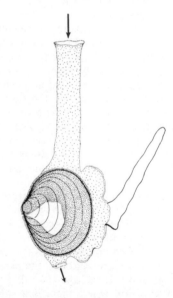

FIG. 106. Erycinacean *Kellia laperoussi*, a Californian species viewed from right side with mantle extending largely over valve, with long anterior inhalant, and short posterior exhalant siphon. Creeping foot fully extended, byssal groove at base.

inhalant siphon is very much longer so that the animal frequently lives deep within obscure cavities. The sizeable foot produces the byssus thread but is also a creeping organ resembling that of a gastropod. Like all such bivalves, *Kellia* is viviparous retaining the developing young in the mantle cavity to be liberated as late veligers ready for almost immediate settlement.

Perhaps the commonest shore bivalve is the minute reddish *Lasaea rubra*, only some 3 mm long, attached by single byssal threads in clusters (Fig. 107) within cavities such as empty barnacle shells or rock crevices or among greyish tufts of the marine lichen, *Lichina pygmaea*, high on the shore. Much is known about this animal which, with some turn of speed, moves upward and also away from light to enter deep shelter where it is only briefly submerged during any tide. Then, the only period when it can feed and digest, the crystalline style becomes a firm rotating rod and the digestive cells become loaded with absorbed material, the former to diminish and the latter gradually to empty

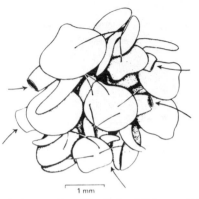

FIG. 107. *Lasaea rubra*, aggregated individuals. (From Morton, by permission of the Marine Biological Association of the United Kingdom)

1 mm

after the sea recedes. This bivalve also is hermaphrodite, indeed it is possibly self-fertile, and retains the young still longer so that they emerge as miniatures of the adult and can immediately establish themselves in the adult environment.

Galeomma turtoni (Fig. 108), over 1 cm long and confined to the south-west and commonest on rocky offshore bottoms is a most unexpected bivalve with the two valves set at an angle of about 30° like the peak of a roof and widely gaping below. This space is occupied by a broad fused extension of the inner mantle lobe leaving space for protrusion of the foot. This is long and highly mobile with a short rounded hind region containing the byssal gland. These animals crawl like very active limpets and will move up the sides of a jar and on to the under side of the surface film. They normally ascend rocks and may then, the foot withdrawn, hang suspended by a few very strong threads.

Omitting various small offshore species, we come to *Montacuta ferruginosa* and *M. substriata*, only about a millimetre long and associated with burrowing sea urchins. The former occurs with the common heart urchin, *Echinocardium cordatum*, which can be dug at good low tides. Young individuals are attached to spines on the under surface but larger ones are free in the anal region of the burrow. The shells are oval and reddish. The more rounded *M. substriata* is always attached to the larger but offshore *Spatangus purpureus*. Although usually byssally attached both can move. The mantle never extends over the shell. *Mysella bidentata*, associated with, but never apparently attached to, the mud-burrowing brittle star, *Ophiocnida bracheta* and possibly other invertebrates is more mobile. A related Californian species lives attached to the legs of sand crabs. All of these bivalves feed on detrital and faecal particles.

The most striking of these bivalves, again confined to the south and found only at the very lowest tides is *Devonia perrieri* (Fig. 109) about 5 mm long and attached to the body of the small holothurian echinoderm (sea cucumber), *Leptosynapta inhaerens*. Rather like *Galeomma*, this has a permanent gape on the underside with mantle and foot protruded, the latter flat and forming a sucker-like attachment. The mantle extends over much of the shell. The related *Lepton squamosum* occurs in or near the burrows in muddy sand or

189

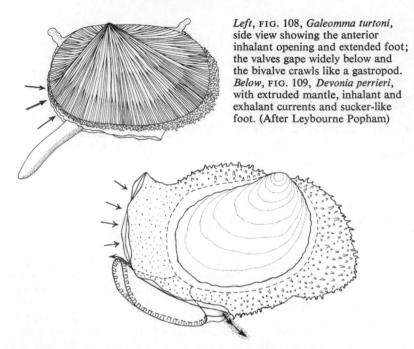

Left, FIG. 108, *Galeomma turtoni*, side view showing the anterior inhalant opening and extended foot; the valves gape widely below and the bivalve crawls like a gastropod. *Below*, FIG. 109, *Devonia perrieri*, with extruded mantle, inhalant and exhalant currents and sucker-like foot. (After Leybourne Popham)

gravel of the burrowing 'shrimps' *Upogebia deltura* and *U. stellata*. Little, however, is known about its mode of life although it leads on to the larger *Pseudopythina* which is attached to the underside of similar crustaceans in the Pacific. In other exotic species the permanently enclosed shell is greatly reduced. The final stage on this line of evolution is, however, attained in *Entovalva*, the only parasitic bivalve, living within holothurians.

In striking contrast to these largely minute coin shells is the solitary British cyprinid, *Arctica* (*Cyprina*) *islandica*. This has an impressively massive shell up to 12 cm long, very thick and covered with brown to black periostracum which with the toothed hinge, rounded external ligament and forward directed umbones render it unmistakable. It occurs in sand and sandy mud from low shore levels to fair depths on both sides of the north Atlantic and is a major food for bottom living fish. The rounded shell is pulled through the substrate by a powerful, hatchet-shaped foot. There are no siphons; like the astartes and carditids the animal lies vertically, the hind end with the two openings flush with the surface. This is a successful plankton feeder protected by an unusually thick shell.

The one shell with which *A. islandica* might be confused because also globular and with dark periostracum is the equally isolated heart cockle, *Glossus* (*Isocardia*) *humanus* (Fig. 110). In the words of a writer in 1888, this 'is certainly a shell of exceptional appearance, its cordate-globular form rendering it both striking and elegant.' Instead of bending inwards, the um-

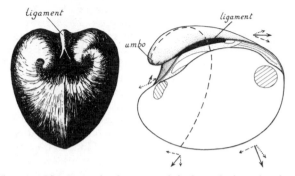

FIG. 110.   Heart cockle, *Isocardia humanus*: *left*, frontal view showing umbones curled back with spit ligament; *right*, interior of right valve showing the mode of growth. The radial component (dotted arrows) is influenced by the tangential component (broken arrows) the resultant direction of growth indicated by *solid arrows*; broken line indicates curvature of growth in the middle of the valve, this becomes backward along hinge line. (After Owen)

bones are 'so spirally twisted as to form a nearly complete whorl'. Linnaeus called it *Cardium humanum* from its resemblance to a human heart, in France it is called 'coeur-de-boeuf' and in Holland 'zots-kappen' or fool's cap. There is only the one species in western Europe and a few others in the Far East, but there are many fossil species.

The curling umbones split the prominent ligament anteriorly, as shown in the figure, while this continues to grow at the hind end. Each valve, it will be noted, is curling in the horizontal plane like a pair of gastropod shells the one dextrally, the other sinistrally, coiled. Gareth Owen has shown this as due to an additional, *tangential*, component in shell growth which, as shown by the arrows, has the effect of bending the radial component in a forward direction. This becomes greatest in the hinge region, causing both the anterior split and the posterior extension. The eventual consequence is formation of an unusually compact shell with the viscera split into two partially coiled masses.

This bivalve lives in pockets of mud at moderate depths and occurs from Iceland to Morocco. Although more elaborately constructed, the siphons are as short as those of *Arctica* but the foot is smaller and less powerful, incapable of pulling the globular shell through anything denser than mud while the opening thrust of the ligament has only about one-eighth the power of that of *Arctica* which has to push the valves open against the pressure of surrounding sand.

The same shell form occurs in the jewel shells (Chamidae) which are unknown in the north Atlantic but common on coral reefs and on rocky shores elsewhere especially in the Pacific. With the same coiling, they are firmly cemented – indifferently by either valve – the under valve deeply cupped with a coiled umbonal cavity, the upper one flat. They can withstand any storm. Such growth form takes us back in time to the Mesozoic, the age of reptiles, when quiet shallow seas were occupied by an extraordinary range of long

191

extinct rudist bivalves (Hippuritacea) also attached by one valve (Fig. 161). Many grew to enormous size and formed reefs. The largest (*Hippurites* and *Radiolites*) had cone-shaped lower valves, in extreme cases up to one metre high, with a flat opercular cap; in other words the former had an enormous transverse component in shell growth and the latter none at all! Long, downward projecting teeth and muscle attachments maintained the cap in position when the valves closed; how they were opened is unknown. The ligament was pulled out vertically and ceased to function.

The cockles (Cardiacea) are a dominating group. No bivalve is better known than the edible cockle *Cerastoderma* (*Cardium*) *edule*, only one out of eleven British species from somewhat over a centimetre long to the impressive prickly cockle, *Acanthocardia echinata* (Fig. 111) which may be 11 cm long. Few sandy shores throughout the world are without cockles: the largest, the east African giant cockle is the size of a coconut while shells of the great cockle, *Cardium elatum*, up to 15 cm across, can be picked up on beaches in the Gulf of California.

The typical cockle is almost globular with radiating ribs and prominent inward directed umbones which grind into one another when the valves open. The short siphons, incorporating the middle (sensory) lobe of the mantle margin, are fringed with tentacles and carry eyes. These very superficially burrowing, often exposed, species are in constant danger from predators, against which they react vigorously by way of the enormous foot. This is retained, bent back within the mantle cavity, to be extended with impressive force. When exposed, the prickly cockle presses the tip of the foot against the surface and then, suddenly straightening out, it makes leaps of up to 20 cm to escape starfish and other enemies (Fig. 111). The edible cockle is less

FIG. 111.   Spiny cockle, *Acanthocardia echinata*, leaping for up to 20 cm when touched by tube feet of starfish. (Drawing by Professor Gunnar Thorson, by permission of Mrs Ellen Thorson)

spectacular in its reactions but all cockles need a powerful foot to propel their globose shells over and through the sand they inhabit.

The edible cockle lives between tide marks and populations can be enormous, as much as an estimated 460 millions in a surveyed bed in south Wales. The young settle out of the plankton into 'nursery' areas of soft sandy mud to form a compact layer under the surface. They rapidly extend marginally into sandy areas but in the centre are literally squeezed out to be carried by currents to stock other sands. Life for cockles is precarious – eaten by starfish and flatfish, bored into by snails, collected by gulls and oystercatchers, at the mercy of winter storms and frosts and equally of summer heat. Fishermen take a major toll of animals three to four years old and over 3 cm long, notably in south Wales and in the Thames estuary; the catch is boiled and then riddled to separate the meat from the shells. Populations inevitably fluctuate but no bivalve is more virile.

All our cockles have a somewhat similar rotund form but many in tropical seas are compressed, not laterally but from end to end and, culminating in the heart cockle, *Corculum cardissa*, completely flattened in this plane, which lies on the surface of tropical reefs with the short siphons pointing upward and the foot occasionally emerging below. Light penetrates the exposed translucent shell providing for the needs within the tissues of single-celled, brown-coloured symbiotic plants. These are the resting stages of usually motile dinoflagellates and are known as zooxanthellae.

What is here of minor consequence assumes over-riding significance in the second family of cockles, the Tridacnidae. These are inhabitants exclusively of mid-tropical Indo-Pacific seas and include the largest bivalves ever evolved. There are six species ranging in length from about 10 cm in *Tridacna crocea* (Fig. 1) that bores into coral rock, hinge undermost, to *T. gigas*, the giant clam (Plate VIB) the largest recorded shell of which measures 137 cm (4½ feet) in length, the two valves weighing over 500 pounds. These clams are among the greatest beauties of coral reefs, the vividly coloured upward-directed tissues forming a scalloped platform which obscures the valves below (Fig. 1). Here the byssus has been retained, all young animals being so attached although it is gradually lost in the larger species which come finally to rest solely by their great weight. Hinge and umbones are on the *underside* alongside the foot, a consequence of the forward extension of the siphonal tissues over the entire upper surface. This in turn causes mantle and shell to rotate through an angle of almost 180° in relation to the visceral mass and foot with only the posterior adductor muscle persisting (a very different mode of attaining this condition than in oysters and scallops but here also involving byssal fixation).

These extended tissues, protected by pigment from the effect of mid-tropical sunlight, are packed with countless millions of symbiotic zooxanthellae. These are literally farmed, exposed to the light needed for starch production and obtaining the nitrogen, phosphorus and sulphur required for elaboration of proteins from the metabolic waste of the clam. This retains the normal means of feeding and digestion. The accessory source of food represented by the plant cells explains the abundance of tridacnids in impoverished coral reef waters where their total mass often exceeds that of all other bivalves. It may also account for the enormous size attained by some species, greater than could be attained by an exclusively ciliary feeder. Tridacnids are actually restricted to both shallower and warmer waters than many corals, only spawning when the temperature reaches about 30°C.

The carpet or venus shells (Veneracea) are supremely successful bivalves occurring the world over, often in great numbers, between tide marks and in shallow water. The solid, somewhat compressed shells are pleasant to handle and mechanically superb. The nineteen British species, fully described in all books on shells, range in length from over 12 cm to a few millimetres; some are rounded, like species of *Venus* and *Dosinia* or oval like *Venerupis*. Essentially shallow burrowers with a broad hatchet-shaped foot, different species occur in all grades of substrate up to coarse gravel and even between stones or rocks when they become attached by byssus threads. Species of *Petricola* bore into rock (p. 208). All are filtering plant plankton with interesting differences in the siphons, constructed like those of cockles but without eyes and in some cases longer and partially separate. Straining tentacles around the inhalant opening are better developed in species living under conditions where there is more sediment in the water as indicated in Fig. 112. Venerid bivalves are widely eaten, especially in North America where the hard-shell clam, *Mercenaria mercenaria*, is rightly prized. This was accidentally introduced into Great Britain about 1960 and has recently been successfully cultivated, finding ready sale in France.

One very small venerid, *Turtonia minuta*, occurs in vast numbers on the shore attached by byssus like *Lasaea* but at somewhat lower levels. It is beautifully adapted for this epifaunal life producing few but large eggs which in some unknown manner make their way into the inhalant chamber to be

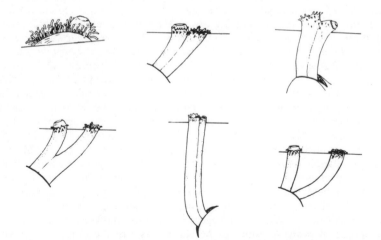

FIG. 112.   Siphons of various species of venerid shells (Veneracea) showing variations in length and degree of union. (From Ansell, by permission of the Marine Biological Association of the United Kingdom)

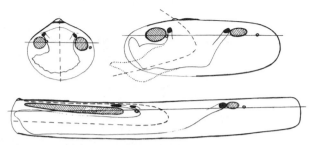

FIG. 113. Figures of *Glycymeris*, *Siliqua* and *Ensis*, to be viewed with Fig. 81, here showing major internal structures (adductors, foot, pedal muscles). Enlargement of posterior regions of the shell in the two last is *not* accompanied by corresponding enlargement of enclosed animal but by change in disposition of the foot which becomes bent (compare broken lines) to point forward so that animals burrow vertically. Horizontal line indicates anterio-posterior axis between mouth and anus.

enclosed in capsules and attached to byssal threads. These are later lengthened so that the eggs develop *outside* the shell. Much as in *Lasaea*, the young hatch out as miniature adults ready to start life in the adult environment.

Apart from the peculiarly constructed lucinids, bivalves mentioned in this chapter have all been shallow burrowers or else, by retention of the byssus, epifaunal. Penetration to greater shelter demands either a long shell or else long siphons. The first solution is achieved by the well-known razor shells (Solenacea), species usually of *Ensis* and *Solen* with the stouter butter clam, *Siliqua*, of north American Pacific coasts. They are widely distributed in intertidal sand or mud in which they burrow vertically. The formation of such a shell, with hinge and ligament at the extreme anterior end, has already been discussed (p. 81). What now becomes significant is the effect of such change on the form and so habits of the enclosed animal. Posterior enlargement of the shell does not here involve, as it does in byssally-attached bivalves, corresponding enlargement of the enclosed body; it is the *disposition* of this which is affected. This becomes apparent when we view the second set of figures (Fig. 113) of the series *Glycymeris/Siliqua/Ensis* this time displaying *internal* changes (more fully shown for *Ensis* in Fig. 115). As the shell extends so does the body, the enlarging foot bending into a forward-facing U. It becomes a piston working within a cylinder formed by the tubular mantle cavity because the margins are now fused apart from the terminal pedal opening and a smaller, fourth, opening farther back that acts as a safety valve. The foot shoots out under the internal pressure of blood and is then as efficiently withdrawn by contraction of the pedal retractors. No better example could be sought of the action of muscle against a fluid, as opposed to the more usual rigid skeleton. Such, indeed, is all that does occur if a razor shell is suspended, but when this is laid upon sand the foot immediately hooks down into this, dilates terminally and the muscles shorten to pull the cylinder down the length of the stationary piston. Each downward probe is accompanied by a loosening discharge of water from the mantle cavity and descent is dramatically efficient

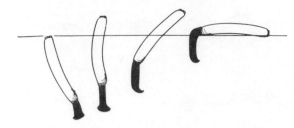

FIG. 114.   Stages in the burrowing of a razor shell, *Ensis*. (From Morton & Yonge)

(Fig. 114). Every second of exposure is one of danger from birds when the tide is out, from fish when it is under water.

The fringed siphons are very short, the animals relying for safety on sudden descent, the smooth shell which is typical of all bivalves that move rapidly through the substrate offering the minimum of resistance. Upward movement involves reverse procedures, namely initial dilation and anchoring by the end of the foot and then distension of the upper regions which push the shell up. All movements are vertical, down or up. The viscera with the gills and full length of the gut, are confined to the posterior (upper) third of the shell, the remainder housing the enormous foot and the much elongated anterior adductor (here larger than the posterior one). Waste is carried upward to be discharged through the inhalant siphon. These are most beautifully, but at the same time irrevocably, adapted animals (Fig. 115).

The five British species can all be mentioned: three species of *Ensis* which live in sand, the largest *E. siliqua* up to 20 cm long and 2·5 cm deep. This is very straight whereas the smaller *E. ensis* and *E. arcuatus*, some 10 and 15 cm long respectively, are curved, to a greater extent in the former. *Solen marginatus*, straight and almost circular in cross section, lives, like all species of this genus, in mud. The much smaller *Cultellus pellucidus*, with delicately translucent shell often no more than 1 cm long, is common in dredgings from muddy sand. All species are widely distributed, largely if not exclusively, in European seas.

There are no less than 24 British species of wedgeshells or tellins (Tellinacea). This is a group of dominating importance exploiting, with far greater success than the lucinids, the rich possibilities of organic detritus. This involves deep and often active burrowing with separate and extremely mobile siphons (Fig. 116). The commonest species are the intertidal tellins of sandy beaches, *Tellina tenuis* and *T. fabula*, the former always at a higher level. Both are about 2 cm long, extremely compressed and of beautifully varied colour. After death the powerful ligament spreads the valves flat like the wings of a butterfly. Like many other tellinids they lie on the left valve when buried and careful examination will reveal differences between the sculpture of the valves, especially in *T. fabula*. These animals are easy to dig and study. The large, extremely compressed foot is highly active in downward and then horizontal burrowing. The separate siphons derive exclusively from the muscular inner

196

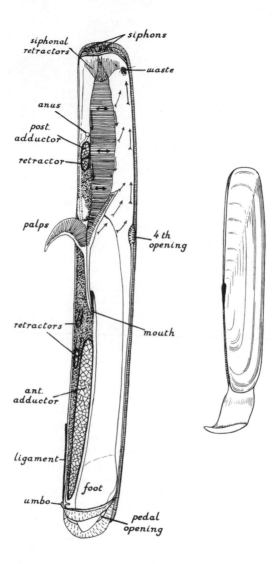

FIG. 115. *Left*, razor shell, *Ensis arcuatus*, structure after removal of left valve and mantle lobe; *right*, the tellinid razor shell, *Pharus legumen*, showing centrally placed hinge and ligament with foot protruding.

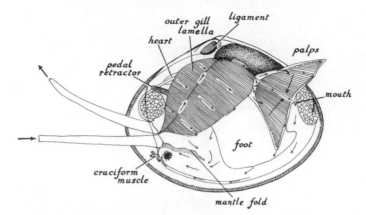

FIG. 116. Tellinids viewed from right side to show major structures with exposed palps and extended siphons: *above, Macoma balthica* (deep burrower in muddy sand); *below, Donax vittatus* (fully exposed sandy beaches).

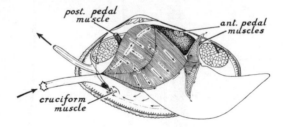

mantle fold with a complex pattern of longitudinal and circular muscle layers. In consequence they act independently and are exceptionally mobile. The exhalant one is much the shorter, extending directly to the surface, if always as far, but the other attaining the surface and then reaching along this actively to pull in bottom deposits, very like the action of a vacuum cleaner. It also, of course, draws in any suspended plankton at these levels. Action of the lateral cilia on the gills is here aided by muscular movements in the siphon, the speed increased by the narrow bore. Masses of material can be seen through the translucent walls of the siphon pouring into the mantle cavity.

The palps are unusually large, when spread out only a little smaller than the gills in *Tellina* but actually larger than them in *Macoma* (Fig. 116), *Scrobicularia* (Fig. 118) and *Abra*, all of them dwellers in mud or muddy sand where organic debris is most abundant. As material pours into the mantle cavity there is frenzied activity on gills and palps followed by a sudden expulsion of apparently all that entered, but of course, with the effective passage of edible matter by way of the gills and palps to the mouth. Then the process is resumed.

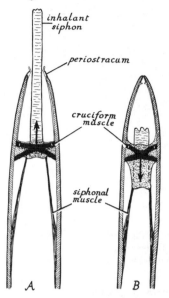

FIG. 117. Under surface of a tellinid showing the base of the separate siphons with the cross tie of the cruciform muscle: A, siphons extended; B, withdrawn.

A remarkable feature of all tellinaceans is the presence at the base of the siphons of crossed muscular connections, the so-called cruciform muscle. This represents a tie for the siphons, the anterior attachments take the strain when the siphons extend and the posterior ones when they are withdrawn (Fig. 117); an enclosed sense organ may give information about the extent to which the siphons are extended or withdrawn at any time. The alimentary canal is modified, the cuticular lined stomach acts as a gizzard, the style revolving within it.

The somewhat larger and thicker *Macoma balthica* (Fig. 116) takes over in muddy, often estuarine, areas; as its name indicates it extends far into the low-saline waters of the Baltic. Although with the same long groping inhalant siphons, it also crawls freely on the surface apparently moving first towards and then away from the sun, so keeping in the same place. Other species occur the world over, all usually in dense concentrations although spaced out like all such bivalves which feed over a defined area. The related *Scrobicularia plana* is one of the larger British bivalves, very flat and almost circular, growing to a diameter of 6 cm or more. It replaces *Macoma* in mud flats where there is much freshwater and burrows down to 20 cm below the surface. The translucent siphons appear almost indefinitely extensile, the inhalant tube reaching the surface and then extending along this for up to 12 cm and literally pulling off surface deposits up to 2 mm in diameter. The siphon extends in one direction, then in another, the mud surface becoming marked with radiating grooves (Fig. 118). Food, consisting of detritus with bacteria and bottom-living diatoms, is here so rich and so effectively redistributed at every tide that *S. plana* rarely moves either, like *Tellina*, below the surface or, like *Macoma*, upon it. The much smaller species of *Abra* found often in

199

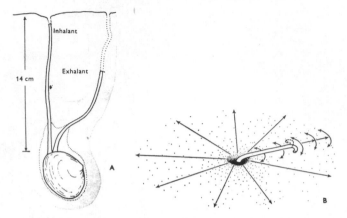

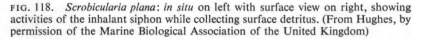

FIG. 118. *Scrobicularia plana*: *in situ* on left with surface view on right, showing activities of the inhalant siphon while collecting surface detritus. (From Hughes, by permission of the Marine Biological Association of the United Kingdom)

enormous numbers in offshore muds and muddy gravels display even more frenzied feeding activities and here the extended palps are much larger than the gills.

Of very different habits are species of *Donax* (Fig. 116) represented by *D. vittatus* and *D. variegatus*, both with smooth and beautifully coloured shells, the former widely distributed, the latter only in the south. These are inhabitants of exposed beaches, the last areas where detritus collects, but they are undoubted tellinids with a cruciform muscle and characteristic siphons. The anterior region of the shell is enlarged, an unusual feature but here housing the powerful, hook-shaped foot. All depends on this organ, because, living close below the surface in the surf zone, these bivalves are in constant danger of being uncovered. The instant reaction is immediate re-burial, accomplished by the foot in seconds. The siphons are short, serving to draw in suspended matter; here the gills are large and the selecting palps small.

These are the most active of bivalves and, particularly in warm and tropical seas, small donacids, such as the coquina shells of American Atlantic beaches, are characteristic members of the surf fauna. They move up and down with the breaking waves, retaining position by virtue of their powers of instant burrowing. Like the little mole crab, *Emerita*, which often lives with them, they feed on the material raised by the surf, the one by ciliary means, the other by a meshwork of hairs on the antennae fine enough to filter out bacteria.

Coarse sand and shell gravel is inhabited by the larger and equally beautiful species of *Gari* (*Psammobia*). The only species likely to be found in intertidal sands, and in the south of England, is *G. depressa* known as the setting-sun-shell owing to the lines of pink which radiate from the umbo. All such bivalves resemble *Donax* although the foot is relatively smaller, the gills larger and the palps reduced. In other words they are suspension feeders with wide and shortish siphons. Burrowing is shallow and they are in danger from predators and notably from starfish which some species elude by leaping. The foot is bent round under the shell and then suddenly straightened.

The larger and longer species of *Solecurtus* occur in deeper water and have peculiar features including extension of the mantle cavity at the base of the siphons, but not much is known about their habits. The cruciform muscle is very conspicuous. A final tellinid, almost invariably classified with the Solenacea because it has a razor-like shell, is *Pharus legumen*, about 12 cm long and shown in comparison with *Ensis arcuatus* in Fig. 115. Inspection immediately reveals the centrally-placed ligament while the short siphons are separate and of the characteristic tellinid pattern; all that is missing is the cruciform muscle, here probably unnecessary because the siphons are so short. Another instance of convergence. This bivalve is not uncommon but is difficult to obtain because it inhabits a narrow zone of sand which is seldom exposed for digging but is also too shallow for dredging. The American jack-knife clam, *Tagelus*, is similar but lives rather deeper and always in mud with longer siphons extending separately to the surface.

The remaining deep burrowers, coming from a diversity of origins but achieving surprising final similarities in appearance and habits, have all massive fused siphons protected by thick periostracal layers. This is because their siphons also comprise the periostracal-forming region of the outer mantle fold as well as the other two folds. These deep burrowers include species of the Myacea, Mactracea, Saxicavacea and Adesmacea (pholads) although certain Antarctic Laternulidae (p. 223) would also qualify. Adult movement is excessively slow or even impossible but the siphons can be deeply withdrawn into the protection of the widely gaping posterior margins of the valves. Although frequently bitten off by fish, the siphons readily regenerate (this is equally true of the Tellinacea where the siphons of *Tellina tenuis* are a major food of young fish).

The Myacea, in the form of the basket-shell, *Corbula* (Fig. 87) have already been mentioned. This is a common shallow burrower in muddy sand or gravel below tidal levels. The rounded shell is about 1 cm in diameter and unmistakable because the left valve, the margins of which are uncalcified, fits into the right one. The very short siphons are surrounded by periostracum below the outer row of tentacles which fringe the middle fold. The foot is long but burrowing is a very slow process. This animal must seldom emerge in nature once it is buried when it invariably attaches by a single byssal thread. In all respects, apart from the lateral asymmetry, this is a typical lamellibranch bivalve with a large gill and long palps. The well-developed cleansing mechanism involves accumulation of pseudofaeces posteriorly and periodic contraction of the quick muscle component in the adductors.

From such a condition one line of evolution has been towards byssal attachment as in *Sphenia binghami*, of much the same size and occasionally dredged off the south and west of Great Britain. It is byssally-attached often within empty shells with some change towards the mussel form with a reduced anterior adductor. The other line leads to loss of byssal attachment and to deep burrowing as in *Mya arenaria* (Fig. 119), the sand gaper and the very similar *M. truncata*, the blunt gaper. Both are northern species occurring in both the Atlantic and the Pacific although the former has been artificially introduced into the Pacific. This is the much prized soft-shell clam. It is a notable bivalve, 15 cm or more in length, oval-shaped and covered with a dark brown periostracum; the other species is shorter with the hind end truncated instead of rounded and living in a coarser grade of muddy gravel. In both the thick siphons (Fig. 119) are much longer than the shell, the

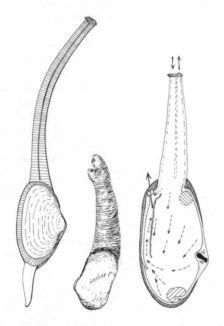

FIG. 119. Deep burrowers: *left, Mya arenaria; centre, Panomya norvegica; right, Lutraria lutraria*, showing interior of mantle cavity with cleansing currents conveying pseudofaeces into a waste canal bounded by a membrane; extrusion through the 4th aperture.

attachment of the retracting muscles forming a deep siphonal embayment or sinus at the hind end of this. The adult habit is slowly acquired. Young animals are byssally-attached (Fig. 120) with an active foot. Later they assume a vertical posture descending deeper as they grow larger probably more as a result of expulsion of water through the anterior pedal gape than by the action of the foot which diminishes in size and activity. When dug out large individuals cannot re-burrow. The contained animal is essentially similar to that of *Corbula*.

Species of *Lutraria* (Fig. 119), the otter shells, are very similar in shape and size and in siphonal length. There are three British species usually in sand although only *L. lutraria* occurs within tidal levels. The periostracum is pale so that shell and siphons are much lighter in colour than in *Mya* while viewed internally the shell valves are easily distinguished. Those of *Lutraria* have a prominent spoon-shaped chondrophore (for ligamental attachment) in each valve whereas in *Mya* this is only present in the left valve. These otter shells are deep burrowing mactrids having the same relationship to the enormously prolific shallow burrowing trough shells, species of *Mactra* and *Spisula*, as *Mya* does to *Corbula*. Again the shallow burrowers have periostracal encased siphons, the prerequisite for elongation in deep burrowing, and largely fused mantle margins. All mactrids have an additional (fourth) opening

FIG. 120. *Mya arenaria*, 4 mm long showing relatively larger foot at this stage, smaller siphons and byssal attachment. (After Kellogg)

at the hind end where pseudofaeces are extruded instead of through the long inhalant siphon (Fig. 119).

A third deep burrower, *Panomya norvegica* (Fig. 119) is very occasionally dredged in northern European waters although the smaller but very similar *P. ampla* is common in shallow water in the north Pacific which is also the home of the largest of all such burrowers, the closely related *Panope generosa* or 'geoduck'.* Here shell and fully-extended siphons attain an overall length of 90 cm (3 feet). This bivalve was once common intertidally in muddy sandy bottoms in British Columbia and the State of Washington but because it is so edible it is now largely absent where it was once dug. The animal is much

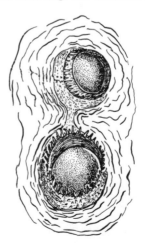

FIG. 121. Siphons of the deep burrower *Panomya ampla* viewed *in situ* on surface of mud. Inhalant (lower) opening fringed with inner and outer rows of tentacles, exhalant opening with inner bounding membrane which concentrates and directs the outflowing current.

* North American Indian word, possibly meaning 'dig deep'.

larger than the shell can accommodate (the same is true of *Panomya*) with the pallial muscles as broad as the adductors with which they merge. The large and very thick shell is essentially a means of attachment for these enormous muscles. Siphonal openings, very like those of *Panomya* (Fig. 121), can occasionally be detected at very low tides when an impressive current is observed to emerge through the exhalant opening, a striking indication of the power of the lateral cilia on gills far below. Little is known about the early stages in life but the adult, only to be dug with knowledge of correct procedures and expenditure of great energy, has long been incapable of doing more than slowly descending with increasing size, again probably by downward expulsion of water. The foot becomes relatively small. *Panomya* and *Panope* are both members of the Saxicavacea, a group comprising bivalves of very varied habits, much the commonest being species of *Hiatella* (*Saxicava*); byssally-attached, but also boring into rock a habit which leads on to the subject matter of the next chapter.

Chapter 16

Borers in rock and timber

*

ROCKS on shores of limestone, sandstone or mudstone are frequently bored into by animals; in tropical seas boulders of coral rock are usually riddled with borings. Although by no means the only animals responsible, bivalves are the most numerous and varied of borers. The two valves with the elastic ligament with the attaching foot or byssus provide an obvious means of boring, the achievement of which confers the major boon of protection against most predators. With such an advantage it becomes less surprising that species of seven different superfamilies have become adapted for what is certainly a difficult mode of life. Moreover this endpoint of efficient boring has been reached by two different routes, one by way of epifaunal byssal attachment the other of infaunal deep burrowing.

The commonest British borer is probably *Hiatella (Saxicava) arctica* (Fig. 122), up to 3·5 cm long and popularly known as the red nose on account of the pink-tipped siphons. It occurs on all levels on the shore and in shallow water in both the north Atlantic and the north Pacific. In habit this is primarily a 'nestler', like various bivalves mentioned in the last chapter, although allied in structure to the deep burrowing *Panomya* and *Panope*. It lives within sheltered crannies in rock and also in the hollow holdfasts of laminarian oarweeds.

The very solid, often irregularly ridged, shell of a nestling *Hiatella* is easily recognized. The reddish-tipped siphons project clear of the crevice; they are massive and only with difficulty withdrawn between the broad and gaping

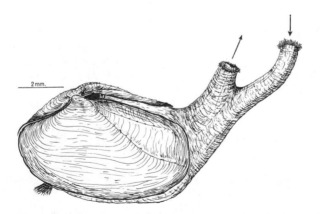

FIG. 122.   Red nose, *Hiatella arctica*, siphons fully extended and byssus projecting.

205

hind margins of the valves. Formerly the nestling individuals were regarded as a separate species from the borers but it now appears that the two may differ only in habit. If larvae settle on to a relatively soft homogeneous rock surface they will bore into this but if the rock be hard and creviced then they will nestle. The borers penetrate mechanically as revealed by the much-eroded valves. They do not produce a byssus. Force for boring is provided by water pressure within the mantle cavity forcing the valves apart, the siphons being closed and the animal braced against the wall of the boring by dilation of their basal regions (Fig. 123). Although the process may seem rather crude the

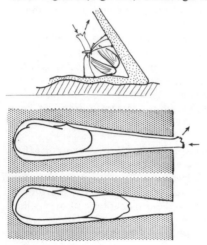

FIG. 123. *Hiatella*: *above*, 'nestling' individual secured by byssal threads within empty barnacle shell; *below*, boring individuals, one with siphons expanded while feeding, the other with siphons contracted and dilated giving purchase while boring. (After Russell-Hunter)

resultant boring is highly efficient. The excavated tunnel is circular in section showing that the animal must rotate within it as it bores.

Date mussels, species of *Lithophaga* and closely allied to the common mussel, are probably the commonest rock borers although confined to calcareous rocks and to warm and tropical seas. They are familiar objects in the Mediterranean where these 'dattero di mare' are frequently present in fish soups in southern Italy. In both dark brown colour, due to thick periostracum, and in shape they closely resemble dates. They are borers pure and simple, the bullet-like shape perfectly adapted for penetration through rock. Here the byssal threads are retained and disposed in two bundles, in front and behind (Fig. 124). The byssal (formerly pedal) retractor muscles are similarly disposed

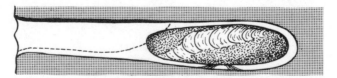

FIG. 124. Date mussel, *Lithophaga*, within boring showing byssal attachment. (After Otter)

and act independently; when the posterior group contract they will pull the animal forward on the anterior group of attaching threads, then the anterior muscles will contract and pull the shell back on the hind group of threads, and so the process will go on.

However, despite this to and fro movement, date mussels do *not* bore mechanically, the periostracal covering is usually intact. Mantle tissues protruded between the valves at the front end (Fig. 125) are applied to the head of the boring. In a still somewhat obscure manner the rock is softened, the resultant layer of paste scraped off by the valves. These borings provide

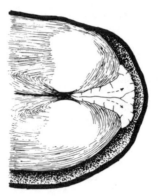

FIG. 125. Date mussel, head of boring with mantle tissues applied to calcareous rock.

evidence of earth movements, notably at Pozzuoli, north of Naples, where limestone columns, the bases of which are now around sea level, are perforated at a height of from 4 to 6 metres by the boring of *Lithophaga* indicating subsidence to this depth and subsequent return near to the original level (Fig. 134).

Closely related bivalves, species of the more elongate *Botula*, the Californian pea-pod shells, do bore mechanically but into mudstones. The two groups of byssal threads and the operative retractors are larger while the periostracum is extensively eroded. Neither *Lithophaga* nor *Botula* rotate in the boring which conforms to the cross-sectional outlines of the shell, i.e. with a ridge along the roof left between the two umbones. The strangest boring mytilid is the recently discovered *Fungiacava* which lives symbiotically within mushroom (fungid) corals. The excessively delicate shell is enclosed in an envelope of mantle tissue, the animal literally 'dissolving' its way through the coral skeleton. The large inhalant siphon opens into the gastric cavity drawing in the plant plankton which the carnivorous coral neglects.

Amongst the highly successful but very standardized venerids (p. 194), species of the genus *Petricola* are byssally-attached nestlers and from that habit some have become borers. The former habit is displayed by the rounded *P. carditoides*, a Californian species which occupies rock crevices which it may enlarge as it grows. The elongated rock-boring *P. pholadiformis*, the American piddock, was introduced – again with American oysters – into Great Britain in 1890 and is now well established around south-eastern shores, particularly in the Thames estuary. It occurs off both the Atlantic and Pacific

FIG. 126. *Left*, *Petricola carditoides*, a 'nestling' species from California; *right*, *P. pholadiformis*, boring species introduced from America into G. Britain. Note modified shell. (Drawings by V. Warrender)

coasts of North America and also in Europe. It bores with great efficiency into softer rocks, also into London Clay and into peat. The borings are characteristic because the siphons emerge through openings separated by a plug of rock scrapings aggregated in the mucus which is produced in quantity by all species of *Petricola* (Fig. 126). The sequence of boring activity is similar to the digging cycle in other venerids (p. 142), the major scraping action being produced by contraction of the posterior pedal retractors which forces the anterior margins of the shells with their chisel-like projections down and across the head of the boring.

A further 'nestler' which has become a borer is the smallest of the tridacnids (p. 193), *T. crocea* which, attached by an unusually massive byssus grinds its way down, umbones undermost, with the margins of the shell valves keeping level with the surface of the coral rock into which it invariably bores. The brilliantly coloured siphonal margins containing symbiotic plant cells extend widely over this (Fig. 1). Boring is mechanical, the massive byssal muscles contracting, first on one side then on the other, the ridges on the thick tridacnid shell ground down flat.

Two superfamilies consist exclusively of borers. The first is the very small group of the flask shells (Gastrochaenacea). These occur in numbers in coral rock but also live in temperate waters, one species, *Rocellaria* (*Gastrochaena*) *dubia*, being found in the south-west boring into the limestone blocks composing the Plymouth breakwater and also into red sandstone. The shell is

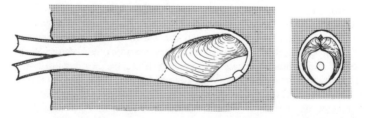

FIG. 127. Flask shell, *Rocellaria* (*Gastrochaena*) *dubia* shown within boring, cavity extended by calcareous tubes secreted by siphons. *Right*, frontal view showing position of pedal opening. (After Otter)

PLATE 13. *Above, Acteon tornatilis*, a sand-burrowing opisthobranch, showing the plough-like, flattened head lobes; from South Wales. *Below*, sea-lemon, *Archidoris pseudoargus*, with spawn; exposed at low tide; from South Wales.

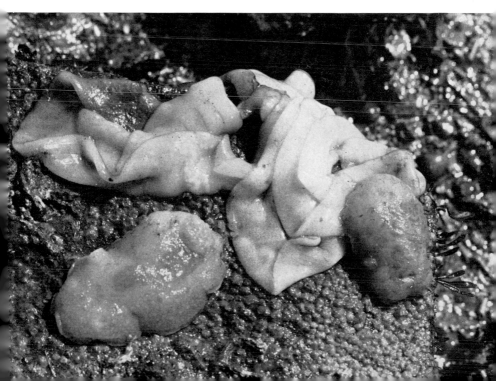

PLATE 14. *Above*, chitons, *Acanthozostera gemmata*, up to 14cm long, on their typical substrate of eroded coral rock; Great Barrier Reef of Australia. *Below*, giant clam, *Tridacna gigas*, about 1m long, half exposed at low tide, with siphonal tissues withdrawn; colony of soft (alcyonarian) coral attached to one valve; Great Barrier Reef of Australia.

up to 2·5 cm long and is quite unmistakable being cut away on the side in front and tapering behind (Fig. 127). But, despite its external appearance, it is heteromyarian with the anterior adductor greatly reduced, indicating a byssally-attached stage in its evolutionary history. The borings also are unmistakable, not only flask-shaped but with separately projecting calcareous openings formed by the naked siphons. The outer regions of the borings have a similar limy covering. In some species, certainly in those that bore into coral rock, the borings may be extremely deep and, although the siphons are long, the animals probably move about within the boring. The animal holds on to the head of the boring by the foot which is modified to form a sucker projecting forward through the pedal gape. Boring is mechanical and probably accomplished (because conditions are not too well known) by contraction of the anterior pedal retractor muscles. The opening thrust of the long ligament and hydrostatic pressure in the mantle cavity are also significant. There is no rotation within the boring.

The remaining rock borers have attained that habit by way of deep burrowing. *Platyodon cancellatus*, a close relative of *Mya* (p. 202), bores into soft mudstones along the Californian coast. The shell, more rounded in section than that of *Mya*, is up to 6·5 cm long, concentrically ridged and much eroded in the umbonal regions. The thick periostracum covering the siphons is thickened near the tip to form four 'scales' which enlarge the siphonal region of the boring as the animal grows. Unlike all previous borers, where the pedal retractors are responsible for penetration, boring in *Platyodon* is due to the

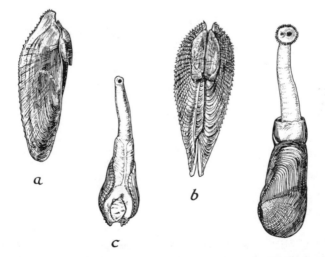

FIG. 128. Rock-boring piddocks: from *left* to *right*, *Pholas dactylus*, interior of right valve; upper view showing plates between valves; smaller *Barnea parva* from under surface with pedal opening; lateral view of paper piddock, *Pholadidea loscombiana*. (From Jeffreys, *British Conchology*)

alternate contraction of the adductors, the valves rocking about a dorso-ventral axis as described below.

The most highly adapted group of borers are the Adesmacea comprising the rock boring pholads and the even more specialized shipworms (Teredin-idae). The pholads or piddocks (Fig. 128) are well represented in Great Britain as they are generally in temperate seas. The largest is the handsome common piddock, *Pholas dactylus* up to 15 cm long, with the smaller white piddock, *Barnea candida* less than half that length and little piddock, *B. parva*, only some 4 cm long. There are also the massive oval piddock, *Zirphaea crispata*, and the distinctive 'paper' species *Pholadidea loscombiana**. Only *B. candida* and *Z. crispata* occur generally, the other three being southern species confined in Britain to southern and south-western shores. The two species of *Barnea* occur up to mid-tidal levels, the others extend from low water level to depths of 6 to 8 metres.

These are very beautifully adapted bivalves knowing no way of life other than boring and penetrating a wide range of material extending from stiff clay and peat, occasionally including waterlogged timber, to rocks. In the nature of things they all live between tidemarks or in shallow water. They never, except as settling larvae, possess a byssal apparatus and both in struc-ture and in the mode of boring appear to have evolved from deep burrowers.

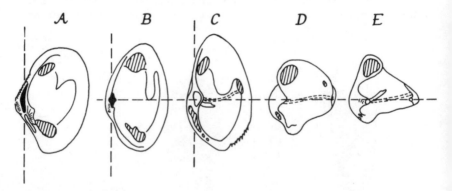

FIG. 129. Stages in the evolution of the boring bivalve shell in the piddocks and the shipworms: A, Venerid *Mercenaria*, valves move only on the antero-posterior (here upright) axis; B, *Mya*, some rocking on the dorso-ventral axis (here horizontal); C, rock boring *Zirphaea* (pholad) with limited movement still on original axis; D, E, wood-boring *Xylophago* and shipworms, movement solely about dorso-ventral axis. (After Nair & Ansell)

This is indeed what some of them, notably *Zirphaea*, remain although clay is penetrated in the same manner as rock.

Boring is mechanical by the scraping action of the modified and ridged shell valves. To a greater extent than in *Platyodon*, this involves rocking of the

* These shells are particularly well illustrated and described in *British Bivalve Seashells*.

valve about a dorso-ventral axis, the result of changes indicated in Fig. 129. In typical shallow burrowers such as the soft-shelled clam, *Mercenaria mercenaria* (p. 194) the valves move only about the antero-posterior axis of the hinge line with its long ligament and interlocking teeth (A). In deep burrowers such as *Mya* – leading on to *Platyodon* – where the ligament is more condensed and the valves gape posteriorly, some degree of rocking at right angles to this occurs, the two adductors contracting independently (B). But in the pholads (C) this tendency is taken further, the ligament greatly reduced or

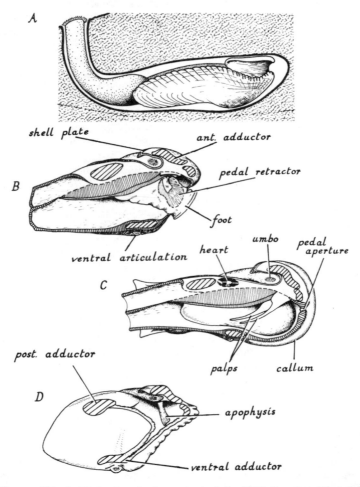

FIG. 130. A, piddock, *Pholas dactylus* drawn *in situ* (after P. H. Gosse); B, *Pholadidea penita*, actively boring with large foot; C, ditto but ceased to bore, pedal opening almost closed by callum, foot degenerated; D, interior of left valve. (B-D, after Lloyd)

lost and the valves gaping at both ends and rocking on the double ball joint of the umbones. The valves are cut away in front much as in *Rocellaria* (Fig. 127) allowing permanent protrusion of the sucker-like foot. Above this wide pedal gape each valve is curled back along its upper margin so moving attachment of the anterior adductor above the hinge line for the greater efficiency of the rocking movements. The upper surface so exposed is covered, according to the species, by one or more shell plates (Fig. 130, B) not found in any other bivalve*. Another new structure, the apophysis, consisting of a curved calcareous rod extending down from within the umbonal region is present in each valve (Fig. 130, D). The pedal muscles are attached to these so providing a straight pull against the head of the boring when the foot is attached. An additional (accessory ventral) adductor, formed by cross connection and enlargement of an area of the pallial muscles, appears about the middle of the under surface and slightly behind the dorso-ventral axis. This muscle works with the posterior adductor to supply the greater force needed when the front halves of the shell separate and their outer ridged surfaces scrape the rock surface. This is the effective action; contraction of the anterior adductor merely draws these halves of the shell together against little resistance. The united siphons are large with only the basal half, actually the extended mantle cavity, covered with periostracum, in this respect differing from other deep burrowers (p. 202).

The boring cycle in these highly adapted animals differs significantly from the burrowing cycle (p. 162). Starting with the piddock free in its boring and the valves open (Fig. 130, A), blood is forced into the foot which extends forward and dilates to attach by suction to the head of the boring. Contraction of the pedal muscles pulls the valves against this. The siphons now close and first the accessory and then the posterior adductor contract, scraping the anterior halves of the valves against the rock surface. This is followed by contraction of the anterior adductor while the siphons reopen. Blood is withdrawn from within the foot which loses attachment after which the animal rotates in one direction or the other for a maximum distance of about 30°, a process which, taken first in one direction and then in the other, produces a completely circular boring like that of *Hiatella*. Scraped fragments enter the pedal gape to accumulate as pseudofaeces at the hind (upper) end of the mantle cavity from whence they are regularly expelled by a wave of muscular (peristaltic) contraction starting at this end of the cavity and proceeding to the tip of the inhalant siphon which opens for the forcible expulsion of the waste.

The long, spinous, hard and yet also delicate shell valves of *Pholas dactylus* (Fig. 128) are not infrequently found along the strand line. In life this species has the unexpected, and biologically unexplained, capacity for luminescence. It glows within its boring with a greenish-blue light. A luminous mucoid secretion is liberated into the exhalant siphon from three regions, a narrow band along the anterior margin of the mantle, a pair of bands extending along the interior walls of this siphon and from two triangular areas near the siphonal retractor muscles.

---

* Which led to their former association with chitons as 'multivalves'.

Pholadidea (Fig. 128) has unique features. The shell terminates at the hind end in a trumpet-shaped collar into the shelter of which the siphons contract. It bores as do the other pholads holding on with a large foot (Fig. 130, B),

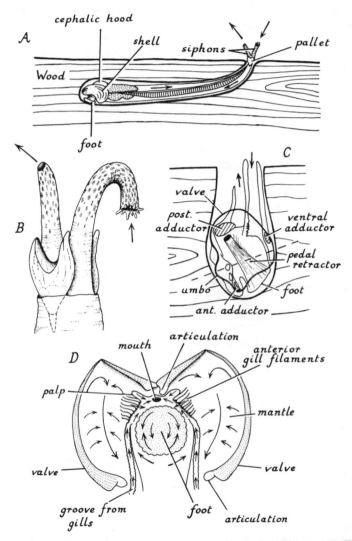

FIG. 131. Shipworms: A, appearance within wood of a boring shipworm; B, *Teredo navalis*, siphons and pallets; C, wood piddock, *Xylophaga dorsalis*, diagrammatic half section of animal in boring; D, *Lyrodus pedicellatus*, shell valves separated to exposed rounded foot with mouth, minute palps and anterior gill filaments, arrows indicate ciliary currents. (B, D, after J. B. Morton; C, after Ansell & Nair)

213

until it reaches maturity when the shell is about 4 cm long. Foot and pedal muscles then atrophy and the pedal opening is reduced to a fine aperture by ingrowth of the surrounding mantle here covered with a callum (Fig. 130, c) consisting of periostracum secreted round its margins. The object of boring, namely protection, has been achieved; the animal now lies passive in the boring, engaged in feeding and reproduction.

In the wood-boring Teredinidae (Fig. 131), clearly derived from pholadiform ancestors, the rounded shell (Fig. 132) is divisible into a hinder winglike lobe known as the auricle, a central rounded area which forms the bulk of the valve and a triangular lobe, sharply cut away below which extends for only the upper half and below which the rounded foot protrudes. The outer surface of the middle and anterior regions are covered with rows of sharp ridges which are continually being added to during life. Viewed internally (Fig. 131) there is no trace of ligament (and no remnant of the original opening movements of the valves) while rocking movements are perfected by the addition of a second ball and ball joint in the middle of the underside of the shell (Fig. 131) so completing the series A to E (Fig. 129). There is no accessory adductor while the very much larger posterior one is broadly-attached to the auricles. The shell has lost all protective functions, enclosing only a very small part of the body, but has become a highly efficient cutting tool, a kind of living centre bit, for boring into timber.

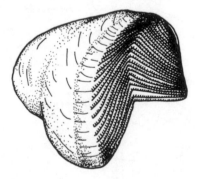

FIG. 132. Right valve of shipworm *Bankia*. (After Turner)

The extent of the long naked body of *Teredo navalis* is shown in the X-ray photographs of animals *in situ* within timber (Plate 15). The opening into the boring is inconspicuous, dumb-bell-shaped and with a calcareous lining that also covers all but the working end of the boring. This lining is said to have given Brunel the idea of a similar lining to the tunnel he drove under the Thames. Unlike other borers, shipworms are attached just within the opening. By this means the siphons are withdrawn; their retractor muscles could not function if still attached to the shell valves which become increasingly distant as they bore into the wood. The naked siphons are separate and capable of great extension. On withdrawal the lined opening is closed by means of a pair of calcareous pallets (Fig. 131) which are unique to the shipworms. Each consists of a stalk which is embedded in the tissues at the base of the siphons and a terminal indented blade; they are pushed out of the opening when the siphons extend. The closure they effect is so efficient that shipworms can survive for long periods when the timber they inhabit is out of water, a matter of obvious significance for wooden ships. Borings that open on the upper surface of submerged timber in still water are often piled high with accumulating mounds of wood fragments. These come more as faeces through the gut than as pseudofaeces through the mantle cavity. The siphons maintain passages through these mounds by forming delicate calcareous tubes around themselves, a reminder of the capacity for secreting lime which is latent in all outer mantle surfaces.

These are notable bivalves known since the dawn of history owing to their devastating effect on wooden ships and timber structures in sea water. Long considered to be the worms they simulate, only in 1733 did the Dutch zoologist, Snellius, engaged in studying the damage inflicted on dykes in the Netherlands, identify them as bivalve molluscs.

There are abundant species the world over, most numerously in the tropics. In British waters and in the North Atlantic generally there are four species apart from a few, including species of the related *Martesia*, which may turn up in floating timber. All were formerly regarded as species of *Teredo* but of British species only the Linnean *T. navalis* remains within this genus. *Lyrodus pedicellatus* is indistinguishable from it in shell form but the pallets differ. The larger *Nototeredo norvagicus* is the commonest species with *Psiliteredo megotara* confined to floating timber. The species can best be identified by the pallets. The world over fourteen genera are now recognized, including species of the widely distributed *Bankia* with long segmented pallets which enable the siphons to be more deeply withdrawn. The largest is the giant shipworm, *Kuphus*, up to two metres long. It probably starts life in timber, certainly ending it encased in a massive tube embedded in mangrove mud.

Shipworms are best described in terms of their life history. In some species the eggs are expelled for fertilization in the sea; in others sperm is conveyed from the exhalant siphon of one individual into the inhalant siphon of another to pass through the gills and fertilize the eggs in the exhalant chamber where (unlike oysters) they are incubated. For periods varying in different species from 24 hours to many weeks during which they can be transported over great distances, the veliger larvae remain in surface waters. They then settle and do so more probably in shade, which may be provided by a wooden vessel or a wharf, than in more exposed conditions. Although they may alight on any surface they only remain there if this be of wood. Some constituent in this stimulates metamorphosis and the production by the briefly-crawling foot of a single byssal thread. So attached there is immediate change in shell form and boring starts with the minimum of delay; it is all-important that the minute animal should find protection. The shell and foot change in form and function, pallets appear and become attached near the opening of the boring. As the 'head' end bores the naked body elongates between advancing shell and fixed pallets. Boring proceeds essentially as in the pholads, the ridges on the anterior end of the shell scraping the softer wood surface whenever the

215

larger posterior adductor draws the auricles together. Movements of 180° first in one direction and then in the other cut a perfectly circular tunnel, somewhat wider, however, in diameter than the shell which can at any time be withdrawn from the head of the boring. The one new feature is a flap of mantle, the cephalic hood (Fig. 131), which overlaps the upper surface of the valves and assists in pressing the scraping surfaces firmly against the wood.

All scraped fragments enter the pedal gape (Fig. 131) but then pass into the mouth, not carried back to be ejected as pseudofaeces. Wood, unlike rock, may be edible, at any rate when an animal is able to convert its major constituent, cellulose, into the simple sugar, glucose. Like the Tridacnids (p. 193), however, despite possession of an accessory source of energy, the shipworms continue, to greater or less degree, to feed in the usual manner of a bivalve. This demands description of the gills.

In these elongated animals the visceral mass, containing the gut, heart, kidneys and reproductive organs extends back for a distance equivalent to about three times the length of the shell. Still further behind the body consists of an ever-elongating tube divided by the gills into lower, inhalant and upper, exhalant chambers (Fig. 133). The simplified gills consist of a single very

FIG. 133. Shipworm, section behind visceral mass, gills consisting of a single modified lamella on each side.

shortened filament on each side with a food groove running along the lower margin. Food is collected in the normal manner by sieving the planktonic content from the water entering through the inhalant siphon. In some shipworms the gill filaments form a continuous series forward to the mouth but in all British species the series is interrupted in the region of the visceral mass to be resumed by a few filaments on either side of the mouth (Fig. 131). Functional contact between the two sets of gill filaments is made by way of a ciliated groove. In *T. navalis* and *L. pedicellatus* the palps are small and functionless but in *N. norvagicus* which lives closer inshore where the water usually contains more sediment, they are larger and must serve the usual selective function. In all shipworms ciliary currents on either side of the under surface carry waste, pseudofaecal, particles backward. But wood in these animals is *not* waste.

Thus both plankton and wood fragments enter the mouth but not necessarily at the same time because shipworms alternate in their activities. The siphons must be closed during boring when increased pressure within the mantle cavity is needed to force the shell against the head of the boring. When boring ceases the siphons open and filter feeding is resumed, plankton instead of wood fragments now entering the mouth. The alimentary system is similarly adapted for dealing with both types of food. The elongated stomach has ciliary mechanisms, absent in that of the pholads, for separating wood and plankton. The latter passes into normal tubules of the digestive gland, but wood fragments are shunted into a long 'appendix' where they are stored and may possibly experience some preliminary digestion although this process is certainly completed within a distinctive type of wider digestive tubules into which only wood is passed. Both appendix and wide tubules are unique to shipworms. The process of digestion involves the action of enzymatic cellulases that convert cellulose into the simple carbohydrate glucose. It remains somewhat uncertain whether these enzymes are produced by the animal or by bacteria, but probably by the former. Bacteria are certainly contained in a series of structures, unique to the shipworms and named, after their discoverer, the glands of Deshayes which occur in the gills and elsewhere. However these are not in the digestive system although they may well have another very significant function. Shipworms can be maintained, boring and growing, in seawater from which all plankton has been filtered. This could be explained if these bacteria fix the nitrogen needed to build up protein from the glucose obtained by digestion of wood. The final residue of digestion, largely of indigestible lignin, passes from the anus into the long exhalant cavity to be finally voided through the exhalant siphon. True faeces are much more abundant than pseudofaeces in shipworms.

Many new problems present themselves when bivalves bore into timber. After penetrating the surface, shipworms normally follow the grain of the wood (see X-ray photograph in Plate 15). During boring water must be forced through the pedal gape ahead of the animal and into the air vessels that run along the grain. Unlike pholads, which can bore straight through other individuals if encountered at right angles to their path, shipworms very rarely enter a foreign tunnel. In some way they are aware of its presence and withdraw the shell (of smaller diameter, remember, than the boring) and resume movement in another direction. They do this repeatedly in heavily infested wood which finally becomes a honeycomb of intertwining passages (Plate 15) and then gradually crumbles away.

When the shell is withdrawn water must pass through the pedal gape into the space between this and the head of the boring. One must emphasize the constant water pressure in the mantle cavity which is aided by muscular movements from the siphonal end forward during boring. Moreover constant moisture of the wood ahead appears to be necessary for lubricating and cooling the actively scraping valves. With this probably come bacteria and fungi which aid in the disintegration of the wood. Although shipworms are able to pass from one block of wood to another if the two are firmly attached, they never emerge from wood, probably because they are unable to bore through the superficial softer layers. The calcareous lining to the boring which is laid down by the soft surface of the extended mantle becomes continuous over the

217

head end when the animal ceases to bore, due to lack of space or to age because shipworms are short-lived. The complete limy tubes can be removed intact from heavily infected wood. If growth ceases for lack of space, the enclosed animal may still draw in water and plankton, the final condition much as in *Pholadidea*.

Owing to the prior need to describe shipworms, we have neglected animals which in many respects represent an earlier stage in their evolution, namely the wood piddocks, species of *Xylophaga*. The rounded *X. dorsalis* with the shell, but *not* the body, of a shipworm occurs in water-logged timber and may turn up anywhere around British coasts. It is common on both sides of the north Atlantic and descends to considerable depths. Some species are abyssal. Boring essentially as do the shipworms, these wood piddocks excavate only a rounded boring into which they neatly fit but to which they are in no way attached and there are no pallets. They feed solely on plankton, unable either to swallow or to digest wood fragments. Unlike shipworms they may live in other media such as the insulating covering of deep-sea cables. These are animals that live in isolated groups, a very few individuals or even just a solitary one present in one piece of timber, the next such population possibly far distant. This raises problems in reproduction. Shipworms occur usually in great populations together, the spawning of one stimulating that of others until the entire adult population is liberating sexual products. Clearly this is not feasible in *Xylophaga*. All these animals are initially male then change to female (in the shipworms with a possible change back to male if they live long enough). That is they are protandrous, sometimes alternating, hermaphrodites. With the shipworms, some are young and male, others older and female and no problems arise. But if a young and therefore male *Xylophaga* liberated sperm it is highly improbable that a female would be available. Instead, as discovered by R. D. Purchon, sperm are stored in a receptacle, unlike anything known in other bivalves, to remain viable until the animal enters the female phase. The eggs then produced are fertilized by these stored sperm.

Viewing the shipworms, including the wood piddocks, as a whole, an interesting series can be described. It begins with *Xylophaga* which, like the pholads, bores solely for protection and not invariably, although usually, into wood, which in any case it cannot digest. The series proceeds with shipworms which attain full protection but initially feed primarily on plankton, with gills, palps and digestive system concerned with that form of diet. The giant *Kuphus* which possesses no appendix very dubiously feeds on wood and certainly can only do so when young. Specialization in the shipworms culminates in those that gain most of their energy from the wood in which they live. The gills are reduced to separate hind and front sections, the palps are functionless and the digestive system with modified stomach, long appendix and wide digestive tubules is specialized for digesting cellulose from wood.

Shipworms are, of course, animals of economic importance still doing great damage to wooden structures in the sea. Protective measures include copper sheathing, impregnation with poisons, usually in creosote, detonation (which will kill the animals *in situ*) and many other methods. As animals they are completely fascinating; the writer knows of no better instance in the animal kingdom of adaptation to a specialized mode of life which involves changes in the shell, foot, pedal and adductor muscles, mantle cavity, alimentary canal and, particularly in *Xylophaga*, reproduction. So very much more could be written were space available.

FIG. 134.   Pillars in the 'Temple of Jupiter Serapis' (so described) at Pozzuoli, near Naples, showing zone of borings by date mussels. Plate from the 'Observations' made thereon by Charles Babbage in 1828 (published in 1847).

Chapter 17

Anomalous bivalves and scaphopods

*

FINAL branches of the strangely proliferating tree of bivalve evolution are represented by an assortment of particularly sluggish and retiring animals, all essentially burrowers in habit although with some interesting divergences from this. In one direction they culminate, evolving in profound depths, in the highly modified carnivorous septibranchs and in another in the appearance of the remarkable exotic 'watering-pot shell' where the animal occupies a long calcareous tube with only the merest vestige of the valves to indicate that this is formed by a bivalve. These denouements of bivalve evolution carry us on, without separation into a new chapter, to description of the invariably tube-dwelling, although burrowing, elephant's tusk shells or scaphopods, the most isolated of molluscan classes.

These anomalous bivalves comprise a number of superfamilies without interlocking hinge teeth but with the probably compensating appearance of a characteristic ligament which often contains a calcareous inclusion, not fused to the valves and known as the lithodesma. It may well be a means of maintaining alignment of the valves in the absence of teeth. The mantle lobes are closely united although usually with the presence of an additional small fourth opening (such as we noted in *Ensis* and in *Lutraria*). There is only a limited number of species to consider and we start with species of the family Lyonsiidae, represented by *Lyonsia norvegica* (Fig. 135), a northern species as its specific name indicates and dredged from moderate depths where it lives in muddy gravel. The thin, elongate shell, up to 4 cm long, is easily recognized by the thick periostracum roughened to the touch by incorporated sand grains while the inner surface is characteristically glossy. If the ligament be intact the calcareous central streak of the lithodesma will be apparent. This is a burrower but a particularly lethargic one. Placed on the surface of its particular substrate it penetrates this in the usual manner but extremely slowly finally taking up a vertical position with the tips of the very short, separated siphons flush with the surface. An interesting feature is the presence of a single byssus thread which, attached to pieces of gravel, doubtless aids in stability although giving a further impression of general immobility.

Related animals occur in shallow water and between tidemarks. Two Californian species, *Entodesma saxicola* and *Mytilimeria nuttallii* indicate the range of habits and something more of the structure of these peculiar animals. The former is somewhat longer than *Lyonsia* but the valves are deeper, often irregular and they gape posteriorly where the separate siphons project (Fig. 135). These appear to be fused at the base but the fused region is actually an extension of the mantle cavity, its outer surface, like the shell, covered with thick, sand-engrained periostracum whereas the siphons themselves are naked.

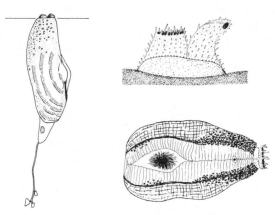

FIG. 135. *Left, Lyonsia norvegica,* normal position in sand attached by byssal thread (after Ansell); *above right, Mytilimeria nuttallii,* siphons projecting from ascidian colony; *below, Entodesma saxicola,* under surface with emerging byssus, exposed mantle covered with periostracum and adherent sand grains.

This animal has a massive byssus and lives, often intertidally and always alone, in holes and between boulders, immobile and largely obscured by encrusting sand grains. Byssal attachment saves it from being torn off and broken up during storms although the irregular shells show frequent signs of damage. Here again byssal attachment has led to a reduction of the anterior adductor muscle.

Mytilimeria has taken this epifaunistic mode of life a stage further by coming to live within colonies of compound ascidians (sea-squirts) which form encrusting masses several centimetres thick on the surface of rocks. This has much more far-reaching effects on the bivalve than the somewhat similar habit noted in the small mussel, *Musculus marmoratus* (p. 170). The presence of *Mytilimeria* is revealed by the projecting siphons (Fig. 135) and, when these are withdrawn, by the presence of slits about 1 cm long on the surface of the dark-coloured ascidian colonies which may house many bivalves each with a globular shell about 2·5 cm in diameter. The young must settle on the surface of the ascidian colony – another instance, as in the shipworms, of selection of the adult environment by the settling larvae. The presence of a settled bivalve inhibits ascidian growth locally so that the animal sinks inward as the colony grows to be finally completely enclosed within it. Attachment is by way of the sticky periostracum; there is no byssus. The ascidian colonies live much the longer so that dead bivalve shells are often found within them. *Mytilimeria* is common between tidemarks and in shallow depths and in its distinctive manner represents an obviously successful exploitation of its sluggish habits and sticky periostracum by association with animals of widely different nature.

The family Pandoriidae consists of related animals but all laterally flattened, rather like small somewhat elongated scallops although lying on the left instead of the right valve. This valve is cupped whereas the upper (right) valve is flat (Fig. 136) or even slightly concave. What appear to be teeth on the valves have actually to do with attachment of the ligament. Species of *Pandora* occur widely throughout the northern hemisphere, always on sandy bottoms where they may be extremely abundant; in general habit they resemble both scallops and the tropical window pane shells.

FIG. 136.   *Pandora albida*, on surface of sand. (From Allen)

There are two British species, *Pandora albida* (*inaequivalvis*), (Fig. 136), and *P. pinna*. The former, up to 3 cm long, occurs off western coasts from low spring tide level downward but is commonest on sheltered sandy beaches around the Channel Isles and along the coast of Brittany. The much rarer *P. pinna* is only taken below 30 metres. These animals are inhabitants of very sheltered waters, never burrowing in captivity and if they do so in life it can only be very superficially, because the separated siphons are extremely short. The foot seems more likely to be used as a means of uncovering the animal if buried during a storm than for burrowing.

The next family, the Thraciidae, is represented in British waters by no less than five species with an added variety of one of these. But none is common and only two occur between tidemarks and these at the lowest levels. They are all typical bivalves with white or cream-coloured shells, oval or rounded in outline, the right valve always slightly the larger so that the umbo of the smaller valve grinds into and sometimes penetrates through that of the larger. The shells are often sizeable ranging in length from 2·5 to 9 cm, the surface usually very smooth and also extremely fragile. The shell of the globose *Thracia convexa*, up to 6·5 cm in diameter, which occurs in gravel at some depth off the west coast, is almost paper thin and will collapse unless handled with the greatest care. The species most likely to be encountered is the atypical *T. distorta* which has a thick irregular shell up to 2·5 cm long with pronounced growth lines. Unlike the other species, all of which burrow, this is a byssally-attached epifaunal nestler of very similar habit to *Hiatella arctica* (p. 205) although it never bores. The young settle into rock crevices and there grow to conform with the space available. In the words of Jeffreys (1865), 'The distorted growth of this species shows that it does not excavate the holes in which it lives. It sometimes appropriates the labours of other animals, but never unjustly or consciously, like a plagiarist. The original and short-lived fabricators of the dwellings subsequently occupied by the *Thracia* are beyond the power of complaint . . .'

The mode of life in the burrowing species is more obscure. Personal observations many years ago in the Bergen Fjord on what was probably *T.*

phaseolina revealed that the animal burrows quickly into the normal substrate of shell gravel by means of the broad, very thin foot. A little later the tips of the separate siphons broke the surface each dilated into a terminal sphere (Fig. 137). This distension had been reported for the inhalant siphon of *T. distorta* by Forbes and Hanley in 1853 and thought to be associated with expulsion of water. But in the animals observed these distended tips were pulled back into the substrate enlarging the opening and consolidating the sides with mucus. The process was repeated several times until firm

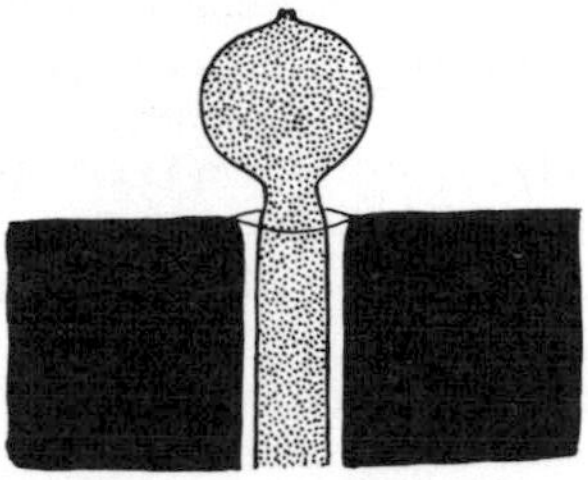

FIG. 137. *Thracia phaseolina*, terminal distension of siphon when constructing mucus-lined tube.

mucus-lined inhalant and exhalant tubes were formed. The siphons were then withdrawn although occasionally protruded to re-establish the linings which finally became so firm that they could be withdrawn intact, each some 2 cm long. The surface of the shelly gravel was finally broken only by a series of openings about 2 mm wide and about 1·3 cm apart; into one an inhalant stream entered, out of the other an exhalant current emerged. The openings of the siphons remain closed during tube formation when water pressure dilates their extremities. They only open after they withdraw when the tentacles fringing the inhalant siphon extend and feeding and respiratory currents are established.

Formation of a mucus-lined tube is reminiscent of conditions in the Lucinidae (p. 187) where the inhalant tube is formed by the modified foot and an exhalant tube by a temporarily extended siphon, and yet again of the pelican's foot shell, *Aporrhais* (p. 88) where, however, the inhalant and exhalant tubes are formed by the proboscis and for exclusively respiratory needs. This habit has the major advantage of allowing these thraciids to live well below the surface and feed on suspended matter without exposing the naked siphons. Tellinaceans such as *Tellina tenuis* where the inhalant siphon searches the bottom for organic detritus must expose their naked siphons which are avidly consumed by young bottom-living fish such as plaice. But these far more numerous bivalves are highly mobile whereas these thracids are suspension feeders with no need to move in search of food and can remain in one place indefinitely. It could be that they have survived – succeeded seems hardly the word – just because of this ability to withdraw these very vulnerable siphons. But much probably remains to be learnt about these retiring bivalves.

The next family, the Laternulidae, contains some impressive members, notably in the southern hemisphere and off Antarctica where species of *Laternula* are the dominant deep burrowers, equivalent in size and general appearance to northern species of *Mya, Lutraria* or *Panope* and *Panomya* – another instance of convergence. In British waters there is only the related *Cochlodesma praetenue* which is very like a thracid in general appearance, oval in outline and up to 3·5 cm long. It occurs in fine gravel, sand or sandy mud from the lowest tidal levels to fair depths. Like all related bivalves it can be distinguished by the presence of a crack extending downward along the hind margin of the umbonal region and possibly associated with the posterior gape of the somewhat unequal valves which are rocked about the condensed ligament by independent contractions of the two adductor muscles, as in *Mya* and pholad and teredinid borers (p. 214). Like *Pandora* this bivalve lies on its side but about 7 cm below the surface and indifferently on either valve. The separate and very extensile siphons resemble those of *Thracia* in their ability to form mucus-lined tubes although here the entire siphon dilates to do this and not merely the tip. Moreover only the inhalant tube reaches the surface, the other extending for about the same length but horizontally into the substrate (Fig. 138), reminiscent of conditions in the Lucinidae (p. 187).

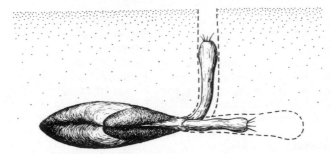

FIG. 138. *Cochlodesma praetenue*, lying *in situ* under surface, mucus-lined tubes shown by broken lines. (After Allen)

Of course the two inhabit very similar substrates although the latter are deposit feeders; however *C. praetenue* appears to be the more active with new tubes formed every 12 to 72 hours.

So far we have been dealing with the usual variations on a particular bivalve theme but now proceed to the first of the two very different culminations, the one leading to the functional replacement of the ciliated ctenidia by a muscular septum and the associated change to a carnivorous habit. The British fauna contains several examples of such unexpected bivalves but for evidence as to how such bivalves evolved we must move into profundal depths. There, amongst the commonest members of an impoverished bottom fauna, we encounter species of the bivalve family Verticordiidae. These are all excessively small and also, due to scarcity of food, probably extremely slow growing, but what particularly concerns us is that although they retain re-

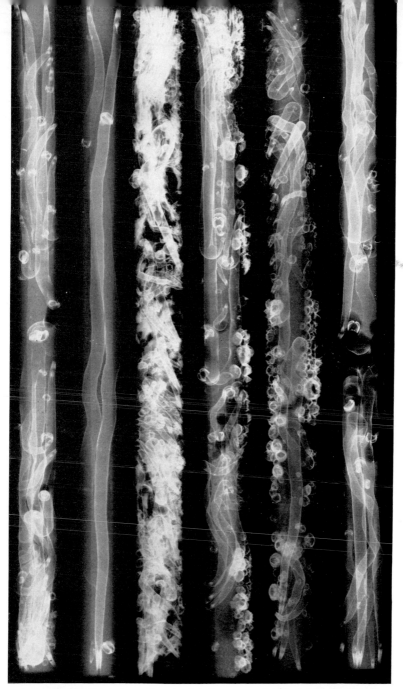

PLATE 15. Radiographs of dowels of timber variously infected by the shipworm, *Lyrodus pedicellatus*. Note speedier growth when infection is slight and the animals follow the grain (second from left); also the inter-twining but never inter-communication of the borings. Acorn barnacles cover the surfaces of the second and third dowels from the right.

PLATE 16. *Octopus vulgaris: above*, female occupying cavity in aquarium tank in Plymouth. This she retained against all comers, prior to laying eggs. *Below*, eggs hanging in strings from the ceiling of a rock cavity.

duced gills these are no longer concerned with ciliary feeding. General structure is shown in the drawing of a typical example, *Lyonsiella perplexa* (Fig.
139), kindly supplied by John Allen who has a unique knowledge of these obscure animals. Coming from the great depths of the sea these animals cannot
be examined living but the large foot indicates mobility while relatively large
food masses (which at those depths can only be of animal origin) can obviously

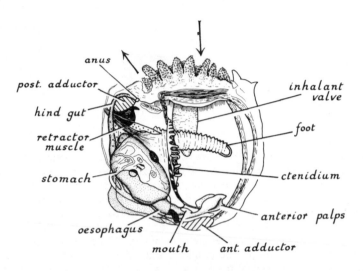

FIG. 139. *Lyonsiella perplexa*, showing general structure of this largely abyssal
family, carnivorous with modified gills and palps. (Supplied by Allen)

enter through the wide inhalant opening, a process probably assisted by the
encircling ring of tentacles. The large valve will prevent subsequent loss. Very
obviously still present, the ctenidia are reduced to a series of widely spaced
filaments on each side and the reasonable assumption is that they act as a
kind of conveyor belt taking food from the inhalant opening to the mouth
which, in life, will be directly below it. There it will be pushed in by the here
very muscular palps, a process which has been personally observed in the
larger and more shallow-living septibranchs mentioned below. In all such
bivalves the palps have lost the ciliated grooves and ridges and with it their
former selective powers. Food passes through a very wide oesophagus into
a capacious stomach the very mixed contents of which indicate a very catholic,
although inevitably non-herbivorous, diet.

From such animals we pass to larger and more accessible bivalves, species
of *Poromya* where the gills are completely replaced by a very differently
operating muscular septum although traces of filaments persist. One of these,
P. granulata, about 1 cm long and living in muddy bottoms at depths of
around 160 metres and below was personally studied many years ago in the

FIG. 140. *Poromya granulata* (septibranch): *left*, mantle cavity opened showing, from above downward, inhalant siphon, foot surrounded by septum perforated by lattice-like pores, enlarged muscular palps. *Below*, siphonal openings viewed from above.

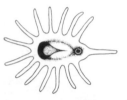

Trondhjeim Fjord. Conditions here are shown in Fig. 140. The mantle cavity is here horizontally divided by a delicate muscular partition or septum which is perforated by two pairs of delicate lattice-like grids formed of what certainly appear to be short' lengths of ctenidial filaments bearing lateral (certainly current-producing) cilia but without the frontal or latero-frontal cilia found in the lamellibranch bivalves. The observed disposition, when buried, of the outspread siphonal tentacles on the mud surface must be much the same in the verticordiids. The palps are muscular flaps and the bag-like stomach, lined throughout with cuticle, may contain intact crustaceans waiting to be crushed up in this gizzard-like structure. *Poromya* is beyond question a true carnivore pulling in dead, moribund or just possibly very slowly moving animals by sudden updrawings of the septum, which occur about once a minute. A large valve, similar to that in *Lyonsiella*, prevents any loss of food.

Poromya does not appear to be recorded as a British species although it may well occur in deep water off the northern coasts of Scotland. But a number of species of the even more specialized *Cuspidaria* occur in northern British waters some being found in depths as shallow as 20 metres in the Clyde sea area including Loch Fyne and the Kyles of Bute. The shell is unmistakable with the hind end drawn out into a characteristic narrow siphonal extension varying in length in different species, to the greatest extent probably in *C. rostrata*, again from the deep water of the Trondhjeim Fjord (Fig. 141). However all species function in the same manner.

In *Cuspidaria* (Fig. 142) there is no trace of ctenidial remnants in the impressively massive septum which is secured like a hammock at its four corners with additional lateral attachments. It adheres closely to the foot which penetrates it anteriorly and is perforated by paired series of valve-like pores, four in *C. rostrata* and five in the largest British species, *C. cuspidata*. When at rest the septum is updrawn with the pores open, the cilia around their

FIG. 141.   *Cuspidaria rostrata* (septibranch), lateral view.

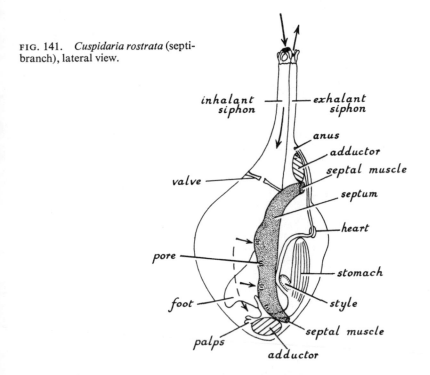

margins producing a gentle flow of water into the exhalant chamber. At more or less regular intervals, about four times a minute in *C. cuspidata*, the septum bellies out and gently descends. Then the pores close by contraction of their surrounding sphincter of muscles and the whole structure is pulled suddenly upward. The resultant inrush of water through the large inhalant, and then expulsion of water through the restricted exhalant, aperture are very obvious in the intact animal – a striking contrast to the continuous inflow and outflow through these openings in ciliary feeding bivalves. Food, consisting largely of very small crustaceans and worms, intact or in pieces, is drawn into the inhalant chamber.* The valve prevents it from escaping or being forced out when the septum next descends. It is then pushed into the wide mouth by the purely muscular action of the palps. Cilia are restricted to tracts that remove accompanying sediment. The barrel-like stomach with a thick cuticular lining and encircled with muscle – totally unlike the elaborately ciliated stomach of the typical bivalve – forms a gizzard in which this animal food is crushed. The crystalline style is reduced to a dubiously functional remnant and the gut, as in carnivores generally, and unlike that in typical bivalves, is very short.

* Robert and Alison Reid now find that the inhalant siphons respond to low-frequency vibrations created by potential prey, usually small crustaceans.

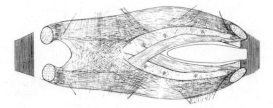

FIG. 142. Septum of *C. rostrata* viewed from above showing complex musculature with four pairs of simple pores and terminal and lateral attachments to shell, foot with anterior adductor on right, posterior adductor on left.

This is a striking culmination to this particular line of bivalve evolution. These septibranchs must be envisaged as evolving in deep water below the influence of light where plants cannot exist. Animals that feed on plant plankton only penetrate into these depths if they become modified as carnivores. This is true of the few sea squirts found in great depths and also applies to the deepest-living scallops, species of *Propeamussium*, although they retain the gills and the precise mode of feeding has never been determined. But in the septibranchs the whole method of feeding has been profoundly altered and with such success in *Cuspidaria* that they have been able to work their way back into shallow water and successfully compete with other animals consuming what are probably largely detrital animal remains. *C. cuspidata brevirostris* is not at all uncommon on muddy gravel in Scottish waters. We have, of course, already encountered 'pumping ctenidia' in protobranchs such as *Malletia* (Fig. 85) but there the 'septum' is composed of modified distended filaments and the stomach has not become a crushing gizzard although certain areas of the surrounding digestive tubules are modified for ingesting relatively large objects such as diatoms. Resemblance between the mode of feeding has suggested some connection between protobranchs and septibranchs but it is just another instance of convergence. How, we may fairly ask, does the septum originate? It continues to perform the same function of food collecting (though not the original one of respiration here assumed by the mantle surface) as does the ciliated ctenidium. Unfortunately nothing is known about how the septum is formed in the embryo although the eggs of these hermaphrodite animals are large, suggesting direct rather than larval development. It has been suggested that the septum represents the enlargement, to the almost complete exclusion of everything else, of the muscular elements particularly in the ctenidial axes. The other view is that it is a new structure created by the forward extension of the septum which divides the siphonal openings. What John Allen has recently found out about verticordiids such as *Lyonsiella* supports the former view as does the fact that the mode of water flow by way of the inhalant opening, 'up' through pores in the septal partition and out through the exhalant opening remains unchanged, all pointing to yet another instance of the molluscan ability to modify existing structures for new functional needs. We see in the next chapter how profoundly the mantle cavity has been altered to meet the still more demanding needs of animals such as squids and cuttlefish.

Such a striking change in food and in the mode of feeding and digestion leaves the external form essentially unaltered: septibranchs are unmistakably bivalves. This is far from the case in the clavagellids, a very small and completely exotic group which represents the other culmination of evolutionary change within these anomalous bivalves. These animals occupy tubes of their own construction. The simpler 'tube-shell', *Clavagella*, which occurs associated with coral reefs in the Red Sea and elsewhere, settles in a crevice. The left valve becomes cemented while the somewhat larger right valve excavates or enlarges a burrow which the fused siphons proceed to extend, keeping pace where necessary with the growth of the coral and in the process, laying down a calcareous tube. The strangest aspect of this remarkable procedure resides in the cementing of the one valve which presumably gives the purchase for boring (supplied elsewhere, as we saw in the last chapter, by the foot, by byssal attachment or by distension of the mantle cavity with water). However, it was probably from some such beginnings that the still more remarkable 'watering-pot' shells, species of *Penicillus* (formerly *Aspergillum* or *Brechites*)

FIG. 143. Watering-pot shell, *Penicillus* (*Aspergillum*) *javanum*, enclosing tube, siphonal end uppermost and perforated 'rose' below, this also shown from below. The minute bivalve shell is embedded in the tube. (After Hornell)

must have evolved. Here the minute although symmetrical shell valves are suitably described as being 'soldered' on to a massive tube (Fig. 143). This may be up to 20 cm long, frilled at the upper end but the other terminating in a rounded, somewhat convex and much perforated plate like the rose of a watering can. Julia Ellen Rogers in her *Shell Book* (1908) may be quoted,

'A strange beast is this which outgrows its bivalve shell, and builds greater after a plan quite distinct from the bivalve pattern; all the organs of the body are changed to suit life in the new abode. The molluscs occur in numbers in sand and mud near low water mark; disturbed they retire within their stony citadels whence they are with difficulty extricated.' Matters are not quite so extreme as she puts them; the animal retains the gills and normal bivalve organs. The tube is formed by an outpushing of the mantle surfaces. How the perforated basal plate is formed we have no idea because these animals seem perversely rare in areas where they have been scientifically sought although, referring to Indian shores, James Hornell* wrote that 'They are common on our sandy shores, washed up after storms; they may also be found at very low spring tides embedded upright in the sand.' It is a major mystery how from first settlement of the presumably planktonic larva, the adult shell is formed; possibly this does not take place until the animal is fully grown because while the tube could be remodelled during growth it is hard to see how the perforated 'rose' could gradually enlarge. Indeed how this unique structure is formed is a complete mystery although the persisting foot, with no apparent function other than cleansing, could find yet another function here. Again, what is the function of the rose? These animals are undoubted ciliary feeders and they would appear to be motionless although unattached; just possibly they may erect themselves by forcing water through the perforations. But there is no bivalve about which we know so little and about which we would like to know more.

In these unattached water-pot shells open at both ends, the bivalves come superficially nearest to the equally anomalous tusk shells, members of the Class Scaphopoda. Here the possibilities of the molluscan body plan have taken a new direction involving a wrapping round of the viscera and head by the mantle and shell, the two sides of which fuse to form a tube. This is characteristically narrow at one end and wider at the other and usually slightly curved like the elephant's tusk after which the scaphopods are popularly named. They are not unsuccessful in their exclusively infaunal mode of life to which, however, they are structurally so committed that, to an even greater extent than in the chitons, further evolutionary diversity is denied them. They are an old group, originating in the Devonian, in the middle of the Palaeozoic, and have not altered significantly, at any rate in shell structure, since then. They would appear early to have evolved a structure adequately fitting them for infaunal life.

There is one common British species, *Dentalium entalis*, never found living on the shore although the empty shells may be washed up. They are unmistakable, very solidly constructed, pure white and slightly curved tubes up to about $3\frac{1}{2}$ cm long and 4 mm across at the wider end. Even in dredging the bulk of the shells taken are usually empty, they take so long to break up. This is a northern species just reaching as far south as the northern coasts of the English Channel. There are four other British species. *D. vulgare* is a stouter and more southern edition of the commoner species; two species of

---

* 'Indian Molluscs' by James Hornell. Bombay Natural History Society. 1951.

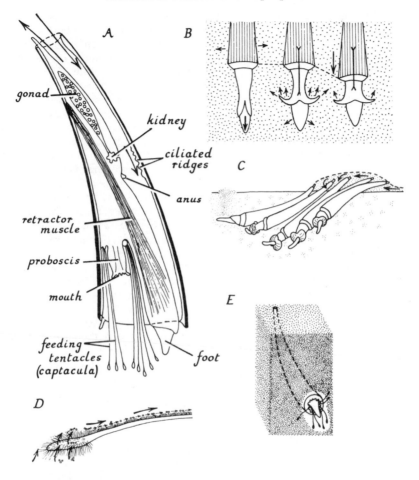

FIG. 144. Structure and habits of Scaphopods: A, *Dentalium*, longitudinal view showing major structures; B, diagrams showing stages in the 'digging cycle' (after Trueman); C, successive stages in twisting motion during burrowing (after Dinamani); D, terminal region of captaculum in *D. conspicuum* (after Dinamani); E, *D. pseudo-hexagonum* shown *in situ* indicating extent of excavated feeding cavity. (After Gainey)

Siphonodentalium with translucent and very tapering shells occur off far western coasts while the much smaller, rather bottle-shaped, *Cadulus jeffreysii* is another northern and far western (i.e. deep sea) species. But all scaphopods are immediately recognizable for what they are. Knowledge of the living animal covers *D. entalis* with related species from the Indian and Pacific Oceans.

231

All live at moderate to very considerable depths on sandy or sandy mud bottoms. They can be observed in aquaria where they speedily burrow when placed on their accustomed substrate. The basic structure, differing so clearly from that of all other molluscs, is shown in Fig. 144. Owing to enclosure by the enfolding mantle and shell, both 'anterior' head and 'ventral' foot point in the same direction to emerge from or be withdrawn within the wider opening of the slightly curved shell, the concave side of which is 'dorsal'. The head consists of a muscular proboscis from the base of which extend a series of long club-ended tentacles unlike anything else in the molluscs and known as captacula. They are both feeding and sensory organs. The pointed foot with paired retractors (shell muscles) attached high up on the shell is also unique in possessing a pair of epipodal lobes some distance behind the tip. The tubular mantle cavity is devoid of ctenidia, the only cilia being carried on a series of transverse ridges in the middle of the cavity. There are the usual internal organs although the circulatory system is so far reduced that there is no heart. There is a radula and a sizeable stomach and a coiled gut which opens at the anus about half-way along the cavity. As in primitive gastropods, the terminal gonads open by way of the paired kidneys.

So much for structure; how does the animal function? Burrowing takes place by a digging cycle essentially similar to that in the bivalves. With epipodal lobes closely adpressed and forced forward by blood pressure and narrowed by contraction of the surrounding muscles, the pointed foot probes downward (Fig. 144). When they are fully extended the lobes erect to form a pedal anchor. The retractor muscles then contract and the shell is pulled down. This in turn becomes the anchor and the process is repeated without, however, quite the efficiency of the bivalves but also without the accompanying need because these tusk shells do not penetrate to any depth; the narrow end must always project above the surface. The process of burrowing is oblique and may be accompanied by rolling although always ending with the concave, dorsal, surface uppermost (Fig. 144).

When finally at rest, at any rate as personally observed in *D. entalis*, there is a sudden expulsion of water through the projecting opening every 10 or 12 minutes followed by a sudden inrush and then a decreasing inward flow. The major water movements are due to those of the foot, the slower inward flow to the action of cilia on the ridges. There is no continuous inhalant and exhalant flow as there is in the bivalves. Respiration takes place through the thin walls of the mantle (as it does in septibranchs) while the ciliated ridges possibly also convey sediment to the captacula and so to the mouth.

Food comes primarily from the substrate. Somewhat as we observed in the pelican's foot shell (p. 88), a 'feeding cavity' about the size of the expanded foot is established around the buried end of the shell (Fig. 144) in this case, however, not by the action of the proboscis but by that of the foot which probes in a circle round the shell opening pushing the sand clear of this. Indeed, unlike other molluscs, the foot does appear to play some part in feeding, its generally ciliated surface carrying material into a furrow leading to the proboscis. But the captacula are the major feeding organs. Their enlarged tips (Fig. 144), bearing the usual molluscan combination of cilia and mucus-producing glands, probe into the walls of the feeding cavity to collect detrital particles including, certainly in *D. entalis*, the chambered limy shells of foraminiferan protozoans. The radula conveys food into a crushing gizzard. The faeces eventually voided will be expelled through the terminal opening. When the local supplies of food are exhausted, the animals can move upwards, just as do razor shells, by reversal of the movements of the digging cycle, the foot, with extended epipodal lobes, forming an anchor while blood pressure forces the shell upward. Penetration can then proceed at a somewhat different angle to expose new feeding areas the possibilities of which are then explored by the sensory captacula, well supplied with nerves and the only organs that come into intimate contact with their surroundings.

Many molluscan shells have served as currency. Cowries have done so in India and Africa and shell-beads or wampum – white from the shells of the venerid *Mercenaria* and black from those of the whelk *Buccinum* – circulated in New England. More surprisingly, until the middle of the last century, tusk shells formed the currency over a wide area of the north-west of America, from Alaska south to the northern end of California and inland as far as the Dakotas. The units of currency were usually strings of five or ten shells; the greatest, however, a fathom long, the distance between outstretched arms. So many strings were paid for a wife, so many to compound for murder (much cheaper for a woman than for a man) and so forth. The shells were also used extensively for personal adornment, sometimes through the nose, by both men and women. The origin of so many shells when the animals usually inhabit deep water is somewhat of a mystery although they do occur in shallowish water off the west coast of Vancouver Island where the Nootka Indians collected them by means of long spears with a bundle of wooden prongs lashed to the end. With additional poles attached until this reached bottom, the spear could then be jabbed into this to secure the occasional tusk shell, an extremely laborious but because of the value of the product, certainly not an unprofitable fishery.

Chapter 18

Cuttlefish, squids and octopods

*

THESE striking animals, some of which attain the greatest size ever achieved by an invertebrate, are members of the Class Cephalopoda*. They are superficially just about as unlike snails or bivalves as any animals could be. All are marine and usually predacious carnivores, pursuing and rapidly consuming living prey. Apart from the tropical *Nautilus* (Fig. 147) of the Indo-Pacific, the shell is either internal or has been lost, permitting a stream-lining of the body so that, over short distances, squids are the fastest moving of all marine animals. They have remarkable sense organs – with eyes the equal of those of vertebrates – and a highly developed nervous system with an elaborate brain enclosed in a protective cartilaginous cranium. With the activities this controls goes high metabolism with more efficient means of digestion, respiration, circulation and excretion than in other molluscs although it is in these matters that the limitations to cephalopod efficiency ultimately lie. Cephalopods occur in all oceans, most commonly in shallow waters where they may be enormously abundant, but are also present in the midwaters and abyssal depths of the open oceans. Modern cephalopods represent the final evolutionary outcome of a group of primitive molluscs in which the shell became modified to form an organ of buoyancy. Although certain gastropods such as *Ianthina* and the heteropods (p. 96) have become pelagic, this is the basic cephalopod habit in distinction to the passive, bottom-living epifaunistic chitons and snails and the initially infaunal bivalves and invariably infaunal scaphopods. Our first task must be to relate them to these other, more obvious, molluscs.

Recent speculations have derived the cephalopods direct from monoplacophorans possessed of a more highly-spired shell than *Neopilina* (Fig. 6). We have already seen how in the gastropods the viscera became increasingly concentrated in an attenuated shell which, for their more efficient disposal, became coiled first in a plano-spiral as in *Bellerophon* (Fig. 17), the coiling initially directed forward (probably so relieving pressure on the all-important posterior mantle cavity) and only changing as a result of torsion with the accompanying appearance of the first gastropods with mantle cavity now in front. We may imagine the same process taking place but with the apical regions of the visceral mass from time to time withdrawing and the covering mantle proceeding to form a series of internally concave partitions within the cavity of the shell (Fig. 145). Such partitioning is precisely what happens in certain gastropods such as the elongated, cemented vermetids (Fig. 35) where the animal only occupies the most recently-formed regions of the shell. However, in the cephalopods there was much more to the process than the mere

---

* Pronounced with a hard 'c' in Great Britain, with a soft 'c' in the United States.

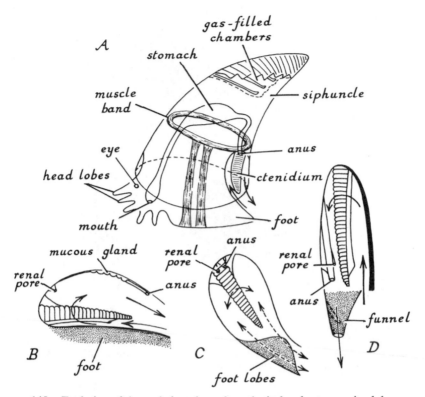

FIG. 145. Evolution of the cephalopods: A, hypothetical early stage, animal drawn out apically with appearance of gas-filled chambers and siphuncle (curvature in this direction would lead to an orthocone, *not* to *Nautilus.*) (Modified after Yochelson *et al*); B-C, changes in the mantle cavity, horizontal with ciliated gills in B, becoming vertical in C with foot lobes forming funnel and respiratory current possibly reversed; D, cavity vertical, reversed current produced by funnel; anus and other openings moved to other side of ctenidia.

formation of shelly partitions. The water which occupied these chambers had to be replaced by gas secreted from the blood. This involved continued connection of the tissues with the cavities, a contact which became restricted to a tube lined with living tissue and containing artery and vein. This siphuncle persists in two modern cephalopods and is best displayed in a longitudinal section through the shell of *Nautilus* (Fig. 146) where it is seen to pass through the centre of every partition. We shall see later how it functions; we can only speculate as to how and by what series of stages, each selected as being advantageous to the possessor, it originally evolved.

It is, however, clear that these evolving cephalopods became progressively lighter until the volume of gas was great enough to counterbalance the weight

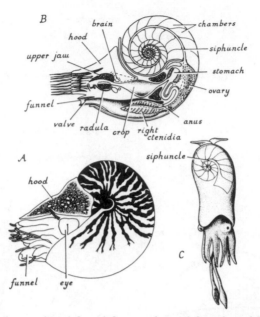

FIG. 146. *Nautilus*, A, viewed from left, tentacles and funnel partially protruded (after Wells); B, longitudinal section showing major structures; C, *Spirula spirula*, normal posture showing internal gas-filled shell.

of the shell and tissues. The animal acquired, as we say, neutral buoyancy so that, without effort, it could rise clear of the sea bottom to which it had previously been confined. One must assume that during these preliminary evolutionary stages the animals changed from a herbivorous to a carnivorous mode of life because the only food in the water above the bottom must have been animals demanding very different modes both of capture and of digestion than for the plants patiently scraped by the broad, many-toothed, surface of the primitive radula. The head of these first cephalopods was presumably furnished with prehensile lobes (Fig. 145), possibly enlargements of those already possessed by monoplacophoran ancestors. From these lobes the arms and tentacles, armed with suckers and hooks, of modern cephalopods could have evolved. The radula, although retained as a conveyor belt (as it exclusively becomes in certain gastropods) gives place to biting jaws as the means of feeding upon prey held within a chamber of encircling arms.

But further significant changes were occurring. While the head developed tentacular lobes for seizing food, the foot was reduced and – a completely new departure in molluscan evolution – became functionally associated with the mantle cavity behind it. This led to the gradual development and eventual perfection (after some hundreds of millions of years) of a jet propulsive mechanism. The mantle cavity remained – and still remains – a respiratory chamber. Owing to the upward extension of the shell it became deeper (Fig. 145) and if the cephalopods did arise directly from monoplacophorans then these animals must already have evolved ctenidia and these must have been restricted to the posterior end (i.e. the cephalopods must have started from much the same beginnings as the gastropods). The ctenidia are once again revealed as a supreme molluscan achievement. They serve as organs of respiration in chitons and gastropods (sometimes in the latter also as organs of feeding), as the most successful of all organs of ciliary feeding (while retaining their respiratory functions) in the bivalves, and now, with adequate increase in respiratory surface and blood circulation, they meet the much greater respiratory needs of the cephalopods. And in addition, through the agency of the modified foot, the exhalant current of deoxygenated water becomes a powerful and exactly directed jet stream.

This all leads to the appearance of molluscs with a very much reduced 'under' surface, with 'anterior' head, 'ventral' foot and 'posterior' mantle cavity pointing in the same forward direction and the 'dorsal' visceral mass (and shell where retained) in the other. The animals have really become U-shaped with anterior and posterior ends coming close together and the previously intervening ventral foot effectively eliminated, reducing to curving lobes around the entrance into the mantle cavity, although in gastropods mouth and anus point in the same direction, this is because the mantle cavity has twisted round to lie in front of the large, previously intervening, foot. However where the foot is greatly reduced – as in the cemented vermetids (where, we may recollect, the pedal glands persist to secrete mucus for food capture) – the body form does resemble that of a simplified immobile cephalopod. So there is a problem of orientation which we may resolve by referring to the front end (comprising 'morphological' anterior, ventral and posterior surfaces) and the hind end (morphologically dorsal surface) of cephalopods.

Initially the front end pointed downward and the hind end upward (Fig. 145). Neutral buoyancy had been achieved but how was the animal to take off from the bottom and move about in the water during what must initially have been short journeys in search of food before returning to rest on the bottom? Here the foot – the most versatile, because the simplest, of molluscan organs – acquires a new form and a new mode of activity. No longer needed for crawling, it becomes reduced in a pair of backwardly-directed flaps which come to overlap one another over the entrance into the mantle cavity. The rhythmical contraction of their intrinsic muscles may initially have been concerned with assisting circulation within the deep mantle cavity. Cilia, which are not present on cephalopod ctenidia, were probably unable to produce the necessary circulation which had to be provided by contractions of the muscular foot. When this change took place we can never know but this is certainly what occurs in the one survivor of these early nautiloids, namely the chambered or pearly *Nautilus* (Fig. 146).

In this animal there are two pairs of gills whereas all other cephalopods have only the one pair, hence the former distinction between tetrabranchiate and the dibranchiate cephalopods. One view is that the two pairs have been reduced to one in the course of evolution but an equally feasible explanation is that, as in the gastropods, there was originally one pair and that the cephalopods had the alternative of increasing the efficiency of this one pair by folding of the surface of the filaments and internally developing a system of ramifying capillaries or else keeping the simpler condition but doubling the number of gills, the former proving the better alternative. It is certainly true that the enormously active squids and cuttlefish have one pair of gills and the sluggish *Nautilus* has two pairs.

At any rate effective circulation within the respiratory cavity is all-important and that is the function of the overlapping pedal flaps in *Nautilus*: by their rhythmical pulsations they draw in water marginally and expel it through the tube formed by their overlapping surfaces. Basically this is a means of producing a respiratory current entering laterally, passing between the gill filaments and then out along the middle line (Fig. 149). But because of its greater power and because the stream can be directed with increasing accuracy by what has now become the cephalopod funnel, it becomes a jet stream and the foot the agent both of its generation and of its direction. Such must always have been the state of affairs when the mantle cavity was enclosed within a shell; only with the loss of this – in all modern cephalopods other than *Nautilus* – does the mantle wall take over the first of these functions. At the same time the funnel becomes a fused tube solely concerned with concentrating and directing the jet stream.

A point to note is that with this new mode of circulation water passes between the gill filaments in the opposite to the primitive direction. A new series of strengthening rods appears on the opposite side to the primitive ones. While these changes were occurring (over what long periods we cannot even guess) the anal and other openings moved into the new exhalant cavity so that their products were carried directly away. This change-over is indicated in Fig. 145. This is yet another instance of the almost indefinite adaptability of the plastic molluscan form.

A vast three-dimensional environment was presented to the members of this new molluscan class which they were to exploit with ever-increasing success, one group succeeding another, until the present time. These animals became pelagic in habit and exclusively concerned with what moved about in the water around them. They developed elaborate sense organs notably those concerned with vision and with gravity, with an associated nervous system far and away more complex and efficient than that in any other group of molluscs. Initially, as we noted, the animals must have pointed downward, swimming upright with the partitioned cap-like shell above. In these early nautiloids (the first cephalopods of which *Nautilus* (Fig. 146) is an undoubted survivor) the chambered gas-filled shell was often coiled above the body, usually in a bilaterally symmetrical plano-spiral (as in *Nautilus*) but sometimes in an asymmetrical turbinate spiral, the animal presumably returning to life on the bottom. In others the shell became extended into a straight tube or orthocone. The consequent change to horizontal disposition involved a redistribution in weight if the animal was to be stable but the more streamlined form gave them greater speed for capture or escape. The largest orthocones were some 5 metres long. Animals with coiled shells must have remained associated with the bottom, like *Nautilus*, those with straight shells were probably the first cephalopods capable of rapid horizontal movements like modern squids.

We have endeavoured so far in this chapter to indicate the stages in which the primitive mollusc described in Chapter 2 gradually acquired weightlessness in water and also the means of propulsion. These early cephalopods were thus able to leave the bottom for brief forays in pursuit of what must, at any rate initially, have been somewhat sluggish animal prey which the enlarged head tentacles could seize. In this manner the nautiloids came into existence, an offshoot of which was to give rise later in the Palaeozoic to the ammonites. These were to flourish abundantly until the end of Mesozoic as their remains – and no invertebrates have ever been better perpetuated in fossil form – bear striking testimony. They began coiled but with a more compressed and keeled shell better adapted for movement through water than any nautiloid shell, and so many remained. Others, however, re-invaded the bottom, possibly crawling like modern octopods, although in the absence of any knowledge of the animals the mode of life in many cases can only be surmised. Although an extremely abundant group, evolving to produce over 600 genera, the largest species over two metres in diameter, they became extinct with the contemporary dinosaurs by the end of the Mesozoic.

With the sole exception of the one surviving nautiloid, all modern cephalopods belong to the Sub-class Coleoidea. These are linked with the nautiloids by way of the belemnites, another extinct group so very common in fossil form, characterized by a straight spindle-shaped shell which, unlike those of nautiloids and ammonites was *internal*. These animals appear and very largely become extinct within the Mesozoic. But the enclosure of the shell was the key to sustained success. The belemnites were survived by animals with further reduced but still initially highly functional internal shells. These are represented by the modern ten-armed cuttlefish and squids (the Decapoda) and the eight-armed octopods. The third, very small, group of the vampire squids (Vampyromorpha) of deep water does not concern us.

After this essential digression on fossil cephalopods, we resume discussion of the living animals and need first to be more specific about *Nautilus* to which such frequent reference has already been made. This is as fortunate a survivor from remote time as the monoplacophoran, *Neopilina*, the primitive slit-shelled gastropods or protobranchiate bivalves such as *Nucula*. It is, however, by no means a recent discovery, the first scientific description being that of the Dutch naturalist, Rumphius, working on the island of Amboyna in what is now Indonesia in 1705. Although living in deepish water, the gas-filled shells rise to the surface after death – sometimes in very great numbers and so probably following reproduction – to be cast up on adjacent or, where pronounced surface currents prevail, sometimes remote shores. Here they were collected by early navigators although the first shells must have reached Europe overland. After removal of the surface layers with acid to expose the underlying nacre, these beautifully symmetrical shells of the pearly *Nautilus*, up to 15 cm in diameter were mounted in gold, sometimes set with gems, to form drinking cups or magnificent ornaments. The chambered shell early excited comment. Although somewhat shaky in his facts, Oliver Wendell Holmes pointed the moral when he wrote,

Year after year behold the silent toil
That spread his lustrous coil;
Still, as the spiral grew,
He left the past year's dwelling for the new,
Stole with soft step its shining archway through,
Built up its idle door
Stretched in his last-formed home, and knew the old no more.

Thanks for the heavenly message brought by thee,
Child of the wandering sea,
Cast from her lap, forlorn!
From thy dead lips a clearer note is born
Than ever Triton blew from wreathed horn!
While on mine ear it rings,
Through the deep caves of thought I hear a voice that sings:

'Build thee more stately mansions, O my soul . . .'

There are six living species the commonest being *Nautilus pompilius* Linnaeus, which occurs in the southern Philippines and further south through the Melanesian islands but the most recently studied species is *N. macromphalus* which occurs off New Caledonia where it can be viewed alive in the fascinating aquarium run by Dr Réne Catala at Noumeá.

The chambered *Nautilus* lives at moderate to fairly considerable depths and has long been caught by native peoples using weighted traps made of split bamboo (Fig. 147) baited with fish or crustaceans and set during the hours of darkness. The animals appear to spend the daytime on the bottom resting on the outer curve of the final whorl of the shell, more or less as represented in the figure, and with the funnel slightly projecting to maintain a gentle respiratory flow. Only when swimming is the head protruded and the funnel extended as a functional organ of jet propulsion. On the upper surface a large

FIG. 147. *Nautilus*, posture on bottom with Philippine fish-trap. (From Dean)

240

pigmented 'hood', formed from two large arms, covers the numerous tentacles (shown extended in the animal on the left of the figure) which, certainly when viewed in aquaria, appear to be withdrawn when the animals are at rest on the bottom. There are 38 tentacles arranged in various groups, including a small pair near the eyes, and totally unlike those of other cephalopods, without suckers or hooks although prehensile. Each can be withdrawn into a sheath to be protruded when food is approached to form what has aptly been described as a 'cone of search'. After seizure the food is held by the inner row of tentacles while it is being bitten into by the jaws.

On either side of the head at the base of the tentacles below the hood is the conspicuous cephalopod eye but here only with a pin-hole opening instead of the highly developed lens of other cephalopods. But these animals are not pouncing on active prey; they are seizing much more slowly-moving animals or carrion, which they recognize by smell. Unlike other cephalopods they will accept dead as well as living prey. The mantle cavity with its two pairs of ctenidia and the anal and other openings lies below the tentacles but facing in the same direction. Its opening is encircled by the downwardly (originally backwardly) directed flaps of the formerly mid-ventral creeping foot which forms the means of jet propulsion in these animals as it must have done in all nautiloids and later in the ammonites. Conditions, as we shall see, are significantly different in the coleoids. In *Nautilus* the mantle cavity is contained within the shell (Fig. 146) and so cannot alter in size, water is drawn into it at the base of the funnel while the undulating flaps of this are forcing water outward. Progression is normally with the rounded surface of the shell foremost, i.e. 'backwards', but the funnel is mobile and can point to either side or backward, the animal moving in the opposite direction to that in which the jet stream is directed. In nature, although not in the less natural conditions of the aquarium, these animals are locally reported as swimming 'as fast as a fish'.

Buoyancy is a matter of supreme importance permitting an alternation between bottom life by day and surface life by night. This is controlled by the activities of the siphuncle which extends through all the cavities. It consists of living tissue surrounded by horny and calcareous layers but as these are porous the passage of fluid or gas is completely controlled by the living tissue. During growth a new cavity is formed by withdrawal of the body mass with accompanied outward extension of the shell margins so enlarging the body chamber. The mantle tissue covering the rounded upper surface of the body then proceeds to form a new partition which consists of the normal, largely nacreous, inner layer of the shell but perforated by a new, basal, addition to the siphuncle. The new chamber is initially full of fluid which it is the function of the siphuncular tissues gradually to remove by way of the blood. From this source also, as in the swim bladder of fish, comes the gas which will here replace the water. The amount of fluid in the chambers diminishes in amount from those most recently formed to the oldest which are usually completely filled with gas. The buoyancy of the animal varies between day and night; it is lighter at night when it leaves the bottom (becoming 'positively' buoyant) than during the day when, becoming 'negatively' buoyant, it sinks to the bottom. The one change involves an increase, the other a decrease, in the volume of gas within the chambers. These changes represent the result of work done by the tissues of the siphuncle. However, unlike the gas bladder of fish where the volume is kept constant by addition of gas as the animal swims deeper and its absorption as it rises in the water, the gas pressure in the shell chambers of *Nautilus* is constant. With increased depth there must obviously come a point beyond which the shell can no longer resist the effect of ever increasing pressure (representing the addition of one atmosphere for every 10 metres added depth). This depends on the mechanical strength of the shell and siphuncle which is so effective that 'implosion' (when the shell shatters utterly) is resisted down to depths of between 500 and 600 metres, i.e. considerably deeper than those in which the animal lives.

Before proceeding from the exotic chambered *Nautilus* to other cephalopods initially of British shores, we should mention the only other species with a chambered gas-filled shell. Among the commonest objects washed up on the higher regions of exposed tropical beaches are flat, loosely coiled shells about 2 cm in diameter, partitioned with a siphuncle running along the inner margin. These come from within the bodies of the little deep sea squid, *Spirula spirula* (Fig. 146) which have floated to the surface on the death of the animal. Their numbers indicate how common this must be. Very occasionally these shells turn up on the west coast of Ireland or of Scotland so that *Spirula* has a slight claim to being a member of the British fauna. The animal itself is never washed up; it is either eaten or else disintegrates long before this could happen. The first animals were taken in deep nets during the pioneer oceano-graphic voyage of HMS *Challenger* between 1872 and 1876. These were studied with the greatest interest but the then conclusion that the shell was partly exposed was due to damage. More recent voyages have produced an abundance of these animals, some of them brought up still living, and revealed that the shell is entirely enclosed within the rounded summit of the body and that the animal swims with this end uppermost in much the same manner as we postulated for the earliest cephalopods. Although totally unrelated, they have the same mechanism of buoyancy control as in *Nautilus* but live much deeper, down to about 1200 metres where there is a pressure of 121 atmospheres. Experiments show that the shell (with siphuncular tissues intact) does not implode until the pressure is considerably greater than that. *Spirula*, therefore, is a deep living or bathypelagic animal which must execute regular up and down movements like those of *Nautilus* but conducted far below the surface.

In other respects very different from *Nautilus*, *Spirula* like all other living cephalopods belongs to the Coleoidea which comprise, as we noted, the ten-armed cuttlefish and squids and the eight-armed octopods. The former have a pair of long, retractile tentacles with suckers confined to their spatulate tips situated within the ring of eight shorter arms (Fig. 148) which, like those of octopods, carry suckers along the entire length. Although in terms of number of species they represent only a small proportion of all the cephalopods that have appeared since the remote origin of such animals in the early Palaeozoic, these modern coleoids are amazingly efficient and represent an unexpectedly

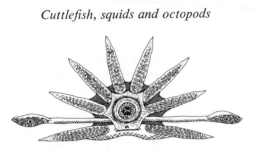

FIG. 148. *Sepia officinalis*, viewed head on showing mouth with jaws and surrounding eight tentacles with suckers and within them the pair of long arms with suckers on their club-shaped extremities. (After Tompsett)

high peak of evolution within the molluscs. In them the restrictions of the enclosing shell – still so evident in *Nautilus* – have been cast aside, the animal becoming linear, with head, foot and mantle cavity now all at the one end and the original dorsal summit of the visceral mass at the other. They have become capable of movement with almost equal facility with either end 'in front'. While in *Nautilus* the funnel generates a relatively gentle jet stream, in these extremely active animals a much greater current is produced by the unenclosed and now highly muscular walls of the deep mantle cavity with the funnel, now a fused and very mobile tube, responsible for its direction and, by control of its lumen, also its strength (Fig. 149).

We begin with the cuttlefishes, represented in shallow British waters by the

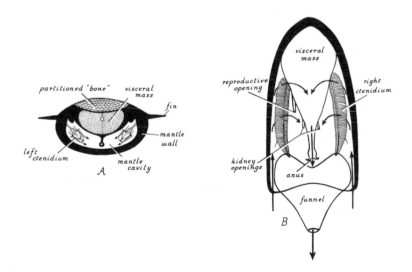

FIG. 149. *Sepia*: A, section through middle of body; B, longitudinal view of underside showing water circulation in the mantle cavity.

243

Living Marine Molluscs

widely distributed *Sepia officinalis*, an impressive animal up to 30 cm long with a broad flattened body extended laterally into rippling fins (Fig. 150) and the relatively narrower *S. elegans*, less than half as long, which is restricted to southern shores although both species extend into the Mediterranean. There are also species of the much smaller, rounded, indeed almost globular, *Sepiola*, the commonest being *S. atlantica* which is only a few centimetres long with short, lobe-like lateral fins which is sometimes extremely common along sandy beaches where these animals may be caught in shrimp nets although they are also taken by trawlers far offshore. *Sepietta oweniana*, which lives close inshore, is about three times as large with *Rossia macrosoma* (distinguished from the others because the mantle edge is not attached to the head) larger still. Both of these two last are commonest in Scottish waters. Of these animals attention must largely be restricted to the first named, the largest, commonest and much the most thoroughly studied. The broad back is sustained by the almost equally broad and completely enclosed 'cuttlebone' (Fig. 150), a familiar object washed up on the strand line and used for a

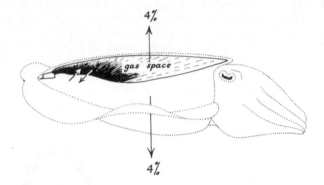

FIG. 150. *Sepia*, diagram showing lateral appearance with undulating fin and internally the chambered cuttlebone filled with gas anteriorly but with a variable amount of contained liquid (shown black) behind. In sea water the cuttlebone gives a net lift of 4% of the weight of the animal in air so balancing the excess weight of the rest of the animal. (After Denton & Gilpin-Brown)

variety of purposes including a source of lime for canaries and other cage birds and for maintaining the condition of the beak. It forms the supporting skeleton but, as indicated by the manner in which it floats on the surface before being stranded, it is full of gas and is just as much of a hydrostatic organ as the chambered shells of *Nautilus* and *Spirula*.

The broad upper surface of a living cuttlefish is the scene of an extraordinary play of colours which has been a matter of scientific comment and enquiry since it was first reported on by Aristotle, the first and among the greatest of marine biologists, who found cephalopods of particular interest. Naked molluscan tissues tend to be richly coloured, as in the sea-slugs (Chapters 10 and 11) and in the tridacnid clams with their widely exposed siphonal

244

tissues (Fig. 1). In cephalopods this coloration is largely due to cells known as chromatophores which can undergo almost instantaneous colour change. Each consists of a bag of colouring matter with radiating strands of muscle which, on nervous stimulation, contract and pull out the spherical cell into a flat plate with its pigment fully exposed. When they relax the cell becomes a minute sphere, its contents effectively invisible. There are three layers of chromatophores, the most superficial contain a bright yellow pigment, those in the middle layer have orange-red contents while the deepest ones appear brown with a tinge of red or maybe almost black. Other, unchangeable, colour cells known as iridophores give, by reflection, a greenish-tinged superficial iridescence. Where these cells are so densely aggregated that they obscure the underlying chromatophores they produce permanent whitish patches on the fins and the back.

With the radiating muscles of each pigment cell under direct nervous control, change between the extremes of contraction and expansion occurs within a fraction of a second when the body surface may alternately flood with colour and then blanch. The pattern of expansion and contraction depends on conditions (Fig. 151). When actively swimming the animals assume a 'zebra' pattern (a), the central region down the back dark brown with alternate stripes of dark and light on each side. The significance of this 'disruptive' pattern becomes obvious when these animals are viewed in their natural habitat among the linear dark green leaves of the eel grass, *Zostera*, which grows in sheltered sandy areas. There they are magnificently depicted by the French artist, M. Méheut in his *Étude de la Mer* where they blend with the pattern of light and shade cast by the dark green leaves appearing like the sinister forms of tigers, their banded bodies similarly, although permanently, adapted for concealment in the broken light of tropical jungles.

Moving on to a bottom of sand or shelly gravel, the colour cells contract and the animal assumes a pale zebra pattern (b) resembling the tone of the background with which it proceeds to harmonize more completely by assuming a light mottled pattern when it settles on the bottom. This normally occurs during the daytime when the fins excavate a cavity into which the animal settles, aiding disguise by throwing sand over its back. Placed in a dark tank with a tightly fitting lid, the animals immediately darken (c) by full expansion of all the pigment cells but gradual introduction of light is followed by their contraction first across the base of the head and then to produce a broad band of light coloration across the middle of the back (d). The effects of disturbance, visual or mechanical, can be remarkable. They consist of a series of effectively instantaneous colour changes involving a total paling accompanied sometimes by the very transitory appearance of longitudinal black stripes (e), all, it would seem, tending to alarm an approaching predator. In last resort the body flattens and two vividly black spots (f) appear against a completely white background, this possibly followed by instantaneous change into almost total blackness. This 'dymantic' display is disconcerting to the human eye and surely no less so to an attacker.

These are protective devices which culminate in the emission of a smoke screen by the expulsion of a cloud of ink (sepium) produced in the ink gland

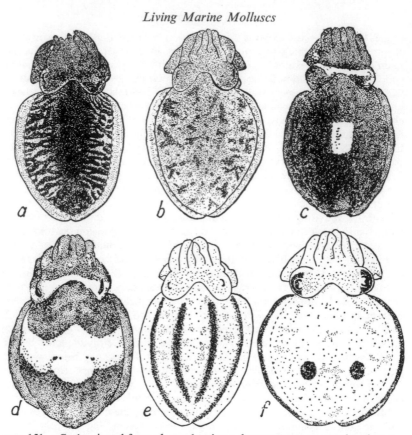

FIG. 151.   *Sepia*, viewed from above showing colour patterns assumed under conditions described in text. (From Hardy after Holmes)

(Fig. 153) which opens near the hind end of the gut. Ink is discharged by way of the anus into the mantle cavity and then expelled through the funnel. No animals other than coleoid cephalopods possess such means of distracting their enemies. Although in an aquarium tank discharge of ink obliterates all signs of the animal (and of everything else) in nature, certainly in squids, it distracts the pursuer while the cephalopod makes good its escape, in a somewhat different direction.

Such are amongst the protective devices of animals sought as food by fishes or dolphins and other toothed whales but themselves amongst the most efficient of predators. When approaching some marked down prey, *Sepia* assumes a characteristic posture with the two uppermost arms held almost vertically (well shown in Méheut's paintings), a pair of sickle-shaped ones extended laterally, and the others ready to grasp the prey first secured by the long tentacles which are shot out with sudden precision from pits on either side of the mouth within the ring of eight outer arms. Cuttlefish approach their prey with caution, the funnel bent back so that they move head foremost. But any cause for alarm and the funnel straightens with a sudden jet that shoots the animal 'backwards'. As the prey, usually crustaceans or fish, is approached waves of colour suffuse the head and arms presumably to distract the prey while the long tentacles are positioned ready to shoot out and secure this, the two working together like a pair of tongs. Both species of *Sepia* have been observed blowing jets of water upon the sand to reveal buried shrimps which, with prawns, are sometimes agile enough to dodge attack several times before final seizure: crabs, however, are wisely approached from the rear. Finally secured, the prey is bitten into by the powerful jaws (Fig. 152)

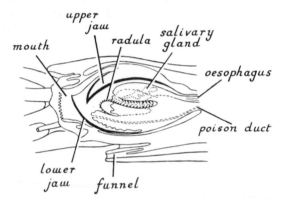

FIG. 152. *Sepia*, longitudinal section through buccal mass with funnel below and including base of tentacles. (After Blochmann & Hamburger)

resembling the inverted beak of a parrot, poison is injected and the food finally cut to pieces and swallowed discarding only a few skeletal fragments. The picture is very different, as we shall see, in Octopods.

Although living in much shallower water, these cuttlefish are not dissimilar in habits to *Nautilus*, tending to bury themselves in sand during the daytime to emerge and feed at night. It is then that Mediterranean fishermen catch them by casting a light down into the water which attracts the animals on which the cuttlefish prey. The animals are actually heavier by day and lighter by night, to such an extent indeed that if kept in total darkness for two days they become too light to remain on the bottom. These changes are due to alternations within the cuttlebone which is a hydrostatic organ equivalent functionally to the chambered shell of *Nautilus*. The mode of operation here, as in *Spirula* and in *Nautilus*, have recently been most beautifully elucidated by E. J. Denton.

Cut in two lengthways the bone is seen to consist of a series of thin chambers separated by delicate calcareous walls maintained by frequent pillars. During life, which is relatively brief, one or two chambers are added weekly. As shown in Fig. 150 the greater part of these cavities is filled with gas, liquid occupying only the hinder and older regions, a necessary provision to maintain the

247

horizontal posture of the animal (otherwise the heavier head end would tip the animal forward). The presence of so much gas cancels out the weight of the dense tissues and the animal achieves about neutral buoyancy. This can be made positive and the animal raised from the bottom without other effort by increasing the quantity of gas. This happens during darkness and the opposite process when light returns causing the animal to sink to the bottom. These changes in the volume of gas are the consequence of pumping water out of or into the posterior chambers in the cuttlebone, this by the action of tissues extended like a membrane over them and serving the same function as the siphuncular tissues in *Nautilus*. The operative power is supplied by osmotic differences between the liquid in the cuttlebone and in the blood. No less than in *Nautilus* the hydrostatic organ must be capable of withstanding external pressure: in the case of *Sepia* implosion occurs at around 24 atmospheres of pressure representing a depth of about 250 metres, much below the shallow sandy bottoms where these animals live.

Structure in these animals is highly elaborate. It involves magnificent sense organs concerned with sight, detection of gravity and of chemicals (a sense of taste rather than smell) with a strikingly complicated brain and the means of rapid digestion of their animal prey. In other molluscs the blood moves leisurely through large sinuses so bathing, but not penetrating into, the tissues and as much used for transferring pressure from one part of the body to another as for the conveyance of oxygen and digestive products. But in cephalopods the major blood vessels eventually divide into a far more efficient system of minute capillaries which ramify through the tissues. Frictional resistance within them absorbs the pressure produced by contraction of a very muscular ventricle. An added pair of 'branchial hearts' (Fig. 153) at the base of the gills is needed to force the blood through a second series of capillaries which replaces the open blood channels within the gill filaments of all other molluscs. They ensure more efficient absorption of oxygen from the

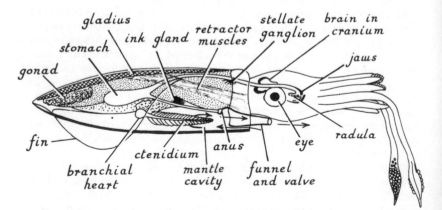

FIG. 153. General anatomy of a squid (e.g. *Loligo*) viewed from right side.

powerful streams of water now forced between the much folded surfaces of the filaments (Fig. 149). At the other end of this enhanced metabolic activity, waste products are removed by way of a much enlarged and more efficient pair of kidneys.

Cephalopod eggs are very large, each of them containing yolk adequate for full development, the young emerging not as larvae but as miniatures of the adult with some yolk still available for further growth. This fact impressed Aristotle who placed the cephalopods in his highest category of 'Anaima' (invertebrates) owing to this possession of 'perfect eggs'.

Young cuttlefish have innate capacity for attack, initially on minute crustaceans but later on larger ones and on fishes, but have to learn by experience that crabs must be approached from behind. Unlike squids which often occur in great shoals, cuttlefish are more solitary animals only seeking their fellows when sexually mature. Initiative comes solely from the male and involves the zebra pattern. When another male is approached this pattern is intensified with the sickle-shaped fourth arm on the side of approach flattened and displayed. The other male assumes a similar colour and posture and conflict may follow with retreat of the less aggressive animal. Absence of such colour response is followed by copulation – even with another male if he fails to respond – the male facing the female and rushing suddenly upon her, a procedure repeated several times over. This involves the transference of sperm from male to female which is an obviously complicated matter when the reproductive organs of both sexes continue to open into the respiratory chamber! In the male (and all cephalopods are of separate sexes) sperm are usually packed into elaborate chitinous cylinders known as spermatophores. By uncertain means – probably by insertion of the appropriate arm into the mantle cavity – these sperm packets enter basal regions of the fourth arm on the left side. This arm is the 'hectocotylus' and is the means whereby the spermatophores are transferred into a sperm receptacle at the base of the head in the female. There they burst, the freed sperm fertilizing the eggs either in the mantle cavity or within the oviducts before they are released.

This remarkable procedure is, of course, basically not so very different from what occurs in the prosobranch gastropods, such as *Littorina* (Fig. 28) where the sperm make their way into a large penis at the right side of the head which later passes them into the oviducal opening in the mantle cavity of the female. It is indeed an argument in favour of the view that the arms of cephalopods are outgrowths of the head and *not* (as the name cephalopod implies) of the foot. That organ is probably entirely converted into the funnel (or siphon – hence the alternative name of siphonopods). In other cephalopods the hectocotylus is inserted into the mantle cavity of the female, in the extreme case of certain octopods, including the 'paper nautilus', *Argonauta* (Fig. 158), the entire arm, here housing free sperm, is detached and left with the female. It was these detached arms, regarded as parasites, that were named as 'species' of the genus *Hectocotylus* by no less a person than Cuvier. He noted that 'Here we have the body of a Polypus which has for its parasite a worm so like the arm of a Polypus that the illusion could not be greater. Let it be judged how many theories might be founded on this extraordinary resemblance. Never has the imagination been exercised on so curious a subject'*.

Egg laying follows, taking some days to complete during which the female starves. Each egg, enclosed in a tough case, is blown separately through the funnel and secured by a stalk usually to seaweed or other marine growth but with eventual production of bunches of up to 300 'black grapes', although colourless ones may be produced.

Squids differ from cuttlefish in their exclusively pelagic habit, the body streamlined and rounded in section with the usually triangular fins restricted to the hind end and acting essentially as stabilizers without the mobility of the rippling cuttlefish fin (Fig. 153). The skeleton is reduced to an elongate chitinous 'gladius' of value only for muscle attachment and for support. The commoner squids are enormously abundant forming a major source of human food in some seas. The commonest British species, *Loligo forbesi*, widely distributed all around the coasts, is now extensively fished, much of the catch frozen for export to Italy. This animal reaches a fully extended length (including the tentacles) of some 60 cm. The related *L. vulgaris* (the common squid of the Mediterranean) occurs only in the south-west. The 'small squid' *Alloteuthis subulata*, only about 15 cm long is widely distributed and commercially valuable but the 'hard squid', *Todarodes sagittatus* and the 'soft squid' *Todaropsis eblanae* distinguished from *Loligo* by the shorter, more posteriorly situated, fins, are caught only for bait. The southern *Illex coindeti* (Plate 12) occurs in the English Channel. The occasionally stranded giant squids, species of *Architeuthis* and *Ommastrephes* are mentioned later.

In the squids the cephalopod structures become supremely adapted for the needs of mid-water life. These involve above all capacities for instantaneous action both for the capture of prey and for escape from predators for which the unprotected body is a constant temptation. The former involves accurate location of prey by means of the magnificently developed eyes and its seizure by sudden projection of the long tentacular arms, all under the control of a highly developed nervous system. The escape reaction is a matter of the streamlined form – with the arrangement of the clustered arms the two ends are equally tapered – and the ultimate modification of the mantle cavity as a precision instrument of jet propulsion. Ejected ink clouds further confuse the pursuer while the squid turns pale and disappears. Although already encountered in the cuttlefish, this is the more appropriate place for dealing with these ultimate stages in the evolution of the originally purely respiratory functions of mantle cavity. Left unsupported by any external protecting shell, the walls of the cavity have acquired a unique investment of alternating circular and radial obliquely striated muscle fibres which are responsible for the instantaneous and, where necessary, rapidly repeated jet stream now discharged through a fused and highly mobile funnel. Recovery after each contraction is assisted by the elasticity of the associated connective tissue fibres.

Unlike *Nautilus* (although resembling the cuttlefish and octopods), the mantle cavity changes greatly in volume, water being drawn in at the sides of

* Translation from *A History of Comparative Anatomy* by F. J. Cole.

Cuttlefish, squids and octopods

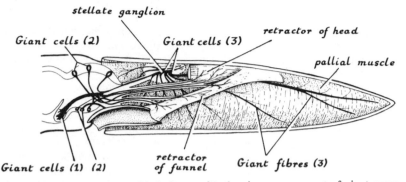

FIG. 154. Diagram of a squid, *Loligo pealii*, showing arrangement of giant nerve fibres controlling movements of the mantle muscles and retractors of head and funnel.

the funnel (Fig. 153) the cavity of which is closed by a valve. Complete, where necessary extremely rapid, dilation of the cavity is followed by instantaneous contraction of every component of the muscular walls, the jet concentrated within the lumen of the funnel the expanded base of which blocks possibilities of egress elsewhere. Undisturbed by the presence of either prey or predator, the squid cruises gently backwards with the funnel under the head discharging water in a forward direction. This degree of movement is essential to maintain an adequate flow of water over the elaborately folded gill filaments.

Unlike cuttlefish, squids are never at rest. Viewed, for instance, in the large tanks of the famous aquarium at Naples, they move constantly to and fro backwards in one direction, then with a turning of the funnel so that water is discharged in the opposite direction, forwards in the other.

This modification of the respiratory chamber as a precise organ of jet propulsion involves a very exact and effectively instantaneous mechanism of nervous control. The speed of a nerve impulse depends on the diameter of the nerve fibre so the greater the need for instantaneous reaction the greater this must be. For instance the ventral nerve cord of an earthworm contains giant nerve fibres which carry impulses direct from one end of the animal to the other and ensure immediate withdrawal when the exposed head end is endangered. The same means are employed to produce the instantaneous contraction of all units in the elaborate mantle musculature in squids where three series of such giant nerve fibres are involved, the largest with a diameter of 1 mm. Their original description and functional interpretation was the work of J. Z. Young who has also been responsible, directly and through collaborators, for a vast volume of recent research into the brain, sense organs and behaviour of cephalopods. We shall have something to relate later about his work at Naples on behaviour of *Octopus*. These giant nerve fibres not only provide the controlling mechanism of the cephalopod jet apparatus, they have also provided material of immense value in the interpretation of nerve action in general. The fluid contents of the fibres has been analysed and, by replacing

251

them with experimental solutions, the all-important properties of the bounding membranes have been demonstrated.

The giant nerve fibre system begins with a pair of first order fibres (Fig. 154) their cell bodies (containing the nucleus) disposed one on each side of the brain but cross connected so that they act as a unit. These are fired into action by nerve impulses coming from the sense organs, usually the eyes but also the organs of touch or of balance. These first order fibres make contact with a number of second order giant fibres which enervate the retractor muscles of the head and of the funnel. They also connect with the conspicuous stellate nerve ganglion a roughly triangular mass of very superficially situated nerves near the opening of the mantle cavity. This is the control centre for the mantle musculature. Third order fibres pass to all regions of the mantle wall, those going to more distant parts of greater diameter than those of shorter length so that the impulse is received simultaneously by every region. Thus any stimulus received by the first order giant fibres fires off the entire system which involves expulsion of the jet with accompanying withdrawal of the head and funnel to complete the stream-lining of the body as the animal shoots backward in the first movement of the escape reaction.

It is hardly surprising that with such a precision mechanism at their disposal large squid can move at speeds of around 20 knots while the jet produced by the small flying squid, *Onchoteuthis banskii*, usually of tropical seas but occasionally turning up in temperate waters, is powerful enough to propel these animals clear of the water and maintain them in the air, supported by the outstretched lateral fins, for distances of 50 yards and over. Like flying fish they are doubtless attempting escape from enemies such as tunny and other predatory fishes.

These elaborately organized animals have surprisingly short lives. The common *L. forbesi* is actually an annual, populations in the English Channel spawning mainly in the winter. The eggs hatch in 30 to 40 days to grow at rates of around 25 mm a month, the males to reach about 30 cm and the females 25 cm in length. *L. vulgaris* spawns off the Dutch coast in the summer but does survive to spawn again the year after. More is known about spawning activities in the common Pacific squid, *L. opalescens*, an animal of considerable economic importance which occurs in vast shoals off the west coast of North America. This spawns only the once, when around three years old. The scene is one of intense drama caught in the photographs and descriptions of Commander Cousteau and Philippe Diolé* of the mass spawning in shallow water off the coast of southern California north of San Diego. Visibility was almost completely blocked by innumerable writhing bodies and intertwined tentacles, the animals usually paired with the male seizing the female from beneath and plunging the hectocotyized arm into the opening of the oviduct deep within the mantle cavity. All such animals were translucent, the occasional unpaired male still brilliantly and variously coloured and desperately seeking a partner. Such frenzied activities continue for some three days with the females sinking to the bottom in preparation for egg laying which occupies a like period. Elongated translucent gelatinous egg capsules,

* *Octopus and Squid* by Jacques-Yves Cousteau & Philippe Diolé.

in shape like small cigars, are successively ejected through the funnel, each with a terminal filament with which it is tethered by the arms to any projecting object on the sea bed. After some twenty such capsules have been produced and secured the females follow the males to death leaving the countless grouped egg masses, described as resembling great flower heads, out of which a new generation of squids will hatch about a month later.

Giant squid, not the terrifying octopods of Victor Hugo's imagination, are the monsters of the deep and the worthy prey of the largest toothed cetaceans, sperm whales. The first real evidence of their existence came from the oceanographical voyages of Prince Albert 1 of Monaco around the end of the last century when tentacles up to 8 metres long were taken from the stomachs of these whales, their skin marked with imprints of great suckers clinging on when in final conflict. These great cephalopods are inhabitants of mid-oceanic depths where they cannot be caught and from which moribund individuals occasionally rise to be washed up on adjacent shores, most frequently around Newfoundland. The largest specimen ever measured and later named *Architeuthis longimanus* appears to have been 19 metres long, the tentacles alone measuring 16 metres. This animal was washed up in New Zealand. But other species, although shorter overall, have bodies twice as long. However, our concern must be with animals that can be claimed as members of the British fauna because still living when found. On 7 January 1937, a giant squid, *Architeuthis harveyi*, was actually taken alive by a trawler off the Bell Rock near Arbroath on the east coast of Scotland, so much alive indeed that the crew were glad to see the last of it overboard although they were able to retain portions of the tentacles one about 6 and the other over 5 metres long. This was only the fourth record of this species in Scottish waters although a few others have subsequently appeared.

A still living specimen of another large squid, *Ommastrephes* (*Sthenoteuthis*) *caroli*, albeit not much over 2 metres long, was washed up at Looe in Cornwall in 1940. The first recorded stranding of this species was on the coast of Holland in 1661 and the Cornish stranding was the 25th record of its appearance around British coasts. So far as the meagre evidence goes, these animals appear to live around the edge of the continental shelf up to depths of around 400 metres. The fact that the majority of strandings have been off the east coast of Great Britain probably indicates the direction of the subsurface currents in which moribund animals are carried.

No such means exist for bringing up squid from profound depths. Smaller, often bizarre in shape, they are rich in many-coloured luminescent organs or photophores, in extreme cases situated in the eyes, themselves on stalks, so acting as searchlights probing the utter darkness for food. A characteristic pattern of illumination may also provide the means of sexual recognition. Here the problem of buoyancy is solved in some by accumulation of ammonium salts within an enlarged body cavity.

Octopods have evolved along different lines from decapods. With their bag-like bodies devoid of fins and without skeletal support, their eight arms all with suckers to the base and possessing a very discriminating sense of touch, they are essentially bottom-living animals. There are two British species, the widely distributed but definitely northern, lesser octopus, *Eledone cirrhosa* (Plate 12), with a single row of suckers on the arms, and the more southern *Octopus vulgaris*, the common octopus of the Mediterranean and of both African and Central American coasts which reaches as far north as the English Channel although in very variable numbers. This animal has a double row of suckers on the arms. Comparisons of size are usually made in terms of the span of the arms which does not usually exceed 70 cm in *Eledone* but may reach up to four times this in *Octopus*. The former usually lives in shallow coastal waters and is seldom encountered on the shore except when washed up, but during the summer months *Octopus* may be found at low tide in pools or crevices along the south coast. All such animals seek shelter, a habit exploited to their disadvantage particularly by the Japanese who catch them in rounded earthenware pots which they instinctively enter.

Much of their life is spent in concealment from which they emerge to feed. Movement is normally by way of the arms but danger will elicit, as in the decapods, an escape reaction involving a sudden change in colour with discharge of a jet stream often accompanied by a cloud of ink, the animal shooting backwards with tapering arms extended behind. But the precision control provided by giant nerve fibres is absent. Feeding differs because, at any rate after capture, speed is less significant. Attack is usually in two stages, a preliminary gliding approach to within some 20 cm of the prey and only then a sudden pounce involving backward discharge of a jet stream through the bent funnel. However, judging from observations in aquaria, approach to unfamiliar objects is cautious, the possible prey being first touched with the tip of a long extended arm before the sudden pounce is made. After seizure the prey is not cut up but pierced by the jaws, killed by injected poison and then held within the enclosing arms while digestive enzymes are pumped into it. After a few hours a captured crab will be released superficially intact but with the entire contents digested and sucked in, an instance of so-called 'extra-intestinal digestion'.

Colour change, indeed surface changes of various types, plays a major part in life. There is a general tendency for octopods to resemble the background

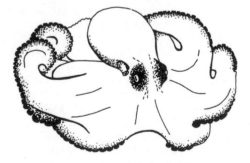

FIG. 155. *Octopus vulgaris* showing 'dymantic' response. (After Wells)

against which they live. Expansion or contraction of the pigment cells is influenced by the wavelength of the light reflected from the bottom. Many colour patterns may be assumed, some of them associated with changes in the texture of the skin but all tending to make the animal less apparent against the particular background. There is an invariable darkening before prey is attacked. As in *Sepia* there is a dymantic response to danger (Fig. 155). When faced by large moving objects, *Octopus vulgaris*, in the words of M. J. Wells*, 'flattens out, pales, and expands the dark chromatophores in rings around the eyes and along the edge of the interbrachial web'. The effect is to enlarge the animal in the eye of the predator and so possibly avert attack or delay it long enough for the octopus to escape behind a distracting cloud of ink.

Like all cephalopods, octopods grow rapidly and are probably sexually mature when three or four years old. Sexual behaviour is almost the opposite to the mass hysteria of spawning squids. It is a solitary affair affecting only the two participants who even manage to keep as far apart as possible (Fig. 156).

FIG. 156. *Octopus vulgaris*, copulation, the male extends the modified 4th arm on the right side into the mantle cavity of the female, depositing a spermatophore. (After Wells)

Unlike·*Sepia*, the common octopus makes no obvious display. The modified 'hectocotylized' fourth arm on the right side is fully extended, initially no more than caressing the female but eventually, after some preliminary resistance on her part, to be inserted into the mantle cavity. Copulation may continue for some hours during which the spermatophores are passed into the oviducts where they burst with liberation of the contained sperm. These are now available for the fertilization of the eggs which the female begins to lay. These are attached, like small grapes, to long strings which hang down

* *Brain and Behaviour in Cephalopods.* by M. J. Wells.

from the roof of the crevice where the female lives (Plate 16). The process takes about a week to complete and involves production of up to 150,000 yolk-laden eggs – representing, like the inflorescence of a century plant, an enormous and probably invariably final reproductive feat. But the work of the female is not immediately concluded, unlike the decapods and in probable relation to the vulnerability of these isolated egg masses, she guards them assiduously, feeding hardly at all, while hosing them with jets of water from the funnel to keep them clean and aerated. In aquaria breeding females die when this last labour is accomplished and this probably happens in nature.

The young octopods hatch out with eight suckered arms and mantle cavity, all in miniature; only some 3 mm long the animals come immediately to the surface where they spend an initial period of planktonic life. This lasts for at least a month and possibly much more and explains the occurrence of the common octopus along the northern shores of the English Channel where these animals rarely, if ever, breed. The most northern breeding stocks are those on the coast of Brittany where the water temperature is normally just high enough for breeding and it is the larvae there produced that are carried in water currents past the Channel Islands and then either westward towards the coasts of Devon or eastward towards those of Sussex. There they drop out of the plankton to begin adult life on the bottom and there they persist while the water remains warm but usually die during the cold winter months.

Occasionally this does not happen. In certain years, notably 1899–1900, 1913, 1922 and again in 1950 these octopods were both abundant and large, so much so in 1899–1900 as fairly to be described as a plague, sweeping the area for food, driving crabs up the beaches in their attempts to escape being eaten, and ruining the shell-fisheries. Each such period of exceptional abundance was preceded by one or more mild winters when the young octopods could survive to feed and grow during the following summer. In 1900 local populations on the south coast appear to have been further increased by a mass invasion from the French coast where they had been present in over-whelming numbers the previous summer. This instability of numbers is typical of what happens at the margins of the distribution of any species, spectacular in the case of *Octopus* owing to the size and striking appearance of the invading hordes.

Because of their bottom-living habit which can easily be simulated in aquaria and their less delicate skin so that they can withstand greater handling, octopods can be kept in captivity over much longer periods than can decapods. Indeed, if undamaged when captured, they quickly settle down if a cavity made out of bricks is provided into which they can retreat. They are, moreover, as B. B. Boycott puts it, 'resistant to the insults of experiment'. Thus their habits can be observed and their behaviour analysed. And this is supremely well worth doing because in these coleoids we are dealing with animals having an impressive array of sense organs from which messages pass to an elaborate central nervous system from which all the varied activities of the animal are directed. We have already noted the strikingly efficient means of controlling the mechanism of jet propulsion in the decapods and also nervous control of the means of colour change which plays so large a part in cephalopod behaviour. Long series of observations and experiments by J. Z. Young and others working with him at the Stazione Zoologica at Naples, have revealed that this animal can learn from experience and further study of the brain has shown what areas are concerned with these 'higher' functions.

Much the most obvious sense organs in the cephalopods are the eyes, set on each side of the head and so with largely separate areas of vision. They are camera eyes (in distinction to the mosaic eyes of crustaceans and insects) like those of vertebrates. But in their origin and in much of their organization the two are totally distinct; the final similarity is a consequence of the limited means available to living organisms. All molluscs have this type of eye starting as no more than the light-sensitive pigmented cups found on the tentacles of limpets to acquire a simple lens and become enclosed in the higher gastropods where they are most highly developed in actively pelagic heteropods such as *Carinaria* (Fig. 42). The pallial eyes that line the mantle margins in bivalves such as scallops or fringe the siphons in cockles have a similar structure. It is an obvious, if major, step both in size and complexity to the eye of the coleoid cephalopods, a large globular structure contained in an orbit within which it can be partially rotated. Although so similar to the vertebrate eye, it differs in mode of formation, an inpushing of the outer surface, not an outpushing of the brain, so that the retinal surface is not overlain with blood vessel, as it is in our eyes. The differently formed lens is a rigid structure pulled closer to the retina to accommodate for distant vision, a process achieved by deforming the curvature in the vertebrate lens. In a manner totally unlike anything that happens in vertebrates, the characteristic slit-like pupils of the eyes are always maintained in a horizontal position due to reflex association with the gravity organs and messages received by the brain are interpreted on the basis of this alignment. While this is clearly associated with pelagic life where gravity is the only constant factor, it has been retained in the octopods which are secondarily adapted for life on the bottom.

All molluscs, apart from a few that are cemented, possess simple gravity organs in the form of statocysts, essentially small cavities lined with sense hairs and containing a solid body or statolith which responds to the pull of gravity to stimulate the particular sense hairs on which it presses. Where, as in so many of the molluscs, the animal is in close contact with the substrate the information so obtained can be of minor significance but obviously this changes in pelagic gastropods such as heteropods where, like the eyes, these organs enlarge. So they are expectedly large and complex in the supremely pelagic cephalopods. Encased in hard capsules they lie beneath the hind surface of the brain and provide essential information about the position of the animal in relation to the pull of gravity. They are also enlarged to include an organ of balance equivalent to the semicircular canals within our inner ears which provide information about angular acceleration in different directions. Cephalopods are the only animals apart from vertebrates to obtain this information.

The eye, aided by the statocyst, is the supreme sense organ in the decapods, feeding as they do by sight and seizing often rapidly moving prey with impressive precision. The bottom-living octopods have developed a new sense of touch by way of the constantly exploring arms which by the degree of distortion of the margins of the suckers can distinguish between rough and smooth surfaces although, lacking a jointed skeleton within the arms with a consequent inability to determine the relative positions of different regions upon them, they are unable to distinguish between objects of different shapes. Added to the sense of touch is an apparently widely-diffused power of chemical discrimination, a generalized combined sense of smell and taste. *Nautilus*, with the pin-hole eye incapable of form vision, relies on smell for the detection of its immobile or only very slowly moving prey and has only a simple statocyst. There appears to be no auditory sense in any cephalopod.

The brain to which information collected by these sense organs is conveyed and which controls the subsequent and often very elaborate motor activities is an impressively massive lobed structure. Because in the very early Palaeozoic the cephalopods separated from the remainder of the molluscs to become pelagic animals in which the head, foot and mantle cavity became closely associated at the one end, the nervous system must soon have begun to concentrate at this end. When the cephalopods began to evolve, this system may still have been in its probably original state of a series of cross-connected cords containing scattered nerve cells. It is certainly from some such system that the condition in *Nautilus* and the higher cephalopods can best be derived. This is in contrast to the concentration of pre-existing ganglia which occurs in the head region of the (largely terrestrial) pulmonate gastropods where they form a ring round the oesophagus at the front end of the gut. There is a similar concentration in the viscera in scallops and related, and equally 'headless', bivalves. Description of the brain in the cephalopods must involve some technicalities but will be made as simple as possible*.

In *Nautilus* the still obviously molluscan brain (Fig. 157, A) consists of anterior and posterior nerve cords running under the oesophagus and united laterally with each other and also with the optic lobes which are enlargements of the nerves originally connected with the eyes. They are also cross connected above the oesophagus. The anterior cord innervates the arms (probably arising from the head rather than from the foot), the hinder and more certainly pedal cord being concerned with the undoubtedly pedal funnel. The whole is contained within a more delicate and more open cranium than that of the other cephalopods in which the brain is greatly enlarged and its constituent lobes consolidated and so is much less obviously molluscan. Referring particularly to that of *Octopus*, viewed from above (Fig. 157, B) this forms a somewhat elongate structure connected laterally with what are now relatively enormous optic lobes where the vast amount of visual information is received. This affects the impulses which travel along the motor nerves which control muscular contraction on that side and so the posture of the animal. The mass of the brain consists, as in *Nautilus*, of regions above and below the oesophagus but with the former greatly enlarged. Taken as a whole the brain may be said to consist of ascending tiers of nervous responsibility. Appropriately the lowest regions (below the oesophagus and not shown in the figure) are occu-

---

* It is all very clearly described in *Brain and Behaviour in Cephalopods*.

pied by the 'lower' motor centres from which nerves pass to the mantle (involving the giant nerve fibres in the corresponding region in the decapods), to the arms and also to the chromatophores which play so significant a role in the life of these animals. But without aid from higher regions only the simpler activities can be organized.

Above the oesophagus, as shown in longitudinal section (Fig. 157, c), the impressive brain mass is divisible into lobes which contain 'higher' motor centres which supervise the activities of those already mentioned and upper regions with more over-riding functions. Within the former, anterior and posterior basal lobes have the ultimate control over movements of head and arms and of mantle and funnel respectively involving the complicated activities involved in swimming, walking and seizing prey. Lateral basal lobes (not shown) have similar responsibilities where colour change is concerned. In front lies the buccal lobe which receives sensory nerves coming from the mouth region and is also the origin of motor nerves controlling the interacting activities of beak, mouth region, radula and adjacent regions of the gut, comprising all structures to do with feeding (see Fig. 152). Higher again are centres of further functional significance, namely the inferior frontal lobe which receives information from the organs of touch in the continuously groping arms (this lobe is absent in decapods) while associated lobes (not shown) deal with olfactory information. Finally no sensory nerves pass directly into the highest regions of all – the superior frontal, vertical and subvertical lobes which, when sectioned, are found to contain vast numbers of minute nerve cells.

The functions of these lobes have been revealed by experiment. Electrical stimulation of motor areas is followed by predictable responses such as the change in posture and colour involved in the dymantic display, while stimulation of other areas produces almost instantaneous change in texture of the skin from a smooth to a warty surface. Or, under anaesthesia, different lobes can be surgically removed and the resultant changes in behaviour and appearance noted. But neither method reveals the significance of these highest centres, their stimulation produces no obvious effect and their removal makes no significant difference to activities which continue to include normal movement, feeding and, if made at the appropriate time, reproductive behaviour. But it has been learnt from experiments on captive *Octopus*, with significant additional information from *Sepia*, that these so-called 'silent' areas are association centres concerned with learning; they are regions where, with this vast multiplicity of interacting nerve cells or neurones, the animal stores experience from the past that can be called upon to modify later activity, just as the cerebral cortex does in vertebrates including ourselves. These animals can learn from experience because they can remember. Information on this has been obtained from a great volume of very carefully controlled experiments, only to be briefly mentioned here.

Decapods such as *Sepia* can learn by sight, octopods also by touch. Thus over a period of ten days at a rate of four trials a day, cuttlefish can be trained to discriminate between an available prawn and one behind glass on which a white disc has been painted. Memory builds up of the accompanying frustration if the latter is attacked. This has an increasing influence on behaviour In the same way, *Octopus* learns to discriminate between an unaccompanie crab and one with an associated white square attack on which involve exposure to an electric shock. After a period when it approaches the latte situation with caution, the animal finally comes to distinguish with certaint between the two situations, attacking the solitary crab but not even emergin from its home when the prey is presented with an accompanying square.

Using the same general procedure, octopods can also be taught to distinguish similar objects of different sizes and between different shapes, e.g. between horizontal and vertically placed rectangles although, as revealed when the gravity organ is excised, this depends on the slit-like pupil remaining hori- zontal. These animals readily attack hermit crabs but can learn to avoid those having associated sea anemones on the occupied shell. The cephalopod skin is highly vulnerable to the sting cells of the anemones and after initial attacks, these protected hermits are left strictly alone. When sight is cut out, octopods reveal their ability to learn by the experience gained by way of the organs of chemical and tactile sense on the suckers. The object is 'tasted' or 'felt'. As a consequence of experiments in which the animals were rewarded by food for a correct decision and punished by an electric shock for an incorrect one, *Octopus* can be shown capable of learning to distinguish between similar objects differing only in physical texture. All such memories can be retained for some weeks, visual information passing for storage by way of the optic lobes to the silent areas of the superior and vertical lobes while in *Octopus* the inferior frontal lobe system is concerned with memory of what has been touched. In experiments on blind animals involving removing areas of the upper brain, all but this inferior frontal area may be removed without affecting the animal's capacity to distinguish between objects by way of the sense of touch.

Nothing surely would have amazed Dr Martin Lister more than the dis- covery of these higher faculties in the molluscs the shells of which he was among the first to arrange and to name. True, his knowledge of cephalopods was largely second-hand, coming from the work of the Italian, Redi, but he did dissect a specimen of *Loligo*, probably *L. vulgaris*, although so poorly preserved in brine that he was almost consistently wrong in his interpretation of structure but was successful (quoting again from E. J. Cole) 'in finding a "small cerebrum" contained in a small cartilage, but he could discover no trace of a "spinal cord" although he carefully searched for it.'

There are exotic octopods including pelagic species down to depths of around 6000 metres where movement is transferred from the mantle cavity to the arms united almost to their tips by a membrane, the suckers within this tent-like structure modified as organs of touch and for collecting finely- divided food. The animals tend to become gelatinous and translucent and to lose not only muscle but the now useless radula, chromatophores and ink gland while even the eyes may be greatly reduced. Nearer the surface dwell the argonauts, species of the 'paper *Nautilus*' with the female forming a delicate shell, not, of course chambered, by means of the greatly extended web of the first pair of arms. Although in aquaria they can crawl like other octopods

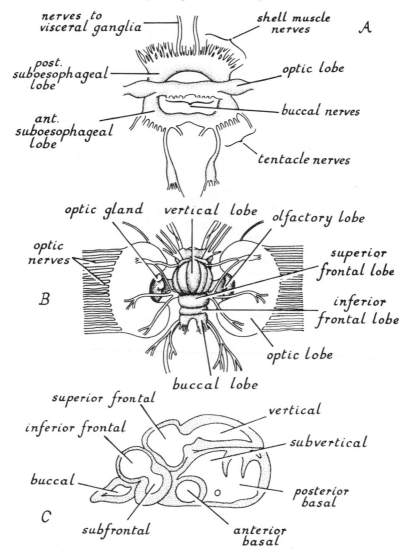

FIG. 157. Brains of cephalopods: A, of *Nautilus* viewed from above, anterior sur-
face below; B, of *Octopus* viewed from above (regions under oesophagus not seen);
C, longitudinal section through the upper regions of this brain, anterior end to left.
(After Wells)

(Fig. 158) and may even leave the shell, in nature they swim somewhat
languidly by jet propulsion, arms directed back but suckers and beak forward.
Feeding would seem to depend on the chance of prey touching the extended

and silvery web. When this happens the fourth arm on that side immediately sweeps across to seize it. The male is minute and, as we already have had reason to note, deposits his entire and, in terms of his body size, literally enormous modified arm – the originally described *Hectocotylus* – within the mantle cavity of the female. She, in her turn, will subsequently pass the fertilized eggs into the cavity of the shell in the protection of which they will develop.

FIG. 158. *Argonauta* or 'paper Nautilus', female crawling on bottom. (From *The Octopus; or, The 'Devil-fish of Fiction and of Fact'* by Henry Lee, 1875)

Epilogue

*

THE theme of this book has been the extraordinarily diverse results of molluscan evolution. True, we can never know the structure of the first molluscs and the solitary surviving monoplacophoran, *Neopilina* (Fig. 6), may be very misleading because everything we learn from other molluscs indicates an originally simple structure and *Neopilina* is a complex animal. Moreover, apart from the cephalopods, so much that is significant in molluscan evolution occurred before the fossil record began and although molluscan shells do furnish magnificent fossils – no invertebrates have a more comprehensive fossil history – these do not always tell us very much about the animals that formed them. However, the presence of a slit in early coiled shells certainly indicates that they possessed paired gills with anus and kidney ducts opening into the respiratory chamber and so had need for sanitation. The presence of a pallial sinus in bivalve shells reveals that the animal had long siphons and was infaunal in habit. A siphuncle is sure evidence of a gas-filled cephalopod shell and of a pelagic mode of life.

The peculiar fascination of molluscs resides in the duality of shell and animal. As we saw in Chapter 1, the shell was the only reality up to the eighteenth century and later. Dr Philip P. Carpenter, the eminent malacologist of Warrington, England, wrote in his *Lectures on Molluscs or Shell-fish and their Allies*, prepared for the Smithsonian Institution of Washington in 1861 that, 'It is only of late years that enquirers have even attempted to gain information about the animals of shells. The very beauty of the shell has contributed to this result. Every sailor could collect shells, and every lady could lay them on cotton in a drawer: the animal was a nuisance, liable to rot if not carefully extracted, only to be preserved in bottles of spirit, and then presenting nothing but a shrivelled or shapeless mass, fit only for the dissector's knife. Even the figures of living animals in the works of scientific voyagers are by no means infallible, it being not uncommon to find voracious proboscids figured with a vegetarian snout, or to see the shell turned the wrong way on the back of the crawler . . . we must be content to wait many years before this branch of natural history is as satisfactorily established as other branches of popular science.'

When the contained animals in so very few of the exotic shells had even been seen it is not surprising that the shell should have seemed the more important. Malacology we saw really to have been founded when the discerning eye of George Cuvier perceived a common basis of animal structure within the external diversity of snails, bivalves, chitons and cuttlefish and so united the former Testacea with certain groups within Linnaeus's 'Mollusca' into a structurally coherent group of animals, their relationships later to be illumi-

263

nated by the Darwinian concept of evolutionary change. It then became possible to explain the extraordinary internal structure of gastropods by postulating the occurrence of torsion – and what a flash of comprehension that represented! Later this process was found continually being re-enacted in the life history of archaeogastropods.

An idea of the basic dichotomy of molluscan animal and shell was conveyed in Fig. 5. For the sake of clarity, an artificial distinction has to be made between the original pre-molluscan animal and the mantle and shell which were imposed on this to protect the massed viscera and the respiratory cavity. Correct or not, in this way the molluscs can be brought into being, a bilaterally symmetrical animal with superimposed mantle producing a radially symmetrical shell.

The unique nature of this arrangement becomes more apparent when we compare the shell of a mollusc with that of a crustacean such as a lobster. There the shell covers everything, each appendage, however small, the eyes, the much branched gills, even the greater part of the gut including the stomach. So encased, growth involves periodic moulting of all these surfaces and replacement by a larger shell, each such 'ecdysis' a period of major hazard. The molluscan shell imposes no such constraints; on the contrary it is moulded internally to fit the growing animal. It may alter in shape during growth to suit adult habits; we may recollect the pelican's foot shell (Fig. 37) or the finally, although mysteriously, produced water-pot shell (Fig. 143).

Bilaterally and radially symmetrical animals differ widely in potential. The former move with head in front, sense organs and centralized nervous system controlling the activities of paired appendages used in crawling, swimming, walking, or finally flying. Radial symmetry confers no such capacities, it brings to mind the slow multi-directional movements of starfish or sea urchins, the apparently undirected pulsations of jellyfish and the total immobility of sea anemones, sea fans or stony corals. But of its major advantages in passive strength every coral reef bears witness.

Early equipped with a most effective and highly adaptable radular apparatus, molluscs began their evolutionary career with very limited capacities for movement owing to lack of paired limbs or appendages and also because of the resistance of the rounded shell to anything more than very slow movement. They had to rely very much on the protection supplied by this thickly calcified shell. As evolution proceeded, some molluscs remained in this state of balance but others sacrificed protection for motility; others again lost all powers of movement to live completely attached within the protection of a more massive shell.

The chitons, so admirably fitted for life on uneven hard surfaces, represent a condition involving extended length which is usually associated with greater mobility. Here, however it is associated with retention of the protective shell which becomes calcified in a series of articulating plates with the gills also multiplied in numbers within the narrow palliai grooves into which the mantle cavity becomes extended. The end result has been complete success within a limited environment. Chitons may dominate life on suitable rocky platforms such as those formed by dead coral rock (Plate 14).

Epilogue

Following the strange process of torsion that brought them into being, the snails went to the opposite extreme of compact rotundity. The visceral mass and mantle cavity were twisted so that the anus came to point in the same direction as the mouth while the sensory capacities of the head and of the mantle cavity came gradually to blend. Reorganization of the mantle cavity with loss of the organs on the right side – and so of the primitive slit – with development of a left/right respiratory circulation represented a highly successful compromise between 'animal' and shell. The very 'commonness' of shore winkles, top shells and dog whelks is evidence of supreme success.

Because this represented a continued compromise it could lead in many directions. That most often taken was towards the limpet form with its concentration on protection at the expense of mobility. This has occurred so frequently – several times in both archaeogastropods and mesogastropods, in the neogastropod *Concholepas*, in the opisthobranch 'umbrella' shells and in pulmonate siphonariids (to say nothing of other limpets evolved in freshwaters). Here the hard substrate to which the foot tenaciously adheres becomes part of the protective covering, and the surrounding ring of pallial tentacles play an increasing role in sensory perception. Powers of movement are reduced or may be lost as in slipper limpets or in the hitherto unmentioned *Hipponyx* (horse-hoof shell) which cements a layer of shell on to the rock to become a horizontally-disposed bivalved gastropod like a small rock scallop (Fig. 159). Although immobile it feeds by way of a protruding snout and, with

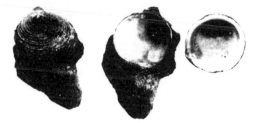

FIG. 159. *Hipponyx antiquatus*, a gastropod 'limpet' with an under 'valve': *left*, intact shell; *centre*, 'lower valve'; *right*, conical limpet shell forming 'upper valve'. Californian species.

a far-extending penis, fertilizes adjacent females just as do acorn barnacles. While there is clearly no evolutionary future for any type of limpet, present success could hardly be greater with species covering every rocky shore outside the ice-scoured polar regions and with dredges pulled over infested oyster beds brought up filled with chains of slipper limpets.

Radial symmetry has taken complete control in the worm-like cemented vermetids (Fig. 35) where the lengthened shell loses both cohesion and mobility. The foot provides no more than an opercular plug to the uncoiled tube, its one-time lubricating mucus glands producing food-entangling strings which are pulled in by the formerly scraping radula.

The other side of the story is told by the opisthobranchs where the protective shell is replaced by chemical repellants with accompanying warning coloration. The external symmetries imposed by the two processes of coiling and torsion are lost and with them the mantle cavity with its contained ctenidium and associated organs. This led to the explosion of diversity in form and habit described in Chapters 10 and 11. The effect of past history persists in the asymmetry of internal organs such as kidneys and gonads. To the horizontally-disposed bivalved *Hipponyx* must be added as an extreme instance of this resumed bilateral symmetry, the 'bivalved gastropods', species of the minute green Juliidae with vertically-disposed bivalve shells (Fig. 160).

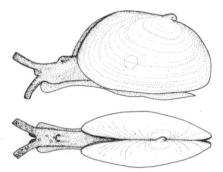

FIG. 160. Side and upper view of a 'bivalved gastropod', *Tamanovalva limax* from Tamano, Japan. Position of solitary adductor indicated, also aborted spiral on the left 'valve'. Shell 6 mm long. (After Kawaguti & Baba)

These tropical opisthobranchs live on species of the green alga, *Caulerpa* which they closely simulate. During development the flattened univalve shell with aborted spiral is pushed to the left while an extension of the mantle on the other side forms a matching valve and a connecting ligament and a single adductor draws the valves together. Although formed in a totally different manner, the end result is strikingly similar to the bivalve shell.

Many opisthobranchs can swim by means of pedal lobes some becoming pelagic, notably the sea butterflies, both ciliary-feeding thecosomes (Plate 7) and naked gymnosomes. The latter are actively predacious carnivores like the larger mesogastropod heteropods, such as *Carinaria* (Fig. 42) sacrificing the protective shell for better development of a muscularly active body.

Nevertheless it is the bottom-living neogastropods which most fully exploit the possibilities of predatory life and this without any reduction in the shell or significant increase in the powers of movement. Surprisingly, the effective modifications are within the gut! The probing proboscis and the tearing radula culminate in the violently ejected introvert with poisoned harpoon-like barbs of the cone shells. The protection of a compactly coiled shell is combined with powers of seizing prey as effective as those of predacious fish or crustaceans. Foot and shell yield place in adaptive importance to radular apparatus and other anterior regions of the gut. These numerous cones represent almost complete integration of animal and shell.

In the bivalves, mantle and shell impose their form on the contained animal. Despite the various gastropod essays into infaunal life, it is the bivalves that enter and move most successfully through sand or mud. Initially they must have fed on organic debris and bottom diatoms by extensions of the lips – much as does *Nucula* – but later came to exploit the full potential of the molluscan ctenidium and from it evolved the most successful of all ciliary feeding mechanisms. This is only displaced in two groups, partially in the wood-boring shipworms and completely in the deep-water carnivorous septibranchs. The mantle became organized so that both intake and expulsion of water take place at the hind end giving the ability for downward and forward (in razor shells also upward) movement leading to mechanical and chemical penetration of rock and timber. In a real sense the front end, although hardly the non-existent head, resumes a measure of control. Knowledge about the environment is now supplied by sense organs largely round the mantle margins fringing the regions where water enters. Much of the adaptive ingenuity in the bivalves is furnished by the foot with its varied capacities as an organ of movement, of adhesion, of byssal formation (with all that has been responsible for) and of cleansing.

There have been many adventures in the course of bivalve evolution and attachment has been the first step in many. Cementation leads to great lateral asymmetry in the jewel shells (Chamidae) which have a deeply concave half-coiled under valve and a flat upper valve producing what amounts to a gastropod attached, upside down, by the summit of the shell with the operculum uppermost. And this is precisely what many of the once very numerous and spectacularly large mesozoic rudists (Hippuritacea) were like (Fig. 161)

FIG. 161. Mesozoic rudist, *Requi-enia*, attached by lower, deeply coiled (left) valve with similarly coiled but flat upper 'opercular' valve. Coiling due to a tangential component in shell growth, very pronounced transverse component in lower valve, none in upper valve; adductor muscles indicated.

Attachment by byssal secretion from the base of the foot has yet more remarkable consequences leading to increasing posterior enlargement of both mantle and viscera to culminate in the single-muscle (monomyarian) condition when the animals acquire an almost radial symmetry with the viscera reorganized around the centrally-placed adductor. When such, now horizontally-disposed, bivalves lose attachment they acquire a new symmetry with definite upper and lower valves while greater need for cleansing the deep lower half of the mantle cavity culminates in the production of a jet stream, powered by the enlarged catch muscle and directed by the muscular inner folds of the mantle margin. By flapping the stream-lined valves, scallops can now swim.

Taking byssal attachment and a horizontal posture a stage further brings us to the closely adpressed saddle oysters with a calcified byssus passing straight down through a deep embayment in the under valve. A double – almost a triple – asymmetry has been achieved. What could then be more unexpected than evolution to a crawling habit? But the foot, retained as a means of cleansing the mantle cavity (Fig. 99) has been able to resume its original function in the aptly named *Enigmonia aenigmatica*. This is a true bivalve limpet (in form *not* in feeding habits) with the umbo of the upper valve moved from the margin to an apical position and shown, in its natural habitat crawling on a mangrove leaf, in the last figure in this book (Fig. 162). It is a typical inhabitant of mangrove swamps in SE Asia. Such is the plasticity of molluscan form that bivalves such as this species, the Chamas and the extinct rudists (Fig. 161) appear like gastropods while *Hipponyx* (Fig. 159) and the bivalved opisthobranchs (Fig. 160) simulate bivalves.

The scaphopods, with mantle and shell wrapped round the extended animal leaving the upper end open for respiratory flow and the lower one for feeding activities, combine the two symmetries although only to the extent of fitting the animals for limited penetration into soft substrates and leaving no scope for further adaptation. More restricted even than chitons, these tusk shells indicate the extent to which success in the larger groups is due to their capacity for keeping the options open.

We know more about the course of evolution in the relatively more recently evolved cephalopods. Here, as ingeniously as anything that has ever occurred in evolutionary history, the protective shell became an organ of buoyancy which lifted these slowly-moving benthic animals clear of the bottom into mid and surface waters. Their continuously functioning respiratory cavity – its contained gills as truly ctenidial as those of bivalves – became an increasingly efficient organ of jet propulsion, the stream first produced and directed by a funnel of overlapping pedal lobes which still persists in *Nautilus*. While the early story is of increasing shell size notably in the Ammonites, eventually all such animals (bar the fortunately surviving *Nautilus*) were carried to extinction although enclosure of the shell in the Belemnites proved the beginning of the answer to the problem of survival. In the finally-evolved coleoids the shell serves as a means of buoyancy in cuttlefish but only of support in the supremely active squids and is lacking in octopods which made a successful return to benthic life.

In these most active of marine invertebrates, symmetries have been reconciled. Head, foot and mantle cavity all face forward and the apex of the horizontal body contains the viscera above and prolonged mantle cavity below (Fig. 149). A hovering squid represents the climax of molluscan evolution. Motionless with downward-directed jet (like a hovercraft) and gently undulating fins, it can pivot in the vertical plane around a central point within the body. Arms and tentacles in front complete a perfect spindle so that, with instantaneous efficiency, a squid can move 'forward' for predation or 'backward' for escape. Unlike the no less naked opisthobranchs, loss of an external shell has not been accompanied by that of the mantle which survives the shell it initially formed to produce, out of the respiratory chamber, a superb organ of jet propulsion. Reliance is on speed with the distractions of instantaneous colour change and of ink clouds, where the naked sea-slugs employ acid glands and warning colours. Speed demands exact information gained by way of increasingly elaborate sense organs and the control of the mantle musculature through a mechanism of high precision involving three orders of giant nerve fibres. More easily handled, study of the octopods reveals the presence of higher nervous activities including memory.

No group of animals lives to itself. All must have defences against predators and be successful in the search for food whether it be vegetation, suspended plankton or sessile or actively-moving animals. If predators like cephalopods they must at the same time escape from other and larger predators and effectively secure their own prey. They must be as successful in both roles as their competitors maintaining pace with them in the evolutionary race. The significance of this as applied to cephalopods has been stressed by Andrew Packard after long experience with them at the Stazione Zoologica at Naples. His arguments are worth more than the brief mention we can give them.

Cephalopods and fish occupy the same marine environments, octopods alongside shore fishes, cuttlefish with pipefishes and other dwellers amongst eel grass, squids with pelagic fishes in all zones from the surface to the abyss. The similarly stream-lined bodies are powered in fish by segmentally arranged muscle blocks and by the elaborate mantle musculature in squids. Both possess highly efficient, but again totally different, methods of food capture and of its subsequent digestion. Both contain species that briefly become airborne by way of the similarly stabilizing paired fins of fish and lateral fins of squids. Such developments have been accompanied by elaboration of sense organs, achieved with almost unbelievable parallel success with the eyes*. Both may be able to change colour although their pigment cells differ in structure and operation; in deep water both may be similarly equipped with elaborate photophores. The buoyancy mechanism evolved from an outgrowth of the gut in fishes is emulated by one originating within the shell in cephalopods and more recently supplemented in some by an enlarged body cavity containing ammonium salts.

The argument is that the cephalopods had to keep pace with the fish if they were to survive – that the fish represented the pressure of natural selection where their fellow predators were concerned. Only if cephalopods could emulate fish could they survive and only variations leading to that end, such as enclosure and reduction of the cumbersome shell and elaboration of the mantle cavity as an organ of jet propulsion, would be selected because enabling their possessors to secure prey and to elude enemies as successfully as did fish. The striking efficiency of the jet propulsive mechanism can best be explained on this basis – it is almost as though, increasingly hard-pressed by competition first with mesozoic marine reptiles, then fish and then also with

---

* Did not Bergson take this as the supreme argument in favour of his views on *Creative Evolution*?

marine mammals such as toothed whales, the full possibilities of molluscan genetic variability were forced into the open.

Success appears as a final consequence of the buoyancy mechanism, a product of the superimposed mantle and shell, which originally lifted the first cephalopods off the bottom into an increasingly competitive world inhabited by other rapidly evolving pelagic animals. This was eventually to produce the superbly efficient cuttlefish and squids. With the passing of the external shell, the still-functioning molluscan respiratory cavity reached its apotheosis as the supreme organ of jet propulsion.

Although, aided by their exceptional speed of growth and impressive fecundity, these animals do vigorously survive, this is not a story of absolute success. Unlike the vertebrates, unlike the equally molluscan snails and bivalves, cephalopods have never penetrated into freshwater to say nothing of passage on to dry land so successfully overrun by snails and slugs. The essential prerequisite for survival in freshwaters is the ability to regulate the osmotic pressure of the blood. This is the function of the molluscan kidneys, adequate for the needs of the less demanding snails and bivalves but not for those of the highly metabolic cephalopods. A drawback, common to all molluscs, is the lower efficiency of the copper-based blood pigment, haemocyanin, compared with the iron-based haemoglobin present in vertebrates with less efficient variants in some marine invertebrates. The oxygen-carrying capacity of the blood in highly active squids and cuttlefish is so low that, despite an elaborate circulatory system with additional branchial hearts to boost pressure, the available oxygen is barely sufficient to meet basic demands in the sea; it could never cover the additional demands involved in osmotic regulation in freshwaters.

Passage on to land is impossible owing to lack of adequate skeletal support, external or internal, and also the permeability of the delicate skin. Nevertheless, despite denial of such ultimate triumphs, the course of evolution in the Mollusca with the interacting components of bilaterally-symmetrical animal and radially-symmetrical mantle and shell has resulted in a far greater diversity of form and habit of life than is to be found in any other group of marine invertebrates.

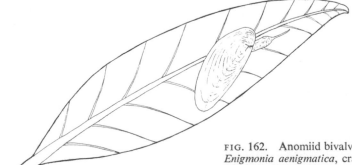

FIG. 162. Anomiid bivalve 'limpet', *Enigmonia aenigmatica*, crawling on the leaf of a white mangrove tree, *Avicenna*, at Singapore.

Selected book list

*

THE following very restricted list is confined to contemporary books on marine molluscs, all it is thought now in print, which are likely to be available to readers in English-speaking countries. Going back in time would render the list unwieldy – and where, indeed, would one stop? However, certain old books of particular significance were mentioned in the Introduction and in Chapter 1. All the listed books are written for the general reader; those concerned with the scientific study of molluscs, who will also it is hoped find interest in this book, have adequate sources of information about more erudite works and about the numerous scientific journals partially or exclusively concerned with the publication of molluscan studies.

General

BARTSCH, PAUL, *Mollusks*, Dover Publications, New York.
MORTON, J. E., *Molluscs*, Hutchinson University Library, London.
PURCHON, R. D. *The Biology of the Mollusca*, Pergammon Press, Oxford, London, etc.
SOLEM, G. ALAN, *The Shell Makers*, John Wiley & Sons, New York.

Concerning Cephalopods

COUSTEAU, JACQUES-YVES & DIOLÉ, PHILIPPE, *Octopus and Squid: The Soft Intelligence*, Cassell & Co., London.
LANE, FRANK W., *Kingdom of the Octopus*, Jarrolds Publishers, London.
WELLS, M. J., *Brain and Behaviour in Cephalopods*, Heinemann, London.

Shells

ABBOTT, R. TUCKER, *Kingdom of the Seashell*, Hamlyn, London.
CAMERON, RODERICK, *Shells*, Weidenfeld & Nicolson, London.
COX, IAN (edited by), *The Scallop: Studies of a shell and its influences on humankind*, 'Shell' Transport & Trading Co., London.
DANCE, S. PETER, *Shells and Shell Collecting*, Hamlyn, London.
FEININGER, ANDREAS & EMERSON, WILLIAM K., *Shells*, Thames & Hudson, London.
STIX, HUGH & MARGUERITE & ABBOTT, R. TUCKER, photographs by H. LANDSHOFF, *The Shell: Five Hundred Million Years of Inspired Design*, Abrahams, New York.
These two last contain some of the most magnificent photographs of shells, in colour and black and white, ever produced. Although expensive, each is a joy to possess.

Selected book list

Shell Collections

DANCE, S. PETER, *Shell Collecting: An Illustrated History*, Faber & Faber, London.

DANCE, S. PETER, *Rare Shells*, Faber & Faber, London.

Marine Molluscan Faunas

British

BARRETT, JOHN & YONGE, C. M., *Collins Pocket Guide to the Sea Shore*, Collins, London.

BEEDHAM, GORDON E., *Identification of the British Mollusca*, Hulton Educational Publications, Amersham, Bucks.

EALES, N. B., *The Littoral Fauna of the British Isles*, Cambridge University Press.

FRETTER, VERA & GRAHAM, ALISTAIR, *British Prosobranch Molluscs*, Ray Society, London.

GRAHAM, ALASTAIR, *British Prosobranchs*, Linnean Society of London, Synopses of the British Fauna (New Series), Academic Press, London & New York.

MCMILLAN, NORA F., *British Shells*, Frederick Warne & Co., London.

TEBBLE, NORMAN, *British Bivalve Seashells*, British Museum (Natural History), London.

THOMPSON, T. E. *Biology of Opisthobranch Molluscs*, Ray Society, London.

THOMPSON, T. E., & BROWN, GREGORY H., *British Opisthobranch Molluscs*, Linnean Society of London, Synopses of the British Fauna (New Series), Academic Press, London & New York.

American

ABBOTT, R. TUCKER, *American Seashells*, 2nd edition, 1974, D. van Nostrand Co., Ltd., New York.

HUMFREY, MICHAEL, *Sea Shells of the West Indies*, Collins, London.

KEEN, A. MYRA with MCLEAN, JAMES H., *Sea Shells of Tropical West America; Marine Mollusks from Baja California to Peru*, Stanford Univ. Press, California.

KEEN, A. MYRA & COAN, EUGENE, *Marine Molluscan Genera of Western North America. An illustrated Key*, Stanford Univ. Press, California.

KEEP, JOSIAH (revised by JOSHUA L. BAILY, JR), *West Coast Shells*, Stanford Univ. Press, California.

MORRIS, P. A., *A Field Guide to Shells of the Atlantic and Gulf Coasts and the West Indies*, Houghton Mifflin Co., Boston.

MORRIS, P. A., *A Field Guide to Shells of the Pacific Coast and Hawaii*, Houghton Mifflin Co., Boston.

Australia and New Zealand

ALLEN, J., *Australian Shells*, Georgian House, Melbourne.

Selected book list

CERNOHORSKY, W. O., *Marine Shells of the Pacific*, Vol. I, 1967; Vol. II, 1972, Pacific Publications, Sydney, Australia.

COLEMAN, NEVILLE, *What Shell is That?*, Hamlyn, Sydney, Auckland, London, New York, Toronto. (Admirable colour plates of Australian molluscs, many living, from diverse habitats.)

MACPHERSON, J. HOPE & GABRIEL, C. J., *Marine Molluscs of Victoria*, Melbourne University Press.

POWELL, A. W. B., *Shells of New Zealand*, Whitcombe & Tombs, Christchurch.

WILSON, B. R. & GILLETT, K., *Australian Shells: Illustrating and Describing 600 species of Marine Gastropods from Australian Waters*, A. H. and A. W. Reed, Sydney.

South Africa

KENNELLY, D. H., *Marine Shells of Southern Africa*, Thomas Nelson & Sons (Africa), Johannesburg.

KENSLEY, BRIAN, *Sea-Shells of Southern Africa – Gastropods*, Maskew Miller, Cape Town.

Index

*

Index

279

Index

Protobranchia, 154-6, 160, 166, 228, 239
Pseudoconch, 115
Pseudofaeces, 152, 158, 159, 162, 171, 201, 203, 212, 215-17
Pseudopythina, 190
Pseudovermis mortoni, 141, Fig. 77
Psiliteredo megotara, 215
Pteria, 147, 172
P. hirundo, 172
Pteriacea, 172
Pterocera (Lambis), 89
P. chiragra var. *arthritica*, Fig. 10
Puget Sound, 62, 80
Pulmonata, 35, 69, 121
Puncturella noachina, 54, Fig. 21
Purchon, R. D., 218
Purpura, see *Nucella*
Purpurin, 102
Pycnodonta, 179
Pyramidellomorpha, 119, Fig. 63

Radiolites, 192
Radula, 26, 38, 49, 61, 80, 90, 94, 96, 113, 118, 119, 124, 125, 131, 136, 137, 139-41, 144, 233, 236, 260, 261, 264-6
   Docoglossan, 50, 60, *Pl. 2*
   Rhipidoglossan 30, 50, 60, *Pl. 2*
   Stenoglossan (rachiglossan), 97, *Pl. 3*
   Taenioglossan, 69, 75, *Pl. 3*
   Toxoglossan, 107, 108, Fig. 55
Rapana thomasiana, 104
Ray, John, 13
Ray Society, 19
Razor shells, 142, 146, 195, 233, Figs. 81, 113-115
Réamur, 58
Redi, 260
Red nose, see *Hiatella*
Red Sea, 173, 229
Reproduction, 31
   Calyptraeidae, 81-4
   Cephalopoda, 250, 255, 256
   Chitons, 39
   Littorinidae, 76
   Mesogastropods, 68
   Opisthobranchia, 118, 136
   Oysters, 180
   Shipworms, 214, 215
   Trochacea, 66
Reproductive system, 31, 39, 48, 74, 111, 144, 152, 249
Requienia, Fig. 161

Respiration, 27, 47, 155, 232, 237, 238, 251
Retusa, 112
R. obtusa, 112, Fig. 59
R. obtusa var. *pertenuis*, 112
Rhinophores, 127, 133, 136-41
Rissoidae, 79
Rocellaria (Gastrochaena) dubia, 208, 212, Fig. 127
Rock oyster or scallop, see *Hinnites*
Rogers, Julia Ellen, 229
Rondelet, 52
Rossia macrosoma, 244
Rostangidae, 131
Royal Society, 13, 16, 18
Rudists, see Hippuritacea
Rumphius, 108, 239

Sacoglossa, 124
Saddle oysters, see Anomiacea
Sanitation, 46, 63
Santiago de Compostela, 13, 173
Saxicavacea, 201, 204, Figs. 119, 121, 122, 123
Scallops, 13, 146, 166, 167, 173, 174, 180, 193, 221, 228, 257, 258, 268, Figs. 93, 96
   Swimming of, 268, Fig. 97
Scaphander, 94
S. lignarius, 116, Fig. 56
Scaphopoda, 35, 220, 230-3, 268
Scissurella costata, 50, 53, Fig. 21
S. crispata, 50, 53
Scotland, 242, 243
Screw-shells, see *Turritella*
Scrobicularia, 198
S. plana, 199, Fig. 118
Scutus breviculus, 53
Sea anemones, 131-3
Sea butterflies, see Gymnosomes and Thecosomes
Sea-pansies, 141
Sea-slugs, see Opisthobranchia
Sepia, 246-8, 255, 260
S. elegans, 244
S. officinalis, 244-8, Figs. 148-152
Sepietta oweniana, 244
Sepiola atlantica, 244
Septibranchs, 166, 220, 225-9, 267, Figs. 140-142
   Carnivorous feeding of, 224-9
Septum, 160, 224-8
Sex change, 61, 81, 180, 218

285

Index

THE FUTURE FOR
RENEWABLE ENERGY

THE FUTURE FOR RENEWABLE ENERGY

■ PROSPECTS AND DIRECTIONS

EUREC Agency

© 1996 EUREC Agency

Published by James & James (Science Publishers) Ltd
Waterside House, 47 Kentish Town Road, London NW1 8NX

A catalogue record for this book is available from the British Library

ISBN 1 873936 70 2

Typeset by Edgerton Publishing Services, Huddersfield, UK

Printed by Biddles Ltd, UK

The illustration of the house on the front cover is of the IEA5 Solar House, Pietarsaari, Finland (reproduced by permission)

CONTENTS

Dedicated to
Professor Werner Bloss (1930–1995),
first President of EUREC Agency

AUTHORS AND ACKNOWLEDGEMENTS

1. Biomass
Authors: **S. McCarthy**, Hyperion, Ireland, **M. Walsh**, Hyperion, Ireland, **G. Gosse**, AFB/INRA, France

Acknowledgements: **J. Beurskens**, ECN, The Netherlands, **C. Charonnat**, ADEME, France, **C.D. Dalianis**, CRES, Greece, **A. Faay**, Rijksuniversiteit Utrecht, The Netherlands, **D. Hall**, King's College London, UK, **J. M. Jossart**, UCL, Belgium, **R. Maggy**, UCL, Belgium, **J. Luther**, FhG-ISE, Germany, **G. Palmers**, EUREC, **F. Rosillo-Calle**, King's College London, UK, **F. Sanchez**, IER-CIEMAT, Spain, **Y. Schenkel**, Station de Génie Rurale Gembloux, Belgium, **J. van Doorn**, ECN, The Netherlands; **ADEME France, EUBIA (European Biomass Industry Association)**

2. Ocean Energy
Authors: **P. Fraenkel**, IT Power, UK, **A. Lewis**, University College Cork, Ireland

3. Photovoltaics
Authors: **R. Van Overstraeten**, IMEC, Belgium, **R. Mertens**, IMEC, Belgium, **J. Luther**, FhG-ISE, Germany, **A. Luque**, IES-UPM, Spain, **W. Bloss**, ZSW, Germany

Acknowledgements: **D. N. Assimakopoulos**, University of Athens, Greece, **P. Baltas**, CRES, Greece, **J. Beurskens**, ECN, The Netherlands, **M. Cendagorta**, ITER, Spain (Tenerife), **G. Chimento**, Conphoebus, Italy, **H. Gabler**, FhG-ISE, Germany, **M. Garozzo**, ENEA, Italy, **L. Guimarães**, Universidade Nova de Lisbõa-FCT, Portugal, **P. Helm**, WIP, Germany, **R. Hill**, NPAC (University of Northumbria), UK, **M. Imamura**, WIP, Germany, **P. Jourde**, GENEC/Cadarache, France, **W. Kleinkauf**, ISET, Germany, **R. Lo Cicero**, Conphoebus, Italy, **A. Louche**, ERASME, France, **P. Lund**, HUT, Finland, **M. Macias**, IER-CIEMAT, Spain, **P. Malbranche**, GENEC/Cadarache, France, **D. Mayer**, ARMINES/Ecole des Mines, France, **S. McCarthy**, Hyperion, Ireland, **B. McNelis**, IT Power, UK, **J. C. Müller**, CNRS-Labo Phase, France, **J. Nijs**, IMEC, Belgium, **F. Öster**, ZSW, Germany, **H. Ossenbrink**, JRC, Italy, **G. Palmers**, EUREC, **J. Poortmans**, IMEC, Belgium, **G. Peri**, ERASME, France, **A. Räuber**, FhG-ISE, Germany, **J. Sachau**, ISET, Germany, **F. Sanchez**, IER-CIEMAT, Spain, **H. Schock**, ZSW, Germany, **P. Siffert**, CNRS-Labo Phase, **W. Sinke**, ECN, The Netherlands, **M. Stöhr**, WIP, Germany, **T. C. J. Van der Weiden**, Ecofys, The Netherlands, **W. Wettling**, FhG-ISE, Germany, **G. Wrixon**, NMRC, Ireland, **A. Zervos**, CRES, Greece; **EPIA (European Photovoltaic Industry Association)**

4. Small Hydro Power
Author: **P. Fraenkel**, IT Power, UK

Acknowlegements: **ESHA (European Small Hydro Association)**, **B. Buyse**, Ecowatt, Belgium

5. Solar Thermal For Buildings

Authors: **A. Gerber**, FhG-ISE, Germany, **V. Wittwer**, FhG-ISE, Germany, **J. Luther**, FhG-ISE, Germany

Acknowledgements: **A. Argiriou**, University of Athens, Greece, **M. Becker**, DLR, Germany, **A. Gombert**, FhG-ISE, Germany, **H. M. Henning**, FhG-ISE, Germany, **S. Herkel**, FhG-ISE, Germany, **P. Lund**, HUT, Finland, **D. Mayer**, ARMINES – Ecole des Mines, France, **M. Macias**, IER-CIEMAT, Spain, **H. Ossenbrink**, JRC, Italy, **W. Platzer**, FhG-ISE, Germany, **J. Reinländer**, ZSW, Germany, F. Sick, FhG-ISE, Germany, **K. van der Leun**, Ecofys, The Netherlands, **K. Voss**, FhG-ISE, Germany; **BASF AG**, Ludwigshafen, Germany, **Bayer AG**, Leverkusen, Germany, **Preussag AG**, Germany, **Deutsche Bundesstiftung Umwelt**, Osnabrück, Germany, **INTERPANE**, **Philipp Holzmann AG**, Neu Isenburg, Germany, **Solar Diamant**, Wettringen, Germany, **DLR Institut für Technische Thermodynamik**, Stuttgart, Germany, **Institut IB GmbH**, Hannover, Germany, **Foco Ltd**, Athens, Greece

6. Solar Thermal Power Stations

Authors: **M. Becker**, DLR, Germany, **M. Macias**, IER-CIEMAT, Spain, **J. Ajona**, IER-CIEMAT, Spain

Acknowledgements: **A. Argiriou**, University of Athens, Greece, **R. Aringhoff**, Pilkington Solar International (formely Flagsol Co.), Germany, **P. Heinrich**, Fichtner Co., Stuttgart, Germany, **R. Köhne**, DLR, Stuttgart, Germany, **J. Luther**, FhG-ISE, Germany, **D. Mayer**, Armines/Ecole des Mines, France, **W. Meiecke**, DLR, Köln, Germany, **R. Rippel**, Siemens/KWU Co., Erlangen, Germany, **M. Sanchez**, CIEMAT-PSA, Spain, **M. Schmitz-Goeb**, Steinmüller Co., Gummersbach, Germany, **U. Sprengel**, DLR Stuttgart, Germany, **H. J. Cirkel**, Siemens/KWU, Germany, **M. Geyer**, PSA Almeria, Spain, **E. Hahne**, Technical University Stuttgart, Germany, **F. Staiss**, DLR, Stuttgart, Germany; **IEA-Solar PACES (Solar Power and Chemical Energy System)**

7. Wind Energy

Authors: **P. D. Andersen**, RISØ, Denmark, **E. L. Petersen**, RISØ, Denmark, **P. H. Jensen**, RISØ, Denmark, **J. Beurskens**, ECN, The Netherlands, **G. Elliot**, NEL, UK, **J.P. Molly**, DEWI, Germany

Acknowledgements: **W. Kleinkauf**, ISET, Germany, **M. Hoppe-Kilppner**, ISET, Germany, **P. Fraenkel**, IT Power, UK; **EWEA (European Wind Energy Association)**

8. Integration

Author: **P. Lundsager**, DANREC, Denmark

Acknowledgements: **A. Zervos**, CRES, Greece, **P. D. Andersen**, RISØ, Denmark, **E. L. Petersen**, RISØ, Denmark, **J. Halliday**, ERU-RAL, UK, **G. Palmers**, EUREC

Linguistic corrections: **G. Elliot**, NEL, UK, **R. Hill**, NPAC, UK, **J. Halliday**, ERU-RAL, UK, **P. Cowley**, IT Power, UK, **P. Fraenkel**, IT Power, UK

General acknowledgements: **European Commission, Directorate General XII for Science, Research and Development, European Commission, Directorate General XVII for Energy, W. Palz**, European Commission, Directorate General XII, **A. Van Wijk**, Rijksuniversiteit Utrecht and Ecofys, **C. Vanderhulst**, EUREC

The addresses of the authors are given in Annex I.

PREFACE

Every second, three new-born children require a safe and affordable energy supply. The world's primary energy requirements may almost double by 2020 and more than 80% of the world population will then be living in developing countries.

Current energy investments are not consistent with the challenges which our energy supply system is facing. The centralized approach to power generation will not be able to supply power to a major part of the world's population in an economically affordable way. In addition, the environmental impact of conventional power supply is only beginning to show its real cost.

Therefore, intensive research, development, demonstration and market development in new energy technologies are justified. Renewable energy has already seen many important developments in recent decades. The impressive potential for cost reduction, together with the expected rise in oil prices in the future, and the environmental costs linked with the conventional energy-supply system, make it clear that renewables will become fully competitive for mass use in the coming decades.

This work presents a consensus on research and development (R&D) efforts to make these technologies mature for mass use. It is a result of cooperative action by more than 1000 experts from all EU Member States. A balancing exercise was carried out between regional preferences and between industrial-oriented and fundamental R&D by experts with scientific, technological or industrial backgrounds. EUREC Agency, the European Association of Renewable Energy Research and Development Centres (see Annex 1), provided the ideal platform for such a challenge. The book has been discussed in detail with industry and the utilities before publishing. It can therefore be considered as a widely accepted proposal for the further development and exploitation of renewable energy sources. Achieving this before the publication of *The Future for Renewable Energy* proves its recognition as a reference that will enable policy makers to organize an efficient and focused R&D policy at regional, national and European levels.

The cultural and local climatic differences within the EU make it a unique home market and basis for industrial development in this field. The leading position of the European Union in the development of renewable energy worldwide should be confirmed and strengthened in the future. In addition to the energetic and environmental benefits provided, the development of renewables will stimulate employment and export opportunities – both vital for the EU.

We want to thank all the scientists, industrial companies and utilities for their contributions. It was a particular pleasure to encourage them to look through the glasses of a policy maker and express their points of view.

Take-up of new technologies in our society is a process of mutual adaptation: people need to get used to the new environment brought by new technologies, while new technologies need to supply the services required within the given socio-economic and environmental framework.

Each important milestone in the history of energy use by human kind has changed the style of society dramatically. It can be expected that during the next decades, the new energy-provision systems will again strongly influence the structure of society.

The same enthusiasm with which the first important oil resources were discovered is now driving the research and industrial community towards the search for clean, safe, affordable and inexhaustible energy sources. Creativity and bright ideas will always be the most valuable energy source human kind can count on for its progress.

Professor R. Van Overstraeten   Geert Palmers
President   Secretary General
EUREC   EUREC

Leuven, Belgium, September 1996

EXECUTIVE SUMMARY

INTRODUCTION

The use of renewable energy sources and rational use of energy are the fundamental vectors of a responsible energy policy for the future. Because of their sustainable character, renewable energy technologies are capable of preserving resources, of ensuring security and diversity of energy supply, and providing energy services, virtually without any environmental impact. They thus contribute to the environmental protection of present and future generations. It has become clear that the 'business as usual' scenario, implying considerable increases in world energy demands, is not sustainable in the medium term.[1-3] It is the environmental concerns that will probably require the use of renewable energy sources, in combination with very ambitious energy conservation schemes, rather than the exhaustion of fossil fuel reserves, that will also become increasingly important several decades from now.

Today, renewables already represent more than 7% of the primary energy production of the EU, without Austria, Finland and Sweden. In these three new European Member States, almost two thirds of the primary energy production is from renewable sources. It is estimated that, taking the contribution of these three countries into account, renewable energy represents almost 10% of the primary energy production in the EU-15.[4,5] Because of the importance of fossil fuel imports into the EU, it is clear that the role of renewables in the EU is still modest compared to the consumption levels: only hydroelectricity and biomass exceed a 1% contribution to European consumption. It is therefore important to focus on their potential for development. Renewable energy can clearly contribute to decreasing the dependency on imports of the energy provision of the EU.

- Present energy technologies cannot be regarded as sustainable.

- The development of renewable energy technologies and an increase in energy efficiency are essential to realize a sustainable energy system.

- The EUREC position papers presented as the chapters in this book give roadmaps and goals for a strong and coherent research, development and demonstration policy for renewable energy technologies.

Appreciable progress has been made in the development of renewable energy and related technologies. Although in general they are not yet cost competitive on a micro-economic level today, various scenario studies (e.g. World Energy Council,[6] Shell,[7] United Nations[8]) foresee a total contribution from all the renewable energy technologies in the range of 20–50% of the world primary energy supply by the middle of the next century.

On a European level, different scenarios are showing that it is realistic to project a contribution of 15% for the European Union by 2010.[9]

Reaching such objectives implies immense efforts. The introduction of renewable energy technologies is perceived as more difficult because of the different character of the resources, e.g. the low energy density and the fluctuations in time and space of the resource, and their relatively high cost at the moment. Nevertheless, the potential for cost reduction is obvious, taking into account the early stage of development and the low production volumes of these technologies. Furthermore, the structural changes of a non-technical kind, needed if renewable energy is to play a significant role not too far in the future, are well known and can be overcome if a strong policy is developed. In July 1996, the European Parliament adopted the Mombaur resolution,[10] calling for such a strong and coherent action plan for renewable energy at a European level.

This book focuses on the scientific and technological developments which are required for renewable energy technologies that are able to replace conventional energy sources to the considerable extent reflected in the aforementioned scenario studies. More specifically, this book offers realistic sets of goals based on roadmaps for research, development and demonstration aiming at the required technological developments to achieve the 15% goal in the EU. Actions for market development and the structural changes needed will also be discussed. An extensive description of these goals and of the R&D roadmap has been written for each of the following technologies:

- Biomass
- Ocean energy (marine currents and waves)
- Photovoltaics (PV)
- Small hydro
- Solar thermal energy for buildings: heating, cooling, lighting and domestic hot water systems
- Solar thermal power stations
- Wind energy
- Integration of renewable energy technologies into the power supply system.

The work presented is the result of a joint effort of about 40 prominent research institutes in Europe, members of EUREC Agency (see Appendix 1). In addition, it has been discussed with the different European industrial associations for each technology and with several utilities. This Executive Summary lists all relevant elements for policy makers and formulates a series of recommendations. It offers a basis for the setting up of a strong and coherent policy for the development of renewable energy sources at a European and a regional level. It is also intended to initiate a discussion between research centres, industry and policy makers, aiming at a consensus on the priorities in research on and development of renewable energy technologies.

We are convinced that the position papers and this Executive Summary will help in rationalizing the research on, development of and demonstration efforts concerning renewable energy technologies in the European Union and strengthen the leading position of the European industry and R&D institutes.

I. BENEFITS OF RENEWABLE ENERGY AND THEIR SIGNIFICANCE FOR EUROPE

Benefits of renewable energy technologies

Renewable energy technologies have the following benefits:

- An energy policy based on renewable energy allows a sustainable energy supply.
- The use of a broader range of sources implies the security of energy supply.
- Increased employment, mainly in small and medium-sized enterprises, and stimulation of agriculture and rural employment in the case of biomass, e.g. in cooperation between farmers, industry and local authorities.
- Decentralized production of energy stimulates regional development; this applies in particular to developing countries.
- Availability of reliable and appropriate technologies for transfer to, and cooperation with, developing countries.
- The long lifetime of energy systems.
- The modular character of the technologies allows gradual implementation, which is easier to finance; it offers the possibility of a rapid scale-up when required, and it gives a short lead time between investment and return.
- The cost of energy is mainly determined by the investment, implying a higher cost stability and thus lower financial risks.
- The short time between decision and implementation.
- The reliability of electricity supply in decentralized applications.

In addition, it should be noted that, in general, the energy pay-back time for renewable energy technologies is only a small fraction of the system lifetime.

At the same time, renewable energy technologies can contribute to the solution of problems inherent with conventional energy sources such as:

- limited indigenous energy supply for most European countries;
- selective depletion of fossil fuels;
- serious contribution to global warming;
- air pollution;
- nuclear waste, danger from proliferation of nuclear technology and risk of nuclear accidents;
- high liability related to decommissioning of obsolete installations.

The disadvantages of the present energy supply system are often quantified in terms of external or social costs. These costs range between 0.03 ECU/kWh up to 0.3 ECU/kWh,[11,12] depending on the inclusion of external costs due to CO_2 emissions. At present, these external costs are not accounted for in the price of energy.

Further development of renewable energy technologies is therefore in accordance with the economic, energy and environmental policies of the European Union.

Industrial developments and employment

Europe is at the forefront in the world for several renewable energy technologies. The manufacture, installation and maintenance of renewable energy technologies generates several tens of thousands of direct and indirect jobs in the EU, involving several hundred companies, mainly small and medium-sized enterprises.

For the new renewable energy technologies (i.e. not including large hydro-electric power stations and the classic use of biomass), the worldwide annual turnover of the industry is estimated to be higher than ECU 5 billion, of which Europe has a one third share. The following examples show the current trends:

- About 90% of the world's manufacturers of medium- and large-sized wind turbines are European, although gradually more competition is coming from the USA and Japan. The European wind energy industry is one of the fastest growing industries, with annual growth rates of 50% during recent years.
- The EU accounts for about one third of the annual worldwide PV-module production and use. Several thousands of PV building integrated systems (rooftop and façades) have been installed in Europe from Finland to Spain, mainly in the framework of national programmes. On this basis, the European industry has built up a leading position in the field of photovoltaics integrated in buildings.
- Europe also has the lead in applications of PV for developing countries.
- European R&D is clearly leading in the field of marine energy, offering an important future commercial potential worldwide.
- European know-how on solar thermal power stations is certainly among the foremost worldwide. Development of the next generations of such power stations in Europe will be led by the Plataforma Solar de Almería, Spain.
- European industry is leading in several biomass conversion technologies (e.g. gasification in Scandinavian countries and biogas production in Denmark), and the R&D in Europe on energy crops for electricity, heat and liquid fuels is also in a leading position.
- EU countries dominate the world market for small hydro equipment. Of the 150 small hydro contracts (greater than 1 MW) awarded in 1991–1992 worldwide, 86% were awarded to European firms.
- The market for solar thermal domestic hot water systems is estimated to be 500 million ECU/year. The European glass industry leads in glass coating and windows technology.

As a substitute for imported fossil fuels, renewable energy technologies clearly contribute to the substantial creation of new employment opportunities in the EU. This new employment will be found in the design, manufacturing and maintenance of the energy conversion systems.

- Renewable energy technologies offer great opportunities for new industrial and agricultural activities and create new employment.

- European industry and R&D institutes are leading in several technologies, although increasing competition is experienced from the USA and Japan.

Potential and applicability in Europe

In theory, the renewable energy potential in Europe can meet several hundred times the total energy requirements, e.g. the total solar radiation reaching the land area of the EU is several hundred times the energy demand of the EU. But, although the potential is high, these resources have some characteristics that are different from conventional energy sources, which at first sight make them less attractive, such as the relatively extensive land use for some renewables and their fluctuating availability. These particular characteristics will be discussed first.

Land use

It is often said that, owing to the diffuse nature of many renewable energy resources, large areas for energy harnessing are required. The following considerations show that this is not the case. For biomass, it is estimated that the land released or not needed for food crops in the frame of the Common Agricultural Policy in the EU, could cover a biomass production of more than 10% of the final energy demand of the EU.[2] Photovoltaics can be integrated aesthetically into roofs and façades of buildings, acoustic barriers of highways, etc. without occupying any additional area. For example, the total installable PV-rated capacity mounted on rooftops and façades in the UK represents an annual electricity production exceeding the total electricity demand in the UK.[13] Also, solar thermal cooling and heating techniques can be integrated into the building concepts and require no additional space. Solar thermal power stations and process heat production plants are applicable in the sunbelt (Mediterranean countries, Northern Africa and the Middle East) with much direct sunlight; land availability is not a problem there. The utilization of ocean energy also requires virtually no land and can in some cases increase the amenity of the sea space. A 100,000 MW wind power plant, needed to supply 10% of Europe's electricity would cover a total land area no greater than the island of Crete.[14] In addition, a part of the installations could be installed offshore. Onshore wind farms also have the advantage of dual land use. 99% of the area occupied by a wind farm can be used for agriculture or remain as natural habitat.

Recent studies have shown that the land necessary for the generation of energy, making use of renewable energies, is no higher than it is for conventional sources if the full life-cycle land use (i.e. all stages from fuel preparation to generation and waste treatment and storage) are taken into account.[15]

Fluctuating supply

Owing to the fluctuating character of the renewable energy resources, as well as that of the demand pattern, an integrated approach with a different control paradigm will be necessary to meet the energy requirements at all times if renewable energy technologies are used intensively.

Biomass technologies, and also solar thermal power to a lesser extent, have an intrinsic storage capability. Therefore, they can serve as base-load power generators. Moreover, fuels derived from biomass can be used in the existing energy infrastructure, e.g. in the cofiring of biomass with coal and the use of liquid biofuel for transportation. Small hydro can readily achieve load factors in the 70–90% range and, in addition, ocean energy is less random; hence both are suitable to contribute to base-load power needs. Hydropower can also be used as fast peak load or spinning reserve. Experience with wind energy shows that the predictability of the power output increases with the number and spatial spread of the installed wind turbines so that to some extent they can also be considered as base-load power generators.[16]

For wind energy and photovoltaics, penetration levels of 20% of the European grid capacity can be reached without need for storage, simply by connecting to the grid and using the grid as virtual 'storage' medium. This penetration level may be considerably higher by making use of load management techniques and including storage, additional loads (e.g. pumping, desalination, etc.) and energy savings. Furthermore, the combined use of complementary sources such as hydro, photovoltaics and wind will additionally decrease the fluctuating character of power production from the combined renewable energy systems.

Despite their varying supply, it is clear that renewable energy sources can replace firm capacity and meet a large fraction of the future energy demand. The contribution of renewable energy to the total energy demand will be able to increase gradually to values up to 50% by the middle of next century worldwide. The current energy infrastructure over this period will have to be adapted and optimized to accommodate the decentralized renewable energy sources.

- The renewable energy potential in the EU can meet several hundred times the total EU energy requirements.

- The land requirements for energy generation making use of renewables is not higher than for conventional sources if the full life-cycle land use is taken into account.

- Renewables can progressively replace conventional capacity and cover up to 50% of the EU energy demand by 2050, provided that this opportunity is fully integrated in the energy policy.

2. REALISTIC TECHNOLOGICAL GOALS FOR RENEWABLE ENERGIES IN EUROPE

In the Introduction, it has been stated that a 15% contribution to the European energy production in 2010 is a realistic objective. In order to fulfil this objective and to ensure a continued growth afterwards, goals for technology development, cost and implementation have been assessed in the position papers presented in the following chapters. These goals are based on the R&D roadmaps and on the growth potential of the industrial production capacities, as described extensively in the position papers. Appendix 1 at the end of this chapter summarizes the status, the main challenges and the realistic goals for the different renewable energy technologies in Europe.

The scenario studies mentioned in the introduction indicate ranges of contributions of renewable energy to the future world energy demand, depending on the assumptions made by the different authors:

World Energy Council (2020 – Western Europe):[6]   15–20%
United Nations (2050 – Western Europe):[8]   61%
Shell (2060 – World):[7]   > 50%
Madrid Conference (2010 – EU):[9]   15%

The focus of this study is not on scenarios, but on the construction of RD&D (Research Development and Demonstration) 'roadmaps'; nevertheless, the assessment of the technical potential of renewable energy based on these 'roadmaps' clearly confirms the ability of renewable energy to make major contributions by the beginning of next century and, more specifically, the ability to approach the 15% contribution at the European level by 2010.

Section 3 of this Exectutve Summary outlines the priorities of the roadmaps for each technology, formulated as recommendations to policy makers.

3. RECOMMENDATIONS

A number of recommendations are presented which are essential for attaining the RD&D goals described in the position papers and summarized in Appendix 1. We make a distinction between recommendations that are common to all renewable energy technologies and recommendations that are specific for a particular resource. The common recommendations are listed here and the specific ones are given in Appendix 2 at the end of this chapter.

General recommendations

Research, development and demonstration

- Coherent and continuous support of research, development and demonstration (RD&D) as proposed in the following chapters, with a yearly total budget of at least ECU 1 billion.
  - Continuous support of RD&D with regular review of priorities taking into account the developments in related fields.
  - Lining up of regional and European RD&D programmes and encouraging European and international cooperation.
- Develop standards for the different renewable energy technologies. These should be related to engineering issues, safety, certification requirements, warranties, etc.

Educational capacity building

- Training and education at all levels by means of a Renewable Energy Educational Plan.

Targeted market action programmes (examples)

- Large-scale integration of renewables into buildings (districts) (district heating, domestic hot water systems, PV, etc.) .
- Coordinated action for biomass energy development on set aside and erodable land by alignment of agricultural and energy policy, stimulating rural development.

- Development of large-scale wind parks in high resource areas.
- Early and aggressive introduction of renewable energy technologies in those places in Europe where they are particularly advantageous.

Economic measures

- Introduce methods which include external costs in financial decision making.
- New ways for the financial support of the introduction of renewable energy with focus on attracting private capital (buy-back rate of electricity at 100% of purchase price, subsidies for lending rates, a 'renewable energy levy' on kWh price, tax credits, green funds, arbitrary amortization of renewable energy systems).
- Allow free competition in electricity production and in electricity distribution, combined with a renewable energy obligation.

Stimulate European renewable energy industry

- Strengthen industrial linkages to stimulate renewable energy business, to take up new technologies in industry and to create new employment opportunities.
- Intensify the scientific and industrial cooperation with southern Mediterranean countries

Preparation of the energy infrastructure

- Electricity systems, e.g. the grid structure, should be designed and optimized to accommodate renewable energy.

Developing countries

- Integrate renewable energies in European and bilateral development programmes, and coordinate efforts made in different programmes and make optimal use of experience gained.
- Renewable energy should get the highest priority of energy investments in developing countries.
- Initiate a market action programme within the framework of the European Renewable Energy Export Council (EREEC[17]).

4. CONCLUSIONS

The potential of renewable energies is enormous as they can meet many times the energy demand. They have the advantages of sustainability, of environmental acceptability and of availability in every region. The diversity of technologies matches the geographical and climatic diversity of Europe and is able to provide energy in the form of electricity, heat and fuels. Many renewable energy technologies are already available as reliable industrial products and represent an important market, involving many small and medium-sized enterprises throughout Europe. Their economic competitiveness will be strongly improved by boosting production capacities to mass-production levels and by further technological developments. The external or social costs of renewable energy (selective depletion of fossil fuels, nuclear hazards, global warming, etc.) are negligible compared to those of conventional energy sources. For a fair comparison, these external costs should be included in the market price. The substitution of renewable energies for import of fossil fuels reduces the import dependency of EU energy provision and creates substantial employment opportunities for Europe.

Renewable energies are quite different from conventional energies and often do not fit well into the existing energy business (production and distribution) models. More effective introduction can therefore only be obtained with the support of the European Commission and of national and regional authorities.

This book, which describes the state of the art of the different technologies and discusses the R&D still to be done, can be the basis of a European and regional policy on renewable energies. This policy should result in a strong European industry, in important employment creation, and in environmentally friendly energy production that is less dependent on changing political situations and is, in addition, self-sustainable.

APPENDIX 1. STATUS, MAIN CHALLENGES AND REALISTIC GOALS FOR RENEWABLES

Technology	Status	Main challenge	Realistic goals
Biomass			
Environmental and social issues	R&D	Sustainability and public acceptability	**RD&D** • Demonstration of environmentally/socially acceptable large-scale energy farming
Lignocellulosic crops	R&D	Yield and sustainability	• Improvement and optimization of the production techniques at the agricultural and forestry level
Conversion: thermochemical			
· combustion	Commercial	Emissions, Efficiency	· Increased efficiency of the existing systems by 2000 by at least 50%
· gasification	Demonstration	Clean gas, proven application in gas turbines	· Gasification efficiency › 40% (electricity) › 80% (Combined Heat Power) and improvement of gas cleaning
· fast pyrolysis	R&D	Proven application in engines, Fuel quality	· Demonstration of flash pyrolysis unit and related technologies of several thousands of tonnes/year by 2000
Conversion: chemical	Commercial	Cost	· Competitiveness of liquid biofuels from 2010 on.
Conversion: biochemical	Commercial	Productivity, Efficiency	

Cost goals:

Energy crops: Short rotation forestry   ‹ 30ECU/odt
                                                                   (odt = oven dry tonnes)
                    Herbaceous energy crops   ‹46 ECU/ odt
                    Rape methyl ester and bioethanol   ‹ 0,3 ECU/l

Implementation

	2010	2025
Heat:	› 20%	› 35% contribution by biomass to heat demand in EU
Electricity	› 5%	› 15% of electricity generation using biomass in EU
Biofuels		› 5% of European demand for gasoline and gasoil

Technology	Status	Main challenge	Realistic goals
Ocean Energy			
Marine energy	R&D	Reliability, sealing, maintenance	**RD&D** · Demonstration of grid-connected marine current turbines in 200-800 kW range by 2005 · Several 100 MW installed capacity in 2010
Wave energy	Demonstration	Reliability , sealing, maintenance, Conversion efficiency Survivability Construction cost	**RD&D** · Demonstration of third generation offshore in 2010 **Implementation** · 200 MW installed by 2010 with 20MW/y growth, mainly first and second generation devices

Technology	Status	Main challenge	Realistic goals
Photovoltaics			
Crystalline Si	Commercial	Cost of Si-feedstock, cell and module	**RD&D** · 16% efficient multi- and 18% efficient monocrystalline cells in production by 2000
Amorphous Si	Commercial	Conversion efficiency and stability; Manufacturability	· Amorphous Si modules of 10% stable efficiency by 2000
Thin film crystalline	Pilot production		· Pilot production of thin film crystalline before 2000
Systems	Commercial	Cost of systems & energy efficiency of loads	· Standardized, low energy consumption reliable systems by 2000
			Cost By 2010: Cell cost < 1.0 ECU/Wp Module cost < 1.5 ECU/Wp System cost < 3 ECU/Wp **Implementation** · Grid-connected PV integrated in buildings competitive by 2005 · PV production level > 1 GWp/year in EU by 2010 · Installed PV capacity 5 GWp in EU by 2010
Small hydro	Commercial	Cost & regulatory framework	**Implementation** · 1000–2000 MW new small hydro power installed by 2005 in EU, with similar or greater capacity of exported European equipment
Solar thermal energy for buildings: **heating, cooling, lighting and domestic hot water systems**			**Implementation** By 2010–2020
Solar and energy-efficient building techniques	Non-optimized systems commercial;	System improvement, reliability, Large-scale production	· Reduction of energy demand for heating by 50% (about 17% of the final energy use in EU) · Heating demand < 70 kWh/m²a
Domestic hot water (DHW) & active heating systems	Collectors commercial; only large scale seasonal storage available;	Mass production of improved systems; Integration of systems into the old building stock	· Solar Ratio (contribution of solar energy to the energy demand) for heating 30% (about 5% of final energy use in EU) · Solar Ratio of 50% for DHW (about 17% of final energy use in EU)
Solar cooling, thermal storage, solar assisted thermal driven heat pumps	Demonstration	Combination of passive and CFC-free cooling systems; Development of new cycles combined cooling/heating systems	· Solar Ratio for cooling > 50% in new buildings (Southern & Central EU) · Wide-spread storage applications for solar district heating and seasonal storage for low-energy houses
Low-energy concepts	Demonstration	Development and demonstration of total low energy systems (cogeneration)	· Houses with a low non-renewable energy demand for heating and cooling · New houses < 20 kW/m²a ; Old stock < 50 kWh/m²a

Technology	Status	Main challenge	Realistic goals
Solar thermal power stations		General: Credibility for utilities and finanicial institutions	**Demonstration**
Parabolic through	Commercial	Demonstration/commercial application	· Demonstration plant and first commercial use of hybrid system and combined cycle by 2005 (steam, air, molten salt)
Central receiver	Demonstration	Demonstration of technology	· Demonstration plant and first commercial use of hybrid system and combined cycle by 2005
Parabolic dish	Pilot plants	Demonstration of technology	· Demonstration and first commercial units with power blocks of 1MW-5MW by 2005
			Cost
			· Parabolic through and central receiver: < 0.1 ECU/kWh for second-generation technologies
			· Parabolic dish: < 0.15 ECU/kWh by in case of mass fabrication
			Implementation
			· 3.5 GW by 2005
			· 23 GW by 2025 for conservative scenarios or more (e.g. 60 GW) in case of more accelerated scenarios and with Mediterranean-wide interconnecting grids
Wind Energy	Commercial	**Cost** Free operation of wind power markets	**RD&D** · Harmonized EU standards and legal-institutional framework by 2000 - 2005
		Credibility for utilities, financial institutions	· Reduction of uncertainty of generation costs by 10% by 2000
		Public acceptance	· Realistic output prediction up to 36 h ahead for wind parks in 2000
			· Technical & economic solution for integration of 100,000 MW wind power in the European grid by 2010
			· Introduction of European Standards for noise, siting and stealthing by 2005
			· Proven, mature and competitive application of wind power in remote hybrid systems etc. by 2005
			Cost:
			· Reduction of kWh cost by
			30% by 2000
			40% by 2005
			50% by 2030
			Implementation
			· 11,500 MW in 2005
			· 25,000 MW in 2010
			· 100,000 MW in 2030

Technology	Status	Main challenge	Realistic goals
Integration			**RD&D**
Local	Demonstration		· Develop and demonstrate proven & cost-effective concepts, principles and solutions for Integrated Hybrid Renewable Energy (IHRE) systems
Regional	R&D		· Improve support technologies, e.g. energy conversion & management technologies
			· Flexible, modular & updateable tools for planning, design and evaluation
		General: Integration of renewables in European grids	· Ensure necessary quality of deliverables (power, reliability, predictability)
		Increase technical and economical credibility	· Harmonized European Standards, legal structures and institutional framework
		Open markets and increased industrial collaboration	· Agreed rates & principles for the quantitative evaluation of IHRE technology
		Acceptance by implementing agencies	· Proven and competitive applications of RE cogeneration and IHRE technology within 2010
			Implementation by 2010:
			· Integrated hybrid renewable energy systems with 100% recognized capacity value
			· Communities and regions in EU up to 100% supplied by renewable energies
			· Substantial part of global increase in energy demand covered by integrated hybrid renewable energy systems

APPENDIX 2. SPECIFIC RECOMMENDATIONS FOR THE DIFFERENT RENEWABLE ENERGY TECHNOLOGIES

Biomass

Research, development and demonstration

- R&D should strengthen the links between energy and agriculture and forestry, and the production of chemicals in parallel.
- Development of advanced conversion systems, focus on advanced gasification, combined heat and power generation, co-combustion and flash pyrolysis.
- Focus on the environmental and social acceptability of biomass production.
- Large-scale demonstration projects: energy farming, logistics and conversion technologies.
- Development of methodologies for the assessment of land availability.
- The route of gasification of woody biomass to methanol should be continued to be examined as a long-term option.
- RD&D should be stimulated on production of ethanol by means of biochemical processes and on the reduction of the cost of biofuel.

Other

- Develop and verify financial models for biomass systems.
- Study of legal, administrative and planning issues for the establishment of biomass systems.
- Stimulation of cofiring of biomass with coal.
- Stimulation of public debate between industry, farmers, local authorities, utilities, etc.

Ocean energy

Research, development and demonstration

- Establish properly funded, well defined and well selected wave and marine current pilot projects.
- More detailed resource assessment based on actual measurements of ocean energy

Photovoltaics

Research, development and demonstration

- A number of actions to reduce the cost of crystalline Si PV modules below 1 ECU/Wp and of PV systems below 3 ECU/Wp. These activities not only include R&D on substrates, cells, modules, manufacturing technologies, system components and integration techniques, but also mass production at the 100 MW level.
- The installation of a pilot plant for promising polycrystalline thin film technologies.
- The concentration option at the research and at the demonstration level, and the development of tracking and concentrator technologies.
- Long-term R&D on novel materials and cell concepts, and R&D on thin films.

- A large number of well chosen demonstration actions; building integrated projects in all EU Member States with special emphasis on cost reduction of system integration.

Other

- Strategic considerations to valorize strengths of European PV community such as the support of PV integration in buildings and an active market development to trigger increases in production volumes.

Small hydro

Research, development and demonstration

- Concerted action by EU to develop R&D programme on low head hydro aiming at cost reduction.

Other

- Development of improved institutional and regulatory framework in the EU for run-of-river hydro.

Solar thermal energy for buildings

Research, development and demonstration

- Development of new materials and components for effective façades and windows (smart façades and windows), heat transformation systems (long-term and thermo-chemical storage, thermal-driven heat pumps, thermal-driven cooling systems) and daylighting.
- Development of solar-assisted district heating schemes.
- System development for integration of new technologies into buildings; old stocks and new ones.
- Total energy concepts for low energy houses; cogeneration, combined heating and cooling systems.
- Integral planning and education.

Other

- Standardization of test procedures for collectors, stores and systems.
- Improved standards and regulations.

Solar thermal power stations

Research, development and demonstration

- Quantification of cost/performance benefits of parabolic-through and central-receiver systems integrated in 100 to 200 MWe solar/fossil hybrid combined cycle plants and 1–5 MWe plants with dishes.

- Design of such plant systems.
- Implementation of demonstration plants, initially in Southern Europe, later on in North Africa, using proven technology.
- Identification of the next technological steps for components and systems; design and optimization of these components and systems.
- Testing of new designs, improvement and qualification of the second generation.
- Evelution and development of appropriate systems for industrial cogeneration in the power range of 30 MW.
- Development of market penetration strategies.

Other

- Governmental programmes to initiate solar thermal power stations in the Mediterranean area.
- Establish consortia with international partnerships.
- Establish joint ventures and cooperations between South and Central European utilities.

Wind energy

Research, development and demonstration

- Actions to reach the cost reduction targets by improvement of wind turbine efficiency, by reducing the cost of existing wind turbines and by development of new concepts and components, by decrease of manufacturing costs, project preparation cost and operation and maintenance cost.
- Actions aiming at a decrease in production uncertainty by improved production prediction, improved performance prediction and availability.
- Activities aiming at an increased power quality and predictability, and investigation of large-scale grid integration issues.

Other

- Development of harmonized European Standards, legal structures and institutional framework.
- Activities aiming at the mitigation of environmental and societal consequences of wind power.

Integration

Research, development and demonstration

- Increased R&D effort in cogeneration issues for energy supply systems with multiple renewable energy technologies, in particular control, dispatch and prediction issues.
- Initiation and support of well defined and monitored pilot and demonstration projects aiming at the increase in technical and economic credibility of the integrated hybrid renewable energy technology.

Other

• Secure European industry's international competitiveness by facilitating industrial competition and promoting industrial collaboration and coproduction of integrated hybrid renewable energy systems.
• Contribute to the acceptance of integrated hybrid renewable energy systems from implementing agencies, donor and financing institutions by actions leading to agreed rates and principles for the quantitative evaluation of such systems.

REFERENCES

1 Raskin P and Margolis A (1995). Global Energy in the 21st Century Projections and Problems. Stockholm Environment Institute.
2 Houghton J T et al. (1995). Climate Change 1994, Radiative Forcing of Climate Change and An Evaluation of the IPCC IS92 Emission Scenarios. Intergovernmental Panel on Climate Change. Cambridge University Press.
3 Rio de Janeiro Climate Convention (1992).
4 Following the EUROSTAT Convention. Data on renewable energy contribution in the EU-15 are not yet available, but estimates have been made based on data of previous years, in reference (5). Note that the mentioned 7% corresponds to more than 10% if it assumed that all electricity is produced from oil equivalents with an efficiency of 38.5%, as is done by the World Energy Council and the UN; see also reference (5).
5 Palz W (1995–96). Renewable Energy in Europe: Statistics and their problems, Yearbook of Renewable Energies, p. 146. James & James, London.
6 New Renewable Energy Resources (1994). World Energy Council, London.
7 Kassler P (1994). Energy for Development, Shell Selected Paper, London.
8 Johansson T B et al. (1993). Renewable Energy – Sources for Fuels and Electricity. Island Press, Washington DC.
9 An Action Plan for Renewable Energy Sources in Europe (1994). Proceedings of Madrid Conference, March 1994. European Commission DG XVII, Brussels.
10 Mombaur Resolution of the Committee on Research, Technological Development and Energy of the European Parliament, A4-0188/96.
11 Hohmeyer O (1992). The Social Costs of Electricity – Renewables versus Fossil and Nuclear Energy. International Journal of Solar Energy, 11, 231–250.
12 Hohmeyer O (1993). Economic Thinking, Sustainable Development and the Role of Solar Energy in the 21st Century. Parliamentary Hearing on 'Energy and Environment: Towards sustainable development', Paris, 25–26 November 1993.
13 Potential Generation Capacity for UK, ETSU 31365-PI.
14 Garrad A (1991). Wind Energy in Europe, Time for Action – a strategy for Europe to realize its enormous wind power potential. European Wind Energy Association.
15 Energy Systems Emisions and Material Requirements (1989). Report to USDOE by Meridian Corporation.
16 See Grubb and Meyer in Reference (8)
17 EREEC, European Renewable Energy Export Council, established on 3 July 1996 in Brussels by the European Photovoltaic Industry Association (EPIA), the European Small Hydro Association (ESHA), the European Solar Industry (Solar Thermal) Association (ESIF), the European Biomass Industry Association (EUBIA) and the European Wind Energy Association (EWEA).

1. BIOMASS

1.1 INTRODUCTION

Biomass is the world's fourth largest energy source today and it contributes 14% of the world's primary energy demand. In developing countries it represents 35% of the primary energy supply. In 1991 biomass contributed 2% of the EU primary energy requirements (25.4 Mtoe) and the potential for 2005 has been estimated at 75 Mtoe in the ALTENER programme. In the new EU Member States, Austria, Finland and Sweden, biomass accounts already for more than 14% of the primary energy supply. Biomass is a versatile source of energy in that it can produce electricity, heat, transport fuel and it can be stored. In addition, production units range from small scale up to multi-megawatt size.

Development of biomass energy use can also contribute to other non-energy policies of the EU, in particular:

- **Environmental policy.** The life-cycle of biomass has a neutral effect on CO_2. It also offers the possibilities of a closed mineral cycle and a closed nitrogen cycle. Biomass is also an attractive fuel from an environmental point of view because it is renewable. The environmentally hazardous sulphur dioxide (SO_2), which is produced during combustion of fossil fuels and contributes to acid deposition, is not a major problem in biomass systems because of the low sulphur content of biomass (< 1% compared to 1 to 5% for coal).
- **Agricultural policy.** CAP (Common Agricultural Policy) and the search for alternative uses of set-aside land. It is estimated that 20 million hectares of agricultural land and 10–20 million hectares of marginal land are likely to be available for non-food production by the year 2000.
- **Social policy.** Estimates show that 11 jobs are created per MW (installed biomass plant). 5% of additional coverage of the community energy needs, on the basis of biomass would lead to 160,000 additional jobs (Wright report[1]).
- **Regional policy.** Biomass can be used as a decentralized energy source where conversion plants are located close to the source of biomass. This would lead to stabilization of employment in rural areas and regional development.

Already a surprising number of actions have been undertaken with promising results:

- In Austria, the contribution of biomass for district heating has increased sixfold,[2] in Sweden eightfold[3] during the last decade thanks to positive stimulation at federal and local level.
- In the USA, already more than 8000 MWe installed capacity based on biomass has been installed, primarily stimulated by the PURPA Act.[4]
- In France, direct combustion of wood represents almost 5% of the primary energy use.[5]

This chapter focuses on the needs for research, development and demonstration and formulates a set of goals. For the different levels of biomass systems, from crops and conversion technologies to biomass end products, a 'roadmap' for R&D is discussed.

As an introduction, the status is summarized.

1.2 PRESENT SITUATION

This section summarizes the current status of biomass covering biomass crops, conversion technologies and end-products. It includes an introduction to the crops used, technologies available and end-products of the conversion process.

Figure 1.1 gives an overview of the different *filières* from biomass to end-products.

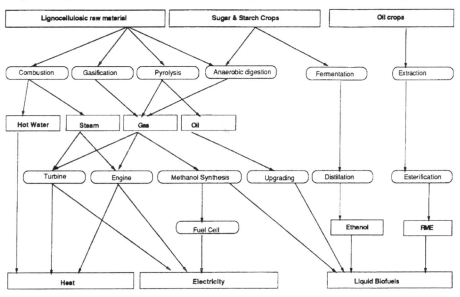

Figure 1.1. The different filières from biomass to end-products

1.2.1 Biomass material

The main biomass resources include the following: short rotation forestry (willow, poplar, eucalyptus, e.g. Figure 1.2), wood wastes (forest residues, sawmill and construction/industrial residues, etc.), sugar crops (sugarbeet, sweet sorghum, Jerusalem artichoke), starch crops (maize, wheat), herbaceous lignocellulosic crops (miscanthus), oil crops (rapeseed, sunflower), agricultural wastes (straw, slurry, etc.), municipal solid waste and refuse, and industrial wastes (e.g. residues from the food industry). Current and future biomass resources in the EU are given in Table 1.1.

It can be seen from the table that in the long term, energy crops will be an important biomass fuel (if they fulfil their potential). At present, however, wastes, in the form of wood wastes, agricultural wastes, municipal or industrial wastes, are the major biomass sources and are, arguably, the priority fuels for energy production. There is also an added

Figure 1.2. Short Rotation Forestry (Conde-sur-Suippe – O. Sebart/ADEME)

Table 1.1. Current and future EU biomass resources[6–8]

Raw material	Current resources (dry) (Mt./yr.)	Future resources (Mt./yr.)
Short-rotation forestry	5	75–150
Wood wastes	50	70
Energy crops	–	250–750
Agricultural/wastes	100	100
MSW/refuse	60	75
Industrial wastes	90	100

environmental benefit in using residues, such as municipal solid waste and slurry, as feed-stocks because these are potential pollutants.

Research on biomass energy crops is concentrating on generating reliable data on potential yield, environmental impact, limitations and economics. Developments are achieved through networks of research groups, such as the Miscanthus Network, the Sweet Sorghum Network, etc. There are also a number of other European and national projects which carry out research on a range of biomass materials.

1.2.2 Conversion processes

The conversion technologies can be divided into thermochemical, chemical and biochemical conversion processes. These include the following:

- Thermochemical processes:
  - Combustion (co-combustion and cofiring)
  - Gasification

- Pyrolysis
- Liquefaction
- Chemical processes:
  - Esterification
- Biochemical processes:
  - Acid hydrolysis
  - Enzyme hydrolysis
  - Fermentation.

1.2.2.1 Thermochemical processes

COMBUSTION

Combustion can be defined as the direct burning of biomass to produce heat that can be used directly (heating or drying) or indirectly (steam turbine) transformed into electrical energy. This can be represented by:

$$C_6H_{10}O_5 \quad + \quad O_2 \quad \rightarrow \quad 6CO_2 \quad + \quad 5H_2O \quad - \quad 17.5\,Mkg.$$

Biomass   +   Combustion fuel   Carbon dioxide +   water   +   heat

The majority of biomass-derived energy comes from wood combustion and this will continue to remain important because of improvements in combustion efficiency (fuel–electrical energy) of > 30% and a reduction in pollutant emissions. The major development in the area of combustion will probably be in large combined heat and power plants (CHP). Direct combustion processes are commercialized already and the firing of biomass powder in ceramic gas turbines is being actively explored. These could be commercialized in 5–10 years.

The amount of heat produced depends on the humidity of the biomass source, the level of excess air required and the degree to which the combustion process is accomplished. Today, combustion technology is extremely well advanced, permitting widespread industrial application. Two types of boiler are distinguished:

- boilers with fixed or travelling grates;
- boilers with fluidized beds.

The former type is very common, ranging from the household boiler to large-scale 50 MW industrial furnaces, and can accommodate combustible material that is comparatively heterogeneous in terms of humidity values and granularity. On the other hand, these boilers do not adapt readily to variations in load.

When a fluid is passed upward through a bed of solids with a velocity high enough for the particles to separate from one another and become freely supported in the fluid, the bed is said to be fluidized.

GASIFICATION

This process is incomplete combustion of a solid and gas, to produce a mixture of combustible gases, mainly carbon monoxide and hydrogen, diluted in nitrogen, except when gasification is performed with oxygen. The most efficient and economical use of the product is in the production of electricity via gas.

Among a series of processes, focus is on the BIG-STIG (Biomass Integrated Gasifier-Steam Injected Gas Turbine) process. In this system, steam is recovered from exhaust heat and is injected back into the gas-turbine combustor and then passed through the turbine. This allows more power to be produced from the gas turbine at higher electrical efficiency. But still today, IGCC is the most advanced concept in terms of efficiency. Electricity generation by IGCC is at the demonstration phase.

Combustion is basically a technology to convert the chemical energy of a feedstock into heat, while gasification is a technology to convert a solid chemical energy carrier into a gaseous carrier of chemical energy. The gas obtained in gasification still can be combusted in a second step, resulting in the liberation of the chemical energy of the gas in the form of heat.

Biomass gasification is offered commercially by several companies for heat applications. As a long-term option, the gasification–methanol route has a promising economic potential.

PYROLYSIS / CARBONIZATION

Pyrolysis is a process of decomposition through the effect of temperature in the absence of oxygen. The products obtained by pyrolysis of lignocellulosic matter are: solids (charcoal), liquids (pyrolysis oils) and a mix of combustible gases. The proportions of each of the products is dependent on the reaction parameters, i.e. the temperature, heating rate and residence time of the process. Pyrolysis has been practised for centuries for the production of charcoal (carbonization); this process requires relatively slow reaction temperatures to maximize solid char yield at around 35%.

In recent years more attention has been paid to the production of pyrolysis oils, which have the advantage of being easier to handle than the starting biomass and have a much higher energy density. Yields of up to 80% weight liquid may be obtained from biomass material by using fast or flash pyrolysis at moderate reaction temperatures.

These liquids, currently referred to as bio-oils or bio-crudes, are intended to be used in direct combustion in boilers, engines or turbines. Nevertheless, it is generally agreed that some improvements are necessary to overcome unwanted characteristics, such as poor thermal stability and heating value, high viscosity and corrosivity.

The degree of upgrading depends on the final utilization of the oils and, if minor adjustment (reduction of viscosity by careful heating to less than 100°C or dilution with water of alcohols) is enough for direct combustion in adapted engines, further chemical/catalytic deoxygenation engines are needed to obtain transportation fuels.

The upgrading to a hydrocarbon transport fuel by deoxygenation may be effected by catalytic hydrotreating at high pressure or by zeolite cracking at atmospheric pressure. Both processes have been developed at laboratory scale.

The main advantage of fast pyrolysis for the production of liquids is that fuel production is separated from utilization for electricity.

LIQUEFACTION

This is a low-temperature (250–500°C), high-pressure (up to 150 bar) process in which a reducing gas, usually hydrogen, is added to the slurried feed. The product is an oxygenated liquid with a heating value of 35–40 MJ/kg, compared to 20–25 MJ/kg for pyrolysis oils. Interest in liquefaction is lower owing to the high cost of pressure reactors, the need for feed preparation and problems with feeding slurries. Some R&D is being carried out on batch reactors and catalytic hydro cracking.

1.2.2.2 Chemical processes

ESTERIFICATION

Esterification is the chemical modification of vegetable oils into vegetable oil esters that are suitable for use as biofuels in engines. Vegetable oils are produced from oil crops (e.g. rapeseed, sunflower) using prepressing and extraction techniques. The by-product of the oil production is a protein 'cake', which is a valuable feedstuff for animal feeding.

Esterification is then used to adapt the vegetable oil to the requirements of the diesel engine by conversion to vegetable oil esters. This process eliminates glycerides in the presence of an alcohol and a catalyst (usually aqueous sodium hydroxide or potassium hydroxide). Methyl esters are formed if the alcohol used is methanol while ethyl esters are formed if ethanol is used. The most common vegetable oil ester is RME (rape methyl ester), which is used as a biofuel in diesel engines.

The productivity of the process is represented below. This example considers an initial biomass (raw material) quantity of 3000 kg of rape seed. During the extraction process this would be converted to approximately 1000 kg of rape oil and 1900 kg of protein feedstuff. In the esterification process the rape oil would be treated with methanol to produce 1000 kg RME and 110 kg of glycerine.

Extraction:	Rape seed	→	Feed stuff	+	Rape oil
	(3000 kg)		(1900 kg)		(1000 kg)
Esterification:	Rape oil	→	Glycerine	+	RME
	(1000 kg)		(110 kg)		(1000 kg)

Vegetable oil esters have a good potential and can be used in mixtures with diesel fuel from 1% up to 100%. Compared to conventional diesel, RME produces far lower levels of most exhaust emissions that have been linked to a range of health problems, e.g. respiratory problems and cancer. Rapeseed oil does not contain sulphur, so there is no production of sulphur dioxide, which impares lung function and contributes to acid rain. There may, however, be problems with odour (similar to cooking oil) when pure RME is used as a fuel.

1.2.2.3 Biological/biochemical processes

These include anaerobic digestion, acid and enzyme hydrolysis and fermentation.

Anaerobic digestion of wastes to produce methane is a well established technology for waste treatment. Methane can be used for direct burning or for internal combustion engines. The average production rate is 0.2–0.3 m^3 biogas per kg dry solids. 80% of the industrialized world 'biogas production' is from commercially exploited landfill. R&D is mainly concentrating on factors affecting microbial population growth. High-solids digesters are being developed for the rapid treatment of large volumes of dilute effluents (wastes) from agro-industrial processes. This process has the advantage of using a low-cost feedstock and offers substantial environmental benefits as a waste management method.

The main product from acid and enzyme hydrolysis, fermentation and distillation is ethanol, which is used as a transport fuel, on a European level mainly in the form of ETBE (a mixture of ethanol and isobutane) – see Figure 1.3. In the USA however, ethanol is used as a mixture called gasohol (ethanol mixed with gasoline), while in Brazil either pure ethanol or gasohol is used.

The techniques of acid hydrolysis, fermentation and distribution are all commercialized for sugar and starch substrates at present and acid hydrolysis should be economical

Figure 1.3. Distillery of Artenay, France (B. Martelly / ADEME)

in about five to ten years. Enzyme hydrolysis is at the prepilot stage, and it is expected to be commercial in five to ten years and economical in 10 to 15 years. The economic competitiveness is expected to be increased by improvement of industrial productivity and efficiency and the use of new species. Acid and enzymatic hydrolysis of cellulosic materials are not commercial technologies and, furthermore, they need a strong R&D development before commercial demonstration.

1.2.3 Biomass end-products

Biomass as an energy carrier can be used in solid, liquid or gaseous form. It can be transformed into different energy forms such as liquid fuels, heat and electricity. This section summarizes the main end products of biomass conversion technologies. It covers:

* biofuels: bioethanol, ETBE, diesters, gasohol, biomethanol, pyrolysis oil;
* heat and electricity.

1.2.3.1 Bioethanol

Bioethanol is ethyl alcohol obtained by sugar fermentation (sugarcane) or by starch hydrolysis or cellulose degradation followed by sugar fermentation and then by subsequent distillation. The raw materials can be sugars or starch feedstocks such as wheat, sugarbeet, potato, Jerusalem artichoke and sweet sorghum. Maize grain in the USA and sugarcane in Brazil are the most utilized biomass material for alcohol production.

Bioethanol can be used in undiluted form (cf. the Proalcool Programme in Brazil) or mixed with motor gasoline (gasohol is the term used in the USA to describe a maize-based mixture of gasoline (90%) and ethyl alcohol (10%). It should not be confused with gasoil, an oil product used to fuel diesel engines). If bioethanol is used at 100%, engines should be adapted, while for mixed utilization non-adapted engines can be used. It can be used to substitute for MTBE (Methyl Tertiary Butyl Ether) and added to unleaded fuel to increase octane ratings. In Europe, the preferred percentage – as recommended by the Association of European Automotive Manufacturers (AEAM) – is a 5% ethanol or 15% ETBE mix with gasoline. Ethanol could in the future also be produced from lignocellulosic feedstocks.

1.2.3.2 ETBE (Ethyl Tertiary Butyl Ether)

This is a product derived from the reaction of equal parts of ethanol and the hydrocarburant isobutane, whose physico-chemical properties are superior to bioethanol in terms of improved octane characteristics (a more effective substitute for lead), lower volatility, low water solubility (enabling transportation by pipeline), better heat efficiency and non-corrosion.

According to the AEAM, ETBE can be added (instead of MTBE[9]) to unleaded motor gasoline to obtain a mixture of up to 15% without creating technical problems. The resultant mixture exhibits the same performance characteristics and engines do not have to be modified. ETBE can be manufactured in plants currently producing MTBE. The first industrial ETBE plant came on stream in 1990 at ELF France, using bioethanol supplied by the French producers Beghin-Say and Ethanol Union.

1.2.3.3 Methyl esters

The most promising product at present is RME, a methyl ester based on vegetable oil, which is obtained from rapeseed or sunflower and further processed by cross-esterification of fatty acids and alcohol (methanol). Results from the THERMIE Programme on biofuel utilization have shown that no special problems have been detected with conventional diesel engines working on mixtures of up to 50% rapeseed methyl ester.

1.2.3.4 Biomethanol

Biomethanol is a fuelwood-based methyl alcohol obtained by the destructive distillation of wood or by syngas production through gasification. Biomethanol is a substitute product for synthetic methanol and is extensively used in the chemical industry (methanol is generally manufactured from natural gas and, to a lesser extent, from coal).

1.2.3.5 Bio-oil

Bio-oil is directly produced from biomass by fast pyrolysis. The oil has some particular characteristics but has been succesfully combusted for both heat and electricity generation. The largest plant built today produces 2 tonnes/h but plans for 4 and 6 tonnes/h (equivalent to 6–10 MWe) are at an advanced stage of planning. In the long term, pyrolysis oil could be used for transportation fuel. Although this is already technically feasible, the processes required to upgrade the oil are far too expensive at present.

1.2.3.6 Heat and electricity

Heat and electricity may be produced from the combustion or gasification of biomass material or the use of pyrolytic oils or RME in oil burners. Biogas produced from biomass may also be used to produce heat and electricity. Biomass represents stored energy and is easier to manipulate than other renewable energy sources (e.g. wind, solar, water) in that it can be used at chosen times (e.g. peak hours). The following heat and electricity markets have been identified for potential penetration by biomass:

- District heating systems.
- Modern furnaces for chipped wood or wood gasifiers for collectives or singly situated homes
- Warm water/ space heating systems for processing industries.
- Additional bio gasifiers or burners added to existing coal-fired power stations.
- Cogeneration (combined heat and power) units for process industries.

1.2.4 Economics of biomass systems

1.2.4.1 Liquid biofuels

Although RME can be burned to produce electricity, its main potential is seen to be as a transport fuel. The cost of production of RME (Table 1.2) can be significantly reduced if the by-products of the process (i.e. glycerine and animal feed) can be sold. Bioethanol can also be used as a motor fuel or can be further processed to produce ETBE (a higher value product). Table 1.3 outlines the production costs of bioethanol, Tables 1.4 and 1.5 the costs of pyrolysis and bio-oil.

Table 1.2. Production costs of RME[10]

Specific investment	ECU 24 million
Capacity	150,000 tonnes/year
Biomass costs (rapeseed)	
with EU support	160 ECU/tonne
without EU support	350 ECU/tonne
Overall costs	
with EU support	0.45 ECU/litre (by-product sales included)
without EU support	0.90 ECU/litre

For comparison, the price of fossil transport fuels at the refinery gate before taxes is approximately 0.07 ECU/litre for gasoline and diesel. The price of ethanol is approxi-

Table 1.3. Production costs for bioethanol, based on sugarbeets[10]

Specific investment	ECU 100 million
Capacity	1.15 million hlitre/year
Biomass costs (sugarbeet)	20–22 ECU/tonne
Overall costs	0.50 ECU/litre

Table 1.4. Costs of pyrolysis and upgrading by hydrotreating[11]

Biomass costs	50 ECU/dtonne
Yield	30 wt% hydrogen on wood
Output	1 tonne/hr hydrocarbons
Investment	16,700 ECU/tonne hydrocarbons
Cost	15 ECU/GJ or 640 ECU/tonne hydrocarbons

Table 1.5. Production of pyrolysis liquid[11]

Specific investment	3300 ECU/litre/h bio-oil
Capacity	7.5 tonne/h wood or 5.6 tonne/h bio-oil
Biomass costs	6 ECU/GJ
Overall costs	115 ECU/tonne bio-oil or 0.14 ECU/litre bio-oil

mately 0.28 ECU/litre. All liquid biofuel prices are greater than fossil fuel prices at present. However, there is a major difference in that high tax duties are imposed on transport fuels. If liquid biofuels were tax exempt, then they would become competitive in the transport fuel market.

1.2.4.2 Heat

Biomass is generally considered only for heat production in relatively small-scale processes. Table 1.6 gives the details of a 1.5 MWth hot water boiler. Combined heat and power generation is considered to be a key potential market for biomass use. Table 1.7 outlines the economics involved in a CHP plant which uses willow as a feedstock.

Table 1.6. Costs of heat production – hot water boiler (1.5 MWth)[5,12] *(Assumptions: lifetime = 20 years, interest rate = 16%, operation = 3000 hr/y, maintenance: 4% of investment)*

Specific investment	130 ECU/kWth
Capacity	1.5 MWth
Biomass costs (SRF-poplar)	55 ECU/odt
Overall costs	0.025 ECU/kWhth

Table 1.7. Costs of CHP plant (fluidized bed)[12]

Specific investment	1600 ECU/kWe
	η = 29%, lifetime = 25 years
Capacity	17 MWth + 10 MWe
Biomass costs (SRF-willow)	55 ECU/odt
Overall costs	0.076 ECU/kWe ; Heat at zero cost.

1.2.4.3 Electricity

Many economic evaluations of bioelectricity systems which utilize biomass as a feed-stock have been carried out. Tables 1.8 to 1.11 outline the costs involved in a range of different bioelectricity plants which are fuelled by a range of different biomass fuels.

Table 1.8. Direct combustion of solid biomass[12]

Specific investment	2000 ECU/kW
Capacity	2–3 MW
Efficiency	20%
Biomass costs	50 ECU/dt*
Overall costs	0.11 ECU/kWh

*   This value refers only to energy crops or short rotation forestry which are grown exclusively for combustion. Agricultural and forest residues may be obtained for less than this.

Table 1.9. Advanced technologies[12]

	Ceramic gas turbines	Gasification and aero-engine derived gas/steam turbine /cc
Commercialized	2000–2005	–
Biomass cost	50 ECU/toe	50 ECU/dt
Fuel cost	(80 μm powder) 150/toe	–
Conversion efficiency	40%	35%
Investment	330 ECU/kW	2600 ECU/kW (1st unit)
		1100 ECU/kW (10th unit)
Capacity	10–500 kW	10 MW
Overall costs of energy	0.05 ECU/kWh	0.057 ECU/kWh

Table 1.10. Thermal power stations fuelled by bio crude oil[12]

Specific investment	1200 ECU/kW
Efficiency	35%
Cost of bio-oil	170 ECU/toe (large unit)
Environmental credit (desulphurization)	40 ECU/toe
Biomass costs	50 ECU/dt
Fuel cost	0.062 ECU/kWh (base load)

Table 1.11. Aero-engine derived gas turbine fuelled with upgraded bio crude oil[12]

Commercialized	2000
Investment	1550 ECU/kW at 50 MW, efficiency = 38 %
	7000 ECU/kW at 0.3 MW, efficiency = 20%
Biomass cost	50 ECU/dt
Fuel costs	170 ECU/toe (bio-oil in large units)
Capacity	300 ECU/toe (bio-oil - upgraded)
Overall costs	0.3–50 MW
	0.075 ECU/kWh (base) at 50 MWe

It should be noted that the *filières* mentioned and the corresponding costs cannot be compared without additional considerations, because not all technologies are at the same level of development. E.g. the costs mentioned in Tables 1.10 and 1.11 are the best estimated available at the moment, although it should be noted that in these cases, the industrial implementation is still very limited or does not yet exist.

1.3 REALISTIC GOALS FOR BIOMASS R&D

1.3.1 Long-term goals

The long-term goal of biomass R&D is for it to be competitive with fossil fuels, without subsidies and with a level playing field of full costs, and to increase its contribution to the energy demand of the EU to > 20% of the projected primary energy demand in 2025 and > 30% in 2050. Different studies have shown that these goals are realistic when the right policy measures are taken.[13,14]

In parallel, it is necessary for gradual increases of biomass energy contributions to be realized in an environmentally sustainable way and accepted by the public.

1.3.2 Intermediate goals

1.3.2.1 RD&D goals

- Environmental sustainability of the applied biomass energy systems.
- (i) Yields for lignocellulosic crops on large-scale basis by 2005–2010;
    Biomass crop yields vary according to climate, soil, local preferences and other parameters such as water and nutrient requirements. Therefore each crop will be more suitable for one region than another, and the indicated goals are in this sense indicative goals:

Short-rotation forestry	15–25 odt/ha
Sweet sorghum	20–35 odt/ha
Miscanthus	20–35 odt/ha
Jerusalem artichoke	25 odt/ha

- (ii) Improvement and optimization of the production techniques at the agricultural and forestry level (plant breeding, fertilizers, etc.)
- (iii) Demonstration of highly productive energy plantations such as willow, poplar, robina, miscanthus, sweet sorghum, etc. on a large scale by 2005–2010.
- Conversion systems and other goals:
    - Improvement of efficiency of existing conversion systems by at least 50% by 2000.
    - Introduction of gasification with efficiencies > 40% (electricity) and > 80% (Combined Heat and Power).
    - Completion of commercial gasification units, full cycle from feedstock through electricity on a scale of 30 MW by 2002.
    - Demonstration of a unit for flash pyrolysis and related technologies, such as upgrading, of several thousands of tonnes/year by 2000.
    - Competitiveness of production of liquid biofuels from 2010 on.

1.3.2.2 Cost goals

For the production of energy crops, the following goals are realistic by 2005:

Short-rotation forestry	< 30 ECU/odt
Herbaceous energy crops	< 46 ECU/odt
RME and bioethanol	< 0.3 ECU/litre

The delivered end-products should be cost-effective compared to present-day and pro-jected fossil fuel costs, especially for electricity and liquid fuels from 2005 on. This target price will be reached more rapidly if the full cycle costs are incorporated into all fuel costs.

1.3.2.3 Implementation

The stated goal for the implementation in the long term can be specified and intermediate goals can be put forward:

	2010	2025
Heat (contribution to EU heat demand):	> 20%	> 35%
Electricity (contribution to EU electricity demand):	> 5%	> 15%
Biofuels (contribution to EU gasoline and gasoil demand):		> 5%[15]
	> 5%	> 10%[16]

1.4 ROADMAP FOR BIOMASS R&D

1.4.1 Biomass materials

At present, the most available and cheapest biofuels are biomass wastes (chip wood, thin-nings wood, waste timber, agricultural waste, waste from food industries). Energy crops are not readily available except, for example, in Sweden (willow) and France (sugarbeet, rapeseed and wheat), but will become biomass fuel in the future.

1.4.1.1 Energy crops
STATUS
The ideal biomass crop is defined as one which has a high yield, low production inputs, high energy value and low moisture content at harvest (in crops to be 'burnt' for electric-ity and/or heat production). In addition to this, its impact on the environment should be low and it should be easily integrated into existing agricultural and forestry practices. Research on biomass crops will be based on generating accurate and reliable data (such as chemical constituents, reactivity, energy content, etc.) on the following energy crops:

Cynara	Miscanthus	Sugarbeet
Eucalyptus	Poplar	Sweet sorghum (Figure 1.4)
Jerusalem artichoke	Rapeseed	Willow
Kenaf	Robinia	Wheat

Figure 1.4. Sweet Sorghum (ADEME)

R&D TOPICS

The information which must be generated in the R&D of 'energy crops' will be:

* plant physiology;
* plant pathology;
* energy crops behaviour and yield under a reduced employment of synthetic chemicals (pesticides and fertilizers);
* genetics of the crops;
* yields and yield limiting factors (water use, temperature, soil preferences etc.;
* energy content;
* life-cycle analysis (LCA) of each crop including greenhouse gases and energy;
* harvesting, drying and storage technologies;
* environmental impacts;
* quality parameters for relevant processing;
* productivity models for each crop;
* economic models for the production of each crop;
* public acceptability.

Specific R&D activities which should be undertaken are:

* recycling of biomass wastes as fertilizers on biomass plantations;

- maintenance of existing projects and networks;
- inter-network task force;
- demonstration of large-scale plantations to assess the supply problems which must be overcome for large-scale biomass systems;
- development of standards for biomass feedstock;
- development of harvesting, drying and storage facilities.

OBSTACLES

The major obstacle to the large-scale implementation of biomass systems will be the guaranteed supply of biomass feedstock. To guarantee supply of energy crops, the characteristics of the crops should be fully understood at laboratory, field trial and large-scale demonstration levels. The commercial viability will be based on the margin to the farmer (farm gate price production cost) and this must compete with the lowest margin crop in conventional farming. Acceptance of new crops into the agricultural system can only be achieved if the farmer is confident with the new crop or has experience with the crop for other uses (e.g. rapeseed oil). All demonstrations and field trials should involve agricultural organizations.

Acceptability of the biomass *filière* depends on the producers (farmers) and the industry, but also on the habitants of the region, environmental bodies, etc. It will consist of a compromise between all these players, who may have different interests.

Another obstacle to the growing of biomass for energy on set-aside land is the possible emergence of new crops which will be grown for non-food and non-energy purposes (e.g. paper pulp and chemicals). These crops will be suitable for growing on set-aside land and the products may have higher value than biomass fuel, therefore allowing the processor to pay more for the biomass. The price offered for the energy crop must compete with prices offered for other crops that may also be grown on set-aside land.

1.4.1.2 Residues

STATUS

The term 'biomass material' includes the energy crops mentioned in Section 1.4.1.1 and a variety of agricultural, domestic and industrial residues. At present these 'residues' are readily available often at very low, zero or, in some situations, negative cost. Some debate exists over the use of these residues and the decision to use them is generally site-specific, e.g. forest fires are a real threat in Southern Europe thus necessitating the routine collection of forest residues which are therefore a potential biomass fuel. However, in other more northern areas, where forest fires are not a threat, residues are not harvested, because they are considered to be a valuable part of the nutrient cycle of the forest and also contribute to soil structure. In these cases forest residues are usually not considered as a biomass fuel. In some regions, residues from the food industry are potential biomass fuels.

R&D TOPICS

Important R&D topics for large-scale utilization of biomass residues for energy purposes are:

- the optimization of the entire waste treatment structures on a national and regional level to determine the most suitable use of various available treatment technologies and desired development of new conversion technology for various streams (especially gasification;

- comparison of energy production with other applications of the biomass, such as fodder, material, and increased recycling;
- the effect on the market price of residues when a large demand is created;
- methods for collection of forest, domestic and industrial residues;
- effects of residue collection on nutrient levels in the forest;
- surety of supply of residues;
- economics and environmental impact of biomass system fuelled on residues;
- nutrient recycling, particularly in low input systems such as forestry.

OBSTACLES
Supply of domestic, industrial and some agricultural residues (e.g. slurry) is generally constant and so surety of supply may be guaranteed. The major obstacle to the use of residues is the cost of collection. Agricultural residues are generally produced in small quantities at sources which may be scattered over a wide distance; the cost of collection of these may rule out their use as a biomass fuel. Industrial residues are produced in larger quantities and their collection may be economically feasible. Collection infrastructures already exist for municipal waste and so this type of 'residue' fuel has most potential.

1.4.2 Logistics

STATUS
In this chapter, the term 'logistics' is used to refer to the processes that occur between the production of the biomass material and its conversion into energy. They include the following:

- harvesting
- chipping
- collection
- transport
- storage
- drying
- densifying.

The harvest methods used depend on the crop being grown and are usually automated. Some energy crops may be harvested using existing machinery, while new harvesters may have to be developed for other more 'novel' crops. Chipping is used for woody crops e.g. short-rotation forestry and is generally carried out *in situ*. Collection of forest residues may be carried out at the same time as harvesting and may be manual because of the dispersed nature of the resource. Transport may be carried out by road or rail or (in some cases) by barge. The transport process used is dependent on the vehicles available, the distance to the conversion plant and the nature of the biomass. Storage and drying methods vary according to the biomass material and the conversion process requirements. The logistic chain of a biomass system is strongly dependent on the location (climate, type of crop, soil) but also on the conversion technology used. It may be very cost-intensive and/or labour-intensive, and the economics of each process is site specific, e.g. the existence of railways or waterways is crucial.

R&D TOPICS

Specific research topics in the logistic chain are:

- Drying: efficient drying techniques also need to be demonstrated for various types of biomass. Drying of biomass should be preferably be done with waste heat. Steam drying, flue-gas drying, fluid-bed drying and drying with mechanical vapour recompression should be tested for varieties of fuels. Explosion risks (especially for flue-gas drying) and the regulation of constant moisture content of biomass are crucial research topics.
- Harvest and pre-treatment: the aim should be the minimization of costs. Different harvesters may need development and testing for specific crops: chip harvesting, whole-stem harvesting, harvest of grasses, etc. Machinery that can be used in conjunction with the existing equipment of the farmers in a given region is favoured. Research should be performed in conjunction with equipment suppliers.
- Biomass behaviour: losses of organic matter during storage, losses of biomass during harvest, drying behaviour and in-field drying of biomass should be tested under various circumstances.
- The 'streamlining' of transport, storage and drying operations for biomass systems.
- Economic evaluations and assessment of the environmental impact of harvest, transport, storage and preprocessing (e.g. drying) stages.

OBSTACLES

The main obstacles to the development of the processes that are included in 'logistics' are economic. The development of improved harvesting, collection, transport, storage and drying systems is capital-intensive. Biomass resources (with the exception of municipal and industrial wastes) tend to be in rural areas where rail infrastructures may not exist and where roads may be of very low standards; these factors can limit the efficiency of the transportation stages of a biomass system.

1.4.3 Conversion processes

1.4.3.1 Combustion

STATUS

The main development has been with fluidized bed combustors. These combustors have a high efficiency, can burn a mixture of fuels and fuels that can contain up to 60% moisture. The largest boilers are grate systems (up to 100 MWth) which can produce about 200 t steam/hr.

Direct combustion is already commercialized and the firing of biomass powder in ceramic gas turbines should be commercialized before the year 2000. These turbines will have a capacity of 100–500 kW.

Products are:

- heat
- high-pressure steam, which can be used via turbine to produce power or combined heat and power.

The most promising developments in combustion for efficient biomass conversion is co-combustion. This can be done in existing coal plants of a large capacity (which allows high efficiencies for production of electricity). However, new boiler concepts, where biomass is combined with coal, peat, RDF or other fuels, offer high efficiencies because of their larger scale and low risks in the power supply since more than one fuel can be used (e.g. to compensate for seasonal influences); see Figure 1.5.

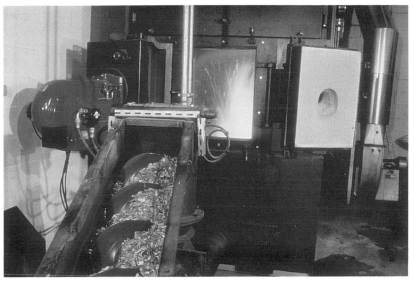

Figure 1.5. Combustor with fuel conveyance (Sébart/ADEME)

R&D TOPICS

Most R&D is on technical aspects, e.g. stoking, combustion air and fuel conveyance. There have been large improvements in combustion efficiency (> 30%), in reduction of pollutant emissions (e.g. fly ash) and in the development of CHP plants. R&D will also be required for Stirling engines and pressurized combustion systems. Table 1.12 gives the status and R&D needs of the main heat and electricity markets.

The main R&D tasks lie in the field of co-combustion: the assessment of possibilities of co-combustion in different situations, development and demonstration of advanced boiler concepts. Specific research topics on combustion are corrosion alkalis and chlorides and prevention options, slagging prevention and applying difficult biomass fuels such as straw, RDF and grasses in different combustion systems.

Table 1.12. Heat and electricity markets

	Municipal and industrial residues	Agricultural residues	Forest residues	Energy crops
Heat only	OK	OK	OK	High cost
CHP	OK	Economic demonstration required	OK	High cost
Power stations	RD&D*	RD&D*	OK	RD&D

* This reflects the average situation. It should be noted that in some parts of the EU and the USA this technology is at a more advanced stage

OBSTACLES

The main barriers to overcome are the high cost, making use of the economy of scale. The developments will be helped if up-front investment is available. The involvement of industry in the development will be an important issue and part of the R&D should concentrate on demonstrating the environmental and energy benefits of the technologies to industry. One issue which must be assessed in the studies will be how well the utilities meet the CO_2 and other emission standards.

1.4.3.2 Gasification

STATUS

The most advanced process is the BIG-STIG (Steam Injected Gas Turbine) process (up to 50 MWe). All gasifiers using air as the agent are already commercialized (updraught, fluidized bed, downdraught).

The most effective and economical use of the gaseous product is the production of electricity via gas turbines if combined with steam cycles. Gasification produces a higher yield than combustion with respect to electricity production for lower-power plants (50 kW to 1–10 MW) with internal combustion engines. For higher power (1–10 MW to 50–100 MW) combustion systems with steam turbines are more efficient than gasification systems. For very large-scale power plants (50–100 MW) gasification can reach exceptionally high levels of efficiency through a combined gas turbine–steam turbine system.

R&D TOPICS

- R&D in gasification is aiming at large-scale (1000 tonne/day) oxygen and/or air blown systems.
- Development of efficient systems for electricity production, namely IGCC and STIG to achieve efficiencies of 42–47%.
- There are still some emission problems (e.g. hydrocarbons and NO_x, Cl^- and alkali metals), which are being addressed.
- Development of gas cleaning methods, especially for use in gas turbines.
- Small-scale energy production (100 kWe–2 MWe).
- Development of stringent standards for fuel quality.
- Tolerance of gasifiers to different types of biomass.
- Operation of gas turbines fired by low calorific gases.

Once efficient and cost-effective gasification has been achieved, the synthesis gas can be used for methanol production instead of combustion for electricity production. The relative demand and cost advantages are unlikely to become evident until after 2010, when liquid fuel may increase in price or environmental requirements may restrict the use of gasoline or petroleum additives.

OBSTACLES

Gasification is sensitive to changes in feedstock type, moisture content, ash content and particle size. The gas can be used for internal combustion engines provided it is cleaned of tars, carry-over dusts, and some of its water content, as well as being cooled. If cleaning does not take place, tars may precipitate on inlet valves and clog up gas/air mixers. Dust can clog carburettors, cause engine damage and act as a grinding powder between the piston and the cylinder wall.

1.4.3.3 Pyrolysis

STATUS

Flash pyrolysis will produce the largest percentage of bio-oil (60–80% by weight). Slow or conventional pyrolysis will produce more charcoal (35–40%) than bio-oil. Flash pyrolyis is at a demonstration stage. Upgrading processes are at a far lower degree of development than pyrolysis processes. A pyrolysis unit is shown in Figure 1.6.

Bio-oil is expensive as a transport fuel (especially if no environmental credits are taken into account), but as a liquid, bio-oil presents the advantage of easy handling, transport and storage.

* Combustion of bio-oil for heat and electricity represents at present an economically promising use of biomass.
* Charcoal can be used in small gasifiers (kW range).
* As a transport fuel (diesel substitute), bio-oil needs a stabilizing step and maybe upgrading.

RESEARCH TOPICS

R&D is concentrating on:

Figure 1.6. Union Fenosa Flash Pyrolysis Plant (La Coriña, Spain), upscaled from the laboratory scale pyrolyser designed and constructed by the University of Waterloo, Canada

- improving the production of bio-oil (for MW power stations) and upgrading using catalytic hydro-treatment;
- solving the corrosive and toxic problems;
- modification of diesel engines which will be run with pyrolysis oil;
- development of recovery of fine chemicals.

1.4.3.4 Esterification
STATUS

The process for the production of RME is well developed and the product is commercially available in France, Germany and Italy. EU non-food oilseed production is confined to 700,000–1.2 million ha under the GATT Blair House Agreement (1993) and this allocation is being quickly taken up by Member States. In 1994 the total EU area of oilseeds for non-food purposes was 0.62 million ha as compared to 0.2 million ha in 1993. Most of this is accounted for by rapeseed, which increased to an estimated 0.4 million ha. The major producers are France and Germany with respective areas of 173,000 ha and 152,000 ha (1994).

Bio-diesel is expensive as a transport fuel (costing approximately 0.20–0.25 ECU/litre more than its mineral equivalent). In the countries where RME is commercially available it is competitive with fossil diesel as a result of tax exemptions. The Schrivener Directive (1995), which is still under debate, proposes that biofuels be made economically competitive through a reduction in excise duty.

RESEARCH TOPICS

R&D should further concentrate on:

- testing RME in different types of engines;
- testing of engines for emissions (particulates) and reduction of odour problems;
- improved energy ratios and greenhouse gas benefits;
- reduction of production costs, especially by using the by-products (glycerine, cake) more efficiently.

OBSTACLES

The main obstacles to the development of esterification processes are the high production cost of RME, the limited amount of raw material which is allowed to be grown in the EU as a result of the GATT Blair House Agreement and the opposition of Member States to the Schrivener Directive. In addition, the lack of competitiveness of biofuels in comparison to fossil fuels mitigates against the injection of capital into the development of improved esterification methods.

1.4.3.5 Biological/biochemical conversions
STATUS

Acid hydrolysis, fermentation and distillation of sugar/starch-based substrates are all already commercialized. Enzyme hydrolysis may be commercially available in 5–10 years. Acid and enzymatic hydrolysis of cellulose-based substrates are not commercial technologies. There is still an economic gap between the price of fossil fuels (0.15 ECU/litre) and the price of liquid biofuels (0.4–0.6 ECU/litre for ethanol in Europe).

The gap is expected to be reduced by improvement of industrial productivity and efficiency, and use of new species. Methane (used for power) and compost are other products commercially available from biochemical processes.

The main product is ethanol, which can be mixed with gasoline up to 10% in normal engines. 100% ethanol can be used in adapted engines. ETBE (a mixture of ethanol and isobutane) can be used as a lead substitute (up to 15%) in diesel/gasoline engines.

RESEARCH TOPICS
- Development of advanced methods for the chemical hydrolysis of cellulose and lignocellulosic materials.
- R&D in fermentation/distillation includes the use of novel yeasts, bacteria and fungi.
- Pretreatment is being investigated to increase the ease of hydrolysis. The most cost-effective hydrolysis process developed so far is steam explosion.
- R&D in acetone–butanol fermentation is being carried out, but there has been no breakthrough as yet.
- A one-step hydrolysis/fermentation stage, where the hemicellulose and cellulose are treated at the same time, is being investigated.
- Niche markets should be identified and demonstrations should be established to highlight the benefits of the technologies. Example of niche markets are environmentally sensitive areas such as waterways and leisure areas.
- Development of new types of bio-reactors.
- Development of new strains of micro-organisms for fermentations.
- Development of cheap enzymes for enzymatic hydrolysis of lignin.

OBSTACLES
The main obstacle to the development of bioconversion technologies is the lack of investment in RD&D. In the absence of this investment, coordination activities should be initiated, and these should involve the USA.

1.4.4 Integration of biomass systems in the regions

This R&D will develop methodologies for the integration of biomass at a regional level. Studies will be required to identify niche markets where biomass can be used, interfaces which can be used in existing infrastructures, and detailed designs describing complete processes from the biomass planting to the generated energy. Detailed designs should be completed for selected regions and a number of pilots/demonstrations should be installed. Existing programmes should be carefully analysed, where farmers, local authorities, inhabitants of the region and industry have collaborated to implement successful projects. Integration has to be carried out in association with the local drving forces. These groups may be instrumental in the implementation of small-scale decentralized biomass systems.

Specific research topics are:

- Assessment of how biomass crops and residues can be integrated into current agricultural practices, addressing the following issues:
  - logistics of regional biomass systems;
  - distances of biomass sources to the conversion plant and available modes of transport for biomass material;

- biodiversity of crops;
- supply/demand curve of the purchaser.
• The interface between the agricultural supply of energy crops (3 months/year) and the industrial demand (12 months/year) will require major development. Therefore the following steps are necessary:
  - development of a methodology for the integration of biomass systems at a regional level;
  - application of these methodologies to selected *filières* and regions and to the definition and set up of pilot projects at a regional level.

Additionally, development of a general approach for analysis of land availability and possibilities for different energy crops. This could be done by means of a GIS (geographic information system) coupling physical (soil, climate, etc.) and economic (income of farmers, data on local energy system, etc.) parameters.

1.4.5 Environmental and social aspects

It is clear that, if biomass is to play an important role in the future energy supply, its production, conversion and end-product use must be environmentally acceptable, and also accepted by the public. Ensuring the environmental sustainability of biomass systems will be an important factor for the development of biomass energy. Therefore, social and environmental aspects should have a high priority in future R&D.

1.4.5.1 Environmental aspects[13]

Negative environmental effects may include loss of biodiversity, water pollution from agrochemicals, loss of fertility, exotic species becoming a weed, etc. But with careful management and planning, these effects can be limited or even avoided. Technical solutions exist, but they have to be applied correctly. The potential positive effects far outweigh the negative effects: afforestation can protect fragile regions by preserving wildlife habitats, reducing erosion and conserving watersheds and aquifers.

R&D should generate the information required to carry out an environmental impact study on biomass. This information is described in detail in the EU Directives. Environmental impact assessments should be completed for selected crops and conversion technologies in selected regions. The assessment of the environmental impact of biomass material includes the following issues:

• the effect of growing monocultures of energy crops on wildlife habitats in the area – preservation of biological diversity;
• evaluation of the benefits of poly-cultures, mixed species and clones;
• reduction of use of pesticides through the introduction of disease-resistant cultivars or the employment of biological control mechanisms;
• reduction in use of fertilizers through the use of improved management practices and introduction of higher yielding cultivars;
• the assessment of the environmental impact of the logistics of biomass systems, which includes the following issues:

- use of waste ash from conversion plants as a fertilizer in plantations;
- environmental impact of transport, storage and pretreatment of biomass sources;
- the assessment of the environmental impact of conversion processes, which includes the following issues:
  - reduction of emissions such as CO, particulates and nitrogen oxides;
  - recycling/disposal of wastes (for example, solid waste (ash) of combustion and gasification can be used as fertilizer, while the potentially carcinogenic liquid waste of pyrolysis can be injected back into the system or treated by aerobic biological systems);
- life-cycle analyses of complete biomass systems integrating biomass production, logistics and the conversion process, and especially verification in practice.

1.4.5.2 Social aspects

Public acceptance can only be gained if biomass systems are built up gradually, taking into account the given social context. In general, it is necessary to establish guidelines for acceptable practices taking into account environmental and social issues and to inform all involved partners properly. The public debate between industry, farmers, local authorities, utilities and environmentalists should be stimulated. Major concerns and opportunities should be addressed, such as the potential for profitability and job creation, and the environmental concerns.

This should allow a balanced policy and balanced planning, allowing a sustainable development of biomass energy.

1.4.6 Bioenergy for developing countries

In contrast to the industrialized countries, biomass is the main energy source of developing countries. A rough estimation is that biomass represents 45% of the primary energy of developing countries, but in some African countries this proportion can reach 80%. However, this biomass resource is usually not converted efficiently and safely: huge amounts of energy are lost and pollution by unburned elements can be tremendous.

Safe and efficient technologies do exist in Europe, where many references show that these technologies are reliable, efficient and safe for the environment. Such technologies are:

- combustion techniques for heat and/or electricity production (high-pressure grate and fluidized-bed boilers, staged combustion, suspension burners, etc.);
- carbonization systems producing high-quality charcoal and recycling the extra energy;
- gasifier/genset units for low-power decentralized electricity production, with the possibility of cogeneration;
- biogas techniques for heat and/or electricity production;
- steam engines and gas-turbine engines;
- biofuel conditioning systems (chipping, milling, drying, briquetting).

Furthermore, Europe is also contributing to the development of advanced biomass energy technologies such as:

- fluidized-bed gasification coupled with a gas turbine–integrated gasification combined cycle;
- flash pyrolysis reactors for the production of pyrolysis oils;
- fuel-cell technologies for transport.

Developing countries are mainly tropical and equatorial countries; most of them have big potentials for biomass production with high yields. A more efficient use of their biomass would contribute dramatically both to a better global environment and to improving the local socio-economic conditions. This requires the transfer of European technologies to developing countries, a process which has almost failed up to now. Technology transfer can only be efficient and effective if it leads to:

- building local technical capability;
- technological innovation in developing countries.

Indeed the question is not just about getting the hardware, but also about installing the right hardware or adapting it to local conditions. This requires technical skills and knowledge, which eventually lead to technical capacity.

To achieve these two objectives, we would recommend the following actions:

- Implement in developing countries biomass energy projects based on modern proven European technologies (cogeneration plants, modern carbonization, etc.), after necessary adaptation to local conditions.
- Involve the industrial sector in both commercial and R&D projects, which is essential to successful technology transfer, through international industrial collaborations (joint ventures, BOT, BOO, etc.).
- Integrate major externalities into the assessment of biomass energy projects (employment generated directly or indirectly, environmental impact, greenhouse gases life-cycle analysis,etc.).
- Conduct market surveys for the development of promising advanced technologies.

Regarding biomass production in developing countries, two aspects should be analysed as top priorities:

- the use of biomass residues for energy production;
- the possible competition between agriculture and energy plantations, and the role of degraded and disused land.

Biomass residues are largely available from agriculture, agro-industrial, forestry and wood-industrial activities. Part of these residues should be used to retrofit organic matter to the soil (particularly agricultural residues). However, most of the other residues are not currently used: sometimes just landfilled or dumped in the rivers, or burned in open air. There is thus a considerable loss of energy and a very negative impact on the environment. A better use of biomass residues must be developed; this involves:

- comprehensive surveys (region by region, sector by sector) of biomass residues actually available for energy production;

- a comprehensive survey of agro- and wood-industrial sectors, identifying their energy needs now and in the future, as well as the regional and national energy contexts;
- transfer of efficient and safe conversion technologies (see above).

In the future, we could also face a dramatic problem of competition for land between agriculture, forest and biomass-energy plantations. A considerable research effort has to be carried out in this field aiming at:

- a better understanding of land-use competition issues, which could be transposed into models designed to prevent potential confilict;
- a survey of degraded and disused land areas and analysis of their potential for growing energy crops.

This brief overview of what R&D efforts could be directed to developing countries is certainly not comprehensive or detailed. We just hope that it gives some useful guidelines for public and private actions, as well as some material for reflection.

1.5 STRATEGY

Biomass energy development can contribute to a considerable extent to the objectives of the energy and non-energy policies of the European Union:

- creation of employment using biomass and regional development;
- contribution to EU energy demand;
- contribution to EU environmental objectives.

1.5.1 Studies and surveys

- The existing successes and problems should be fully analysed.
- Regional surveys should be carried out to identify how biomass can be used to create employment at a regional level and how biomass can be integrated into existing agriculture and energy infrastructures.
- Economic studies are needed to define the required developments, so that biomass can compete commercially with conventional systems.
- Environmental impact studies in accordance with EU Directives should be carried out.
- Socio-economic studies are needed to identify the non-technical barriers to biomass.

The environmental impact studies and socio-economic studies should aim at the establishment of guidelines for acceptable practices taking into account environmental concerns and the social context.

1.5.2 Research, development, pilot systems and demonstration

Pilot systems should be selected to evaluate technologies which have been developed on a laboratory scale. A detailed monitoring programme over a number of years will be required to generate the relevant technical, environmental and economic data based on the experience of successful large-scale schemes. Demonstrations will be used to develop systems based on the experiences gained in the pilot phases. More regions would be selected to demonstrate the different technologies and crops.

Specifically, the following actions are proposed:

- Rapid development of *energy farming on a large scale* in various contexts (dry climate, wet conditions, etc.) with a representative number of crops, such as poplar, willow, miscanthus, eucalyptus, etc. Large field trials should provide practical experiences on a semi-commercial scale with farming organizations involving year-round supply and various harvest and storage techniques.
  These large-scale field trials can simultaneously provide clean biomass fuel for development of various conversion systems, such as co-combustion, gasification and pyrolysis.
  Focus should be on monocultures, since such systems are easy to realize and most knowledge can be gained from them, as well, if possible, on mixed species and clones.
- Development of a methodology for the *assessment of land availibility* in the EU with a detailed approach coupled to GIS, based on physical data (soil, climate, etc.) and economic parameters (local farmers' income and farm size, etc.). This should provide a basis for implementation strategies for biomass in the EU: crop selection, identification of low-cost production sites, optimization of scale and economics.
- Development of advanced conversion systems:
  - Further improvement of the efficiency of existing conversion systems should proceed. Advanced combustion (CHP) and co-combustion should receive more attention.
  - Further development of advanced gasification technologies aiming at efficiencies > 40% (electricity) and > 80% (Combined Heat and Power), and development of gasification units, full cycle from feedstock through electricity on a scale in the range of 30 MWe.
  - Demonstration of a unit for flash pyrolysis and related technologies, such as upgrading, of several thousands of tonnes/year.

Parallel to the large-scale field trials of energy crops, low-cost biomass residues can be used to develop advanced conversion systems, on a commercial or semi-commercial scale.

Over the medium term, both crops and conversion technologies should be developed so that competition with fossil fuels for power and heat production is possible. A combination of high conversion efficiencies and high crop yields is therefore required:

- The route of gasification of woody biomass to methanol should be continued to be examined as a long-term option.
- RD&D should be stimulated on the production of ethanol by biochemical processes, which could be economic by 2005, and on the cost reduction of RME.

1.5.3 Other measures

Finally the following recommendations are made for policy makers:

- Stimulation of cofiring of biomass with coal (typical mixing of 10–20%) now.

• Stimulation of public debate among industry, farmers, local authorities, utilities and environmentalists, addressing, for example, the potential for profitability and job creation and environmental concerns. This should allow a balanced policy and balanced planning allowing sustainable development of biomass energy.

1.6 REFERENCES

1   Wright D (1992). Biomass: a new future? Internal document 2111, CEC Forward Studies Unit.
2   Biomass technologies in Austria, Market Study THERMIE Programme (1995). Action BM62, European Commission DGXVII, July.
3   Energy in Sweden 1994, NUTEK (The Swedish National Board for Industrial and Technical Development).
4   Klass D (1995). Biomass in North American. In: P. Chartiers, A.A.C.M. Beenackers, G. Grassi (ed.), Biomass for Energy, Agriculture and Industry, Vol 1, 8th EC Conference, pp. 63–73. Pergamon Press, Oxford.
5   Ballaire P (1996). Internal Publication, ADEME.
6   Wrixon G T, Rooney A, Palz W (1993). Renewable Energy 2000, Springer Verlag, Berlin.
7   Mitchell C P (1995). Resource Base. In: P. Chartiers, A.A.C.M. Beenackers, G. Grassi (ed.), Biomass for Energy, Agriculture and Industry, Vol 1, 8th EC Conference, p. 116. Pergamon Press, Oxford.
8   Mauguin Ph, Bonfils C, Nacfaire H (ed.) (1994). Biofuels in Europe: Developments, applications and perspectives 1994–2004, Proceedings 1st European Forum on Motor Biofuels, 9–11 May 1994, Tours.
9   MTBE (Methyl Tertiary Butyl Ether) is obtained from fossil methanol (natural gas) and added to unleaded fuel to increase the octane rating. MTBE output is currently growing at the rate of 10% annually in France. MTBE is the principal competitor to bioethanol and ETBE as an octane booster, with more than 10 million tonnes produced annually worldwide. The price of MTBE is linked to that of methanol, which exhibited major price fluctuations of between 95 and 190 ECU/tonne between 1987 and 1992. As a result, manufacturers may favour ETBE, the market price of which is generally more stable. European regulations currently specify maximum MTBE (and ETBE) content in engines as 10% by volume.
10 Private Communication, ADEME (1996).
11 Bridgewater A, Grassi G (1991). Biomass pyrolysis liquids upgrading and utilisation. Elsevier Science, Brussels and Luxembourg.
12 Grassi G (1996). Private Communications, EUBIA.
13 Hall D O, House J I (1995). Biomass Energy in Western Europe to 2050. Land Use Policy, 12(1), 37–48.
14 Johansson T B J, Kelly H, Reddy A K N, Williams R H (1993). Renewable Energy for Fuels and Electricity, pp. 593–652. Island Press, Washington DC.
15 AEBIOM (European Biomass Association) (1995). Strategy for Biomass, Paris, June.
16 ALTENER Decision, Council Decision no. 93/500/ECC of 13 September 1993, OJ L235 of 18 September 1993.

GLOSSARY

CAP	Common Agricultural Policy
BIG-STIG	Biomass Integrated Gasifier Steam Injected Gas Turbine
GIS	Geographic Information System
IGCC	Integrated Gasification Combined Cycle
RME	Rape Methyl Ester
ETBE	Ethyl Tertiary Butyl Ether
MTBE	Methyl Tertiary Butyl Ether
AEAM	Association of European Automotive Manufacturers
odt	Oven dry tonnes

2. OCEAN ENERGY

2.0 INTRODUCTION

As the land surface becomes more crowded and its easily accessible resources are removed and used up, so we need to look increasingly to the sea to provide for our future needs. In particular, concern to find large, clean, renewable energy resources to combat the environmental problems looming from excessive use of fossil fuels makes it timely to start serious work on developing and perfecting methods for extracting energy from the oceans. The oceans represent a huge energy resource consisting of stored solar energy (and gravitational energy) in various forms, causing the ceaseless movements of unimaginable numbers of cubic kilometres of water. This energy is generally diffuse but in many cases, as will be shown later, significantly more concentrated than other forms of renewable energy already being successfully exploited on land.

In the past, even had the need been as great as it is now, it was technically difficult to exploit energy from the sea because of the difficulties in constructing equipment that could survive long periods in such a harsh and difficult environment. However, recent developments in offshore engineering, in particular in relation to the exploration and development of off-shore hydrocarbons, have introduced new capabilities. Rigs can now be constructed which routinely survive decades of exposure to the open sea, through improved understanding by engineers of how to design structures that can and will successfully survive the violence of extreme storms and the corrosiveness of sea water. In fact, such rigs survive so well that a new problem has arisen of how to get rid of them when the oil has been depleted and their usefulness has expired!

The need for large clean-energy resources and the new capabilities in offshore engineering combine to offer some interesting and potentially important new challenges to find economical and reliable techniques for exploiting the energy of the seas. There are in fact a number of energy forms present in the sea which may be exploited in different ways; these can be summarized as follows:

- **Wave energy.** The waves are a product of the effect of wind blowing across hundreds or thousands of kilometres of open ocean and transferring kinetic energy into the surface of the sea. Waves are therefore a form of kinetic energy and can be accessed by using various harmonic devices that are generally tuned to respond to wave movement by accepting some of the energy of wave motion.
- **Marine current energy.** Marine currents are caused mainly by the rise and fall of the tides (resulting from the gravitational interactions between earth, moon and sun) which cause the whole sea to flow, but other effects such as regional temperature and salinity differences and the Coriolis effects caused by the rotation of the earth are also major influences. The kinetic energy of marine currents can be accessed in much the same way that a wind turbine extracts energy from the wind, using various forms of kinetic-energy converter.

- **Tidal barrages.** It is possible to construct barrages in estuaries or other semi-enclosed inlets from the sea with a large tidal range; such a barrage will admit water through turbines to an artificial lagoon at high tide and then release the water through turbines to the sea when the tide is lower. Systems of this kind are essentially a specialized form of low-head hydro power. By far the largest and most famous example is the 240 MWe installation at La Rance in France, built during the 1960s. Various studies have been completed on other potential sites such as estuaries with high tidal range, including the potential 7 GW Severn Tidal Barrage in the UK, but they generally appear costly and there is considerable uncertainty about the potential environmental impact of such large schemes, so that there are no indications that any more schemes are to be built.
- **OTEC (ocean thermal energy conversion).** This is a technique to utilize temperature differences in the ocean as a means to convert solar heat gained by the surface of the seas into useful energy. In certain deep tropical oceans the surface waters can be 20 to 30°C warmer than the water at great depth, which is often at around 5°C, and a heat engine can be utilized to work between this limited temperature difference as a means to extract energy from the warm surface waters. The main kinds of device proposed for this purpose are based on the Rankine Cycle, as used by conventional steam engines.
- **Offshore wind.** This is in fact an adaptation of onshore wind technology. Generally stronger and more consistent winds are found at sea than onshore and, of course, many of the environmental problems of onshore wind exploitation such as land-utilization and alleged 'visual intrusion' can be avoided by installing wind turbines some distance offshore. However, the added costs of installing wind turbines out at sea have so far tended to exceed the benefits, although there is good reason to believe that, as good onshore wind sites become scarcer, it will eventually make sense to install wind turbines in shallow offshore locations and a few pioneering installations of this kind have already been completed.
- **Osmotic pressure differences.** At every point where a river pours fresh water into the sea, there is a huge release of energy caused by dilution of sea water by fresh water (in effect this is a return of energy given by the sun to water vapour that has been evaporated from the sea and then which returns via the hydrological cycle from land to the sea). The available energy is extremely large (approximately 2.65 MW per m^3/sec of fresh water mixing with sea water[1]). This level of energy dissipation is in effect the equivalent of a water fall 270 m high at each point where a river of fresh water meets the sea. Unfortunately, no practical method for extracting this copious energy has so far been invented, although in principle several techniques have been suggested, such as an osmotic pump or utilization of the differences in vapour pressure of sea water and fresh water to run a vapour turbine.

This chapter deals with the two most promising marine energy resources of greatest relevance to Europe, namely *wave energy* and *marine current energy*. Tidal barrage technology is mostly highly site-specific and consists mainly of unique civil engineering projects, and there are few indications that it is regarded anywhere as having much potential with its present costs and possible environmental disadvantages. There are no potentially exploitable OTEC resources in European waters. Offshore wind (although based in the sea) is technologically much the same as onshore wind, which is dealt with in Chapter 7. Osmotic pressure differences are worth noting as a potential resource, but remain at present unpractical, although perhaps some fundamental research may eventually result in the development of credible methods for exploitation in the distant future.

Both wave energy and marine current energy have an existing research community in Europe and promising results have been obtained in developing techniques for their exploitation. This chapter outlines the achievements in these fields to date and the general directions that future R&D might follow in order to arrive at practical and economic techniques for utilizing these major energy resources to the benefit of Europe and the rest of the world.

2.1 MARINE CURRENTS

2.1.1 Introduction

Recent studies indicate that marine currents have the potential to supply a significant fraction of future EU electricity needs and, if successfully exploited, the technology required could form the basis of a major new industry to produce clean power for the 21st century.

The exploitation of marine currents has only recently been considered as a realistic energy supply option following major improvements in offshore engineering technology. In earlier eras, although the boundless energy in the movement of the sea has always been apparent, the means to extract it were not realistically available.

Kinetic energy from the sea can be harnessed using techniques similar in principle to those for extracting energy from the wind, by using submarine kinetic energy converters similar to 'underwater windmills'. Because water is so much denser than air, the velocity necessary for a given power density (kW/m^2) in water is only about 11% of the equivalent velocity in air. For example, a power density of 1 kW/m^2 is present with a marine current of only 1.3 m/s but the same power density in air needs a wind velocity of about 11.7 m/s. Therefore quite low water velocities (which occur naturally in many places) represent potentially exploitable power densities.

Various studies[1–2] confirm that the tidal/marine current resource is only sufficiently concentrated for effective use in certain places where fast-moving currents can be found, (generally it is believed that velocities in the range 1 to 3 m/s, which is 2 to 6 knots, are needed). Many such places exist, mainly where sea water is accelerated by the coastal topography, such as in straits between islands and the mainland, the entrances to sea lochs and fjords and around major headlands and peninsulas.

One recently completed study[3] identified and analysed 106 European locations with strong marine current resources (Figure 2.1), and has estimated that these could supply 48 TWh per year to Europe's grid network (equivalent to 12,500 MW of installed capacity at the expected capacity factors). This is on the basis of power systems utilizing nothing but present-day technology.

It should be added that tidal and marine currents, apart from offering a large new renewable energy resource, may have some unique advantages, such as:

• This method of large-scale electricity generation has negligible environmental impact (no pollution, no noise, no land use and little or no visual impact).
• The energy resource availability can be as accurately predictable as the future movements of the tides, so that planned base-load power contributions are possible.
• The energy intensity from flowing water is more intense and concentrated than for most other forms of renewable energy and tidal currents generally also offer signifi-

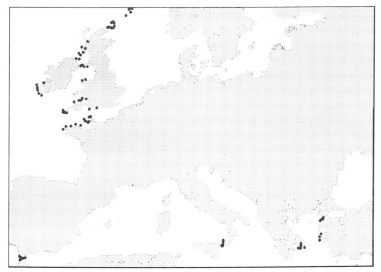

Figure 2.1. Principal European locations analysed under EC-JOULE2 CENEX Project and found to have potentially exploitable currents (sites marked with spots)

cantly better than average capacity factors in the 40 to 60% range (i.e. average output as a percentage of rated (peak) output).

2.1.2 Present situation

2.1.2.1 Basic principles

The most obvious technique for the exploitation of tidal and marine currents is to use a turbine rotor mounted on a suitable support structure normal to the direction of flow of the current, and hence to drive a generator through a suitable speed-increasing mechanism.

Any such rotor should preferably be mounted near to the surface because marine currents vary in velocity as a function of depth, with maximum velocities being found in the upper half of the flow (declining to zero velocity in the boundary layer at the sea bed). Since energy availability is proportional to the cube of the velocity, in typical flow profiles over 75% of the energy tends to be concentrated in the upper 50% of the flow. Provision of a suitable support structure to hold a rotor high enough above the seabed is probably one of the primary technical problems (or providing suitably secure mooring if the turbine is mounted below a raft or pontoon).

Figure 2.2 illustrates the magnitude of extractable power as a function of rotor size in different stream speeds. The most appropriate design velocity is believed to be in the range 2.0–3.0 m/s (4–6 knots).[5,6] Below this velocity range there is insufficient energy density, while above it the forces are likely to be too excessive for turbines to continue to be efficient and cost-effective. Also, sites with peak mean velocities in the order of 2m/s (4 knots) are quite widely available, while sites with velocities peaking higher than 3 m/s are few and far between.

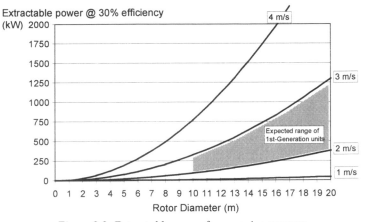

Figure 2.2. Extractable power from marine currents

As with windmills, the most likely types of turbine to be used for marine current exploitation will be either axial flow propeller-type turbines or possibly the vertical axis cross-flow or 'Darrieus' turbine, (see Figure 2.3). This is because these two mechanisms have the highest efficiency as kinetic energy converters. Also, as with windmills, such turbine rotors can readily be made to drive a generator via a suitable mechanical transmission system. Other devices such as Savonius Rotors, Panemones and oscillating hydrofoil devices have been hypothesized, but they all suffer from being significantly less efficient and from being more difficult to extract shaft power from than the first two types given above. Similarly, other possibilities for power transmission may prove viable; for exam-

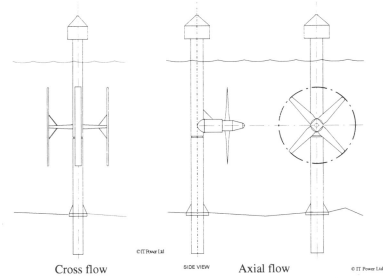

Cross flow   SIDE VIEW   Axial flow   © IT Power Ltd

Figure 2.3. Conceptual designs of cross-flow and axial-flow turbines mounted on a monopile as used in the CENEX Technology Assessment study[4]

ple, the use of high-pressure water (sea-water hydraulics) to transmit the power from the slow-moving rotor to a high-speed Pelton water motor and generator has been proposed.[2,5,7]

The size of individual turbine units will normally be limited by engineering considerations . The depth of water available also limits the rotor size. Various analyses[5,6] suggest that devices of around 200 to 800 kW will be the optimum practical size for first-generation systems (based mainly on standard industrial components) in order to utilize the water depths and velocities commonly available at many of the more promising high current locations (e.g. 20 to 50 m) and to optimize the cost-effectiveness (gaining maximum economy of scale without reaching sizes demanding drive train components that do not presently exist). Such turbines would have rotors in the 15 to 25 m diameter size range.

2.1.2.2 Comparison with tidal barrages, wind and hydro technologies

Marine current exploitation is sometimes confused with tidal barrage technology and it also has certain features common to wind and to low-head hydro technology. In fact, many engineering features and concepts that are 'prior art' in the latter two areas of technology are of direct relevance to marine-current exploitation. Therefore, because marine-current exploitation is based on well established principles, systems can be conceived that could partly be engineered from existing components developed for other purposes. It follows that there is significantly less uncertainty about the technology at this early stage than applies to most totally new methods of energy production. In fact the main question is not 'will it work?', but 'can it be engineered to function reliably and at a low enough cost to be economically attractive?'.

2.1.2.3 Applications

Energy extraction from marine currents offers a number of options. The most straightforward is to drive a gearbox and generator for the direct production of electricity to be fed via a marine cable to the grid. Another option is the pumping of sea water at high pressure either to generate electricity through a conventional high-head hydro-electric system (including the possibility of pumped storage if suitable coastal topography permits) or for other purposes such as the production of fresh water by reverse osmosis. Other more exotic applications might be to use tidemill energy for mineral extraction from sea water, the production of hydrogen (by electrolysis of sea water), etc.

In most cases marine current turbines would be deployed in clusters to reduce the high cost overheads per turbine of interconnecting with the grid and of site preparation and maintenance, in much the same way as a wind farm optimizes the economics of wind power.

2.1.2.4 Experience to date
BACKGROUND (UP TO 1990)
Attention began to be given to the possible use of marine currents as an energy resource in the mid-1970s, after the first 'oil shock'. Notably the MacArthur Workshop on Energy from the Florida Current (i.e. the Gulf Stream) in 1974 produced a range of concepts,[8] some more plausible than others. In 1976 the British General Electric Company (GEC) undertook a study, part-funded by the UK government, and concluded that marine cur-

rents deserved more detailed investigation.[7] Soon after (1977–1982), the Intermediate Technology Development Group in the UK undertook probably the first practical research programme, which involved performance testing of Darrieus rotors in water and culminated in a successful device with a 3 m rotor, which was deployed experimentally for over a year on the River Nile at Juba to demonstrate the use of river currents for pumping irrigation water. An initial assessment was also completed at that time, independently of GEC to assess the UK tidal stream resource and the results matched reasonably well those predicted by GEC.[9]

The 1980s saw a number of small research programmes, mostly theoretical, to evaluate tidal and marine currents. The main countries where studies were carried out were the UK,[10] Canada[11] and Japan.[12] Perhaps the most notable practical development during the 1980s was the successful deployment on the sea bed in the Kurashima Straits (off Japan) of a 3.5 kW model (approximately 1.5 m diameter) Darrieus turbine. This ran for about one year from 1988.[11]

UK TIDAL STREAM REVIEW (1992–1993)

The first attempt to assess a national tidal current resource was the *Tidal Stream Energy Review*.[2] This identified specific sites in UK waters with adequate current velocities to deliver an aggregate 58TWh/year of electricity to the UK grid. It confirmed that there is a tidal current resource, capable theoretically of meeting some 19% of present total UK electricity demand, but not economically (about 20 TWh/yr was estimated as being accessible on the assumptions used at a unit cost of less than ECU 0.13/kWh).

10 KW PROOF OF CONCEPT PROJECT (1992–1994)

A consortium consisting of Scottish Nuclear Ltd, I T Power Ltd, and NEL developed a 'proof of concept' experimental tidal current system. This involved an axial-flow 3.5 m diameter rotor suspended below a floating catamaran pontoon (Figure 2.4), and it developed some 15 kW in 2.25 m/s current velocity in Loch Linnhe, Scotland, in May 1994.

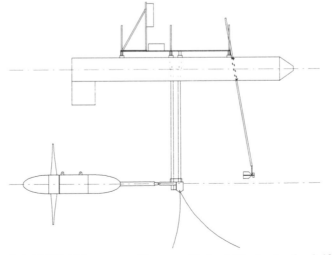

Figure 2.4. 10 kW tidal stream turbine, tested in Loch Linnhe, Scotland, 1994
(O. Paish, IT Power)

The results and practical experience confirmed the concept of tidal-stream power generation, with the conclusion that, although there are many problems of detail design to be solved, there are no fundamental difficulties standing in the way of the development of larger, practical turbo-generators.

EU-JOULE CENEX PROJECT JOU2-CT93-0355 (1994–1995)
Under the JOULE-II energy research programme, DG XII of the EU supported a technical and resource assessment of marine current energy in Europe.[3,5]

The Resource Assessment[3] involved the compilation of a database of European locations with the most promising marine current resource. Over 100 offshore sites of interest were identified as having potential for energy extraction (Figure 2.1), the sites ranging from 2 to 200 km^2 of sea-bed area, many with power densities sufficient for over 10 MW of electricity generation per square kilometre of sea area. However, there remains a severe lack of detailed marine current data for an accurate assessment of the true generating potential of the resource.

The Technology Assessment[5] reviewed a range of options for the construction and deployment of arrays of tidal-stream turbines. The study principally examined conventional technology from related areas (wind, hydro power, maritime, and offshore) and produced design and cost guidelines on which to base future development work. The study found that electricity cost is dependent upon the size of machine, the choice of economic parameters (lifetime, discount rate), an estimate of O&M costs, and the load factor obtainable at a particular site. The load factor can vary widely between sites – typically from 20% to 60%. Figure 2.5 shows the effect of load factor on electricity cost, and indicates, in round figures, that 0.15 ECU/kWh may be achievable for a 2 m/s rated current, and 0.07 ECU/kWh for a 3 m/s rated current under favourable circumstances.

TIDEMILL FEASIBILITY FOR ORKNEY & SHETLAND (CEC DGXVII REF. 4/1040/92-41)
(1994–1995)
Under the Regional and Urban Energy Programme, DG XVII of the EU part-funded a feasibility study for supplying Orkney and Shetland with electricity from tidal stream tur-

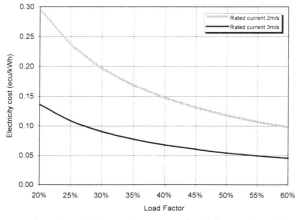

Figure 2.5. Levelized electricity cost vs load factor for a 15m axial-flow turbine

bines.[6] Island communities, which frequently have higher than normal conventional energy costs, are likely to be the most attractive initial market for electricity from tidal streams. On-site stream measurements were used in conjunction with a computer model to produce the tidal-stream characteristics for two sites. These indicated in both cases that load factors of 45–55% would be achievable for 200 kW turbines rated for a 2 m/s current.

Costings were developed for three sizes of turbine (10 m, 15 m and 20 m rotors) to cover everything, from manufacture and installation to subsea cabling and grid-connection. The results indicated total costs in the region of £750,000 (ECU 920,000) for an installed 15 m, 200 kW, turbine, equating to about 10 p/kWh (ECU 0.13/kWh) for a site load factor of 50%, life-time of 15 years and discount rate of 5%. Consideration of a cluster of eight turbines of 20 m diameter brought the electricity cost down to below 6 p/kWh (ECU 0.08/kWh), although there were greater uncertainties inherent in the larger turbine design.

The study included an environmental impact assessment to cover the full social and environmental consequences of sea-bed-mounted turbines at the chosen sites. It became apparent during the study that tidemill developments would have negligible impact on both the onshore and offshore environments.

2.1.2.5 Conclusions from recent projects

GENERAL

There are no significant *technical* reasons why the marine current resource should not be exploited in the near future on a large scale, since the engineering principles that can be applied are mostly well established. However, factors that can only be resolved through a technical R&D programme are whether adequate longevity and reliability can be built into a tidal stream system at a low enough cost.

RESOURCE

A large marine-current resource with numerous potential sites exists in Europe (106 sites studied so far in Europe with an aggregate generating potential of the order of about 60 TWh/yr)). Countries with promising sites include the UK, Ireland, France, Spain, Italy and Greece. There are many areas of sea offering potential for extraction of more than 10 MW per km^2.

SUPPORT STRUCTURES

There are three main methods for supporting turbines: floating moored systems, sea-bed mounted systems and intermediate (i.e. tension buoy) systems. First-generation systems using existing engineering know-how would probably be sea-bed-mounted monopile structures limited to relatively shallow waters (circa 20 to 40 m depth). Floating systems and totally submerged systems for use in deeper waters would follow as second generation systems.

TURBINE SYSTEMS

There are two main types of turbine that might be considered, namely axial flow (propeller) type rotors and cross flow (Darrieus/Voith Schneider) type rotors. Subsets of these include fixed-pitch or variable-pitch rotors, but studies so far indicate a major cost advantage for fixed-pitch rotors, at least for 'first generation' systems.[5]

ECONOMIC ASSESSMENTS

The 'UK Tidal Stream Energy Review'[2] indicated unit costs for tidal-stream turbines connected to the UK main grid (including all connection costs) in the range sterling pence 7p
to 100p (approximately 10 to 120 ECU cents) for large machines depending on siting and
financial parameters. Approximately 20,000 GWh/yr of potentially extractable electrical
energy were identified from UK waters at a cost of under 10 UK pence (~12 ECU cents).

The 'Technical and Resource Assessment of Low-head Hydro-power in Europe'(EU-
JOULE contract JOU2-CT93-0415)[3,5] found minimum unit costs in the 5 to 10 ECU
cents range under the most favourable siting conditions.

The 'Feasibility Study of Tidal Current Power Generationfor Coastal Waters: Orkney
and Shetland'[6] indicates that a 200 kW system could be installed, connected to the grid
and commissioned in Orkney or Shetland for a capital cost in the order of UK £750,000
(ECU 920,000). However if a field of ten such machines was installed, the cost per
machine would fall to almost half this cost. A small field of ten machines could deliver
electricity at a cost in the order of 6 to 12 pence (ECU cents 10 to 15).

All these studies were based on the use of existing engineering components as far as
possible and included all the costs of grid-connection.

ENVIRONMENTAL IMPACT

The consensus is that the environmental impact of submerged marine current power systems will be minimal. The main constraint relates to conflict with shipping and navigation.

2.1.3 Realistic goals for marine current energy development

2.1.3.1 Design requirements

Whatever the design concept, in the end the essential requirement will be to find optimum
methods to achieve cost-effectiveness and reliability.

Some key targets to be achieved are:

• long periods between maintenance and m.t.b.f. (accessing marine current turbines is
  likely to be difficult and costly);
• corrosion resistance combined with durability;
• effective sealing of enclosures;
• good efficiency over a broad range of velocities;
• reliable interconnection between individual turbines and with the shore;
• secure and economical methods of deployment and recovery.

Bearing in mind that this is perhaps the most immature of renewable energy technologies,
it is less easy to predict the possible rate of successful development of the technology, so
any development goals need to be seen in this context.

2.1.3.2 Long-term goal (by 2005–2010)

The long-term goal is to see the large-scale commercial take up of marine current technology (i.e. installation of several fields of turbines aggregating hundreds of megawatts of
installed capacity) .

Given effective initial support for the short- and medium-term goals that are described below, the first commercial field of marine current turbines could be installed within 10 to 15 years (sooner if given high priority).

2.1.3.3 Medium-term goal (by 2000–2005)

The development and demonstration of the first small field of grid-connected marine current turbines in the 200 to 800 kW size range, to test and demonstrate workable technology. It seems feasible, if the technology continues to show promise, for this to be achieved in a minimum of five years and certainly within ten years.

2.1.3.4 Short-term goals (immediate)

PILOT PROJECTS TO TEST AND DEMONSTRATE MARINE CURRENT TURBINES
The main short-term goal should be to test and demonstrate several pilot projects to gain operational experience, to find out the true costs and to confirm the assumptions behind feasibility studies so far completed.

There has already been identified a need for two types of system, one which could be seabed mounted and surface piercing for relatively shallow seas (20 to 30 m depth) such as in the UK, Ireland and Northern France, and one for deeper waters such as in the Mediterranean and various oceanic locations. The latter might be suspended from a buoy or vessel or be seabed mounted but totally submerged.

The practical turbine size for pilot projects would be from 5 to 10 m diameter with ratings in the 20 to 100 kW range.

SUPPORTING ACTIVITIES
Any programme to develop the technology needs to be supported by a range of activities in three main areas as follows:

- **Resource exploration and assessment.** Collection of detailed resource data for sites of interest. Most data on marine currents presently available were collected from the point of view of marine navigation. Such data are only useful to give indicative results for the energy potential of different sites. Therefore, there will be a need for much more detailed measurements to obtain three-dimensional velocity profiles as a function of time. Practical measurement is costly and difficult, so validated modelling techniques based on some minimized set of practical measurements will be an essential tool for the more detailed site assessments.
- **Engineering studies (experimental and theoretical).** Future R&D required to make marine current turbines a commercial reality will require further experimental work to examine detailed variation of forces and system behaviour over an extended period and under all possible conditions, together with more elaborate design studies involving both new concepts and solving problems of detail design. The latter may require a certain level of laboratory-based experimental work.·
- **Economic and market studies.** An essential input to the engineering design process will be confirmation of the economic criteria that will need to be met for commercial success, which will of course vary with different markets. It may also be preferable to aim the technology initially at niche markets (such as remote island communities or

drinking water production through reverse osmosis desalination). Therefore, it seems important to undertake various supporting studies to clarify the non-technical constraints to be met to satisfy real market needs.

It is recommended that work on the three main areas listed should start in the immediate future if realistic technology is to be demonstrated within the next five years.

It should be noted that this research programme is likely to enjoy effective synergy with other research programmes into marine technology and it can therefore be reasonably expected that fruitful 'spin-off' results will be achieved in addition to the main programme goals.

2.1.4 R&D 'roadmap'

A summary of R&D topics to be pursued, and their inter-relationships in achieving the short-term goals, is illustrated below in Figure 2.6.

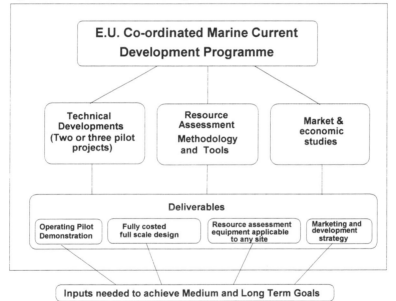

Figure 2.6. R&D roadmap – routes to achieving short-term goals

2.1.5 Strategy

2.1.5.1 Pre-competitive R&D

A consortium of European organizations already involved in this area should be strengthened and expanded so as to attract an enhanced commercial and private-sector financial involvement. European organizations with prior experience in this field (in alphabetical order) include those listed in Table 2.1.

Table 2.1. European organizations with prior experience in the field of marine current energy (An asterisk indicates a member of the EUREC Agency)

Name of organization	Nationality	Type of organization
ENEL	IT	State electricity utility R&D department
I T Power Ltd*	GB	Renewable energy consultancy
International Centre for Island Technology (Heriot-Watt University)	GB	Research organization attached to university
NEL*	GB	National Engineering Laboratory
PowerStream Plc	GB	Hydro-turbine manufacturer/designer
Seacore Ltd	GB	Offshore piling & boring contractor and manufacturer of offshore structures
Scottish Nuclear Ltd	GB	Electrical power utility partially privatized
Tecnomare SpA	IT	Offshore engineering consultancy
University of Grand Canary	SP	University R&D department
University of Patras	GR	University R&D department

2.2 WAVE ENERGY

2.2.1 Introduction

The total gross wave-energy resource arriving at the coast of Europe is significant with a magnitude estimated to be about 1000 TWh annually.[13] This resource is strategically located, mainly around the western periphery of Europe, and could make a significant contribution to the energy budgets of these regions. The establishment of the proposed Single Market for Electricity and more extensive grid integration gives this resource the potential to contribute to the energy budget of Europe as a whole. Estimates of the recoverable resource are difficult to make as there has not been any systematic assessment for its exploitation and few practical wave-energy devices have been constructed. A reasonable estimate would be about 120 TWh per year.

Large numbers of patents have been filed over the years for wave-energy devices, but research programmes have narrowed the number of practical devices. The most common of these is based on an air chamber or oscillating water column system whilst others incorporate a float in their operation. Prototype devices have to be reasonably large and the high cost of these has discouraged commercial investment in such high-risk projects. A device, developed in Norway, based on low-head hydro technology, has reached commercial maturity. but has limited application because of its operational principle.

The research programme instigated by DG XII in 1991 with a series of preliminary actions has resulted in two Pilot Plant projects, one involving a shore-based and the other a nearshore oscillating water column system. These projects are currently funded by the Third Framework JOULE Programme and are expected to be constructed by late 1995 or early in 1996.

Real ocean waves have wave heights and wave periods that vary continuously but there are mathematical expressions that allow calculation of the wave power in terms of representative statistics. The most commonly used statistics are the significant wave height H_s and zero crossing wave period T_z or energy period T_e. The power available per metre of the shoreline is given by a relatively simple expression:

Power = kW/m.

Typical wave heights on the European Atlantic coast are 2 m with wave periods around 10 seconds, while extreme waves have heights of 10 m and periods of 15 seconds. The energy is transferred by the waves as a combination of displacements of the water surface and movements of water particles below the surface. This energy transmission is largely confined to a depth of about one quarter wavelength below the sea surface.

The north-west European coastline from Cape Wrath in Scotland to Cape St Vincent in Portugal has one of the most energetic wave climates in the world. There the waves collect the wind energy from a large area of the North Atlantic Ocean and transfer this to the shore. The North Sea, Mediterranean and Baltic coastlines experience less energetic wave climates except for limited locations such as the north and west coast of Denmark, the southern tip of Italy and a number of the Greek Islands. This can however be of advantage, as the extreme forces experienced in these locations will be reduced.

A systematic assessment of the European wave-energy resource is being addressed by one of the current JOULE projects. The European Wave Energy Atlas will have data for the whole coastline at the 20 m depth contour available on a PC-based system. Until this is available, an estimate can be made using published data. By making assumptions about averaged wave energy flux, it can be estimated that the total wave-energy resource is equivalent to about 1000 TWh per year.

This can be roughly distributed as:

- North-west European coastline   75%
- North Sea coasts   1.5%
- Mediterranean coastline   23.5%

This is the total estimated resource available along a line parallel to the whole coastline of the areas mentioned and includes waves from all directions. It will not be possible to convert all this resource because of environmental and other constraints but this figure gives an order of magnitude to the upper limit. It is estimated that the recoverable or technical resource from this total (including machine efficiencies) could be around 120 TWh but Mollison[14] suggests that the recoverable resource from the North West European Shelf could be as high as 400 TWh.

The resource is therefore not a constraint in the development of wave energy.

2.2.2 Wave-energy devices – present situation

2.2.2.1 Wave-Energy Convertor (WEC) systems

There have been a large number of device concepts proposed for the utilization of wave energy over the years. Few devices have been tested in the sea at full scale and only one large device can be considered to be close to commercial reality. It is technically feasible to construct wave-energy convertors that will perform efficiently at sea. However, a number of detailed factors that affect the economics are still unknown, given the lack of operational experience with research prototypes. Tank testing of scale-model convertors has been carried out in a number of countries and mathematical descriptions have been developed. Further tank testing and mathematical modelling is required and proving of these modelling exercises will require full-size prototypes to be tested at sea. Component reliability and survival of the devices in storm-wave conditions will also require to be determined in full-scale trials.

Wave-energy convertors consist essentially of two major components:

- the interface element that is acted on directly by the waves;
- the power take-off system that damps the interface motion.

The interface elements are normally of two main types :

- floats that heave or roll in response to wave action;
- air chambers, within which the pressure varies either by direct contact with the water surface or indirect contact through a membrane.

Falnes has summarized the major generic types of convertor. The power take-off systems can be classified under three main headings:

- high-pressure hydraulics – usually oil;
- low-pressure hydraulics – usually using sea water;
- air turbines.

Most of the power take-off systems for current practical devices are designed to generate electricity with a small number proposing the use of mechanical power to desalinate sea water.

Most renewable energy technologies have very few options for the principle of energy conversion. Wind energy requires a turbine which can have either a vertical or a horizontal axis; photovoltaics can utilize only limited materials and must be mounted in arrays; biomass requires chemical conversion or combustion for utilization (usually with conventional technology) and hydro power has limited options all based on impulse or reaction turbines. Wave-energy conversion by contrast has almost an infinite number of potential possibilities and, even after a number of years of research, the options are not clear for the optimum system. There are, however, a limited number of practical systems that are more mature and could be considered for further development.

2.2.2.1.1 OSCILLATING WATER COLUMN SYSTEMS (OWC)
This device can be considered the closest to commercial maturity, as the principle of operation is simple and the construction uses conventional technology. As such, these systems can be considered as first-generation devices. The OWC device consists of a large chamber which has a free opening to the sea. This chamber encloses an air volume which is compressed by the wave pressure. The increase in pressure causes a flow from the air plenum through a turbine generator.

This air flow alternates in direction as the wave pressure rises and falls and the air-turbine system must be capable of generating with this reversing flow. A valve and ducting arrangement can be used to rectify the flow or alternately a self-rectifying turbine utilized (such as the Wells Turbine). A typical size for a 500 kW power generator is a chamber with a waterline plan area of 150 m^2 and a shoreline width of 10 m.

2.2.2.1.2 FLOATING DEVICES
A large number of floating devices have been proposed, but the system which has the best potential for electricity production at economic levels in the medium term is the CLAM

device.[15] This device consists of a float with air bags mounted around the periphery and the wave pressure causes the bags to breath air into a reservoir through an air turbine.

This air turbine is again the Wells self-rectifying system and is used to generate electricity. The typical size for a 250 kW device is about 60 m in diameter.

In the longer term other floating devices such as the Salter Duck will be required to convert the higher power levels available further offshore. Technology developments are required for this device to be realized, particularly in relation to the power take-off, mooring and electrical cabling systems.

2.2.2.1.3 POINT ABSORBER ARRAYS (PAS)

Most of the wave-energy convertors listed above are designed to be deployed in lines parallel to the shoreline to intercept the wave energy. The point absorber (PA) concept uses a large array of small devices to capture the energy, a little like a radio receiver. Studies have shown that such arrays can be highly efficient.[16] The point absorber has the advantage of small size and suitability for modularized line production. The disadvantages are the reliability of moorings and interconnection. The majority of this type of device incorporate a float performing a water pumping action, in some cases with a seabed mounting for reaction. Examples of these devices are the DWP Float, IPS Buoy and Hosepump Buoy.[13]

2.2.2.2 Technology benchmarks - present situation
2.2.2.2.1 PILOT POWER PLANTS

The Oscillating Water Column Device is the most developed of all wave-energy devices with a number of small (< 500 kW) pilot plants constructed. Devices of this type have been constructed in Norway, Japan, China and India.

Operating experience with these pilot plants is limited and in most cases the full potential of the system has not been realized. The Japanese plant at Sakata has only limited power-generation capability and the Norwegian plant has been abandoned after a mechanical failure.

A 500 kW pilot plant of the TAPCHAN type has been constructed in Norway and this has worked with reasonable performance over a period of six years. The disadvantage of this system, which involves waves overtopping a tapering channel, is that the number of potential sites in Europe is limited because of tidal effects.

Two single-chamber OWC pilot plants are to be constructed in Europe with support from the JOULE Programme, one in the Azores in the North Atlantic constructed with a concrete chamber and one off the North of Scotland using steel. Both pilot plants will utilize Wells Turbine systems for electricity generation with the Azores plant at the shoreline and the Scottish plant being constructed in the nearshore region.

2.2.2.2.2 POWER TAKE-OFF SYSTEMS

Power take-off systems for the first generation of wave power plants consist of air-turbine generator combinations. These turbines are of the self-rectifying type invented by Wells. The existing small pilot plant at Islay, Scotland, incorporates a 70 kW machine, and a 500 kW machine was built for the defunct power plant in Norway. Electrical generation and grid connection for these systems is through synchronous generators with turbine speeds allowed to vary.

2.2.3 Goals for wave-energy development

2.2.3.1 Long-term goal (by 2010)

The resource available for wave-power convertors in Europe is large and therefore not a barrier to potential development. A number of studies related to renewable energies suggest that goals for the contribution to primary energy supply could be up to 15%.[17,18] This means that renewables will be expected to make a contribution to electricity supply of up to 300 TWh per year by the year 2010. It would be reasonable to expect wave energy to realistically contribute about 1 TWh per year as this only represents 1% of the technical wave energy resource.

- The installed capacity of WECs to be 200 MW with annual installation rate of about 20 MW. (Largely first- and second-generation devices).
- The demonstration of third-generation offshore devices.

2.2.3.2 Medium-term goal (by 2000–2005)

- The construction and operation of multi-megawatt demonstration plants based on the first-generation devices (OWCs).
- The construction of pilot power plants based on arrays of second-generation (Point Absorber) WECs.
- The development of technology to allow pilot plants for third-generation (offshore devices) to be deployed.

2.2.3.3 Short-term goal (immediate actions)

The immediate actions must be:

- The construction and operation of a number of first-generation (OWC) Pilot Plants on the European coast over a period of about 3–5 years.
- Supporting research into optimization of devices and design methods.
- The technology development and construction of a number of second-generation (Point Absorber) WECs.
- Further research on the development of technologies for offshore WECs (e.g. moorings, linkages, bearings, electrical connections).
- The development of efficient power conversion systems for all devices.

2.2.4. Research and development roadmap

A summary of R&D topics to be pursued, and their inter-relationships in achieving the short-term goals, is illustrated in Figure 2.7.

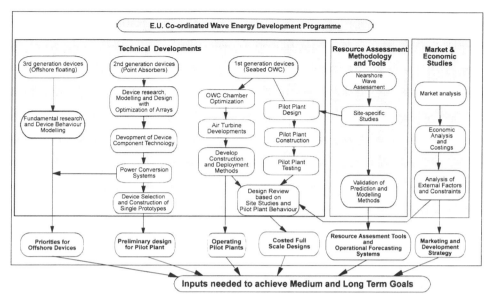

Figure 2.7. R&D roadmap to achieve short-term goals

2.2.5 Strategy

2.2.5.1 Pre-competitive R&D

There is an existing network of research groups involved in the JOULE Programme. These would need to be grouped into a coherent set of interlinked 'expert' subgroups with specific experience in the areas required to achieve the short-term goals. The main groups which would be relevant are listed in Table 2.2.

Table 2.2. European organizations with prior experience in this field

Name of organization	Nationality	Type of organization
Danish Wavepower	Denmark	Research consultancy
Hydraulics & Maritime Research Centre	Ireland	Research organization at university
University of Limerick	Ireland	University R&D group
University of Trondheim	Norway	
INETI	Portugal	Research organization
Technical University of Lisbon	Portugal	University R&D group
Chalmers University	Sweden	University R&D group
Technocean Ltd	Sweden	Development company
I.P.S. Ltd	Sweden	Development company
NEL	UK	Research organization
University of Edinburgh	UK	University R&D group
A.R.T. Ltd	UK	Development company
Heriot Watt University	UK	University R&D group
Queen's University	UK	University R&D group
Coventry University	UK	University R&D group

2.3 REFERENCES

1 Sørensen B (1979). Renewable Energy. Academic Press, London and New York.
2 Tidal Stream Energy Review, (1993). Prepared by Engineering & Power Development Consultants Ltd, Binnie & Partners, Sir Robt. McAlpine & Sons Ltd and I T Power Ltd. for the Energy Technology Support Unit of the Department of Energy, Report No. ETSU T/05/00155/REP.
3 Marine Currents Energy Extraction: Resource Assessment (1995). Final Report, EU-JOULE contract JOU2-CT93-0355, (Tecnomare, ENEL, IT Power, Ponte di Archimede, University of Patras).
4 Bryden I G, Bullen C, Paish F (1995). Utilising Tidal Currents to Generate Electricity in Orkney & Shetland, 5th International Offshore & Polar Engineering Conference, The Hague. ISOPE, Colorado, USA.
5 Marine Currents Energy Extraction: Technology Assessment (1995). Final Report, EU-JOULE contract JOU2-CT93-0355, IT Power & Tecnomare UK.
6 Feasibility Study of Tidal Current Power Generation for Coastal Waters: Orkney and Shetland (1995). Final Report, EU contract XVII/4 1040/92-41, ICIT (with IT Power and Aalberg University).
7 Wyman P R, Peachey C J (GEC Hirst Laboratories)(1979). Tidal Current Energy Conversion. Proceedings of the Future Energy Concepts Conference. Institution of Electrical Engineers, London.
8 Stewart H B (ed.) (1974). Proceedings of the MacArthur Workshop on the Feasibility of Extracting Energy from the Florida Current, Palm Beach.
9 Fraenkel P L, Musgrove P R (IT Power & Reading University) (1979). Tidal and River Current Energy Systems. Proceedings of the Future Energy Concepts Conference. Institution of Electrical Engineers, London.
10 Continued work by ITDG and subsequently by IT Power on river current water pumping systems (1981–1984).
11 Field Testing of a 2.4 m Diameter Vertical-axis Watermill (1983). Report NEL-034, National Research Council Hydraulics Laboratory, Ottawa, Canada.
12 Kihoh S, Suzuki K, Shiono, M (Nihon University) (1990). Power Generations from Tidal Currents, Tokyo, Japan.
13 Lewis AW (1992). Wave Energy: Current Research Activities and Recommendations for a European Research Programme. Final Report for DGXII/E, Ref. JOUR-0128-IE. Commission of European Communities, Directorate General for Research and Development, Renewable Energies.
14 Mollison D (1989). The European Wave Power Resource, Proceedings of Conference on Wave Energy Devices, Coventry, UK, 30 November 1989.
15 Thorpe T (1992). A Review of Wave Energy. ETSU Report R-72, UK Department of Trade and Industry.
16 Randlov P, Thomas G P, Nielsen K, Salter S, Beatty W, Thorpe T (1993). Final Report for JOULE Wave Energy Preliminary Actions. Sub-Project B, Technologies and Devices. Commission European Communities, Directorate General XII/E (also in Proceedings of 1st. European Wave Energy Symposium).
17 TERES (1994). The European Renewable Energy Study. ALTENER Programme, Commission European Communities DG XVII.
18 MADRID (1994). An Action Plan for Renewable Energy Sources in Europe. Proceedings of Conference for Declaration of Madrid. Published by European Commission, DG XII, XIII, XVII, European Parliament, STOA Programme, IDAE (Spain), Fondation Canovas del Castillo.

FURTHER READING

Barber N F (1960). Water Waves. Wykeham Science Series.
EC (1989). Energy in Europe: Major Themes in Energy. Special Issue of Periodical for World Energy Conference in Montreal. European Commission DG XVII, Directorate General for Energy, Cat. No. CB-BI-89-004-EN-C.

EC (1990). Energy and the Environment. Communication from the Commission to the Council. COM (89) 369 Cat. No. CB-CO-89-574-EN-C.

Falnes J, Lovseth J (1991). Ocean Wave Energy. Energy Policy.

Lewis A W (1984). Wave Energy: An Evaluation for the European Community. Graham and Trotman, London.

GLOSSARY

OTEC	Ocean Thermal Energy Conversion
GEC	General Electric Company
NEL	National Engineering Laboratory
WEC	Wave Energy Convertors
OWC	Oscillating Water Column Systems
PAs	Point Absorber Arrays

3. PHOTOVOLTAICS

3.1 INTRODUCTION

Solar radiation, converted directly into electricity, offers a clean and virtually inexhaustible power source, able to generate in theory the total world electrical energy demand.

The main specific advantages of photovoltaics are the reasonable conversion efficiencies obtained for both direct and diffuse radiation, the fact that photovoltaic modules can be efficiently integrated in buildings, minimizing the visual intrusion, their modularity and their static character. Moreover, photovoltaic modules are characterized by a high reliability, a long lifetime and low maintenance costs. Because of the intermittent nature of the energy source, use has to be made of storage, connection to the electric grid or a combination with other renewable technologies.

Today, the cost of PV electricity is still too high for bulk power production in European utility grids; however, for peak-power applications and local grid support, PV electricity may became cost-effective in the near future – especially in southern Europe. PV electricity already has an important natural market in worldwide off-grid applications. For several years this market has been expanding at a rate of approximately 15% per annum.

The enormous potential of PV electricity generation justifies the intensive research efforts needed to reduce the cost. Because of the modular nature of photovoltaics, cost reductions will enable a gradual market growth, from stand-alone application to bulk power generation by means of grid-connected systems. Cost reductions will be a result of real mass production and new technological developments.

This chapter presents the goals in terms of technological performance and cost, on which the members of the European Renewable Energy Centres Agency have agreed. It gives an overview of the wide range of research topics still to be investigated, from material and cell level right through to system level for the different promising technologies.

As an introduction, the current technological and cost status are summarized.

3.2 PRESENT SITUATION

3.2.1 An overview of PV systems

Terrestrial photovoltaic systems can be described according to three types of applications: stand-alone, hybrid, and grid-connected.

3.2.1.1 Stand-alone systems

Depending on the application, a stand-alone system either has to make use of a battery for storage or can operate without a battery.

With battery. Stand-alone systems involving battery storage, are generally used in remote locations that have no access to a public utility grid; see Figure 3.1. The load can be dc or ac.

Up to about 1 to 2 kWp, electrical loads can be direct current (dc). The main advantages of the use of dc are simplicity and high reliability. Standard 12/24 V dc systems are used to feed equipment and components for the motor vehicle, boat and camping markets. A dc system with a battery represents the standard configuration for most small lighting and electrification applications.

Some typical examples are:

* PV vaccine refrigerators, utilizing a PV array of 100–300 Wp, a battery and associated charge controller and a compressor controller and a 12 or 24 V compressor refrigerator specially designed for photovoltaic power and vaccine use.
* Solar home systems, supplying small amounts of energy in off-grid households. These comprise one or several PV modules mounted onto a suitable support structure (such as a roof), a battery and a charge controller.
* Battery charging systems, ranging from low power Ni–Cd chargers up to community battery charging stations.

Figure 3.1. Lighting of a Dutch parking lot during all seasons by twelve PV-powered streetlights (160 Wp) each) (courtesy Marine Solaire, NL)

Alternating current (ac) systems with a battery represent the standard configuration for larger applications (above 1 to 2 kWp). In such cases, a conventional fixed frequency 50–60 (USA) Hz inverter is used to feed ac loads continuously 24 hours per day. The advantage of such systems is that off-the-shelf household ac appliances or equipment can be used.

Without battery. Systems without a battery in a power range from 600 Wp to 3.5 kWp have had widespread application for water pumping applications. In this case the water reservoir itself provides the storage. These systems usually have a variable-frequency inverter directly connected to the PV array. The variable-frequency inverter regulates the pump speed in order to make maximum use of the available PV power. The main advantages of such systems are high efficiency, rugged design, and the possibility of operating many off-the-shelf standard ac pumps.

3.2.1.2 Stand-alone hybrid systems

A hybrid system is a stand-alone system used in combination with another power source. The other power source can be used as a back-up generator (e.g. a diesel generator) or is used to provide a more continuous energy supply by using complementary sources (e.g. a wind turbine). Since such systems combine different power sources, they require a more complex controller than stand-alone systems.

3.2.1.3 Grid-connected systems

In a grid-connected system, the PV power generator feeds the grid via an inverter. Grid-connected systems normally do not include batteries.

The number of grid-connected PV plants in the 1–5 kW range has increased through the 'PV-on-roof-tops and façades' programmes that are operating in several European countries, e.g. Germany, Switzerland, The Netherlands and Austria (see Figure 3.2). This trend is expected to continue in the future. The number of multi-hundred kW and MW-size plants is also increasing.

3.2.2 State of the art of PV-technology

The state-of-the-art information presented here is limited to commercially available components. For those PV technologies that are not yet commercially available, the state-of-the-art is summarized in Section 3.4.

3.2.2.1 PV modules

The only modules currently on the market are based on the use of crystalline silicon, amorphous silicon or CDTe. International production of photovoltaic modules is of the order of 80 MWp/annum (1995). During the last few years production has increased by approximately 15% per annum.

PV modules available in the European Union are predominantly flat-plate types with 18 to 180 monocrystalline or multi-crystalline Si cells in a module. Power outputs range from about 26 W to 240 W at STC (1000 W/m^2, 25°C cell temperature). A normal module efficiency is 11–13%. The best module efficiencies are in the range of 15–16%.

Figure 3.2. Building-integrated PV is regarded as highly promising for future power production. Cost reductions, quality improvements and integration of PV into the building process are key issues to be addressed in order to reach large-scale application in the next century (courtesy Riesjard Schropp/Ecofys, The Netherlands)

Most commercial PV modules have a lifetime of at least 20 years. The energy pay-back time for the present generation of crystalline silicon modules (not optimized with respect to energy pay back) is in the range of 2–6 years from sunbelt region to continental climate.[1,2]

Commercially available modules of amorphous Si have stabilized efficiencies of 5% to 6%. Here the energy pay back is estimated to be 1–3 years.[3]

More than 80% of the PV module market is based on crystalline silicon. Amorphous modules are only used for low power applications such as calculators, garden lights, small power lighting for rural electrification, etc.

3.2.2.2 Power conditioning

Power conditioning devices used in PV systems are mainly power converters and inverters.

Power converters. Power converters are dc-to-dc regulation devices placed in series with the PV array. They make use of a high-frequency switching regulator, which usually operates at 20 kHz or higher to minimize the size and weight of the magnetic (i.e. transformer) components and capacitors.

Inverters.[4] The inverter's main functions are: inversion of dc voltage into ac, wave shaping of the output ac voltage, regulation of the effective value of the output voltage. They are designed to operate the PV array continuously near its maximum power point. The technology for high-switching-frequency inverters (typically 20 kHz or higher) is made possible by switch-mode power devices. Transistors, power MOSFETs and bipolar transistors predominate as the power switches in low-power inverters. High-power inverters generally use thyristors. A device that has recently emerged is the IGBT, insulated-gate bipolar transistor. IGBT inverters capable of several hundred kW, running at frequencies up to 50 kHz, are now available. A high-switching-frequency inverter presents an output wave form very close to the pure sinusoidal one, with very little filtering at the output; this eliminates the need for bulky, expensive, and energy-consuming power filters.

Inverters generally have full-load efficiencies ranging from 90% to 96% and from about 85% to 95% for a 10% load. Since their fixed losses are usually greater than their resistive losses, they exhibit a steadily decreasing efficiency as the input and output power are reduced.

3.2.2.3 Batteries

The only widely available battery systems are lead–acid and Ni–Cd batteries.[5] The performance of these batteries is summarized in Table 3.1.

Table 3.1. Performance of Pb–acid and Ni–Cd batteries

	Pb–acid	**Ni–Cd**
Cycle life	600 to 1500 cycles	1500 to 3500 cycles
Efficiency (Ah ratio)	83 to › 90%	71%
Self discharge	3 to 10%/month	6 to 20%/month
Range of operation	−15 to +50°C	−40 to +45°C

3.2.3 Cost of PV systems

3.2.3.1 Cost of major components
FLAT-PLATE PV MODULES
The current total production cost estimates of PV modules, resulting from a survey of European suppliers[6] is as shown in Table 3.2. The retail price depends, among other factors, much on the quantity supplied.

Table 3.2. Production cost of flat-plate PV modules

Crystalline Si modules	above 3 ECU/Wp
Thin film a-Si	above 2.1ECU/Wp

INVERTERS
Current prices of inverters are listed in Table 3.3.[7]

BATTERIES

Table 3.3. Typical prices of inverters

1 kW	1.0 ECU/W
2–5 kW	0.5 ECU/W

The typical prices of lead–acid and Ni–Cd batteries are shown in Table 3.4.[5]

Table 3.4. Typical prices of Pb–acid and Ni–Cd batteries

	Pb–acid	Ni–Cd
Investment cost (ECU/kWh$_{capacity}$)	160–200	690–1590
Specific energy cost (ECU/kWh$_{from\ battery}$)	0.11–0.33	0.20–1.06

3.2.3.2 Overall system costs

GRID-CONNECTED SYSTEMS

Roof-top programmes. Typical system costs in Dutch,[8] German[9] and Austrian programmes were reported to be around 13 ECU/Wp. For larger numbers of identical systems, today's prices in the range of 8 to 12 ECU/Wp can be achieved. Interesting in this case is the opportunity to replace conventional building materials by PV modules. These 'avoided costs' are not taken into account in these prices. The relative breakdown of the different components in the costs of a representative 1 kWp roof-top system is shown below:

Module:	53%
Inverter:	22%
Mounting:	12%
Rest:	13%

Central PV station. For grid-connected PV systems up to 500 kWp the costs range from 8.20 to 16.20 ECU/Wp.[10] The total plant costs for the 1 MW central station size grid-connected PV plant in Spain, with fixed-tilted array segments, were 9.63 ECU/Wp and 11.22 ECU/Wp depending on the module choice. The high cost is a consequence of the very limited experience with central PV power stations.

STAND-ALONE/HYBRID SYSTEMS

The cost of such systems depends strongly on their configuration.

Generally, the PV module costs average around 30% of the system cost, as compared to about 50% for the grid-connected systems.

3.2.3.3 PV energy costs

Based on the above-mentioned system costs, it is possible to make estimates of the actual kWh-cost for different PV systems

GRID CONNECTED SYSTEMS

- **Roof-top systems.** Energy costs are of the order of 0.35–0.90 ECU/kWh for western Europe and 0.25–0.60 ECU/kWh for southern Europe. The range depends on how the avoided costs related to the replacement of conventional building elements are accounted for. (The assumptions for the calculation of the energy costs were: capital cost = 5%, lifetime = 20 years. Operation and maintenance cost a 1%/year of investment; residual value = 1%. For western Europe and southern Europe, irradiation levels of 1100 kWh/m^{2}year and 1750 kWh/m^{2}year respectively were assumed.)

- **Central power station.** For southern Europe, an energy cost of 0.35 ECU/kWh is a realistic value.[10]

These kWh prices should be compared with the customer tariffs which are in the range of 0.15–0.19 ECU/kWh.

STAND-ALONE SYSTEMS
The energy costs depend strongly on the application.

It is clear that PV electricity still cannot compete with electricity from the grid (baseload), but, because of its nature, PV can be applied in an economically viable way in many other situations. In general, this is the case for relatively small consumers at a relatively large distance from the grid.

3.2.4 PV industrial and market developments

The turnover of the PV industry is currently estimated to be about 900 million ECU world-wide. The market volume of about 80 MW grows steadily at an average of 15% per annum. European manufacturers represent a share exceeding 30% in 1994. The total European production-line capacity is over 30 MWp, and shipments total over 20 MWp, of which about 50% is exported outside Europe.[11,12] Most of the manufacturers foresee the installation of extra capacity in the future. European manufacturers employ more than 1600 people in Europe and more than 1000 outside Europe. The roof and building-mounted façade grid-connected market represents the fastest-growing PV market in Europe. Figure 3.3 shows the growth of the world PV module shipments.

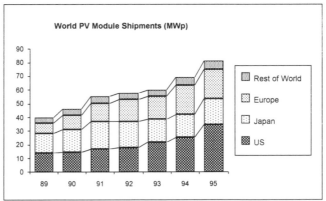

Figure 3.3. World PV module shipments (MWp) (source: PV News)

3.3 REALISTIC GOALS

3.3.1 Final goal

The final goal of all research and development in PV is to obtain a power generation system which is able to convert solar energy into electricity at a cost/kWh which is comparable with other generation or delivery schemes at the specific location. In this case the use of PV power generation may be favoured because of its advantage of being a clean and environmentally benign technology. In order to keep this advantage, non-toxic materials that are widely available should be used.

3.3.2 Intermediate goals

Because the technology is still expensive, owing largely to the extremely small market of PV compared to that for other electricity-generation technologies, PV is far from being competitive with bulk electricity generation in an industrial environment. However, the cost of electricity generation can differ by orders of magnitude, depending on the size of the system and on the location. PV is already competitive in certain market niches, and is often an economic solution for rural electrification. As the cost of PV systems is reduced, more and more market segments will be gained.

Furthermore, owing to the decentralized nature of PV compared to the centralized production by conventional methods, a satisfactory comparison is not straightforward.

The medium-term goal is to open larger areas of applications by reducing the overall cost of PV systems. This can be achieved by developing mass-production techniques for solar cells and modules, by introducing standardized and simpler systems, by developing balance-of-system components with lower energy consumption and by the developments of cost-effective mounting and building integration techniques.

Also, there are still many materials and processing technologies that show a large potential but which have not yet been studied in depth. There are technologies that have proved to be excellent in the laboratory but that have not yet been tried out in industrial production. For the well proven technologies there is still a large gap between laboratory efficiencies and industrial efficiencies.

3.3.3 Realistic targets

Goals for performance of components, cost and implementation put forward in this section are based on estimates of the potential for performance improvements and cost reductions of the proposed R&D topics described in Section 3.4, and on the growth potential of the industrial production capacities.

3.3.3.1 Goals for R&D

Individual goals for the performance of the major components of a PV system are given in Table 3.5.

3.3.3.2 Cost goals

For module and system costs, the goals in Table 3.6 can be put forward:

3.3.3.3 Implementation goals

Module cost reduction from more than 3 ECU/Wp now to less than 1.5 ECU/Wp in the medium term will open progressively larger areas of applications. Note that the break-even point for grid-connected roof-integrated applications in Europe corresponds to a cost

Table 3.5. Goals for performances in the short and medium terms

Item	Short term 2000	Medium term 2010
Solar cell efficiency		
c-silicon		
laboratory	24%	26%
production (mono-multi crystalline)	16–18%	› 20%
thin film (polycrystalline, amorphous)		
laboratory	18%	20%
production	› 10%	› 15%
advanced devices (tandem, concentrator)		
laboratory	› 30%	35%
production	› 20%	25%
Module lifetime	› 20 years	› 30 years
maximum degradation during lifetime	‹ 10%	‹ 10%
Inverter efficiency		
100% load	› 97%	› 98%
10% load	› 90%	› 95%

Systems. Availability on short term (2000) of
· reliable systems for developing countries
· building specific modules satisfying building physical, aesthetical and safety requirements
· reliable concentrators
· lower energy consumption balance-of-systems components

Table 3.6. Goals for module and system cost in the short and long terms

Item	Short term 2000	Medium term 2010
Module cost	‹ 2.5 ECU/Wp	‹ 1.5 ECU/Wp
of which cell cost	‹ 1.5 ECU/Wp	‹ 1.0 ECU/Wp
System cost		
grid-connected	‹ 5.0 ECU/Wp	‹ 3.0 ECU/Wp

of about 1.5–1.75 ECU/Wp at module level. Therefore, it is realistic to expect that grid-connected PV integrated in buildings will achieve a competitive position as of 2005. This will become an important market, next to the one of autonomous electrification systems for rural regions, rich in sunlight.

The achievement of the long-term goals will clearly result in a large market for photovoltaic electricity generation. For example, by reaching these cost goals, 50% of the annual electricity consumption of a typical European household could be provided by a PV system adding only 2.5% to the overall building cost.[12]

Consistent with these system costs, one can expect a PV electricity generation cost below 0.15 ECU/kWh in the medium to long term for grid-connected residential systems.

A realistic module production volume for 2010 is 500–1000 MWp. The capacity installed in the European Union by the same time would be expected to exceed 5 GWp. Reaching this annual production goal would generate direct employment of several tens of thousands of man-years.

3.4 DISCUSSION OF R &D 'ROADMAP'

There is general agreement that there is a large potential for cost reduction particularly if the following three considerations are borne in mind:

- Even conventional technologies can lead to substantial cost reduction when they are applied to mass production. Present manufacture is still on a level which involves a significant amount of manual handling.
- Improvement of the efficiency of solar cells has a strong impact on the electricity generation cost since it results in the reduction of all area-related cost components which are a large part of the total investment.
- New technologies are expected to emerge from the intensive research and development efforts, especially in the field of thin-film approaches that may lead to reduced materials consumption and to large-scale deposition techniques.

This section describes in detail the proposed R&D topics that have the potential to bring down the cost according to the stated goals. These R&D efforts can be considered at four levels:

- Source material, substrate and cell fabrication
- PV-modules
- Concentrators
- PV system technology.

3.4.1 Source material, substrate and cell fabrication

3.4.1.1 Crystalline silicon

It is important to note that today the European photovoltaic industry is essentially based on crystalline silicon technology (Figure 3.4). This situation is likely to continue for at least the next ten years. Therefore, because of its industrial importance, the R&D of this technology should receive high priority.

ADVANTAGES AND DISADVANTAGES
The advantages of the crystalline silicon technology are the following:[13]

- well established Si industry (micro-electronics);
- wide availability of Si (SiO_2);
- uniform material quality (electrically, mechanically, chemically);
- environmentally benign, non-toxic;
- simple technology, involving no complex processing;
- production can be easily automated or upgraded by the modular structure of the production equipment;
- relatively high conversion efficiency;
- cells have a very good stability when they are properly encapsulated; the lifetime can easily reach 30 years.

The disadvantages are the following:

Figure 3.4. A 10 × 10 cm^2 multi crystalline silicon wafer

- relatively thick substrates from expensive material, which are cut from a Czochralski ingot or from a cast block;
- modules are not obtained by monolithic integration, but cells are restricted to certain sizes and have to be tabbed and interconnected.

RESEARCH TOPICS[14]

Efficiency of laboratory cells. The goal is to obtain the highest possible efficiency without taking cost considerations into account. This research is important in order to determine the ultimate performance. Later on, research has to be carried out to make the process economical in industrial production.

Progress can be expected from:

- fine tuning of the existing high-efficiency structures by experimental work and by 2D and 3D simulation work. The most efficient crystalline Si solar cell is the PERL (Passivated Emitter Rear Locally Diffused) structure, developed at the University of New South Wales (Australia), yielding efficiencies of 24%. It is generally accepted that if all design parameters are fully optimized, the PERL structure is able to yield 26% efficiency under one sun illumination.
- long-term basic research leading to:
  - the implementation of more efficient light trapping;
  - the use of unconventional carrier generation processes: The impurity PV effect uses sub-bandgap photons to create electron-hole pairs. Theoretical improvements of 1 to 2% absolute in the conversion efficiencies have been shown in recent studies.
    In Auger generation the excess energy $E_x = h\nu - E_g$ is used to create a second electron–hole pair, leading to quantum efficiencies above unity. Calculations show that the effect is negligible for the silicon band structure and the terrestrial solar spec-

trum. For silicon alloyed with germanium, however, this effect may play a more important role.

Efficiency of industrial cells. In order to reach the break-even point of PV in grid-connected roof-integrated applications, a cost level of about 1.75 ECU/Wp should be reached. This cost goal corresponds to 1.3 ECU/Wp at the cell level and can be translated to specific targets at the different levels of cell manufacturing. For wafer and cell fabrication the corresponding cost goals are 0.85 ECU/Wp and 0.45 ECU/Wp respectively.

Source material. Today, most silicon cells are made from reclaimed material from the micro-electronic industry. This situation may continue for a number of years because of the expanding electronic industry and also because the wafers used for PV are becoming thinner and the efficiencies are increasing. Advanced slicing results in a pitch below 400 micron and a conversion efficiency above 17% is realistic. The consumption of silicon therefore can be reduced to less than 10g/Wp, corresponding to a poly Si cost of 0.2 ECU/Wp (based on a cost of 20 ECU/kg). This price level is compatible with the cost goal of 1.75 ECU/Wp.

However, the evolution of demand from the electronics industry may endanger the availability of Si feedstock material for PV. Therefore, efforts have to be made to obtain a cheap PV feedstock independent of the microelectronics industry. Two approaches can be followed: a conventional one, i.e. a relaxed Siemens process giving the best chances for sustainable feedstock production, and a less conventional way, in which new cheap alternatives are investigated.

Ingot formation. Since the competition between mono-Si and multi-Si is not yet decided, further development of ingot formation techniques for both mono- and multi-Si should be continued:

- Mono-Si ingots are currently prepared by the Czochralski process. The required developments concern the reduction of consumables (crucibles, gases, etc.) and the increase of the throughput.
- Multi-Si fabrication techniques can be subdivided into three groups:
  - Casting: this technique is clearly the lowest cost option because of the potential for higher throughput and the possibilities for scaling up. Production speed could be increased by using larger ingots or continuous casting methods.
  - True directional solidification: these techniques yield slightly higher efficiencies. Again increased throughput and lower consumption of consumables is required.
  - Electromagnetic casting: the advantages of this technique are the absence of crucible wear-out and melt contamination by the crucible and the potential for higher throughput. Large-scale production of silicon using this method should be demonstrated and the homogeneity of the material should be improved.

Slicing. Multi-wire saw cutting is becoming the standard technique. The advantages over inner diameter saws is the fact that extremely thin wafers can be sliced with low kerf loss, small surface damage and low breakage.

The evolution towards thinner wafers imposes the requirement of appropriate handling and manufacturing equipment which allows processing with high mechanical yield. A pitch of < 300 μm is a realistic goal.

Cell processing. The cost goal on this level is in the range 0.45 ECU/Wp.This necessitates cell processes with low material cost and with a minimum number of operations (< 10), and in which each operation only takes 1 to 2 s. Moreover these requirements should be met without compromising the cell efficiency.

The required future efficiency goals for industrial cells are 18 to 20% on mono-Si and 16% to 18% on multi-Si. It should be noted that the difference in efficiency between the laboratory and industrial cells is still of the order of 8% to 10% absolute. The reasons for this difference are mainly due to:

- material quality and cell dimensions;
- the need to use production methods with high throughput and low costs;
- difficulty in implementing efficient texturing schemes;
- achievable line widths of metallization.

This important difference illustrates the large potential for improvement in industrial production.

The developments needed in order to reach the anticipated efficiencies and cost goals in industrial production are summarized as follows:

- Substrates: larger size (10×20, 15×15, 20×20 cm^2) and thinner wafers (170–200 µm), limited by the yield of the production process.
- Optical confinement: Techniques used are chemical texturing, laser texturing, mechanical texturing and photo-electrochemical texturing. The challenge is to obtain good texturing in an economical way, especially on multi-crystalline substrates.
- Junction formation: Novel cell processes, such as advanced screen-printed cells or the buried contact cell, often use a selective emitter. Further work is needed to integrate such an emitter in a cost-competitive way.
- Back surface field (BSF) and back metal contact: To reduce the surface recombination at the rear surface, which becomes more important for thin cells with a high diffusion length, the following approaches are proposed and implemented:
  - p + BSF
  - gridded back with passivated non-contacted areas
  - floating junctions.
  More work is needed to achieve low surface recombination combined with efficient optical reflection or light trapping.
- Front contact formation: Two routes are followed:
  - laser or mechanical scribing of a pre-diffused and nitride (or oxide) covered wafer, followed by a self-aligned electroless deposition of Ni, followed by Cu. Advantages are the fine line width and the large height/width ratio. The grooving approach can also be used for the rear contacts.
  - Further improvement of screen printing technology (Figure 3.5).
    With novel screens and pastes, infrared firing and a tighter control of the production environment, line widths of less than 100 µm giving a reproducible fill-factor approaching 80% could be obtained in production.
    Alternative printing techniques, such as gravure offset printing, have been proposed but not yet demonstrated for solar cells. Offset printing could considerably improve the aspect ratio of conventional screen printing for small finger width.

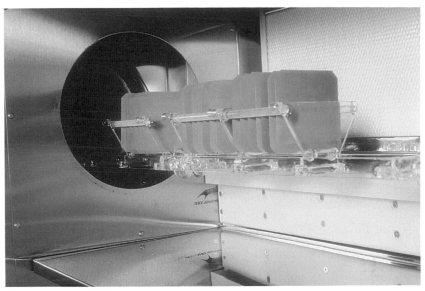

Figure 3.5. Industrial pilot line for crystalline silicon solar-cell production using advanced screen printing technology (IMEC, Belgium)

- Processing with low thermal budget: Homogeneous emitters without etch-back can already be delivered by rapid thermal processing, simultaneously with a back surface field and/or with surface passivation. Further research will lead to the processing of complete high-efficiency solar cells in a single short thermal cycle.
- Use of manufacturing science in industrial cell processing: Statistical process control and design of experiments are tools for achieving a cost-effective process with minimal sensitivity to unavoidable small changes in the production environment.
- Environmental aspects of the processing: More attention should go to the recycling of chemicals and the reduction of chemical waste production.
- Crystalline silicon cells with different designs (Emitter Wrap Through, Back contact Triode, etc.), especially in relation to module design (see also Section 3.4.2).
- Non-ingot-type crystalline Si cells.

Ribbon type: The manufacture of Si crystals in ribbons eliminates the losses of cutting and grinding. Efforts are needed to increase the material quality and the throughput.

Deposition of thin film of polycrystalline silicon on cheap substrates: This approach consists of the deposition of a thin polycrystalline silicon film (CVD, LPE, etc.) on top of a cheap substrate: ceramic, UMG-Si, glass, ribbons etc. The main challenges are:

- reaching a sufficient crystal quality without an extra remelting step, with a high-rate deposition;
- finding cheap substrates that do not lead to excessive contamination of the deposited Si film by out-diffusion from impurities;
- making an assessment of the need for conductive substrates in relation to the module technology;

- achieving a sufficient crystal quality and grain size without an extra remelting step by a high-throughput low-cost deposition method;
- realization of an efficient and upscalable bulk passivation technique that results in diffusion lengths higher than the layer thickness;
- achieving a low surface-recombination velocity at the Si layer/substrate interface;
- realization of effective optical confinement schemes to keep high short-circuit currents.

3.4.1.2 Hydrogenated amorphous silicon

STATUS

Among thin-film solar cells, cells based on amorphous silicon and related alloys (a-SiGe, a-SiC) are the most advanced. The technology for basic single-junction and tandem cells is mature and fully commercialized. For indoor low-power consumer products (pocket calculators, watches, etc.) a-Si cells are used almost exclusively. a-Si modules are increasingly penetrating the market for consumer power (< 50 W), such as street lights, battery chargers, electric fences, etc. There are several production facilities in Japan, the USA and Europe with capacities around 0.5–3 MW. Larger plants are under discussion. Theoretical conversion efficiencies are around 18%, demonstrated initial small-area efficiencies have been around 13% for single junctions and close to 14% for triple-stack structures. No major improvements regarding record initial efficiencies have been achieved for several years, suggesting a practical efficiency limit for a-Si based solar cells of around 14–15%. The potential for scale-up has been demonstrated with initial module efficiencies of around 12%, relatively close to small-area efficiencies (Figure 3.6). Improvements in reduction of performance degradation have led to stabilized module (30 × 30 cm^2) efficiencies of 10.2% (USSC). Commercially available modules offer stabilized efficiencies of 5–6%.

ADVANTAGES AND DISADVANTAGES

The advantages of amorphous silicon-based solar cells are:

- Low material costs: because a-Si has a high optical absorption coefficient and therefore cells can be made very thin (< 1 mm), and the raw materials (Si, C, Ge) are abundant and cheap.
- Low toxicity of cell materials: there are no disposal hazards and no fire hazards due to release of toxic materials.
- Low energy consumption for module production, mainly due to low-temperature processing. Module-related energy pay-back times well below one year may be achieved with advanced large-scale integrated manufacturing processes.
- Large-area thin-film technology promises a drastic cost-reduction potential. Projected module costs for large-scale production (> 10 MW) are 1 ECU/Wp or lower.
- Cells and modules may be produced in arbitrary shapes, sizes, and designs for integration in façades, rooftops, or tiles. They may be designed as opaque or semi-transparent.

The principle disadvantages are:

- The technology is rather complex. Vacuum and batch processing is used. High-purity feedstock gases and cleanliness for the deposition process are required. Multi-layer

*Figure 3.6. In-line system for large-area
deposition of amorphous silicon solar cells
(Universidad Nova de Lisboa, FCT)*

and multi-junction structures for the more advanced cells require highly accurate and complex process control.

- Investment costs are high owing to the complex technology and to standard safety requirements regarding handling of partially explosive or toxic processes and feed-stock gases (H_2, SiH_4, CH_4, GeH_4, PH_3, etc.), during production.

- In addition to extrinsic degradation mechanisms (layer inter-diffusion, pinholes), there exists an inherent, principally unavoidable, instability of the amorphous Si and alloys. Exposure to sunlight produces recombination centres with the result that the initial performance of a cell degrades by typically 10–25%, until a stabilized state, typically after a few months, is reached.

- The stabilized module efficiency is relatively low. Commercially available modules have 5–6% efficiency, while record module efficiencies of advanced multi-layer structures are around 10%. Prospects of achieving more than 12% stabilized module efficiency are low. To achieve 10% module efficiency in a cost-effective, high-yield production process is a tough challenge.

RESEARCH TOPICS

Thin-film technologies promise an important cost-reduction potential. In order for this potential to materialize, it is imperative that R&D efforts are devoted to increasing the efficiency and that the acceptability is increased through a certification procedure, recognizing its ability to render services equivalent to, and cheaper than, crystalline silicon technologies.

Although intrinsic degradation is principally unavoidable, the material stability can be improved at least slightly. Research is focused on variation of deposition processes, alternative deposition techniques, and alloying with carbon and germanium.

More promising for the enhancement of efficiency and the reduction of degradation are cell engineering concepts. Carrier collection can be enhanced – carrier recombination reduced – by:

- a reduction of cell thickness with corresponding higher electric fields;
- SiC buffer layers at the p/i interface to prevent back diffusion of electrons;
- graded bandgaps across the i-layer when alloying with C or Ge to improve electric field distribution;
- graded doping profiles across the i-layer to improve electric field distributions in degraded (stabilized) material.

Optical absorption can be enhanced by light trapping with textured front and back contacts or textured substrates. Optimization of the surface texture of the transparent conducting oxide, to maximize light trapping and minimize sharp edges with associated short-circuit current and pinhole problems, is a key element for enhanced cell performance and efficiency.

To combine both high absorption and high carrier collection, tandem and triple-stack modules are being developed, which promise the highest stabilized efficiencies of a-Si-based solar cells. Research is concentrated on optimization of the complex multi-layer structure and on control and scale-up of the associated complex deposition processes.

3.4.1.3 III–V semiconductor solar cells
STATUS

III–V solar cells have achieved the highest laboratory solar-cell efficiencies reported to date for both non-concentrator (GaAs by NREL, 25.1%) and concentrator (GaAs by VARIAN at 200 suns, 27.5%) solar cells. They have reached practical efficiencies close to the physical limits for both one-sun and concentrator illumination. Only slight improvements in efficiency are still possible as a result of design refinements and of improvements in material and processing technologies.

GaAs can be considered to have an advanced laboratory status and to be progressing towards acquiring a maturity at the industrial stage; several companies in the USA, Japan and Europe can produce these cells, almost exclusively used for space applications. However, as GaAs efficiencies are not much higher than those of Si, it is unlikely that this material can compete in cost with concentrator Si cells.

The potential of III–V semiconductor solar cells is shown to full advantage where very-high-efficiency solar cells are used, alone or in combination with concentration, together with a more efficient use of the solar spectrum. This can be achieved by dividing the solar spectrum into different energy ranges, each range being absorbed by a different material with an appropriate bandgap and active junction. The implementation of this concept revolves around two basic configurations. One is based on the spectrum-splitting approach, which makes use of dichroic filters in optical series to split the sunlight into two or more parts. Most promising though is the tandem configuration, where different bandgap materials with active junctions are stacked in optical series, with the higher-bandgap material placed first in the optical path. The implementation of this approach has involved the mechanical stacking of individual solar cells and monolithically grown structures. Monolithic structures of AlGaAs/GaAs (Varian, 27.6%) and of GaInP/GaAs (NREL, 27.3%) have reached the highest one-sun efficiencies ever reported. For concentration operation, however, the highest efficiencies have been obtained with mechanically stacked, four-terminal cells (Boeing, 32%).

ADVANTAGES AND DISADVANTAGES
Advantages are:

- high efficiency;
- low efficiency loss with temperature (this is of interest for concentration applications);
- low degradation under radiation conditions (this is of interest for space applications).

Disadvantages are:

- high cost;
- the use of dangerous components (this is, however, of less importance in concentration applications because of the lower quantities used).

RESEARCH TOPICS
For mechanically stacked and splitting systems the challenge is to develop further both high-bandgap and low-bandgap devices. A further advance would be to grow the top cell on a removable substrate to reduce cost and to reduce the optical losses produced in thick-top devices.

For monolithic structures the challenge is to grow in the same structure two devices of different materials with both lattice and current match, as well as to grow a suitable lattice-matched tunnel diode for the interconnection of the two devices. Quaternary III–V semiconductors need to be taken into consideration because they allow variation of the lattice constant and the bandgap independently.

For concentrator applications the development of high peak current, low resistance and low optical absorption, tunnel diodes are still to be improved.

For all cases, it is necessary to develop further ideas that result in increasing efficiency or reduction of the cell fabrication cost: production of crystalline films without consuming a crystalline substrate; simplifying the device structures without a loss of efficiency; better use of back reflectors and photon recycling, etc.

In the area of the production of the cells, it is important to reduce the costs of the epitaxial processes.

3.4.1.4 Other compound materials

Although polycrystalline thin-film solar-cell devices of both chalcopyrites and CdTe have been made with efficiencies in excess of 15%, these materials are relatively unexplored in terms of classical semiconductor properties and grain-boundary behaviour. CIS-based PV materials and CdTe, however, have yielded the best results and are the most developed compound materials for PV applications approaching commercial demonstration. Owing to their high absorption coefficient, these direct semiconductor materials are suited for thin-film solar cells. $CuInSe_2$ has a bandgap energy of 1 eV, which can be increased by addition of gallium as a substitute for indium. $CuGaSe_2$ has a bandgap of 1.6 eV. The most promising preparation techniques for CIS-based materials are vacuum evaporation, sputtering and CVD techniques.

$Cu(Ga,In)(S,Se)_2$

STATUS

During the last decade the efficiencies of thin-film solar cells based on multinary chalcopyrite compounds of the type $Cu(Ga,In)(S,Se)_2$ have improved continuously and have achieved the best results of all thin-film devices of more than 17%. Efficiencies of more than 15% have been realized in different laboratories by using different ratios of Ga/In and S/Se and different deposition techniques. The best results have been achieved by deposition of the chalcopyrite film by thermal co-evaporation of the elements at substrate temperatures around 550°C. The results mentioned above have all been realized in a laboratory scale with a maximum cell area of 4 cm^2. Stability tests so far do not show any degradation of device performance. Several companies and institutions have just started or will shortly begin construction of preproduction lines for 30×30 cm^2 with low capacities in the 10 kW/a level. As yet, CIGSS modules are not commercially available.

Projected costs of $Cu(In,Ga)(Se,S)_2$ modules have been estimated by several authors.[10,13,15] They calculated material costs to be 0.1–0.33 ECU/Wp and module prices to be within 0.28–1.7 ECU/Wp at different production capacities.

ADVANTAGES AND DISADVANTAGES

The principal advantages are:

* the high degree of freedom for optimal adaptation to the solar spectrum owing to easy tuning of electronic parameters by material variations;
* highest conversion efficiencies up to above 17%, with no degradation, have already been realized;
* low materials costs, because the chalcopyrite absorber has a high absorption coefficient as a result of a direct bandgap; therefore films can be very thin, in the range of a few microns;
* low toxicity of device materials and final product;
* high scalability of processes for large-area fabrication with high throughput;
* low energy consumption of fabrication processes and therefore low energy payback time for thin-film modules, well below one year assuming large-scale production;
* module design very flexible and adaptable to consumer application as a result of flexibility of patterning for monolithic integration of the module.

The principal disadvantages are:

* rather complex technology for film preparation;
* scalability to high capacities with high yield not yet proven;
* availability of raw materials high but partially limited;
* relatively high investment costs for preparation plants ;
* very thin CdS film (20 nm) is still seen as a problem; experiments to replace CdS with a non-Cd-containing compound are at an advanced stage with comparable film and device qualities and will be considered in the upscaling activities.

RESEARCH TOPICS

Fundamental R&D has to be continued intensively and results have to be transferred for upscaling activities. The main points are material research and modification (e.g. related chalcopyrites and other polycrystalline semiconductors, Cd-free films), modifications of device structures (e.g. superstrate), process-simplification and patterning-related aspects. Strategies for recycling the modules have to be developed.

The goal within the next four years is to develop process conditions and deposition techniques with high yield to realize module efficiencies of more than 10% on areas around 0.1 m^2. The key points are absorber deposition and therein substrate temperature, simplification of laboratory techniques, and the achievement of high tolerances of process conditions with respect to device performance, material yield and throughput. All different techniques have to prove their suitability for further scaling up to areas of 0.4–0.8 m^2 with pilot plant capacities in the low-MW/a range. Fabrication costs for pilot production are expected to be 1–2 ECU/Wp. Environmental, health, safety and energetic aspects during raw material and module production and lifetime of the product have to be taken into consideration with respect to large volume manufacturing.

CdTe/CdS

STATUS

Intense research activities have led to substantial progress in the development of highly efficient CdTe/CdS cells. Different deposition methods with promising economy have been applied. As well as closed-space sublimation and chemical deposition methods, spraying, electro-deposition and sintering of screen-printed films have been applied successfully.[16] Laboratory cell efficiencies of 15.8% have been reported which prove the potential for economy, especially in view of the simple basic structure.

Present production is for consumer applications only. Future module costs for large-scale productions may be the same as expected for other thin-film technologies. Under these conditions competitiveness with conventional electrical power production can be achieved. Energy pay-back time is assessed to be of the order of one to two years.[17] CdTe/CdS modules operating under both external and internal accelerated tests show stable efficiencies.

ADVANTAGES AND DISADVANTAGES

The general advantages of CdTe are the ease of growth and the close to optimal bandgap (1.4 eV). Because of its beneficial growth properties and simple basic structure, different deposition methods with promising economy have been applied.

General disadvantages of CdTe and CdS are:

- Toxicity of Cd, Te and their chemical compounds used for preparation: once deposited in the semiconductor these elements can undergo reactions in connection with humidity and heat (fire). That is why toxic compounds could potentially contaminate the environment during fabrication, operation or recycling.
- Owing to the reactivity of these elements, the stability of such PV materials is a further problem.

Both toxicity and stability problems can be solved for normal operation by means of good encapsulation techniques that prevent humidity building up inside the solar cells. Apart from accidental fires, there is then no hazard in the operation.

- Limited availability of the compounds used: Te is one of the 85 rarest elements present in the earth's crust with an occurrence rate of less than 0.03%. On the other hand, the materials used are basically available in quantities necessary for PV production. However, the supply of Te has to be substantially increased if it is hoped that CdTe PV modules will cover even a small proportion of the current global consumption of electricity.

RESEARCH TOPICS

Although polycrystalline CdTe solar cells have demonstrated a high efficiency, a major difficulty has been obtaining a high enough p-type carrier density to lower bulk and contact resistances. Basic R&D efforts have to be undertaken to improve further the cell characteristics and to increase cell efficiencies. Most important are continued studies for improving p-type conduction of CdTe, leading to more stable I–V characteristics. This can be improved by an annealing process in oxygen. Diffusion of Cu into CdTe or annealing of CdS with hydrogen also reduces the series resistance.

Another concern related to this is the formation of low-resistance contacts to p-CdTe because of the large work function of this material and the difficulty of obtaining high p-type doping. Very good contacts have been obtained by diffusion of Li into CdTe, which significantly increases the hole density near the surface, or using contact materials like HgTe with a larger work function. Both methods still suffer from out-diffusion or grain-boundary diffusion of Li and Hg. Contacts to p-type CdTe remain problematic and require a relatively large technical effort.

The most important objective is to increase the module yields in large-scale module production, improving and simplifying the manufacturing processes and decreasing the production costs. The most important fabrication criteria are as follows: high material utilization rate, non-expensive equipment, low energy requirement, high specific throughput, high growth rates, good process control, wide growth window, low processing temperature, low vacuum.

Significant progress has been made using the rapid, large-area CSS (closed space sublimation) technique. Some criteria, such as the need for non-expensive equipment, low energy requirement and simple manufacturing techniques, are fulfilled by sintering techniques and spray pyrolysis, which still offer great potentials for technical improvement.

Environmental aspects of photovoltaic module manufacturing, especially for CdTe and CdS, demand a minimum of material use, high yields and safe handling, as well as recycling of wastes. CdTe–CdS modules have just failed the toxicity characteristic leaching procedure (CTLP) test. It is believed, however, that reduced material quantities in the deposition processes could overcome this problem. Concepts have to be developed for disposal and recycling of modules at the end of their lifetime.

New materials

The cost of conventional silicon solar cells justifies the search for materials that can be deposited in thin film formation on cheap substrates like glass. Potential candidates are:

- WS_2, WSe_2, $MoSe_2$
- Dyes on semiconductor particles as used in some photo-electrochemical cells
- Organic polymers or conjugated oligomers
- Naturally occurring chalcogenide compounds
- FeS_2 (pyrite)
- $FeSi_2$.

3.4.2 PV modules

More than 35% of the module cost is concerned with module-related technologies. Therefore major efforts are necessary to reach the cost goals aimed for.

First, efforts should concentrate on standardization, reliability and on some environmental issues in order to make PV-modules acceptable on the market as a mature product:

- Standardization: in order to avoid disappointment for users and to facilitate the financial planning of PV systems, a standard and realistic energy rating concept should be established.
- Reliability: in order to secure reliability, certification is important. It already exists for crystalline silicon and should be developed for amorphous silicon.
- Introduce reliability analysis for PV systems (see also Section 3.4.3).
- Environmental issues:
  - life-cycle assessment of material and energy flows should further identify the environmental risks of PV-modules, especially in the case of thin film modules;
  - the possibility of reprocessing recovered wafers from used or reject modules, aiming at important cost and energy savings, should be considered.

Some further improvements of the conventional module production process could still result in limited cost reductions:

- Cell selection: for systems using only one module, mismatch between modules is not a concern, and selection procedures are allowed to minimize cost per Wp instead of the variance between the cells. Study of the potential for cost reductions by optimizing cell selection procedures and production tolerance is needed.
- Cell interconnection: optimization of the use of bypass diodes is important for projects where partial shading cannot be avoided. Better automation is needed to reduce labour costs. A break-through would be possible if contacts for tabbing and stringing could be made on the same side of the wafer (point contact or equivalent).
- Cell encapsulation: a break-through is needed with respect to reduction of material costs and to production automation. A reduction in material cost would be more easily attainable with thin films than with crystalline silicon, because the substrate can be an integral part of the encapsulation. The potential for cost reduction by using encapsulation technologies that lead to higher module output (e.g. entech cover, the use of bifacial cells) needs to be investigated. For applications with a power of over 100 to 200 Wp, the availability of larger modules is important. Production of larger modules not only leads to reduction of production costs (lower material costs, less labour and more efficient production equipment) but also to a higher power per m^2. Also, larger modules might require specific, non-conventional encapsulation techniques to avoid stress failures (hardening of encapsulants by techniques other than temperature and pressure).

However, although the module technology has matured to the point where these issues have become important, innovative developments are still necessary in order to reach the required cost reductions.

Promising innovations that need more investigation are building specific PV modules, modules with integrated inverter, and innovative design of cells and interconnection schemes (e.g. avoiding the conventional tabbing by applying new cells to a predeposited metal pattern on glass or other materials).

BUILDING SPECIFIC MODULES

Further development in building specific modules, combining solar-module technology and roof-sealing techniques, should result in an architecturally, technically and economically satisfying product, meeting the following requirements:

- resistant to harsh weather conditions (e.g. the water resistance of frameless laminates should be investigated) and able to withstand decades of sunlight exposure;
- mechanically robust and durable;
- resulting in a watertight roof that does not require further sealing, and which avoids condensation at the back side of the module;
- easy to install, fitting into existing tiled roofs;
- easy to repair;
- having electrically reliable connectors;
- allowing aesthetic integration, preferable adaptable to different kinds of roof or walls;
- fulfilling building material safety codes.

Therefore testing and further optimization of existing concepts, such as PV tiles and PV walls, together with the development of new concepts, is necessary. Close collaboration between the building industry and architects is essential.

The potential for cost reduction by simplification of design, by the use of cheaper materials or by the use of mass-production techniques has to be assessed.

The economy associated with multifunctional integration and replacement of conventional building elements is an important consideration. Therefore, opportunities such as structural glazing, natural daylighting and combination with thermal applications should be adopted as much as possible.

MODULES WITH INTEGRATED INVERTER (AC MODULES)

By fully integrating a grid-connected inverter into the module, it becomes an independent grid-connected unit. This new approach has considerable cost-reduction potential (up to 20%[18]). R&D-efforts should focus on:

- improving the design of an AC-module inverter and developing a more cost-effective connection system suitable for large-scale applications in buildings;
- testing the performance of AC modules with special attention to thermal stress (due to the placement of the inverter at the back of the module), current harmonics and possible interaction;
- evaluating the cost-effectiveness of this new approach in comparison with the single-inverter approach.

Finally, future cell technologies (e.g. CIS) can be expected to open the way for new concepts for encapsulation, such as flexible modules. Further progress in these new cell technologies is required.

3.4.3 Concentrators

BACKGROUND

A different approach from the flat-plate module consists of the concentration of sunlight onto photovoltaic cells (Figure 3.7). Hereby, a potential for cost advantage can be obtained by the use of a small area of high-efficiency solar cells in combination with relatively low-cost concentration devices. Concentrators require direct sunlight, and therefore their potential applications are found in favourable climates. The efficiency of concentrator devices has often been rather good, but the cost of the early plants was too high, most probably because of the small market size; there were also several reliability issues.

Today there are several small firms in the USA that offer concentrators commercially, but the market for concentrators remains insignificant, so these must mainly be considered as R&D companies. Nevertheless, prototype concentrators, such as 'EUCLIDES', shown in Figure 3.7, can be further developed into commercially standard modules of typically 30 kW$_p$.

ADVANTAGES AND DISADVANTAGES

Advantages are:

- the potential for cost reduction;
- the compatibility with relatively expensive cells;
- good semiconductor material supply availability;
- the environmentally benign nature (less than one year energy pay-back time).

Figure 3.7. Prototype concentrator 'EUCLIDES'
(Instituto de Energia Solar, UPM Spain)

Disadvantages are:

* the relatively large size of the modular unit;
* the presence of moving elements that require some maintenance;
* the requirement for direct radiation limits the application to favourable climates;
* the higher cost of prototype development resulting from the larger unit size.

RESEARCH TOPICS
The research on concentrators is inherently linked to structural research, involving the following topics: structure, sun-tracking, cells, cell bonding, cooling, optics and housing.

Structure. Two important requirements are low cost, including installation costs in the field, and reduction to acceptable limits of the deformations under the various stresses caused by wind and gravity. Experience of the wide variety of structures is very limited and it is difficult to make a sound comparative analysis.

Passive trackers, based on differential heating of fluids by the sun and piston movements, are popular nowadays. Their accuracy should still be improved.

Cells. R&D concerning concentration cells must concentrate on high efficiency, even if relatively complex processing is required. Additional conditions for research on the one-sun cell are that the series resistance must be considerably reduced and the size of the cell for concentration use should be smaller than for flat panel, because of the specific series-resistance factor and the difficulty of collecting too much current from the cell.

Bonding and connecting. The bonding of concentration cells must be able to extract large currents, which implies the need for low series resistance, appropriate thermal expansion coefficient in relation to the semiconductor and good thermal contact with a heat sink.

Cooling. Cell cooling is also a crucial aspect of concentrating devices. Active and passive cooling have been used for this task. Passive cooling is by far the most attractive and in most cases it is sufficient.

Optics. The optical element most often used in PV concentration is the Fresnel lens, either point focus or linear. In the case of linear Fresnel lenses, arched Fresnel lenses are the most attractive. In most cases they are made of ultraviolet-hardened acrylic, and they have shown good performance so far (some have more than ten years of field experience). Techniques used are casting and compression. This first is designed to produce stress-free lenses that keep their shape better, while the second is designed to be cheaper.

Early research on concentrators, mainly in the USA, included investigation into the use of parabolic mirrors. These were discarded because of their poor performance. Yet the mirror has been widely and very satisfactorily used in solar thermal applications and seems to exhibit higher cost-reducing potential. At the moment the mirror option is receiving more attention again. The optical design is most crucial in static concentrators, where the use of anidolic (non-imaging) optics is mandatory.

Housing. The housing is an almost sealed box containing the lenses and the cells, used mainly for protection against dust. Dust may be deposited in the grooves of the Fresnel lenses and degrade their operation. Housing is one of the most expensive parts of the concentrating module (often more than the optics and the cells), so it deserves some thought. Apart from imaginative solutions not foreseen here, R&D here should be concerned with the manufacturing and assembling industrial procedures.

A different concept is that of static concentrators. These do not require sun tracking, and collect diffuse light fully or in part, thus being applicable to central European climates. They are small, of a size comparable to flat-plate modules. Static concentrators most probably require bifacial cells to be cost-competitive. Other options based on luminescent dyes are also objects of research.

3.4.4 PV system technology

Considerable cost reductions will be required for all system components in order to improve the competitiveness of PV systems. R&D efforts should aim at the enhancement of system reliability and at a reduction of cost of the overall PV system.

3.4.4.1 General requirements

An important challenge at the system level is the transfer of the modular character at the array level to the system level with a guaranteed reliability and at an acceptable cost. The quality of supply in decentralized PV applications should be comparable to that of a utility grid, implying high reliability, with simple routine operation and maintenance.

Requirements contributing to these goals are as given in the following sections.

RELIABILITY, MODULARITY AND STANDARDIZATION
It is very important to establish a technical framework to take full advantage of a comprehensive technology and in order to concentrate the R&D activities of as many companies and research institutes as possible.

This includes:

* compatible addressing of components from different manufacturers;
* standardization of monitoring and supervisory control through the use of standard protocols;
* standardization of interface connectors for multi-manufacturer appliances;
* simplified system structures with only parallel subsystems.

In order to deal with the diversity of applications in a cost-effective way, unit kit construction of plants is needed, in combination with computer-aided methods. By means of a modular systems technology, using a limited set of flexible insertable units, it should be possible to configure the most diverse supply systems, e.g. for stand-alone applications. In addition, with the use of contemporary microprocessor technology in combination with communication bus structures, the modularization of supervisory control can be eased.

GUARANTEED POWER
High reliability of the autonomous power supply is of extreme importance for commercial applications (e.g. telecommunications) and certain residential and public applica-

tions. One concept to increase the acceptance of PV-energy is to guarantee a certain reliability of supply. R&D efforts should be undertaken in the field of:

- system lay-out procedures;
- cheap and reliable monitoring techniques for online system error detection;
- maintenance and repair schemes.

TECHNICAL QUALITY
It should be stressed that there is still an open field for reaching an international understanding on quality issues for the balance of system components and the appropriate electrical appliances. R&D efforts should be undertaken in the field of:

- quality recommendations for components and systems and recommendations for repair and maintenance;
- methods for testing technical quality;
- dissemination of information on quality recommendations and testing methods.

ANALYSIS AND INTERPRETATION OF MONITORED PV-SYSTEM DATA
A number of PV systems of various sizes and for various applications have been monitored. A quantitative interpretation of the results is, however, still missing for most systems. Low system performance is not understood in many cases and so the potential for system optimization is not exhausted.

3.4.4.2 Power conditioning

As the main advantages of photovoltaic electricity generation are its scalability and applicability for very different applications, an important challenge for a power-conditioning technology will be to transfer these advantages to the system level.[19] Therefore, there is a tendency to use parallel, low-power inverters, corresponding to the modular construction of photovoltaic electricity generation itself. Also, more emphasis is put on self-commutated pulse inverters, just as is in conventional technologies. Most stand-alone applications require self-commutated inverters and this type of technology is also most suitable for all other applications, especially as it is becoming increasingly cost-effective, it leads to considerably reduced electromagnetic compliance problems, and it is most suitable for parallel operation.

The cost reduction, correlated with the increased production, can achieve savings similar to those for PV modules.

POWER ELECTRONICS
The main emphasis is on the reduction of material, i.e. miniaturization and the reduction of losses, which also means a reduction in cooling and thereby in casing size. In this respect, the following developments are still needed:

- reduction of passive elements for smoothing and filtering by use of high switching frequencies up to the MHz range;
- avoidance of 100 Hz fluctuations by use of three phase inverters;
- reduction of semiconductor switching losses by zero-voltage and zero-current switching;

- integration of power semiconductor and driver circuits;
- development of innovative circuit topologies, integrating both voltage set-up and conversion to alternating current.

SIGNAL PROCESSING
Here the emphasis should be put on:

- methods for robust pulse inverter parallel operation without external synchronization;
- supervisory control methods for operation in all sensible electrical system configurations;
- control methods for fast frequency and voltage support;
- a method for compensation of harmonics by pulse patterns;
- development of programmable microprocessor single chips;
- use of power-line modulated communication techniques.

The development of specific integrated circuits especially requires a considerable amount of pre-industrial work. However, in order to find successful solutions that can be incorporated by many manufacturers, industry will have to be involved in developments as early as possible.

3.4.4.3 Integration of systems

Integration of PV systems is defined as the adaptation of PV systems to, and their application within, a specific context. The adaptation has to take into account not only the specific requirements of PV technology itself, but also the requirements of the context in which PV integration is undertaken. In Europe, the main contexts for PV system integration are buildings and utility grids or other existing energy-supply structures.

The whole task of supplying power in a decentralized way using photovoltaics has to be considered in all phases from the development to installation, expansion, operation, maintenance, repair and recycling. Therefore, the following topics will be of importance in the future:

- supervisory control methods for operation in all sensible electrical system configurations;
- on-line concentration of distributed monitoring data;
- strategies for the organization of installation, expansion and combining of plant complexes, maintenance, repair and recycling.

Recommendations for further work on grid connected and stand-alone PV systems include the following.

GRID-CONNECTED SYSTEMS
Utility interconnection issues are an important aspect for these systems. To ensure wide acceptance of the systems, inverted-grid interface criteria and minimum output power quality must be standardized.

For residential grid-connected systems, the following requirements, additional to those associated with the development of building specific PV modules, have been identified:

- Integration of PV into the global residential energy supply: the global energetic benefits of solar components should be further exploited, using combinations of solar thermal collectors, passive solar energy and PV.
- Aesthetically pleasing appearance and acceptance by the public: a positive, but realistic, attitude should be promoted among occupants of solar houses. This can be achieved, for example, by providing clear information on yield, by timely repair of malfunctioning solar systems, etc.
- Design rules for architects: development of clear design rules, adapted to the specific needs of architects. In addition, technical information, details of cost and reliability of the system and suggestions relating to the demands of building code authorities should be made available.
- Simplifications of mechanical and electrical installations in buildings.
- Easily adaptable supervisory control methods.
- Combination with rational use of energy.
- Dynamic tariffs with information distribution.
- Normalization and certification in relation to islanding.

STAND-ALONE AND HYBRID SYSTEMS
For these systems R&D should focus on the storage and auxiliary energy requirements for autonomous PV systems.

To maintain the widespread use of these systems and to increase the demand for them, the battery lifetime must be increased. Furthermore, batteries often do not live up to the expectations of either the designer or the user. Steps to improve this situation include:

- establishment of adequate design specifications and procedures for operation and maintenance to allow long-term reliability;
- a concerted investigation to determine factors affecting the field operation of batteries;
- methods for active limitation of charge and discharge;
- redundant storage structures and having respect to dynamic problems;
- small rotating mass storage units with low losses.

Furthermore, R&D efforts should be undertaken in the fields of:

- alternatives to lead acid battery systems;
- auxiliary or complementary energy converters in autonomous PV systems, i.e. wind energy for autonomous operation, thermoelectric or thermophotovoltaic converters, very small diesel engines, etc.;
- development of advanced balance-of-system components with low energy consumption.

For many stand-alone applications, PV is already perfectly suited to providing certain energy services. R&D should be concentrated in the fields of PV lighting, PV cooling, PV water treatment (pumping, disinfection, wastewater treatment), PV telecommunication, PV information and signalling. It will be important to support families of small systems for different purposes with as many common properties as possible, in order to achieve the scale effect for PV applications. This will include:

- quality standards;

- operational plans involving authorities and financial institutions;
- integration with conventional planning methods;
- innovative organization of operation and maintenance.

3.4.4.4 PV systems for developing countries

In the context of a comprehensive PV promotion strategy, system deployment in developing countries (DCs) is an entirely distinct issue because of the particular local constraints and very specific application priorities. In the developing world, four aspects are particularly relevant:

- the climate;
- the specific familiarity of those involved with technical products in general;
- the relatively poor transport and communication infrastructure;
- the generally low financial liquidity of potential PV system purchasers, combined with the absence of appropriate financing schemes in most cases.

The widespread dissemination of PV systems in the developing world (Figure 3.8) still requires R&D, both at the PV system and at the PV integration level. PV integration in the developing world differs from integration in industrialized countries. In contrast to the latter and as a prerequisite for its success, the former very often demands the establishment of an infrastructure that is not uniquely related to PV, but whose existence is nevertheless necessary before PV technology can be introduced in a sustainable way. R&D is required to analyse the best ways to establish this infrastructure.

Figure 3.8. 1 kWp photovoltaic-powered water pump at Tioribougou, Mali (McNelis, IT Power)

PV SYSTEM LEVEL

R&D is required to assure that PV systems meet the following combination of criteria:

- Modularity and extendibility of stand-alone systems ranging from about 10 Wp to 1 kWp. Current experience in DCs reveals that the most important power range is 50 to 100 Wp.
- The possibility of using components that are not particularly suited for PV systems, but that are locally available (thus leading to a better total reliability of components and replacement procedures) and much cheaper than special PV components (thus allowing for a more widespread dissemination of PV technology).
- High reliability under tropical, semi-arid and arid climate. Robustness and ability to support mechanical shocks.
- Low price and simplicity. Operation must be easy and restricted to the very essential operation modes.
- The technology must be adapted and must allow for production and/or repair in DCs.

In addition R&D on reliable PV village-grid systems, which to date have only been successful in very few cases, is still necessary before these systems can be implemented on a large scale.

PV INTEGRATION LEVEL

Compared to activities in industrialized countries, R&D on PV integration in the developing world places less emphasis on technical issues. The focus is rather on the relationship between PV technology and those involved in related applications, as well as on the corresponding organizational and financial issues:

- The training of, and provision of information for, illiterate users or those only able to speak/read local languages, requires the possibility of exploring new media, such as videos, comics, etc. and developing the corresponding education tools.
- Manuals and other tools for training of skilled staff (e.g. maintenance and repair technicians) need to be adapted to the specific background and local culture of the people involved.
- Schemes for the organization of PV installation, maintenance and repair schemes, adapted to cope with local transport and communication infrastructures, need to be developed.
- Novel financing schemes adapted to the local micro-economic structure have to be developed.

3.5 STRATEGY

From the previous sections, it can be concluded that there is no doubt about the technical potential for making the use of photovoltaics economic in comparison with conventional electricity generation technologies.

The strategy for further development of photovoltaics should be based on the following actions.

AN INCREASED R&D EFFORT ON CELLS, MODULES AND SYSTEMS

These efforts should be developed with a good balance between medium- and long-term research. This effort should preferably be made in close cooperation with industry to lower the barriers for industrial implementation.

Priority should be given to the following activities:

- Further development of PV modules based on crystalline silicon. Because of its almost ideal properties and its industrial importance, crystalline silicon will remain the preferred PV material for the next decade. Moreover, recent analysis indicates that a module cost of 1 ECU/Wp is feasible if production occurs on a sufficiently large scale. The R&D efforts should focus on:
  - Closing the gap between laboratory and industrial cell efficiencies.
  - Reduction of fabrication costs by increasing throughput and manufacturing yield, by reducing consumption of energy and raw materials and by introducing more automation. In this respect the effort in PV-applied manufacturing science should be increased in order to prepare for future large-scale cost-effective production.
  - Further development of multicrystalline silicon, because of its larger potential for cost reduction.
  - Development of a reliable supply of appropriate polysilicon feedstock material, with a cost lower than 20 ECU/kg.
  - The improvement of cell assembly and module encapsulation techniques aiming at low costs. A specific R&D effort should be oriented towards the development of modules suitable for cost-effective integration into buildings.
- An action aiming at the installation of pilot plants of a few hundred kW/year for the production of CdTe- or CIS-based modules, with emphasis on:
  - demonstration of the potential to upscale laboratory results to the industrial level, meeting the imposed cost requirement;
  - the development of environmentally benign production techniques and, if necessary, of methodologies for module recycling;
  - the manufacturing of thin-film modules optimized for cost-effective integration into buildings.
- Although amorphous silicon solar cells are produced on an industrial scale, the efficiency of large-area cells is still too low for large power production. More fundamental R&D is needed on the stability of amorphous silicon and a-Si based alloys.
- R&D on polycrystalline Si thin film on cheap substrates.
- R&D and demonstration on concentration cells and systems both of Si and of GaAs.
- Long-term R&D on novel materials and cell concepts. Examples are porous Si, novel Si alloys, TiO_2 films sensitized by molecular antennae and other emerging materials.
- An increased and focused R&D effort on system components to increase the reliability and efficiency and to decrease costs. Power conditioning and low energy consumption by system components must receive more attention.
- Building integrated PV systems should have top priority, because of the high potential for Europe; the total installable building roof-top-mounted PV exceeds 600 GWp, which could generate yearly about 500 TWh.

A LARGER NUMBER OF WELL CHOSEN DEMONSTRATION ACTIONS

- Building integrated demonstration projects in all EU Member States should be continually encouraged.

- A closer link between R&D efforts and demonstration actions of the EU should be established.

MARKET DEVELOPMENT
- An active market development inside and outside Europe is essential to trigger increases in production volumes necessary for further cost reduction
- Therefore the following market stimulation measures should be considered:[4]
  - the price paid for electricity exported to the grid should be equal to the price of electricity purchased from the grid;
  - banks should be encouraged to accept PV as a part of the building mortgage package;
  - subsidy of the discount lending rate;
  - tax reduction;
  - PV imposition with building permits.
- Strategic considerations, taking into account the market and technological developments in the rest of the world, have as important a role to play in ensuring that the European PV community retains its competitive position in the future. Additional initiatives have to be taken at a European level in order to support PV integration in buildings.
- Since PV will often be the best energy source in developing countries, those countries also form an important market for European PV products and PV manufacturing technologies. Photovoltaics therefore has to be made a substantial part of the European aid programme for developing countries.

REMOVAL OF NON-TECHNICAL BARRIERS
The necessary efforts should be made to overcome non-technical barriers, such as a lack of an appropriate legal framework and economic regulations and the limited political motivation to support the required developments.

The monopoly of the electricity producers should be seriously questioned and different bodies should be responsible for the production and distribution of electricity.

3.6 REFERENCES

1 Palz W (1992). Energy Pay-Back Time of Photovoltaic Modules. In: H. Scheer et al. (ed.), Yearbook of Renewable Energies 1992. James & James (Science Publishers), London.
2 Hagedorn G (1989). Hidden Energy in Solar Cells and Photovoltaic Power Stations. ECPVSEC-9, p. 542. Kluwer Academic Publishers, Dordrecht, Netherlands.
3 Van Engdenburg B C W, Alsema E A (1993). Environmental Aspects and Risks of Amorphous Silicon Solar Cells. Report no. 93008, Department of Science, Technology and Society, University of Utrecht.
4 Imamura M, Helm P, Palz W (1992). Photovoltaic System Technology: European Handbook. H. S. Stephens & Associates, Bedford, UK, on behalf of the European Commission.
5 Schmidt J (1994). Photovoltaik Strom aus der Sonne, p. 129. J. Müller Verlag, Heidelberg.
6 Mertens R, Nijs J, Van Overstraeten R, Palz W (1992). Technical Goals and Financial Means for PV Development, Proceedings of EPVSEC-11. Harwood Academic Publishers, Switzerland.
7 FhG-ISE (1994). Book accompanying seminar 'Grundlagen und Systemtechnik solarer Energiesysteme'.
8 Wiezer F, Sunke W, Shone A J N, van der Weiden P C J (1994). Introduction of PV on private dwellings in the Netherlands, Proceedings of EPVSEC-12, p. 1142. H. S. Stephens & Associates, Bedford, UK.

9 Kiefer K, Hoffmann V, (1994). 1000 Dächer Mess- und Auswerteprogramm. FhG-ISE, Freiburg.
10 Kapur V K, Basol B M (1990). IEEEE PVSC -21, Kissimmee, pp. 467– 470. IEEE, New York.
11 DG-XVII-EPIA (1995), PV 2010 – Photolvoltaics in 2010. EC DG XVII – EPIA (European
   Photovoltaic Association). Study prepared under the ALTENER Programme.
12 Palz W, van Overstraeten R (1995). Strategic Options for PV Development in Europe, 13th
   European Photovoltaic Solar Energy Conference, Nice.
13 Siemens Solar (1993). IEEE PVSC -23, Louisville.
14 Mertens R (1994). Silicon Solar Cells, Proceedings EPVSEC-1994, p. 1. H. S. Stephens & Associates, Bedford, UK
15 Wrixon G et al. (1993). Renewable Energy 2000. Springer Verlag, Berlin and Heidelberg.
16 Zweibel K (1995). Thin films: Past, Present, Future. NREL report.
17 Reetz Th (1993). Prozesskettenanalyse zum CdTe-Solarmodul. Forschungszentrum Jülich,
   Bericht KfA-STE-1B-2/93, Jülich.
18 Dunselman C P M, van der Werden T C J, de Haan S W H, ter Herde F, van Zolingen R J C
   (1994). Ecofys Research and Consultancy. In de Haan S W H et al. (ed.), ECN, Feasibility and
   development of PV Modules with Integrated Inverter AC-modules. EPVSEC, p. 313. H. S.
   Stephens & Associates, Bedford, UK
19 Kleinkauf W, Hempel H, Sachau J (1992). Developments in Inverters for Photovoltaic Systems
   – Modular Power Conditioning and Plant Technology, EPVSEC, Montreux.

GLOSSARY

PV	Photovoltaic
Wp	Watt peak
IGBT	Insulated Gate Bipolar Transistor
PERL	Passivated Emitter Rear Locally Diffused
CVD	Chemical Vapour Deposition

4. SMALL HYDRO POWER

4.1 INTRODUCTION

Hydro power is the largest and most mature application of renewable energy, with some 630,000 MW of installed capacity currently producing over 20% of the world's electricity (some 2200 TWh/yr). Hydropower already contributes about 17% of EU electricity (avoiding thereby the emission of some 67 million tonnes of CO_2 annually)[1]. There is however still much room for further development as most assessments assume this is only around 10% of the total world viable hydro potential.

This paper is limited to *Small-Scale Hydro Power* (SHP), since large-scale hydro power is technically mature and its R&D requirements, which are mainly refinements by the specialist large companies active in this field, are generally being well taken care of. Indeed, the development of SHP has tended to be neglected perhaps partly because of the widely held but false impression gained from the maturity of large hydro, that there is not much scope for technical development and improvement of any hydro power systems. There is, however, considerable scope for improving the cost-effectiveness of SHP, especially with low head systems, both through technical and non-technical innovations.[2]

There is no general international consensus on the definition of SHP; the upper limit varies between 2.5 and 25 MW in different countries, but a value of 10 MW is becoming generally accepted and has been accepted by ESHA (The European Small Hydro Association).[3] This paper will therefore use the definition for SHP as any hydro systems under 10 MW. SHP can be further subdivided into mini hydro, usually defined as < 500 kW and micro hydro < 100 kW.

Small-scale Hydro Power (SHP) is mainly 'run of river' (i.e. not involving significant impounding of water and therefore not requiring the construction of large dams and reservoirs). Moreover, SHP mainly involves smaller manufacturers, generally SMEs. Few of the large companies producing large-scale systems are very active in manufacturing and marketing small systems, even though a few include small systems in their product range (usually simply scaled-down from their larger systems). Europe has a lead in this field and total employment in Europe in this field is estimated at 10,000 with a total turnover of 400 million ECU/year.[4]

SHP, whichever size definition is used, is one of the most environmentally benign forms of energy generation, based on the use of a non-polluting renewable resource, and requiring little interference with the surrounding environment. It also has the capacity to make a significant impact on the replacement of fossil fuel since, unlike many other sources of renewable energy, it can generally produce some electricity at any time on demand (i.e. it needs no storage or backup systems), at least at times of the year when an adequate flow of water is available, and in many cases at a competitive cost with fossil-fuel power stations. For example, a 5 MW SHP plant typically replaces annually 1400 tonnes of fossil fuel, and avoids the emission of 16,000 tonne of CO_2 and over 100 tonnes of SO_2, while supplying the electricity needs for over 5000 families.[5]

Moreover SHP has a huge, as yet untapped potential, which would allow it to make a significant contribution to future energy needs, and it depends largely on already proven and developed technology, although there is considerable scope for development and optimisation of the technology. Table 4.1 shows the estimated distribution by region of global SHP capacity in 1990, together with two projections of possible future SHP development, for 2000 and 2020, under alternative 'Business as Usual' and 'Accelerated Development' Scenarios (adapted from the World Energy Conference Committee study on Renewable Energy Resources[6]). Hydro is generally seen as the renewable source having one of the largest potentials for development in the next few decades. For example, to meet the ALTENER target of 8% of EU electricity from renewables by 2010 will involve hydro making much the largest contribution. The European Renewable Energy Study[7] envisages, for example, that hydro output for the EU 12 countries will grow from 165 to 185 TWh/yr (under the 'Existing Programmes' scenario) between 1990 and 2010; in the same period, the total electricity generated by renewable energy technologies will increase from 191 to 305 TWh/yr, i.e. hydro will move from contributing 86% to 60% of electrical energy generated by renewable energy technologies, which is still by any measure by far the largest contributor.

Table 4.1. Estimates of realizable small-hydro potential by region[6] for the present and for two future development scenarios (capacities given in MW)

Region	Present 1990	'Business as usual' 2000	'Business as usual' 2020	Accelerated development 2000	Accelerated development 2020
North America	4302	4861	6152	6829	12,906
Latin America	1113	1992	5751	2125	6557
Western Europe	7231	8822	12,587	11,478	21,692
E. Europe & the CIS	2296	2801	3997	3645	4197
Middle East / N. Africa	45	81	233	86	266
Sub-Saharan Africa	181	324	935	345	1065
Pacific	102	124	177	162	306
China	3890	6963	20,101	7428	22,915
Rest of Asia	343	614	1772	655	2021
Totals:	19,503	26,582	51,705	32,753	71,925

Unfortunately the development of SHP, both in Europe and elsewhere, has been handicapped by generally failing to receive similar support to that which has been given to other forms of renewable energy; possibly because:

- there is a common perception that the technology is mature and fully developed and that therefore it does not need any significant level of institutional encouragement support (i.e. market forces alone will be sufficient to take it forward); for this reason it is commonly excluded from programmes designed to assist other forms of renewable energy development. However, in reality, there still is potential for development and improvement of SHP.[1,4]
- economic analysis of hydropower projects generally gives no significant credit for the exceptionally long useful life and low running costs of SHP, while the high 'up-front' costs tend to make it seem financially unattractive unless low discount rates are available.[8]

- there are numerous other institutional barriers, mainly resulting from the difficulties inherent in gaining permission to abstract water from rivers in many countries, and also due to perceptions that hydro plant might adversely effect fishing, boating and other riverine leisure interests (although in practice well designed hydro systems can avoid causing any serious environmental impact on fish or anything else). Difficulties in gaining affordable connections to the grid are also common, although this situation is tending to improve.

With a new international climate of concern about global environmental dangers, SHP clearly deserves to be more strongly promoted and more widely and effectively developed, yet the progress so far seems disappointing to many who are involved in advancing its use.

4.2 PRESENT SITUATION

4.2.1 Basic principles

The main requirement for hydro power is to create an artificial head of water so that water can be diverted through a pipe (penstock) into a turbine from where it discharges, usually through a draft tube or diffuser back into the river at a lower level. Various types of turbine exist to cope with different levels of head and flow. There are two broad categories of turbines:

- impulse turbines (notably the Pelton), in which a jet of water impinges on the runner that is designed to reverse the direction of the jet and thereby extract momentum from the water;
- reaction turbines (notably Francis and Kaplan, Figure 4.1), which run full of water and in effect generate hydrodynamic 'lift' forces to propel the runner blades.

It is normal to achieve optimum energy conversion efficiencies in the range 60% to 90% with all types of hydro turbine. The larger the turbine, generally the higher its efficiency; hence good-quality designs of several hundred kW or greater tend to approach or even exceed 90% optimum efficiency. In contrast, a micro-hydro turbine of, say, 10 kW might have an efficiency in the order of 60% to 80%. Part-load efficiency varies considerably depending on turbine type; usually it is possible to achieve good efficiency over quite a broad power range, but to do so generally involves some cost and complexity.

Sizing of turbines depends on the flow characteristics of the river or stream to be used; generally the maximum flow rate of a European river in flood can be several orders of magnitude greater than the minimum flow rate. The energy capture depends on the sizing strategy; the larger the turbine at a given site the poorer its load factor (or capacity factor) as it will only run at rated power for a shorter period. A turbine sized to use the minimum flow only can have a load factor or capacity factor approaching 100%, but it obviously will extract less energy per annum than a larger turbine.

Resource assessment for hydro turbines has been developed to a high standard and can be based (preferably) on actual flow measurements or on computer-based analysis of rainfall, catchment area and run-off.

Biwater

Francis Turbine Generating Set

Net Head 98.3m
Design Flow 0.6m 3/s
Electrical Output 475kW
Manufactured March 1993

Biwater Hydro Power, Clay Lane, Warley,
Oldbury, West Midlands B69 4TF

*Figure 4.1. Francis Turbine Generating Set for a medium-head scheme in
Scotland (IT Power Ltd)*

4.2.2 Experiences to date

4.2.2.1 Background

Small hydro has been exploited for centuries. Many tens of thousands of small-scale hydro power systems (i.e. water mills) were in regular use by the 18th century, right across Asia and Europe, mostly for milling grain. These ranged from simple Norse wheels (25,000 of which are still in use in Nepal) to sophisticated waterwheels, fitted with speed-governing mechanisms even in the 18th century, and often capable of as much as 70% efficiency.

In the 1880s hydro turbines were first used to generate electricity for practical purposes, and in Europe the turbine took over from the waterwheel almost completely by the end of the century. Until the 1930s small turbines were increasingly used in Europe and North America and it was during this period that the basic turbine technology in use today was developed.

With the penetration of subsidized grid electricity into remote rural areas, there was a steady trend away from small hydro from the 1930s until the 1970s. Even rural areas without mains electricity generally found it cheaper and easier to install diesel generators than to bother with the complications of installing hydro-electric systems. It should be noted that although turbine technology has not changed much, the control systems in use for SHP systems until recently were costly, tended to be troublesome to maintain and often failed to keep the system functioning under as good control as is normally expected for running modern electrical appliances.

The first oil crisis of 1973 was a major catalyst in prompting developed and developing countries alike to look to their indigenous energy resources for electricity generation. Both grid electricity and oil-based fuels became increasingly expensive in most countries up until the mid 1980s. Governments continued to encourage the development of small hydro resources, and there was a revival of the industry, with a few new turbine manufacturers appearing. However, the fall in conventional fuel prices in real terms through the 1980s and into the 1990s and the subsequent 'dash for gas' has tended to cause a slow-down in the interest in developing hydro systems again.

Small hydro was initially seen as applicable only in rural areas far from the grid, but it is increasingly proving an attractive option for supplying electricity to the regional grid.

4.2.2.2 Present state of the art

Hydropower has been technically feasible for decades and given a favourable site it can be economically attractive (sometimes even offering the least-cost method of generating electricity). Least-cost hydro is generally high-head hydro since the higher the head, the less the flow of water required for a given power level, and so smaller and hence less costly equipment is needed. Therefore, in mountainous regions even quite small streams, if used at high heads, can yield significant power levels at attractively low costs. Norway, for example, produces some of the cheapest electricity in Europe from its numerous high-head hydro installations. However high-head sites tend to be in areas of low population density where the demand for electricity locally is relatively small, and long transmission distances to the main centres of population can often nullify the low-cost advantages at the hydro plant busbar. Easily engineered high-head sites are also relatively rare, with most of the best ones in Europe being already developed.

Low-head hydro sites are of course statistically much more common and they also tend to be found in or near concentrations of population where there is a demand for electricity, but unfortunately the economics of low-head sites tend to be less attractive. In fact, most low-head sites, at best, are marginally attractive economically compared with conventional fossil-fuel power generation (if no allowance is made for the external 'added costs' of using fossil fuels) and for this reason many such sites exist but have yet to be exploited.

Paradoxically, under modern conventions for financial and economic appraisal, a young hydro installation tends to appear to produce rather expensive electricity (since usually the high up-front capital costs are written off over only 20 or 30 years, yet such systems commonly last without major replacement costs for 50 years or more), whereas, in contrast, an older hydro site where the capital investment has been completely written off is usually extremely competitive economically, as the only costs relate to the low O&M costs (many SHP systems these days are operated under automatic control without human supervision). We therefore have situations, such as in the UK (see Figure 4.2), where new hydro projects find it difficult to attract government funding under the NFFO scheme because their unit energy costs are too high (typically in the order of 6 to 8 ECU cents/kWh) when calculated using the prevailing discount rates especially when amortized over only 15 to 20 years, while old hydro plants in the same country produce electricity at unit costs in the region of 1 to 2 ECU cents. In short, the institutional and financial framework existing in most countries does not favour the take up of new hydro plants,[4] even if old ones seem economically attractive.

4.2.2.3. Industry and employment

European manufacturers dominate the world market for SHP equipment. It is worth noting that of 150 small turbine contracts (greater than 1 MW) awarded in 1991–1992,

Figure 4.2. Benson Weir on the River Thames: typical of many low head hydro opportunities in Europe

throughout the world, only 21 were assigned to non-European firms.[3] Total employment from this sector in Europe has been estimated at 10,000 workplaces[10] and turnover at present is of the order of 400 million ECU.

4.2.2.4 Distribution of small hydro power within Europe

Table 4.2 indicates the approximate scale and distribution of SHP within the EU at this time.

Table 4.2. Developed small hydro in EU countries[11]

Country	No. of plants	Capacity (MW)
Austria	~1400	~430
Belgium	20	21
Denmark	60	11
Finland	235	~300
France	~1400	~1000
Germany	~4600	1380
Greece	10	41
Italy	369	285
Ireland	28	5
Luxembourg	7	1
Netherlands	7	36
Portugal	50	150
Spain	853	876
Sweden	~1200	~320
UK	70	20
Total	~10,309	~4876

4.3 REALISTIC GOALS FOR SHP DEVELOPMENT

4.3.1 Long-term goal (by 2005–2010)

SHP currently accounts for 1% of all electricity in the EU, i.e. approximately 15 TWh/yr.[9] This has been estimated as about 20% of the ultimate SHP economic potential in the EU,[4] making an extra 60 to 70 TWh/yr to be obtained from about 4000 MW of new SHP capacity by 2010 could be achieved given a more favourable regulatory environment.

4.3.2 Medium-term goal (by 2000–2005)

1000 to 2000 MW of new SHP capacity installed in the EU by 2005 (with a similar or greater capacity of exported European equipment)

4.3.3 Short-term goals (immediate)

There is some scope for coordination of efforts to develop more cost-effective low- and ultra-low-head SHP systems, but the main general needs are considered to be:[4]

- establishment of definitive data on existing installations and further potential as an aid to setting realistic targets for future developments;
- definitive evaluation of the real environmental impact of SHP compared with fossil fuelled and nuclear power plants;
- development of standard specification for design and installation 'packages' for export to developing countries;
- harmonization of equipment standards at the European and at the international level.

4.4 R&D ROADMAP

The main area where the take-up of SHP could be improved is non-technical, by improving the institutional and economic framework for SHP projects. There may also be scope for gradually obtaining a more favourable economic and institutional infrastructure to encourage the wider take-up of SHP, such as finding methods of finance and arrangements for electricity procurement more compatible with SHP and by streamlining and simplifying the procedures for gaining permission for water abstraction from European rivers, as well as improving procedures for the sale of electricity to the grids.

The main technical thrust for SHP development is to improve the cost-effectiveness of the technology for use on the more common low-head sites (high-head hydro technology is generally fairly well developed although the latest micro-hydro technology using electronic control systems remains rare in developing countries, where it could find its largest markets). Only by improving the cost-effectiveness can sites previously considered on the margin of being economic become attractive enough for widespread exploitation.

There are four main technical areas where research can assist the future dissemination of SHP technology, not only in Europe but worldwide, as indicated in the headings of the four sections which follow.[4,9]

4.4.1 Data collection on resource and on existing installations

Development of standardized methodologies for resource assessment and for evaluation of installations as an aid to setting more precise and realistic targets for future development.

4.4.2 Technical RD&D

To these ends, a number of approaches have been proposed in recent years and are beginning to be followed to good effect; in particular:

- **Standardization.** Cutting overheads by reducing the need for specially designing site-specific systems.
- **Use of existing civil works.** With low-head systems in particular, the civil works often represent the greatest cost, but many weirs already exist for flood-control purposes on most well developed European rivers. The majority of flood-control weirs do not have hydro generating equipment, yet a large proportion of these could have hydro systems added. Here the cost is reduced to just the marginal cost of fitting a hydro-electric system to an existing weir. It has been estimated that there is in the order of 3 GW of untapped but potentially economic SHP capacity of this kind on existing weirs in the EU.[9]
- **Use of variable speed turbines at low heads.** Recent developments in power electronics allow the possibility of turbines not needing to run at synchronous speed, so that the turbine can be constantly regulated to run at an optimum speed. This permits much simpler (and less costly) turbines (such as fixed-pitch propeller turbines) to be used without serious loss of efficiency compared with conventional single or double regulated Kaplan turbines normally used.
- **Use of induction generators.** These are less costly than conventional alternators, although their use involves some complications.
- **Use of electronic control and telemetry.** This permits unattended operation yet allows remote monitoring of the system to detect any incipient faults (e.g. potential bearing failures, vibration, cavitation, etc.).
- **Use of submersible turbo-generators.** These use similar technology to submersible electric pumps and have low maintenance requirements and can eliminate the need for a power house, or any direct supervision by an operator, thereby avoiding significant cost.
- **Use of new materials.** Plastics, new anti-corrosion materials, bearings and seals all offer possibilities for more cost-effective turbines, penstock pipes, etc.
- **Computer optimization of small systems.** This permits more accurate sizing aimed at optimizing the financial return from a site.
- **Inflatable weirs.** These provide an increasingly popular technique for raising and stabilizing the head on sites with otherwise very low heads, which can of course increase the power and energy capture *pro rata* with the percentage increase in head.·
- **Head enhancement.** Surplus flow of water can be used to create an extra suction at the draft tube on ultra-low-head hydro plants in order to artificially raise the effective head – this can lead to reduced efficiency but increased cost-effectiveness when sufficient surplus flow is available.

- **Innovative turbines.** Various novel types of turbine have been developed recently and work has been done on using mass-produced and hence inexpensive pumps as turbines.
- **Avoiding the use of cofferdams during installation.** Various system concepts and installation techniques can avoid or minimize the use of cofferdams, which are generally a particularly costly element of a hydro system installation.
- **Simplification and improvement of trashracks.** Trashracks and trash removal can in many cases represent a major cost element in an SHP plant; various innovations such as self-cleaning trashracks or self-flushing intakes are being developed to mitigate this problem area.
- **Improved techniques to avoid interference or damage to fish.** This is an important issue in many rivers, one of the most common objections to new hydro systems being that they may harm or interfere with fish. Novel forms of fish ladder and screening, as well as the use of acoustic devices, promise more cost-effective solutions to this difficulty.
- **Refurbishment of old sites.** This is one of the most promising and cost-effective ways to increase the European hydro generating capacity, as many thousands of old sites developed in the early part of the century have been abandoned (particularly in Eastern Europe) and many can be readily refurbished with modern equipment at marginal cost. For example, there are more than 3000 obsolete or abandoned hydro plants just in the eastern part of Germany (the former DDR).[9]

4.4.3 Development of standard specifications for design and installation packages and harmonization of engineering standards

One of the reasons for the high costs of present generation SHP systems is that each one tends to be a unique design exercise, even if reasonably standard components are used. There is much scope for developing standard installation packages to suit reasonably common siting situations so as to reduce the design overheads per site. There is also a need to improve the harmonization of SHP specifications, as there are at present numerous variations with which the technology may be presented or promoted and there is a major difficulty for potential users in evaluating the results they might expect when they seek to assess different options.

One of the most promising areas in the short term for an expansion of hydro capacity in Europe is through a combination of adding low-head hydro plant to existing weirs and flood-control structures and of rehabilitating old and abandoned hydro plants. There is scope for facilitating this by developing standard installation designs to fit the most common types of weir and obsolete plants, so that the design inputs involved in specifying such equipment are simplified and made more economic.

4.4.4 Evaluation of the real environmental effects

In common with other renewable energy technologies, there is a mixture of reality and mythology surrounding the perceptions of environmental impact from SHP systems. In many cases, even though this is an environmentally clean method of power generation, there are false perceptions often stemming from the adverse environmental effects widely publicized in connection with large hydro projects. There are also, of course, a number of genuine negative environmental factors that can result even from SHP, (for example, on issues such as noise, aeration, fish damage, trash collection and disposal and on residual river flow parallel to the hydroplant) and these can be made more or less severe depending on the installation design. It would be advantageous to explore these in detail to produce definitive and broadly acceptable conclusions of use for both designers and planners to assist in the future approval of SHP installations.

Development of standardized methodologies for resource assessment and for evaluation of installations should be used as an aid to setting realistic targets for future development.

4.5 STRATEGY

Small hydro offers one of the most practical and immediately realizable routes to expanding the use of renewable energy resources in Europe (and at the same time boosting European exports as a result of strengthening the technically advanced European small hydro manufacturing industry), yet it is handicapped more than most renewables by an unfavourable regulatory framework and generally limited official support for the technology. This is perhaps partly due to the fragmented nature of the industry and the involvement of mainly SME manufacturers with limited lobbying and self-promotional capacity compared with the activists in other renewable energy fields. Hence a prerequisite for the future expansion of this industry is a need to raise official awareness of the benefits of small hydro and to develop a more objective view of the true environmental impact of small hydro projects, and this needs to be an essential component of any strategy to develop the use of hydro power in Europe.

Other factors that relate to the aforementioned need to raise the public profile of small hydro concern the development of effective and realistic standards to meet the requirements of minimizing any environmental problems, while avoiding loading SHP developers with unfair or onerous cost burdens that can result from unnecessarily stringent conditions. Also, there is a need for the tariff rates on offer to SHP owners and developers for the purchase of electricity to reflect the low environmental impact and high potential load factors from SHP rather than to reflect those for large hydro or conventional fossil-fuel generation.

Hence the initial strategic requirement is for small hydro to feature more strongly in national and EU energy planning with a view to its stronger encouragement. The regulatory and financial framework for SHP needs to be considered and improved and where possible harmonized across the EU.

Lastly, contrary to popular mythology, the fact that hydro represents a long-established and mature technology does not mean there is no further room for technical development. A resurgence of SHP development in Europe needs to be backed by technical improvements designed to meet current and future requirements such as those suggested earlier, so SHP should feature as a valid area for R&D support in national and international programmes. Table 4.3 has been adapted from the recommendations of the expert group at the Madrid Conference for 'An Action Plan for Renewable Energy Sources in Europe'[4] and indicates the possible weighting of the roles of key participants in furthering the successful development of SHP in Europe. It shows that, while there is a continuing need for R&D, the main thrust needs to be in the areas of demonstration, dissemination and commercial development to ensure market penetration.

Table 4.3. Weighting scale for role of participants in development of small hydro in Europe (1 = low, 2 = medium, 3 = high) (adapted from reference 4)

Key participants	Research	Development	Demonstration	Dissemination	Market penetration
Research centres (public)	1	1	2	1	–
Industrial/ professional associations	–	–	–	3	3
Financiers	–	1	1 / 2	–	3
Utilities	2	2	3	3	3
Local authorities	–	–	2	2	2
Regional authorities	1	1	3	3	2
National authorities	3	3	2	2	2
EU institutions	1	1	3	3	–
Consumer associations	–	–	1/2	2	3
Civil society (NGOs, environmentalists, etc.)	–	–	1	3	2
Media	1	1	1	3	2
Manufacturers	2	2	3	3	3
Consultants	1	2	2/3	1	2
Installers / developers	–	–	–	2 / 3	3
Training /education centres	–	–	1/2	2/3	–

4.6 REFERENCES

1   Layman' s Guidebook on how to develop a Small Hydro Site (1994). European Small Hydro Association and Commission of the European Communities, DG XVII, Brussels.
2   Tung T T P, Bennett K J (IEA Small Hydro Task, Canada) (1995). Small Scale Hydro Activities of the IEA Hydropower Programme. Hydropower and Dams, September.
3   Babalis G A (General Secretary of ESHA) (1994). The Status of Small Hydropower in Europe. Hydropower and Dams, September.
4   An Action Plan for Renewable Energy Sources in Europe: Working Group Report on Small Hydro (1994). Madrid Conference, March.
5   According to studies by the Spanish Institute for Diversification and Conservation of Energy (IDAE) and quoted in Reference 3.
6   Strange D L P (Energy Mines and Resources Canada) (1992). Draft Small Hydro Chapter, World Energy Conference Committee on Renewable Energy Resources, Opportunities and Constraints, 1990-2020.
7   The European Renewable Energy Study (1994). ALTENER Programme, CEC DG XVII.
8   Rao K V, Gosschalk E M (1995). The Financial Case for Hydropower. International Water Power & Dam Construction, October.
9   IT-Power, Stroomlijn and Karlsruhe University (1995). Technical and Resource Assessment of Low Head Hydropower in Europe, JOULE Project JOU2-CT93-0415.
10 Energy in Europe: Annual Energy Review, Special Issue 1993. Commission of the European Communities, DG for Energy (DG XVII), Brussels, quoted in Reference 4.
11 Based on References 4 and 9, but with additions from various sources including personal communication from two hydro turbine manufacturers (1995).

GLOSSARY

SHP	Small-Scale Hydro Power
ESHA	European Small Hydro Association
SME	Small and Medium Size Enterprises
O&M	Operation and Maintenance
NFFO	Non Fossil Fuel Obligation

5. SOLAR THERMAL ENERGY FOR BUILDINGS

Heating, cooling, lighting and domestic hot-water systems

5.1 INTRODUCTION

Thermal energy for buildings in a wider sense (passive, active, lighting) is a very complex and important area. About one third of our final energy is used in this sector.

Beside the utilization of solar energy in active and passive systems, it is very important to save energy by using it rationally. In addition, the intelligent use of 'thermal' solar energy can reduce cooling loads and electricity (for example, for lighting and and solar thermal process heat, which replaces electric power for washing machines, etc.).

Today, solar gains through windows already reduce the energy demand for heating in central Europe by 5% and the use of daylight in office buildings reduces the demand for electric lighting and cooling. This potential can be improved dramatically.

Conventional solar thermal systems for domestic hot water, space heating and air conditioning may become much more important when the total energy demand of buildings is reduced by available technologies like opaque insulation and improved windows. Especially solar district heating systems will play an important role in minimizing the use of fossil energies, owing to their high potential of cost reduction.

Since the demand for heat will be of the same order as that for electric power in future houses, completely new energy concepts have to be developed. Newer cogeneration systems, e.g. fuel cells, storage systems and thermally driven heat pumps are foreseen as becoming interesting components of future houses and having the potential to change the total energy market.

5.2 PRESENT SITUATION – SOLAR ENERGY IN BUILDINGS

5.2.1 Active systems for low temperature heat

5.2.1.1 Domestic hot-water systems

Solar domestic hot-water systems (SDHWS) are technically mature and available practically everywhere in Europe. Considering the climate, solar irradiation, demand for hot water, suitability of buildings and the financial resources of inhabitants, the potential for the use of solar domestic hot-water systems in general is a large multiple of the number of systems actually in operation.

Analysis of statistical figures like collector area per head of population (e.g. Cyprus 0.5 m^2; Greece 0.13 m^2; Austria 0.06 m^2; Italy 0.006 m^2; Germany 0.005 m^2; EU average

0.009 m^2; values from 1992) shows that favourable climatic conditions have less influence on acceptance than socio-economic boundary conditions. The success in Cyprus is explained by the absence of any other local source of energy. As a consequence, loans for investment in solar systems are publicly subsidized. The factor of ten between the value for Austria on one hand and those for Italy and Germany on the other, is more difficult to understand. Apparently the background to the success of SDHWS in Austria is a mixture of:

- demand for SDHW by tourists in periods with 'good weather';
- fewer administrative and legal obstacles for the building industry;
- exceptionally strong private initiatives for the production of cheap components.

However, the market for SDHWS in central Europe is growing steadily.

The production of SDHWSs and their components has achieved a good level of quality throughout most of Europe. The tight market has eliminated dubious producers and suppliers. Lifetime expectancies are usually fulfilled. International standards have been implemented for the systematic testing of collectors, storage units and complete systems. Several test facilities offer tests according to these standards. However, the technical and economic success of a SDHWS depends less on the quality of the components than on exact dimensioning to meet the user's demand. For the usual requirement for hot water at about 50°C in family homes in central Europe, 1.5 m^2 flat-plate collector area per head and 80 litres of hot-water storage volume per head allow for a solar fraction of about 60% of the annual energy demand for hot water. Evacuated tube collectors are justified only if higher temperatures are demanded by the user (e.g. hot water for the kitchen in a restaurant). For larger buildings (e.g. hotels, hospitals, appartment blocks), the collector areas and storage volumes required per head are smaller, but good dimensioning needs detailed analysis of demand and local climatic conditions. The experience gained over more than two decades has shown that SDHWSs should be designed to be as simple as possible and not be oversized. The environmental benefit of a given volume of investment for renewable energy is larger:

- if many single houses are equipped with small systems yielding low solar fractions instead of a few homes equipped for a solar fraction close to one;
- if large buildings are equipped with central systems instead of several free-standing houses with individual systems.

Bottle-necks against market penetration are:

- In some regions, the image of SDHWS has been spoiled by dubious suppliers.
- Deficits in knowledge about SDHWS in the plumbing trade result in oversized systems and faulty installation.
- Integration of SDHWS into roofs or façades that already exist or are not designed for this purpose is difficult and expensive.
- There are no large enterprises for production and supply. Public funding schemes pay for installed equipment but not for avoided emissions.
- Prices for fossil fuels do not include external costs resulting from their use.

5.2.1.2 Heating systems for buildings

The initial market penetration of solar domestic hot water systems has led to considerable interest in extended systems for space heating.[1] An important stimulus was the development of low- and matched-flow systems with highly stratified storage tanks. This concept allows a simple system configuration, resulting in good energy performance and high reliability. Applied to low-energy houses, such solar heating systems allow a solar fraction of about 30–60% of the total thermal load (DHW and space heating), depending on the collector area and the climatic conditions, even with storage volumes limited to about 1–5 m^3 of water. These system sizes are sufficient to smooth out fluctuations over hours or over the daily cycle in the solar irradiance. However, higher solar fractions lead to considerably larger storage volumes, up to 50 m^3 or even more, and are appropriate only in a limited number of applications. The solar fraction depends on the temperature level in the building heat-distribution system. Therefore, good results can only be achieved with a total system concept that treats solar energy as a main energy input. Basically, a small solar fraction leads to a good annual system efficiency and less excess heat during the summer months. This leads to less thermal stress on the collectors under stagnation conditions and therefore to a longer system lifetime. As an alternative, the summer excess heat may be used for low-temperature thermal processes to generate electricity (e.g. Stirling engines).

Higher market penetration of solar space heating systems may be possible with:

- increased storage capacity (phase-change materials, chemical storage materials);
- improved solar collectors (absorber coatings, convection barriers, rear insulation, concentration).

The output from materials research can therefore be a significant input for use on a larger scale. In non-residential buildings with high air exchange rates, solar energy utilized by air collectors can reduce the heat demand. Collectors may profit from new absorber coatings, which allow ambient air to pass through the absorber without degrading it.

5.2.1.3 District heating systems

One of the most promising applications for large-scale use of solar heating is in connection with district heating systems. In a solar district heating system, a large collector array is connected to a district heating network that distributes the heat to the load. Three major types of solar district heating systems can be distinguished: central solar heating plants with seasonal storage (CSHPSS), central solar heating plants with diurnal storage (CSHPDS), and central solar heating plants without any storage (CSHPxS). Several hundred m^2 of collectors may be considered as a minimum size for a large-scale solar heating system and the upper limit today is above thousands of m^2. The heat load should correspond to at least 20–30 residential units. The collectors may be centrally located, e.g. as a collector field, which is often the case for very large installations, or on the building roofs.

District heating is a proven heating technology, mainly used in colder climates such as those in northern Europe. The main component of a district heating system is the heat distribution system, for which well established approaches exist. In traditional, large heat networks with cogeneration plants, the outlet temperature is between 90 and 120°C and the return temperature 60–80°C. For smaller loads and networks, e.g. group heating, low-temperature heat distribution approaches exist, in which the temperature levels are 60–70/ 35–50°C. These low-temperature networks can use simpler and cheaper piping constructions and are very suitable for solar heating. If directly connected to the district heating network, some 10–15% of the annual heat load could be supplied by a CSHPDS or CSHPxS system, whereas with CSHPSS, solar fractions up to 75–80% of the yearly demand would be possible.

Several district solar-heating plants have been constructed in northern and central Europe. The number of operational systems today is about one hundred. Most of the solar district heating systems have been constructed in Scandinavia and Denmark, but recently interest has grown also in Austria, Germany and Switzerland. For instance, within the German Solar THERMIE 2000 programme for promotion of solar heating, large-scale solar heating has been given a priority. Operating systems can be found in Austria, Denmark, Finland, Germany and Sweden.

The largest existing solar district heating plant is in Falkenberg, Sweden. The system comprises a collector area of 5500 m^2 and a 1100 m^3 insulated steel tank for diurnal storage. The solar heating system covers some 6% of the 20 GWh/a heat load. Recently planned demonstration plants include a 5600 m^2 roof-integrated system in Friedrichshafen, Germany with a 12,000 m^3 reservoir. This system could supply about 50% of the heat demand of 570 residential units. Interesting approaches in Austria include the combination of solar heating and biomass, e.g. at Deutsch Tschantschendorf, where 370 m^2 of roof-integrated solar collectors and a 2 MW biomass boiler provide heat for some 50 residential units within a small district heating network. In such systems, solar energy provides most of the summer heat demand and the biofuels cover the winter demand.

Thus, a renewable energy fraction of 100% may be obtained without seasonal heat storage. This combination also increases the efficiency of the biomass use, as the partial loads typical for summer can be avoided.

The solar yield from a solar district heating plant is often less than that of hot-water or swimming-pool systems, as the temperature levels are considerably higher. In northern and central Europe, 300–450 kWh/m^2 per year could be expected.

The cost per unit area of a solar district heating plant is typically much less than that for individual systems. The large solar systems can be integrated directly into existing infrastructures, so these systems can also use existing components, e.g. the heat distribution network. Savings and improved collector performances are obtained by the use of large collector modules or roof-integrated structures. In 1982, when the first major solar district heating systems emerged, the investment cost was in the range of 400–500 ECU/m^2. At present, the level is at about 200 ECU/m^2 when the system size exceeds 1000 m^2, which leads to 0.05–0.06 ECU cents/kWh. These costs are valid for systems without seasonal storage, which automatically have a lower solar fraction. Storage systems today are mainly at the experimental stage. Cost-effective solutions are the main focus for further development.

5.2.2 Cooling and air conditioning

Summer air conditioning of buildings (i.e. cooling, dehumidification) is very attractive for the application of active thermal solar energy systems,[2] since there is a high correlation between solar gains and cooling loads. Active cooling is very common in large buildings (office buildings, lecture rooms, hospitals) in southern and central Europe; in southern Europe, there is also an increasing demand for cooling in residential buildings.

The dominant technology for building air-conditioning systems is electrically powered compression.

Two main aims have motivated the search for alternative cooling techniques during the last ten years: the replacement of cooling systems involving ozone-depleting refrigerants (e.g. CFCs) and the demand for rational use of energy in order to save resources and to decrease CO_2 emissions. Both motivations led to intensified development of thermally driven cooling systems that can be operated with low-temperature heat sources, such as district heat, waste heat or heat from solar thermal collectors.

Thermally driven cooling techniques may be classified into four groups depending on the phase state of the sorbent (liquid or solid) and the type of cycle (open or closed). In the following, the current situation for these four classes is presented.

5.2.2.1 Closed cycle with liquid sorbent

This class includes the classical absorption-cooling machines employing a working pair, which is either water/lithium bromide or ammonia/water. Single-action machines are well developed and available in a power range from below 100 kW up to several MW; they exhibit efficiencies (COP = Coefficient of Performance) of typically 0.6–0.7 and require driving temperatures of 80°C or higher. Double-action machines, requiring higher driving temperatures (150°C), yield COP values of about 1.1–1.2, but they are presently available only for powers greater than 100 kW. Absorption-cooling machines are typically used for building air conditioning, in combination with cogeneration plants or district heat. Some demonstration projects of coupling with solar collector fields have been carried out. In general, evacuated tube collectors have to be employed to drive the cooling process.

5.2.2.2 Closed cycle with solid sorbent

So far, only one Japanese solid-sorption cooling machine is known to be commercially available. The machine has also been installed in some pilot projects in Germany, but no practical results have become available yet. Several research groups in Europe are investigating new materials and systems for thermally driven cooling based on solids; the main physical principles are reversible thermo-chemical reactions (e.g. ammonia/salt) and adsorption. Similar research focuses on metal–hydride systems.

In open-cycle sorption cooling, the process steps of absorption and desorption are separated in time. Desorption is achieved by solar energy when available. The sorbent is stored and available for absorption on request. Thus, open cycles can easily respond to time lags between the solar energy supply and the cooling demand. The cooling effect is achieved by using the sorbent to dry air, so the process is usually called 'desiccant cooling'. The air is then adiabatically (re-)humidified as the temperature falls. This pre-conditioned air may either be cooled further by other processes or be supplied directly to the building. As the drying of air is the essential process step in desiccant cooling, the application of this technology is limited to air conditioning for buildings.

5.2.2.3 Open cooling cycles with liquid sorbent

Sorbents for open-sorption cooling cycles are hygroscopic solutions of salts in water (e.g. $LiCl–H_2O$ or $CaCl_2–H_2O$). Within the desiccant cooling cycle, the sorbent periodically absorbs water vapour from humid air and desorbs (regenerates) by evaporating water. The apparatus for absorption requires large contact surfaces between the solution and the air. The heat of absorption has to be removed by air or water cooling (at temperatures near ambient level). Conventional adiabatic humidifiers are available for (re-)humidifying. The apparatus for desorption by evaporation of water requires a (solar) heat supply. This can be provided either by bringing (solar) heated air into good contact with the solution (e.g. by spraying) or by exposing the solution directly to solar irradiance in solar stills. For desorption, temperatures in the range from 50 to 100°C are sufficient. Therefore, conventional solar air collectors and advanced solar stills (e.g. those with an evaporating wick) are suitable for this purpose.

5.2.2.4 Open cycle with solid sorbent

This class of systems (in general referred to as desiccant cooling systems) was proposed in the literature many years ago. Recently, several manufacturers have started to produce building air-conditioning systems based on this principle. The technique is starting to penetrate the market. In Germany, several units are operating and yielding very promising results. Annual average COP values of these systems range between 0.8 and 1.0. Again, heat from cogeneration plants or district heat is utilized in these applications. Some projects to incorporate solar collectors into open-cycle solid-sorption cooling systems are in the starting phase. As in the case of liquid sorbents, this combination seems to be very attractive, since temperatures from 55°C on can be used to regenerate the sorptive materials.

For desiccant cooling cycles with liquid sorbents, R&D is required on:

*   components:
    *   absorber (materials, geometry, cooling by water or air);
    *   desorber (materials, geometry, heat supply by air from solar air collectors or by direct irradiance into solar stills);
*   process
    *   design of cycle and components for fluid transport;
    *   analysis of performance;
    *   test and demonstration.

5.2.3 Passive systems

5.2.3.1 Window technology

Windows and glazing in general play a significant role in buildings. These multi-purpose architectural elements have several important functions in the building envelope. The most obvious is the effect on visual and thermal comfort in the building, but also sound reduction, weather protection, security and aesthetic appearance are to be considered in the selection of a specific window.

There has been a considerable improvement during the last ten years in window technology. The technical state of the art is represented by glazings with U-values around 1.0 W/(m^{2}K). The lowest U-value (centre-of-glazing value) for a triple-glazed unit (xenon filling, two transparent heat-mirror coatings) is 0.4 W/(m^{2}K). The colour neutrality for these products is satisfactory. The light and solar transmittance is sufficiently high (around 60% for triple-glazed units).

The edge sealing is reliable and durable, but also forms a thermal bridge. Metal-based spacers are responsible for comparatively high thermal losses. New products with improved thermal performance are beginning to appear on the European market, but probably the required change in the production lines is impeding a broad market introduction.

A second weak component of a modern window is the frame. Frame technology, especially that of plastic and metal frames, has improved; frames with U-values around 1.5 $W/(m^2K)$ are offered on the market, closing the gap to the previously thermally superior wooden frames. However, the size of the profiles leads to 30% frame area for an average window, which seems excessively large. Integration of the window into the building is another weak point. Complete system solutions are required.

5.2.3.2 Transparent insulation materials

Insulation is used to reduce the heat losses, e.g. of a building wall. Three physical effects lead to heat losses: convection, radiation and conduction. The goal of using transparent insulation materials (TIM) is to reduce these effects as far as possible, but still use solar radiation as an energy source.

The TIM market is limited, both in size and choice. Four commercial products are on the market:

- Okalux plastic capillary structures made of polycarbonate and acrylic; U-values below 1.0 $W/(m^2K)$ accompanied by high total solar-energy transmittance are achieved for a typical material thickness of 100 mm; price roughly ECU 500 per m^3.
- Arel polycarbonate square-celled honeycombs; properties and price similar to the Okalux product; availability on the market questionable at present.
- Technotop polycarbonate square-celled honeycomb; nearly identical to the Arel product; no price information.
- BASF Basogel; granular Aerogel product; may be used as translucent filling, e.g. between two glass panes; Interpane glazing product commercially available; future availability questionable owing to low sales (reasons: marketing activities are nearly absent); U-value below 1.0 $W/(m^2K)$ for 20 mm; associated light transmittance low (40–50%); price around 1500 ECU per m^3.

In spite of the small current market, new developments are being undertaken, because the hypothetical market potential is huge:

- Schott glass tube modules are at a prototype stage; production and handling technology is being improved in a development project.
- Other manufacturers or institutions are undertaking steps to produce simpler and cheaper TIM on the basis of existing products or technology related to TIM.

5.2.3.3 Daylighting

Little is known today about the extent to which daylighting can actually reduce the energy reduction of buildings. Studies exist for specific cases in Europe. More general investigations have been carried out in the USA. However, they are not transferable to European conditions. A current EU project under the SAVE Programme aims to investigate these issues for the first time. It is recognized that technical daylighting solutions will contribute to energy savings only in combination with a daylight-responsive control system for daylight and artificial lighting.

Most practitioners today use CIE representations of the sky luminance distribution for prediction and planning purposes. These representations are, however, not always accurate. They perform well for clear and dark overcast skies, but do have their limitations for intermediate and bright overcast conditions. The Perez representation is a major step forward, but is not yet standardized.

From an architectural point of view, improved daylighting means improving the extremely unsatisfactory illuminance distribution throughout a room that is daylit by a side window only. In general, this means the addition of lighting apertures in other walls or the ceiling. Buildings thus will gain a less uniform appearance. Atria are frequently used to introduce daylight, not only from the outer façade but also from the building core. From an economic point of view, it might be argued that these architectural elements belong to the building structure, so that the passive daylighting measures are free.

Technical solutions aim to redirect the light incident on a side window so that it penetrates more deeply into the room. They usually require a window to be divided into viewing and lighting areas. Current technologies are based on specular reflection, total reflection and refraction. Typical examples are:

- lamella systems in a variety of forms
- prismatic systems
- holographic films
- transparent insulation materials
- heliostats.

Most of these systems are expensive.

There are several powerful computer tools available for accurate lighting calculation, visualization and prediction of the energy impact of daylighting measures. They have not yet been integrated into standard planning practice.

5.2.3.4 Passive cooling systems

In southern European countries, the cooling energy demand represents the largest energy requirement for HVAC (heating, ventilation, air-conditioning) systems in buildings. In the residential sector, the energy demand for cooling is around 30 kWh/m^2 year. In offices and commercial buildings, the cooling demand is much higher owing to internal heat gains and the solar energy gains through glazing.

Energy can be saved by any or all of:

- a reduction in the cooling loads by means of an appropriate design of the building;
- the use of alternative low-energy cooling systems based on environmental heat sinks;
- the improvement of the efficiency of conventional cooling systems;
- reduction of internal loads;
- use of evaporative cooling systems.

The benefits of passive cooling techniques as alternatives to conventional air conditioning are summarized as follows:

• environmental benefits: reduction of CO_2 caused by avoiding consumption of electricity and indirect environmental benefits associated with the reduction of CFCs;
• indoor environmental quality and occupant health;
• cost saving: saving in investment, maintenance and running costs;
• reduced strain on national grids by reducing the peak electricity demand.

During the last decade, research on passive cooling has received attention in the EU DG XII PASCOOL and other programmes.

This research had led to a much better understanding of the processes involved in the energy flows in buildings, and to the development of improved technologies, as well as an increase in the level of the energy demand and supply. During this period, new technologies have emerged, such as new glazing systems, PV technology and controlled ventilation systems. As an indirect result, our knowledge of the indoor environment has increased.

Progress on design and evaluation tools has been very rapid as a result of more precise knowledge of the physical properties of the materials and processes involved, new software tools and more powerful personal computers. As a result of these efforts, new cooling-oriented tools are being developed, e.g. updated versions of PASSPORT+.

5.3 REALISTIC GOALS

The final goal of all research and development on the utilization of solar thermal energy for buildings is to obtain materials, components and systems that are suited to use solar thermal energy at a cost per kWh which is comparable with fossil fuels.

Realistic goals for 2010–2020 in the different areas of application are summarized in the following.

5.3.1 Solar and energy-efficient building technologies

• Status: new materials for windows, daylighting and insulation and non-optimized systems are commercially available.
• Main challenge:
  – system improvement, reliability, large-scale production;
  – qualification of products (certification);
  – development of very accesible simulation tools for building engineers and architects.
• Realistic goals:
  – reduction of the energy demand for heating by 50% (about 17% of the final energy in the EU), average heating demand < 70 kWh/m^{2}a;
  – reduction or avoiding of cooling loads.

5.3.2 Domestic hot-water systems (DHWS) and active heating systems

- Status:
  - collector systems are on the market, high potential for new materials and components to improve efficiencies and reduce costs;
  - seasonal storage for large installations (district heating), lack of seasonal storage systems for single houses.
- Main challenge:
  - mass production of improved systems, integration of systems into the existing building stock;
  - overcoming the problem of mismatch between solar gains in summer and heating demand in winter by cheap seasonal storage, thermochemical storage systems and solar-assisted heat-pump concepts.
- Realistic goals:
  - solar ratio for heating 30%, solar ratio of 50% for domestic hot water.

5.3.3 Solar cooling, thermal storage and solar-assisted, thermally driven heat pumps

- Status:
  - first demonstration projects, large potential for new materials and systems, hybrid applications.
- Main challenge:
  - combination of passive and CFC-free cooling systems, development of new cycles (closed and open), combined cooling/heating systems (summer/winter);
  - development of chemical storage techniques (summer/winter).
- Realistic goals:
  - solar ratio for cooling > 50% in new buildings (southern and central Europe).

5.3.4 Low energy concepts

- Status:
  - first demonstration projects.
- Main challenge:
  - development and demonstration of integrated low-energy systems (cogeneration).
- Realistic goals:
  - houses with a low non-renewable energy demand for heating and cooling; new houses < 20 kWh/m^{2}a, existing stock < 50 kWh/m^{2}a.

5.4 DISCUSSION OF R&D PERSPECTIVES

5.4.1 Materials

5.4.1.1 Optical coatings
SELECTIVE COATINGS
Coating technology is a key to the use of solar energy, since it allows surfaces to be modified in order to optimize their optical properties for efficient reflection, absorption or

transmission of solar radiation. There are four main applications of coatings in solar thermal systems: absorbers, reflectors, low-emission (low-e) coatings on glazing and switchable coatings for window applications.

Solar absorber coatings used in active solar systems for photo-thermal solar energy conversion are mainly produced by electroplating, for example black chrome or black nickel coatings. Current and future research will focus on their substitution by coatings with better optical performance, produced with more environmentally acceptable technology like physical vapour deposition and sputtering. Another important aspect will be the application of novel absorber coatings in glazed or unglazed air-collector systems. Here, the major issues are the required durability and the aesthetic quality to ensure a higher acceptance by architects. High temperature applications for solar thermal power plants or thermophotovoltaic systems will be a smaller but important market in the future, which requires new solutions.

Reflecting devices are mainly needed as components of solar thermal power plants, booster mirrors or CPC mirrors for lower working temperatures. The biggest problem is still their long-term durability. Metal-coated polymer films exhibit the best performance-to-durability ratio. Aluminium mirrors could compete, if suitable anti-corrosion coatings, which do not impair the optical properties, were developed.

The biggest market for coatings on glass is the heat-reflecting 'low-e' layer to reduce energy losses. The silver-based sputtered coatings, the so-called 'soft coatings', exhibit excellent optical performance, but have stability problems which require a dry, inert climate in the window gap. This is not necessary for the hard coatings based on fluorine-doped tin oxide, which is deposited by pyrolysis during the float-glass production, but their optical performance cannot compete with that of the soft coatings. The production of pyrolitic coatings requires major efforts to meet environmental standards. Future research will concentrate on the optical limits of infrared reflectance versus visible or solar transmittance, including broadband anti-reflection layers. A big issue is the development of a low-e coating with sufficient temperature stability to withstand the tempering process for safety glass.

5.4.1.2 Switchable layers

The main goal of switchable layers is the reversible switching of transmission to control the radiation flux and thus to prevent overheating. The different systems can be distinguished by their switching mechanism. Thermotropic layers[3,4] change from a clear and directly transmitting state to a scattering state after reaching a certain temperature. The operating principle is as follows: at low temperatures, at least two materials with different indices of refraction are mixed in such a way that the material appears homogeneous to the incident light. At a certain temperature, which can be varied and defined by the chemical composition, the two phases separate into small domains and scattering centres are created. The direct transmittance of the system decreases dramatically and, if there are not too many absorbing components in the system, most of the light is reflected. Again, a thermotropic system has advantages and disadvantages. Important advantages are the low cost of the materials used and the simplicity of the system. On the other hand, the predetermined switching temperature may cause problems in the optimum use of the same system in winter and summer. Recently, results from different systems have been published and it is expected that the first large-area prototypes will come onto the market soon. In addition, long-term stability (mainly against ultraviolet) has to be examined very carefully. The transmittance of eletrochromic coatings is changed by applying an electrical voltage, driving ion currents in and out of the electrochromic layers. The need for transparent conducting layers (e.g. ITO) and ion-conducting layers still causes problems, but there are concerted efforts worldwide to overcome them. Electrochromic systems (EC) are among the most prominent candidates for large-area switchable films.[5] During the past year, first prototypes with an area of about 1 m^2 came onto the market. The characteristic data for such windows reveal that the maximum solar transmittance is 50–60%. This low transmittance is mainly due to the two low-resistance transparent electrodes, which are needed for homogeneous switching over the whole area, as well as some absorption in the ion conductor, the other two active layers and the glass panes. Therefore, these systems will mainly be interesting for switching visible light, but they are not optimal for solar-gain systems. In addition, the system alone has a poor U-value. For applications in a building, it has to be combined with an additional pane with an air gap and an additional low-e layer, which further decreases the total solar transmittance.

A novel approach is the catalytically switched device, which changes the transmittance by means of protons provided by the catalytic dissociation of hydrogen (usually as an additive of less than 1% to an inert gas circulating through the window). The colouration is reversed by adding oxygen. This device will be subject to further R&D in the near future.

These new principles should allow the construction of smart windows with a wide dynamic range in solar transmittance.

The next step is the direct combination of low-e coatings and switchable films, which is possible with both the thermotropic and the catalytic electrochromic systems. For the catalytic system, the conventional gap in a double-glazed window can be used as an insulating layer. A small variation in the gas mixture is sufficient for the switching process. Thus, the whole smart window with a low U-value and a high switching range needs only two glass or plastic sheets. If anti-reflection layers, which are under development, are added, a variable solar transmittance in the range between 80% and 10% is possible. First experimental results confirm these estimates. Similar experiments are being carried out on the thermotropic system. As a long-term goal, the application and combination of these different technologies could enable a breakthrough in the passive use of solar energy.

5.4.1.3 Heat transformation materials

In order to gain a realistic overview,[6–8] of the potential of thermally driven heat transformation concepts (heat pumps, cooling machines, thermochemical storage), extensive screening of sorption systems is necessary. In particular, many material combinations between solids and refrigerants have not yet been investigated. The main important physical processes in this context are:

- adsorption (e.g. by amorphous and crystalline highly porous silicates and carbons; refrigerants include water, ammonia and alcohols);
- thermochemical reactions (e.g. ammine salts and salt–hydrates);
- metal hydrides.

Each of these process types has particular advantages and disadvantages and a specific range of possible applications. Research on any of these processes must focus on the following main topics:

- measurement of thermodynamic equilibria of possible material systems (equilibrium states (e.g. isosteres) and enthalpies);
- development of mathematical formulae for the description of equilibria, based on theoretical and/or semi-empirical models;
- evaluation of favourable applications based on thermodynamic data;
- experimental investigation of kinetics (diffusion, heat and mass transfer, reaction velocity)
- evaluation of thermal, chemical and physical stability and reversibility of the processes.

An objective of major interest is the establishment of a database that contains the thermodynamic and physical data of investigated sorption systems and further important information such as environmental, toxicological and economic aspects.

5.4.2 Components

5.4.2.1 Light guiding and control units

In general, research should focus on components that promise a high market penetration. This means that they should be applicable in fenestration systems. In large areas of Europe, diffuse light makes up the major part of daylight. Taking into account that, even under overcast sky conditions, there is an outdoor illumination of 10,000 lux, while the indoor requirements are around 500 lux, it is worth while to investigate improved approaches for diffuse-light guiding, even at the cost of reducing the global efficiency. In order to reduce losses and avoid overheating, physical principles for highly efficient light deflection should be applied. Therefore, the following developments should be encouraged:

- The reflectance of transparent covers, solar receivers and emitters can be changed by modifying the surface of the components. In the case of transparent covers, periodic surface structures with a period smaller than the light wavelengths can enhance the transmittance of the cover and thereby reduce the losses. This is a broadband effect and is therefore useful for the solar spectrum. Nevertheless, for longer wavelengths the reflectance reduction is negligible. Thus, monolithic selective receivers and emitters become manufacturable. They are very interesting for high temperature applications.
- The fundamental feasibility of the innovative concepts proposed above has been demonstrated, but the technological approaches and the applicability of such components are not well known. Therefore, intensive research is needed on models of the spectral behaviour of micro-structured materials (effective medium theories, rigorous diffraction theory), the production technology of these structures in dielectrics (e.g. embossing) and metals (ion-etching, electro-forming) and characterization of the optical properties and the durability of such systems, depending on the applications.
- Current technologies for redirecting light deeper into rooms show a number of deficiencies: some are quite complicated and expensive, some are of limited performance, and in many cases the thermal properties cause new problems. R&D is necessary to understand:

- improved bi-directional transmission and reflection properties;
- glare prevention;
- optimization and control of the total energy transmission;
- replacement of specular reflection by total reflection as the operating principle;
- development of (mass) products for light deflection and glare control;
• Diffuse-light guiding components: Diffuse light is the primary natural light source in many parts of the world, including central and northern Europe. It is, however, more difficult to handle than direct light. Efforts should be undertaken to direct diffuse light from a large solid angle into a small solid angle (at the expense of total intensity). It could than be handled in a similar way to direct light.

5.4.2.2 Improved window systems

Improved and intelligent windows are an important component to minimize the energy consumption of houses. On the one hand, highly insulating windows with low U-values (high R-value) are necessary to reduce the heat transmission losses during the cold season, but, on the other hand, components with high solar transmittance are desirable for solar gains during the same season. In addition, overheating problems can occur during summer. These demands are conflicting, unless smart windows with variable characteristics are introduced. The combination of new technologies like anti-reflection layers, low-e coatings and switchable films may allow smart windows with a wide dynamic range in solar transmittance to be produced (Figure 5.1).

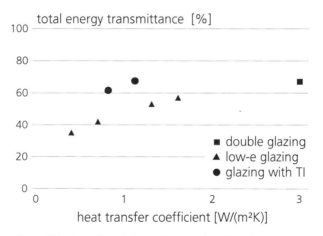

Figure 5.1. Optical and thermal properties of various type of glazing

The R&D strategy is to develop complete solutions, not only materials. A new product on the market shows the way. Combining glazing technology (transparent heat mirrors, gas fills and edge sealing) and TIM has led to a 50 mm thick argon- or krypton-filled TIM glazing by Okalux, with a U-value below 1.0 $W/(m^2K)$ combined with high solar-energy transmittance.

Better market acceptance requires:

- lower system complexity and system prices;
- better reliability and product homogeneity;
- effective shading or overheating protection techniques;
- improved handling on the building site.

5.4.2.3 Transparent wall insulation

R & D on transparent insulation materials has led to improved thermal and optical properties.[9] Therefore the materials available today are suitable for high-performance façade systems. The limited application to date is partly a result of the system costs and partly because steps are still needed to guarantee sufficient performance and lifetime of whole systems. Future work has to tackle the interaction of both topics:

- The main advantage of TI walls is the simple – while passive – working principle, allowing a long lifetime with little maintenance. Mechanical shading devices do not comply with these criteria. Therefore efforts are necessary to integrate switchable layers – already mentioned above – into the constructions. Special thermotropic glazings are suitable as passively switching front covers. A similar approach may be possible for a transparent plaster with thermotropic properties. Both measures strongly affect the construction of the TI façades as well as the system costs.
- Only the transparent part of the façade utilizes solar energy. Similarly to advanced glazings, the energy performance of the whole system can be improved significantly by reducing the frame area and improving its thermal properties.
- The installed façades realized have shown significant problems with condensation. New developments have to consider the hydrophobic properties of most TI materials to overcome these problems.
- Because most TI materials are made of plastics, sufficient fire protection must be ensured by the combination with other materials in the façade construction. Otherwise, the market of multi-storey buildings cannot be exploited.
- The R&D results on phase-change materials can contribute to TI walls with a better system performance.
- TI façades are new on the market. Therefore, information on long-term stability and energy performance is needed.
- Applying product life-cycle analysis, TI façades have to be optimized with respect to their embodied energy and their total environmental impact.

A high solar fraction in building heating with TI walls strongly depends on the energy concept of the total building. Design guidelines should be established to allow easy estination of the effect of a TI application on a building.

5.4.2.4 Heat transformation components

Based on the results of materials research programmes (Section 5.4.1), the development of components for thermally driven heat transformers adapted for a certain application has to follow. Two main components are of special interest in order to increase the potential use of solar thermal energy in buildings: thermally driven cooling machines that are adapted to the specific conditions of a combination with solar collectors and high-efficiency seasonal storage concepts with high energy densities.

The main developments on thermally driven (i.e. sorption) cooling machines should focus on the following objectives:

- development of small-scale cooling machines in the power range below 50 kW, which are well suited to the cooling requirements of typical commercial and office buildings with a high energy-saving standard. High values of the solar fraction are obtainable in this power range without the need for extremely large collector areas.
- development of cooling machines that may be driven by heat at temperatures down to about 60°C in order to allow operation with flat-plate collectors with acceptable overall efficiency.
- development of double-action machines that may be driven as single-action cycles with solar energy, but as double-action cycles with auxiliary heat (fossil fuels): this requirement is very important in order to yield significant primary energy savings.
- development of machines that can be used for cooling in summer and for heating in winter (thermally driven heat pump).

A main bottle-neck for a broad use of active solar energy for heating – the main energy load in buildings in central and northern Europe – is the lack of efficient seasonal storage techniques. The sorption technique is a possible solution to this problem, in particular for low-energy houses and in combination with low-temperature heating systems. In these storage systems, solar thermal energy is used for regeneration of the sorbent in summer. In the heating season, the solar collector serves as a low-temperature heat source for driving the evaporator in the sorption system. Research mainly has to focus on the choice of appropriate sorption materials, on the design of heat exchangers inside the storage unit, on the integration of domestic hot-water production into the concept and on the development of control strategies.

5.4.3 Systems

5.4.3.1 Collector and storage systems
SDHWS
A few R&D topics on SDHWS remain:

- Processes for mass production of collectors.
- Technology for prefabrication and installation of large-area collector units on roofs and façades (for façades applying experience from PASSYS).
- Simple and cheap measuring systems for the evaluation of emissions avoided by SDHWS (or kWh produced from the solar source).
- Schemes for integrating solar thermal energy into contracts for energy supply to buildings (contractor = investor, interested in optimal operation of the SDHWS).

Strategy for market penetration of SDHWS is concerned with following:
- Guaranted solar results.
- Public support and policy, required to correct prices for non-renewable energy.
- Payment for avoided emissions instead of subsidies for investments.
- Elimination of administrative and legal obstacles (building regulations, regulations on the distribution of energy cost in multiple-occupant buildings).
- Fulfilment of the R&D requirements listed above.

5.4.3.2 Heating

The R&D efforts in large-scale solar heating should support the following main objectives:

- to increase the contribution of solar heat;
- to improve the solar collector performance;
- to decrease the collector and storage costs.

For solar collectors, short- and medium-term R&D needs to include further improvements in solar collectors, systems, and materials technology to increase the output and to reduce the costs. The following research topics can be identified:

- improvement of collector h_0 through anti-reflective coatings and use of booster reflectors in collectors to increase the exploitable solar radiation;
- new lighter materials for collector covers;
- reduction of the collector heat-loss factor with new materials (e.g. TIM);
- development of roof-integration and prefabrication techniques;
- minimization of parasitic and system losses by system optimization;
- new system combinations for solar heat and other fuels.

These improvements represent a total cost reduction potential of 30–50%, which means a medium-term bottom-line cost of 0.03–0.04 ECU/kWh for large-scale solar heating.

There is important medium- and long-term R&D needed on energy storage technologies to enable higher solar fractions. Most of the research should be focused on improving both the technical and economic aspects of storage. Possible research topics include the following:

- improvement of liner materials for underground storage at higher temperatures (max. 100°C);
- development of systems to protect storage walls against humidity (surface water, vapour);
- search for materials with higher storage densities (e.g. thermochemical storage);
- testing of available insulation materials at different temperatures and pressures;
- search for low-cost storage designs and insulation materials;
- divalent storage systems (e.g. combined heat and cold storage in aquifers or gravel/water/ice pits with heat-exchanger coils);
- improved loading systems;
- improved insulation materials for above-ground storage;
- improved insulation materials for higher pressure (80–150 kN/m^2).

With these measures, improved approaches for thermal-energy storage in connection with district solar heating systems can be conceived. Consequently, the typical solar contribution of less than 15% in present systems could be increased to 75%. As the storage component always adds costs to the solar system, special attention should be given to economic aspects.

5.4.3.3 Passive cooling

Research in passive cooling should be aimed at developing techniques, tools and design guidelines to improve and promote passive cooling application in buildings.

Two of the most effective alternative passive-cooling technologies are based on improving the thermal insulation of the building envelope, and on the dissipation of the building's thermal load to a lower temperature heat sink.

To enable progress beyond the present state of the art, it is necessary to increase efforts along the following lines of development:

- thermal comfort and indoor air quality;
- interaction between building and environment;
- better knowledge of the effect of mass, ventilation, building shape, shading and micro-climate for free-floating and air-conditioned buildings;
- algorithms and tools to assess the cooling potential of natural cooling techniques;
- promotion of retrofitting with innovative passive cooling systems on case objects;
- development, improvement and performance evaluation of natural cooling systems.

5.4.3.4 Active cooling

Two types of thermally driven cooling technology are already available: cooling with absorption cooling machines and desiccant cooling systems employing solid sorbents. For both types, case studies and pilot and demonstration projects have to be carried out, in order to gain more experience in the combination with solar energy. The main objectives are:

- Development of optimized control strategies: air-conditioning systems in general exhibit high electricity demands for auxiliary components, in particular for ventilators. Control strategies have to consider all energy fluxes and should focus on minimization of the overall primary energy demand.
- Development of simulation tools for system design: solar-assisted air-conditioning systems represent a complex thermal network, consisting of the building (including occupant behaviour), the cooling system and the solar system (collector, thermal storage). System layout and comparison of different technologies require detailed computer models to obtain an accurate prognosis of overall system behaviour and energy needs.
- Reliable information on the system economy.

5.4.4 Simulation tools

Several dynamic building simulation tools with different features are available in Europe (e.g. ESP-r, TRNSYS) but some problems still have to be solved.

5.4.4.1 Standardization

- The input data for the design tools should be more standardized and be compliant to European and national standards. In particular, data for transparent components should be available with all their thermal and optical properties. These databases should be

provided by manufacturers and proof institutes and should be available via the Internet or World Wide Web.
- Dynamic simulations as a design tool should be accepted by EC/national standards bodies for the evaluation of building energy consumption.
- Integrated databases of materials, both for building-simulation tools and tools such as CAD for architects, should be available.
- Standardized weather data (test reference years for all EC members), based on the same principles of data selection and generation, should be available.

5.4.4.2 Research

- Building simulation tools should be used at an early stage of the design, when the architect is deciding on the geometry. Tools have to be developed that are quick and easy to use on the one hand, while, on the other hand, the same tool should be used for a detailed analysis of the building. The goal is to intensify the link between architects and engineers in the integrated planning process.
- Newly developed mass-flow simulation tools and computational fluid dynamics (CFD) should be verified by comparison with comprehensively monitored buildings. This is necessary because natural ventilation concepts become more and more important in passive-solar building concepts (see Sections 5.2.3.4 and 5.3.3).
- As a result of the enormous progress in the field of building control (domotic, EEC bus), these facilities should be used and applied even in the design phase. Therefore, building simulation tools should focus on the control of buildings, in order to simulate the interactions between user behaviour and climatic conditions more correctly.
- Sensitivity analysis of results is needed as a function of input to gain confidence intervals for the results. This should identify the critical points in the building design.

5.4.5 Implementation and education

Some of the main objectives of the energy planning policy in the European Union and in the Member States are to promote the efficient use of energy by exploitation of local energy resources, especially renewable energy sources, and to implement measures that improve energy efficiency.

Results from monitoring and feasibility studies carried out in the framework of several EU projects (PASSYS, Large-Scale Solar Heating) have shown that there is a major potential for energy saving in the European building sector.

During the last 20 years, a large number of basic research projects have been undertaken, many demonstration and monitoring studies have been carried out, and much information has been obtained. The knowledge and technology to achieve the targets of energy conservation and solar thermal applications are available, and they are being continuously updated and improved with new elements. It is important to promote the knowledge and information obtained and disseminate it to all interested persons.

Education and training in the more efficient and convincing processes encourages people to apply these technologies and to implement efficient policies for the related issues. Educational procedures should be addressed both to involved professionals and to students, to promote a more complete technical understanding and to make them aware of energy issues. To achieve this goal, continuing education and training of engineers, scientists, technicians and users should be ensured. To facilitate implementation of the basic principles, the main techniques and systems, the necessary resources – available information and tools – should be provided in a complete and simple form. An efficient, well formulated and updated educational infrastructure is essential for more productive exchange of knowledge on this subject.

Lack of education about the associated technologies and the available tools limits effective transfer of the knowledge and results obtained from research, development and demonstration. The rapid development of the technology and tools related to building science makes it extremely difficult to absorb, filter and translate the new approaches into educational material. This is one of the main reasons for the delay in passing on new technological achievements to professionals and also for the confusion in their application. For the successful execution of this task it is important to provide suitable educational and informative material – books, brochures, manuals, design tools, etc.

5.4.6 Advanced solar buildings

Buildings are generally among the longest-lasting products of the economy, if planned in the right way. The buildings planned today will reach an age when severe problems will occur with fossil energy resources, both from a climatic point of view and for sustainability reasons. Therefore advanced solar building concepts[10] must encompass both residential and non-residential buildings.

5.4.6.1 Residential buildings

- Integration of medium-scale (e.g. for multi-storey buildings) and large-scale active solar systems (solar district heating).
- Cost reduction for solar houses by prefabrication and improved integration of solar components in the HVAC system.

5.4.6.2 Non-residential buildings

- Solar-assisted ventilation systems for air heating.
- Solar-assisted cooling for climates with a high number of cooling degree-days (southern Europe).
- Advanced daylighting systems including intelligent control of artificial lighting.
- Smart windows.

Besides the development of materials and components, R&D is mainly concerned with integration of solar components into the building envelope and state-of-the-art HVAC systems (Figure 5.2).

5.5 STRATEGY

The thermal energy demand of buildings is the application area where the highest amount of fossil energy can be saved by rational use of energy, achieved by the combination of passive and active solar systems in intelligent systems. The house of the future will need much less thermal energy. The thermal and electricity demands will be of the same order of magnitude.

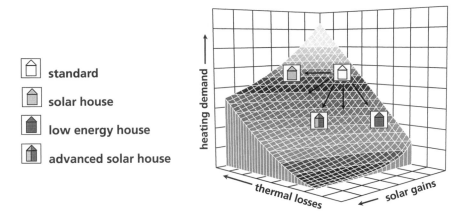

standard

solar house

low energy house

advanced solar house

Figure 5.2. Heating demand of a building as a function of the heating losses and the solar gains of the building envelope

For these low-energy buildings, totally new concepts for the energy supply are necessary (cogeneration, thermal storage).

The strategy for saving fossil fuels by rational use in combination with solar energy utilization should be based on the following activities.

5.5.1 Research, development and demonstration

- An increased R&D effort on new materials that are able to meet the demand for high quality, long-term stability and low cost.
- An increased R&D effort on systems and system integration into the building.
- Development of energy systems, where the required total energy is minimized.
- R&D on cogeneration and storage systems.
- R&D on solar cooling and air conditioning by closed and open absorption cycles.
- Demonstration of improved systems for the existing building stock:
  - in free-standing houses;
  - in high-density housing;
  - in villages.
- Demonstration of low-energy concepts for towns and cities.

5.5.2 Market development

- New regulations on the energy demand in houses can stimulate many activities that are close to financial viability (for example: low-e coated windows).
- Support of collector installation by governments. An annual market increase of 10–20% has already been achieved by such measures in Germany, Austria and Switzerland.
- Integration of large collector fields into district heating systems – the most economic way of using solar thermal energy – would stimulate a dramatic increase in collector production.

5.5.3 Overcoming non-technical barriers

* Development of an appropriate legal framework and economic regulations.
* Increased political motivation to support the required developments.
* Adequate representation in courses at universities and technical colleges and improved information for architects and engineers.
* Royalties for architects and engineers which reward the planning of energy efficient buildings.

5.6 REFERENCES

1 Fink C, Streicher W, Schnedell K, Weiss W (1994). Zwischenbericht zum Projekt Teilsolare Raumheizung, Gleisdorf.
2 Sayigh A A, McVeigh J C (ed.) (1992). Solar Air Conditioning and Refrigeration, Pergamon Press, Oxford.
3 Chahroudi D (1974). Transparent thermal insulation system, US patent 3 953 110; filed 1974.
4 Wilson H R, Raicu A, Nitz P, Ferber J (1995). Thermotropic Glazing, Proceedings of Window Innovations Conference, Toronto, Canada.
5 Wittwer V, Granquist C G, Lampert C (ed.) (1995). Proceedings of Optical Materials Technology for Energy Efficiency and Solar Conversion XIII, Freiburg, International Society for Optical Engineering, Vol. 2255.
6 Meunier F (1992). Solid Sorption: An alternative to CFCs. Proceedings of the Symposium on Solid Sorption Refrigeration, Paris, pp. 44–52.
7 Sorption Solar Cooling (1994). Renewable Energy, Vol 5, Part I.
8 Critoph R E (1988). Performance Limitations of Adsorption Cycles for Solar Cooling. Solar Energy, 41, No 1, 21–31.
9 Braun P, Goetzberger A, Schmid J, Stahl W (1992). Transparent Insulation of Building Facades - Steps from Research to Commercial Applications. Solar Energy, 49, No. 5, 413.
10 Luther J, Voss K, Wittwer V (1996). Solar Technologies for Future Buildings, 4th European Conference on Architects and Urban Planning, Berlin.

FURTHER READING

Achard P, Gicquel R (1986). European Passive Solar Handbook. Commission of the European Communities, EUR 10.683.
Antinucci M et al. (1992). Passive and Hybrid Cooling of Buildings – State of the Art. International Journal of Solar Energy, 11, 251–271.
Henning H-M, Erpenbeck T (ed.) (1996). Solar unterstützte Klimatisierung von Gebäuden mit Niedertemperaturverfahren, Forschungsverbund Sonnenenergie Köln.
International Symposium on Passive Cooling of Buildings, Athens, Greece, 19–20 June 1995.
Kangas M T, Lund P D (ed.) (1994). Thermal Energy Storage – Better Economy, Environment, Technology. Proceedings Calorstock 1994, Espoo, Finland.
Santamouris M, Wouters P (1994). Energy and Indoor Climate in Europe – Past and Present. European Conference on Energy Performance and Indoor Climate in Buildings, Lyon, France.

GLOSSARY

COP	Coefficient of Performance
CSHPDS	Central Solar Heating Plant with Diurnal Storage
CSHPSS	Central Heating Plant with Seasonal storage
CSHPxS	Central Solar Heating Plant without storage
HVAC	Heating, ventilation, air conditioning
ITO	Indium Tin Oxide
SDHWS	Solar Domestic Hot-Water System
TIM	Transparent Insulation Material

6. SOLAR THERMAL POWER STATIONS

6.1 INTRODUCTION

Solar energy has a high exergetic value since it originates from processes occurring at the sun's surface at an equivalent temperature of 5777 K. The irradiation of energy into the sphere around the sun amounts, at the location of the earth (not accounting for atmospheric attenuations), to a rarefaction $f = E/E_{sun} = 2.165 \times 10^{-5}$ or to the so-called solar constant of 1.37 kW/m^2. To improve this situation by technical means, solar thermal technologies use concentration devices, the more efficient ones moving the exergy closer to the original value. Line-focusing parabolic-trough facilities with concentrations of about 50 suns can produce temperatures ranging up to 400°C. With point-focusing facilities (central receiver/tower or parabolic dish) and concentrations of the order of 1000 suns, temperatures from 300 to 1500°C can be achieved.

Of all renewable technologies available for large-scale power production today and in the next few decades, besides wind applications, only solar thermal concepts are able to contribute a considerable share of clean energy delivery. However, it is amazing how unknown the present-day potential of solar thermal electricity generation is, even within communities concerned with renewable energy.

Solar thermal technology complies with some of the prime objectives of EU Research Technology Department programmes because:

- its development will enhance the implementation of solar thermal power plants, thus protecting the environment and reducing the impact of the provision and use of energy, in particular the emissions of CO_2;
- it will reduce the electricity generation cost of solar thermal plants, and thus contribute to ensuring durable and reliable energy services at affordable cost;
- it will provide European industry with a better technological basis, thus opening possibilities, not only to the internal market of southern European countries, but also to the export of equipment and services in the field of solar thermal power plants.

This paper deals with three areas of solar thermal technology:
- Parabolic-trough technology
- Central receiver or tower systems
- Small stand-alone or grouping for medium- to large-size grid connected parabolic dishes.

6.2 PRESENT SITUATION

6.2.1 An overview of solar thermal concentrating systems

All solar thermal systems for electricity generation use the concentration of sunlight to attain the required temperature levels needed for the operation of a thermodynamic cycle. The three main concepts of solar energy concentration originate from the ideal design to collect uniform radiation, the parabolic dish (Figure 6.1(c)). Consequently the highest concentrations are available from such tools. However, the modular unit size is limited to diameters of 10 to 20 m because of the aberration effect due to deviations from the ideal shape and because of constructional reasons. This implies that a power station with parabolic dishes would consist of many electricity delivering units, each, say, 25 kW_e (12 m diameter). Because of the high concentration, temperatures above 1000°C can be realized. An significant gradient of cost reduction with size (25 kW_e × 1000 units = 25 MW_e) cannot be expected, except in terms of using the same infrastructure, facilities and personnel. Otherwise, the modularity of the concept makes it ideal for small, stand-alone applications.

The paraboloidal idea modified towards more large-scale utilization is the central receiver concept (Figure 6.1(b)). It uses in essence parts of different paraboloids, represented by the so-called heliostats. The various rows of heliostats around the centrally located tower, which holds the energy receiver, belong, because of their different focal lengths, to various virtual paraboloidals. The advantage of this concept of collecting solar energy in the original radiative phase is clear and enables the formation of units up to 200 MW_e. The limit is determined by the efficiency of the most distant heliostats in transferring solar radiation to the top of the tower. Concentration can be performed from a few hundreds to about one thousand suns, which covers the temperature range from 300 up to 1000°C.

The parabolic trough concept (Figure 6.1(a)) represents the highest degree of concentration simplification. Only in cross section is the ideal form of curvature maintained, and extends linearly like a trough. This results in a line-focusing with a lower concentration capacity and a temperature range from 200 to 400°C. This concept has a high modular potential for collecting energy in many long, parallel rows and a gradient of cost reduction in adding rows. As a result of the modular build-up and the simplicity of this concept, this was the basis of the first successful solar thermal power-plant realization. In California, a total of 354 MW_e is fed into the grid; the unit sizes start at 15 MW_e and go up through 30 MW_e to 80 MW_e, while a reasonable size limit might be 200 MW_e.

6.2.2 Status of the technology

6.2.2.1 *Parabolic troughs*

The concept of parabolic troughs has been the only solar thermal technology in the world commercially available for electricity production. The SEGS plants in California, using this technology represent with their 354 MWe peak power supplied to the grid, more than the 80% of all solar electricity generated. The approximately 2.5 × 10^6 m^2 of current parabolic trough collector technology, using oil as heat transfer fluid (HTF), has fed over 4000 GWh of electricity into the Californian grid since 1985 (Figures 6.2 and 6.3).

SEGS plants have used the technology developed by the company LUZ International since 1984 and are a good demonstration of a continuous reduction of costs together with an increase in efficiency at the same time. The most important changes have been the increase in the aperture width of the collector from less than 3 m to almost 6 m, the structure concept, the high-temperature selective coating on the absorber of the vacuum receiver and, especially as a result of optical and thermal improvements, the increase in the operating temperature, so as to be able to feed a more efficient turbine directly without a back-up system in series. Unfortunately, these efforts were not enough to withstand the reductions in conventional fuel costs and the decreases in tax subsidies. Thus the company collapsed. However, the technology is still available. Its use has been documented throughout the continuous and reliable operation of the nine plants in California, during

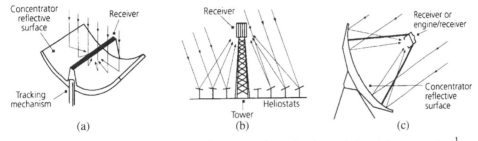

Figure 6.1. *The three main concepts of concentrating solar thermal electricity generation.*[1]
(a) Parabolic trough (Line focusing C = 30 to 80; Unit 30 to 80 MW; trough curvature in one direction); (b) Central receiver (Point-area focusing C = 200 to 1000; Unit 30 to 200 MW; elements of different paraboloids with various focal lengths); (c) Parabolic dish (Point focusing C = 1000 to 4000; Unit 7.5 to 25 kW; Ideal parabolic shape limited by aberration)

Figure 6.2. *LS3 parabolic trough with 5.8 m aperture and 100 m length*

Figure 6.3. Parabolic trough plant (5 × 30 MW$_e$) at Kramer Junction, USA

which time there have been major improvement programmes for collector design and the
O&M procedures, carried out in collaboration between the Kramer Junction Operating
Company and US Sandia National Laboratories. In addition, key component manufacturing companies in the field of solar energy have made advances; for example SOLEL in
Israel has improved the absorber tubes and Pilkington (formerly FLAGSOL), the German
reflector producer, has developed the process know-how and system integration, as well
as initiating new project developments in the sun belt.

It is important to note that the SEGS plants, by Californian law, are obliged to supply
at least 75% of the thermal energy fed to the turbine by solar collectors and up to 25% by
fossil firing. Their operational strategy is that of a peak power plant. Tariff structure and
fiscal subsidies are the main elements in understanding how solar plants produce electricity economically: SEGS plants receive 55% of their income in summertime, when they
capture 16% of annually available solar energy to be sold at peak hours.

Figure 6.4 shows the reduction path of the solar-only levelized electricity cost (dividing the power block investment and the O&M cost proportionally to the number of full
load-hours with conventional fuel) since the implementation of the first solar thermal
plants with parabolic troughs (Acurex and MAN, at the PSA). The achievements of LUZ
(SEGS Plants) are also depicted in this figure. The most promising alternative of a solar
thermal plant with thermal oil technology, as remarked in the Assessment Study, recently
financed by ENDESA and the EU (DG-I), is a combination of the solar field with a
combined cycle power block (Integrated Solar Combined Cycle System, ISCCS). The 80
MW$_e$ SEGS-like plant, solar-only mode, in Morocco is also shown in the graph. Although
the advantage of the ISCCS Plant is clearly shown in Figure 6.4, it is still a little outside
the competitiveness range of gas-fired fossil plants. On the other hand, the expected levelized electricity costs of next-generation plants with improved parabolic-trough collectors and direct steam generation (DSG) may be located within the competitiveness range
defined by the International Energy Agency (IEA) projections concerning the cost
increase of conventional plants running with natural gas (data from the IEA has been used
in producing Figure 6.4).

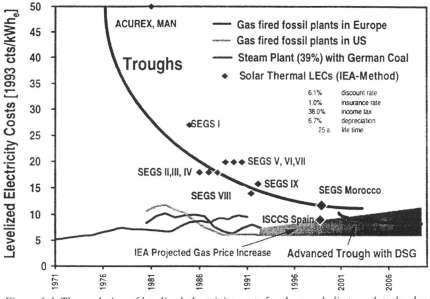

Figure 6.4. The evolution of levelized electricity costs for the parabolic trough technology
(Source: M. Geyer)

6.2.2.2 Central receivers

The central-receiver or tower concept has been proven to be technically feasible in different projects, using steam, air, sodium and molten salts as heat transfer media in the thermal cycle and different techniques for the heliostats, over 15 years of experimental evaluation on the Plataforma Solar de Almería. At Barstow, CA a 10 MW$_e$ pilot plant (Solar One – Figure 6.5) operated with steam until 1988 and is presently under modification to be operated with molten salt (Solar Two). In parallel, European activities have related to the utilization of air as transfer fluid, with heat transfer into tubes substituted by direct radiation into a porous, air-containing volume (Germany), and of molten salts as the transfer fluid (Spain). Furthermore, activities at the Plataforma Solar de Almería have included specific programmes aimed at making heliostats and their control more economic. There have also been experiments on new receiver concepts and large-scale technical feasibility investigations (e.g. project PHOEBUS, Technology Program Solar Air Receiver TSA – Figure 6.6 – and project SOLGAS, which uses a well proven saturated-steam receiver with vertically located tubes for cogeneration/combined cycle applications) and these, without doubt, will stimulate the development of future generations of solar thermal power plants. The situation is such that Europe is leading this technology, especially regarding receivers, heliostats and field controls.

For the heliostats, which are the most expensive item, Figure 6.7 shows the trend of the central-receiver technology, decreasing from the order of US $1000 to $100 per square meter of reflective surface.

Figure 6.5. Solar One 10 MW_e tower plant at Barstow, USA, operating up to 1988 as Steam plant, from 1996 on as molten salt/steam plant

Figure 6.6. PHOEBUS Technology volumetric air receiver test (2.5 MW_e element) at the Plataforma Solar de Almería, Spain, 1994

6.2.2.3 Parabolic dishes

The parabolic dish concept, if used for large-scale power production, needs a combination of units either in the thermal phase, connecting the receiver-heated media to a central heat exchanger, or in the electrical phase, connecting each receiver separately to an engine and a generator. The development in both Europe and the USA, with the exception of the 400 m^2

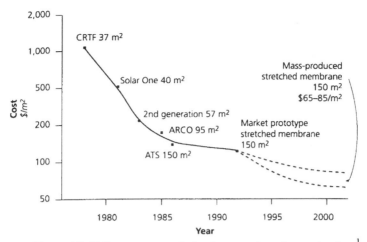

Figure 6.7. Heliostat cost trends for the central receiver technology[1]

Australian dish concept, exclusively turned to small and autonomous operations with coupled receiver/Stirling or receiver/turbine engines. Activities undertaken to date and those in progress (Brayton cycle, heat-pipe receiver, Stirling motor, MHD at the focal point, etc.) have enabled record yields to be achieved (30% maximum efficiency, giving 25 kWe). As no cooling water is needed to operate the system, it is especially suitable for applications in arid regions. The possibility of hybridization with a gas burner expands the range of utilization, increases the capacity factor, lowers the specific investment cost and guarantees the energy supply to the consumer, even in cloudy periods.

Through a programme sponsored by the US Department of Energy (DOE), Cummins Power Generation (CPG) and Sandia National Laboratories have recently entered into a joint venture to develop and commercialize economically competitive dish–Stirling systems for remote power applications. CPG plans to develop and test 5 kW$_e$ systems that could be used for water pumping and village electrification, or be connected to an existing utility grid. In Europe, Schlaich, Bergermann und Partner (SBP) has developed a successful 7.5 m diameter design. Three of these units have since 1992 been under steady operation conditions at the Almería facilities, displaying excellent performance (Figure 6.8). Figure 6.9 shows the cost trends for the dishes and these also show a decrease to about US $100 per square meter of reflective area.

6.2.3 Performances and efficiencies

From the start of the Plataforma Solar de Almería, when parabolic-trough and central-receiver concepts were intended to be compared, comparative evaluation of performance has ultimately turned out to be difficult. To account for the auxiliary contribution from fossil fuel was a special task, which depended on concept selection, as well as on the details of site and on consumer requirements. As a general result, the following can be stated:

- Performances and efficiencies of all three solar thermal technologies are broadly described by DLR studies[2–4] both for ideal desert and for realistic Mediterranean conditions, including infrastructure restrictions.

Figure 6.8. Three dish/Stirling units (each 9 kW) under continuous operation at the Plataforma Solar de Almería, Spain, since 1992

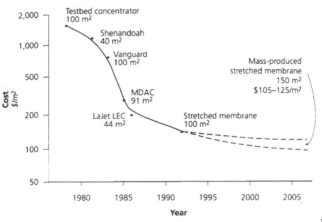

Figure 6.9. Dish cost trends for the parabolic dish technology[1]

- Dishes capture most of the available beam radiation. Central receivers and parabolic troughs lose a significant portion of the available radiation as a result of cosine and optical effects.
- Central receivers and parabolic troughs present greater possibilities for hybrid concepts, and especially for combined cycles, and thus for greater system efficiencies and mid/full-load operation.
- Both central receivers (especially) and parabolic troughs still have considerable possibilities for significant cost reductions resulting from up-scaling.
- For the temperature range of the applications foreseen in the near future (steam at 400–600°C), there is no clear reason for selecting either central-receiver technology or parabolic troughs. Both are worth developing and their capabilities demonstrated.

- Dishes are the best selection for small (< 1 MW$_e$) plants, especially for stand-alone operations.
- Annual efficiencies (from beam solar to electricity) for dishes can reach 20%, while parabolic troughs and central receivers in solar-only mode reach around 15%. If operation is in hybrid and combined-cycle mode, the efficiencies will increase considerably.
- The great operational experience of the SEGS plants can also be applied to central receivers, specifically with respect to hybridization strategies, operation and maintenance issues (for example, by the Kramer Junction Company to Solar Two).
- Typical investment costs (and actual and mid-term costs) for all three technologies are in the range of 2000 to 4000 ECU/kW$_e$.

6.3 REALISTIC GOALS

Electrical power is a strategic asset, essential to maintain and create wealth in both industrial and developing nations. In order to attain a sustainable growth, the expected increase in electricity demand in the lesser developed countries of the sun belt means that significant use should be made of their available renewable resources and especially of solar energy.

From the results of the DLR study[3] the potential for new and fossil-fired replacement power plants in solar-suited Mediterranean areas ranges from 90 GW$_e$, between the years 1990 and 2005, to 100 GW$_e$, up to 2025.

Two most promising alternatives are able to make a significant contribution to providing solar thermal electricity with available technology and at affordable costs:

- Rankine-Cycle solar power plants at site locations where no gas is available as a back-up fuel and where mid-load operation (3000–5000 full-load hours) is desired;
- integration of proven solar field technology into conventional combined cycles, the so-called Integrated Solar Combined Cycle System (ISCCS) concept, at locations where gas is available and a base-load operating strategy requires maximum fuel efficiencies.

6.3.1 Technology and cost goals

6.3.1.1 Parabolic troughs

The large increase in performance attained by LUZ in the late 1980s did not rule out the possibility of further substantial improvements. According to preliminary results, the levelized electricity costs of a solar thermal-power plant would be substantially reduced (well below the 0.1 ECU/kWh) by four steps representing the second generation of the parabolic-trough technology:

- improvements in the collector field due to better optical and thermal properties of the receivers and mirrors, lighter and tilted structures, lighter mirrors and better controls;
- improvements in the process by substitution of synthetic oil by water as a one-cycle/two-phase heat-transfer medium between the solar collector field and the power block, known as Direct Steam Generation (DSG);

- improvements in the system integration by reduction of parasitic loads, optimization of start-up procedures, better control strategy and optimization of the solar field linkage and solar/fossil hybrid operation;
- coupling with combined-cycle power plants (ISCCS).

6.3.1.2 Central receivers

The efforts devoted in Europe and the USA toward cost-effectiveness of the central-receiver technology should be directed towards cost values lower than 0.1 ECU/kWh by means of:

- improvements in the heliostat field and receiver due to better optical properties, lighter mirrors and structures, as well as to better control;
- improvements in the process by selection of heat transfer media and receiver concepts (volumetric air and advanced salt receivers);
- improvements in the system integration by reduction of parasitic loads, optimization of start-up procedures, better control strategies, optimization of the solar field linkage and solar/fossil hybrid operation;
- coupling with combined-cycle power plants.

6.3.1.3 Parabolic dishes

The application of dishes for stand-alone installations seems to be the means to reach the most attainable, near-term goal, which is to attain 0.15 ECU/kWh by means of:

- improvements in mirror and receiver due to better optical properties of the mirrors, and to lighter mirrors and structures; improved hybrid heat-pipe receivers and development of a control system for fully automatic operation;
- improvements in the process by using solarized Stirling and Brayton engines with heat-pipe receivers;
- improvements in the system integration by reduction of parasitic loads, optimization of start-up procedures, better control strategies and hybrid operation of the Stirling and Brayton engines.

The essential component and subsystem objectives for improvements are as shown in Table 6.1.

6.3.2 Market assessment

As heliostats and collectors can only concentrate direct-beam radiation, the locations suited for implementation are those places where a level of yearly direct-beam radiation over 1700 kWh/m^{2}a) is available. This is the case for countries in the so-called sun belt of the earth (latitudes between 40°N and 40°S). A number of well-known institutions, such as the World Bank, the Intergovernmental Panel on Climate Change (IPPC), the European Commission (CEC), have reported fast-growing electricity demands in the sun belt of the world and have recently become interested in solar thermal power projects to protect the environment and to assist less developed countries.

Table 6.1. The essential component and subsystem objectives for improvements

	2005	2025
Parabolic trough		
Collector/Receiver Improvements Power Blocks up to	Concept Optimization and Application 200 MW$_e$	
One Cycle for Heat Transfer and Prime Mover by Direct Steam Generation	Demonstration Plant and First Commercial Unit	Commercial Units
Combined Cycle	Demonstration Plant and First Commercial Unit	Commercial Units
Central Receiver (Tower)		
Molten Salt for Heat Transfer and Storage	Demonstration Plant	Commercial Units
Volumetric Air Receiver with 90% efficiency	First Commercial Units	Commercial Units
Power Blocks up to	200 MW$_e$	
High Temperature (600 to 700°C) Storage (Thermal or Chemical)	Development and Demonstration	First Commercial Unit (Chemical)
Combined Cycle (e.g. Water/ Steam: SOLGAS)	Demonstration Plant and First Commercial Unit	Commercial Units
Parabolic Dish		
Power Farms up to	100 KW$_e$ and I MW$_e$	Commercial Units
Heat Pipe Sodium Receiver and Hybrid Firing	Development, Demonstration and First Commercial Unit	Commercial Units
Turbine Applications	Development, Demonstration and First Commercial Unit	Commercial Units

6.3.2.1 Parabolic troughs

Over the last three years several project studies for new parabolic troughs have been carried out. These include:

- Spain, where the Spanish utility ENDESA financed and collaborated with FLAGSOL on a pre-feasibility study for parabolic trough technology.
- Morocco and Spain, where the Moroccan Ministry of Energy, the Moroccan Renewable Energy Centre CDR and ENDESA particpated in a technology assessment study on the transferability of parabolic trough technology to the Mediterranean, conducted by FLAGSOL and sponsored by the European Union's DG I and ENDESA.[5]
- Greece, where the Regional Development Organization of Crete collaborated with FLAGSOL on a pre-feasibility study for a 50 MW$_e$ parabolic trough (SEGS-type) plant with the support of the European Union's DG XVI and the Greek National Ministry of Economy.
- Tunisia, where a feasibility study for a new parabolic trough plant has been published recently.
- Iran, where a joint German–Iranian expert group is going to carry out a feasibility study for a 100 MW$_e$ parabolic-trough (SEGS-type) plant.

- Israel, where a pre-feasibility study for an 85 MW$_e$ ISCCS plant has been executed by SOLEL, funded and contracted by the Israeli Ministry of Energy and Infrastructure.
- India, where the Government of Radjasthan solicited an expression of interest from industries worldwide for the implementation of a 35 MW$_e$ SEGS-type power plant, the feasibility study for which was financed by the German Bank KfW and executed by Fichtner.
- Mexico, where a pre-feasibility study of a 128 MW$_e$ ISCCS plant has been carried out by a US project development group and a request for financing under GEF funds was expected from the Mexican governement in spring 1996.
- China, where initial plans for a 10 MW$_e$ parabolic trough plant have become known.
- Nevada, where new US policies and local political interest, together with a California-based project development group technology, indicate the revival of the parabolic trough project opportunities..

All these studies are based on the state-of-the-art parabolic trough collector technology with synthetic oil as the heat-transfer medium.

6.3.2.2 Central receivers

The implementation of central-receiver systems has captured the interest of many utilities. Currently, the following assessment studies are being performed with participation by the local utilities:

- Feasibility study for a 30 MW$_e$ volumetric central receiver plant in Jordan (PHOEBUS).
- Feasibility study for a 24 MW$_e$ solar receiver thermal output cogeneration plant in Huelva, Spain (SOLGAS project).
- Refurbishing Solar One into Solar Two, while preparing the assessment studies for Solar Parks with some 100–200 MW$_e$ plants with salt-in-tube receivers in Nevada, California and Arizona, with the goal to reach 2400 MW$_e$ in the year 2050.
- Feasibility study for a 100 MW$_e$ plant in Sacramento, California.
- Feasibility study for a central receiver plant in Israel.
- Proposal for the construction of a water/steam central receiver with 21 MW$_e$ thermal output, to refurbish an existing heavy-oil power plant into a solar/gas combined cycle plant in Huelva, Spain.

6.3.2.3 Parabolic dishes

To supply, for example, two thirds of the rural population of Morocco with electricity and sufficient power for water pumping, about 300 MW$_e$ would be needed. If this demand is provided by hybridized dish systems, the saving of fossil fuels could amount to 10% of the total consumption. Apart from the environmental impact, this would also reduce the migration of the rural population into the cities. Since 40% of the working population lives from agriculture, this is a particularly urgent problem.

If not only Morocco, but also the north and south Mediterranean countries – except France, Albania and the former Yugoslavia, where the insolation is too low for an economic application – are considered, the economic potential for dish/Stirling systems increases by more than an order of magnitude. This is because any power demand around a few MW_e or below can be delivered by a field of dishes.

6.3.3 Market perspectives

Because it possesses the respective research groups, industrial entities and test sites, Europe is in the lead in attaining the above-mentioned solar thermal goals. By the demonstration, 15 years ago, of electricity production with the first generation of parabolic trough collectors and central receivers, the Plataforma Solar de Almería PSA instigated the subsequent industrial developments. By demonstrating the improvements of these technologies, there is a unique chance to initiate the next breakthrough and give European industry the world leadership in this technology and consequently take advantage of an excellent chance in this enormous potential market. To achieve a broad market expansion, European cooperation is required to provide a greater than critical mass.

To assess the size of this potential market of solar thermal electricity generation, an evaluation of the following is appropriate:

- the available solar resources (theoretical potential);
- the available area (available potential);
- the electricity demand size and structure (technical potential);
- the existing technology at given costs (economical potential); and
- the socio-political context (realistic potential).

Such an exercise has already been performed for the Mediterranean region[3] and, as a result, the prospects for solar thermal power plants can be summarized as:

- There is a total potential of 90 GW_e until 2005 and additionally 100 GW_e up to 2025, as stated at the beginning of this chapter, and of this there is a very high potential for solar thermal electricity generation (anticipated 3.5 GW_e (2005); 23 GW_e (2025); 60 GW_e in the case of Mediterranean-wide interconnecting grids).
- Wherever the insolation is high, solar thermal electricity generating costs may already today account for 0.15 ECU/kWh, and may drop to 0.10 ECU/kWh in the long term. (Compare with Figure 6.4 and costs between 20 and 14 US cents/kWh; for example, the SEGS IX plant at Harper Lake, CA, with 25% fossil-fuel firing, approximately 0.11 ECU/kWh.)
- Levelized electricity costs of less than 0.10 ECU/kWh are expected from the new SEGS-type and ISCCS-type plants in the mid- to base-load condition.
- In the southern Mediterranean area, the available potential is very large; presently, a limiting factor is the relatively low demand for electricity.
- An interconnected international network of grids – both within and extending beyond the immediate Mediterranean area – could reduce the imbalance between solar irradiance and electricity demand.
- The introduction of solar thermal installations in the marketplace must be accelerated. The Mediterranean area represents only a part of the earth's sunbelt, but it can assume a pilot function.
- A solar thermal plant reduces the CO_2 emissions by about 2000 tonnes per year per MW_e of installed electric power; equivalently, each GWh produced with solar energy avoids 700 to 1000 tonnes of CO_2.

From this analysis it results that, in the Mediterranean area, the African countries have the largest potential for the systems considered (grid-connected power plant with parabolic troughs or central receivers and stand-alone applications with dishes). However, in order to reduce the risks of a first demonstration, it seems convenient to start by implementing a parabolic-trough Rankine-cycle plant (SEGS type) or a combined-cycle plant using solar steam generated by a trough or central receiver system.

It is worth remarking that solar thermal technology, as well as having the potential to supply the electricity demand, has the advantage of a positive social impact by improving living conditions and protecting the environment from the pollution caused by conventional fuels.

In summary, the state and expectation of solar thermal technology are:

* Both trough and tower systems can already perform at 10 to 200 MW_e sizes with costs below 0.20 ECU/kWh. They have the clear perspective to reach competitive conditions below 0.10 ECU/kWh after some second-generation improvements.
* The trough system already feeds 354 MW_e into the California grid, under special conditions and with a 25% fossil energy input. Similar circumstances are imaginable in southern Europe.
* The tower system has an outstanding reduction potential because of its ability to concentrate radiation onto one single unit (the receiver on top of a tower). This applies especially when modular sizes providing more than 100 MW_e of electrical power can be built.
* The dish system may after some development very soon perform well under normal competitive conditions within the smaller sizes (< 1 MW_e). This addresses the market segment below the trough and tower-unit sizes but still being larger than typical photovoltaic applications.
* With the evolution of high-voltage dc power transfer, the grid connections over some thousand km between solar beneficial areas and non-solar industrial regions will develop more and more realistically and thus favour the installation of solar thermal power plants also for this reason.

The following main goals should be achieved:

* to build large solar/fossil and integrated solar/combined cycle power plants with the current technology of central receivers and parabolic troughs within the next few years (southern Europe and North Africa).
* to secure for European industry the leading technology position;
* to improve the confidence of the utilities and of the funding institutions in solar thermal technologies.

6.4 A ROADMAP OF R&D

For all three technologies the trend in collector costs is towards about US $100 per m^2 in mass production. Especially for the two larger-size concepts, the parabolic trough and the central receiver system, hybrid operations or applications of solar energy in combined-power stations are highly recommendable in order to achieve promising competitive conditions. The following approaches are of importance for economic operation:

- Retrofit of existing power stations, with common power conditioning units and infrastructure, by making use of solar energy, will help the introduction of renewable energy.
- In conventional boilers the heat exchange between the flue gases (with linearly decreasing temperatures) and the evaporating fluid (with constant saturation temperature) requires a high mean temperature difference, causing significant exergy losses. This effect, known as the pinch-point problem, also occurs in solar-energy systems, when sensible heat is transferred from a primary circuit (e.g. thermo-oil in troughs, molten salt or air in towers) to a steam-power conversion cycle. The direct application of solar energy for evaporation avoids this pinch-point problem and makes the overall system more efficient. At the same time, steady operation at saturation temperature eases the load on the solar parts of the receivers. This is mainly a factor for the parabolic-trough system and the water/steam central receivers.
- In addition to the above-mentioned constant-temperature solar input, central-receiver systems can provide higher temperature-sensitive energy, e.g. for superheating.
- Generally hybrid plants will be more economic than solar-only facilities. Therefore, operation will not be solely dependent on solar conditions; by using fossil firing, operation times can be prolonged and process demands accomplished. Expensive storage with developmental needs could be reduced or even rendered unnecessary. In the long term, however, storage will be an absolute requirement.

To ensure progress from the present state of the art to an advanced second generation of components and systems, it is necessary to define the lines of development leading to improvement. These are outlined in the following for all three solar thermal technologies.

6.4.1 Parabolic trough systems

Taking as the base case the levelized energy values (given in a pre-feasibility study for parabolic trough systems financed by ENDESA and the EU for a solarized combined cycle), a working group has analysed the effect of the next generation improvements and concluded that it is possible to attain a 30% reduction by improvements in the collector and by the introduction of direct steam generation. This reduction stems from a considerable reduction in investment and a remarkable improvement in performance.

The main items responsible for performance improvement are:

- Solar collector improvements:
  - 8° tilt of the collector axis to reduce cosine losses;
  - increase of the mirror reflectivity from 0.94 to 0.96;
  - increase of the receiver absorptivity from 0.96 to 0.97;
  - reduction of the receiver thermal emissivity from 0.19 to 0.15;
  - improvements in mirror cleaning procedures.
- Process improvements:
  - further advances in the present loop concepts;
  - replacement of thermal oil by direct steam generation;
  - process control.
- Overall system improvements:
  - reduction of parasitic loads;

- advanced and more integrated power block;
- improvement of the start-up procedure;
- improvement of the coupling between the solar field and the power block.

The main cost-reduction topics considered are:

- Solar field:
  - upscaling from 80 to 200 MWe for current versions;
  - no thermal-oil system (direct steam generation).
- Heat transfer fluid system:
  - simplified plant configurations (no steam boiler between the solar field and the power conversion);
  - simplified heat transfer loops (direct steam generation);
  - reduction of the number of components (pumps) and of parasitic loads.

As preliminary calculations have shown, direct steam generation may be responsible for an increase of one third of the possible performance gains and for half of the possible cost reductions. The substitution of thermal oil by water and steam also has advantages concerning the elevation of temperatures above 400°C. If there is any leakage, water is free from pollution effects.

However, it has to be stated that the technology of direct steam generation in horizontally oriented tubes still gives technical problems. Though some laboratory-scale experiments have been performed during the last few years or are planned within projects which are currently under way (GUDE, ARDISS, PAREX), many of the open technical questions cannot be investigated on a laboratory scale. Thus a real-size test facility to study the process under working conditions will be erected at the PSA in Almería (Spain) within a first phase to the end of 1997, and a second phase with testing proposed thereafter.

6.4.2 Central receiver systems

Two components of the central receivers, the heliostats and the receivers, have substantial development issues with respect to technical performance and cost factors. They are, therefore, important subjects of investigation in terms of their second-generation potential. The development of heliostat concepts is tending to larger units, to front-surface mirrors, to polymer materials and/or to stretched-membrane constructions. Cost decreases to about US $100 per m^2 are viable under mass production conditions.

While heliostats will profit, both in cost and quality, from mass fabrication, the receiver, which is a single unit on top of the tower, will also be improved by a technologically more efficient and simple solution, leading to lower weight and safer operation.

The state of the art is represented by the heat exchanger/tube technology with different choices of heat transfer media, such as steam, air or molten salts.

The main items responsible for performance and cost improvements are:

- Heliostat improvements:
  - optimization of concepts (rectangular versus stretched membrane);
  - optimization of glass and polymer performance properties;
  - optimization of structural hardware.

- Receiver improvements:
  - optimal application of material properties;
  - tube safety and reliability aspects;
  - development of molten-salt internal-film technique;
  - demonstration of volumetric air receivers for higher temperatures and efficiencies.
- Overall system improvements:
  - start-up procedures and internal consumptions;
  - solar-field/power-block coupling;
  - unit sizes of more than 100 MW_e, operating on power blocks that are several times larger;
  - molten-salt receiver systems at high heat-flux rates and operation with storage within the heat transfer cycle;
  - volumetric air-receiver systems at high heat-flux rates with coupling of aiming-point strategy and mass-flow regulation.

In addition, it has to be pointed out that direct steam generation in vertically oriented tubes is a proven part of this technology. The incorporation of cost-effective storage systems within the molten-salt heat transfer cycle represents a major advantage for this technique. The volumetric receivers are convincing low-weight/high-performance/low-cost solutions.

6.4.3 Parabolic dish systems

The parabolic-dish concept is obviously already very mature and close to industrial demonstration. Nevertheless, as with central-receiver concepts, a mass-fabricated stretched-membrane technique could further reduce the collector costs. A step prior to commercialization would be the successful operation of a large plant over a long enough period. The experience gained would guarantee technical reliability and cost reductions. For suitable autonomous small-size solutions in stand-alone operation the proper interaction with demand profiles require flexibility. Therefore, the addition of a fossil-fuel combustion chamber, heating up the helium engine cycle in parallel with solar operation, is planned and one possible solution is currently under development, to be pursued in the future.

Tubular receivers with improved lifetimes are used in conventional designs. Heat-pipe receivers, however, show a high potential to reach considerably longer lifetimes as a result of their excellent heat-transfer properties and their ability to equalize the extreme thermal gradients. They are also suitable for hybridization. In that direction, the work that still remains is in the following areas:

- improvement of performance and reliability of dish/Stirling systems for decentralized power production, using improved heat-pipe receivers with long life expectatation;
- increase in availability of such systems for a possible 24 h/d operation by hybridization with an adapted combustion system suited for both natural gas and biogas;
- a considerable decrease in investment costs for the receiver as a result of new manufacturing methods for the wick structure of the heat pipes;
- demonstration of technical maturity, both generally and particularly for special applications such as water pumping or desalination.

6.5 STRATEGY

Many recent studies, performed in both European and non-European countries, have indicated that an implementation of solar thermal power plants is technically feasible, economically affordable and, from an environmental viewpoint, necessary in order to reduce CO_2 emissions.

Studies have also concluded that there are good prospects for solar plants in all the countries of the so-called 'sun belt', especially in the Mediterranean area. The large potential of the technology has given rise to an increasing interest in these countries, thus promoting many feasibility studies aimed at the implementation of solar thermal power stations. However, facilities of this sort are not only of interest for countries with high solar radiation. Industrialized countries with low solar radiation can also make profits by transferring this technology to lesser developed countries with good solar conditions.

The recommended strategy is to start with a *demonstration* of the existing technology in the Mediterranean area and to carry out *research* on the next steps. This means:

- Quantify cost/performance benefits of solar systems integrated in 100 to 200 MW_e combined-cycle plants with central receivers or parabolic troughs and in 1–5 MW_e plants with dishes.
- Design such hybrid solar/fossil-plant systems.
- Implement demonstration plants, initially in southern Europe and later on in North Africa, using the most proven technology: oil-cooled parabolic-trough plants, water/ steam central receivers and dishes with Stirling engines.
- Identify the next technological development steps for components and systems; design and optimize these.
- Test these designs; improve and qualify the second generation.

In addition, it is necessary to improve the social environment, so as to ease the implementation of these demonstration plants. The following recommendations and actions are derived from different studies and planning activities:

- government programmes to initiate solar thermal power stations in the Mediterranean area as a signal for long-term planning of power plant economy;
- consortia with international partnerships;
- joint ventures and cooperation between north and south European utilities and other entities;
- financing mechanisms in the frame of the World Energy Conferences, Rio 1992 and Berlin 1995, including financing under GEF funds;
- solar incentives for CO_2 compensation measures;
- research and developments, leading to further progress in solar thermal technologies.

6.6 REFERENCES

1 Johannson T B, Kelly H, Reddy A K N, Williams R H (ed.) (1993). Renewable Energy Sources for Fuels and Electricity. Island Press, Washington.
2 Becker M, Meinecke W (ed.) (1992). Solarthermische Anlagen-Technologien im Vergleich. Turm-, Parabolrinnen-, Paraboloidanlagen und Aufwindkraftwerke. Springer-Verlag, Berlin.

3 Klaiss H, Staiss F (ed.) (1992). Solarthermische Kraftwerke für den Mittelmeerraum, Bd. 1 und 2. Springer-Verlag, Berlin.
4 Becker M, Klimas P (ed.) (1993). Second Generation Central Receiver Technologies, A Status Report. Verlag C.F. Müller, Karlsruhe.
5 Assessment of Solar Thermal Trough Power Technology and its Transferability to the Mediterranean Region (1994). Executive Summary of ENDESA/FLAGSOL Study.

FURTHER READING

Étude de Faisabilité d'une Centrale Solaire en Tunisie (1995). Les Cahiers du Clip, No. 4, June.
Klaiss H, Meinecke W, Staiss F. (1994). Comparative Assessment of the Costs and Benefits of Solar Thermal Concentrating Technologies for Power Generation. Proceedings of the International Conference of Comparative Assessment of Solar Power Technologies, Jerusalem, pp 33–55.
Lotker M (1991). Barriers to Commercialization of Large Scale Solar Electricity. Sandia Report, SAND 91-7014.
Solar – Thermal – Electric Five Year Program Plan FY 1993 through 1997. US Department of Energy.
Winter C-J, Sizmann R L, Vant Hull L L (ed.) (1991). Solar Power Plants. Fundamentals, Technology, Systems, Economics. Springer-Verlag, Berlin.

GLOSSARY

C	Concentration factor
SEGS	Solar Energy Generating System
PSA	Plataforma Solar de Almería
ISCCS	Integrated Solar Combined Cycle System
DSG	Direct Steam Generation
IEA	International Energy Agency
HTF	Heat Transfer Fluid
DOE	US Department of Energy
GEF	Global Environment Facility

7.   WIND ENERGY

7.I INTRODUCTION

Europe has a very large untapped resource of wind energy. The total exploitable wind-energy potential of Europe equates to approximately half of the total electricity consumption of the countries in the European Union.

The technology related to grid-connected wind turbine generators (WTGs) is becoming mature. Wind energy today is competitive at specific sites with favourable conditions. Wind energy is expected within the time frame of 2005 to 2010 to be economically fully competitive with fossil-fuel and nuclear-based power production.

Like other new renewable energy sources, wind energy is clean and safe. Wind turbines do not produce greenhouse gases. Wind energy has very low external and social costs. Wind energy has no liabilities related to decommissioning of obsolete plants.

Wind power is a promising and competitive new renewable source of energy. However, scientific research is able to make a significant contribution to:

* the further development of wind energy technology;
* the European windpower industry's international competitiveness.

The aim of this chapter is to suggest a strategy for such R&D activities. Particular attention is paid to activities suited to European-level R&D programmes.

The chapter is structured as follows. First, the state of the art of wind-power utilization is described in terms of technology maturity, markets, economy and environmental aspects. Then follows a brief discussion of the strategic goals for a European wind energy policy. From these strategic goals the paper suggests six interdependent goals for an European R&D strategy on wind energy.

In Section 7.4 the the R&D activities needed to achieve these goals are outlined. Finally, the a strategy for the R&D activities is recommended.

We have attempted to write this chapter as briefly and concisely as possible, concentrating on facts and on the outline of the activities needed. Consequently, we do not debate in a traditional scientific way and omit specific citations of the references quoted.

The paper deals with three areas of wind power technology:

* grid-connected large-size WTGs;
* hybrid energy systems with intermediate-sized WTGs;
* stand-alone small WTGs for battery charging, water pumping, etc.

However, the main emphasis is on the large-size grid-connected wind turbines.

7.2 PRESENT SITUATION

7.2.1 European wind energy resources

Europe has a very large resource of wind energy. Wind energy could, in theory, provide all of Europe's electricity.

The total exploitable wind-energy potential of Europe equates to approximately half of the total electricity consumption of the countries in the European Union.

Areas potentially suitable for wind energy application are dispersed throughout all the countries of the European Union. Major areas that have a high wind-energy resource include: Great Britain, Ireland and the north-western continental parts of the EU: Denmark, northern Germany, south-western Sweden, The Netherlands, Belgium, and north-western France. Other areas are north-western Spain and a majority of the Greek islands. In addition, there are many areas where wind systems associated with mountain barriers give rise to high energy potentials. Some of these wind systems extend over large areas: the Mistral between the Alps and the Massif Central in the south of France, the Tramontana north of the Pyrenees in France and south of the Pyrenees in the Ebro Valley. In other cases such wind systems are of smaller geographical extent, but may nevertheless give a large wind resource locally. Of particular interest are mountain valleys, passes and ridges where natural concentrations of wind occur (e.g. mountainous parts of Germany, Austria, Portugal, Italy, Sweden and Finland).

7.2.2 Status of technology

The technology related to grid-connected wind turbines is becoming mature.

Wind-energy conversion technology exists in a range of sizes and for a range of applications. Usually the technology is categorized in three areas.

The first area is medium- to *large-size grid-connected WTGs*. The size of commercially available grid-connected horizontal-axis WTGs has evolved from 50 kW the early 1980s to 500 to 800 kW today. The next generation of commercial wind turbines in the 1000–1500 kW size are being tested, and they are scheduled to reach the market in 1996. The concept of an (economically) optimum size of wind turbine has been discussed extensively, but conclusive evidence of the existence of an optimum size is still lacking.

Europe has a competitive advantage on commercial MW-size wind turbines, because development of these has only take place in Europe. Examples are shown in Figures 7.1 and 7.2.

Grid-connected WTGs often are placed in a windfarm, which is operated as a single plant. Plant size has evolved from a few MW in the early 1980s to tens or hundreds of MW today.

Many different design concepts are in use, the most used at present being three-bladed, stall- or pitch-regulated, horizontal-axis machines operating at near-fixed rotational speed. Other concepts, such as gearless designs and variable rotor speed designs, present promising advantages. European companies are leading in exploiting these possibilities. Modern WTGs are reliable with a technical availability of typically 98–99%.

The technology and software (for example the European Wind Atlas and the computer code WASP) for evaluating the available wind resource are now available. The European Commission has played a key role by funding the research leading to the development of these tools. In several other regions of the world specific evaluations of resources have

Figure 7.1. The 'Näsudden II' wind turbine installed at Näsudden on the south tip of the Swedish island of Gotland. Installed power 3 MW, rotor diameter 80 m, hub height 78 m, rigid hub, full-span pitch control, constant two-speed conversion system

Figure 7.2. The 'Nordic 1000' turbine, located at Näsudden. Installed power 1 MW, rotor diameter 53 m, hub height 58 m, teetering hub, total control, constant- and variable-speed conversion system

been carried out. European-developed siting software is now being employed on a regular basis to identify the most energetic wind turbine sites.

Currently, the uncertainty of the energy production of wind power plants is of the order of 15% on average. It is estimated at present that a penetration (supply fraction) of wind energy on a large grid can be as much as 15–20% without special precautions being taken with respect to power quality and grid stability.

WTGs can be used competitively as a dispersed energy-production technology in areas with dispersed electricity consumption. WTGs can be installed rapidly. Wind power plants of, for example, 50 MW can be in operation in less than a year from signing the contract.

The second area is *intermediate-size wind turbines in hybrid energy systems* combined with other energy sources such as photovoltaics/hydro/diesel and/or storage used in small remote grids or for special applications such as water pumping, battery charging, desalination, etc. (10 kW to 150 kW size range). This size range tends to be too expensive for grid-connected applications. Wind–diesel and wind–solar hybrid systems have been demonstrated and evaluated, but remain generally as the least attractive wind-technology size range in terms of economic viability.

The third area is *small stand-alone turbines* for battery charging, water pumping, heating, etc. (< 10 kW size range). In the area of small battery-charging wind turbines, the size range 25 to 150 watts (i.e. rotors of 0.5 m to 1.5 m diameter), is by far the most successful commercially. Probably, some 200,000 small battery-charging wind turbines are now in use.

By far the most widely used form of wind-energy technology remains the mechanical farm windpump. One to two million units are in regular use worldwide and over 50 manufacturers are known to be active. However, this is generally an obsolete technology. A few modern developments are supported by national overseas aid programmes. The general interest in these machines seems to be increasing.

7.2.3 Markets

At the end of 1994 global installed capacity of modern grid-connected wind turbines was some 3700 MW, of which 1700 MW was in the USA and 1650 MW in Europe.

The worldwide annually added capacity of WTG (the world market) is rapidly increasing; from 541 MW in 1993 to 742 MW in 1994, of which approximately 450 MW per year was in Europe. The worldwide added capacity in 1995 is estimated to be 1200 MW. With an approximate cost of 1 MECU per MW of installed wind power, the world market in 1995 has a value of 1200 MECU.

Active installation programmes as part of government policy exist outside Europe in the USA, China, India, Canada and many other countries. More than ten major European banks and more than 20 European utilities have invested in wind energy, as well as a large number of individuals and companies, with more than 100,000 in Denmark alone.

Financial organizations, utilities and industry increasingly consider wind power as a new viable and reliable source of energy in the grid's supply portfolio. However, the pattern and economics differ significantly between the European countries, depending on the track record of wind power in that country.

Several international organizations have made estimates of future wind-power implementation. The World Energy Council (WEC) has produced two scenarios for wind-power installations in the year 2020. In a 'Current Policy' scenario WEC estimate 180,000 MW of installed wind power capacity by 2020 (1.5 % of the world's electricity demand). In an 'Ecologically Driven Scenario' WEC estimate that wind energy will provide 5% of the world's electricity demand by 2020, corresponding to 474,000 MW of installed wind-power capacity.

Present worldwide production of small battery chargers is probably of the order of 30 to 50 thousand units per year, of which 90% (in number) have a power rating under 100 W. The main producers of small battery chargers are in the UK (marine and caravan leisure markets) and China (for semi-nomadic cattle raisers in the Mongolian region).

The main application for mechanical farm windpumps is drinking-water supply. The markets for this type of machines include the USA, Argentina, South Africa and New Zealand. The present market for windpumps is probably in the region of 5000 to 10,000 units per annum from around 50 manufacturers.

7.2.4 Industry and employment

In 1994 the European wind-power industry produced around 550 MW of wind turbines in the 100 kW to 750 kW range. The total turnover of the industry was approximately MECU 450 in 1994 and this is steadily increasing.

In 1995 approximately 20,000 Europeans are estimated to be employed in relation to European wind power activities, primarily in the wind-turbine and supporting industries.

90% of the world's manufacturers of medium- and large-size wind turbines are European. More than 25 manufacturers are presently serving the European market, but, as the industry matures, a concentration on a few strong companies can be expected. In Germany 85% of the market is shared by the six largest companies.

At present, European wind power industry is the world leader, but it is experiencing increased competition from America and Japan.

Small machines represent a relatively low level of economic activity, especially in Europe. The annual turnover of small wind-generator industries is probably less than 4 to 5 million ECU in Europe. However, during the last decade, the UK, The Netherlands and the Italian governments have supported significant R&D into windpumps, which then feature in their development assistance programmes. In 1994 the Danish government launched a demonstration programme for small machines (< 25 kW) for domestic application. At present total employment in the area of small wind turbine manufacturing and research in Europe is of the order of a 'few hundred' persons.

7.2.5 Wind power economy

It is estimated that wind power in many countries is already competitive with fossil and nuclear power when external/social costs are included. International organizations without preference for wind power (for example, the International Atomic Energy Agency – IAEA) estimate that wind power in a short-term time frame (2005 to 2010) will be competitive with fossil and nuclear power in a narrow economic sense, without taking into account wind power's competitive advantage in external or social costs.

The economics of grid-connected wind power can be evaluated from two different perspectives. The first is that of public authorities or energy planners, making assessments of different energy sources. Here the focus is on levelized cost in, for example, ECU/kWh. These calculations do not include factors determined by society or governments, such as inflation or the taxation system.

The second perspective is that of the private or utility investor, where inflation, interest rates, the taxation system, amortization period, etc. must be included and consequently the economics of wind energy differs greatly from country to country. Here the focus is on cashflow in each project and on payback time and present value of the investment.

For this chapter the two perspectives basically differ with respect to amortization period and interest rates.

The generation cost from wind energy is then basically determined by the following parameters:

- total investment cost, which consists of:
  - ex-works cost of wind turbines;
  - project preparation costs, cost of the infrastructure, etc.;
- operation and maintenance cost;
- average wind speed at the particular site;
- availability;
- technical lifetime;
- amortization period;
- real interest rate.

Ex-works cost has been estimated by surveying all commercially available Danish, German and Dutch machines/versions on the Danish and German markets. The study shows average ex-factory costs of 870 ECU/kW of installed capacity and 360 ECU/m^2 rotor-swept area. These averages include some deviation, partly due to different market structures of the two countries. Thus for the lowest-cost machines the figures are 610 ECU/kW and 300 ECU/m^2 respectively. If tower height and rotor diameter are taken into account, the WTG with the lowest ECU/kW ratio may not be the most economical one.

The above ex-works costs represent only single-machine projects. When machines are acquired for windfarms, rebates can be negotiated.

Project preparation cost depends heavily on local circumstances, such as condition of the soil, road conditions, proximity to electrical grid sub-stations, etc. Investigations indicate that project preparation costs amount to approximately 225 ECU/kW for new 450 kW to 600 kW machines located on flat onshore sites. This does not include grid reinforcement costs and long-distance power transmission lines. Project-preparation costs can be reduced by windfarm operation of wind turbines. As a rule of thumb, total investment cost can be estimated to be 1.3 times the ex-works turbine cost for flat onshore sites.

Operation and maintenance costs include service, consumables, repair, insurance, administration, lease of site, etc. Recent Danish and German investigations found that the annual operation and maintenance cost for modern 450–500 kW wind turbines are approximately 1–1.5 ECU cent/kWh, of which the half is insurance premium. For ten-year-old 55 kW machines the O&M costs are typically 2–3 ECU cent/kWh. The annual operation and maintenance cost is often estimated as 2–3% of a wind turbine's ex-works cost.

The *availability*, namely the capability to operate when the wind speed is higher than the start-up wind speed of the machine, is typically higher than 98% for modern European machines.

Technical lifetime or design lifetime for European machines is typically 20 years. Individual components have to be replaced or renewed at shorter intervals. Consumables, such as oil in the gearbox, braking clutches, etc., are often replaced at intervals of one to three years. Parts of the yaw system are replaced at intervals of five years. Vital components exposed to fatigue loads, such as main bearings, bearings in the gearbox and generator are expected to be replaced halfway through the total design lifetime.

Choice of *amortization period* depends on:

- the perspective of the economy calculation (levelized-cost method or private-economy perpective);
- the type of investor and the market structure.

For the levelized-cost perspective, the amortization period often is set to the technical lifetime, which is normally 20 years. For the private-investment perspective a 'real' amortization period must be used. Privately owned European wind-power projects are normally financed by 10–20% of equity and 90–80% bank loan over 8 to 12 years.

The *average annual wind speed* on the site is of paramount importance to the cost of energy. As a rule of thumb, a wind turbine's power increases with the wind speed to the third power and thus the cost of energy decreases accordingly.

In the best locations in The Netherlands, northern Germany and Denmark annual output of over 1000 kWh/m^2 is often achieved (1000 kWh/m^2 corresponds to an annual wind speed slightly higher than 5 m/s at a height of 10 m with average new technology). In the

UK sites, where wind speeds of 8, 9 and 10 m/s are common, an annual output of over 2000 kWh has been recorded. Average annual wind speed for wind turbines installed in Denmark over the last three years is 4.7 m/s at a height of 10 m, corresponding to an average annual output of 793 kWh/m^2.

The *levelized cost of wind energy* can be exemplified assuming the following

Ex-works cost	870 ECU/kW or 360 ECU/m^2
Total investment	133% of ex-works cost
Annual O&M cost	2.5% of ex-works cost
Availability	99%
Technical lifetime	20 years
Amortization period	20 years
Local average wind speed	5.0 m/s at 10 m (roughness class 1)
	6.9 m/s at 50 m
Real interest rate	5%
Levelized cost of energy	0.055 ECU/kWh

For privately financed projects, the cost of energy can be exemplified by assuming the following:

Amortization period	10 years
Real interest rate	7.5%
Cost of energy	0.091 ECU/kWh

Wind energy has very low external and social costs, and no liabilities related to the decommissioning of obsolete plants.

7.2.6 Certification

The certification process in principle verifies that a product or a process conforms to well known reference documents, such as standards, legal requirements or contract specifications. The requirements for type approval and certification of a wind turbine vary in the different countries in the European Union. Some countries have national legal requirements for type approvals, which must be met before permission for erection can be given by the local authority. Other countries have no national requirements. Local authorities may also have requirements that must be fulfilled, and other issues based on agreements between the consumer and the wind turbine manufacturer may exist. Obtaining a certificate from a recognized certification body can be of crucial importance for a project. Such a certificate provides increased confidence in the proposed project, which is important in assessing the risk for owners, investors and insurance companies.

In future certification of WTGs, the EU countries will be governed by directives and standards given by the EU – when they are fully adopted.

7.2.7 Environmental impact

Wind energy's environmental impact has been investigated thoroughly in both Europe and America. The investigations have concluded that wind energy is a clean and safe source of energy.

- **Atmospheric emissions.** No direct atmospheric emissions are caused by the operation of wind turbines. The indirect emission from the energy used to produce, transport and decommission a wind turbine depends on the type of primary energy used.
- **Energy balance.** The energy invested in production, installation, O&M and decommissioning of a typical wind turbine has a 'payback' time (energy balance) of less than half a year of operation.
- **Social costs and liabilities after decommissioning.** Electricity from WTGs has very low external or social costs and no liabilities related to decommissioning of obsolete plants. Almost all parts of a modern wind turbine can be recycled.
- **Land use.** Windfarms have the advantage of dual land use. 99% of the area occupied by a windfarm can be used for agriculture or remain as natural habitat. Consequently, a limited area of land is not a physical constraint for wind-power utilization, as it could be for biomass-produced energy. Wind energy is diffuse and collecting energy from the wind requires turbines to be spread over a wide area. As a rule of thumb, wind farms require 0.08 to 0.13 km^2/MW (8–13 MW/km^2).
  On typical flat onshore sites installation of WTGs has no erosional effects and the installations do not affect vegetation or fauna. In most countries wind-power developers are obliged to minimize any disturbance of vegetation under construction of windfarms (in combination with road works, etc.) on sensitive sites such as mountainous sites.
- **Noise emissions.** Acoustic emissions from wind turbines are composed of a mechanical component and an aerodynamic component, both of which are a function of wind speed. Analysis shows that, for most turbines with rotor diameters up to 20 m, the mechanical component dominates, whereas for larger rotors the aerodynamic component is decisive.
  The nuisance caused by turbine noise is one of the most important limitations on siting wind turbines close to inhabited areas. The acceptable emission level strongly depends on local regulations. An example of strict regulation is the Dutch regulation for 'silent' areas, where a maximum emission level of 40 dB(A) near residences is allowed, at a wind speed of about 5–7 ms^{-1}. At this wind-speed level the turbine noise is distinctly audible. In Europe a typical distance between wind turbines and living areas is more than 150 to 200 m.
- **Visual impact.** Depending on the characteristics of the landscape, modern wind turbines with a hub height 40 m and a blade length of 20 m have a visual impact on the landscape. This visual impact, although very difficult to quantify, can be a planning restriction in most European countries. A more objective case of visual impact is the effect of moving 'shadows' from the rotor blades. This is only a problem in situations where turbines are sited very close to workplaces or dwellings. The effect can be easily predicted and avoided through proper planning.
- **Impact on birds.** Studies in Germany, The Netherlands, Denmark and the UK have concluded that WTGs do not pose any substantial threat to birds. Bird mortality due to wind turbines is only a small fraction of the background mortality. Only isolated examples have been reported, such as the Spanish wind farm of Tarifa near the Strait of Gilbraltar, which is on a major bird migration route. However, disturbance of breeding and resting birds can be a problem on coastal sites.
- **Interference with electromagnetic communication systems.** Wind turbines in some areas can reflect electromagnetic waves, which will be scattered and diffracted. This means that wind turbines may interfere with telecommunication links. An investiga-

tion by the UK British Broadcasting Company (BBC) concluded that WTGs' interference with electromagnetic communication systems is not a significant problem.

The IEA has provided preparatory information on this subject, identifying the relevant wind-turbine parameters (diameter, number and cross section of blades, speed, etc.) and the relevant parameters of the potentially vulnerable radio services (spatial positions of transmitter and receiver, carrier frequency, polarization, etc.). In the planning of windfarms, areas where wind turbines could interfere with telecommunication are normally avoided.

- **Safety of personnel.** Accidents with wind turbines involving human beings are extremely rare and there is no recorded case of persons hurt by parts of blades or ice loosened from a WTG. Insurance companies in the USA, where most of the experience with large windfarms has been, agree that the wind industry has a good safety profile compared with other energy-producing industries. The International Electrical Committee (IEC) has issued an international official standard on wind-turbine safety.

A typical windfarm is shown in Figure 7.3.

7.2.8 Public acceptance

Opinion surveys in areas of the European Union with wind farms or many wind turbines (such as Denmark and the UK) indicate that 70 to 80% of the population is 'general supportive' or 'unconcerned' with respect to the WTGs in their neighbourhood. In a referendum in a Danish municipality with a very large number of wind turbines, 77% of the votes favoured more wind turbines. However, public acceptance of windpower can affect planning restriction and is consequently also a political issue. The political debate is often

Figure 7.3. The 'Dobbelsteen' wind farm on the Maasvlakte near Rotterdam, The Netherlands. It consists of 10 NedWind machines of 0.5 MW each. Installed power 5MW, rotor diameter 35 m, hub height 39 m, rigid rotor, stall-controlled, constant-speed conversion system

quite polarized. On the one hand, the general public in many countries favour renewable energy sources such as wind power. On the other hand, deploying a windfarm in a local community sometimes raises local resistance due to the neighbours' uncertainty and negative expectations about the visual intrusion and noise emission due to WTGs. This has been called the NIMBY (Not-In-My-Back-Yard) dilemma. Experiences from all over the world indicate that the potential neighbours' participation in planning and ownership of a windfarm can secure the public's acceptance and active support of wind power.

7.2.9 Research, development and demonstration activities

According to the International Energy Agency, government funding for wind energy research, development and demonstration has increased dramatically over the last six to seven years. From a level of about US $90 million in the mid-1980s to US $180 million in 1995. The figures include programmes in the 14 OECD/IEA member countries participating in 'The Implementing Agreement for Co-operation in Research and Development of Wind Turbines Systems'.

7.3 REALISTIC GOALS

This section first briefly discusses the strategic goals for a European wind energy policy. From the overall strategic level, goals for a European R&D strategy on wind energy are established. For each goal realistic targets are proposed.

7.3.1 Strategic goals

- The first strategic goal for wind power RD&D activities in the EU should be to achieve an installed capacity of 100,000 MW by 2030.

The total exploitable, wind-energy potential of Europe equates to approximately half of the total electricity consumption of the countries in the European Union. 'How much of the potential should be exploited and when?' are the strategic questions for a European wind-energy policy.

In Annex I of the Council of the European Communities' Decision of 13 September 1993 concerning the promotion of renewable energy sources (the ALTENER Program) the Community establishes a number of targets to be achieved by 2005. Two of these are:

- Increasing the contribution of renewable energy sources from 4% to 8% of the total energy demand.
- Trebling electricity production from renewable sources.

In 1991 the EU's electricity production from renewables was 180 TWh, with 86% from large hydro, 8.6% from mini hydro, 3.5% from biomass, 1.6% from geothermal, and 0.6% from wind and PV. If wind alone were to account for this trebling (with 360 TWh annually), an installed capacity in the order of 150,000–200,000 MW should be in place by 2005.

In the European Wind Energy Association's strategy paper 'Wind Energy in Europe; A Plan of Action' (October 1991) it was recommended that the European Commission adopt the goal to utilize about 20% of the total readily exploitable wind potential by the year 2030, despite the difficulties now being faced. This is equivalent to about 10% of the European Union's present electricity demand.

To achieve this a wind-power capacity of 100,000 MW must be installed. The area needed for this is less than 0.3% of the territory covered by the European Union, and a part of the installations can be offshore. Onshore wind farms have the advantage of dual land use. 99% of the area occupied by a wind farm can be used for agriculture or remain as natural habitat. Consequently, a limited area of land is not a physical constraint for wind-power utilization.

The EWEA scenario proposes realistic goals for wind-power deployment in the EU countries (Table 7.1).

Table 7.1. The goals of the EWEA scenario for wind energy deployment in the EU

Year	Installed power in MW
1994	1400 (has been exceeded)
2000	4000
2005	11,500
2030	100,000

• The second strategic goal for wind power RD&D in general is to provide developing countries and areas with sustainable energy at a competitive cost.

Wind-energy application in Europe has a very important demonstration/promotion function for further application in other parts of the world. Wind power is not only applicable in the industrialized countries of Europe and America, but is also an ideal technology for the electrification of developing countries. Wind-power application in developing countries can include all types of systems: grid-connected windfarms, hybrid energy systems, and stand-alone applications such as battery chargers. Wind power has proved to be a reliable technology adequate to fuel small remote grids and special applications such as desalination, as well as large grids. It is modular, and more power can be added quickly as the demand increases; and it is a cost-effective technology in many developing areas and nations. Finally, the technological complexity of operating and maintaining wind turbines does not differ from that of other electrical machines in rural, developing communities: desalination plants, water pumps, etc.

Consequently, wind power today is being included in the energy planning of developing nations such as China, India and Egypt.

7.3.2 Goals for a European R&D strategy on wind energy

From these two strategic goals, six interdependent goals can be put forward.

1 **Goals.** Installation of 100,000 MW of wind power competitive with fossil and nuclear power generation, maintaining European industry's international competitiveness
   Means. Reduction of wind power's production costs.

Compared with traditional energy sources, wind energy today is competitive at specific sites with favourable conditions. However, to install 100,000 MW of wind power in the

EU, economically fully competitive with fossil-fuel and nuclear-based power production requires a further cost reduction for wind power.

If the strategic goal for wind power in Europe is realized, Europe will be one of the world's largest markets for wind turbines. The European wind-power industry must be competitive in this market as well as on the other international markets for wind turbines. The European wind-power industry competes on a range of parameters, but production cost is – and will be – the most important parameter.

Based on the cost per kWh of average European wind turbines in 1994, realistic targets are cost reductions of 30% by 2000, 40% by 2005, and 50% by 2030.

2 **Goal.** Free operation of the markets for wind turbines and wind power
  Means. Establishment of harmonized European standards, legal structures and institutional frameworks.

As mentioned in the European Commission's Green Paper 'For A European Union Energy Policy', the free operation of the market has to be the principal instrument of any policy. A goal for a European policy on wind-energy utilization must be the free operation of the markets for wind turbines and wind power. Also non-EU based players must have access to this market.

The key role of the European Commission, as well as national authorities, is to ensure that these markets function to satisfy the general interest. The means must be harmonized European standards, legal structures and institutional frameworks.

Realistic targets are:

- European planning procedures suggesting and ranking feasible sites (on flat coastal and inland sites, in the mountains and offshore) for 10,000 MW by the year 2000 and 100,000 MW by 2010 (suggestion of sites only).
- A European certification and accreditation system facilitating a free market for wind-power technology by 2005.
- A European standard for performance (test and measurement) by 2000.
- A European standard for risk assessment for investment in renewable energy by 2000.
- A transparent, harmonized cost and tariff system, facilitating a free market for wind power, by 2005.
- A European code of practice for integration of wind power into the grid system and the reinforcement of the grid to make integration possible.

3 **Goal.** Increase the credibility of the technology from the perspective of the financial and insurance institutions
  Means. Minimizing the financial and technical uncertainties of wind power.

Wind is a reliable source, which can be predicted with a defined degree of uncertainty. Financial and insurance institutions increasingly consider wind power as a reliable source of energy and have increased confidence in the economic performance of the industry. However, the pattern and economics differ significantly between the European countries, depending on the track record of wind power in that country. If wind power is to be utilized widely, the technology's credibility from the perspective of the financial and insurance institutions must be increased. To achieve this, the financial, and consequently the technical, uncertainties of wind power must be minimized. Both the wind resource and the performance of wind turbines must be predicted more accurately. In particular, better prediction of the wind resource offshore and in mountainous terrain is needed.

As realistic targets, uncertainty of generation cost for flat terrain should be reduced to 10–15% by 2000 and to 5–10% by 2010. For complex (mountainous) terrain, such as regions of the Alps, uncertainty should be reduced to 20–30% by 2000 and to 10–15% by 2010.

4 **Goal.** Increase wind power's credibility from the perspective of the utilities
  Means. Ensuring wind energy's power quality and predictability. Reduction of wind power's transmission costs and grid costs.

European utilities increasingly consider wind power as a new viable and reliable source of energy in the grid's supply portfolio. However, in countries with no experience with wind power the electrical utilities are reluctant to accept wind power. This is often rooted in utilities' concern about technical issues, such as power quality, power predictability, and grid integration. Futhermore, Europe's electrical utility sector is facing a significant restructuring process, so that less attention is being given to the introduction of wind power and other renewable energy sources.

Because wide use of wind power in Europe requires the active participation of the European utilities, wind power's credibility from the perspective of the utilities must be increased. The most important means for this end are:

- ensuring wind energy's power quality and predictability;
- reduction of wind power's transmission costs and grid costs.

Realistic targets are:

- An electrical output prediction 24 hours in advance for wind farms with a standard deviation of 10–15% by 2000 and 5–10% by 2010.
- Arriving at technical and economic optimal solutions/plans for integration of 100,000 MW of wind power into the European grid by 2010.

The latter target concerns only the *planning* of the integration of 100,000 MW, not the installation itself. Plans for integration must be in place in good time before the actual deployment of the hardware.

5 **Goal.** Maintain and increase public acceptance of wind power in Europe
  Means. Minimizing the environmental and social consequences of wind-turbine deployment and operation.

Opinion surveys indicate that the majority of citizens in most European countries are generally in favour of renewable energy sources such as wind power. Opinion surveys in areas of Denmark and the UK with wind farms indicate that 70% to 80% of the population is 'generally supportive' or 'unconcerned' with respect to the turbines. However, the benefits of wind energy are on a global or national level, whereas the costs often are carried by local communities with large windfarm installations. If not dealt with properly, this can cause a Not-In-My-Back-Yard (NIMBY) dilemma.

If 100,000 MW of wind power is to be installed in Europe over the next 35 years, it is essential to maintain and increase the public's acceptance of wind power. The means for this are primarily of a political nature and therefore outside the scope of this book. However, minimizing the environmental and social consequences of wind-turbine deployment and operation is partly based on scientific research and development.

Realistic targets are to arrive at European standards and codes of practice for noise emissions, siting and 'stealthing'.

6 **Goal.** Application of wind power outside major grids in the EU and in developing countries
   Means. Exploration, development and demonstration of ample and reliable technologies of hybrid systems, battery chargers and windpumps; technology transfer.

Applications other than large grid-connected wind turbines are relevant both for areas within EU and, especially, for developing areas and countries. The basic technology and components by and large exist, with a potentially very large market.

It is generally believed that the largest impediment to a more widespread use of wind power in hybrid systems and for special applications is rooted in the hesitant stance of potential customer groups (aid organizations, the World Bank, local utilities and industries, etc.) towards the technology because of its lack of a solid track record.

Therefore, we recommend a programme to build up confidence in the technology by a short-term focus on exploration, development and demonstration of ample and reliable technologies of hybrid systems, battery chargers and windpumps. Technology transfer should also be included in such a programme.

A realistic target is a proven, mature and competitive application of wind power in remote hybrid systems and as battery chargers and windpumps by 2005.

Table 7.2 summarizes the goals, means and targets discussed above.

7.4 ROADMAP FOR R&D

Other books and reports have analysed general hindrances for wind-power implementation in Europe and have put forward strategies and suggested actions to be taken by the European Commission and national governments. This chapter limits itself to contributions from scientific research in order to achieve the overall goals.

Even though wind-power technology has matured dramatically during the last 15 years, there is still a need for further R&D. Technological improvements today are much harder to achieve than ten years ago. Nonetheless, wind-power R&D has not yet reached a level of 'diminishing returns'. As the absolute effect (measured in reduction of kWh cost) of an R&D effort is decreasing, the technology's volume is exploding, resulting in a very impressive return on the effort.

100,000 MW of installed capacity would annually produce approximately 170,000 GWh. With existing technology the production cost on average sites is of the order of 0.05 ECU/kWh. Consequently, our short-term goal of a 10% reduction in this cost would save the European economy 850 million ECU annually. This amount is a very good return on the Community's investment in wind-energy R&D.

Pursuing the above goals involves the following RD&D areas:

Table 7.2. Strategic goals, means and realistic targets

Strategic goals	Goals and means	Realistic targets
	– 100,000 MW of wind power installed competitively to fossil and nuclear power – maintain European industry's international competitiveness ⇒ decrease production cost	* Reduction of kWh cost with 30% by 2000, 40% by 2005, and 50% by 2030
	– free operation of the markets for wind turbines and wind power. ⇒ harmonized European standards, legal structures, and institutional framework	* European planning procedures suggesting and ranking feasible sites (onshore, offshore, mountains) for 10,000 MW in year 2000 and 100,000 MW in 2005 * a European certification system facilitating a free market for wind-power technology by 2005 * a European standard for performance (test and measurement) by 2000 * a European standard for risk assesment for investment in renewable energy by 2000 * a transparent, harmonized transmission cost and tariffs system facilitating a free market for wind power by 2005
100,000 MW in EU by 2030	- increase wind power's credibility from the perspective of the financial and insurance institutions ⇒ decrease uncertainties	* For flat terrain, uncertainty of generation cost for flat terrain should be reduced to 10–15% by 2000 and to 5–10% by 2010 * For mountainous terrain, uncertainty should be reduced to 20–30% by 2000 and to 10–15% by 2010
	– increase wind power's credibility from the perspective of the electrical utilities – integration of wind power in the European grid ⇒ assure power quality and predictability and decrease transmission cost	* An electrical output prediction 24 hours in advance for wind farms with a standard deviation of 10–15% by 2000 and 5–10% by 2010 * Within 2010 a technical and economical optimal solution for and planning of integration of 100.000 MW of wind power in the European grid.
Sustainable and competitive power for developing nations	– public acceptance of 100,000 MW installed wind power capacity in Europe ⇒ mitigate environmental and societal consequence of wind power	* Introduce European standards for noise, siting and stealthing by 2005
	– application of wind power outside major grids in the EU and in developing countries. ⇒ exploration, development and demonstration of ample and reliable technologies of hybrid systems, battery chargers and windpumps ⇒ technology transfer	* A proven, mature and competitive application of wind power in remote hybrid systems and as battery chargers and windpumps by 2005

- Meteorology
- Aerodynamics and aeroacoustics
- Aeroelasticity and loads
- Concept and component studies including new materials
- Operation and maintenance (logistics) studies
- Power control
- Power quality, grid interface, transmission and storage issues
- Other applications
- Certification
- Testing and measurement procedures
- Technology transfer.

7.4.1 Cost reduction

The target for cost reduction can be achieved through a number of activities connected with the components of the production cost:

1 Efficiency
2 Investment cost
   a choice of design or concept
     – further optimization of existing concepts
     – change of concept
   b manufacturing cost
     – improvement of productivity in manufacturing
     – internationalizing of the industry and its manufacturing
     – increased volume
   c project preparation cost
   d optimization of land use by reducing noise
3 Service and maintenance
4 Wind conditions.

1 Wind turbine efficiency can be further improved through more advanced aerodynamic profiles and blade design. We estimate that the potential cost reduction due to this in the short term and with present technology is modest; nevertheless, new knowledge could change this position. Furthermore, this cost reduction, by and large, is free of cost to implement.
   • basic aerodynamic research including both CFD and empirical investigations;
   • R&D in profiles and blades and experimental verification of the aerodynamic characteristics;
   • specialized WTGs to match wind conditions on each site.

2 The investment cost of wind turbines depends on both the chosen concept and on the actual design.
   a It is estimated that the costs of the *existing WTG-concept* can be reduced substantially through a better understanding, description and modelling of the wind loads and the dynamic behaviour of turbines, as well as through an optimization of the relationship between production and loads. Further development of the design basis

for wind turbines (partial coefficients, safety factors, etc.) is expected to reduce the machine cost.

- basic aeroelastic research including modelling and experimental verification;
- precision of partial coefficients;
- decrease safety factors by lowering uncertainty on loads;
- improved load models for optimization of existing concepts;
- better knowledge of material properties, especially of new materials.

Within the area of *new concepts and components* we believe, based on existing studies, that the largest long-term potential for cost reduction lies in change of concept from existing designs (20–30% on generation cost). Experience also indicates that grid-integration cost can be decreased by use of other generator types and new control systems, both aiming at better power quality. Under previous programmes MW-size WTGs have been developed and brought to a prototype stage (within the WEGA-II action). Prototype test and demonstration of MW-size machines are likely to introduce unforeseen load types. Testing and verification of MW-size machines are expected to be very costly. This is a new challenge for European test stations. We believe that direct industrial participation in this area is essential.

- basic RD&D in gearless concepts and variable speed;
- cost-effective designs for multi-MW machines
- concept studies, proof of concept by means of development, construction, and field testing of components and complete wind-turbine systems;
- parallel with concept development, aeroelastic models need to be extended and verified in order to be able to scale up and design cost-effective machines for both onshore and offshore use;
- new materials – recycling and integration of recycling in the design phase.

b Manufacturing costs are expected to follow at least the general development in industrial productivity in Europe: improved logistics, automation, new manufacturing methods, etc. It is also expected that the ongoing internationalization of the European wind industry will result in cost reductions. Finally, it is expected that manufacturing costs will be reduced as a result of the increased volume of the worldwide market for wind turbines.

Parts of this kind of cost reduction are outside the influence of an R&D programme, but some activities can be carried out:

- improve manufacturability;
- development of specialized manufacturing techniques for composite blades;
- monitoring and implementation of materials research.

c Project preparation costs depend heavily on local circumstances, such as the condition of the soil, road conditions, availability of electrical sub-stations, etc. It is expected that project preparation cost and cost of infrastructure (measured in ECU/kWh) will be halved in an intermediate time frame. This is partly due to increased machine sizes, improved quality, and expanded wind operations of wind turbines.

- development of technology and techniques for installating WTGs without cranes, roads, etc.
- monitoring the WTGs' impact on the natural environment on the site.

3 Within the area of operations and maintenance (O&M – including insurance, administration, etc.) a substantial cost reduction is expected. The O&M cost in ECU/kWh will decrease with an increase in the size of the wind turbine and the ongoing improvement of wind-turbine technology. This is due to the relatively larger energy production with

only a small increase in the initial cost and in the O&M costs. Also, as wind turbines develop, this will lead to a decrease in the O&M costs with an increase in the lifetime of the wind turbine and its main components.

It is expected that operation and maintenance costs in ECU/kWh in the intermediate time frame can be halved. Most of this cost reduction is outside the influence of an R&D programme, but some activities should be carried out:

- changing perspectives of the overall O&M with respect to safety, reliability, performance, economy, etc.;
- analysis and mitigation of lightning damage and definition of the lightning risk;
- monitoring technical experiences from wind-park operations of WTGs.

4 Wind-power economics is strongly dependent on wind conditions. The biggest potential cost reduction lies in siting wind turbines on the windiest sites. However, the siting of wind turbines depends on many societal interests, which must be considered. Especially, the impact of WTGs on birds and visual amenity need special attention.

It is not expected that offshore siting of wind turbines will result in kWh cost reductions. Although better wind conditions prevail, this is offset by higher project preparation and foundation costs. Offshore siting of wind turbines primarily contributes to enlarging the available area. Offshore siting is only interesting for MW sizes of WTGs, because foundation costs for these are relatively smaller.

Siting wind turbines in mountains is interesting for two reasons. First, a large portion of the area covered by the states in the European Union consists of mountains, and implementing the goal of 100,000 MW of wind power requires siting in these areas. Second, because of local effects, high average wind speeds can be found in places such as mountain passes (e.g. the Californian wind sites: San Gorgonio Pass, Altamont Pass, etc.). Placing wind turbines in such areas could become very competitive.

RD&D activities which should be carried out are:

- accurate measurements and modelling of wind resources offshore and in mountains;
- further improvement of tools for micrositing offshore and in mountains;
- consideration of optimized sites as opposed to maximum-wind turbine sites;
- demonstration projects with offshore MW-size WTGs;
- demonstration projects with WTGs in mountains.

7.4.2 Market issues

Securing the free operation of the market is the principal instrument for the Union's energy policy. The activities leading to free operation of the market for wind turbines and wind power comprise two areas, namely:

1 Market and competition issues.
2 Physical planning issues.

1 It is necessary for the free operation of the market and for development of optimized wind turbines that the rules for type approval and certification are the same in all countries in the European Union. This includes quality assurance systems for wind-turbine production and installation, quality systems for certification bodies and quality systems for measuring bodies.

In addition to the basis for type approval and certification of wind turbines, it is also of vital importance to maintain common rules and to ensure that wind turbines erected are in accordance with their type approval. Activities needed here are:

- investigation of financial cost/benefits and legal issues concerning transmitting substantial amounts of wind-generated electricity across national boundaries within Europe;
- conceiving and implementing European quality assurance systems;
- continuous upgrading and harmonization of measurement methods and procedures throughout the EU;
- mandatory certification in EU;
- harmonization and updating of a European technical basis for certification;
- easy-to-use calculation tools (programs, standards, etc.) for loads and strength;
- R&D leading to a European certification system;
- R&D leading to a European standard for performance, tests, measurements, and energy-prediction methods;
- R&D leading to a European standard or recommendation for risk assessment for investment in renewable energy.

2 Solid physical planning must be initiated:

- improved determination of Europe's wind resources offshore and in mountains;
- RD&D facilitating European planning procedures suggesting and ranking sites for 100,000 MW, both offshore and onshore, including mountainous terrain.

A typical offshore windpark is shown in Figure 7.4.

Figure 7.4. Offshore wind park Ijselmeer near Medemblik, The Netherlands. It consists of four Nedwind machines of 0.5 MW, rotor diameter 40 m, hub height 42 m, rigid hub, active stall control, constant-speed conversion system

7.4.3 Reduction of cost uncertainty

In pursuit of the target of 5–10% uncertainty on kWh production cost for flat terrain and 15–20% for complex terrain in 2000, activities in three areas should be carried out:

1 Improved production (annual or lifetime) prediction (meteorology).
2 Improved performance prediction (aerodynamics and measurements).
3 Failures/availability (operations and maintenance).

1 Production prediction is usually based on average annual or lifetime wind speeds. The research area of meteorology contributes primarily here:
   • improved prediction of turbulence, gust and extreme levels for different types of terrain; including mountainous terrain and offshore sites;
   • better meso-scale models;
   • improved 3D turbulence modelling;
   • development of user-friendly turbulence models;
   • verification of the effect of WTGs in parks;
   • establishment of credible, harmonized production prediction systems;
   • existing databases should be made exchangeable;
   • verification of the prediction models used.
2 The area of testing and measurement procedures includes: performance (power curve, power quality, acoustics, etc.), wind-potential assessment (anemometry), load monitoring, extrapolation to lifetime loads, strength and fatigue evaluation, and finally fatigue test on components (blade, hub, etc.).
   Within this area the following activities are vital:
   • improved measurement techniques;
   • improved reference procedures;
   • reference anemometer calibration facilities;
   • development of cost-effective calibration methods;
   • meeting industry's demand for faster, cheaper and more confident tests;
   • establishing reference procedures for proving tests (fatigue and static strength tests for blades).
3 Within the area of operation and maintenance the following activities should be initiated:
   • monitoring and clarification of O&M costs and the cost of consumables;
   • analysis and mitigation of lightning damage and definition of lightning risk.

7.4.4 Grid issues

In order to pursue the short-term target of a realistic electrical output prediction up to 36 hours ahead for wind parks and the intermediate-term target of a technical and economic optimal solution for integration of 100,000 MW of wind power into the European grid, activities within three categories are suggested:

1 Improved short-term production prediction.
2 Improved power quality.
3 Grid integration, long distance transmission and storage.

1 Improved short-term production prediction requires meteorological RD&D on:
   - R&D on better local physical models;
   - R&D on better numerical weather-prediction models;
   - RD&D and verification of models for short-term prediction and integration of inter-mittent energy sources in grids;
   - making existing databases (which can provide the input to the models) exchange-able;
   - inclusion of the models in utility planning tools;
   - implementation of planning tools at utility dispatch centres.
2 Improved power quality applies to electrical grid items such as:
   - RD&D on methods for meeting utilities' and consumers' demands for high-quality power;
   - further improvement in controlling power quality in order to minimize grid-connec-tion cost and optimize wind capacity to the grid (micro scale);
   - improvement of methods to meet grid-connection requirements: controllability of output, reduction of higher harmonics, etc.
3 The area of large-scale grid integration of wind power, long-distance power transmis-sion and storage has a long-term perspective. Activities that should be initiated, are:
   - definition, investigation and optimization of grid integration costs;
   - European investigation of grid limitations in the windiest areas to assess needs for grid reinforcement;
   - investigation of perspectives on long-distance power transmission;
   - RD&D on transmission technology, leading to reduced costs;
   - investigation of perspectives on energy storage for integration of intermittent energy sources;
   - monitoring the real, definite capacity of wind power under different wind-power share aspects;
   - investigation of wind power's position under the 'common carrier' principle.

7.4.5 Public acceptance

Public concern is often about the environmental effects of wind power, such as visual intrusion, impact on birds and birds' habitat, acoustic noise emission, safety, shadow/ flicker, etc. This is partly an educational or political problem on a national and regional level, and therefore outside the scope of this book. However, some of these problems have partly technical solutions, which can be dealt with in this context on a European level. Goals and research activities are:

1 Safety of personnel must be assured:
   - the achievement of objectives and goals discussed in this chapter must not reduce the safety of wind power (with regard to personal injury).
2 Decrease of wind turbines' noise emission and perception of that noise:
   - fundamental research on aeroacoustic noise emission;
   - improved mechanical design aiming at less noise emission;
   - new models of noise propagation, incorporating topographic and meteorological variables;
   - a better understanding of the variation of wind speeds, and the consequential back-ground noise levels, as a function of wind speed at the turbine and of topography;

- studies on attitudes to noise from wind turbines, as opposed to noise generally.

Aeroacoustics is a relatively new field of research. If an R&D effort with this area is to have even a small chance of being of any use within the next decade or two, a very large effort must be made. Even so, this is a 'high risk' strategic research area with a long-term horizon for practical use. Thus this area is suitable for concerted action.

3 Mitigation of the visual impact of wind turbines in 'open land':
- development of methods for 'stealthing' wind turbines in the open land;
- off-shore siting of wind turbines;
- development of links between techniques of landscape assessment used in planning and the methods of environmental economics.

4 Mitigation of the influence of wind turbines on birds and other wildlife:
- research on the impact of windfarms on birds, and ecosystems more generally, to refine the identification of unacceptable locations;
- development of a European Best Practice for siting windfarms with respect to birds.

5 Assessment of the comparative advantage of wind power concerning external and social costs:
- more accurate assessment of wind power's comparative advantage concerning external and social costs;
- evaluation of wind power's value for society.

6 Minimize emissions to the environment from manufacturing, operating and decommissioning WTGs:
- recycling systems for components;
- component development should include life-cycle analyses.

7 Securing public acceptability:
- general European overview of the public's attitudes to wind power – correlated with the presence of WTGs in the neighbourhood;
- research on the public's attitudes to wind power, in particular the extent to which local ownership and control assist acceptability;
- introduction of European standards for noise, siting and 'stealthing' by 2000.

7.4.6 Other applications

Applications other than large grid-connected wind turbines are relevant both for areas within the EU and, especially, for developing areas and countries. The basic technology and components by and large exist, with a potentially very large market.

We generally believe that the largest impediment to a more widespread use of wind power in hybrid systems and for special applications is rooted in the hesitant stance of potential customer groups (aid organizations, the World Bank, local utilities and industries, etc.) towards the technology as a result of:

- lack of awareness;
- lack of a solid track record;
- lack of resources for project identification;
- lack of financial tradition.

We therefore recommend a programme to build up confidence in the technology by short-term focus on, and demonstration of, simple and reliable systems. In an intermediate and long-term perspective more advanced systems and technologies must be applied.

In highly industrialized countries wind energy utilizations other than feeding the grid should also be investigated. This should include the possibilities of local use and benefits to increase the public acceptance of wind power.

We recommend that initiatives are taken in three areas:

1 Technology development:
   • further development of simple and reliable systems and technologies;
   • development of ample applied technology such as batteries, pumps and desalination systems;
   • development of certification standards for stand-alone wind systems (but without constraining innovative designs);
   • work on improving reliability of small wind systems, especially when located in turbulent terrains;
   • simplified and less costly procedures for site assessment for small systems;
   • development of specialized wind-powered stand-alone systems with a storable product, including for example ice production, desalination, cooling, heating, etc.
2 Demonstration and technology transfer to developing countries:
   • exploration of possibilities and application outside major grids;
   • feasibility and implementation studies;
   • verification of the technology through demonstration projects;
   • development of technology more suitable for licensing to manufacturers in developing countries.
3 Finally, we believe that an EU programme for development and deployment of wind turbines (grid-connected and hybrid systems) in developing countries is needed, equivalent to the suggested 'Power for the World' programme on photovoltaics. This programme must involve local governments, European industry, and its local subsidiaries, together with joint ventures.

7.5 STRATEGY

In the above we have outlined activities essential to meeting the overall goals for wind power technology and its implementation. In this section we will suggest an outline of a strategy for the European Commission's RD&D activities on wind power. The suggested strategy contains three elements.

First, the European Union's and the European Commission's responsibilities and political possibilities are briefly discussed. Second, the strategy suggests a priority between above-mentioned activities; what is needed during the next three to five years. Longer-term needs are not considered here. The strategy is based in a match between the suggested activities and the Commission's programme structure.

Finally, as the Commission does not operate a wind-energy research organization of its own, this strategy identifies types of key contractors and other key stakeholders appropriate for carrying out the proposed activities.

7.5.1 European-level responsibilities and political possibilities

Many governments and international organizations have initiated programmes for research, development and demonstration in the area of wind power. However, on a European level we find that the European Union has an important role.

The European Union's role in energy policy (i.e. wind energy) is suggested in the Commission's Green Paper 'For a European Union Energy Policy'. Based on this, it is the EUREC Agency's position that European-level research, development and demonstration programmes on wind energy should be guided by the following:

1 European actions should address common problems and potentials faced by European authorities, industry, utilities and energy planners.
2 At a programme level the actions should not distort competition in the market place. However, to secure an impact of the activities, it is important that programmes at the project level facilitate close cooperation between research organizations and individual companies.
3 Activities requiring an effort exceeding the potential and capability of an individual country should be preferred.
4 It is our position that the Commission's strategy and programme formulation should include the point of view of the European wind-power industry and electrical utilities, as well as research institutions and national authorities.
5 The Commission does not operate any wind-energy research institute of its own, nor are the Commission's R&D programmes able to provide 'basic funding' for any existing European wind-energy research institution. We find this an advantage. The Commission can draw on experience within existing institutions.
6 European RD&D programmes should not 'pick the winner' among WTG concepts or technologies, but let the industry and its customers make the necessary choices on the basis of the free operation of the market and set the speed with which new concepts are introduced. Consequently, the Commission should support R&D on well known concepts as well as on new ones.
7 Europe has accumulated a 'critical mass' of knowledge and human resources in the area of windpower research and development, both within research institutions and within industry. It is a European-level task to facilitate co-operation between this 'critical mass' on wind technology and related areas of competence, such as aerodynamic or materials research.
8 Wind-energy technology, and the industry, institutions and organizations affiliated to this technology, are still young and small compared with the established, powerful energy sectors (coal, oil, gas and nuclear). It is the Commission's responsibility to ensure that the interests of the wind-energy sector are included in policy-making processes on a European level in the same way as more established energy sectors.

7.5.2 Priority and classification of the activities

Wind-energy technology has developed tremendously over the last decade. Wind-energy technology and the European wind industry have reached a certain level of technological matureness and competitiveness. The European Union's and national RD&D programmes have played an important role in this development. This has created an industrial innovative inertia of its own with respect to cost reduction.

The most important political objective for EU's wind-energy policy is to secure a stable and open market for WTGs. If the presence of a stable European market for wind turbines is assumed, the cost of wind power will continue to decrease as a result of both competition within the wind-turbine industry and the industry's accumulated knowledge along the learning curve. This may call for a higher priority to be given to the R&D Road-map's three 'demand-side' issues; namely:

1   industrial competition and open market issues;
2   decrease of uncertainties;
3   power quality and power predictability; decrease in transmission cost.

It is not an easy task to make a short list of activities suited for the EU's RD&D activities during the next three to five years. Nevertheless, in the following we have tried to do so. Successful accomplishment of the activities listed below will require more funding than is available. A priority between the suggested activites requires detailed evaluation of proposals for each project. We can only recommend initiation of an activity if the project proposals and the contracting organizations have a high standard.

For each of the six goals suggested in the roadmap we recommend the following activities on a European level within the next three to five years:

7.5.2.1 Cost reduction
R&D MEASURES
Basic aerodynamic and aeroelastic research including numerical and empirical investigations, modelling and experimental verification. Development of WTGs specialized to match wind conditions on specific sites. R&D on lowering uncertainties on loads, material properties, and partial coefficients. Basic RD&D in new concepts and components; proof of concepts by means of development, construction and field testing of components and complete wind turbine systems. Parallel with concept development, aeroelastic models need to be extended and verified in order to be able to scale up and design cost-effective machines for both onshore and offshore use. New materials – recycling and integration of recycling in the design phase. Analysis and mitigation of lightning damage and definition of lightning risk. Further improvement of tools for micrositing in mountains.

DEMONSTRATION MEASURES
Demonstration of new concepts, offshore MW-size WTGs, and WTGs in mountains and offshore.

7.5.2.2 Market issues
R&D MEASURES
R&D leading to a European standard for performance, tests, measurements, and energy prediction methods.

DEMONSTRATION AND SUPPORT MEASURES
European planning procedures suggesting and ranking sites for 100,000 MW both offshore and onshore, including mountainous terrain. Conceive and implement European

quality assurance systems. Continuous upgrading and harmonization of measurement methods and procedures throughout the EU. Harmonization and updating of a European technical basis for certification.

7.5.2.3 Reduction of cost uncertainties

R&D MEASURES

Improved prediction of turbulence, gust and extreme levels for different types of terrain, including mountainous terrain and offshore sites. Improved 3D turbulence modelling and meso-scale models. Improved measurement techniques, reference procedures, and reference anemometer calibration facilities. Analysis and mitigation of lightning damage and definition of lightning risk.

DEMONSTRATION AND SUPPORT MEASURES

Credible, harmonized production prediction systems must be established. Make existing meteorological databases exchangeable.

7.5.2.4 Grid issues

R&D MEASURES

R&D in better local physical models and numerical weather prediction models. Make existing databases (which can provide the input to the models) exchangeable. R&D on further improvement of controlling power quality in order to minimize grid-connection cost and optimize wind capacity to the grid (micro scale). R&D on methods to meet grid-connection requirements: controllability of output, reduction of higher harmonics, etc.

DEMONSTRATION MEASURES

Demonstration and verification of short-term prediction models in utility planning tools. Implementation of planning tools at utility dispatch centres.

7.5.2.5 Public acceptance

R&D MEASURES

Fundamental research on aeroacoustic noise emission (suitable for concerted action). Development of better models of noise propagation, incorporating topographic and meteorological variables. More accurate assessment of wind power's comparative advantage concerning external and social costs. Evaluation of wind power's value for society.

SUPPORT MEASURES

Research on the public's attitudes to wind power, in particular with respect to measures ensuring local acceptance (such as local ownership and control).

7.5.2.6 Other applications

R&D MEASURES

Further development of simple and reliable systems and technologies. Development of ample applied technology, such as batteries, pumps, desalination systems, etc.

DEMONSTRATION AND SUPPORT MEASURES

Verification of the technology through demonstration projects. Establishment of an EU programme for demonstration and installation of wind turbines (grid-connected, stand-alone and hybrid systems) in developing countries.

7.5.3 Key players

It is our position that the contractors in the research (JOULE) part should primarily be found among industrial enterprises, universities, national research centres, etc. with a basic funding of their own and a track record of high-class research. Whereas contractors in the demonstration (THERMIE) part should primarily be found among the technology's end-users, such as industrial enterprises, utilities, government bodies, the finance and insurance community, etc.

It is also our position that wind-energy research must be defined and carried out in close cooperation with industry, utilities and other 'users' of the results of this research. This is the most efficient way of defining the activities needed, and of successfully achieving the goals and implementation of the results.

It is our position that in the future RD&D programmes should also facilitate cross-national and cross-sectorial cooperation by requiring project partners from several member countries and from typical user groups, such as industry, utilities, government institutions, etc. On the other hand, we are concerned about mega-projects including too many project partners, such that project administration paralyses the scientific process and devalues useful results of the projects. The Commission's legitimate interest in cross-national and cross-sectorial cooperation must not become a hindrance to efficient research and implementation of results.

Table 7.3 shows key players who should be concerned with specific strategic issues, while Table 7.4 gives estimates of global wind-power installations.

Table 7.3. Key players other than research organizations

Area	Key players other than research organizations
Cost reduction	European wind industry
Market issues	European wind industry
Cost uncertainty	European wind industry, utilities, financial and insurance institutions
Grid issues	European wind industry, electrical utilities, national meteorological authorities
Public acceptance	National governments
Other application	European wind industry, utilities, financial institutions, international organizations (UNDP, World Bank, etc.)

7.6 REFERENCES

Andersen P D, Fuglsang P (1995). Vurdering af udviklingsforløb for vindkraftteknologien (in Danish). Risø National Laboratory, Roskilde. Risø-R-829(DA).

Arkesteijn L, Havinga R (1992). Wind Farms and Planning; Practical experiences in the Netherlands. Conference Proceedings from European Wind Energy Association's Special Topic Conference ' 92: The Potential of Wind Farms, Denmark.

AWEA (1994). Testimony of the American Wind Energy Association before The Senate Committee on Energy and Natural Resources. AWEA, Washington DC, 8 March 1994.

Table 7.4. Estimates of global wind power installations in MW

Country or region	New capacity in 1994	Estimated capacity in 1994	Estimated capacity in 2000
USA	100	1722	2800
Latin America	4	10	400
Americas	**104**	**1732**	**3200**
Germany	307	632	2000
Denmark	52	539	1000
Netherlands	30	162	500
UK	40	170	800
Spain	16	73	800
Sweden	10	40	240
Greece	10	36	200
Italy	7	22	300
Portugal	-	9	60
Ireland	6	8	150
Finland	3	4	50
Other European	4	28	440
Europe	**485**	**1723**	**6540**
CIS	**–**	**–**	**70**
India	141	201	2900
China	18	29	730
Other Asia	–	7	185
Asia	**159**	**237**	**3815**
Australia/N.Z.	**–**	**6**	**80**
Egypt	1	5	150
Cap Verde	2	3	6
Other African	1	2	70
Africa	**8**	**10**	**165**
Total	**756**	**3708**	**13,800**

Beurskens J (1983). Practical Aspects of the Application of Wind Energy (in Dutch). PT/Werktuig-bouw 4/83, April.

Beurskens J (1994). Wind Energy: European Status and Prospects. Contribution to the Conference 'Energy for the Future', Vision Eureka, Lillehammer.

Beurskens J (1994). Wind Energy Systems: Resources, Environmental Aspects and Cost. Netherlands Energy Research Foundation, Petten, The Netherlands.

Carstensen U T (ed.) (1995). Windkraftanlagen Markt – Typen, Technik, Preise. Sonderdruck WIND/ENERGIE/AKTUELL, ISBN 3-9804393-0-5.

Carver H A, Page D I (1994). Public attitudes to the Cemmaes Wind Farm. Paper presented at the BWEA '94 conference.

Cavallo A J, Hock S M, Smith D R (1993). Wind Energy: Technology and Economics. In Johansson T B, Kelly H, Reddy A K N, Williams R H (ed.), Renewable Energy. Sources for Fuels and Electricity, Island Press, Washington DC.

Cohen, J (1993). The IPCC Technology Characterization Inventory – Horizontal Axis Wind Turbines in Windfarms. NREL/US-DOE, November.

Durstewitz M, Ensslin C, Hoppe-Kilpper M, Kleinkauf W (1994). Wind Energy Development in Germany – Results from the 250 MW Programme. Paper presented at 5th European Wind Energy Association Conference and Exhibition, 10–14 October 1994, Thessaloniki, Greece.

The Economist (1994). Power to the People – A Survey of Energy. The Economist, 18 June 1994.

European Commission (1993). Growth, Competitiveness, Employment. The Challenges and Ways Forward into the 21st Century. White Paper. ECSC-EC-EAEC, Brussels/Luxembourg.

European Commission (1995). For a European Union Energy Policy - Green Paper. ECSC-EC-EAEC, Brussels/Luxembourg.

EWEA (1991). Time for Action – Wind Energy in Europe. European Wind Energy Association.

Eyre N (1994). Externalities of Fuel Cycles 'Externe' project. Wind Fuels. Working Document No. 7. European Commission, DG XII.

FDV (Danish Windmill Manufacturers Association) (1994). Perspectiv 2004 (in Danish).

Frandsen S, Christensen C J (1992). Accuracy of Estimation of Energy Production from Wind Power Plants. Wind Engineering, 16, No. 5, 157–168.

Godtfredsen F (1993). Sammenligning af danske og udenlandske vindmøllers økonomi (in Danish). Risø report, Risø-R-622(DA), Risø National Laboratory.

Godtfredsen F (1994). Analyse af danske vindmøllers driftsudgifter 1993 (in Danish). Risø report, Risø-R-776(DA), Risø National Laboratory.

Grubb M J, Meyer N I (1993). Wind Energy: Resources, Systems, and Regional Strategies. In Johansson T B, Kelly H, Reddy A K N, Williams R H (ed.), Renewable Energy. Sources for Fuels and Electricity, Island Press, Washington DC.

Hohmeyer O, Ottinger R (1990). External Environmental Cost of Electricity. Workshop report, Ladenburg, Germany.

IAEA (1991). Key Note Papers. Senior Expert Symposium on Electricity and The Environment, Helsinki, Finland, May 1991, International Atomic Energy Agency, Vienna.

International Energy Agency (1995). IEA Wind Energy Annual Report 1994. National Renewable Energy Laboratory, CO, USA.

IPCC (Intergovernmental Panel on Climate Change) Working Group IIa (1994). Energy Supply Mitigation Options, Review Draft 18, July 1994. IPCC.

Keuper A, Schmidt A,Veltrup M (1994). Die Windenergieindustrie in Deutschland (in German). DEWI Magazin no.5, August.

Molly J P (1994). Windenergie in Deutschland (in German). DEWI Magazin no.5, August.

Nielsen P (1994). 500 MW vindkraft i Danmark - Sådan gik det til (in Danish). Naturlig Energi, September.

OECD/IEA, NEA (1993). Projected Costs of Generating Electricity. Update 1992. OECD, Paris.

Rasmussen F, Kretz A (1992). Dynamics and Potentials for the Two-Bladed Teetering Rotor Concept. Paper presented at AWEA 1992 Conference.

SERI/US-DOE (1990). The Potential of Renewable Energy – An Interlaboratory White Paper. US Department of Energy, SERI/TP-260-3674.

Still D, Little B, Lawrence S G,Carver H (1994). The Birds of Blyth Harbour. Paper presented at the BWEA 1994 Conference.

van Wijk A J M, Coelingh J P, Turkenburg W C (1991). Global potential for wind energy. Proceedings of European Wind Energy Conference 91, The Netherlands 1991.

Windkraftanlagen Marktübersicht '94 (in German). Interessenverband Windkraft Binnenland, Osnabrück.

World Energy Council (1993). Energy for Tomorrow' s World. Kogan Page, St. Martin's Press. ISBN 0 7494 1117 1.

World Energy Council (1994). New Renewable Energy Resources – A Guide to the Future. Kogan Page, London, 1994. ISBN 0 7494 1263 1.

World Energy Council (1995). Local & Regional Energy-Related Environmental Issues. World Energy Council, London, September 1995.

World Energy Council/Commission (1994). Fuel Switching. World Energy Council.

Wrixon G T, Rooney A-M E (1992). Draft Final Report – EUREC Agency Renewable Energy Study. Final report of Contract reference Number 46/92 With the Commission of the European Communities, EUREC Agency.

GLOSSARY

WTG	Wind Turbine Generator
WEC	Wind Energy Converter
O&M	Operation and Maintenance
IEA	International Energy Agency
PV	Photovoltaics
EWEA	European Wind Energy Association
RD&D	Research, Development and Demonstration
EUREC Agency	European Renewable Energy Centres Agency
UNDP	United Nations Development Programme

8. INTEGRATION OF RENEWABLE ENERGY INTO COMBINED HEAT AND/OR LOCAL POWER SUPPLY

8.1 INTRODUCTION

Renewable Energy (RE) technologies are developing rapidly and it is generally antici-pated that the new RE technologies (wind, PV, solar thermal, biofuels etc.) will be increasingly economically competitive with fossil and nuclear plants. Within a time hori-zon of 10 to 20 years some of the RE technologies, such as wind, will be fully economi-cally competitive while others, such as PV, will be approaching full competitiveness. However, when used on their own, each of the RE technologies have shortcomings when compared to the ability of traditional fossil fuel based generation technologies to supply guaranteed power with accepted high-capacity value.

Therefore, in order for the full potential of RE technologies to be utilized, they must be used together in an integrated way in generating units or schemes that may be termed Integrated Hybrid Renewable Energy (IHRE) systems or RE Cogeneration Schemes. IHRE systems consist of RE generating technologies in combination with other RE tech-nologies and energy storage and/or power-conditioning technologies in layouts (concen-trated systems for local power supply or dispersed schemes for regional power supply) adapted to the conditions and possibilities of each specific location, so as to ensure guar-anteed and reliable power.

This chapter formulates a set of realistic goals for RD&D in terms of technological and economic performance, as well as the practical measures necessary for the realization of the goals in terms of actions within RD&D and associated fields. The chapter outlines a strategy for development and gives recommendations as to how the strategy may be real-ized.

8.2 PRESENT SITUATION

8.2.1 Basic issues

There is a growing global awareness that the energy supply of the future must rely to a very high degree on 'clean' and renewable energy technologies, and that a failure to attain this may have very serious consequences.

A very significant increase in global energy consumption is happening, partly as a con-sequence of national policies for a significant increase in standards of living for a large part of the world's population. This increase cannot in the long run be met by a fossil-fuel-based power supply without very serious consequences for the global environment.

It is therefore necessary to develop, within a time horizon of less than, say, 50 years, a sustainable global energy-supply concept that ultimately is based on 'clean' and renewable energy on a scale sufficient to meet the demands. Strategies to support this development should be developed and applied by relevant national, regional and international bodies. The development itself must be driven by those who can afford to do so, i.e. the industrialized countries, and applied to those who cannot.

8.2.2 RE technologies

Renewable Energy (RE) technologies are developing rapidly, but, when used on their own, each of the RE technologies has shortcomings when compared to the ability of traditional fossil-fuel generation technologies to supply guaranteed power with accepted high-capacity value.

Therefore, in order for the full potential of RE technologies to be utilized, they must be used together in an integrated way, in generating units or schemes that may be termed Integrated Hybrid Renewable Energy (IHRE) systems or RE Cogeneration Schemes, depending on whether they are concentrated systems for local power supply or dispersed schemes for regional power supply. An example is shown in Figure 8.1.

It is convenient to discuss integrated application of RE technology in terms of both IHRE systems and RE Cogeneration schemes, although a rigorous distinction between the two concepts is not always possible. Likewise, it is not rigorously defined what is a local community versus a power supply region.

IHRE Systems and RE Cogeneration Schemes consist of RE generating technologies in combination with other RE technologies, including passive designs, energy management and energy storage and/or power-conditioning technologies.

Figure 8.1. Deersum energy project: combined tapping of manure digestion and wind energy (European Commission, Directorate General XVII for Energy – THERMIE Programme)

Layouts should be adapted to the conditions and possibilities of each specific location, so as to ensure guaranteed and reliable power.

In concept, IHRE systems and RE Cogeneration Schemes are envisaged as consisting only of RE technologies for up to 100% local power supply from concentrated IHRE systems and integration of dispersed RE Cogeneration schemes into existing power supplies.

Ultimately IHRE systems and RE Cogeneration Schemes could develop into completely RE-based schemes, which include new types of energy carriers such as hydrogen, in combination with new ways to supply and manage the end-user's energy demand (see, for example, Figure 8.2).

In practice, the power supply will often include fossil-fuel energy sources for support and backup, in particular when IHRE systems and RE Cogeneration Schemes are introduced into supply systems with existing fossil-fuel power plants.

Tools and techniques developed for the IHRE systems should therefore be applicable also in cases where individual RE systems are positioned geographically apart from each other, i.e. where two or more geographically separated RE systems are connected to a common grid, and applied to systems where fossil sources are incorporated.

8.2.3 European status

There is presently a significant increase in the interest shown by governments, planners, utilities and private investors in including RE technologies in the energy supply portfolio. A long-term goal of European policy is a significant contribution (15% at year 2010) from European-based renewable energy. This goal is influenced by rising concern regarding externality costs (CO_2-related and others).

Today's most promising RE technologies are based on wind, biomass and biofuels, and solar energy for both electricity production and heat production. Currently, RE applications mostly deal with one RE technology at a time, such as in wind parks, PV systems, etc.

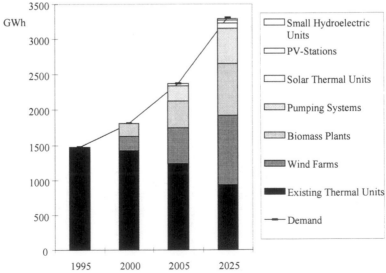

Figure 8.2. Action plan for an intensive penetration of REs in the island of Crete (CE-Project JOU2-CT92-0190)

To date international R&D in hybrid RE systems has mostly concentrated on wind diesel systems; see, for example, Figure 8.3. It is envisaged that future R&D programmes will concentrate more on IHREs, systems in which several RE technologies are integrated.

National capabilities exist in manufacturing, consultancy, application and R&D of RE technologies and increasingly in IHRE technologies. European networks and alliances in the field of RE and IHRE technologies are already established, and more are being formed, very much as a result of EU programmes emphasizing this type of development.

8.2.3.1 RE technologies

Within each of the RE technologies, a world-lead position has been established internationally, at both national and European levels within manufacturing, consultancy, construction, implementation and application, as well as in research & development

The R&D effort in the field of RE is in accordance with national and European policies on energy, and the EU Framework programmes have made available considerable allocations of funding for developing RE technologies. Complementary national R&D programmes also exist, with emphasis on different RE topics, according to national resources and preferences.

RE technologies are not yet fully competitive with existing energy-supply technologies on purely commercial considerations, i.e. when externalities are not included in the comparison. However, it is generally anticipated that the new RE technologies (wind, PV, solar thermal, biofuels, etc.) will be increasingly economically competitive with fossil and nuclear plant and some, such as wind, fully competitive within a time horizon of 10 to 20 years. In high-wind locations, such as the UK, wind is already nearly competitive.

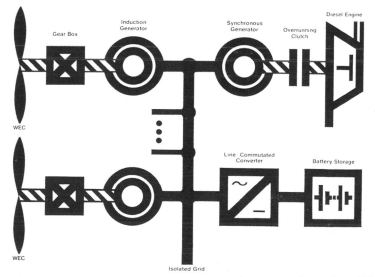

Figure 8.3. Modular autonomous electrical power supply system: advanced wind/diesel/ battery combination on the Irish island of Cape Clear (European Commission, Directorate General XVII for Energy – THERMIE Programme)

European manufacturers, consultants and research institutions are in a good position to contribute very substantially to the enormous effort necessary worldwide during the coming years in RD&D and implementation of RE technologies.

8.2.3.2 Integrated RE systems

There is a growing realization, that RE technologies should be applied in combination with each other, to supplement each other and to improve capacity values.

Today, the situation is that few manufacturers aim specifically at manufacture and supply of RE systems, but there are suppliers of Hybrid Wind Diesel systems (i.e. systems with wind and diesel generation together with another RE technology, typically PV) with development strategies that aim at IHRE systems. Although there is no widespread application of IHRE systems, a number of pilot plants and demonstration projects have been implemented (for example, see Figure 8.4). Their operation adds to the increasing body of experience being accumulated.

The development and application of IHRE systems presently aims at the supply of electricity to grids, heat for use in (district) heating and as process heat, and energy carriers such as biogas and biofuels (and in the long run hydrogen from electrolysis).

The integration of renewable energy in the urban environment using passive and active systems has also been considered during the last few years. A number of pilot projects for modern urbanization ('solar city' concepts), which take into account new climatic techniques in order to develop a new solar and bio-climatic architecture have been designed (Figure 8.5).

Attention has also been given to the possibilities of producing water using IHRE systems, specifically in regions like the Mediterranean where the natural water supply is lim-

Figure 8.4. Two 250 kW wind turbines and two 600 kW combined heat/power plants at Enkhuizen (European Commission, Directorate General XVII for Energy – THERMIE Programme)

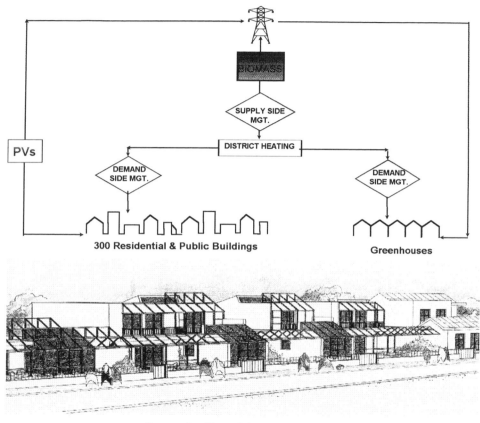

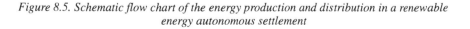

Perspective View of the PV Metal Grid

Figure 8.5. Schematic flow chart of the energy production and distribution in a renewable energy autonomous settlement

ited. A new way of producing water in a sustainable manner and at a cost that people can afford is currently being investigated.

There is a simultaneous development of planning tools in terms of system models on various levels, predicting resources and output, but practically no standards or agreed evaluation criteria have been established.

8.3 REALISTIC GOALS

8.3.1 The vision

For Europe the visions in terms of long-term objectives should be:

1 To ensure a sustainable energy supply in the long run, i.e. an energy supply concept based almost entirely on RE technologies.
2 To ensure a controlled and well planned transition from the present fossil-fuel-based energy supply to the future sustainable one.
3 To contribute on a global scale to the implementation worldwide of RE technologies in the form of IHRE systems and technology developed in Europe as an offshoot of European development.

For European energy R&D policy the corresponding vision should be:

4 To establish a framework for continued, increased R&D and demonstration of large-scale applications and integration of RE technologies.

The overall European strategy should be:

5 To develop tools for planning, design, implementation and evaluation of IHRE technology.
6 To implement pilot and demonstration IHRE systems.

The goals, means and strategy necessary to implement the vision are defined in the following sections, and the whole conceptual setup is shown in Figure 8.6

8.3.2 Strategic goals

Overall strategic goals should be:

1 Development of IHRE systems for up to 100% electricity production (or combined heat and power production).
2 Development of RE Coproduction schemes for integration of RE into existing power supply systems.

This should include development of IHRE technology giving the same power supply reliability and power quality as a conventional system.

On a European level this development should concentrate on

3 Development of regions in EU with 100% RE power supply.
4 Development of smaller IHRE systems for isolated/remote areas.

Technology should be developed *and implemented* to meet the needs in the developing world, in order to avoid conflicts and other consequences of an increasing use of fossil fuels.

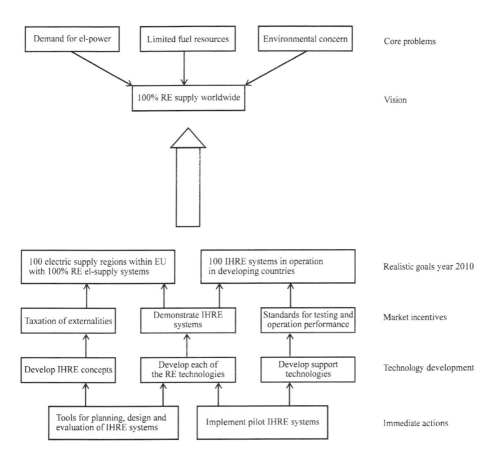

Figure 8.6. Conceptual setup of the proposed strategy

On a global level the development should concentrate on:

5 Development of sustainable and competitive power for developing countries.
6 Ensuring that a substantial part of global increase in energy demand is covered by IHRE and RE Cogeneration technology.

This development will ensure that an increasing proportion of third-world energy demand will be supplied by IHRE and RE Cogeneration technology and it will include the development of a competitive technical and economic performance. In the end, it will contribute to limiting the (growth in) global CO_2 emissions.

8.3.3 Goals and means for a European RD&D strategy

Specific goals for the development of IHRE technology could be:

1 100 electric supply regions within the EU with supply systems operational up to 100% RE-based electricity.
2 100 IHRE systems in operation in developing countries.

These regions and systems should be fully operational no later than the year 2010. They should be of different sizes and have different characteristics. A certain number should be identified immediately as pilot regions and specific action and implementation plans should be put into effect.

On the small scale, the units could be building blocks, new neighbourhoods in residential areas, small rural areas with particular electric and heating needs (e.g. pumping, small manufacturing, water production, refrigeration, etc.), or isolated areas like islands or mountain communities. On a larger scale, one or several 'solar cities' should be identified, where the use of RE in the urban environment should be introduced, and larger rural areas with an approach using energy crops should be considered as base for an RE activity.

Regions in the administrative sense should also be defined as pilot regions, while the large islands of the Mediterranean (e.g. Sardinia, Crete or Mallorca) could also be used as pilot regions.

These goals may be indicative only, but it is necessary to have clearly stated goals. As implementation proceeds and experience is gained, the numbers may have to be adjusted. Maybe, an actual 100% RE-based power supply will only be possible in a few cases, but, on the other hand, the time limit of 2010 may turn out to be pessimistic.

In order to reach these goals, a number of interdependent goals must be reached, and, in order to do this, a number of measures must be implemented. In order to define the actions necessary and to monitor progress, a strategy must be defined that includes schedules, priorities and players.

The strategic and dependent goals and the associated measures are outlined below. There are four groups (Table 8.1) of interdependent goals leading to seven means or measures:

A Secure European manufacture and application
- **Goals**
   a 100 power supply grids and regions within EU with operational power supply systems based, up to 100% on RE technologies;
   b Secure European industry's international competitiveness.
- **Means**
   1 Develop and demonstrate proven and cost effective concepts, principles and solutions for RE Cogeneration and IHRE systems;
   2 Improve support technologies, e.g. energy conversion and management technologies.

B Increase credibility and predictability
- **Goals**
   c Increase the technical credibility of the IHRE and RE Cogeneration technology;
   d Increase the economic credibility of the technology;

Table 8.1. Table of goals and measures

Strategic goals	Dependent goals	Measures
* IHRE Systems with 100% recognized capacity value * Communities / regions in EU up to 100% RE power supplied * Sustainable and competitive power for developing countries * Substantial part of global increase in energy demand covered by IHRE technology	* 100 power supply grids and regions within EU with operational up to 100% RE-based power supply systems * Secure European industry's international competitiveness	– Develop and demonstrate proven and cost-effective concepts, principles & solutions for RE Cogeneration and IHRE systems – Improve support technologies, e.g. energy conversion and management technologies.
	* Increase the technical credibility of the IHRE technology * Increase the economic credibility of the IHRE technology * Increase the predictability of the performance of the IHRE technology * Increase the integration into European grids and regions	– Flexible, modular & updateable tools for planning, design and evaluation –Ensure necessary quality of deliverables (power, reliability, predictability)
	* Free operation of the markets for RE Cogeneration and IHRE Technology * Increased industrial collaboration and Coproduction of IHRE systems	– Harmonized European standards, legal structures and institutional framework.
	*Acceptance by implementing agencies, donor organizations and other international financiers * Application of RE Cogeneration and IHRE technology outside EU including developing countries	– Agreed rates and principles for the quantitative evaluation of IHRE technology including externalities – Proven and competitive applications of RE Cogeneration and IHRE technology by 2010

  e Increase the predictability of the performance of the technology;
  f Increase the integration into European grids and regions.
- **Means**
  3 Flexible, modular and updateable tools for planning, design and evaluation;
  4 Ensure necessary quality of deliverables (power, reliability, predictability).

C Increase compatibility and collaboration
- **Goals**
  g Free operation of the markets for RE Cogeneration and IHRE Technology;
  h Increased industrial collaboration and Coproduction of IHRE systems.
- **Means**
  5 Harmonized European standards, legal structures and institutional framework.

D Increase international acceptance and application

- **Goals**
  - i Acceptance by implementing agencies, donor organizations and other international financiers;
  - k Application of RE Cogeneration and HW technology outside EU, including developing countries;
- **Means**
  - 6 Agreed rates and principles for the quantitative evaluation of IHRE technology including externalities;
  - 7 Proven and competitive applications of RE Cogeneration and IHRE technology by 2010.

The means or measures are described in the following section.

8.4 A ROADMAP FOR RD&D

RD&D areas and tasks involved in pursuing the goals of Section 8.3 are shown in the Table 8.2. The measures to be implemented in order to achieve the goals are briefly described. These measures include actions which may also be dealt with as part of the development of specific RE technologies, and these actions should of course not be repeated as part of the development of IHRE systems and RE Cogeneration schemes.

Table 8.2. RD&D areas and tasks

RD&D areas	Important RD&D tasks
A SYSTEMS & CONCEPT STUDIES * System design & modelling * Component interfacing & interaction * Control & regulation	* Layouts & principles for modular control * Local vs global control * Scheduling & despatch of system components * Standardized protocols for control communication and power exchange * Tools for flexible modelling and design layout of system configuration and control
B COMPONENT STUDIES * Power electronics * Energy storage * Energy carriers	* Converters * Battery technology * Flywheels * Hydrogen storage * Hydrogen in prime movers
C SYSTEMS PLANNING & EVALUATION	* Integrated Resource Planning techniques for IHRE technology * Quantification of externalities * Capacity values / short-term predictions
D CERTIFICATION & EVALUATION	* Standards for certification * Standards for evaluation & prediction of technical/economical performance
E TEST & MEASUREMENT PROCEDURES	* Standards for test, measurements
F APPLICATIONS	* Technology development * Demonstration and technology transfer * Development and deployment in second and third world countries

Instead some degree of coordination between the various technologies should be exercised, so that the various efforts may contribute to each other.

8.4.1 Develop and demonstrate proven and cost-effective concepts, principles and solutions for RE Cogeneration and IHRE systems

In order to reach the goals for application of IHRE systems and RE Cogeneration schemes both inside and outside the EU, cost-effective concepts and solutions should be developed and demonstrated. In the process there will be a substantial contribution to the international competitiveness of the European industry, and support skills.

Development efforts should include work on configuration and architecture of both concentrated IHRE systems and dispersed RE Cogeneration schemes, and the philosophies and principles for integration and dispersion would form part of this. Control and regulation, local as well as global, are important issues which are linked to the interfaces and interactions between components. Solutions applied for specific cases should be demonstrated and monitored.

Preference should be given to activities involving combinations of technology and application in such a way that such projects have the potential to cover the entire range from pre-feasibility study, through feasibility study and demonstration phase (mainly programme financed), to large-scale implementation with (mainly) commercial international financing.

8.4.2 Improve support technologies, e.g. energy conversion and management technologies

In order to improve the ability of IHRE systems and RE Cogeneration schemes to supply guaranteed and reliable power, support technologies such as energy conversion, storage and management technologies should be developed and improved.

Electrical power conversion technologies and storage technologies, such as battery and flywheel storage, are 'hard' technologies to support the RE generating technologies, but 'soft' technologies, such as management of input (RE resources, e.g. biomass, etc.) and output (consumer loads) should also be included.

An important issue is to develop, incorporate and manage secondary loads, such as water (including water desalination), heating, cooling, freezing, etc. The generation and storage (and distribution) of energy carriers such as biofuels and hydrogen should be part of this effort.

Ultimately the development and demonstration of the application of energy carriers in prime movers, such as power generators and vehicle engines, will make a major contribution towards a high utilization of RE-based power supply.

8.4.3 Flexible, modular and updateable tools for planning, design and evaluation

A prerequisite for the increased integration of RE technologies into European grids and regions is the acceptance of the IHRE and RE Cogeneration technologies by decision makers, financers etc. This means that both technical and economic credibility should be increased and substantiated.

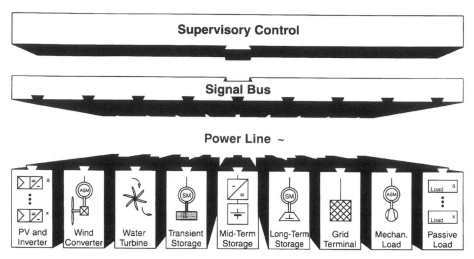

Figure 8.7. Modular photovoltaic and hybrid systems technology: Eurec Agency Megahybrid Project, coordinated by ISET Germany (European Commission, Directorate General XII for Science, Research and Development)

An important part of this will be the development of flexible, modular and updateable tools for planning, design and evaluation of such systems and schemes. This implies the need for tools for flexible modelling of system configurations and control strategies as well as system planning models and integrated resource-planning techniques. Models should be developed for technical development (for example, see Figure 8.7), as well as for techno-economic assessment of performance.

As part of this there is a need for development of agreed criteria for evaluation of technical and economic performance, so that proposed solutions may be compared to other alternatives in a generally agreed and accepted way.

8.4.4 Ensure necessary quality of deliverables (power, reliability, predictability)

As part of increasing the technical and economical credibility of IHRE systems and RE Cogeneration schemes the necessary quality of the deliverables from such systems and schemes should be ensured.

This requires work within areas such as :

1 Interface and interaction between systems, components and users.
2 Verification and documentation.
3 Monitoring of actual installations.

Examples of deliverables in this context are power, reliability and predictability.

8.4.5 Harmonized European standards, legal structures and institutional framework

Another prerequisite for a successful large-scale and high-penetration deployment of IHRE systems and RE Cogeneration schemes will be to ensure a free operation of the markets for such systems and schemes. A major part of this will be to work for a harmonization within Europe. Examples are:

1 Standards to improve quality, performance and compatibility, such as standards for:
   a protocols and interface between components and users;
   b testing and measurement procedures;
   c technical and economic performance.
2 Legal structures such as certification, planning permits, noise limits, etc.
3 Institutional issues such as insurance, financing, etc.

This will also contribute towards increased industrial collaboration and co-production with respect to these systems and schemes.

8.4.6 Agreed rates and principles for the quantitative evaluation of IHRE technology

This is a prerequisite for any widespread acceptance of IHRE systems and RE Cogeneration schemes by implementing agencies, donor organizations and other international financiers and decision makers.

This work includes agreements on:
1 Energy accounting principles and rates.
2 Economic assessment principles and methods.
3 Quantification in economic terms of emission reduction effects and socio-economic effects.

Such agreements will enhance the application of IHRE systems and RE Cogeneration schemes both inside the EU and in the developing countries.

8.4.7 Proven and competitive applications of RE Cogeneration and IHRE technology by 2010

This is very much a matter of implementing conscious and well planned, executed and monitored applications of IHRE and RE Cogeneration technology in the form of actual systems and schemes, i.e. a matter of successful demonstration and application.

In order to obtain the goals in this contexts it may be necessary to include issues such as

1 Subsidies and policies;
2 Establishing of manufacturing capabilities; and
3 Formation of networks for resources including manufacturers, R&D institutions, consultants, etc.

Some of these issues include components of policy and politics.

8.5 STRATEGY

The previous parts of this chapter have outlined recommended goals for Integrated Hybrid Renewable Energy Systems and Renewable Energy Cogeneration schemes, as well as the recommended means in terms of Research, Development and Demonstration (RD&D) needed for the achievement of the goals.

An overview of the main issues that must be addressed in an RD&D strategy for the European RD&D activities on Integrated Hybrid Renewable Energy Systems and Renewable Energy Cogeneration schemes is given below.

Integration of renewable energy involves both technical issues and non-technical issues, such as planning and policies, and therefore the strategy includes the four main issues described briefly below.

It might be advantageous to finalize the detailed mapping of the strategy in a forum where European Commission representatives interact with representatives from the European resource base for the RE and integration technologies.

8.5.1 Policy and politics

Overall guidelines and priorities should reflect a policy of actively promoting and supporting development towards a high degree of integration of RE into the European power supply in such a way that inter-European cooperation is supported without distorting the competitive balance between the parties in the European resource base.

On a political and strategic level those preferences and initiatives that are needed to implement this policy should be supported or implemented. It could include support for strategic work, such as a complete reasoning and argument for IHRE and RE Cogeneration technology ('White Paper') in regional (EU) and global (worldwide) contexts, together with implementation and incentive initiatives for market developments. This initiative could also include a policy for the utilization and transfer to the second and third worlds of European capabilities, technology and experience, that have been, and will be, acquired through European RD&D efforts.

The policy should emphasize a reinforced integrated and interdisciplinary approach, including the continuation and formation of interdisciplinary networks.

The policy should include preference for projects of the 'co-ordinated programme' type, i.e. projects with the potential to cover the entire range from pre-feasibility study, through feasibility study and demonstration phase (mainly programme financed), to large-scale implementation with (mainly) commercial international financing; such projects should also include countries from outside the EU.

8.5.2 Priorities and schedules

Each separate RE technology is presently developing at a rapid and steady pace and the associated needs for RD&D are dealt with in earlier chapters.

In the context of IHRE and RE Cogeneration technology the development needs are primarily in the development of tools necessary for planning and assessment of systems and schemes, and in establishing agreed rates and criteria for their evaluation, including externalities and other social costs/values.

The equally important demonstration needs are primarily for carefully designed, well executed and closely monitored demonstrations of systems and schemes for local and regional integration of RE technologies.

A number of 'demand side' issues should have high priority, such as harmonizing standards and increasing the technical and economical credibility of the IHRE and RE Cogeneration technology.

Technology and concepts exist today that are suitable for application, and an immediate priority should be to identify examples of currently working concepts and to implement them in demonstration projects aimed at creating a (positive) track record. In the long term, development programmes should be implemented to improve tools and other capabilities, and demonstration programmes should be implemented to demonstrate improved concepts and/or applications as they become available.

Competent and critical review of the systems developed and demonstrated is a precondition for a qualified feed-back to the R&D programmes for both integrated systems and for specific RE technologies.

High priority should be given to projects with the potential to cover the entire range from pre-feasibility study, through feasibility study and demonstration phase (mainly programme financed), to large-scale implementation with (mainly) commercial international financing; such projects should also include countries from outside the EU.

8.5.3 Classification

Classification of the goals, means and measures of the recommended RD&D roadmap according to programme and project structures of the EU would benefit from the combined expertise of EU staff and the European resource base. It might be advantageous to finalize the classification in a forum where European Commission representatives interact with representatives from the European resource base for the IHRE and RE Cogeneration technology.

This process would also be useful if and when new programmes and/or project structures are to be considered. In this context it should be recognized that integration projects and programmes may be able to provide very useful feed-back and directions to the specific RE technology programmes.

8.5.4 Key players

The main contractors on the development part should typically be major (national) institutes, while the main contractors on the demonstration part should typically be industry-based (manufacturers) or end-users (communities, utilities). Both types of main contractors will normally have a basic funding of their own.

Subcontractors may be other participants of the 'main contractor type', in which case they may also have their own basic funding. They may also be of the smaller 'consultant type' (or even 'consultant–entrepreneurial type'), which frequently will contribute with expertise, innovation and ideas, but rarely with a great deal of basic funding. Being 'the salt' of many projects, such players (as well as the projects) might benefit from the possibility of 100% financing arrangements.

Cross-national, cross-disciplinary and cross-sector cooperation should be facilitated as an important part of building European capabilities, and operational projects should also be a high priority. It would seem preferable to implement several manageable projects, even if they appear to overlap each other, rather than implementing a few large 'white elephant' projects encompassing everything and everybody.

8.6 REFERENCES

CEC DG VII (1993). A Strategy for the Promotion of Renewable Energy Technologies to Local Authorities. TERES, DG XVII, CEC.

European Directory for Renewable Energy Suppliers and Services (1994). James & James (Science Publishers), London.

IPCC – Energy Supply Mitigation Options (1994). IPCC Working Group Iia, Draft, Juky, Japan.

Open University (1994). Renewable Energy – A Resource Pack for Tertiary Education. The Open University, Milton Keynes, UK.

Proceedings of the Madrid Conference (1994). Working Group Documents. TERES, DG XVII, CEC.

Teknologinævnet – Fremtidens Vedvarende Energisystem (1993). Teknologonævnets Rapporter, 1994/3, Teknologinævnet, DK-1106, Copenhagen, Denmark.

World Energy Council (1993). Energy for Tomorrow's World – The Realities, The Real Options and the Agenda for Achievements, September 1993. World Energy Council, London.

World Energy Council (1994). New Renewable Energy Sources – A Guide to the Future. World Energy Council, London.

World Watch Institute (1986). Electricity for A Developing World: New Directions. World Watch Paper 70, June 1986. World Watch Institute, Washington, DC.

World Watch Institute (1994). The Power Surge. World Watch Institute, Washington, DC.

GLOSSARY

IHRE	Integrated Hybrid Renewable Energy systems
RE	Renewable Energy systems

Annex I.   EUREC Agency

The European Renewable Energy Centres Agency

The European Renewable Energy Centres Agency was set up in 1991 as a European Economic Interest Grouping to provide a forum for interdisciplinary co-operation. EUREC Agency has now close to 40 members. It includes Europe's most respected renewable energy organizations, ranging from academic institutions and national research centres to other organizations responsible for major R&D programmes and projects for education, for training, and for technology transfer activities.

The objectives of EUREC Agency are:

*   To promote international collaboration in science, technology and education.
*   To advise the European Commission, the European Parliament and National and Regional authorities on scientific and technical policy and priorities in R&D programmes.
*   To advise on and to support political initiatives aiming at the increase of the use of energy from renewable energy sources.
*   To assess realistic technical and economic goals for the development of renewable energy technologies in the broadest perspective, taking social and environmental limitations into account.
*   To provide a platform for discussion and exchange of information with related organizations such as associations of utilities, associations of architects and international organizations such as UNDP, the World Bank and UNESCO.
*   To discuss collaborations between EUREC's members and industry, including large and small companies
*   To undertake technical cooperation with institutions in Developing Countries and emerging economies of Eastern and Central Europe including exchange of research staff, joint programmes in R&D and technology transfer.

These activities should lead to a better coordination and rationalization of the efforts aiming at the further development of renewable energy technologies and their integration into the existing energy infrastructure.

EUREC Agency EEIG
c/o IMEC, Kapeldreef 75, B-3001 Leuven, Belgium
Fax : +32 16 281 510

President	(1994-1996):	Professor R. Van Overstraeten
Vice President	(1994-1996):	Professor A. Luque
Former Presidents	(1991-1992):	Professor W. H. Bloss
	(1993):	Professor G. Peri

EUREC Bureau:

Dr M. Becker	(Solar Thermal Power Stations)
Mr J. Beurskens	(Wind Energy)
Dr P. Fraenkel	(Small Hydro Power and Ocean Energy)
Dr G. Gosse	(Biomass)
Professor J. Luther	(Solar Buildings)
Mr McNelis	(Developing Countries)
Professor R. Van Overstraeten	(Photovoltaics)
Professor A. Zervos	(Integration)
Secretary General:	Mr G. Palmers
Secretary:	Mr C. Vanderhulst

The distribution of EUREC members

MEMBERS OF EUREC AGENCY

Dr M. Garozzo
ENEA, Renewable Energy Sources Department, Via Anguillarese 301, 00060 S. Maria di
Galeria (Roma), Italy

Professor D. N. Assimakopoulos
University of Athens, Department of Applied Physics, Ippokratous Street 33, 10680
Athens, Greece

Ir H. J. M. Beurskens
ECN, Westerduinweg 3 postbus 1, 1755 ZG Petten, The Netherlands

Dr F. Oster
Z.S.W., Hessbrühlstrasse 21 C, 7565 Stuttgart, Germany

Professor A. Papathanassopoulos
CRES, 19 km Athinon-Marathona Ave, 19009 Pikermi, Greece

Professor Dr J. Luther
FhG-ISE, Oltmannstrasse 5, 79100 Freiburg, Germany

Dr G. Gosse
AFB, c/o INRA, Station de Bioclimatologie, 78850 Thiverval-Grignon, France

Professor L. Guimaraes
Universidade Nova de Lisbõa, Faculdade de Ciências e Tecnologia, Quinta da Torre, 2825 Monte da Caparica, Portugal

Dr J. A. Halliday
RAL, Energy Research Unit, Bld. R 63, Chilton, Didcot, Oxfordshire OX11 0QX, UK

Mr P. Helm
WIP, Sylvensteinstrasse 2, 81369 München, Germany

Professor Dr E. Hill
NPAC, University of Northumbria, Ellison Place, Newcastle upon Tyne NE1 8ST, UK

Professor Dr W. Kleinkauf
ISET, Königstor 59, 34119 Kassel, Germany

Professor A. Luque
IES, ETSI Telecomunicacion, Ciudad Universitaria 24, 28040 Madrid 5, Spain

Dr D. Mayer
ARDER, c/o ARMINES, Ecole des Mines de Paris, Centre d'Energétique B.P. 207, 06904 Sophia Antipolis Cedex, France

Dr S. McCarthy
Hyperion, Enterprise Centre, Main Street, Watergrasshill, County Cork, Ireland

Mr B. McNelis
IT Power Ltd, The Warren; Bramshill Road, Eversley, Hants RG27 0PR, UK

Mr R. Melchior
ITER, Cabildo Insular de Tenerife, Parque eolico, 38594 Granadilla, Spain, Islas Canarias

Dr J. P. Molly
DEWI, Ebertstrasse, 96, 26382 Wilhelmshaven, Germany

Mr B. Morgana
Conphoebus, Passo Martino, Zona Industriale, Casella Postale 95030, Piano d'Arci/ Catania, Italy

Mr J. M. Jossart
Université Catholique de Louvain, Faculté des sciences agronomiques (ECOP), Place Croix du Sud 2/11, 1348 Louvain-la-Neuve, Belgium

Professor Dr G. Peri
ERASME, c/o Université de Corse, Lab. d'Hélioénergie/Centre Sc. de Vignola, Route des Sanguinaires, 20000 Ajaccio, France

Dr E. L. Petersen
RISØ National Laboratory, Meteorology & Wind Energy Dept., P.O. Box 49, 4000 Roskilde, Denmark

Dr F. Sanchez
IER–CIEMAT, Avenida Complutense 22, 28040 Madrid, Spain

Dr P. Siffert
Laboratoire PHASE (CNRS), Rue du Loess 23 B.P. 20, 67037 Strasbourg Cédex, France

Professor Dr R. Van Overstraeten
IMEC, Kapeldreef 75, 3001 Leuven–Heverlee, Belgium

Professor Dr G. Wrixon
NMRC, University College, Lee Maltings, Prospect Row, Cork, Ireland

Dr T. C. J. van der Weiden
ECOFYS, Kanaalweg 95, P.O. Box 8408, 3503 RK Utrecht, The Netherlands

Professor P. Lund
NEMO, Advanced Energy Systems, Helsinki University of Technology, Otakaari 3, 02150 Espoo, Finland

Mr G. Elliot
NEL, Renewable Energy Group, National Wind Turbine Centre, East Kilbride, Glasgow G75 0QU , UK

Dr M. Becker
DLR, Linder Höhe, 51147 Köln, Germany

Professor D. Hall
King's College London, Division of Life Sciences, Camden Hill Road, London W8 7AH, UK

Professor N. I. Meyer
Technical University of Denmark, Physics Dept, Energy Group Building 309, 2800 Lyngby, Denmark

Mr P. Maegaard
Folkecenter for renewable energy, Kammersgardsvej 16, P.O.Box 208, 7760 Hurup Thy, Denmark

Mr E. Michel
CoSTIC, Rue A. Lavoisier, Z.I. Saint-Christophe, 04000 Digne, France

Dr H. Ossenbrink
Joint Research Centre, European Commission, 21020 Ispra (Va), Italy

Professor Kai Sipilä
VTT Energy, P.O. Box 1601, 02044 VTT Espoo, Finland

FURTHER ADDRESS

Dr P. Lundsager
DanREC, CAT Technology Centre, Frederiksborgvej 399, DK-4000 Roskilde, Denmark

Annex II

GENERAL REFERENCES

European Council (1993). Decision Concerning the Promotion of Renewable Energy Sources in the Community (ALTENER Programme), Official Journal of the European Communities, 18 September 1993

The European Renewable Energy Study (TERES) (1994). European Commission – Directorate-General for Energy DG XVII , Brussels and Luxemburg.

Resolution of the Committee on Energy Research and Technology of the European Parliament (rapporteur Mr. Bettini), Reference A3-405/92, adopted on 19 January 1993.

A European Action Plan for Solar Energy (1993). European Solar Council, The 'Club de Paris' of Renewable Energies, 14 October 1993,

Mombaur Resolution of the Committee on Research, Technological Development and Energy of the European Parliament, A4-0188/96.

PHYSICAL UNITS AND CONVERSION FACTORS

W	Watt
Wh	Watt hour
W_p	Watt Peak (see photovoltaics)
We	Watt of electrical power
Wth	Watt of thermal power
toe	Tonne of oil equivalent
J	Joule

1 TWh = 0.086 Mtoe (energy equivalent)

1 TWh = 0.222 Mtoe (corresponding to a Carnot efficiency of 38.46 % for the conversion of fuels into electricity)

PREFIXES

k	Kilo-	(10^3)
M	Mega-	(10^6)
G	Giga-	(10^9)
T	Tera-	(10^{12})
P	Peta-	(10^{15})

INDEX